When We Were Boys

I desire respectfully to acquaint the American public that Messrs Longmans, Green, and Company, are the only authorized publishers of this novel in America and that editions issued by them are the only ones from which I derive any profits.

William O'Brien

Dublin,
April 12th 1890.

yours sincerely

June 2d 1887   William O'Brien

WHEN WE WERE BOYS

A NOVEL

BY

WILLIAM O'BRIEN, M.P.

LONDON

LONGMANS, GREEN, AND CO.

AND NEW YORK: 15 EAST 16th STREET

1890

TO

JOHN DILLON

IN MEMORY OF

ANXIOUS YEARS AND GLORIOUS HOPES

CONTENTS

WHEN WE WERE BOYS

CHAPTER THE FIRST

THE GARRINDINNY RAILWAY

'Now, lad, look alive. Stow away the sandwiches, and kiss your mother. We'll never catch the nine o'clock!' A loud, hearty voice, and its owner, a bluff, hale-faced man in a burly great-coat, who stood, whip in hand, outside the rustic porch of the miller's house at Greenane, growling at the little family group which was clinging around the neck of a schoolboy of seventeen.

'Good-bye, mother! Nonsense, dear mother! It is only till summer and the holidays.' The youngster spoke it stoutly enough, but not without a choking gulp or two such as afflict home-bred youths, who, in learning to be heroes, have not yet forgotten how to cry.

Ken Rohan was only going forty miles away to school—from one peat-perfumed little Irish rustic town to another. How am I ever to get an age that chats across the wires from continent to continent, and barely lifts its eyebrows if its acquaintance of Pall Mall to-day should turn up by the Mahmoudieh Canal or in a Japanese tea-garden next month or the month after, to understand that, well on in the sixties of the present century, people's hearts could still be wrung by a schoolboy's change of residence from drowsy Drumshaughlin to drowsier Clonard? The railway had not yet arrived at Drumshaughlin, however, to abolish the sweet pains of leave-taking. Everybody was crying, or pretending not to cry—tears in his mother's eyes, tears in his sister Katie's eyes, tears—or as good as tears—in the eyes of his brindled terrier, Snipe, as he rubbed his ugly muzzle against his master's legs; and one may suspect that the indignation, and whip-cracking, and timepiece-consulting, and bluster of the burly

B

miller himself was only another and a more painful way of crying, too. Even lame little Danny, the miller's man, with whom grumbling was as much the sauce of life as vinegar is of an oyster, and who had wasted some of the best eloquence of his life in impressing upon the young marauder that apple-trees were not made to be climbed, nor haycocks to be tumbled in, had a snug wisp of hay ready to tuck around the young marauder's feet on the outside-car, which was Danny's skulking way of presenting a bouquet.

'Will I ever see my darling child again?' Women—especially delicate women—are terrible sceptics that way. They have so much faith in another world that they have little left for this. If her darling child had gone off in scarlatina before the holidays, she would have treasured that doubt of hers all her life as a presentiment.

'Very well. Keep him altogether. Am I to put up the pony?' growled Myles Rohan, the miller, his eyes fixed upon a massy silver timepiece, which his grandfather before him used to consult in his day. Myles liked to think of grandfathers and great-grandfathers, and to trace his old mahogany and silver spoons to them. He could not be persuaded to discard his grandfather's frieze coat until it was in the last agonies of dissolution. 'One would think the boy was bound on a voyage for life.' That is just the bitterness of it in those first rendings of the veil of tender homes. A voyage for life, alas! it is. The summer and the holidays never arrive that bring us back the children who go —never, at least, till they join us for the Long Vacation.

What poor hands we are, too, at farewell speeches on such occasions!—and how lucky, upon the whole, that Nature, in endowing every simple human heart with more poetry than you will find in a volume of verse, and more eloquence than you will hear in a session of Parliament, bestows its gifts for the most part in the dumb alphabet of touches, sighs, and glances! Young Rohan's mother did not at all speak in blank verse, though her heart was bursting like a little Ætna within her to express itself. To remember to say the Prayer of St. Bernard every morning— not to read too hard—to explain to Father Mulpetre that neck of mutton never did agree with him—(such was the poor prose in which she sought to stammer out her soul)—to take care of the coral studs in the washing—to remember that the white-currant cordial was stowed away here, and the red-flannel night-shirts there—above everything, if he did not want to break his mother's heart, never to forget that the postman's knock would henceforth be the most important event of the day at the Mil——

'Good-bye, old woman. Don't be making a fool of yourself,' said the miller, imprinting a kiss on his old woman's cheek in one of those outbreaks of kindly roughness by which old-fashioned medical practitioners effect more cures than they effect by their prescriptions. The boy availed himself of the moment to spring on the car, and it was all over.

A mist rose between his eyes and the old mill, like a sacred nimbus, through which he could dimly see the sweet motherly face as it faded into the shadow of the porch, see Katie's sunny hair and fluttering handkerchief as they sped vainly after him to the furthest verge of the orchard, hear old Snipe's forlorn howl as the miller's whip drove him pitilessly back, hear the old mill-wheel itself mumbling its farewell like a hoarse old friend. A sharp turn of the road—a thick screen of elm-trees, where the rooks were exchanging their gruesome morning's news—and the little glen of Greenane was gone—the glen, with its bare woods and barer mountain cones overhead, and in its bosom the tawny mill-wheel lazily rolling in the playful embraces of the mill-stream, and the miller's quaint old house, with all manner of queer little windows and lawless gables, ensconced in its nest of orchard-trees so cosily that the hydrangeas were blooming at its door and the thrushes singing the songs of spring around it even in the grey of this raw January morning.

A bell began to toll in Ken Rohan's ears. A vague fancy crossed him that the silence of the disabled streets was death—the death of *his* Drumshaughlin—and that this was its passing knell. It was only the bell for early Mass, however, as he very well knew; and the silver-headed old curate—the golden-hearted old curate—the oldest old curate who was ever assumed into Heaven without a parish—was walking up and down the chapel-yard in his square tasselled cap and purple stole, warming his hands and muttering his Latin Office, a living message of good cheer to the people in the graves all around.

'I was on the look-out for you, boy—not going to serve Mass for me any more, eh?' cried the old man blithely, taking the boy's hand gently between his own broad palms. 'Well, well, the boys will grow in spite of us, Myles.'

'Ay, and *go* in spite of us, into the bargain, Father Phil,' said the miller.

'He'll be a good boy wherever he goes—that is, if that rascal of mine will let him. You don't know Jack—my nephew, Jack—Ken?' the old priest asked, a little falteringly. 'No, of course—he came straight from France. Well, you'll see enough of him at St. Fergal's—perhaps too much of him. Keep him straight, Ken, for his old mother's sake, and don't let him make

you ashamed of deserving an old fellow's blessing. Safe home
Myles!—you're a trifle behind time on the road, but Sheela will
make up for it down Cooleeruch Hill.'

Ken's eyes followed the old priest wistfully into the vestry,
where he went to robe for Mass. Through the open doors he
could see the little acolyte, a strange acolyte, flitting about the
altar, the wax-lights burning with such a tranquil faith, and the
sparse old worshippers bowed in the shadowy corners like spirits
in a sweet Purgatory who could see the *splendor della viva luce
eterna* already glimmering in the distance; and he longed, if
only once more, to throw on his scarlet soutane, and serve
Father Phil's Mass as in the old days, and scamper home in time
for a breakfast of fragrant tea and divinely-browned toast at
the Mill.

The bridge, and the town clock, and the tatterdemalion cabins
in the suburbs flew past him like so many old friends reproachfully
casting him off. He had never experienced such a pang of lonesomeness before in leaving the trumpery old town behind him.
He was more astonished still, when they had cleared the last
wreaths of peat-smoke, to observe what a really noble place
Drumshaughlin was—or, rather, not Drumshaughlin itself, which
lay crawling like a tattered mendicant at the feet of Lord Drumshaughlin's haughty-looking castle, but its environment—what
mountains, and misty fastnesses, and glimpses of an untamed sea!
He knew and loved every glen and cliff of them, having a healthy
heart for all beautiful things; but it was only now, when he was
leaving them, that he quite realised that this roar of the mighty
waves was music, and that the hills he used to shoot over and
course hares over were clad in colours like so many Oriental kings.
If you should not be able to find Drumshaughlin on the map, you
will have to take it from me that Drumshaughlin is the capital of
the ancient principality of Beara—that bold peninsula which
forms the northern walls of Bantry Bay and shoots its great ramparts unflinchingly out into the jaws of the Atlantic Ocean. The
principality was the scene of the last stubborn stand of the
Southern Irish during the Elizabethan Wars, and seemed to have
been swept bare up to the bald peaks of the mountains by those
blasts of conquest under which castles, shrines, and woods had
withered away below. A mining-shaft sunk here and there, with
its reddish flow of copper following the gash, looked as though
the conqueror had endeavoured to uproot the very mountains.
There they stood, however, the chain of storm-beaten warrior
peaks that extend for the whole length of the principality from
Glengariff to the ocean—gleaming with the same delicate poetic
mystery and vocal with the same grand organ-voices of the winds

and waves as on the day when Carew's and Raleigh's cannon-shots first affrighted them ; and the green valleys are as green as ever over the graves of the two races, and the withered woods have sprouted again, and the beaten clans have established themselves throughout the bare hills once more, even as the heather has managed to coax sustenance out of their stony hearts.

'It *is* fine !' the boy exclaimed, as a flush of pale rosy light shot through the Caha Mountains like the flesh-tints of beautiful sculptures coming to life. 'There's nothing in the world to beat Beara—is there, sir ?'

'If people could dine and sup off a picture-gallery, 'twould be a plentiful country, sure enough. Hallo, you young rascal, diving into the sandwiches already, eh ?'

The miller's son blushed violently to be caught developing a material appetite so soon on this melancholy occasion. A few minutes before he had been thinking what a chasm, oceans wide, had opened between him and home, and what he would give to have Sheela's head turned the other way ; and here he was already nibbling furtively at ham sandwiches, and sipping the scenery, and guiltily enjoying the whirl through the brisk air, and feeling his heart bound in the tide of novelty, excitement, and adventure that was surging in upon him. If ever you are to understand Ken Rohan, you must understand that he had never before been outside the cordon of his native hills, and that his knowledge of the real world was as scanty as his travels in the worlds of poetry, history, and adventure had been extensive. His little argosy set out for its Golden Fleece with troops of gay zephyr-like illusions swelling the sails. His father was a Jove the Thunderer among men ; his mother a crystal-souled Madonna among women ; but, for the matter of that, were not all women angelic, and all men brave, and all Doctors beings of power, and all Divines divine ? Death and sin, doubt and pain, were the only illusions he could perceive ; and they were obviously illusions. Troubles there were, to be sure, on the face of the bright world ; what would the world be without them, as what would a monthly confession be without some heinous secret like that of a clandestine pipe to be contrite for ? The clouds and sorrows were the clammy mists that so often darkled around the great brow of Hungry Mountain ; they came only that the strong man, like the strong mountain, should toss them aside and laugh in the sun. Two sides there had to be to make a battle ; and the losing side often, perhaps mostly, the more enviable. Much though his blood was stirred by the sight of Ney's Old Guard charging up the hill of Mont St. Jean in all their bravery, he was not sure that he was not prouder of their scanty ranks as they tottered back. And now his own Hill of Mont St. Jean was beginning to flash into view, with all youth's martial music and dancing feathers around him, and the prizes of mastery of this bright, brave world already glittering on the heights in front. To most people who are not Celts of seventeen this will seem an extravagant way of regarding a drive to Garrindinny railway station on an Irish jaunting-car ; but you may as well expect Irish hills to throw off their hues and shadows as Irish youngsters to look at life as a table of statistics. Young Rohan had long been convinced—as he was convinced that any two sides of a triangle were greater than the third—that there were cities and nations of men beyond the furthest blue ranges he could see from the top of Hungry ; but how different to be actually going out into this enchanted world so full of freshness, of surprise, and hope !—where every turn of the road might bring adventures, and every peasant leaning over his half-door smoking a black pipe was the citizen of a strange land ! And so it was that Ken Rohan felt himself dreaming of battles and munching sandwiches while the streaming eyes and aching hearts at the lonely Mill kept their faithful mourning rites for the young conscript, who had gone out to the great wars.

On they sped through the stony, wind-shorn, glacier-polished mountains, by the shores of the great Bay, past the coquettish evergreen groves and toy-like islets of Glengariff—on as though Sheela also was feeling the intoxication of the gun-flashes and the beat of drums. When Myles Rohan intimated that ' they'd never catch the nine o'clock,' he only meant that, give anybody else the reins, or put any other nag between the shafts, and the thing was not to be done ; but Sheela, the jaunting-car, the reins, and the hand that held them being his own, he bowled along with as comfortable an assurance of being in time as if he had a private understanding with the sun to halt in the heavens until Sheela should pass the Cross at Garrindinny. The miller was one of those hearty positive men, whose whisper goes further with a horse than other men's whips, and whom women like to have in a country house by night when there is somebody ill and the doctor at a distance. His son half-dreaded, whole-reverenced him, Sheela knew every turn of his wrist, the peasants doffed their hats to him as if iron manliness in one of their own blood and creed were a portent almost too good to be true ; and, if such tributes made him as self-satisfied, good-natured, and affable as gratified vanity usually makes men, long may we have vanities with so sunshiny a gift of paying their way !

' Why, that's Hans Harman's old shay amongst a thousand !' he cried, pointing his whip at a lumbering one-horse coach that was plodding along leisurely in front of them down Cooleeruch Hill. 'What piece of roguery is bringing *him* over to Garrindinny this perishing morning, I wonder? Maybe it's to evict old Meehul, up on the top of Cnocaunacurraghcooish? I hear he's "expecting the Sheriff" one of these days. But old Meehul is "expecting the Sheriff" all his life as regular as he's expecting his br·akfast—and the breakfast don't always arrive for the poor *angish*, no more than the Sheriff—Easy awhile!—why, to be sure, this is Presentment Sessions' Day at Clonard, and Hans is going across to carry his presentment. What, do you think, is his presentment?'

With due diffidence in presence of superior wisdom, Ken hazarded the suggestion : 'Something, I dare say, sir, he wants the Grand Jury to do for him.'

'And those who are not grand jurors to pay for—exactly. A trifle of a thousand pounds or so to build a bridge into his own demesne, on the ground that the public use it as a short cut. So they do—as a short cut to the Workhouse, or, what's the same thing, to the rent-office, for sorra another thing ever brought a decent neighbour to his hungry door. Was there ever such a bare-faced job?'

'A what, sir?'

'A brand-new bridge over nothing at all at the expense of the county. He'll be putting in a presentment next for a river to run under it! Ken,' said the miller, sternly, 'we'll throw out that presentment!'

'I didn't think you had a vote, sir?'

'They take precious good care I've not, boy ; but they can't strike a man's wits off the Register as they did the Forty Shilling Freeholders. Heeup, Sheela! let's see if we can't manage a small Reform of the Grand Jury Laws on our own hook, old girl!'

Sheela bounded forward with the enthusiasm of an old politician, and was quickly abreast of the chaise.

'Hallo, Rohan, so it's you—hope you're well—glad to see you!' sang out a pleasant voice from the chaise. The voice came from the broad chest of a gentleman of massive and well-proportioned frame, thin, but handsome, clear-cut features, flowing moustaches and full black beard, powdered here and there with grey—all lighted by a smile of frankness and good humour. 'Why, it's like a glimpse of the sun to meet you on the road this chilly morning.'

'Thank you, s-a-h-r!' said the miller, employing the 'sir' as an uplifted sword which might descend, either to cleave a skull or to describe a ceremonious salute, at discretion.

'Not coming over to Sessions to-day? Tell you candidly I hope not, if I'm to carry that little job of mine.'

'Bless you, no, sir—the likes of me may be as good as another to pay for a job; what call should we have to go spoiling one?' returned the miller, with a twinkle of rebellion in the corners of his eyes.

The gentleman in the chaise laughed the good-natured laugh of a man who could give blows on occasion, but, on the whole, found it rarer fun to receive them. 'Rohan, you're a Radical monster—devil a less. Well, well, you'll have your joke and I'll have my bridge—what could be fairer or pleasanter? I know nothing about politics myself—couldn't guess whether Brian Boru was a Whig or a Tory; could you?—Ah! so this is your lad—taking him to school, I hear?— How do you do, sir? Hope you will be a good boy. A youngster may be anything nowadays, if he minds his moods and tenses. Is it to be a marshal's baton or a mitre, which? Fewer marshals' batons going in our day, Rohan, eh?'

'True enough, sir—the people didn't know half how hungry they were then—they have education to tell 'em all about it now, and still the greedy fellows aren't satisfied. Heeup, Sheela!' and Sheela sprang forward, as if chuckling like a Radical over her master's rude pleasantry.

'You're in a deuce of a hurry, Rohan. Boohig is never particular to ten minutes,' said Mr. Harman, with imperturbable good humour.

'Thank you, sir. I find it more comfortable to be too soon than too late,' shouted the miller, and he was gone.

That wildly romantic being, the British shareholder, was the author of the Garrindinny and Great Western Railway. The Bill, as it passed Standing Orders, was an epic poem lit by glimpses of a Glengariff picture-country sighing to be sliced into building-lots, lively with the siren-songs of innumerable shoals of mackerel willing to do all but swim ashore to be cooked, and tragic here and there with the stern groan of some copper or barytes mine sick with desire to yield up its treasure to the first comer. The epic caught the soft heart of the British Public like the poems of Mr. Robert Montgomery. The railway, like the poet, however, met its remorseless Macaulay. Before the line could get within a dozen long-legged Irish miles of Glengariff, its painted paradises, copper ores, or little fishes, the Company was in a state of liquidation in a dingy mausoleum up four pair of stone stairs in King Street, Westminster. The first canto ended with the seizure of the first passenger-train (including the Board of Directors and the materials of the champagne luncheon) by the

Sheriff under a writ of *fi. fa.* on foot of certain transactions with a contractor who had no music in his soul ; and there and then the railway came to an end in the midst of a moaning desert of black bog-mould, naked rocks, and shivery pools—like a story of adventure to be continued in a future number, or a promising young railway cut off in its bloom and buried at the cross-roads of Garrindinny in hopes of a happy resurrection. Traffic still went on upon the completed sections of the Garrindinny and Great Western 1 y the aid of stingy and precarious subsidies from the Court, but in a spirit befitting the obsequies of a great design rather than with any ignoble ambition of scrambling for dividends. Mr. Hans Harman might well take his ease in his chaise. When Sheela scoured up to the cross-roads at steeplechase pace, the old-fashioned engine, which wore most of its bowels on the outside, was puffing up and down about the turn-table, in a broken-hearted, undecided way, as if deliberating whether the Court would allow it coals enough to make the journey, or whether it was really worth while stirring at all for so small cause. Though it was now branded with the barbarous *alias* of ' Erin-go-bragh,' the venerable locomotive had once been christened ' Stephenson ' amidst salvoes of champagne corks, and had screamed through Rugby for many a proud day with the commerce of a world on its back. Fancy the reflections of that iron veteran as it surveyed with a snort of contempt the rails turning carmine with the rust, and an invalided wagon like a lame beggar imploring an alms of cargo by way of starting it in business, and a goat peacefully making its breakfast over the grass-grown siding ; and then to think of being obliged in its declining days to drag its old legs after it all the way to Clonard for no other reason in life than that a wagon or two of empty porter-barrels and weeping emigrants might burlesque the uses of the steam-engine, and a policeman with a crease in his poll might graciously arrive to see them off ! The ' Erin-go-bragh ' had really contracted a hollow, grave-yard moan, which gave it the air of contemplating *felo de se* by an explosion, since upon the Garrindinny and Great Western there was no possible hope of honourably ending its days ty a collision with anything.

The guard and the engine-driver were at this moment soothing themselves, in the spirit of Preference Shareholders, with certain palliatives, which the engine-driver, cleaning his brow with a dirtier pocket-handkerchief, called ' Two raw rammers, ma'am,' at the bar of the adjacent Terminus Hotel. The Terminus Hotel had once formed a sounding strophe in the Garrindinny and Great Western Epic. It had figured in chromo-lithograph, depicting the nobility and gentry descending from crimson-and

gold barouches, and received at the door by a waiter of ancient
lineage with a Louis Quatorze sweep of his napkin ; but the
barouches never came, and the waiter of the *vieille école* drifted
away into a Cork oyster-cellar, with the threads of his black
swallow-tail grown as white as his necktie was black, and all the
blood in his body lodged in his nose in the last stages of despon-
dency ; and the very sign of the 'Terminus Hotel' had disappeared like the rosy adjectives of the Prospectus under a matter-
of-fact blob of green paint, on which a rustic artist had blazoned
forth the golden legend : 'Mick Brine—Entertainment for Man
and Horse ;' and, to crown all, the 'Coffee Room' windows had
their two eyes punched into one, where, behind ranges of bottles
of rare vintages more gloriously coloured than the chromo-lithograph itself, Mrs. Brine, a buxom, sonsy-looking matron, with
indifferently combed hair, was blushingly separating the guard's
change for the raw rammers from his compliments to the crowing
baby in her arms ('Begob, ma'am, 'twas worth making the mis
fortunate railway, if 'twas only to see how thim babbies flock
down out of the sky to you—God bless 'em ! I'll engage that's
about your eleventh now, Mrs. Brine?' the guard was remarking,
genially.——' And two that's in Heaven, Mr. Boohig, plaze God !'
——'Amen, ma'am !' observed the guard, piously).
　　'Now, Boohig—time's up ! How soon are we off?' cried
Myles Rohan, bursting in with his cheery ' God save all here !'
　　'Wisha, the day is young, Misther Myles,' was the leisurely
answer of Boohig. (That was the guard's name, Mick being the
remainder of it.) 'The world will be there afther us. We may
just as well give the neighbours a chance.'
　　'Divil a sounder principle as a general rule, my poor man ;
but listen !' The miller whispered something that made the guard
slap the zinc counter till the raw rammer leaped in an ecstasy.
　　'You don't mane it, sir?—hungry Hans, is it? Ho, ho, by
the bombshells of war, if all the fun isn't gone out of the country,
we'll lave him time enough to study the scenery ! 'Twas only the
other day, being Christmas-time, he tipped me a tin-shilling piece
in mistake for a sixpinny bit—'twas the only slip he ever med in
his life—and what do you think he does but gets the ould Head-
Constable, Muldudden, to report to the Boord that Boohig was
out on a tear for the holidays? Honey isn't sweet enough for
Hans Harman—nor hell isn't hot enough, nayther.'
　　'He'll be down on us in five minutes at latest.'
　　'Not he, sir—he's never in a hurry—he thinks the train
daarn't budge while Lord Drumshaughlin's agent is within a
donkey's screech of it. Daarn't it, though?' chuckled Boohig,
bolting the measure of hot whisky, and, for some obscure reason,

stuffing a jujube into his mouth by way of second course.
'Fifteen minutes past the hour—come along, sir!'

A party of emigrants and their friends were wailing in each
other's arms on the platform. At every southern and western
railway station in those days you could hear that wild, heart-
breaking ullagone of the Irish Rachel weeping for her children
and refusing to be comforted. The whole ghastly passenger traffic
of the country seemed to consist in one long funeral of the population. The principal other passenger was a small nervous man,
whose individuality seemed to be stored in a long, obtrusive, and
yet deprecating, muddy-grey beard, behind which an insignificant
face appeared to be apologising for being in anybody's way; and
a pair of long arms terminating in long skinny fingers pawed the
air at either side as if stuck on as after-thoughts by a schoolboy
caricaturist.

'What, Humphrey! going across to help Harman to his
bridge, eh?' cried the miller, slapping him on the shoulder with
a thwack that made the beard and its appurtenances jump like a
frog under the knife of a vivisector.

'Eh, bless us and seeve us! You do come upon an old fellow
in such ways and say such things—and quite welcome, too, I'm
sure, from an old neebour, Mr. Rohan, sir.'

'So isn't Hans Harman's haul out of the County Cess.'

'Ha, ha, that's your pleasant way of putting it—but humble
people in a small way must live, Mr. Rohan, sir—people that has
no pretinsions to figuring in the peepers, so to say—and I do
assure you, Mr. Rohan, sir, I find his lordship's agent a most
eemiable, public-sperrited gentleman. But goodness gracious!
how unfortunate!' he started off, glancing excitedly at his
watch, and then along the Drumshaughlin Road, as the guard
came tearing along the train, shouting: 'In with ye! All for
Clonard!' and ringing the bell with a fury that raised the wail
of the emigrants' friends an octave higher.

'Going to start, sir—look out for your leg!' cried Boohig,
banging the door.

'God bless my soul!' cried the electric little man, saving his
limb with the spring of an automaton toy; but his eyes still
ranged desperately up the road. 'Was there ever anything so
unlucky? But you don't understand, guard—you don't, reelly.
It's Mr. Harman that's coming over to Sessions. Just think if
he should be left behind! You couldn't do it, guard—no,
reelly!'

'Quarter of an hour late, sir—complaints in the papers, sir—
as much as my place is worth, sir.—Now, then, old woman, out
with your ticket!—Is that handful of turkeys all right in the

van, Mr. Draddy?—Where am I to drop Mrs. Deloohery's hand-box?—At the junction, is it?—All right. Here he's down the road, sir—divvel such *keóil* (music) ever was heard!' whispered Boohig, springing into his van behind the third-class carriage in which Myles Rohan travelled for the time-honoured Radical reason that they would not accommodate him with a fourth.

Ken Rohan heard the guard's whistle sound, heard the old 'Erin-go-bragh' respond with a deep groan like that of a Company in its last agony, saw the trim-polled policeman nod approvingly at the departing train as who should say that he saw no sufficient reasons of State at present for detaining it, saw the emigrants' friends cling to it and shriek at it as if it were tearing the heartstrings out of their bosoms with it; and lo! with feelings like those of Sindbad the Sailor on the roc's back, he beheld the only world he knew moving wondrously away into space, and was preparing himself for the delights of the Valley of Diamonds, when he heard his father sing out with the zest of a hot-blooded schoolboy: 'Here he comes! Look at him—for the honour of God, watch him!' At the same moment a yell came from the platform: 'Pull up, Mick, pull up!—*ainm-an-diaoul*, don't you hear me telling you 'tis Mr. Harman?'

It was, indeed, the handsome figure of the agent that stood calmly beckoning after the train, with the assured serenity of a Neptune calling the unruly winds to heel with a bare whisper of *quos ego.*—The train moved on and on, however—faster, it seemed, than any Garrindinny train on record—and the engine set up an impish screech, as if its old lungs were crowing with schoolboy frolicsomeness like the rest. The servile little herd of mendicants and railway officials gathered together in mute awe to observe what would happen next. If a thunderbolt had crashed down upon that audacious locomotive—if the mailed hand of Britannia had suddenly taken it by the throttle-valve, it would scarcely have surprised Mr. Harman's trembling subjects to see his outraged dignity thus supernaturally avenged. They were not quite certain that, as the train flashed out of sight spouting mockery and defiance, that the avenging lash might not fall upon their own shoulders, they being more immediately within range. It was the first time the agent's will had been successfully baffled within his dominions. He could not have been more amazed if his ancient coach-horse had risen in rebellion between the shafts. Most affronted potentates in his case are addicted to strong language. To the intense relief of the obsequious little indignation-meeting on the platform he burst out laughing.

'It's the biter bitten, boys, that's all,' he cried gaily. 'I'm

the only man that ever preached punctuality at Garrindinny, and
—deuce mend me!—I'm the only one that ever lost his train by
not practising it. Heigho! Nothing for it but to see whether
Mick Brine can't console a hungry man with a rasher. A
devilish good joke it was!' he chuckled to himself, while the
savoury rasher was in process of crisping—'though it has blown
that bridge of mine sky-high till the Summer Assizes. Why
shouldn't a man like Rohan be cured of his infernal Radical
crotchets, and be one of ours!—a landed man, a magistrate, or
whatever more outlandish mountebank he pleases! A fellow
like that is worth a whole regiment of whimpering Humphrey
Dargans.'

Hans Harman was one of the sweetest-tempered of mankind.

CHAPTER THE SECOND

ST. FERGAL'S

KEN ROHAN found Mick Boohig a scarcely less amazing aerial
traveller than the roc. He felt so elated with the speed, and the
novelty, and the crash, that he thought he would never tire of a
railway journey if Boohig were to bear them away and away
through this land of enchantment until their hair should grow
white. Their arrival at Clonard (in whose diocesan Seminary
he was about to be installed as a pupil) was a heavy blow, until
Clonard in its turn blossomed into Wonderland around him, and
he found himself plucking his father's sleeve hither and thither
with a rapturous: 'Just look at this!' and an: 'Oh, I say!'
without the slightest regard for the dignity of his first silk hat
and ecclesiastically-cut garments.

Clonard was a Bishop's See. Its line of prelates extended
back to the times of St. Patrick. Most of their lordships had to
make shift with a mountain cave for a palace, and some with a
gallows for a pulpit. Even still the older portion of the town
had a curious dead-and-gone sort of air. Half-way up the main
street, in the midst of a tangled grave-yard, the battered ruin of a
Franciscan Abbey lay breathing out its everlasting *memento mori*
through its shattered grey traceries, like an old monk on a
contented death-bed, mumbling gentle words of warning to the
living. The principal portion of the population seemed to reside
in the surrounding graves; and the adjoining cabins, though
they still breathed the turf-smoke of the living, wore a certain
moribund aspect of resignation as though preparing for a general

death-bed under the patronage of the reverend Franciscan ruins. There was a delightfully drowsy Spanish luxury about the whole thatched-cloister-life of the place. To think that a monthly pig fair desecrated the Main Street jarred upon one's sensibilities, like a French chorus breaking in upon a Gregorian chant. If Town Commissioners there must be at all in such a place, there was a certain æsthetic comfort in learning that they reaped a yearly crop of hay off a considerable slice of the great, empty market-place. The people ceased their chat in the street, and pulled off their hats when the Angelus bell sounded; and it seemed as if the Angelus bell never did quite finish sounding, unless when a Vesper bell was beginning, or the modest hour-bell from the Calvary Convent tinkling, or the Cathedral thundering out its chimes in full-dress majesty, like a whole sonorous Œcumenical Council. Clonard's simple life from dawn to dark was set to ecclesiastical music, even to the gay cherub choirs of children playing about the gravestones, and the deep monkish caw of the sober old rooks up in their ivied cloisters. The very town band was organised under the invocation of St. Fergal, and played religious and patriotic hymns with equal spirit.

But on the breast of the hill overtopping this dozy, crumbling, thatched, and ragged Clonard of the Penal Days there had arisen a shiny new town of virgin limestone, all of a piece, all of a cluster, as if it had been let down from heaven in a single night fresh from the brain of some not-too-inventive angelic architect— the new Cathedral, the new College, the new Convent, the new Orphanage, the new Presbytery, glittering in naked whiteness all of a row; and around these there had gathered the usual booths that drive a not ungodly trade on the Way of Heaven—a wine-merchant with a speciality for Spanish altar-wines; a tailor with clerical fashion-plates; a fancy warehouse garnished with articles of devotion 'imported direct from Paris;' and a pastry-cook whose function in life it was to supply the funeral baked-meats for a Month's Mind at the Cathedral, or the wedding-cake for the profession of a nun at the Convent, or the apple-pies and waiters for a particularly large dinner-party at his lordship's, the Bishop's. This resurrection of a faith that seemed to have been trampled into the dust ages ago as utterly as the Franciscans' kitchen-fire, was a source of incredible pride to a generation whose grandfathers took to the hills for worship as for an insurrection, and whose great-grandfathers deserved to be hanged for the capital offence of going to school. 'Like the fabled bird of the Orient,' Mr. Mat Murrin, of the *Banner*, used to write, on speech-day at St. Fergal's, where he annually beamed on the proceedings in a cloudy eye-glass that required perpetual furbishing, and a silk hat that

seemed to have spent a long life in endeavouring to get properly
polished, and where Mrs. Murrin's vigorous performances during
the *déjeuner*, and Mat's flowery toast of 'The President' after it,
were amongst the most valued traditions of the place—'like the
fabled bird of the Orient, temple and cloister and educational
establishment have sprung, godlike, and, so to say, full-fledged,
from the ashes of our fathers' shrines, radiant with the immortal
juvenility of our faith and race, crowning the historic hill of
Clonard as with a dazzling limestone tiara, and reflecting the
utmost credit upon our enterprising townsmen, Messrs. Houlihan
and Daggs, the contractors, to whose courteous and hospitable
foreman, Mr. Macdarmody, our representative takes this opportunity of expressing his indebtedness for much interesting information and some slight, though graceful, hospitalities.' Indeed, to
look up at those astonishing masses of shapely masonry, and then
down over the poor little out-at-elbows town out of whose loins
they had all arisen, the most whirling young Zeitgeister who
decrees that the commission of Christianity was exhausted centuries ago in building churches for the Encyclopédists and Mental
Physiologists to tumble down, might well bow his head as
reverently as Mat Murrin before an authentic miracle of living
faith. One peculiarity of all this headlong rush into stone-and-
mortar was that nothing was quite finished. The Cathedral
wanted a spire, and was waiting complacently until the next
generation should build it, like a clergyman out under a shower
of rain without his hat; there was room for another wing to the
College in the architect's designs; old Mother Rosalie, of the
Calvary Convent, objected totally to die until her old eyes should
see an altar and reredos of Sicilian marble gleaming in the
Convent Chapel; the priests' house was only roofed in for the
winter until funds should come in to floor and plaster the top
story; but on the Work went all the same, with funds or
without them. Your Irish banker never refuses to honour *post-
obit* drafts upon the piety of posterity, and your Irish church-
builder never fears to draw them.

 • 'And why should they?' observed Myles Rohan, singing the
praises of the various gems in the limestone tiara as he and his
son rattled up to the College gate on a jaunting-car. 'If they
passed a resolution to rebuild Solomon's Temple in this famished
country, cedar, gold, and all, they'd manage to get the roof on by
hook or crook, my hand to you, and start a Bazaar to defray the
price of the precious stones.'

At St. Fergal's they were ushered into a bare, shiny, beeswaxed little reception-parlour, furnished as ascetically as a cell
in the Thebaid; a rough table, with a jug of cold water—it

looked like ice-water—on the same ; an expanse of uncarpeted
floor suggestive of rigid Lenten regulations ; whitewashed walls
staring you out of countenance with their chastity ; and a morsel
of fire in the grate barely sufficient to act as a satiric sting of the
flesh to anybody who should apply for comfort for unmortified
appetites in that quarter.   Another new pupil and his parents
were seated in awful silence there before them.   It was a tall
shambling youth of rude country strength, writhing in his first
suit of black broadcloth under the double disadvantage of having
all the blood in his body jostling in his cheeks, and his arms and
legs glued irrevocably in the uncomfortable postures into which
modesty had first contorted them.   His father was one of those
' strong farmers' who emerged from the Great Famine fat with
the spoils of their weaker brethren, who had departed without
securing as much as a coffin in that ennobling scramble for the
survival of the fittest.   He was a man with quantities of straggling bright yellow hair breaking out in all directions around a
very florid, very freckled face ; and a pair of exuberant scarlet
hands seemed to be engaged in the opposite operation of bulging
out through a pair of brilliant yellow gloves, and indulging in all
sorts of manifestations not provided for by the glove-maker.
His partner was a comely matron, with the cheeks of a thriving
milk-maid, and a ' real sealskin' jacket (which Myles enviously
estimated would purchase out Mrs. Rohan's entire wardrobe), and
accessories of the highest fashion to match :—to wit, a chinchilla
muff through which hands and gloves of pink and green peeped
in and out, a gown of sky-blue glossy silk, and a coquettish little
hat of the fashionable shade of yellow, set somewhat precariously
upon a lofty chignon amidst clusters of red roses and glass
cherries.   They sat demurely together, as though the jug of ice-
water was slowly freezing them, or the stern beeswaxed floor
gradually awing them into a mood to sink on their bare knees
and confess their sins.   They were much impressed by Myles
Rohan's temerity, when they observed him stride across the room,
and with a few vigorous pokes set the sickly spot of fire ablazing
—he was one of those men who never poke a fire without warming
the heart in it.

' I hope they don't expect people to fast from red turf of a
morning like this ?' he remarked.   ' Wouldn't you come to the
fire, ma'am, and warm your toes ?'

The proposition was not in itself a startling one ; but the
lady in some alarm drew in one honestly proportioned foot which
had strayed outside the fortifications of the sky-blue silk, as if not
quite certain that that was not the topic alluded to.   She blushed
and smiled, and looked at her husband.

'Thank ye. It makes no odds. We're only waiting for a word with the Docthor,' said he of the scarlets-and-yellows, half apologetically and half stiffly.

As he spoke a side door opened with a whiff of warm air, laden with vague, generous suggestions, and in glided the Doctor, like the embodied spirit of those cheerier regions inside—'The Doctor' was the half-awesome, half-caressing Irish title of the Very Reverend Marcus O'Harte, D.D., the President of St. Fergal's—a strong-built, massive-headed, precipitous-looking figure, with masses of storm-cloudy wrinkles piled over his eyebrows in the region to which physiognomists assign quickness of perception and swiftness of action ; an upper-forehead, where the ramparts of the reflective powers were rounded off, as in all fine Celtic heads, into an imaginative arch ; a square mouth, which would be a cruel mouth but for a twitch of drollery that now and again trembled at its corners ; and a wonderful grey eye, which always seemed to pierce you through and through, whether with a sun-ray or a dart of lightning. With a quiet, well-bred shake-hands to the address of Myles Rohan and his son, the Doctor passed as softly as a great cat across the room, with a smile and an open hand towards the strong-farmer group.

'Ah ! Mrs. Deloohery, so happy ! Mr. D., you must have had a smart spin across the Bog this morning. And this is our young friend—Patsy, I believe ?'

'Agustine, Docthor, Agustine,' suggested Mr. D., one of whose peculiarities was that, when he required to blush—all the natural reds being exhausted in his normal complexion—he adopted the plan of turning blue over the red, with distressingly apoplectic-looking results.

'Augustine, oh !—the English Augustine, I presume ? How fortunate ! Would you believe it, Mrs. Deloohery ?—he arrives just within the octave of his patron saint. A most interesting coincidence—isn't it ?' The Doctor chucked Augustine under the chin, just as that modest youth had succeeded in completely ruffling the fur of his silk hat in a desperate endeavour to unruffle it. 'We'll make a man of him, Mrs. Deloohery, never fear,' he added, pleasantly.

From this point the conversation grew confidential, Mr. D. assuming an obstinate and incredulous attitude, while the lady conducted the *pourparlers* with excellent ability, albeit in unambitious English. The Doctor's face hardened into polite but icy firmness as, with his fingers playing with the tassel of his biretta, and his eyes engaged in dreamy admiration of the scenery out of windows, Ken overheard his bland, 'In advance, my dear Mrs. Deloohery - invariably in advance !' Then one of the yellow kids disappeared in a breeches pocket, and the Doctor plunged into affectionate researches as to the numbers, ages, measles, and personal adventures of the house of Deloohery, while unhappy Mr. D., who was accustomed to handle his money without kid gloves, conducted the operation of capturing the necessary number of guineas so clumsily that a gold piece tumbled through the gloves to the beeswaxed floor with a flop, and with painful deliberation rolled across to Ken Rohan's feet; whereupon there was a moment of terrific suspense, and that young gentleman presented the coin with his best bow to the afflicted owner, and the afflicted owner looked as if he did not know whether to box Ken's ears for the courtesy, and the Doctor developed a more devouring interest than ever in young Master Aloysius Deloohery's course of treatment for the rickets.

The yellow kids and their sky-blue spouse were at last satisfactorily ushered to the door, and Augustine led away in the custody of a young ecclesiastic. Doctor O'Harte, wearing an austere smile, held the door open for the departing silks and sealskins. Then he closed it briskly, and turning back into the parlour with both his hands extended, suddenly broke forth :—

'Myles, my old friend, how is every inch of you !' The earlier years of the Doctor's ministry had been spent as curate in Drumshaughlin, and a genial curate was never long in finding out that the chimney-corner at the Mill was the sunniest spot in the parish. 'And this is little Ken that used to serve my Mass and steal my pippins ! Why, the young rascal is grown a man on our hands !' He twirled the stripling round in his strong grasp, like a drill-sergeant, noting with a critic's appreciation that, for all his childishness in the world's ways, and all the clumsiness of his black garments, it was a lithe, broad-shouldered, bright-complexioned lad, among whose fearless brown curls he let his broad hand rest for a moment with a rough, mastiff-like kindness—'Come along out of those arctic regions.'

'Not to tell you a lie, Doctor, your face has a pleasanter look than your fire this morning,' said the miller, with a glance towards the dismal little grate.

There was a roguish twinkle in the Doctor's eye. 'We have to do a good deal of freezing with both of them hereabouts, I can tell you. What are you to do with people like our good friends in the rainbow liveries that were here just now? Excellent Christians, and invaluable to their parish priest, but they think their boy ought to be made a priest cheaper than their three-year-olds could be fattened for the Shrove Fair. That woman fought tooth and nail against making the piano an extra—the piano mind you, nothing less !'

'The piano! Blood alive!—I ask your reverence's pardon,' said the miller, rubbing his hands. 'You ought to teach the young man how to dress dolls, or maybe a stitch in embroidery.'

'They *would* be serviceable accomplishments—over in Schkooil Bog. Come, thou irreverent man, I've got the reputation of a rogue—it's my whole stock-in-trade in this wicked world—you'll spoil my character if you get me blurting out candid opinions of the faithful. Come along. Fact is, you broke in on my breakfast, and the only revenge I can have is to make you swallow a share of it cold.'

He led the way to the President's own snuggery, which, after the penitential room outside, glowed like a sunbright Easter Sunday morning after a lean Lenten season. A jovial fire of oak logs and cubes of black peat was leaping and sparkling on the hearth, and upon a table close to the warmth lay the materials of a half-finished breakfast.

'My regimen, like my ague, is chiefly derived from the Campagna,' said the Doctor, as he pressed Myles Rohan into his own easy chair and tossed aside his biretta. 'A dish of stirabout, soused in fresh milk, to begin with; then a bird, or some snack of that kind, with a glass of white wine; and a bunch of grapes or a chunk of melon to wind up with"—gently drawing the cork of his demi-bouteille of Château Yquem étampé, like a violinist drawing his bow across a delicate instrument.

'Well, sir, it may be an old-fashioned prejudice,' said the miller, 'but I like the look of a teapot on a breakfast-table, and I don't greatly fancy fruit, unless of a Snap-apple Night or so, for the sake of old times.'

'As you will.' The Doctor turned to a dumb-waiter glittering with a neat little silver tea-service, whose urn was steaming merrily over a diminutive spirit-stove. It was a parting 'Testimonial' from the parishioners of Drumshaughlin. 'You ought to be able to recognise it, Myles—at least, I know it's you're responsible for most of the silver. The blackguards say I contributed the complimentary inscription myself.'

'Upon my conscience, Doctor, I never take more than one breakfast, and that's down hours ago; but, if something it must be——'

'I know—the best white wine ever grown——'

'Thank you, Doctor—a glass of grog.' There was a smack and a robust dignity about Myles Rohan's way of pronouncing 'a glass of grog'—an air of art in his apportionment of the water to a shade, and his tender poising of the tumblerful of honest gold liquor between himself and the light—a sturdy virtue and deep content in his way of settling himself out to take in the full aroma—which made the President's costly Château Yquem seem the syrup of babes and sucklings in comparison.

Ken had no invincible objection to 'more than one breakfast,' and was soon helping the Doctor through his game-pie with a heartiness for which, after disposing of a fat grouse and a huge segment of crust, he meanly sought to compound by blushing guiltily when he caught his father's eye fixed, half-comically, half-reproachfully on his performance. The truth is, our faithless young Sindbad was beginning to find the Doctor, with his hearty grips and his plump bird on the point of his fork, an even more wonderful being than Boohig.

'Don't be in dread we'll pamper him much with game-pie, Myles. Father Mulpetre has a theory that neck of mutton and vegetable soup make the best brain food going. 'Twould astonish you what medical authority he can cite for it—I am deeply impressed with his erudition myself when it comes to totting up the butcher's bill at the end of the session. Well, but now, my young friend, enough of gossip and game-pie ; let's hear what better you can do than demolish pie-crust.'

The miller listened with earnest edification while the President, stern as a Grand Inquisitor, subjected his new pupil to the torture with defective Greek aorists, and absurd distinctions between Pythrambic and Asclepiadean metres, and details touching one Aristomenes who, he rather thought, was a Messenian hero, and yet, on second thoughts, reminded him of that leather lunged Athenian cobbler :—in all of which ordeal Master Ken, whose sympathies went with the strong-winged bird rather than with the exact sciences of the ant-hill, figured less heroically than in the historical romance which his sister Katie so often constructed for him of winter evenings at the Mill. He saw the President's face darkening. Now that he looked at it more closely, it was a face that could be harsh and pitiless.

'Hark you, sir,' he said, his eye lightening from under the louring brow with a flash that made Ken Rohan, who was not a sheepish boy, drop his own eyelashes and hang down his head. 'You have breakfasted with your father's friend, not with the President of St. Fergal's. I warn you that your father's friend has no place in the business of this College, and from the President you'll get simple justice, raw and unboiled, just as you earn it— no less, and not a grain more. Come out now and know your schoolfellows. Let me offer you two last words of advice,' he added, in a softer tone, 'for Myles Rohan's son : Never lie, and avoid Jack Harold. Come along.'

Ken's schoolfellows turned out to be better than a hundred callow country lads, who, at the President's entry into the study-

hall, formed a dumb and frightened little mob around the rostrum
of a peevish-looking young ecclesiastic, with beady yellow eyes
and a majestic soutane.

'Hallo, a culprit!' said the President, before whom the
boys shrinkingly gave way. 'What's wrong, Father Mulpetre?'

Father Mulpetre lugged forward a diminutive urchin, in still
more diminutive jacket and trousers, whose little body was quivering with suppressed terror, and his little fists dug into the sockets
of his streaming eyes.

'It's Master Mulloy, sir, who's been detected reading "Robinson
Crusoe" during Mass, instead of his prayer-book ; and '—he added
in a lower tone, meant to be caught by the President alone—'it
cannot be the first time, for I never could understand what made
him so attentive at his prayers.'

'Who saw him do this?' demanded the President, sternly.

Father Mulpetre whispered significantly, 'It would be highly
undesirable to make my informant known.' The yellowish gleams
under the overhanging eyebrows were like stealthy skirmishers
from the sharply-graved, perpendicular furrows which ran into a
knot between the eyes, and which appeared to be the citadel of
Father Mulpetre's character.

'Who saw him do this?' repeated the President, without
moving a muscle.

There was a breathless little pause.

'Master Dargan, like a good boy, thought it his duty to mention to me that he watched him reading about the man Friday
during the entire Mass,' said Father Mulpetre.

'Come to the front, Master Dargan.'

'Good gracious, father, it is Lionel—what a sneak!' whispered
Ken, as a smartly dressed youth swaggered forward with a jaunty
and offended air.

The President's face grew harsher. 'Master Mulloy, since you
love "Robinson Crusoe" so much better than your prayers, you
will please retire to the punishment-room, and on your bended
knees recite "Robinson Crusoe" aloud from this until play-hour is
over. You will probably have got enough of the author by that
time. You did well, Master Dargan, if you saw your comrade do
wrong, to have him corrected'—the youngster readjusted his
smart necktie with complacency—'but as you could not have
detected him reading his prayers out of "Robinson Crusoe" if you
had been attending to your own, I must ask you to bear Master
Mulloy company in the punishment-room during play-hour and read
aloud "The Meditations of St. Alphonsus Liguori," which you will,
no doubt, prefer to works of profane literature. Father Mulpetre

will be good enough to see personally that these exercises are performed to the letter.'

'Hourra!' shouted a rebellious voice, somewhere in the thick
of the crowd.

'Who spoke?' demanded the President, in a voice of thunder.
The rising titter was instantly frozen up, and several boys who
didn't do it blushed crimson under the Doctor's remorseless eye.
'He's a coward, whoever he is, and if I had caught him he should
kneel down and beg Father Mulpetre's pardon every day before
meals for a week.'

'Thank you, Doctor; I am proud to leave my boy with you,'
fervently murmured Myles Rohan, squeezing the President's hand,
when they were out again in the corridor. He was delighted with
the Doctor's code of summary jurisdiction; delighted with the
trim, snow-white dormitories fed with the free air of the hills;
delighted with the elaborate heating apparatus—the Doctor's
favourite *calorifère*—which would do almost anything except
work; delighted with the mystic little chapel, steeped in the dim
religious light of pink and blue panes of glass; delighted and
overawed, beyond all, by the Library which, though the shelves
were of painted deal and its contents chiefly elementary school-
books and moral fiction, oppressed the miller only less than a
church with the shadows of unknown powers. There were two
topics on which Myles Rohan, the most stubborn of men, had the
simple, unquestioning reverence of a child—religion and learning.
Start him upon these and his indomitable spirit might be bridled
and driven with a silken thread.

Dr. O'Harte perceived the direction of his thoughts. 'What
humbugs we schoolmen are, to be sure,' he said, with his
boisterous laugh. 'Here you are, thinking you are surrounded
by ghostly regiments of Greek and Latin Fathers, and imagining
—don't tell me!—that midnight finds us with wasted cheek and
hollow eye poring over the secrets of their dread folios. My dear
Myles, the only books I've studied these years back are the
College pass-books—these and my Breviary, and not too much of
that same.'

For all that the honest miller breathed more freely when they
emerged from the oppressive fumes of all this learning into the
playfields, where he amused a party of young racket-players by
proposing to 'take a hand' against any champion of their naming,
and covered them with confusion by beating their champion all
to love.

'Hallo, the honour of St. Fergal's is at stake!' cried the
President, who, on the playground, had relaxed once more into
the chum and big brother of his boys. 'Just hold my soutane,

O'Hara, will you ?—*pro aris et focis*—I'll try a bout with him myself.'

And, whether it was that Myles Rohan's respect for the clergy pursued him even into the racket-court, or that he had met his match in the muscular President, certain it is that the reputation of St. Fergal's was abundantly retrieved, and the miller managed to become more popular vanquished than victorious, and was being escorted to his car in a sort of triumphal procession, when a peremptory tantarara from the Prefect's trumpet announced that play-hour and ' The Meditations of St. Liguori ' were over and re-called the mutinous young enthusiasts to their allegiance.

'Come, boy, your duty now is to obey Father Mulpetre's trumpet,' said Myles Rohan. ' Be off, and—there now, God bless you !'

If Ken scorned to display a tear before the weaker sex at home, he had no scruple—nor, indeed, choice—about bursting into tears now, when he felt his father's brave hand enfolding his own for the last time ; and as Myles Rohan himself strode sturdily away, I think any jury of his countrymen must have found that a certain globule trembling on the brink of his eyelid was as true and overt a tear as ever was wrung from an honest heart, although he would have pleaded guilty to a larceny of spoons rather than to so lackadaisical a show of sentiment. His was a sort of tenderness which is never savage until it is found out.

CHAPTER THE THIRD

BAPTISING THE BLACKS

WHILE our new pupil was wandering at random about the grounds in the fall of that grey January evening, in dismal lone-liness, an arm was slipped through his, and the spruce young gentleman who had spent his play-hour in declaiming the works of St. Alphonsus Liguori to Father Mulpetre sang out: ' Hallo ! so the old fox has pulled you, too, into this infernal hole ?'

' Who is the old fox ?' asked Ken Rohan, simply, ' and where is the infernal hole ?'

'You're awfully green,' said his jaunty young friend. ' A fox is a fox though his reverence is dressed up in a soutane and wears the degree of D.D. as his tail ; as to the hole—if you don't recog-nise St. Fergal's by the description, you soon will. I'm off next half.'

' Oh !'

'Yes, pa is sending me to Trinity—allowance of a hundred guineas—think of that !—dress clothes and four changes, and all the fellows young noblemen, or swells of the first water.'

'All, Lionel ?' The boy was maliciously thinking of Master Lionel's pa—the gombeen-man.

'These clerical schools ain't the ticket,' rattled out his companion, never heeding the interruption. 'A parcel of damned young bog-trotters, and elderly bog-trotters in soutanes set over 'em with birches to flog 'em to their prayers. It is done cheap and the fellows like it—they are reared up to their stirabout and litanies.'

Ken Rohan opened his eyes wide.

'There aren't three clean pairs of gloves in the whole college. And the accent !—well they might teach a fellow either Irish or English, and do the thing above-board. But, no ! they must go and muddle the two together, like jam and trotter oil, and turn you out upon the world with such a confusion of tongues, that I verily believe if you found yourself in the Strand, the policeman could not understand what language you spoke when you asked the way to Temple Bar.'

'Thank you,' said Ken Rohan, with a smile. He had never before listened to such a torrent of daring profanity, it sounded like a passage out of Voltaire or Mrs. Radcliffe ; but having secretly dipped into the works of these philosophers, and being of a somewhat sturdy turn of mind, he was not greatly perturbed by the conceits of the smart weakling, and watched them as he might the antics of a vivacious young monkey. I do not at all say that he had any prerogative to be thus contemptuous ; indeed, Lionel Dargan, although he was Ken's senior only by a few days —their respective mammas having, among many other rivalries in life, timed the birthdays of their various darlings neck-and-neck—had many years odds of him in knowledge of the world of men, if not, also, of the world of books.

'It's all very well for you fellows that want to be priests,' pursued Master Dargan—'you do—don't you, Ken ?'

'So my mother says.'

'Very well ; they will cram you with Christian Classics and catechism right enough ; but is a chap like me, that hasn't your blessed ambition, to go into life and know his prayers, the whole prayer-book, and nothing but his prayers ?'

'I am afraid "The Meditations of St. Alphonsus Liguori" are still running in your mind,' said our malicious Ken.

'Ay, a good plan the old fox took to make me curse them !' said the other, hissing out the words in a way which, for a little boy, was very naughty.

'Then why did you go peeping over that little beggar's shoulder and peaching?' asked Ken, a little hotly.

'Why? Because peaching is the best policy according to the teaching of Father Mulpetre, and I always use the best weapons that are convenient to me. Do you think it wouldn't be more agreeable to my feelings to hurl an ink-bottle at Father Mulpetre's yellow eyes? But I'm no fighting man, you know; I hate fighting men. They are all bullies and boors. So I find I succeed better by minding my prayers and my lessons and being Father Mulpetre's pet; and whatever succeeds is good enough for me. There now, *you* won't peach.'

'You are a philosopher. I don't understand you. How is Lily?'

The philosopher, who had been tossing his head about with considerable self-satisfaction, suddenly looked into his companion's face with a scowl.

'My sister is all right, thank you,' he answered curtly. 'Hallo! there's the Angelus bell.'

'Isn't that her convent at the other side of our boundary-wall yonder?'

'What the devil is that to you? Here's Father Mulpetre;' and Master Lionel, taking off his cap while the bell tolled, was murmuring his evening prayer when Father Mulpetre surprised him in that pious occupation.

How much of boyish home-sickness, I wonder, comes from a wounded heart, and how much from a mere sense of vacancy?—some little want that is no longer satisfied, some face missed at the accustomed hour, some toys broken and the new ones not yet arrived! Ken Rohan had as honest a heart as beat under any little blue-and-white counterpane in that long dormitory, yet it must be allowed that in the life, bustle, and novelty of his first day from home he had taken an almost criminal delight, and that it was not until all these were shut off with the gaslight, leaving nothing but emptiness and strangeness around him, that he found out how bitter a thing is that first plunge from the glowing fireside which has lighted up our childish hearts into the chilly outer world, whose winds howl in the chimney-top, and whose mysterious voices whisper at the casement out of the darkness. Then, indeed, when he was cuddled up in his blankets, luxuriating in the warmth of an extra pair, which his mother, to his disgust, had insisted upon stowing away at the bottom of his trunk, and which the young rascal now discovered to be a by no means superfluous item of luggage (the Doctor's *calorifère* notwithstanding)—then, you may be sure, the four little oaken partition-walls

of his cell dilated into the likeness of his own special snuggery at
Greenane, its snowy little cot with the strawberry-flowered curtains, its print of Sassoferrato's Madonna looking down on his
slumbers with those eyes of almost earthly unspeakable love and
beauty ; his books, sketches, and fishing-tackle tumbled about ;
old Snipe dreaming placidly away with his nose on the hearthrug ; a rose-tree peeping in at the window ; the apple-blossoms
of the little orchard waving underneath (for, to the feverish
dreamer, it is always summer). He could hear the old mill-wheel
mumbling its eternal rounds, like an ancient litany ; hear the
thrush singing blithely out of the neighbouring glen ; hear the
carters' shouts as the flour-bags bumped merrily down the shoot
from the lofts ; hear his father's lusty orders and great hearty
laugh. Here comes Miss Katie, of the timid blue-grey eyes, and
the sunny hair, and the warbling voice, bright as an escaped sun-
beam ; and whose should be that sweet, pale, ever so little delicate face which bends over his bedside now, the tenderest, noblest,
best in the world, her soul welling up to her eyes with such a
yearning, anxious love—whose, indeed ? Is there so desolate a
wretch in all the deserts of existence as not to guess ? And when
he put out his arms to clasp his mother's neck, and found that he
had been asleep, and saw nothing but the cold moonlight shining
into the dormitory, and heard nothing except his young neighbour
Deloohery snoring the snore of the just – there were bitter tears
upon his pillow, which were the less shameful that Ken Rohan did
not remember crying downright until that day, ever since he heard
the men with the heavy boots carrying away his baby sister in her
little satined coffin when he was quite a chit.

    Old stuff, these schoolboy dreams !—old as the schoolboys'
selves, who have dreamt and fought their fight, and grown grey,
and sickened, and died, generations of them—old as the sun
which used to gild their playground, and shines now upon their
graves. As if there was anything new except bacteriology and
electricity, and men and women were going to love and rave and
struggle to the death about *these* ! Our sleeper's dream is over,
however, for as he lies tossing with whatever liberty a narrow
iron bedstead affords him, thinking of that blessed face, and
thinking also, perforce, how sound a sleeper Master Deloohery
must be, the sound of stealthy footsteps in the dormitory struck
his ears, and presently shadows in the moonlight, and now and
again a confused whispering. He listened with some little
thumping at the heart. The footsteps came softly nearer and
nearer to his own cell. They ceased outside the adjoining little
chamber, where Master Augustine was buried in repose. He
could hear a muffled whisper, 'Here's another Black,' whereat

there appeared to be a moment's consultation, and somebody, advancing on tiptoe into the cell, returned immediately, passing the watchword, 'All right !'

All the footsteps shuffled noiselessly in. What with curiosity —perhaps, with a certain indefinite sense of terror—Ken was now broad awake. His own breathing seemed loud in his ears. There was a short silence ; then a half-suppressed giggle, a quick, peremptory whisper—' Chut ! you brat, you're dropping the paint-pot !' Upon the instant a tremendous bellow echoed through the dormitory. Ken sprang from his bed by an uncontrollable impulse. His figure blocked up the entrance to the adjoining cell, just as the half a dozen youngsters within were rushing wildly out against him. They staggered back before the appari-tion, cowering into a corner. 'Father Mulpetre !' passed from trembling lip to lip.

'Poltroons, no, it isn't,' said the same decisive voice that had spoken before. 'It is only the little miller.'

The moonlight lit the place more brightly than the college gas would have done. Ken's wondering eyes took it in at a glance. The central figure of the scene was Master Deloohery, half pro-jected out of bed. It must have been Master Deloohery, but, inasmuch as his complexion had turned shiny black, the identifi-cation was difficult. As the huge, good-natured creature sat there, rubbing his sleepy eyes—his head looking all the blacker in his white nightdress, his ample mouth wide open with wonder, his teeth shining out of negro darkness, his bewildered senses divided between the midnight spirits gibbering around him, and the unctuous black liquid which was streaming down his cheeks— Ken Rohan felt himself struggling sorely between laughter and indignation.

'What the deuce is all this for ?' he asked, looking around at the midnight visitors, who had now recovered their composure.

'Baptising the Blacks,' was the pert reply of a small imp, who was engaged on the floor ladling up the contents of an overturned paint-pot. It was Master Mulloy, the student of 'Robinson Crusoe.'

It must be known that amongst the rebellious lay boarders of St. Fergal's (who, although in a great minority, had the advan-tage that town-breeding, enterprise, and impudence give to wicked minorities all the world over) their ecclesiastical fellow-students (I suppose from the colour of their cloth) passed by the generic name of the 'Blacks.' It was the custom of the incorrigible section of those young bloods, upon the first night after the arrival every year of a new batch of candidates for Orders, to visit each of the strangers in his sleep, and daub a broad black

sign of the Cross over his face, from brow to chin and from ear
to ear, so that when at daybreak they rushed to roll-call, half
awake and all unconscious of the decoration, they confronted
Father Mulpetre in a guise which was an outrageous mixture of
the Christy Minstrel and the Apostle. The Blacks—braw, big-
limbed, simple-hearted country lads—never dreamt of combining
to thrash their small tormentors. They were four to one in
numbers, thews, and weight. They might have broken every
bone in their small bodies; but they bore it, as big dogs bear
the antics of little ones. This, then, was the annual ceremony
which was going forward when, as the irreverent artist was
engaged giving the last touches to Master Deloohery's nose, a fit
of his unlucky laughter took Master Mulloy in the stomach. The
mug of paint, slipping through his fingers, poured over the face
of the sleeper like an eclipse; and the victim, opening his eyes
out of a dream of ghosts and goblins to see them actually grinning and dancing at his bedside by the light of the moon, put
forth a great voice as aforesaid.

'Do you call that fun?' demanded Ken a little hotly.

'We were waiting for your highness's opinion,' said the same
authoritative voice, with all the gravity in the world. 'A Daniel
come to judgment *en pleine chemise*!'

'It is stupid, and it is inhospitable, whatever you say,' pursued
Ken, feeling a little foolish in spite of his virtue, 'and, if I were
he, I wouldn't stand it.'

'You would call your mamma, like a man, or ring Father
Mulpetre's alarm-bell, *n'est-ce pas*?'

'Try.' Ken was stung by the cool insolence of his in-
terrogator, and the obsequious cackle of his little myrmidons.

· 'Precisely what we intended. You were the very next.'

'You do well to approach fellows asleep.'

'By no means. We are charmed to meet them awake, when
they are insolent.'

'That is to say, it is insolent to object to a daubed face for
your neighbours' amusement?'

'*Après*?'

'And the joke is a really good one?'

'As you shall see.'

'So good that, being six to one, you are going to play it off
upon me whether I like it or no?'

'*A merveille!* The miller develops a comprehension the most
brilliant. Mulloy, here with the paint-pot!'

'Then you'll appreciate the sport yourself better than I do,'
cried Ken; and, with a quick movement, seizing the streaming
paint-brush he dashed it into the handsome face of the White

Chief. At the same moment he heard a hurried step behind him, and, turning, found himself in the grasp of Father Mulpetre.

At a rush the whole band of marauders struggled past or dived under the legs of the Prefect. Master Mulloy left a lock of his abundant hair in the disengaged hand of the good Father, and that was all. There was a moment's wild pattering of feet through the corridor, and all was still. The dark shadow of the priest's soutane had even obscured the tell-tale light of the moon within the little cell. In the hurry and half-darkness the culprits were safe from identification. But Father Mulpetre was content to maintain his hold of the ringleader, who still flourished the guilty paint-brush in his hand.

'You !' exclaimed the Prefect, as he turned his prisoner into the light and scanned him with those sharpened eyes of his : 'This is a pretty commencement, sir.'

Ken Rohan's heart sank. He could not reason himself out of the feeling that he was somehow an offender ; how, then, convince the Prefect, who had the most damning part of the evidence under his eyes ? A thought occurred to him. He espied Master Deloohery, who, from the moment he made sure that there was nothing supernatural around, had occupied himself placidly in washing out his dark disguise. He had just inserted his head in the water-jug.

'*He* knows that I am not to blame, sir.'

'Begar, I know nottin' at all, surr !' spluttered out the in- genuous Deloohery, popping up his dripping head, its shock of brist- ling hair on end, its eyes and nose still shrouded in African gloom— with such an expression of puzzled, smiling, frightened sheepishness on his good-humoured face that, for the life of him, Ken Rohan could not choose but burst out laughing in Father Mulpetre's arms.

'This is a very sayrious matter. I'd have you to know, young man, that levity in this college is a thing I will not permit nor to-le-*rate*,' said the Prefect, laying a severe emphasis, like the whirr of a blackthorn, on the final syllable.

And next morning, when after prayers our culprit was affec- tionately invited by Father Mulpetre to 'step this way' into the President's chamber, there was a sort of pious malice under those jagged little eyebrows of his which told Ken Rohan that he had been already tried and condemned. Very terrible, too, looked the President, pacing up and down the cold ante-room in his huge cloak, muttering a Latin Office out of his Breviary, and very unlike the President who had been helping him to game-pie twenty-four hours ago. It was a weakness, to be sure ; but our young friend, in his moment of desolation, somehow missed his father from his side.

'I see only one way out of this scrape for you,' exclaimed the President, without the least preface, suddenly stopping opposite the spot where Ken Rohan was standing expectantly in, I am afraid, a rather ricketty state of fortitude. 'I see only one way out of this scrape.'

The young fellow glanced uneasily up.

'You must tell who brought you into it.'

'That, sir, is impossible.'

'What did you say? I did not understand you.' Ken felt, without seeing, that a pair of dark and angry eyes were frowning down upon him.

'I mean that whatever I did I did of my own motion.'

'You had associates. Father Mulpetre saw half a dozen others in the room with you. Take care!'

'I was only defending myself against them, sir.'

'Then you can have the less hesitation in telling me their names.'

'I do not know their names, sir.'

'That makes no matter. You can tell their faces.'

'I cannot, sir, and even if I could ——'

'Well? Well? And if you could?' repeated the President, threateningly.

'I beg your pardon, sir. I ought not to have added anything. Indeed, I did not see their faces.'

The Doctor resumed his walk up and down the room, wearing a scowl which he seemed to be able to put off or put on as he did his black cap. The young gentleman in the dock was beginning to think that he had, perhaps, forgotten all about him, and had made two choking attempts at a cough by way of remembrancer that he was still glued to the middle of the floor in a highly uncomfortable attitude, when the President again stopped abruptly in front of him, and said:

'I gave you two bits of advice entering this place. Have you made the acquaintance of Jack Harold?'

Ken started at the suddenness of the inquiry, but answered stoutly, 'No.'

'You remember my other advice?'

Ken Rohan lifted up his young face unflinchingly, and down went the scowl before his honest, blue-grey eye, the conscious flush in his cheeks, and the toss of his rough, light-brown curls.

'I believe you. Never do it again.' And with this enigmatical conclusion the President took the boy, half-rudely, half-kindly, by the shoulders, bundled him into the passage, and slammed the door behind him.

Ken Rohan turned away with a heavy heart. The net

result of his first day in St. Fergal's was the equivocal warning
of the President, the unequivocal enmity of Father Mulpetre,
and, worse than all, the antipathy of that very section of his
schoolmates to whom all the sympathies of a bright and active
nature attracted him.   He had wantonly broken in upon their
sport—brutal though it might be.   He had humiliated their
favourite before their eyes.   That he would have a reckoning to
settle with this formidable young gentleman, reinforced by the
sympathies, if not by the fists, of the lads who looked up to him
as a leader, was not the most comfortable, although it was not
the most tormenting, of his reflections.   Bitterer even than to be
taken for a bully or a prig was to be laughed at as the victim
who had been hoist for the transgressions of his enemies.

The President's apartment gave upon a corridor which served
as a recreation-hall whenever the weather out of doors was forbidding.   At this moment it was full of students.   The elders
in the long black coats (which, with a provident eye to further
developments, were invariably constructed some sizes too large)
were marching decorously up and down the flags in twos, making
the highly harmless and inane observations which naturally occur
to persons engaged in that venerable academic goose-step.   The
bulk of the younger boys were collected right on Ken Rohan's
path, in an excited little crowd, around a senior comrade, whose
air of easy self-confidence, no less than his authoritative voice,
which was heard distinctly above the din of tongues, told our
unlucky young friend that he was face to face with his antagonist
of last night.   A rapid glance discovered to him a lad slightly
but gracefully built, of less than his own height and more than
his own age.   His face and dress had a decidedly foreign cut.
His complexion was of that interesting cast which the French
call *le teint pâle aux cheveux noirs* — with a glow of warm colour
suggesting rather than revealing itself in the centre of his sallow
cheeks.   The faintest tinge of moustache over the upper lip, a
mobile pair of eyebrows, a softly-rounded tapering chin, two
small white hands, and a certain air of foppishness in the details
of his dress, might have given him a character for effeminacy
only that his eyes—quick, bright, and resourceful—his active
build and easy carriage, while they converted all these into the
mere incidents of taste and good-breeding, gave him an air of
indefinable superiority over his fellows.

Ken Rohan thought he had never in his life seen so pretty a
fellow.   He felt his heart beat loud and fast as he marched
straight on towards the noisy little army of the White Chief,
whose looks and gestures warned him plainly that they were
waiting to encounter him.

Before he could come within six paces of them, the young foreigner darted out of the group to meet him.

'You were cheeky last night, and you blackened my face,' he commenced.

'I did,' said Ken Rohan, simply.

The youngsters clustered around with boyhood's relish for mischief. They looked admiringly at their champion. His cheeks were pale, but with the most engaging smile in the world he put out his hand, as he said in his minced Parisian tone:

'*Très bien!* I deserved it. Will you shake hands ?'

His words fell like a bombshell. The boys were puzzled and disgusted. They looked into their leader's face questioningly—cruelly—to read whether it was cowardice that had spoiled their sport. That face was frankness itself. Ken Rohan was too confounded to do anything except place his hand simply in the other's.

'It was a bad pleasantry, that Baptising the Blacks, and we never will do it again. Never !' repeated the White Chief, looking around at his growling subjects. 'You have behaved like one brick. I overheard it all.'

'Overheard ?——'

'You have not remarked a *tintamarre*—what you call it ? one grand row—behind the Doctor's fire-screen while he was asking you whether you would know my face ? *Ma foi*, no ? It was I. I came near to stumble over the coal-scuttle. It had nearly spoilt all, *ce diable de* coal-scuttle.'

Ken Rohan laughed in spite of himself. There was a charm in this young fellow's gay transgressions that was drawing his heart out towards him like a magnet.

'The Doctor played a superb Mentor to your Télémaque. I took a note of the dialogue. We shall have a rehearsal in the grand dormitory to-night as soon as Father Mulpetre has mixed his tumbler of punch for the night. You fellows need not come in evening dress—night-dress will be perfectly *bon ton*. Look here,' he ran on, slipping his arm through Ken Rohan's, and marching him off towards a more retired place. 'I like you. I want that we should be friends.'

'With all my heart,' said the other, his eyes sparkling with pleasure.

'It is a bargain ?'

'It is.'

'In testimony whereof the high contracting parties hereto subscribe their—*provisoirement*. What names shall we subscribe ? What does your sister call you ?'

'Ken—Ken Rohan. And you ?'

'Jack Harold.'

Ken Rohan started back as if he had been struck. The other laughed a joyous laugh.

'Hallo! I was forgetting—the Doctor has forbidden the banns. My cell is marked "Dangerous." I bite. I am a walk- ing leper. Every little barque that puts into St. Fergal's must pitch Jack Harold overboard before obtaining *pratique*. Nay, no apology. You are a good boy, and the Doctor will make you a Bishop——'

'Dr. O'Harte has been very kind to me,' said Ken, a little stiffly.

'*A moi aussi*, I can assure you. I dine with him to-day in his own rooms, and it is not twenty-four-shilling Lafitte *née* Clonard he lays before *me*, I can tell you. Avow it, you are afraid of me ?'

'Of your French—yes,' said Ken Rohan, laughing heartily. This stroke decided him. Why should this generous, bright young fellow be condemned unheard, without offence stated, and ruled out of the society of his comrades like an item in the Table of Sins ? It was a noble advice of the President's, never to lie; but what call had the President to smother the instinct which made his young heart jump at this proffer of friendship, or to bid him fly instead to the bosom of a virtuous Master Deloo- hery ? It was his first rebellion. He felt wickedly, but also triumphantly conscious of the fact. He held out his hand.

'Bah! we part with mutual regrets and go to our prayers; *n'est-ce pas* ?'

'Not if you will it.'

'You are one double-baked brick. Mind, I will tell the Doctor after dinner that we are sworn friends *in sæcula sæculorum*.'

'Amen !'

CHAPTER THE FOURTH

BARON DRUMSHAUGHLIN IN THE PEERAGE OF IRELAND

A NIGHT in the beginning of the London season ; and as, at the lifting of a stone slab with an iron ring in it, the Eastern magician steps into an enchanted palace underground, a thousand palaces open in the clammy yellow gloom of the great city, and Ali Babas who are in the secret step out of a half-frozen London fog into lands of delight, where the roses and fruits of the tropics have travelled by special train to perfume the air, and the soft sun, which caressed the Riviera during the day, turns up to fulfil

D

private engagements by night in the voluptuous rose-gardens of the West End. That, at least, I assume to be the Ali Baba view of the pleasures of being whirled through shuddering streets of a February night in carriages with ogre-like flaming eyeballs— very likely the London season, like British match-making, begins in frost and east winds, only that it may end, like it, in a splendrous June of orange-blossoms and sunbeams. But the great family of Cassims out in the cold this particular night in the regions between Grosvenor Square and Park Lane might well flatter themselves with the reflection that if this were indeed the splendid 'land of the midnight sun '—those dead-cold streets with hideous porticoes like mausoleums—silent, except for the stealthy roll of carriages on their eternal weary rounds, like so many Ixions, with restless burning eyes—dark, except where here and there the house where the minister's dinner-party was breaking up, or Lady Grandleigh's dance commencing, was lighted up like the sacrificial altar in some Temple of Night, whose priests were the funereal footmen posted at the crimson-carpeted doorway— Fashion must be a religion as gloomy as the countenances of the gentlemen descending from their carriages, and as fatuous as their countenances when getting back.

Rashleigh Street was one of those sombre streets which hang on to the skirts of Park Lane like a family of poor relations— one of those streets where you expect to see everybody going out for the night and nobody coming in—a retreat of rusty respectability, where great families bent on economies still seek a lurking-place for the season, and preserve an air of distinction over the locality long after the young Irish doctor has set up his red lamp and brass door-plate, and a hardy French milliner her lay figures, and even a butler's widow her announcement of apartments to let. The name of Rashleigh Street, however, had fallen so low that a hansom cabman from the Euston circuit who was wandering irresolutely through one of the streets of mausoleums was obliged to inquire his way from a friend in the profession—a crawler, who was prowling about an East-Indian Club for a late dinner fare.

'Secon' to the left, Chawls. What was the party's name, ole man ?'

'Lord Drum-summut-or-other'—in a confidential whisper— 'one of them bloomin' Hahirish lords, *you* know !'

'Course I do, Chawls—numm'r eighty-five, next the Mews— pleasant ole gen'leman—dyes—ricketty on the pins—tips a cove most 'ansome—all them Hahirish gen'lemen do, when they've got it. Uncommonly pooty gal, Lady Drum's daughter—'ad her to Lady Chumley's dance last night.'

The slide in the roof of the Euston cab is jerked impatiently open. 'Drive on, and be damned to you!' shouts a voice inside.

There is one muddy ray of light in the blackened front of No. 85, next the Mews. Let us track it through the heavy brown curtains into a den which has the air of a study and the smell of a smoking-room. The gas is lowered to a glimmer, and in the blinking underglow of the fire a hideous plaster bust, which might be that of Demosthenes or of the inventor of the spinning-jenny, or (such is fame) of the late Mr. MacAnaspie, husband of the landlady, appears to be making faces at a man propped up in the arm-chair by the fire. Privilege of introducing you—Gentle Reader, Lord Drumshaughlin—Lord Drumshaughlin, Gentle Reader—Ralph Warbro Westropp, to give him his full title, second Baron Drumshaughlin in the peerage of Ireland. Pray, no compliments at this moment. Don't be shocked if his lordship even snarls. That foot which he nurses so tenderly on the cushion has gout at the base of the great toe. The thin white hand drooping over the arm of his chair twitches and contracts from time to time as if clutching an enemy.

Even now the footstep of his valet, muffled as it is, in the room behind him, breaks through his half-doze, and he turns with a tigerish snort of pain:

'Eh! What! Don't stand mumbling there like an idiot. Didn't I caution you not to torment me?'

'If your lordship pleases, the gen'leman hinsisted on my fetching up his card.'

'Tell him to go to the devil—do you hear?'

'Cett'nly, m' lud; only I was to say the gen'leman's just arrived from Hahireland on impottant business.'

'Eh! Who is he! Here with that card. Stand out from me, or I'll strike you! "Mr. Hans"—show him up, Mundle, show him instantly up. Don't shake hands with me, Harman!' he cried, the moment the door opened again. 'Come around behind that sofa—there! How do you do?'

'If your lordship will allow me—it is easier in the long run to have the leg a little more perpendicular—favours the deposit of tophus. There!—after a moment's burning, you will find that better,' said the newcomer, skilfully re-arranging the ailing leg and its oilcloth bandages on its pillows. 'You know, I'm a bit of a doctor, as I'm a bit of most things, in a small way. What have we got here? Colchicum? Hum—the old thing! I'm a believer in gin-and-water. Alcohol is the Cinderella of the medical profession—does all the real work, and is shoved into the coal-hole whenever company call. Shall I pour your lordship out a dose?'

'Excellent, Harman, excellent.   You're a vastly clever fellow
Did you bring any money ?' he demanded all of a sudden.

'Do I ever come without it, my lord ?' was the purring
half-reproachful answer.

'You come damnably seldom.'

'So do your lordship's rents.   I wish I could get them to
travel as fast to the rent-office as they get from the rent-office to
the Holyhead mail,' said the agent, with a pleasant laugh, as he
leisurely searched among the papers in his pocket-book.

'Eh ? what ?—what ?' cried the other graspingly.   'How much
is it ?   Here with the cheque.'

'The Derreenadiarmuida and Lochawvowl collections are not
closed yet   The fellows poured scalding water on Quish, the
bailiff, when he went to warn them for the November gale, and
there will be some delay until we can have them transported
at the Spring Assizes.   Then your lordship will recollect those
allowances for bog-money to the Trafrask tenants that I wrote
you about, and there is one other deduction.   Would your lordship mind if I turn on the gas a bit ?   I have the figures here.'

'Perdition whip the figures !   I shall have gout at the heart
presently.   The tot, man, the tot—and don't torture me with
your damned bog-money and fiddlesticks.'

'2,778l. 2s. 10d. on the half-gale, out of a possible
3,151l. 16s. 7d., less half poor-rate,' said the agent placidly.

'Capital, Harman, capital !' cried Lord Drumshaughlin,
sinking back among his cushions with a complacent feeling that
his own oath-spangled vehemence had somehow contributed creditably to the result.   'If you and I sometimes burn powder
together in a confidential way, I always do you the justice of
saying you were born for an Irish agent.   Egad, you were—
cradled in a clean balance-sheet, by Jove !'

'With a baptismal certificate out of a blunderbuss,' said Hans
Harman in a grim undertone.

'Poor old Ringrose'—his lordship scampered along without
hearing him—'poor old Ringrose was a good fellow, but a bad
agent, a devilish bad agent.   A sensible man would send me my
half-year's rents and pocket his commission, and be done with it.
Ringrose used to send me driblets of money, as if it were alms,
and long lists of grievances that it would take Attorney Wrixon to
make head or tail of.   And they shot him, after all, poor devil,
just as well as if he had got his rents out of them.'

'They are a singularly interesting people, if you study them
conscientiously, my lord,' said the agent, dashing genially into a
favourite subject.   'They hate shillyshallying as a thoroughbred
does.   Put a bungler on his back, and the more he pats and

coddles, the surer the animal is to throw and trample him. But let him once feel—the horse or the Irishman—the right shake of the bridle——'

'There is Hugg's mortgage, two instalments in arrear—and that thing of Rowell's for livery—some wretched funeral horses Lady Drumshaughlin will insist on hiring—the scoundrel is threatening a debtor's summons'—mused the old lord, in a half soliloquy—'won't let me even have a cob for a gallop in the Park to shake up a man's liver—and then there is the MacAnaspie woman, and that confounded ball——By the Lord, 'twon't go within six hundred pounds of it! Did you say two thousand eight hundred——?'

'The exact figure is two thousand seven hundred and seventy-eight pounds, two shillings, and——'

''Twill never do, Harman, not within leagues of it. You know what an infernally expensive nickname an Irish peerage gives a man, and what an enviable animal is an Irish peer.'

'I only know of one of them that he has one of the most coveted titles, and one of the most eligible landed properties in Munster.'

'Stuff! You talk as if you were on the steps of the Drumshaughlin clubhouse. An Irish peerage is an invitation to dinner without the price of a shirt. There are tens of thousands of retired tallow-chandlers and the like within five miles of us who wouldn't put out a newspaper fellow to make room for me at their dinner-tables, and who could buy a better title at a matrimonial agency. Don't you know as well as I do that the little beggar who blacks my boots is in more affluent circumstances than I?—that is, if his wages are paid; I hope they are.'

'Now your lordship is poking fun at me.'

'Fun! I shouldn't be surprised if you hear the woman who lets these lodgings raising her voice before you leave. She is a Mrs. MacAnaspie—was in the army—always attacks when I have the gout. The woman is capable of turning off the gas. Fun! I wish you could see the tradesmen's young men standing in the hall of a morning—a most unpleasant matter. We have been going too fast, Harman—going to blazes—there's the truth for you. What is to be done? We might buy off this she-wolf and pay the tradesmen, and I think we might manage Rowell—it is something under a hundred and fifty, and the animals were atrocious—fit for the Drumshaughlin mail-coach, by George! But there are lots of other things. Horace has got into a deuced expensive set—I'm afraid the boy is doing bills—his Colonel in the Life Guards Grey almost hinted as much to me the other day

at the Chrysanthemum. Then there is old Dargan and there is
Hugg—every time the fellow's name occurs to me, it gives me a
stab in the ankle—and there is that wicked old sister of mine
that must go marry some mountebank scoundrel of a Ritualist,
or a Spiritualist, who is filing a Bill against me in the Rolls
Court for an undivided third, or the devil knows what, of my
father's personalty, whatever that means—maybe the empty port
bottles that killed him, or the coffin that buried him, though
these were got on credit like the rest. Did I tell you about Plynlymmon's little bill in the London and Westminster? It's 600*l.*,
and will have to be taken up on the 23rd.'

'Plynlymmon? A new name in the discounting way?'

'Ha, ha, not exactly. Don't know Plynlymmon?—an invaluable fellow—saves you no end of bother—but the very devil
at baccarat.'

'Oh!'

'And a brazen fellow at producing knaves of trumps, to boot.
I'll have to shoot him if I ever discover how it's done—but then
I know I never shall, and in the meantime I find watching him
as good fun as a fox-hunt.'

'And probably as costly as the foxhounds, my lord,' suggested
the agent, in a tone of confidential chiding.

'If that were all! But the fellow must get it into my wife's
head that we must have a state dinner and evening party in what
the MacAnaspie calls our apartments. I took the place because
it had W. after the address, and I was in hopes nobody would
ever run us to cover; but here we are going to go out in the
highways and byways to beseech the fashionable public to step in
and inspect Mrs. MacAnaspie's conservatory and learn, possibly
from that lady's own lips, that we live on mutton-chops and do
not pay for them.'

'Can nothing be done to impress Lady Drumshaughlin with
the—ahem!—inadvisability of all this?'

'Just you try! No. It's all settled. My wife is only waiting until the tradesmen are paid something on account to give up
the rooms to them. There is to be a universal hiring-out for the
night—window-curtains, hothouse plants, food, footmen, and all
—I believe we are even to have a loan of a few parlours from a
dancing-master downstairs.'

The agent looked as severe as an habitually-pleasant countenance would admit in view of such primrose prattle.

'Lord Drumshaughlin,' he said, with judicial emphasis, 'as
your responsible man of business, and—may I be permitted to
flatter myself?—as one who has some claim to be considered
devoted to the welfare of your house——'

'Yes, yes. A devil of a twinge! O-oh!—Come to the point, Harman, there's a good fellow.'

'I feel it my duty to warn you that those repeated extravagances, following, as they do, upon a long train of embarrassments inherited with the estate——'

'Quite true—thank you, Harman—that was not what I wanted to discuss with you,' said Lord Drumshaughlin, with a haughty wave of his trembling white hand, 'I must have a thousand pounds on the top of this. How is it to be done?'

The agent bowed without the least discomposure. 'Things have not come to such a pass that Lord Drumshaughlin need go far afield for a thousand pounds, if he wants it,' he said, genially. 'I think I can almost answer for it that Hugg, for instance——'

'Do you think so? By Jove, you are Aladdin, and Hugg is your Wonderful Lamp. Do you know, Harman, only you never did a foolish thing in your life, I'm sometimes inclined to think you know more about Hugg than cashing his cheques – ha, ha!'

'I only wish I could find the money to be generous on Hugg's terms,' laughed the agent. 'Do you know that your lordship is paying him seven per cent. all round?'

'Upon my soul, I would be inclined to make it eight, if he would only drop that infernally unpleasant name of his.' Lord Drumshaughlin rattled on in overflowing spirits at the prospect of a fresh shower of gold at his bidding. Money came to and went from him as lightly as air to the lungs; the details of how it came or how it went were the affair of hired men of business, as unworthy of any inquisitiveness on the part of a man of breeding as it would be of a Duke to descend into the kitchen to higgle over the bill for truffles with his French *chef*.

'Quite seriously, my lord, I sometimes think you have dipped too deep with this fellow already—a satisfactory man of business, no doubt, but you never quite know what these foreign fellows are up to. I fancy we can manage it with old Dargan at five and a half or six. Dargan you can always appease by giving him two fingers in public. You might have his immortal soul, if you cared, for a Commission of the Peace. How all this money is to be repaid is another question,' he added, musingly.

'Is there anything to be done, Harman?—is there no way out of it?'

'Why, of course, there are, my lord—a thousand ways,' said the agent, brightening up with a flash of that resourceful wit of his. 'The Muinteravara tenants are the best pays on the estate —most worthy creatures, really—travel across the Bay more punctually than the Castletown steamer to drop the rent into my lap the first office day after it is "called"—they do, I assure you.'

'Well ?'

'Their rents have not been raised within living memory.'

The invalid started and pushed back the silk skull-cap on his poll, glowering at the agent with blazing eyes. 'What do you mean ? I won't have *my* tenants flayed alive, Harman—do you hear me ? By God, I won't !'

'Quite so, my lord—certainly not——'

'Maybe they'd put a bullet through me, and maybe they've put bullets through better men ; but still they're mine. I have a tenderness for them, and I won't have it—that's all – drop it !'

'I am glad to find that your lordship's views so entirely coincide with my own,' said Hans Harman. 'It is the study of my life to do justice to their many engaging qualities, while reconciling them with the obligations of organised society. A man who tries to do his duty fearlessly between landlord and tenant must expect to be a little misunderstood now and then on both sides. God knows it's no pleasure to me to take one of those poor devils from Muinteravara by the collar, and say : "When your rent for the Inch field was fixed, there was nothing on it but bog-water and *birreenuch* that would give a snipe the neuralgia ; that's a capital crop of rye you've made it grow ; let us halve the price of those eight barrels you sold to Sam Prescott last market-day in Bantry." I sometimes think that there is, perhaps, a good deal to be said for shooting us, as your lordship suggests——'

'Eh ?'——

'For, after all, neither your lordship nor I had any more to do with producing Darby Driscoll's crop of rye than we had to do with producing the sun that ripened it.'

'Yes, yes—we know all that from the agitators, Harman '— tartly : writhing threateningly in his arm-chair.

'Precisely, I was just proceeding to observe that this is all upon the assumption (which I can assure your lordship is growing common enough in Ireland without our joining the agitation) that your property is not your property at all, but Darby Driscoll's—at least, the better half of it—because it is he that digs the ground, and not your lordship. I expect every day to hear the man who cooks my dinner claim a partnership in the joint, or Biddy proposing to join us in the drawing-room, because it is she who dusts it. After all, Lord Drumshaughlin,' said the man of business, speaking more rapidly, and in a tone of confident authority which he sometimes assumed as the *pas de charge* of a winning battle, 'is it the more worthy of your name—is it the more honest—to leave your butcher or your hatter without his honest debt in order that your Muinteravara tenants may drink

Congou tea at 4*s.* 6*d.* per lb. and teach their daughters the piano?
It is cruel to the creatures themselves. Their grandfathers were
industrious men on a stone of potatoes. Their grandmothers had
honest red shins, and were not ashamed to show them without
high-heeled boots. A three-quarter firkin of butter fetches just
34*s.* more in Bantry market to-day than it did when your rents
were fixed. You think the difference, which ought to go into
your pocket, goes into the land because Darby Driscoll has been
peddling all his life over that acre of bog? Not a bit of it. It
goes to buy whisky and silk dresses and the rebel papers—or
maybe a charge of slugs that will be rattling around my ears the
first convenient winter's night that offers.'

Lord Drumshaughlin smiled like an indulgent parent reluc-
tantly forced to confess the failings of his offspring.

'You know very well that, when I accepted the agency after
poor Ringrose's affair, it was on condition of reductions of rent
here, there, and everywhere—but I was all wrong. I see it all
now—I was doing what a foolish mother does when she lets a
sick boy shirk his rhubarb powders. An increase of rent—always
a judicious one—judicious and moderate, above all things—stirs
up the virtue in a lazy Irishman. Our bold peasantry, their
country's pride, are like a bottle of prime physic—they require to
be well shaken if you want to get any good out of them. Look
at the fellow that bought your lordship's Tinnaclash estate in the
Encumbered Estates Court—Deloohery, you may remember, that
preposterous booby in the kid gloves and red necktie—he had wit
enough to raise the rents somewhere about 50 per cent. all round
as soon as he could get down a valuator, and his tenants are the
most punctual and hardworking men I know—I am told they
used to go barefooted and pay no rent in your father's time, and
there had to be a Relief Fund every other year to keep them in
potatoes.'

'Egad, Harman, you know the fellows through and through
—there they are like a photograph—ha, ha! We used to say the
only fat man ever seen in Tinnaclash was the sergeant of police.
Well, well, you understand these things—I'm a child and a fool
in business matters—do the right thing and let us have done
with it. Only nothing harsh, mind you—nothing that will make
a pother in the papers. It's damnably unpleasant, getting pictures of coffins, and that kind of thing.'

'Coffins! Good gracious, papa, what a naughty word! I've
caught you!' warbled a voice as sweet as silver at his ear. A
luminous figure in silky white muslin stood behind him and bent
over him till the head touched his cheek : a head of rippling gold
hair, which seemed to emit a brighter light than the gas-burners,

a healthy, blush-rose face, and great dark-blue eyes that made it hard to see anything else when they were visible. 'Poor old papa, what business have those wretched twitches to be teasing him?'

'Why, Mabel, I thought you were at—at something of the Asphodels with your mother, child.' If it was Mundle's velvet tread that had sounded on the carpet, he would have sworn at him. If Mr. Hans Harman had leant across him for the ink-bottle, he would have screamed—poor crusty, gouty old victim! Yet here was a young lady springing at him in the dark, and tossing his old head unceremoniously about in her caresses, and he was submitting like a Sultan in a bath of rose-water. If there was any one object under the sun that Lord Drumshaughlin loved more than Ralph Warbro Westropp, it was his daughter. 'Wasn't there something or other at the Asphodels'?'

'Something, you droll papa! The Marchioness's ball that Captain Plynlymmon nearly went on his knees to beg cards for!'

'Captain Plynlymmon is a humbug. He'd have gone on his knees to beg you to accept them—and good business enough for him, too,' he broke in testily. 'But how come you here, child? Not beginning to find these things slow already, Mab, eh?'

'Slow! Oh, papa, it was fairyland!—and such fun! Did you ever notice Mr. Neville's style of waltzing?—Mr. Neville of the Greys, you know—Horace's stable-companion, as he calls him. Do you know I gave him three waltzes on purpose to see him go around?—I'm sure those terrible English ladies thought it very wicked—they didn't seem to see the fun at all.'

'Hum!'

'And you are frowning, too, papa—you an Irishman! How lucky I did not call him Reggy!—he's such a dear, awkward, friendly brute. I assure you I was strongly tempted. But, Oh dear me! there came one of poor mamma's dreadful headaches — the heat of the rooms, I suppose; though it all seemed to me delicious—so Captain Plynlymmon brought us home, and mamma's headache is rather better, and I have come to dear old pappy to tell him what a very selfish, bad humour I am in, and to get his absolution.'

Mr. Hans Harman had tried various gentle hints and signals of his presence in *chiaroscuro*. He thought it time to burst out at last into a perfect rocket battery of 'Hem, *hum*, HUMMS!'

I am afraid her ball-room critics would have been confirmed in their ill-opinion if they could have seen how little scandalised she was to find that there had been an unknown listener to her confidential babble. She darted a pretty little startled look in the direction of the voice—she could not help it—and then put out a hand and arm that might have been sculptured of 'rose-misted marble,' saying simply :

'Oh, Mr. Harman, it is you ! I beg your pardon for breaking in—I took it for granted I would find papa alone. How is Harry ?'

'Yes, egad, how is Harry ?' chimed in Lord Drumshaughlin, starting forward in his chair as if he had received a smart blow on the back, and running his fingers guiltily through the few glossy side-locks that still flourished outside the skull-cap. 'The very thing I wanted to ask you, Harman—how is Harry ?'

'His health, Miss Westropp, I am glad to tell you, was never more robust—ahem !'

'Yes, yes, I know what you mean. He won't learn his lessons.'

'That is all over long ago,' said the agent, smilingly.

'Harry never could make much of the Latin grammar since I left Drumshaughlin. We used to sing the Declensions in duets. We had several of the conjugations set to Moore's Melodies, but Harry would insist on turning them into comic songs, and pro ducing, oh ! such a medley !—he had some nonsense or other about "Slap Bang" for that horrid old Pluperfect tense. Well, it *was* horrid, and the poor boy couldn't help it—could he now, Mr. Harman ? Is that all ?'

'All, Miss Westropp ! I never dreamed of framing an indict-ment against my excellent young friend,' protested Hans Harman warmly.

'Of course not. That means that he has been doing some-thing very wicked. Smoking tobacco ? I am sure he smokes tobacco. Or maybe laming my little chestnut after the Beagles ?'

'No man in the hunt has a prettier seat in the saddle.'

'Or raising an insurrection ? We always wanted to take to the hills, and raise the green flag—he and I.'

'In the interests of the poor non-insurgents, I sincerely hope you won't try—he or you. The people would die for him. "The Lord Harry" they all call him.'

'Poor Harry !' The full dark-blue eyes were gazing seriously straight into the fire, while she beat a tiny white hand with her clenched fan. Lord Drumshaughlin's fingers began to drag ner-vously at his old curls—a way he had of appealing against his conscience to his temper. The words were working in his veins like poison. A moment after she was penitently sucking out the poison of her two little words, with all sorts of distracting ques-tions as to who was making most golds in the Drumshaughlin Archery Club's practices now ?—and was the Bachelors' Ball in Bantry really coming off ?—and was Mrs. Motherwell's (the

Rector's wife's) new baby a boy or a girl?—and was little Floy
Motherwell quite over the scarlatina, and was it very bad in town
still? (for, in spite of all the dazzling crush of her first Queen's
Drawing-room, Drumshaughlin was still 'town' to this unspoiled
London *ingénue*). Having coaxed the conversation into those
drowsy regions, she seemed suddenly to bethink herself: 'Of
course you had business together all the time that I've sat chattering here, only Mr. Harman was too gallant to hint it—yes, but
I'm sure you had. Why didn't you turn me out, papa?' and she
bent her head so low that papa must needs draw the culprit gently
towards him, like a miser fondling his treasure of gold. 'Well,
there now, I'm off. But in half an hour you must let us have
Mr. Harman down to supper. Mamma's headache is all but
gone, and I'm dying for all Mr. Harman's news from home.'

'What did you mean by your hints about that boy?' demanded Lord Drumshaughlin, brusquely, as soon as she had left
the room. 'Is it drink?'

'I did not mean to convey anything alarming, my lord—by
no means. Mr. Westropp is a young fellow for whom, in common
with the warm-hearted peasantry among whom he delights to
make himself at home, I entertain feelings of the most sincere——'

'Do skip the superlatives, Harman. It worries me,' interrupted Lord Drumshaughlin, brutally. 'Is there a woman?'

'As your lordship will have me put a painful matter rudely,'
proceeded Mr. Hans Harman, who could be at need either as
diffuse as the Dr. Johnson of the Dictionary or as terse as the
Dr. Johnson of the Mitre Tavern, 'I feel bound to warn you as
his father, that Mr. Westropp spends more of his time about
the stables than is to a young gentleman's advantage; that
Quish, the bailiff, enjoys the principal share of his confidence;
and I am not sure but he is writing love-letters to the miller's
daughter——'

'The devil he is! Thank you, Harman. That's a good
fellow. I was thinking so,' said Lord Drumshaughlin, half to
himself, letting a face seamed with deep yellow wrinkles droop
heavily over his chest. He looked up quite brightly in a moment.
'Harman, I have a liking for that boy, and I won't have him
come to mischief—do you hear? You shall manage his allowance,
and take him to live with you at Stone Hall—won't you?'—his
voice dropped with a sudden spasm of doubt.

The agent bowed his head cheerfully. 'An honour and a
pleasure; but it will be still better if your lordship can find
him something that will interest him—something that will employ him.'

'That will come all in good time,' cried his lordship, with the exultation with which he always either renewed a bill or adjourned a difficulty. 'I have it all mapped out. We can carry our county, I presume?'

'As securely as we can eject a tenant—that is to say, of course, with a hint or two about Disestablishment in our man's address, to keep Monsignor McGrudder in good humour. You would put Mr. Westropp into the House?'

'Good heavens!—nonsense. The Chief Secretary is hungering to get Glascock, his Attorney-General, into the House to talk blarney for him. Old O'Shaughnessy is drinking heavily, and threatening to withdraw the Irish Vote unless the Ministry demand the extradition of Garibaldi, or kiss the Pope's toe, or something. He cannot hold out much longer. If he is not in *delirium tremens*, they will have to stuff his mouth with something. Very well—that is all settled—the Chief Secretary can have the county for Glascock, if he's ready to pay for it. My wife wants an English peerage. So do I. But I want first something in the Colonies for Harry.'

CHAPTER THE FIFTH

SAINT CECILIA

KEN ROHAN was not long in St. Fergal's before he knew that Jack Harold, in the teeth of the President's warnings against him, was a privileged person. Having been bred up to the pretty graces and vices of schoolboy life in Paris (where his father had been, up to the time of his death, a physician in one of the poorer northern suburbs) he could do a number of things which in Clonard might well pass for genius; he could turn the song of 'The Shan van Vocht' into jingling Latin; he could remove the celestial and terrestrial globes and substitute a mock pair, charged with powder, which would explode at a touch from Father Mulpetre; he could make his own songs, sing them, and play them—meltingly on the fiddle, like a charge of cavalry on the pianoforte; he could, as occasion required, enact Brutus in the play of 'Julius Cæsar,' or Dr. O'Toole in the farce of 'The Irish Tutor,' and bring down the house in both; it was he who painted the scenes which were the admiration of rural mammas on speech-day every summer; it was he who modelled the *togas* of the Senators (with the help of the College tailor); he taught those clumsy little Romans what to do with their legs and arms, his own hands attached to the neighbourhood of the heart of Julius

Cæsar the bladderful of blood which he was presently to shed ; on all things, from the colour of gloves to the plotting of a mutiny, he was the glass of fashion and the mould of form at St. Fergal's —a young person whom every mamma, who came once a year to see great Cæsar die, longed to see her darling imitate, even though it was rumoured that Master Harold smoked cigarettes. It is easy for me here to observe that his attainments were rather broad than deep, rather brilliant than accurate ; but boys do not break their idols as they do their toys to know what is in them. Of what consequence was a miserable rule of syntax to a fellow who could chirp Béranger's choruses like a bird ? He used to say himself that the Great Bear was the only constellation on the globe he could get into his head, because he had painted him to the resemblance of Father Mulpetre, with the addition of a yellow moustache and a black pipe ; and the boys admired his ignorance immensely. What, indeed, had a chap like that to do with beggarly little stars ? Dr. O'Harte, no doubt, judged more wisely ; but Harold had a ready wit, a fertile brain, not a bad heart, and a turn for a thousand things ; and was, besides, an ornament and a centre of culture in St. Fergal's. He was, therefore, sedulously maintained there at a reduced pension (his mother having been left poorly off, and his uncle, who paid the pension, being only a country curate). There was some vague consideration as to his assisting in the teaching of French conversation. Except that in ordinary speech he stumbled frequently into what was in fact his native tongue, this condition was never put in practice ; and far from owning any position of dependence, he lived as a benevolent despot among his fellows, and claimed, even from his seniors, the privileges of a valued, though somewhat dangerous favourite.

One of these privileges was the possession for his sole use of the small circular chamber in the small foolscap tower which ornamented an odd corner of the college buildings. He called it 'the Observatory,' and was very proud of it. The name was very likely a tribute to an old-fashioned telescope, which stood there mounted upon a brass carriage, gazing out upon the heavens with a wise look which would never have led you to suspect that one of its eyes was out—the far one. The telescope was bequeathed to Jack by a whimsical old professor who loved stargazing and loved Jack, and by a bad syllogism arrived at the conviction that Jack's interest in the stars must be as great as his own. The poor man denied himself for four years his annual vacation trip to the Lisdoonvarna Sulphur Spa in order to save up the price of his telescope ; and as soon as the telescope arrived— it was a second-hand Guinaud of some pretensions—his rheuma tism mounted to his head, and he mounted to the stars without the help of the telescope. I am afraid you will not think the better of Master Jack for knocking an eye out of his legacy ; but Master Jack was a cherub wholly without wings. He wept over the dead body of his poor old friend ; but, having no enthusiasm about his poor old friend's stars, he gouged out with much neatness the disc at the larger end of the Guinaud, and made the interior the receptacle for a long clay pipe, a paper of cigars, a sixpenny 'Count de Monte Cristo' rolled up small, some keys to the classics, and other contraband articles over which Father Mulpetre had the authority of a moral gauger. The instrument still kept its sightless socket fixed in solemn contemplation on the firmament, with such perfect good faith that Father Mulpetre, who was shortsighted and could never see anything through a telescope except black things, did not for a moment dream that he could see any better by looking through the wrong end. However, Jack Harold's little Alsatia was seldom invaded, even by Father Mulpetre. It was approached by a short spiral iron staircase, and being remote from the bustle of the house and lighted by two funny little windows from the north, was in every respect an eligible retreat for a young philosopher and artist.

'*Hic arma ; hic currus,*' as the young gentleman himself impudently remarked when showing Ken Rohan the Observatory for the first time ; and Ken liked even his impudence so well that he spent more of his time than was good for him in this foolscapped little Mount Ida. It was to him a museum of endless curiosities and novelties. There was a fiddle. There was a fairy little fan, whose leaves glowed with real butterflies' wings of many colours, gummed on by some preservative process of his own (Jack Harold had no respect for the feelings of butterflies). There were many little retorts and blow-pipes, and tall glass phials with nothing in them, and a small battery to match. He loved chemistry just enough to blow out every pane of glass in the two funny little windows on one occasion with an unexpected explosion of carburetted hydrogen. There was always an easel with an infirm leg planted against something or other, and a palette of chaotic wet colours, and strange little bottles of oils, and narrow little tinfoil tubes with clammy drops of Naples yellow or Persian red oozing out of them. He was nothing if not an artist. There was a small escritoire with ever so many appetising little drawers in it, and an appearance of holding something queer or precious in them, every one. He could show you the bullet which killed Baudin. His father, who had been beside him on the barricade, extracted it, and was shot himself the next day in the Rue St.-Séverin. Another of his treasures was a scooped

potato in which he had inserted a dial-plate with clockwork of
the most ingenious description, which would do almost anything
except keep time.

'You have always something new!' Ken would exclaim, in
rapture, upon one of his visits.

'Yes, only mind what you're rummaging about there. That
is fulminate of silver in your hand. It is going to blow down
this little chamber if you don't take care.'

'You made it yourself?'

'I made it myself, and I am sure I made it wrong. I know
it will go off. Lay it down, then!' cried the artist with an impatient little stamp of his foot, looking up from his painting.

'You are the most wonderful fellow in the world!'

'Very well, come and look at my St. Cecilia. I go to stake
my fame there.' He drew off his brush for a complacent survey
of the half-filled canvas before him, a crude copy from memory of
Raphael's picture of St. Cecilia, letting the instruments of earthly
music drop from her hands as her ears drink in the first rapturous sounds of the harmonies of heaven.

'Hallo!' cried Ken Rohan, stopping suddenly.

'What, then? Don't you find her charming, my *ange aux
grands yeux bleus?* The Doctor is going to present her as an
altar-piece for the cathedral. I don't think he shall get her. I
shall keep her for my own private devotions. She is adorable—
not so?'

'You don't mean to say that is St. Cecilia?'

'Not Raphael's—mine. The Doctor has remarked the same
thing! "But St. Cecilia has not blue eyes and yellow hair like
that," he says. He knows every saint and madonna in every
church in Italy, that wonderful Doctor! "Ah!" I respond, "but
you understand blue eyes better in Ireland." He has looked very
serious at that, and has bored me through with that Holy Office
eye of his ; nevertheless, my St. Cecilia has not been burned as a
heretic. But, I say, Ken—how do *you* know that the St. Cecilia
has brown eyes?'

He turned abruptly round towards Ken Rohan, who had
been standing behind him ; his eyes were fixed upon the canvas
with an annoyed sort of interest, and the question brought a red
flush over his forehead

'What! you know our St. Cecilia, and are jealous. Confess
it!' the artist cried half gaily, half maliciously.

'I—I almost think—I hope not, but——'

'Yes—yes—my friend?——'

'You—you don't know anybody that is at school at the
Calvary Convent—there?' pointing through the window towards

an adjacent block of buildings of the same character as the
college.

'But yes! hourra, I am so charmed. The portrait is then
perfect! But, I say, Ken—this is a secret of the most profound
—you shall not betray me?—word of honour?'

'You are joking, you are not going to play this trick upon
people in the house of God?'

'But yes. One need not be ugly to be a saint. I have promised the picture to the Doctor. For the rest, I could not help
it. I fell in love with my St. Cecilia, and could not refuse her
blue eyes ; also, to say true, I forgot how to mix the proper shade
of brown.'

'Then I—I suppose you know her pretty well?—well, enough
to—to do this sort of thing?'

'And why not?' with a malicious little shrug of his shoulders
and eyebrows (which, after the French fashion, worked by the
same spring). 'Look then. You see yonder tourelle on top of
the Calvary Convent?' He pointed towards the little foolscap
turret at the nearest angle of the neighbouring convent ; it
stood not more than three hundred yards from the northern angle
of the college ; with only a high boundary wall and the foliage
of the tops of the trees in the convent grounds visible between.
The same architect, having built the two buildings upon very
nearly the same plans, the two corner towers bore a strong
family likeness to one another, except that the ladies of the
convent had turned theirs into a little conservatory, windows
all over. 'Very well, that is St. Cecilia's shrine. She comes
there whenever there is a poetic sunset to look at it, and, my
faith, the sun in heaven is not so beautiful to look at as herself.
The sunset inflames the glass around her like the gold background
of a Fra Angelico.'

'Oh! is that all?'

'Do not impatient yourself. That is only the raising of the
curtain of my little drama. There flutters about the convent
one old pigeon whom the Reverend Mother loves. His dovecote
rests against the tourelle. I catch the little beast, pour out my
soul into a charming billet, attach it to the pigeon's leg, and—
voilà! a pigeon-post of the most commodious installed between
us.'

'You don't mean to say you did this?——'

'Assuredly I considered it a *chef-d'œuvre* ; but genius obliges
one to be candid, as well as modest.'

'And—and—that she was a party to such conduct?' stammered Ken, falteringly.

'And responded with billet still more charming in English,

E

still more conformable to the rules of your perfidious grammar—why not?'

'Stuff! This is outrageous. I do not believe it!' burst out the other, with flaming eyes.

That curious pallid spot which we have seen once already declared itself in the centre of Jack Harold's cheek. 'You do not believe it! Do you know what that wishes to say in French?' he said, his lip slightly paling and trembling. There was something in his look that strangely touched and disarmed the younger man.

'Jack, I should not have put it that way. Perhaps——'

'There is no perhaps. My dear boy, do not believe half what I say; only you need not always mention that you don't believe it. You are right, perfectly. She never did answer me.'

'But your brave pigeon——'

'My brave pigeon was a fool. In place of flying back to St. Cecilia, the imbecile wobbled about the grounds for some moments and then directed his steps towards the Reverend Mother, who, it seems, was in the habit of feeding him about that hour. The Reverend Mother did not do justice to my genius. She made me a magnificent row. The Doctor held a Grand Inquisition to try whose was the handwriting of the little billet. As for me, I have six, ten, twelve handwritings, as it pleases me; and the pigeon, you conceive, could not peach, though he was stupid enough for anything, that devil of a pigeon. In effect, nobody dared to accuse me; but an excellent young man with a brogue, who is reading for the Church, came very near to be expelled, and he really deserved it—his handwriting was so like.'

'Did you see her often afterwards?'

'Hallo! has not the Grand Inquisition concluded?' He looked up again into Ken's face, which was again burning red. 'I say, Ken; I go to tell the Doctor you are blushing about a young woman. You are in love, sir, and with my St. Cecilia—we shall blow one another's brains out, at your convenience; not so?'

'I can't bear that sort of thing,' said Ken, hotly. 'She's nothing to me. You know that. We were children together—that's all.'

'Oh! that's all,' repeated Jack Harold, with an enigmatical smile. 'Then, I may tell you I meet St. Cecilia several times when the young ladies of the Calvary take their promenades; she passes close to me; she no more sees me than if I wore a coat of darkness. But the pretty little devil, her friend—she of the piquant, little curly head—comes up behind me one day and slips into my ear: "Ha, ha! I'll tell!—who's sending love-letters to the Reverend Mother?" Bah! they wrung the neck of that pigeon—it is my only consolation. St. Cecilia never again is seen in her shrine. But art does not die with a pigeon; it does not lay down its arms before a Reverend Mother. I dream my dream; I construct my shrine; I create my saint—*la voilà!* And, my faith, the Reverend Mother shall yet kneel to my St. 'ecilia, if she expects grace.'

'Jack, you have no right to do this thing. It is a shame.'

'How?'

'In the first place, it is almost a sacrilege——'

'The least in the world. So are half the Madonnas. Well?'

'Well, I—I have no right to forbid it; but Lily Dargan is one of the purest and loveliest children in all the world, and—and——'

'Oh, that!' The artist scanned his young friend's face attentively, dismissing his air of pretty impertinence for one of curious intelligence. Ken Rohan was stumbling for a word when this sharp little exclamation completed his confusion. He felt stupid and worried and cried:

'It—it is not that. You do not understand me——'

'But I do;' and without another word the artist, who had been dipping his brush in a little black puddle on his palette, drew it quietly but rapidly across the face of St. Cecilia. The beautiful vision was gone. The face like a Seraph's, the tender blue eyes with the raptures of heaven in them, the yellow sunshine of the hair, were all buried under a shapeless black daub.

'Heavens! what have you done?' cried Ken Rohan, bounding with pain. It was as though a murder had been done under his eyes, and that he was the cause of it. The painting would have fetched about 1*l*. 5*s*. in the market without a frame; but it was a work of which a schoolboy would be very proud, and which, in Ken Rohan's eyes, if it were only for the likeness, was a work of genius. It was his meddlesomeness and petulance that had brought it to destruction. It was in order to satisfy his stupid scruples—or was it not rather his jealousy?—that Jack Harold had thus at a stroke sacrificed the fruit of all his dreams and genius. And what call had he, Ken Rohan, to have meddled or felt sore? After all, was Jack Harold the first painter of sacred pictures who had sought his inspiration from the beautiful forms around him? His St. Cecilia, too, was as beautiful and innocent as any saint could be; so Ken told himself; that entranced upward look of hers had the light of heaven in it. Was it that it would have cost him the same pang to see Lily Dargan painted in any shape by anybody? but especially by a young fellow with genius and with a pretty moustache? Nonsense! Ken Rohan

only remembered Lily Dargan as a child with whom his sister
Katie and himself used to play about the Mill and up the glen of
sunny days until one of the thousand little Bianchi and Neri wars
of a country town put their two families asunder. She was to
him no more than the pretty Red Ridinghood of his childish
reading. The meaning or the sensation of love was to him as
unknown as the meaning or sensation of gout. Yet here was he
setting up to be the censor of what was and what was not per-
missible in her regard, and ruining a work of unknown value for
the sake of his imbecile whims. 'Heavens! what have you
done?' he cried, in a perfect agony. 'You misunderstood me
cruelly. What a cursed ass I was! It is perfect murder——'

'Only a sacrilege,' said the artist, with a smile, 'and—the
least in the world.'

'Oh! Jack, can you forgive me?'

Jack looked up with a complacent little smile into that earnest
friendly face, so hot and honest. He thought that he knew more
about Ken Rohan's heart than Ken Rohan knew himself.

'There was three-and-sixpence worth of paint in that head of
hair—there was truly. Black does not cost so much. We shall
say twopence-halfpenny for that daub; and one fine pair of eyes
—say tenpence. In revenge you shall feed me with sixpenny
novels, and pay me an indemnity of raspberry jam—you have,
then, such a wealth of raspberry jam!' he pronounced it—'raas-
pairy ghaam.'

'Jack, can't you be serious? God knows how sorry I am!'

'Serious—so serious that I intend never to forgive you—
never, unless——'

'Unless——'

'Unless you shut up on the instant. *Allons!*' and he commenced leisurely with his brush to make a new flesh-ground where
St. Cecilia's darkened face had been.

'In ten little minutes we shall have a perfectly ugly and
respectable St. Cecilia who shall disgust the public with the things
of this world and turn their thoughts towards their prayers.
You see?'

'Jack, you are not really sorry. I do not mean about the
picture—about——'

'About St. Cecilia—I know,' said Jack Harold, with a little
laugh. 'Think you, then, there is but one saint in my calendar?
You shall see.'

And a week or two afterwards, as the boys were pouring
out of a class-room into the exercise-hall, Jack Harold slipped
his arm in his young friend's, and whispered in his ear, 'I
have shown you my St. Cecilia. Come with me to-night and you

shall see my Magdalen.' The young lady thus unceremoniously
described by this young scamp was the first young lady of a
tragedy-comedy-burlesque company which was at that time per-
forming for six nights only—(which, however, swelled ' by special
desire ' to rather more than eighteen)—in the ball-room of the
Palace Hotel at Clonard. The tragedy-comedy-burlesquers, who
were, indeed, the original Olympic company from Cork, made a
very great stir in Clonard, and Dr. O'Harte, who liked that boys
should be boys (as with equal honesty of purpose Father Mulpetre
liked that boys should be jelly-fish), had secured for his youngsters
a discreet glimpse of the glories of Olympus at a special midday
performance. The gods and goddesses were, however, put upon
their best behaviour for the occasion. Daylight makes things
wonderfully dull in Olympus. The play was, by arrangement,
that irreproachable one of ' Virginius ;' the Olympics did not shine
in what was irreproachable ; and the boys came away with the
conviction that their own ' Julius Cæsar ' had quite as much fine
language in it, and that Jack Harold's scenery was infinitely
prettier. Jack Harold himself had the instinct of the artist or
the vagabond too much ingrained in him to deal thus supercili-
ously with the players. In fact he had contrived to make the
acquaintance of the manager in the bar of the hotel before the
performance commenced at all, the manager being an ill-shaven
gentleman with an enormous diamond ring which was not a
diamond and an enormous sealskin coat-collar which was not
sealskin—and when the boys were departing to buy their oranges
and go back to school, Jack was observed leading in Virginius
himself to a frugal 'gloss o' bittah,' as that great person described
his nectar. After pretty fair 'business' for a fortnight, the good
people of Clonard got tired of seeing the Olympics or of paying
to see them. A brilliant idea came into the head of the manager
—he of the seal and diamonds—who rather prided himself upon
great combinations. He published a grand benefit night for the
first young lady, when the company would be assisted, positively
for this occasion only, by A DISTINGUISHED LOCAL
AMATEUR, with four notes of admiration of the most thrilling
character appended. I don't know how it came to pass between
the man of diamonds and Jack and the Doctor—whether the
reduced price of tickets to the midday performance had anything
to do with it ; or whether Dr. O'Harte, who in the case of any
other boy in St. Fergal's would as soon have rammed him into
the kitchen boiler and turned on the hot water as he would have
consented to his appearing upon the public stage, regarded the
Distinguished Local Amateur as a being perfectly *sui generis*, to
whom the society of vagabonds could do no more harm than he

could do to the vagabonds. What is certain is that the grisly man at the college gate raised no objection when the Distinguished Local Amateur passed out that evening after dusk. He growled, though, when Ken Rohan attempted to pass out with him and said he didn't know ; he had no orders. 'You have mine,' said Jack Harold, coolly pulling his friend after him through the wicket and banging it behind them.

How different Olympus looked by gaslight ! Ken Rohan, who had a very sufficient gift of imaginativeness surging up within him, was dazzled. The manager's combination had been a complete success, and he stood at the door like a Napoleon looking on at a winning battle. Every young man who was in love with the first young lady—that is to say, every young man of the least spirit in Clonard—came to honour the first young lady's benefit ; but several hundred people who did not care twopence for the first young lady, nor for the Shakespearean drama, 'walked over one another' (as the manager observed in the bar) in the struggle for places, in order to see who was the Distinguished Local Amateur and what a fool he would make of himself. There were even some august people in the front seats who had fans and wore something which was not full dress, but which yet was not the dress of common men and women ; and among these fine people there were two or three white or blue opera-cloaks. What between this slight perfume of aristocracy and the rakishness of the gasaliers, and the rataplan of the band, and the excitement of the young men of spirit who were hammering their sticks against the front of the gallery whenever they were not hurling derision at a miserable man with a white hat, Ken Rohan felt in the ecstasy of his heart that this was, indeed, seeing life. What a fool he was not to see the dingy old hangings and the tallow-candles that answered for footlights, and the dirty-looking man in the dirty shirt-sleeves, whom you could have seen emptying his pot of porter as Jack Harold lifted a side curtain and disappeared behind the scenes ! What fools there are in the world, to be sure —perhaps luckily for us wise men !

It must be confessed that upon the tragic stage the Distinguished Local Amateur was not a success. I dare not tell in what tragedy of Shakespeare, or in what character of the same, he tempted the public patience ; but the public yawned, with a dim perception that it was not the thing, although they were not in a position to say critically whether it was or not. The fourth act was dropped altogether, to the relief of a rejoicing public, and I believe the young gentlemen in the gallery derived more pleasure from that one white hat than from all the genius of William Shakespeare and of the Distinguished Local Amateur put together. But

in the burlesque he was really fine. It was something about the
freaks of the gods in Olympus, and in the character of Jupiter
Tonans he danced Irish jigs and sang Irish comic songs, with
local allusions in them, which brought down the sticks of the
gallery in a manner that threatened to bring down the gallery itself.

Ken Rohan saw none of it, and heard not one word. He
could see nothing but a pair of soft, dark eyes, with which Cupid
was doing deadlier execution than with the classic bow and
arrows. Cupid was the first young lady in a pair of silver-grey
wings and an adorable lavender tunic. He (or rather she) had
a delightful manner of appearing sad in the intervals of stage
gaiety, and of throwing a pair of languishing dark eyes around
her, as though pining for Psyche. Ken could have sworn that
several times the languishing dark eyes rested on *him*; and
they went as clean through him as an arrow stuck through a
heart on a valentine. I am afraid he was only a little wrong,
and that the eyes rested not exactly on him, but on a young
officer of the Killorglin Militia sitting behind him, who was the
most fashionable young man in Clonard. Ken Rohan would as
soon have thought that the stars in heaven were making eyes at
anybody because they were shining, as that his goddess could
have any thought about the militia. She looked so ethereal
among the silver clouds! But what insolence on the part of that
Jupiter to chuck her under the chin in that familiar manner!

'Well, how did you like the Distinguished?' said great Jove
himself, when, the performance being over, Ken Rohan waited
outside the red curtain as appointed until his friend had washed
off his godhead and rejoined him.

'She's the loveliest being I ever laid my eyes upon,' said Ken,
fervently.

'She! Hallo, this is atrocious—you are a perfect Barbe
Bleue! You carry off my St. Cecilia——'

'Oh, bother!'

'And the moment you lay your eyes upon my Magdalen, you
must devour her also. You monster!'

'Jack, how I wish I could act like you!' he cried, as the two
friends were stealing home under the boundary wall of the
college. 'Do—do you think a fellow might learn?'

'To make a fool of himself—yes, and to take Cupid's innocent
tricks with those pretty eyes of hers *au grand sérieux*. It's after
hours. We shall have to climb over that wall. It is an old
dodge of mine. Here is the spot.'

'Look here, Jack,' cried Ken Rohan, stopping and laying his
hand earnestly on his friend's arm, 'you must help me. I suppose it is wicked—I don't know—but that girl has bewitched me,'

'Tirelalaire, Tirelaula!' hummed his friend.

'For God's sake, do not make fun of me. I would rather you stabbed me.'

'My poor Ken!'

'But, Jack, tell me. Do you think I could ever, after years and years, do something to deserve her?——'

'Perhaps. I perceive only one obstacle——'

'An obstacle!——'

'That her husband might object—Belknap—that drunken man with the death's-head.'

'Her husband?'

'Perfectly. And then she has some daughters—I think three. It is too much. *Allons!* stand on that milestone, catch the branch of that elm-tree, and swing on to the wall, or we shall be here until morning.'

CHAPTER THE SIXTH

IN ASPHODEL-LAND

'RASHLEIGH STREET—where *is* Rashleigh Street?' It was getting late in the smoking-room of the Chrysanthemum Club, and the young men who had loitered over their brandy-and-seltzer since dinner-time were dispersing for the night's business of pleasure. An outsider following their night's adventures closely would be apt to conclude that their time in the smoking-room was the only real oasis of pleasure amidst the dreary solemnities of the night—a joyous Mi-Carême set between two drab-coloured and long-faced Lenten seasons. Who could suppose that these ruddy, high-spirited young fellows, who boisterously pitch at one another's vacuous heads the tittle-tattle of the Newmarket stables or of the burlesque stage-doors in a choking atmosphere of alcohol and cigar-smoke, are the same who at eight o'clock were gloomily sitting down to the silent worship of their dinners, and at eleven will be boring themselves to death in a quadrille with the loveliest girls in England? It was with a yawn, tempered by an admiring glance at his own baby face in a mirror, that young Lord Amaranth rose, and reiterated wearily: 'Where the deuce *is* Rashleigh Street?'

'The Irish house? You don't mean to say *you* are going?' said a man, whose careful juvenility was somewhat disputed by a sharp line or two round the corners of his thin lips, and by a certain air of desperate clean-shaving.

'Must pick up my mother. Promised to be with her to Beaumanoir's at twelve. She wants me to do something for a living, and old Beaumanoir is to vet. me—nothing is to be got without him in the Prince's household, it appears. I dare say the cabman will make out this place ; don't you think so ? '

'Shouldn't be surprised if it was somewhere down the Seven Dials way. That's where most of the Irish hail from. Lay you a pony you don't pronounce your hostess's name properly, Amaranth.'

'Thanks. I am not good at conundrums,' said the young lord, wearily.

'Ah ! here's your man. Neville, *you* can tell Amaranth all about Lady Drum and the Wild Irish Girl, eh ? '

'I can tell all about your infernal impertinence ; so can every man of your acquaintance,' was the reply of the young fellow addressed, in a deep, passionate half-whisper, as he was passing out.

'Jove, Mortlake, you caught it ! ' laughed the young man, in high glee. 'You scarify the people because they don't ask you, and you would scarify them lots more if they did. I say, Reggy, you're going to this house, I know. Will you take me with you, there's a good chap ? '

'Brougham's at the door ; come along,' said Horace Westropp's 'stable companion' in the Life Guards Grey.

Lord Amaranth, being a young man who called in to Lady Drumshaughlin's dance as he had dressed for dinner, or as he would have dashed into the ride at Balaclava—as one of the inevitable drawbacks of a life which, upon the whole, the worship of prize-fighters, and music-hall goddesses, and parasites like Mortlake rendered fairly endurable—bowed to Lady Drumshaughlin at the head of the stairs, as he might have bowed to any woman whose handkerchief he had picked up in the street, and thought he had done enough for duty. He made his way up to the Marchioness of Asphodel, who was enthroned at the hostess's side like a fat guardian angel, and said in a low tone : 'Here we are, mother. Let's get away. Shall I order your carriage ? '

'Not yet. It is too early for the Chamberlain's. You must dance, Cecil—I wish it. Just once will do. My dear, will you let me introduce my son ? ' Lady Asphodel said, beaming like a gracious queen upon Miss Westropp, who was looking fresh as a dewy rosebud in a frock of some soft gauzy stuff, through which there was a faint flush of pink. Young Neville, whose foolish blue eyes were fastened upon Miss Westropp with a candour visible to several old ladies on the ottomans, had the mortification of seeing her swept from his sight on the arm of Lord Amaranth, as he and she vanished into a room where there was fiddling, and some wild affectation of waltzing.

It was an astounding success, Lady Drumshaughlin's first dance. The dinner-party which preceded it had not been quite a success. 'Fancy people like these inviting a Minister, dear !' whispered Lady Asphodel to her withered old crony, Lady Dankrose ; and there was a gleam of austere triumph in Lady Asphodel's fine dark eyes, which seemed to explain why the Minister at the last moment sent his excuses. Half the party did not know the other half,' and yet got uncomfortably sand-wiched together. The dinner was bad in every particular—'a railway refreshment-room could not have turned out worse, by Jove !' one of the grateful guests remarked, as he was strolling home across St. James's Park with a cigar between his teeth—'except the wine—Drumshaughlin evidently knows a hawk from a handsaw in the claret country—his countrymen always do know a good drop.' But neither Lord Drumshaughlin's wine nor his old-fashioned bonhomie could break the ice. Nobody could be got to talk. When the ladies had left the room, he tried a couple of old stories of his own for want of better—stories of more or less creditable fun and daredevilry, that used to make messrooms ring in the days when his blonde curls were more plentiful and shone of their own lustre. But they evoked no more interest than if they were reminiscences of people who died in the last generation. Captain Plynlymmon alone kept the whole thing from going to pieces, and he afterwards confessed to Lord Drum-shaughlin,

'That *was* a sulky team, wasn't it ? But dinner is always a stupid business.'

'I remember a time when it was a pretty jolly business,' said Lord Drumshaughlin, musingly. 'Those English airs are smother-ing us hybrids. We've forgotten how to be Irishmen, and we'll never become Englishmen. There was old Lord Turloughmore—he sat as glum as a gravestone, and looked like calling out any fellow that would venture to address an observation to him. There was a time when he would have called a fellow out if he let the bottle pass, or if he shirked contributing his tale or his stave of a song to the evening's amusement. And Turloughmore's was as popular a house with women as with men.'

'My dear lord, that was in the dark ages. Digestion has become too serious a matter nowadays for violent experiments. The host's business is done when he has put his ideas on the bill of fare, and the guests have done their part when they've discussed it. How very much more reasonable than that barbarous plan of carving up carcases all round the table, like a butcher's shop,

and men shying smart things like butcher's knives at one another
across the room, instead of attending to their dinners. I'm not
sure that the Trappists' plan of droning out a chapter from the
" Life of a Saint " during dinner would not be welcomed as the
perfection of sensible conversation during meals. After all, men
contract to dine and not to talk.'

'Yes, I suppose we've come to find there's nothing in this world
—or in any other—so well worth attending to as victuals,' said
Lord Drumshaughlin, sadly. 'But, egad, you won't get me to
believe that emptiness of head has not something to do with it, as
well as fulness of stomach.'

'It has, and it has not. We're a talkless race, no doubt. All
dances, music, and games, for that matter, are only devices for
eking out the meagreness of human conversation. You must
find a form of human intercourse adapted equally to all under
standings. What is lawn-tennis, cricket, waltzing, pool, but a
confession that men and women cannot interest one another long
without calling in their arms and heels to supply the vacuity of
their intellects ?'

'I don't know. Men used to know how to pass an Attic
hour or two over a bottle of claret.'

'If you mean that formality is the death of dinner wit,
so it is, and a good job, too. A dinner with the wits meant
Dr. Johnson ruining the livers of half the people round the
table to relieve his own. Society has had to protect itself by
making it possible for people to dine without being clever. Conversation at one table is now as like the conversation at another
as the entrées. People no more expect a man to bring out his
wit to dine with him than to bring out his fiddle. Everybody is
the happier, even the wits. They used to get up their talk for
dinner just as Lady Betty did her face. The culture of the complexion remains, because women want to please. That of the
pyrotechnic faculties is gone, because men want to feed and to
pay as little as possible for it in the way of intellectual disturb-
ance. If men agree, where is the use of saying so ? If they
don't, where is the use of their disordering their digestion ? After
all,' observed Captain Plynlymmon, pausing after his own unusual
intellectual exertion in order to make a neat cannon—'after all,
to a host in modern England the best part of a dinner is the
names in the *Morning Post* ; and these were all right, Drumshaughlin, you'll admit.'

Lady Asphodel had frowned down the dinner-party. The
ambition of this unknown foreign woman with the velvety
dark eyes, who had only been presented the same day as her
daughter, and would probably never have been presented at all

if her daughter's eyes had not been of that uncommon shade of blue, aroused a certain chastened scorn in the great lady, who foretold that the dinner was to be a failure. But an evening-party was a different thing, and the Marchioness, who happened to be at the Minister's when he was despatching his excuse for the dinner-party, entreated him to drop in on his way to the Lord Chamberlain's, and canvassed her friends and issued a fiat to her satellites to do likewise. The Marquis of Asphodel was a grand old Whig—an indefatigable student of blue-books, the chairman of a Mission Society, and perfectly deaf. He might have been Prime Minister (so it was understood at The Meads and all through Primroseshire) only for his infirmity, and was, through his wife, a more considerable power behind the screen in the Cabinet than a good many men who sat around the green table. The word had passed in high quarters to be civil to Lord Drumshaughlin. For one thing, the election of an Irish repre-sentative peer in the room of the Earl of Clancurran, deceased, was pending ; and Lord Drumshaughlin's age and popularity among his class marked him out as the most promising candidate. It so chanced that the probability of the Lords proving refractory on the Reform Bill made a vote in the Upper House a matter of some concern to the Ministry at the moment. Besides, Lord Drumshaughlin was universally understood to have his county in his gift, and the Ministry had marked down his county for the Irish Attorney-General as soon as the sitting member, the patriot O'Shaughnessy, should either have gone off in the horrors, or to some small colonial governorship. Thus it was (though by what subtle social machinery I am utterly unqualified to explain, being only able to look at all these fine doings as in a glass, darkly) that carriages found their way to Rashleigh Street that had never rolled through it before, except as a short cut from the Park on a wet afternoon ; and Captain Plynlymmon, who knew he had no more to say to the success than the constable who directed the carriage traffic, wore his impostor's laurels, if possible, more radiantly than Lady Drumshaughlin herself, and beamed fraternal approval over the bright-coloured throng on the stairs.

Lady Asphodel, who had really filled the rooms, and who consented to sit for quite half an hour near the lady of the house, nevertheless made it clear in ways that women only could in-terpret that an impassable frozen zone separated her and her *protégée*. Once only did Lady Drumshaughlin venture across the ice-fields with the remark : ' I trust you do not find the heat of the rooms too much for you, Lady Asphodel ? Did anyone ever see such a crush ? '

' Not, I should say, in Rashleigh Street,' returned the great

lady, with a perfectly sweet stare of surprise. I hope Lady
Drumshaughlin does not misunderstand us,' she said, turning,
with the faintest angry inflection in her soft voice, to her friend,
Lady Dankrose, who was sitting beside her.

'My dear, there is always a risk in taking up that kind of
woman. You know what she was when poor Ralph Westropp
made that singular match—an organ-grinder, I believe it is generally understood. Depend on it, a woman like that will wear
the spangles all her life.' As old Lady Dankrose spoke in the
tone of voice of one who believed everybody to be as deaf as
herself, the ex-organ-grinder must have heard every word that
had been said of her. If she did, it did not dim the glance of
quiet gratitude she was at the moment bestowing out of her fine
dark eyes upon some people who had just struggled through the
portière—the three Miss Nevilles, fine, kindly-looking girls, in
whom a certain high-bred air, which they derived from antique
maternal Winspurleighs and De Groots, blended unaffectedly with
brilliant English health ; and their sober-eyed, quaker-looking
father, Joshua Neville, who was in a large way in the iron trade,
and in a small way in the House—one of the men whose dress-
coats somehow seem to turn drab in assemblies like this.

'Your son has been here ever so long, Mr. Neville. He is
such a favourite with us !' she smilingly said, in a voice that was
pitched for the ears of her patroness. It would be hard to say
why Lady Drumshaughlin did not look exactly like other women
in an English drawing-room, for her manner was unemotional
and unobtrusive almost to humility, her dress quietly perfect,
and even her faintly foreign accent of that neutral Swiss shade
which suits all climates alike. The fact stands, however, that for
the one passer-by who would remark Lady Asphodel's respectable bust, queenly though it was, ten would be attracted by
the remarkable figure beside her. Lady Drumshaughlin was
not at all handsome. Her skin was sallow, her face small and
almost square, her black hair came too far down on her forehead,
and, although her limbs were perfectly well-set, she was rather
undersized, and in some danger of being fat. Her power radiated
from a pair of soft, full, dark eyes, half-sheathed in graceful
silky lashes, and fascinating with the suggestive depths of sleeping power far within—whether sad, or romantic, or passionate,
you never were permitted to see them long enough to make sure.
In proportion as men found her attractive, women disliked her—
a result sufficiently natural, if only because a proper curiosity
had been baffled as to exactly where or why Lord Drumshaughlin
had made her his wife ; but in her relations with women, even
more than with men, there was a certain subtle deference in her

glance, and at times an all but imperceptible tremulousness of the lips, which conciliated women of broader ways of thinking, and half convinced the narrowest that old Lady Dankrose must be mistaken about the spangles. The general bent of society, however, was to make her husband popular at her expense. She had a cheerless time of it in houses of the better class, until her beautiful daughter broke like a fresh summer dawn on the eyes of the august circle of critics in the Throne Room ; maladies like that which drove her from the Asphodels' ball were not so much headaches as heartaches. But now that her daughter, her husband, and her son were all three of them distinctly in favour in the highest quarters, Lady Drumshaughlin began to feel herself independent of Captain Plynlymmon, and was injudicious and ungrateful enough not to be sorry for the chance of showing her teeth—very pretty, but very sharp ones—just for once even to a first-rate power of the rank of the Marchioness.

A curious chance offered her a still more dangerous temptation in that direction. Lord Amaranth, returning for his mother, caught Lady Drumshaughlin's dark eyes of power, and for the first time for the night found himself interested. His dance with Miss Westropp had been a somewhat dreary affair on both sides. He did not get on well with young girls out of the nursery, as he called them. Talking to them, he used to say, was as great a bore as sitting down to write a letter. You had to tear up half a dozen ways of putting a thing before you could get down a sentence ; and then it was such twaddle. A chat with Lady Drumshaughlin, after this bread-and-butter feast, was like a chat with a pleasant hostess after the children had been duly admired and despatched to bed. This graceless young nincompoop was not a bit more brilliant with the mother than he had been with the daughter ; but that a thing was whimsical was in itself the highest attraction it could wear in Lord Amaranth's eyes—it might be a prize-fight between a cat and a monkey, or blows between two politicians in a gaming-hell, or the tittle-tattle about this or that *diva* and the call-boy—whatever furnished excitement to his idle, vicious, brainless life, was to him for the moment the supreme joy of existence ; and he was by no means the less convinced that Lady Drumshaughlin was the most interesting woman in the room that he could perceive how his preference vexed, and in a certain ice-cold, duchess-like way, infuriated, his mother.

Lady Drumshaughlin's woman's instinct had discerned this much sooner. She could talk with a soft brilliance in such a way as half to persuade Lord Amaranth that it was he who had been talking brilliantly ; but, although her first glance towards Lady

Asphodel was one of gracefully diluted malice, her second was one of respectful and almost cringing propitiation. She shuddered at the folly of incurring the wrath of this high dame for the pleasure of taunting her with the preference of her jackanapes son.

'I see your mother is anxious to go,' she said, tapping his arm gently with her fan; 'and,' noting the wilful toss of his head, she added, smilingly, 'and my guests are not all disposed of yet. I shall never forget it for you,' she cried gratefully, as the great lady swept off on her sulky son's arm, with an exquisitely modulated little bow of recognition.

How, indeed, should she be otherwise than happy as the heroine of rooms—*her* rooms—full of the best people in London? It was better than pleasure—success. So confessed with a groan old Lady Turloughmore, who could never gather together in *her* London house more than the materials of a tea-fight. So a hundred people observed to Captain Plynlymmon and Captain Plynlymmon to a hundred people, who, if they were of the feminine gender, whispered, 'Do tell us how it was managed!' and, if of the masculine, said, 'Deuced clever fellow, Plynlymmon; this is in his best style. He supplies these things with the company, you know, just as some confectioner sends in the supper. Apropos, *is* there anything to eat?' There was not a great deal, it must be confessed, and there was hardly any room for dancing; but nobody who was anybody wanted to dance, and everybody who wanted supper knew where to find it better elsewhere. The main point was that they came, and had to struggle long before they could get away again. And what other comfort, except that of having it all over, do hosts or hostesses ever expect from that stony-hearted Goddess of Fashion whose thousands of altars smoke all the night in a thousand temples of Belgravia and Mayfair, with more abject devotion and more costly incense than ever the children of Israel worshipped their old-fashioned Jehovah withal? More decisive even than the verdict of the women in diamonds was the attitude of Mrs. MacAnaspie. That grizzled warrior, from her post of observation behind a piece of tapestry which concealed a backstairs communicating with the kitchen, looked out upon the dazzling scene, humiliated and subdued. She had had some vague plan in her head for collecting the amount of an outstanding account on this occasion, and settling old scores with Lady Drumshaughlin, no less as a woman than as a lodging-house-keeper, by making her appearance with her little bill in the midst of the festivities, like the Handwriting on the Wall. But at sight of all these splendours even the courage of the MacAnaspie (and it was not inconsiderable) oozed away. It was completely overpowering. She hardly dared to assert to herself that it was

her own rooms she was beholding at all. It was a sort of glorified
Number 85, such as it might appear if translated to another and
a better world. Then her vanity as mistress of the house was
touched ; she began to perceive that the fact of its being Number
85 played a larger part than she had at first in her modesty been
disposed to allow in the fairy scene. 'This is pretty well, I
think ?' she remarked, condescendingly, to the gentleman who
came to oversee the supper.

'Hallo, Reggy—what's this, old boy ?' cried a handsome,
soldierly-looking young fellow, resting his hand kindly on the
shoulder of the melancholy Jaques in question, where he stood,
with thunder on his brow, in the penumbra of the window-curtains. 'What's this, old boy ?'

'This ? What ?—why do you ask ?'

'Oh, nothing. Only you look as if you were composing a
tragedy, or going to enact one.'

'Do I ? So I am—at least, I don't mean that—hang it all, I
don't know what I mean, Horace. Let me go and have a cigar
and consume my own smoke, there's a good chap.'

'Nothing has happened to Carabîche ?' asked the other,
growing ever so little pale.

'Confound it, Horace, do you think a fellow's feelings never
rise above a stable ? Psha, I'm an ass. Good-night, and tell
Miss Westropp——'

'Tell her yourself, won't you ?' whispered a witching voice,
as Miss Westropp herself came up, with her smile of fearless
pleasure. 'Tell her yourself, won't you ?'

'It's—it's really nothing particular,' stammered the honest
young soldier, his gold moustache seeming to stand on end with
dismay, and his complexion deepening into a fine bronzed red all
over.

'Try if you can do anything with him, Mabel. If he goes on
like this, he'll lose the City and Suburban, and we'll all be in the
Bankruptcy Court,' and handsome Horace Westropp moved off
gaily in the crowd.

Young Neville, who was always getting himself into meshes,
always tore his way out of them like a young lion. 'I was
watching for you all night,' he said, brusquely.

She answered with a merry laugh : 'Now that you've found
me, suppose we join this dance ? As you won't ask me, I have
only to ask you.'

'I would die for you,' he muttered between his set teeth. He
was one of those Englishmen who are 'content to say nothing,
when they have nothing to say,' but when anything had got to
be said, it was as direct as the point of a bayonet.

'Good gracious, what a thing to say! How you will have frightened the old ladies sitting on that ottoman who have just heard you' (and who were just remarking that that girl was an impudent flirt, and in her first season, too!).· 'Please to remember that I don't want anybody to die, least of all you—if there was nothing else, Horace wants you to win the City and Suburban, you know, and so do I.'

'Do you?' he cried, looking down greedily into her radiant eyes; but seeing how merrily they sparkled: 'You are only laughing at me, of course. Come along—is it a waltz or what?' In his present mood it made little matter. He dashed into the whirl as a man might go over the top of Niagara, only to come up like a water-dog in the Rapids, however, enjoying it hugely. The effect upon his own spirits was considerably better than upon those of surrounding waltzers.

'I could go on like that for ever. Couldn't you?' he cried, when at last the music ceased, and they moved off amidst an indignant public towards the tea-room.

'I don't think they'd let us,' laughed his partner, whose schoolgirl soul had found as much glee as Neville himself in his performance.

'I saw you dancing with Lord Amaranth,' he observed next, as abruptly as usual.

'Did you? He was delightful.'

'Was he?' groaned the jealous monster, with the utmost good faith.

'Yes. He told me he has been twice to the Irish coast in his yacht, and he didn't see anything particularly strange. I believe he expected to find us all dining upon potatoes and whisky, and introducing a faction-fight by way of dessert.'

'I don't know much about Ireland myself, though I rode once at Punchestown in the Grand National.'

'Your countrymen seldom do know much of the country that gave you Burke and Wellington—seldom even know that it did give them to you,' she cried, a little hotly. 'You've got an island where you might have the music of Ariel if you would, and you've never been able to see anything in it except a Caliban.'

'I was never good at history or things,' ruefully confessed Reggy, to whom, truth to tell, the victor of Waterloo was the only one of the personages named who suggested any very definite idea. 'All I know is, that if Ireland would only give me you I'd adore its name every hour of my life.'

'Now, I'll have to leave you,' she said, a little angrily. 'That is not fair.'

'But, by heaven, 'tis true,' he whispered, in low, rapid tones

F

in her ear. 'If it was to be my death-warrant, I must tell you. There now, you think I am a foo', I know.'

'On the contrary, I like you ever so much,' she said, with frank, kind eyes. '.You know I do.'

'Like! I like my bull-dog, and my chestnut, and a thousand things. What is liking when a man is hungering for—yes, for love——'

'There now, you must stop—stop instantly.' She looked at him in amazement, in trembling, as if he had just struck her, or done something equally unlooked for. The colour came and went in her cheek as in a rose that one could imagine panting. But there was something so gentle in his rough, innocent, worshipping face, that her terror dissolved immediately, though her hand was still trembling painfully. 'You have mentioned two things—love and death—that nobody except grown-up people ought to talk about,' she said, with a desperate effort to recover the school-girl view of things which, somehow, in those few instants, seemed to have departed from her for ever. 'Don't look angry—I know you are fully twenty, if not more——'

'Oh, bother!'

'Why won't you let us be frank with one another always?' she said, in a grave voice. 'To me these two things are equally terrible, and I am not sure that love does not cause more misery in this world than death—love, I mean, such as—oh, such as selfish, giddy, heartless women fill their lives, and thoughtless poets fill their books with. How much happier a world it might be if people would only do as much for kindness as they do for love, and how many a million loveless hearts would be the brighter! We shan't talk of disagreeable subjects any more, shall we? and you'll let me talk to my brother's comrade as my own, won't you?' She put out a small hand, and he took it in a dazed, crestfallen way. 'There, now, that's a bargain. I shall go to see you win the City and Suburban, and you are going to get me a cup of tea.'

If Mabel Westropp had been a hardened coquette she could not have more effectually concealed from old Lady Dankrose, whose eyes were sharper than her ears were dull, that the girl whose joyous laugh could be heard cheering her partner, as he crushed his way like a battering-ram to the refreshment counter, was just after rejecting a lover—one who combined the blood of all the Winspurleighs with the wealth of half the mineral trains of Sheffield.

All this passes, with more or less variation, in London houses every night from January to July, and is as commonplace as swallow-tailed coats. What is not so usual is that two uninvited strangers should burst their way into the hall and throttle a serving-man. This was what was just happening when Miss Westropp and the young Guardsman, after leaving the tea-room, which was on the ground-floor, were about to return upstairs. There was an agitated little group of hired footmen, there was some noise and plunging, there was the sound of a heavy body on the floor, and then appeared a ferocious-looking creature like an overgrown bull-dog, with a hairy cap on its head, holding down one of the hired footmen by the throat, while a tossed and wild-looking youth stood at bay in the midst of them.

'Harry!' The word came from Miss Westropp's lips, almost in a scream.

The servants instantly fell back.

'Yes, it's I, Mabel,' said the young fellow, shaking his mane of dishevelled hair. 'These fellows wanted to put me out

Miss Westropp, looking very white, waved the servants off. Young Neville looked on, his blue eyes distended but unconsciously took a step backwards. The two strangers stood for a moment alone in the middle of the group. He who was called Harry was dressed in slovenly grey tweed. His collar was torn, and his hat had fallen off. There was, therefore, full opportunity of seeing what a mass of hay-coloured hair he had, wildly thrown back from a narrow forehead; what a blaze there was in his eye; and how rigid his features were, and how white with passion. His companion was the most extraordinary being that Neville had ever laid his eyes upon. He was a man, and not a bull-dog, as at first appeared. He was a short man, with an enormous head like a cannon-ball beaten out of all shape on an anvil; he wore a spotted blue handkerchief knotted round his thick neck in a noose that suggested recent cutting down from a gallows, before the choking was quite complete; his great chest and rounded shoulders were of enormous width and thickness, which diminished rapidly in the lower part of the body until the bowed legs shrank away into almost nothing in the closely-buttoned corduroy gaiters which compressed his shins. He possessed a pair of eyes which it took him all his days to endeavour to reconcile with one another. They seemed to be for ever setting out in opposite directions, and looking back as they had turned the corner, like two quarrelling schoolgirls making coy overtures to re-establish relations with one another. These sinister features, together with a growth of wiry stubble on his jaws, were not improved by a scalded patch of purplish-crimson which extended around one of his eyes, and over a large neighbouring tract of cheek. The moment Miss Westropp appeared this creature had released his hold of the footman, and he now stood a little behind his master, very much as if he were really a bull-dog after all, and had in some antic vein stood upon his hindlegs with his front paws in his pockets, and a short, thick stick under his arm. You must have seen the motions by which a dog of this breed intimates that he feels ashamed of himself. Some such expression as this wore the bullet head under the hairy cap. It was waggled about from side to side, in a slouching, downcast kind of way, as though the owner were trying desperately to make both eyes look down together ; but every time the head was raised the two eyes would appear again at opposite points of the compass, leering at one another in a hideously comic duet.

This was for a moment. The people going up and down the stairs had scarcely noticed it in the hum of voices and the hunger for supper.

'Come this way,' said Miss Westropp, drawing the young fellow with her to an unoccupied room.

'I suppose Quish may come, too? Did you see Quish, Mabel?' asked Harry, pointing over his shoulder at the dwarf, who dug his paws deeper into his pockets, and leered in the most horrible manner under this embarrassing recognition.

'Come!' said Miss Westropp, imperiously, and laid her hand upon her brother's arm. The dwarf followed them in a sidelong way, with his head down, and his club grasped tightly under his arm.

Neville found himself alone in the crowd.

CHAPTER THE SEVENTH

THE LORD HARRY

As this does not purport to be a melodrama, now is as good a time as any other to tell you who was Harry. He was Lord Drumshaughlin's eldest son, but not his heir-at-law. Ralph Westropp shared some of the mad blood of the Warbros, which drove his maternal uncle, Dick, out to Ravenna philandering with the Carbonari, and gave him his death-wound in putting down a mutiny of the wild Palikars, who broke Lord Byron's heart at Missolonghi. Young Ralph was cornet in a regiment of hussars, when, effervescing with wild blood which he could see little prospect of dispensing in the hussars, he all of a sudden set off to take service with a band of Italian patriots to expel the Austrian from Lombardy. The patriots did not turn out satis-

factorily. They did not understand Westropp's Italian, nor
Westropp their dread of an Austrian uniform. They plucked up
courage enough to get fired upon in the flower-market at Milan, and
while Ralph Westropp was running away with his companions-
in-arms he received a bullet under the shoulder which, without
being too dangerous, sufficiently appeased his passion for blood-
letting. For five miserable days he dragged himself along through
Lombardy, more dead than alive, not knowing particularly where
he was going, except that it was towards the mountains. At
long last he descried the Austrian frontier-post, and crossed over
in safety in the middle of the night by wading up to his armpits
in a frozen little river, which went near avenging Austria more
effectively than the Austrian bullet. As soon as he climbed
upon a rock on the opposite bank he fainted away, and took no
further interest in the matter. He was picked up by a gigantic
Swiss hunter, contrabandist, and innkeeper, one Antonaccio,
who brought him home with him upon his back, calculating that
as he was an Englishman, with soft crested linen, he would probably be worth the trouble. When Ralph Westropp awoke out
of his fever, he found the contrabandist's dark-eyed sister Berta
hovering like a soft spirit around his bedside, and a sunny,
secluded little Alpine valley (the Italians called it Vallinzona)
spread out before him like a live chromo-lithograph under the
rustic windows of the inn. It was one of those rose valleys
which was not yet discovered of the English. (There are now
a Hôtel Splendide and a German Sanatorium, together with a
grape-cure, *petits chevaux*, and a morning and evening band.)
The eternal snow was all far away behind—a mere harmony in
pink, white, and gold to be lit up for sunrise or sunset, like an
illuminated waterfall. In front, in luxurious tranquillity, basked
a green Spring valley in the embrace of delicate blue mountains
perfumed and fanned with pine groves, and musical with cow-
bells and the liquid loves of the nightingales; and in the distance, like a beautiful mirage, golden Italy. Of course, you have
guessed already what happened during the period of convalescence. Would that you had guessed all! Berta's dark, sumptuous eyes had as much romance in them as all the nightingales
had in their throats, and Ralph Westropp was a youth to whom
the admiration of women was as the breath of life, and who was
very apt to mistake his admiration of himself as a return for
their worship. Alas for those days of lazy sunshine in the Vallinzona! Alas for the ugly reptile heads that peer out amidst
those gentle-coloured, pure breathing Alpine flowers!

One night in the winter of that same year, as young Westropp
was strolling home, cigar in mouth, from a dull official reception

in the Rue St.-Honoré, at Paris, he found himself followed into the court of his hotel in the Rue de la Paix by a sinister-looking stranger, behind whose conspirator's cloak he recognised the contrabandist of the Vallinzona.

'I had much trouble in finding you, milor,' said the Swiss, grimly, as he closed the door of Westropp's appartement on the second floor, into which he had shown him. 'I bring you some news.' He bent down and said, or rather hissed, something in milor's ear. The young man turned desperately pale.

'What—what is to be done?' he asked, after a moment or two, in a scared way.

'One thing and that quickly. You know it—marriage!'

'Marriage!' The contrabandist had spoken with insolence. It was mostly the smart of his insulting words—partly also, perhaps, it was that cruel appetite for rending something which unbridled youth shares with young tigers—that moved Ralph Westropp to burst out into a scornful laugh.

The small close-set black eyes of the Swiss glittered like knives. 'Her blood is as rich as yours. We are of the Casciolini, we!'

'My good fellow, let us come to business,' said Westropp, coldly.

'To business! Very well,' cried the Swiss, raging like a wild animal. 'You are going to promise to be at her side at the Mairie, in the Vallinzona, within seven days, for the ceremony, or I am going to kill you here where you sit. Do you understand?'

'You look quite like it,' said Westropp, laughing, as in these days he always would laugh tauntingly at death. 'But I think I will find another way out of it;' and he touched the bell at his elbow. 'Mundle,' he said to his servant, who answered the summons from the next room, 'see this gentleman to the door. The lady, sir, shall hear from me herself.' He had got thus far when his eyes were blinded by a flash, a venomous sting entered his flesh, and he tumbled on the floor, bleeding.

His valet grappled valiantly with the assassin. They rolled together on the ground, and in the collision the second barrel of the contrabandist's pistol exploded in his hand. His other hand, which was upon Mundle's throat, suddenly relaxed its grip, and he fell back, dead. The bullet had entered at his left temple, and buried itself in his brain. The commissary of police, who had just returned from the Opera, remarked with a shrug of the shoulders, after investigating the circumstances:

'My faith, the defunct has done himself justice.'

After which the commissary rejoined his wife, who was waiting for him in a cab, and proceeded to a quiet supper at the Café Mery

This was Ralph Westropp's marriage engagement. His wound was a slight one. As soon as he could extort the doctor's permission, he was away to Switzerland, and bursting his way through the snows of the St. Gothard to make his dark-eyed nurse of the Vallinzona his wife. Whether it was remorse or chivalry, or whim, or all three that urged him on—who can tell? Least of all men could he tell himself. He only knew that there was a certain wild dash of Missolonghi distinction about the adventure that made him think well of himself; and it is always a comfort to a man whose reasonings are bad to think that impulses are pretty sure to be right if they urge him to do anything uncommon. He chose to face all the snows of society, as well as all those less formidable barriers which choked the St. Gothard Pass, to do of his own free will and pleasure what he would have been hacked to pieces rather than do under the pistol of Antonaccio. He came too late. His son had been born a night or two before, and the mother was convulsed with hysteria, which promised to save his chivalry the trial. She lived, however, to be the Hon. Mrs. Westropp, and, in the fulness of time, Lady Drumshaughlin; and the blonde little infant—a blurred copy of Ralph Westropp's beauty, and a sad caricature of his weaknesses—grew up in the wilds and stable-yards of Drumshaughlin to be—Harry.

'Harry, what is the meaning of this?' was Miss Westropp's first question, when they were *tête-à-tête*.

'The—the meaning of it?' he repeated in a faltering, puzzled tone. 'Egad, Mabel, is that your welcome for me?'

'You have behaved shockingly, sir—before all the world, too. You have disgraced us, and disgraced yourself.'

'Is this our own house, or is it not?' The wild light suddenly flamed up again in the young fellow's eyes; his features were gathered together with a concentrated energy which was obviously rare and painful. 'Have they a right to kick me out of my father's house? Answer me that. Have those fellows in livery orders to keep me out? Am I the cholera, that ye're all afraid of me? That's just what I came here to know, once for all. I'll stand it no longer. By God, I won't!'

'This is worse and worse. Harry, you have taken drink——'

'I know I have. So have all the people here, I suppose. We hadn't much dinner, neither Quish nor I—a sandwich at some railway junction, that was all.'

'Oh! what could have tempted you to make this journey?'

'What induced me to stay where I was so long? That's what I want to know.'

'Then you weré not really happy at Mr. Harman's? You have had a quarrel with him, perhaps?'

'A quarrel? No, nothing particular. He beats his wife. I don't care, Mabel; he does beat her ; but that does not matter—it is her own fault—she flew at me like a cat when I offered tc thrash him. It isn't that; but I don't want him nor any man to follow me about as a keeper—with a strait-waistcoat ready, by ——'

'Oh, Harry, those horrible oaths!'

'Well, what have they left me but those oaths? I won't stand it, I tell you,' he cried, with flashing eyes. 'I suppose I'm not very bright, but I know what it is to be trodden into the slime of the earth—a worm would know it; and I think of it sometimes, Mabel, though you mayn't believe it. 'Twas bad enough to be shut up alone with the rats and the ghosts in that old barrack of a Castle; but they must lock me into Hans Harman's nursery like a baby, and cut off my tobacco, and warn Quish not to go near me. As if Quish weren't a better man than Harman, any-way! By heavens, Mabel, I couldn't stand another day of it. So Quish and myself made it up to run away. I said it would be better for me to throw myself from London Bridge or 'list.'

'My poor Harry!' exclaimed his sister, taking his head between her hands and kissing him; whereupon, sobbing out 'Oh, Mabel, you know how they have treated me!' he let his head sink upon her shoulder like a child.

Quish's posture at this moment would have given a painter the subject of an immortal picture. He had stood during the interview with his body half-inserted through the half-opened doorway—sufficiently present to be of assistance at call, and sufficiently in the draught of the doorway to express respectful discomfort. He was silently gnawing the hairy cap with his teeth, with some hideous suggestion of a lover furtively kissing a letter from the beloved one, and his misshapen and discoloured head was wagging more jerkily than ever, with a grin which you might easily enough have mistaken for some devilish diversion, though it was really only Quish's way of looking sentimental and embarrassed.

Young ladies in filmy ball-dresses do not like being embraced by dishevelled brothers in homespun tweed. Is it quite unpardon-able if it was some half-unconscious thought of her tulle, and of mordant tongues set going upstairs, that all of a sudden froze up the tenderness of the sister, and restored the sangfroid of the beauty?

'You ought not to be such a fool,' she said, disengaging her-self a little hurriedly, and beating her beautiful arm pettishly with her fan. 'Indeed, you ought not. What could you have expected to gain by conduct of this kind?'

'Conduct of this kind!' he cried, flaming out again rebelliously. 'Coming to my own father's house to ask him for something to take me to America or somewhere. Conduct of this kind!'

'Making a rowdy scene in your father's house on an occasion like this—that is what I mean,' cried Miss Westropp, her cheek rosed over with a flush of angry recollection; 'breaking into this house in the middle of the night with this—this man, like—like——'

'Like a blackguard, you mean. Go on, Mabel.'

'Have you a glimmer of respect for what is due to the decencies of society—to our position here—to your mother's feelings——'

'I don't care,' he broke in doggedly.

'What have I done that you should involve me in the pain of such a scene? Oh, Harry, it was unkind of you—it was vulgar—it was unmanly!'

'You are not quizzing me, Mabel?' he asked, looking up into her face hesitatingly.

'You are incorrigible!' she cried, in passionate impatience.

'No,' he said simply. 'I know very well now that you mean it. All right, Mabel. We'll go. I'll do it for you. Come, Quish,' he cried, turning sadly towards the door, 'we've got to pack.' After taking a step or two he turned abruptly, as if something had flashed upon him, and he whispered confidentially to his sister, 'I say, Mabel, could you manage the loan of a few shillings for a fellow?—just what will keep us going for the night, you know. I suppose they charge a fellow half-a-crown or so at least for a bed and a bite of breakfast here.'

'Good heavens! You have not come to London without the price of a bed in your pocket?'

'Oh, no, we had enough for that, and more—lashings more; but I didn't rightly know our—I mean your—address, so we were knocking about in a cab for three hours, and we had to call at ever so many public-houses to inquire the way. You wouldn't believe what a heap of money it cost.'

'Dear, dear old Harry! Forgive me. I was a brute!' she suddenly cried, with tears in her eyes, flinging her arms about him, this time with the most callous disregard of consequences to the tulle.

Harry's pale eyes opened in wonderment. Now that the excitement, which had, like fire, fused his features into a glow, had died away, they looked weak and incoherent features enough, after all. He could not clearly make out what had happened to produce this surprising demonstration.

'That's more like your old self,' he said at length, placidly. 'Don't let them spoil you in London, Mab.'

'They shan't, dear—never again—there's my hand on it,' she cried, beaming with a girlish mother's affection. 'We're sworn friends against all the world from this hour.'

'That's right, Mab—you always took my part,' he said, still considerably puzzled. 'And you'll fish out that ten bob or so for us, won't you, Mab?'

'Don't, Harry—not those horrid words,' she cried, with a look of agony. 'Come along. You must not think of going away.'

'Eh! What is it all about?'

'My poor brother, what should you do out in the streets of London by yourself?'

'Quish is an astonishing fellow at finding his way—as 'cute as if he were after a badger at Corrig-na-thurrig.' Quish smiled sadly as one who had heard mention of the brook Cedron by the waters of Babylon.

'Very well. Quish shall stay with us, too. There is plenty of room, and papa will be delighted to see you.'

'Why that's what I was thinking all along, Mab. The governor was never much down upon me. He isn't in bed yet? Just give him the tip that I'm here, won't you?'

'Not to-night, dear, not to-night,' she said, a little hurriedly. 'Poor papa is not equal to much worry, and—and—we must not let mamma know—not just yet.'

'Oh!' was his crestfallen comment.

'We shall have some supper in my little sitting-room—you and I—and you shall tell me all the news. It will be time enough for us to begin plotting to-morrow or after. Come.' And the young lady of fashion, who a few minutes before crimsoned at the apparition of the tweed-suited young man in the hay-coloured hair, took the said young man's arm, and led him boldly forth into the midst of the perfumed mob that was still flowing up and down the staircase like a bright river in the Moluccas.

Young Neville was standing transfixed to the spot where we last saw him; with what object, he knew no more than does the moth why his wings will not carry him out of range of the fascinating flame that is scorching him. It was not jealousy, even of a young man who called his divinity 'Mabel;' for he was one who, if his divinity had chosen to run away with her dancing-master, would have concluded in simplicity of soul that the dancing master must be a man of superior talents to himself, and would no more have dreamed of challenging the dancing-master than of thrashing the jockey who might beat his chestnut for the City and Suburban. Several people slapped him on the back and trod upon his toes in passing without awakening any demonstration on his part. The moment, however, that he saw Miss Westropp advancing towards him leaning upon the stranger's arm, the bronze vermilion overspread his face to the roots of his gold-coloured moustache once more, and he looked around in a startled way, as if with some mad thought of taking to his heels.

Miss Westropp walked straight up to him. 'Mr. Neville, you have not met my brother Harry,' she said, with a smile of heavenly gratitude. 'I do so want you to be friends.'

'Glad to know you,' said Neville, heartily, putting out his hand. 'Horace and I are cronies.'

'What! It isn't you who're running Carabîche for the City and Sub.?' asked Harry, with much interest.

'Yes, Carabîche is a thing of mine.'

'She ought to do it hands down. I don't know what's to beat her,' said Harry, in whose eyes his new acquaintance was a far more interesting personage in the great world of London than the Lord Mayor. 'I am ever so glad to meet you. Come and have a bit of supper with us—Mabel and me. Mustn't he, Mabel?'

For an instant she looked embarrassed and annoyed, but she immediately laughed pleasantly. 'Very well. I dare say it won't be much more improper than my standing here talking to you two young men all this time in place of helping to mind mamma's guests for her.'

In fact, very much the same remark was being made at that moment by Lady Dankrose to her serious young friend, Mrs. Lentenham, as her lean old shoulders were being embalmed in furs and shawls before departing.

'Who on earth is the young person that extraordinary girl has picked up *now*? She has been making eyes all the night at that young fool, poor Lady Margery Neville's son. Did anyone ever see anything so brazen?'

'My dear Lady Dankrose,' said the younger lady, philoso-phically, 'it is the way with all those Irishwomen, more or less, but they don't mean anything wrong—I really believe they do not—it is simply that they fail to see how it looks to us, quiet English people.'

The Hon. Miss Westropp's national eccentricities were not pushed to any further extremities, however, on the present occa-sion. She discovered quickly that her two young bears were sufficiently co-enthusiasts on the common ground of Carabîche to make capital company for one another; and while she was making up for her disappearance by redoubled zeal in her mother's drawing-rooms, Reggy Neville was arranging to bring Harry down to Newmarket, first train in the morning, to see the mare take her gallop.

CHAPTER THE EIGHTH

'IT IS THE REVOLUTION!'

'JACK, are you ever serious about anything?' asked Ken Rohan, as they lounged together one fragrant May evening in the Observatory—Jack in a smart gold-tasselled turban smoking a prodigious clay pipe, and in the intervals of his whiffs making sport in his light way of everything in the heavens above and on the earth beneath—'Are you ever serious about anything?'

'My faith, yes,' said the philosopher. '*Par exemple*, when villain clouds of tobacco-smoke obscure the air, and the hoof of the Reverend Mulpetre makes groan the neighbouring stairs. Apropos, I think you might place the water-jug at the angle of the stairs. It makes dark there, and he shall fall over it with effusion. That shall give the brave man occupation until we can stifle the chamber with sulphuric acid. That is very well. For a serious, you practise the uses of the water-jug very passably.'

'But one cannot pass his life practising upon Father Mulpetre's shins.'

'Why not? To what good are all the revolutions in the world, if not to lay the Father Mulpetres sprawling? It required less genius to take the Bastille than it does to trip up Father Mul, though, of course, it was a much better pleasantry.'

'Don't talk like that,' said Ken Rohan, gravely. He had been once taught to think of the French Revolution as a rush of hell-hounds upon beautiful princesses and shining saints. He had lately come to think of it vaguely as something quite different from that, but, in either view, a solemn and awful thing, deserving of capital letters in thought as well as in print.

'What will you have? What does the world demand of all its civilisations and insurrections? The liberty to laugh. Life is not a bad pleasantry. All which the peoples demand is that the laugh shall not be always against them.'

'There is more than that in life,' said Ken Rohan, whose eye was following the sunset to its couch of pale ethereal ambers and roses.

'Yes, the Sphinx. Not bad as a riddle, but the riddle is the least interesting form of wit. Dull men fall back on it as they do on plain women in a drawing-room. My old friend who legacied me our brave telescope could see some millions of millions of worlds swinging in the ether *là haut*, and he could not get as much honest light out of them all as out of one earthly tallow-candle. Bah! my Ken, what are *you* serious about? To be a priest, and freeze your blood to snow-broth, for example?'

Ken coloured. It was the first time the question had knocked at his heart so brusquely. He used to let his mother settle his profession for him as she settled the cut of his clothes; but of late he had begun to feel that in neither of these departments did her taste precisely square with his own. He had made the discovery that a looking-glass has other uses than to keep a straight crease in his hair, and that the lumpy rustic garments cut by Dawley, the Drumshaughlin tailor, were not the best setting for a well-shaped pair of shoulders, a head of undaunted brown curls, and a correspondingly brown complexion with a wholesome flush of red through it. The Dawley fashion had been fading perceptibly out of his costumes of late. Other and softer shapes, too, had begun to hover dimly in the depths of the looking-glass; and then when he thought of the mystic shadows and faintly-rustling angel-wings that brooded over the Holy of Holies, he shuddered, as though he would merit the fate of Uzzah if his profaning fingers so much as touched the outer timbers of the Ark—'No, I think not,' he said, after a moment or two blushing.

'And I also. A man carries his standard in his face. Yours bears the aurora of a moustache—that Labarum of youth and love.'

'I am done with love—if I have ever begun!' sighed Ken Rohan, whose thoughts still sometimes reverted obstinately to the silver clouds of high Olympus and the glistering celestial garments of an impossible Mrs. Belknap.

'Va! One like you is never done with love until he is done with life. When you have done adoring young women, you will find old ones more adorable, and when the old ones disappear, you will find children the most adorable of all.'

'That is different. Most things *are* adorable even in this unsatisfying world. The trouble is that all persons and all things are not adorable, and adored. You needn't laugh. They easily might, if a handful of mischievous statesmen with their standing armies would let them. What a glorious, glorious thought that was of Dante—*un riso dell' universo*—a universe smiling for joy! Why should not all the world think as kindly of one another as

you and I? Why should not all the world be as liable to a con
scription of love as they are to be sent to kill and to be killed?
Do you suppose you would find a human heart anywhere—in a
cabin or in a prison—that was not made for sunshine as well as
yours or mine, if you could only release it from its dungeon of
suffering and unkindness? And what pleasure in life is there
like that of adoring?'

'You have been reading the Mystics—or the Communists,'
said Jack Harold, yawning.

'The Monastery and the Revolution are, perhaps, more
nearly related than we think—rightly understood, they only
differ as the Contemplative and the Active Orders of the same
creed do,' said the other, his thoughts, like his eyes, buried
in the burning West, where a heavy purple cloud was forcing its
blunt head into the solid rampart of bright gold, and instead of
extinguishing the glory was itself transfused with brilliancy, like
some spirit of ignorance transmuted in the angelic light it had
come to quench. 'Jack, did you ever feel that you had something to do in this world, and didn't know exactly what?—
something that you could live or die for with a swelling heart?'

Jack suddenly removed the long clay pipe from his mouth—
so abruptly that it broke in twenty fragments—and fixed his
eyes intently on his friend. 'Why do you ask?'

'Because I feel it myself like a fever. I cannot describe to
you what it is, except this—that when I was a boy down at
home by the ocean, my grand ambition in life was to get beyond
the Caha Mountains, and when I climbed to the top of them,
and beyond them, there was still a beyond, and a beyond, as far
away as ever. I had the gun then. A bird would rise, or a
hare would start, and I would forget all about the blue haze;
but here, where one has nothing to do but to read and think,
that old feeling of wanting to be beyond the mountains is fastening on me, like some awful physical craving. It sometimes comes
over me like the sound of some dim fierce tumult of millions of
men crashing their way from their prisons towards Power, and
all the world lighting up with happiness and love in their track;
but then it is all so vague! There are such countries and such
continents beyond my poor rustic furthest beyond!—and beyond
and above all these your poor old friend's millions upon millions
of worlds, and these the merest fringe of an Infinite Beyond!—
the greatest cause that ever thrilled Humanity seems so insignificant! It is like hearing in the distance the vague, intoxicating music of a battle. Passionately though one hungers
to be into it, it is hard to know where to strike in!'

'I can aid you, if you will,' exclaimed the other, in a hushed voice.

'Psha ! this is rant, and you are laughing at me. I do forget sometimes that the first axiom of good form is that it is almost manlier to have no feelings than to show them—that that incomparable musical instrument, the human heart, is best shut up in a bag, like a precious fiddle. What on earth could have set me rhapsodising like this ? I suppose it was that sunset—so grand and so shadowy. We, Irishmen, are dreamers.'

'What does all the world do but dream that it is awake—the most absurd illusion going ? For the rest, a dream of freedom is more égaying than a dream of beefsteak. Listen ! You are a little dizzied by that whirl of the universes. It is too much. The eagle itself loses its head in that dazzling immortality of the blue. That of which you have need, it is to turn your eyes from the worlds to our world, and from our world to our Ireland. Suppose this land, and at this moment, were palpitating with a dream of facing her conquerors once again upon the field she has never given up :—suppose our "Dark Rosaleen" were embroidering a banner which she will give to her young soldiers one of these days to spread it to the wind—suppose all the crushed yearnings of Celtic genius, all the passion of Celtic sorrow, were swelling into a battle-hymn which young hearts will leap to hear—suppose you heard the chorus thundering across the Atlantic Ocean from the camps of the greatest army of this century : "We are coming, sweet Queen Rosaleen, a hundred thousand strong !"—suppose that this very hour, in that very valley, tranquil as it looks in the summer sunset, men were planning all that, preparing for it, drilling for it, arming for it, panting for the signal—would you know where to strike in *then* ?'

'This from you, Jack !' cried Ken Rohan, in a state of stupefaction. 'What *can* you mean ?'

' You have demanded is there anything in the world which I take seriously ? I don't complain. You have heard me mock myself at all things visible and invisible. *N'importe.* The sky does not fall because a saucy lark chirps in its face. We cannot help it—neither the lark nor I. The blackbird was a century ago a considerable personage in Irish history. Has it ever struck you that even the lark's song may be as useful a disguise as another in a country where a deeper note would be—Treason !'

' Treason ! '

'Look, then!' He wheeled his little iron bed out of its corner, and, having dropped on his knees, proceeded carefully to displace a portion of the black timber skirting of the wall, which he had skilfully mortised and painted so as to be of a piece with the rest. From a cavity thus revealed in the thickness of the wall he drew forth a circular tin case, from which he extracted a stout roll of stuff wrapped up in oiled silk to preserve it from the damp. Ken's fascinated eyes followed every movement with a tightening feeling at the heart that his fate was about to spring out of the tin case. What did spring out was a flag of emerald green silk, which fell in rippling folds around him. Jack Harold shook it gaily out. In the centre there gleamed the beams of a rising sun—the Sunburst of the rebel flag.

'Good heavens! is this possible?' A subtle intoxication, not unmingled with terror, crept through young Rohan's veins. In Ireland *primâ facie* everything that has to be hidden is sacred. It had been religion—it was the flag—that had to hide in the barren places. It is all part of the mystery here and hereafter that envelops Irish life, and thrills even while it saddens it. The Beara hills, down by the sea, do not teach English. 'Treason!' —a word which in happier lands suggests nothing that is not foul or repellent—calls up to the fervid Irish brain the vision of a hapless young queen, with passion, faith, and genius in her deep eyes, pointing to the red abyss in which generation after generation of the true and brave have gone to their death for her, one after one, with a love-light in their eyes, and whispering, ' Have mine eyes no longer power to stir young blood? Art thou afraid to follow?' If, at the bottom of every Irishwoman's heart, you will find a love-letter, at the bottom of every Irishman's you will find 'The Spirit of the Nation'—which, indeed, is only a collection of love-letters in another shape, from ' the holy, delicate, white hands' of the most unhappy queen who ever inspired a tender passion, to the most romantic nation who ever felt it, and welcomed the delicious smart. Ken Rohan could all but look into the appealing dark blue eyes—all but hear the deep-voiced answering chant of the Irish-American soldiery. 'We are coming, sweet Queen Rosaleen, a hundred thousand strong!' Only to think of being the bearer of that flag at the head of a charging line, with the eternal love of a happy Ireland for the prize of victory!

'You know why one must hide that flag. You know also why the lark finds it necessary to chirp his gay nonsense around its hiding-place.'

'But you of all men, Jack!—who could ever have suspected!'

'Happily, seeing that I do not *dépêche* myself to be cravated with hemp. Nevertheless, it is not surprising. I am a child of revolutions, I. My father, who was a doctor, had his pike ready in '48 as well as his lancet. Like his co-revolutionaries, the only thing he was called upon to make use of was his legs. He fled to France from the Bay of Kenmare with my mother. I was born upon the voyage. The earliest image on my memory is to see the Chasseurs-à-pied charging up our street in Paris—it was the Rue

St.-Séverin—sometimes stopping, then firing, then running forward again.   It was in the days after the Coup d'Etat ; all the Latin Quarter fought with Baudin ; but it turned out a Parisian Ballingarry, you conceive.   My father was shot through the heart binding the arm of a wounded student.   He was very popular in the Quarter ; it is always like that with one who cures people for nothing.   I can remember still the pile of paper *immortelles* upon the coffin, and the hoarse chorus of the "Marseillaise"—your Parisian takes the air with him to his grave. I remember the noise of a volley at the head of the street.   The students wanted to bring the body through Paris.   The troops barred the passage to the Boulevard St.-Michel, and fired upon the convoy.   My faith, there were more bodies than one to be brought to Père Lachaise!   But they had the heart good, our students.   They have never let the violets die upon his grave ; and, when my mother has opened a little café in the Rue Dauphine, they have baptised it La Mère Médécine, and have made it famous.   Born of one revolution, orphaned by another—you conceive that I owe something more than violets to the grave in Père Lachaise.   I learned the "Marseillaise" as early as the Lord's Prayer—if not in place of it.   What joy to chorus it to the nose of Bonaparte's mouchards!   Listen.   We are composing an Irish "Marseillaise."   One of these days all the world will be ringing with the chorus.'   •

The lightsome young Frenchman had never before spoken with such vivacity, and even passion.   Much more he said, in words of mysterious flame from which Ken Rohan's eyes caught fire like torches.   The hours flew.   The gold territory in the western sky had long faded into a dull chrome-colour, and the great crystal moon rose in an ocean of vivid blue.   Every object in the valley underneath them was brought out with a soft distinctness in the radiance.   The town lay slumbering below ; its lights out ; its fires quenched ; as though it had finally composed itself to its long sleep like the ruined Abbey in the midst of it.   The river Ard seemed to be asleep, too, amidst the whispering woodlands. The high-backed bridge which connected a suburb on the opposite side of the river with the town—its staring white walls and massive battlements—seemed almost close enough to have its ancient inscription legible.   Nearer to them the road which ascended the hill from the town to St. Fergal's unrolled its broad white riband, which lost itself for a while in a grove of trees immediately underneath the College grounds, and reappeared higher up, where it climbed the crest of the hill amidst a wild belt of mountain heather, at an elevation of some six hundred feet.   The bark of a dog or the rattle of a corncrake in a neighbouring field seemed to reverberate for miles around in the still-ness.

'Hallo! Look! Did you see that?' cried Ken Rohan, with a start. A rocket had shot up into the air from the grove which skirted the College walls on the town side.

'Hold, then! There ought to be another. How is that?' Jack Harold jumped to his feet, and for a moment or two gazed eagerly out into the night. 'Ah, there it goes!' he cried, as another red train of fire rose out of the grove. 'All goes well. I must be off. Bon soir!—go to bed and forget Rosaleen's bright eyes, and live in the odour of Father Mulpetre's blessing—or wait!'—and as if acting on second thoughts, he drew the younger man to the opposite little window, which commanded a view of the road as it emerged from the grove and ascended the hill behind the College in long snaky curves until it vanished amidst the heather towards the top—'Look there—can you see anything on the road?'

A solid dark mass was projecting itself from the grove; moving steadily forward, until it completely covered the white face of the roadway. Ken Rohan rivetted his eyes upon it as it grew and grew, until the roadway to the crest of the hill was eclipsed beneath that slowly-moving, murky, terrible some-thing; and now through the tense silence came a dull, heavy, measured sound, like the breathing of the monster. The mass was —men, and the sound was of their march—that hoarse, solemn rhythm, which, in the ghostly light, suggested some unearthly religious rite.

'In God's name, what does it mean?' gasped the younger man, his cheek pale and his heart beating loudly.

'What does it mean? It is the Revolution!' whispered Harold, in his thrilling, theatrical way.

It was the summons that comes once in every young Irish life —the summons that has been the death-knell of generations of the brightest and best of them, and may be again. Ken Rohan's temples were throbbing wildly. It was as if a young Highlander of the last century was listening to the news that Prince Charlie had landed. And yet there came weird Lochiel warnings, too, on the night-wind with the sound of that deep, mystic tramp. The Storm-and-Doubt-Period which attacks German youth in their Religion rends the young Irish soul on the question of Nationality—the conflict which not infrequently decides whether the end is to be the Judicial Bench or the Dock, and usually swops the qualities proper to each like a malevolent gipsy sport-ing with the fate of changeling children. Ken Rohan could see vaguely the mocking gipsy eyes glittering out of the perilous road before him. He had the feeling that his wrist was being fastened in that chilly National mortmain—that Castle Dead Hand—which holds Irish youth fast-bound as to a mediæval rack.

'You are going?' he exclaimed, as the other restored the flag to its case and replaced it carefully in its resting-place behind the skirting, and then pulled a soft felt hat down over his eyes.

'My faith, yes—yonder is our blasted heath. It is by the light of the moon we brew our witches' cauldron. The charm is not yet wound up. One night—soon—I bring the tin case with me, and I do not return. "Malbrouck s'en va-t-en guer-r-r-e—il ne revient pas!"' he hummed gaily, recompensing himself for his unexampled spell of gravity by a lively pirouette.

'But everybody is in bed—how do you propose to get over the walls at this hour?'

'Ah, ça! One never gets over walls who can walk through them. Écoutez donc. The cook and I have confectioned a Holy Alliance. She has her faiblesses of heart like all the world, cette belle Johanna. She admits her beloved—(when not playing Romeo, he is the sexton of the Cathedral)—by the postern gate after dark. Our valiant croquemort has an appetite of the most devouring, and makes disappear the doctor's cold meat. I surprise him amidst the delights of digestion. A vigorous combat engages itself. Bref, la belle Johanna and I conclude a treaty conceived in these terms—Article 1. I leave the postern gate open for our valiant croquemort. Article 2. She leaves the postern gate open for me. Nothing more simple in the annals of diplomacy—Come!'

'What, I?' cried Ken Rohan, all flushed and feverish.

'Yes, you. I see it in your face. You are ours, and Ireland's—Only take off your shoes and tread doucement. The rat, that engaging little beast, which has lent Father Mulpetre its eyes, has lent him its ears also. Come!'

CHAPTER THE NINTH

HARRY DOES NOT JOIN THE MINISTRY

LORD DRUMSHAUGHLIN'S first exhibition of feeling, upon learning that his eldest son was in London, was to tear his hair and to trample his skull-cap under his feet, and to do this with an oath, although it was his daughter who broke the news—he who would once have flung down his cloak at a street-crossing to enable a woman to step over dry. 'The villain! the blackguard! the cursed fool!' he cried, stamping about the room, and dragging at his side-locks with murderous effect. 'Send him up here, if

he's sober. I'll horsewhip him, I'll —— No, don't send him up.
I am not equal to these scenes, Mabel. You ought to know it.
But who cares whether I am or not? O-oh!' So, upon second
thoughts, Lord Drumshaughlin sank querulously down into his
arm-chair (arm-chairs, moral or material, were the end of all his
outbreaks of energy), half persuading himself that the gout was
again grinding his toe-joint. It was his favourite illusion that,
when he wanted to be selfish, he was only ill. In support of this
theorem, as well as because they were pretty, he loved to make a
show of his thin white hands, which were transparent enough to
display an interesting tracery of pale blue veins. He who, given
a chivalrous purpose and an inspiring love, might have earned a
name to quicken men's blood, had sunk into the mean-spirited
truant who shirks standing up to his fight by shamming sickness.
His being an invalid did not altogether remove the difficulty, it
is true; but it was somebody else's business to look to it, as it
was to give him his medicine.

'Your mother does not know anything about this, child?' he
asked, after a moment or two, furtively. Nobody could tell why;
but Drumshaughlin, one of the boldest men alive, was suspected
of being afraid of his wife. What was certain was that, after years
of sordid bickerings, which rubbed off all the bloom of his homage
to women, and left his daughter the only being of her sex who
shone in his eyes with any light of holiness, he and his wife settled
into a perfectly respectable agreement to differ, on the terms of
Lady Drumshaughlin going her own way to a secure station in
society, unhaunted by sinister recollections of the Vallinzona, and
her husband being left unmolested in that soft, sensuous, semi-
detached-bachelor club life, which had come to be the only
Paradise his outworn faiths could promise him. He hated
trouble even more than he loved himself, if the two sentiments were
not really one; he was an Ethelred sunk into the habit of buying
off invaders at any price from his Castle of Indolence; and an
indispensable item in the Danegelt exacted by Lady Drumshaughlin was that Harry should be ruled out of sight and mind.

'No; we have not told mamma.'

'Humph, that's right,' he said, lolling placidly back. He still
felt a guilty necessity for maintaining a decent show of discomfort by twisting himself impatiently about in his chair, as one
struggling with moral and physical agony, until he could feel
Mabel's rosy fingers straying caressingly through his hair, when
he could no longer refuse to surrender himself to the luxury of
being perfectly at his ease.

This was not quite what Mabel Westropp wanted. 'Poor
Harry!' she murmured, half unconsciously.

'Yes, yes—Mabel, I request you will not be making these worrying observations. You know he has behaved badly, and there's an end of it.' There was not an end of it, however, for, wholly oblivious of the respect due to the gout, he started to his feet, and strutted nervously about the room, muttering, as if to himself, 'Poor Harry !—quite true—poor beggar !' The last bright trace of what Ralph Westropp might have been was that it invariably cost him more discomfort to shirk a duty than it would cost a resolute man to perform it. Suddenly he stopped, with his ears erect. 'That's Plynlymmon's step. Come along. Don't be all day about it. Come along there, will you ?' he cried unceremoniously, flinging open the door just as his visitor had his hand upon the handle. 'Well, well—what news from the Secretary ?'

Captain Plynlymmon was one of those correctly-groomed, elderly-juvenile men, of station and domestic circumstances almost as undecided as their age, who are as plentiful in fashionable London club-rooms as stays. He came over, so to say, with the Conqueror, in the remote age, when he served as best man at the weddings of the papas of various young men among his present familiars at the Chrysanthemum. All that the new generation could tell of him was that he was a younger son, who came in with a whiff of ancient Devonshire respectability ; that he was popular with all men, like a cigar after dinner, and with some women, who had not sons in danger of baccarat ; that he made upon the whole a creditable appearance in a club window, with his two-shilling hot-house flower in his buttonhole, his easy carriage, Rule Britannia moustache, and tailoring tastes of ancient lineage ; that, if he gave no dinners, he ate them in the proper spirit, and frequently had his name inserted before the *etcetera* in the lists of dinner-parties in considerable houses—that, in short, he was neither better nor worse than the thousand-and-one 'general utility men' whom society uses as it uses its easy chairs—sometimes to fill a corner, sometimes to be sat upon, never in the way, and always decently upholstered.

Lord Drumshaughlin sometimes sat upon his easy chairs without any regard for the furniture. A less experienced worldling than Plynlymmon would have resented the rude, mastiff-like shake of the shoulder with which he repeated : 'Well, well—what news ?' Plynlymmon's face remained perfectly cloudless as, in place of replying, he glided quietly towards Miss Westropp and made the obeisances of an old-fashioned gallant.

'Sorry to find the gout has been at you again, old man,' he then remarked, with a commiserating nod.

'Gout ! Rubbish ! Did you do anything with the Secretary ?'

'Anything ! Everything, thou most break-necked of a steeple-chasing nation,' smiled Plynlymmon, who knew of old that to give him a yard of his way was to get a mile of his own. 'He has fixed half-past one, at the Irish Office, to see you.'

'Plynlymmon, I am vastly obliged to you,' he said, shaking the other's hand with the benignity of a monarch distributing largess. 'Egad, that was a capital thought of mine—it will come off famously. Let me see. It's just half-past twelve. Mabel, tell that boy to put on his hat and step down with me to Queen Anne's Gate.' Lord Drumshaughlin could fight a battle as gaily as most generals if somebody would only take the drudgery off his hands. He could especially remember himself in the *Gazette*.

'I am afraid it is not so smooth sailing as you imagine,' gently interposed Captain Plynlymmon, who could not see his own name erased from the *Gazette* without some soreness. If the truth must be told, he, too, had no more to do with winning the battle than the young gentleman who brushed the Commander-in-Chief's uniform had to do with winning the battle of Waterloo, the battle having been really fought and won over an afternoon cup of Lady Asphodel's tea; but, inasmuch as he was aware that the Marchioness's subtle strategy was a bit of a humbug in its turn—Lord Drumshaughlin's incurable sloth having subjected him to all sorts of torturing obligations for an interview for which he had only to name his hour, if he had taken the business into his own hands—Plynlymmon had his feelings about this rough-riding way of appropriating his share of the stars and ribbons. 'For instance, I have some reason to anticipate that so far as that English peerage is concerned——'

'Eh ! what the devil do you know about an English peerage ?'

'Only that you told me not later than yesterday that life was not worth living with an Irish one,' was the cool reply.

'Did I ?' cried Lord Drumshaughlin, laughing good-humouredly. 'It's quite true, though. I'd willingly let them shoot Lord Drumshaughlin, if they'd leave plain Ralph Westropp. An Irish peer is like an Irish diamond—well enough in its mountains, but of neither use nor ornament in a jeweller's shop.'

'But a Representative Peer is a different thing, and as you happen to be first favourite for election in old Clancurran's place, I am afraid it will require some very judicious handling, indeed, if we are to suggest anything in the shape of a British peerage at this moment,' said Plynlymmon, with a statesmanlike carriage of the head.

'My dear fellow, I don't care a pinch of snuff for a British peerage,' cried the other gaily; 'not just at this moment, anyhow. All I want is something—devil may care what—for Harry.'

'For ——?'

'For Harry—my son, Harry.'

'Not going to throw up the Guards, eh ?'

'Was never in them,' gruffly muttered Lord Drumshaughlin, who was even testier in answering questions than in putting them.

'Ah ! I did not know,' said Plynlymmon vaguely. He stood arranging his cravat, which was of a subdued blue, by the cloudy old mirror over the fireplace; puzzled by this apparition of Harry in a household whose every garret he thought he had explored; and, like all men who subsist on tittle-tattle, piqued by a good mystery as by a good dinner. 'Well, well, old fellow, mind your play with the Chief Secretary,' he said, not yet satisfied that he had quite asserted the dignity of diplomacy, and gently toying with the feathers of a parting shaft. 'Just take two tips from me—never try to bring Jelliland to the point, and don't swear. There, there—you know there's no man relishes better than I do a good round English-bottomed oath of the Spanish Main—it emphasises a good thing, as a salute of twenty-one guns does Royalty—I always thought it was a mistake that swearing should go out with duelling and the prize-ring—they may come in again— but——' warned by a flash-light from Lord Drumshaughlin's eye — 'but Jelliland is a prig, and a Puritan, and that kind of thing — thinks anybody who talks better than himself is talking blasphemy, don't you see ? By-bye !' And Captain Plynlymmon walked through an airy minuet out of the room, thinking to himself : 'Who the dickens is Harry ?'

The Chief Secretary rose from his desk, without quitting his ground, to give Lord Drumshaughlin a courteous little bob and a well-considered little shake-hands, just cordial enough to abdicate any assumption of superiority, coming from a commoner to a peer from whom he wanted something, even from a Cabinet Minister to an Irish peer (for John Jelliland was a humble man), and yet stingy enough to intimate distantly that hand-shaking was a commodity which, like decorations, a Minister could distribute but sparingly. They were the days in which Cabinet Ministers were still joint-stock kings, who had simply divided up the Crown jewels amongst them.

'One moment, my lord—just a line or two,' he said, waving the father and son towards a couple of old-fashioned, stiff-backed chairs, as uncomfortable as a pair of public stocks, and taking up his quill pen again in a thoughtful sort of way.

Is it altogether too horrible to harbour a suspicion that, if you could have looked over his shoulder, you would have found the Secretary simply scribbling, 'Your obedient servant, John

Jelliland,' in a great variety of styles? Ministers have been known to do such things, even as a great physician lingers over a Latin prescription of ipecacuanha, which he is copying solemnly into his diary, when the succeeding patient enters the room.   They say it is found useful in overawing patients and place-hunters with reflections how much more weighty business this great throbbing world has on its mind than their own liver symptoms or views upon a clerkship in the Excise.   John Jelliland was driven almost by a law of nature to innocent expedients of this kind, as stumpy women are driven to increase their height by wearing dresses striped perpendicularly rather than horizontally.   He was a bald, quick, live, round-headed little gentleman, whom it took all the energies of a pair of active, decisive eyes, and all the majesty shed over his proceedings from a lofty bumpy brow, to save from the impression that he was perpetually standing on his toes to redeem the insignificance of his inches.

While the Secretary went on with his work of signing majestic sheets of foolscap—be the same autographs or death-warrants—with a sense of painful responsibility, until his visitors should be reduced to a proper temperature below blood-heat—a Danish dachshund, with dreamy eyes and proudly aristocratic head, that was taking its siesta on the hearthrug, was, by some secret affinity which dog-fanciers alone could exactly account for, attracted to Harry Westropp's side.   The animal rubbed its proud snout conciliatingly against Harry's legs, and submitted approvingly while that young gentleman, with much interest, took its jaws between his hands and examined its gums, and took it by the nape of the neck and shook it ; to all of which indignities the hound responded with a gently wagging tail and a look of respectful homage, such as a successful author called before the curtain bestows on a discriminating public.

'Down, Halmar, *down* !' cried the Minister, in the tone of one with whom it was a grievance to be compelled to repeat a single word.

'I never saw that breed before,' remarked Harry, genially; ' but it's a beautiful little bitch—our red setters arn't in it with her.'

The Secretary darted his keen eyes at the speaker as if he had unexpectedly developed a second head.   He withdrew them instantly—a busy man could only afford a moment's glance at the portent—merely remarking, 'Ah !' and summoning the dachshund peremptorily to his side.

'I'd give a hatful of sovereigns for a pup out of that one, struck in Harry again, with whom Halmar was still carrying on a distant flirtation from behind her master's chair.

The Secretary glanced up again with a little frown of surprise; then, for fear of further inroads on the dignity of the place, hurriedly wrote off a last autograph, and, having sealed up what he had been writing with much care, assumed a look of gentle weariness, in order that he might the more gracefully shake it off as he rose with a smile and cried, 'My dear lord, I'm so sorry—you know how it is with us, slaves of the lamp—I hope your patience is not as tired as my pen.   This is—ahem ?'

' My son,' said Lord Drumshaughlin ; whereupon Mr. Jelliland gave the tip of a finger to the admirer of the little bitch, who had not noticed her master before now, and rapidly made up his mind that the dachshund was the more attractive acquaintance of the two.

They talked about many things except the things which both Lord Drumshaughlin and Mr. Jelliland had in their minds. These they only talked around.   Captain Plynlymmon was quite correct in his hint that Mr. Jelliland was one of those precisians who, in the cat's-cradle labyrinths of diplomacy, deem it impolite to look over the hedge ; and Harry, who understood vaguely that the governor had come to obtain something to do for him, was greatly puzzled to know what the row about the old Earl of Clancurran's will, and the state of Bobby O'Shaughnessy's nerves, and Monsignor McGrudder's Disestablishment resolution at the County meeting, had to do with it.   Like almost all men who have been less than six months Chief Secretary for Ireland, John Jelliland was enthusiastic about his office.   Other men had failed there, he knew; but they had treated Ireland as young physicians treat the blind, lame, and halt, until more eligible patients turn · up.   That was not his way.   He spent his days and nights in the caverns of Irish Blue-books, with the sombre enthusiasm of an old worshipper in the Catacombs ; and he humbly flattered himself that he had it all at his fingers' ends.   He could teach boozy old sunburstical O'Shaughnessy the alphabet of the Inland Navigation question ; he had spent a great portion of the recess in seeing for himself where the Shannon drainage works had burst, and how many hundred thousand acres were flooded—to the great comfort of the flooded-out population; he had conceived vast projects for encouraging Irish self-help by relieving an unscientific Poor-law of the blot of outdoor relief; he could follow the accounts of the Church Temporalities into their most secret windings, and answer offhand what had become of the Tithe rent-charge. These were the things for an Irish Secretary to know, and not Davis's Poems or the History of King Brian Boru, or, for that matter, whether Orange or Green was the first to run away at a twopenny-ha'penny siege of Derry.   He believed in two great books—the Bible and the Blue-book.   The former, because in

Ireland unhappily it was principally used for pitching at people's heads, he kept rigidly for family prayers ; but in the Blue-book, he believed with a fierce and fanatical devotion, lay the secret of the regeneration of Ireland, the all-sufficient anodyne for the pestilent squabbles of the historians and the moonshine of the poets. Once buckled to his work with the consciousness of unswerving rectitude of purpose, and a considerable success as an Under-Secretary in the Indian Department, he was only confirmed in his humble self-confidence when he found the Nationalist papers in Dublin sneering at his Irish policy as one of 'Blue-book jelly,' since there could be no surer mark of the beast than levity in so serious a matter. Besides, the groundwork of his plan was the theory that the less he did that was to anybody's liking the surer he was to have done what was for everybody's good. 'Ask everybody's advice and then follow your own—that is the only way you can make sure of being in the right about Ireland, my dear,' he used to declare in confidential moments to his wife, explaining to her with meek self-satisfaction what a silly alarmist the County Inspector of Police was, or what a shallow, excellently intentioned man the Archdeacon, with his dirges about the Church in danger; and that admirable woman, who believed in John only less than in the wise men recorded in the Book of Judges, wondered greatly how it was that those extraordinary poor people in Ireland could not see things as John and she saw them—a most excellent and lovable couple of the very stamp that are the pith and strength of their own country, and an insoluble puzzle to themselves and others in strange ones.

'You know, I have always been of opinion myself that we will ultimately have to do something that will make a mild splash about the Church—cut off another half-dozen Bishoprics or so, for example—before people in Ireland will settle down to mind their business. Don't you think so?' asked the Secretary, with a polite display of interest in the answer.

'I am not much of a politician, to be frank with you, though they send me a threatening letter now and again,' said Lord Drumshaughlin. 'But I really don't see why the priests and parsons should not divide whatever is going, in an amicable way, and I suspect our man will have to go that far, at all events, if he is to carry the county, or to carry Monsignor McGrudder, which is the same thing. By the bye,' he added, without exactly knowing why he did so, except that it was the first opportunity that presented itself of bringing the immediate object of his visit into view, 'my son has only just arrived from Ireland.'

'Ah!' said the Secretary, shooting a look at Harry from under the corners of his all but closed eyelids—it was a way he had of startling people with the fact that he was most awake when he chose to seem most asleep. 'You have just come over, sir? What are they saying about our Reclaimed Slobs Bill?'

'I don't think they are saying much; I never heard,' was Harry's somewhat bewildered reply.

'Dreaming more about abstractions as usual, I suppose,' said the Minister, smiling indulgently. 'As if the man who would reclaim a hundred acres of the Fergus slob-lands would not be a more useful citizen than Con of the Hundred Battles! I dare say a crusade against the Establishment, now, would be a more popular programme!—*that's* what they're burning for, eh?'

'I don't think it is.'

'You don't think things are ripe enough in Ireland to go that far—not just yet?' asked Mr. Jelliland, with the languid interest of one who knew the answer better than anybody could tell him.

'They're ripe for an Irish Republic. You'll have it one of those days,' Harry answered, without the least consciousness that he was saying anything explosive.

An ugly spasm crossed the Secretary's face, and left a livid track behind it. 'I did not quite catch?' he said, his brow in its most corrugated and menacing condition.

'As soon as the harvest is in, you'll have the Americans across,' proceeded Harry, in his straightforward, unsuspecting way. 'Every fellow worth his salt about our neighbourhood is in it. You should hear the carabineers chorusing : "Hark ! the time is coming when our darling flag of green"—on the very barrack-square at Bantry, by Jingo ! The Major made a row about it, and the fellows actually tossed him in a blanket. Whenever they pass the word for the rising, I don't know who's to oppose them, except the police, and they'll make short work of the peelers, I can tell you.'

This raw country lad had just given the Chief Secretary the worst stab he had ever received in his life. That very morning he had received an alarming report from the Inspector-General of Constabulary, to which, having to place three sheets of official amendments to the Reclaimed Slobs Bill on the paper that day, he gave but scant attention, a portion of his theory of Irish Government being that it was as much the nature of Dublin Castle officials to invent alarms, as it was of the Portadown Orangeman to curse the Pope, or of the Tipperary peasant to move amendments of the Land Laws out of the mouth of his blunderbuss, rather than of his regular Parliamentary representative. He had dismissed the Inspector-General's report with a somewhat contemptuous minute ; but, fight it down as he would, the wild talk of this harum-scarum youngster brought the slighted official warnings grinning and mowing at him like apes, with vague lurid visions in the background of his Reclaimed Slob-land wrapt in a blaze of insurrection. He had a moment of such sickness as the first thrill of a mortal wound must bring— a moment in which his world seemed to be flying into a million fragments in his eyes. But it was a moment only. The next, he was smiling at his own grotesque weakness. Could there possibly be a better proof of his wisdom in snubbing the Castle alarmists than that they should be of the same opinion as this clumsy rustic simpleton, who might well have the insolence to endeavour to hoax a Cabinet Minister with his tale of Fee-fo-fum, after beginning with the impertinence of patronising Halmar. He suddenly withdrew his eyes from Harry with a withering look of disgust.

'Your son has not, I presume, finished his education?' he said, with a scarcely-disguised sneer, which was all the more provoking to himself that an unalterable part of his Irish plan was to have been to shun sarcasm as he would shun profane oaths. Then he wrenched the conversation violently to the subject of the decoration of the new Egyptian Room at the Club (of which Mr. Jelliland was a committee-man), and Lord Drumshaughlin knew that, so far as its object was concerned, the interview was over. Harry did not join the Cabinet.

'What the devil did you mean by that parcel of rebel balderdash?' asked Lord Drumshaughlin, of his son, when they were together in the street.

'Mean! Why, it's true!' said Harry. 'It's the talk of the country.'

'So it is true that Mr. Jelliland is a confounded old prig and pedant; but it is not necessary to tell him so when you're begging your bread from him.'

'That bitch was the loveliest thing I ever laid my eyes on,' said Harry, who was philosophising on the waywardness of fate which assigned such a treasure to such a master. Suddenly he burst forth : 'Oh, governor, I say!' and stopped with an appearance of the liveliest interest to make sure whether the gorgeous equestrian figures in the niches outside the Horse Guards were really alive, or whether they were only statues painted as advertisements for recruits for the Life Guards Blue.

Lord Drumshaughlin stood for a moment regarding him with a pang which brought back old wild moments of conflict between fondness and pain. 'He has inherited one heirloom from the Westropps in spite of us,' he muttered to himself—'the knack of putting his foot in it grandly.'

CHAPTER THE TENTH

THE WILD IRISH GIRL

His disastrous performance at the Irish Office did not at all pluck down Harry Westropp's spirits. He was enjoying London as a child enjoys its first pantomime, and Harry was not more disposed than the child to keep his eye on the clock, calculating how long the performance was going to last. Do the fire-flies worry about the next winter when they are glittering in an Italian dell? Poor Harry was anything but a gorgeous insect, but he could roll in the sun with the best of them, and trouble himself quite as little about the future. With young Neville he had established a friendship of as sudden growth as the storied Beanstalk. The tongue-tied young Englishman was a stranger to the genial Irish liberties with Christian names, not merely as an affectionate method of tutoying their friends, but of playfully gibbeting their enemies (the conqueror of the Boyne being simple King Billy, and the famous Chancellor who carried the Union Black Jack, in the traditions of the people). He was astonished to find himself 'Reggy' after twenty-four hours' acquaintance with the young man in the homespun tweed suit, and was still more astonished to find how naturally he slipped into calling his companion Harry, even as the early Norman invaders lapsed into the delights of Irish dress and Irish wives.—'I am downright jealous. So should you be, too, Mab,' said handsome Horace Westropp to his sister. 'Harry is cutting us both out.'—'I am so glad,' was the reply, spoken with a fervour somewhat puzzling to the young guardsman, who laughed and said : 'Don't be cruel, Mab. Neville is the best fellow in the world.'

The best fellow in the world was not content with trotting Harry about the stables (where the latter feasted his eyes upon more enthralling *chefs-d'œuvre* than the average British citizen can discover in all the picture galleries in Italy). He showed him the little Princes walking in St. James's Park (in whom also Harry's liberal tastes developed a certain degree of interest), and the Christy Minstrels who never performed out of London (and whose plantation walk-round, entitled 'Shoo-fly,' aroused his enthusiasm to the utmost pitch), and the helter-skelter of cab traffic in Trafalgar Square towards theatre hour (which Harry rather took to be some exciting form of public sport, in which the game was to dodge in and out at peril of your neck among processions of flying imps with blazing gig-lamp eyes rushing together from all the points of the compass to test the agility of the public). He had heard of the view from the top of the Monument as a spectacle in much repute with young persons from the provinces; but he was not himself sufficiently acquainted with that part of the country to be a good cicerone; and upon the whole he judged the time would be more judiciously devoted to a visit to the New Circus, and here not only Harry but he himself enjoyed the tinsel wonders like a schoolboy, and, although he had the reputation of being wanting in humour, laughed at the jokes of Meelya-murdering Molloy, the Hibernian clown, with a warmth which surprised nobody so much as the Meelya-murderer himself, whom Harry further proposed to invite out to some light refreshment as a countryman. The two friends dined together at the Chrysanthemum, where they had white wine to begin with, and red wine to follow, and more wine, red and white, than was good for them; and Harry, who had not a good head for liquor, was a little boisterous towards the Green Chartreuse stage of the proceedings; and the young Millefleurs of the Club, who would not have been amazed if Neville had brought the crossing-sweeper to dine with him, languidly agreed that the noisy young man must be the jock of Carabîche, and began vaguely to think of hedging.

Amidst revels and suppers of the gods of this description Quish was somewhat neglected. What with the fine footmen who would insist upon calling him Paddy (upon the theory that men of his nation were restricted to that name, as all Jews were obliged to wear black gaberdines in Venice); and the kitchen-maids, who charged him with ogling them; and Mrs. MacAnaspie, who required him to come in and go out by the back way through the mews, like the sanitary cart; and the policeman who attentively kept him in view whenever he took his walks abroad— Quish was beginning to feel that London was a lonesome and uncomfortable place. He had a wild animal's longing to be back in the jungle. Only for an acquaintance which he struck up with a lean dog which haunted the back yards of Rashleigh Street, with his tail between his legs and an eye always supplicatingly appealing to the public whether he was really worth any further kicking, Quish would probably have done somebody harm—as wild animals that are baited sometimes do. The popular impression in Mrs. MacAnaspie's kitchen was that, like his ragged friend with whom he shared his dinner, he wore a tail. Certainly, the lean dog was not a greater affront to the starched respectability of the neighbourhood than this singular shaggy creature, who scarcely spoke English, and, indeed, scarcely spoke at all. Sad to tell, the Lord Harry, as he used to call his young master, thought but little of all this while he was seeing life at the Circus and quaffing Pommery See at the Chrysanthemum. Stumbling upon him one evening in the dusk in Rashleigh Street, he cried :

'Hallo, Quish! I thought you were gone home long ago.'

Whereat Quish wagged his enormous head in a crestfallen way, with an 'Och, no, then, zurr,' and looked as though his eyes were about to fly out of his head in opposite directions.

The truth is, it was the first time in his life that Harry West-ropp had found a friend who did not reek of the stables; and, in the first joyous moment of his good fortune, young Neville not merely outshone Quish, he effaced him, as the midday sun does a star of the nine-hundred-and-ninety-ninth magnitude. Their friendship was no less rich in pleasure to Neville. Even to one so utterly good-natured and humble in his own esteem, there came the pleasant sensation of being assured that there were men less brilliant than he, and the delightful novelty of strutting about as a superior being, showing the town to a man to whom a music-hall yielded the delights of Paradise, and who was as-tonished at the Lord Mayor. So the days and nights sped with-out the least looking back on Harry's part upon Mr. Jelliland's flesh-pots, nor the smallest further exertion on Lord Drum-shaughlin's part to reverse the decrees of Fate. Until——

One night, after a feast of Whitstable oysters and champagne at the Café Paradiso, as Harry was tipsily picking his way up-stairs with a candle in his hand, Lady Drumshaughlin, who was returning from an evening party, met him plump upon the landing-place, and fell as if a shot had struck her. Captain Plynlymmon, who had been of her ladyship's party, was in wait-ing to receive her as she fell, and remarked to himself, reflec-tively, as he rang for a servant :

'Harry, for a ducat! What a queer chap, and who the mis-chief is he? Her ladyship has a three-volume novel somewhere in those dark eyes of hers, if one could only read it.'

Pondering which problem, he lit a cigar, waved off an officious cabby, and walked home in the moonlight. Three or four nights afterwards, walking home again in the company of the moon and his cigar, Plynlymmon had a new and more incredible element of complication to give him pause:

'The Wild Irish Girl flying from London!—not a dozen prettier girls in the lot—and in the very fruit-time of the season—six good weeks left—the weeks of moonlit gardens, whispering walks—the St. Bartholomew of bachelors. Bah! don't tell me! No woman ever fled from it without a bruise somewhere. But where? or how? or what the deuce do all these people mean with their masques and mystery plays? First the mother, then a Man in the Iron Mask, Harry—and now this unaccountable daughter—why, the family is as full of mysteries as Prospero's Isle !   Upon my conscience, I was never in my life so provokingly out of the know.'

Young Neville heard the news at the Chrysanthemum, where he was perspiring over the composition of a letter of three lines to his stud-groom.

'Fact. The Wild Irish Girl's bolted,' said Mortlake, whose function in life it was to circulate as a sort of stop-press edition of all such items of intelligence.

'You don't say !—by Jove !' exclaimed Lord Amaranth, who represented the buying public of the early and exclusive news-men.

'Not gone,' said another. 'Mortlake's wrong, as usual. Only going—under a vow to bury herself in some Irish bog or other, to teach a hobbledehoy brother of hers pothooks—such a shame ! —the law ought to forbid it :—as bad as burying herself alive in a convent, every bit.'

'A convent it is to be—one under the rule of the Abbey of Thélème,' grinned Mortlake, with an evil sneer. 'Bet my hat nobody tells who the fellow is, except myself ? And I can only guess.'

'Mortlake, you will die of cancer of the tongue.'

'Don't you think you had better look to your own symptoms of softening of the brain, old fellow ?'

'Why did fellows turn the head of that girl ?' asked Lord Amaranth, pettishly pulling flakes off his cigar, as one who had, somehow, been treated badly in the matter. 'Do you know, I always thought the mother was immensely the finer woman of the two ? I could never understand those wild Irish ways of the girl —a man could never be sure what they meant.'

'You can be sure what they mean now,' said Mortlake, emboldened by Lord Amaranth's pique. 'It is always the way with these wild people. The love of the beautiful savage is all very well for a time—it begins like a page of "Hiawatha," and ends by an elopement with the junior footman.'

'Neville has overheard you. He'll smash your face,' said somebody.

He had, indeed, overheard a few vital words of the conversation ; but he was not thinking of Mortlake. Instead of smashing Mortlake's face, he got up, looking straight before him, and walked out of the room, leaving the dabbled page behind him on which he had scrawled :

'Chuddley, the Vet, thinks that instead of the steel balls ——'

He went out into St. James's Street as dizzy as a man who had

just suffered sunstroke, and with no more notion of where he
was going than one in delirium has of his destination when he is
being whirled through endless galleries of grinning human heads.
His legs walked away with him to Rashleigh Street by an independent mechanism of their own.   Ten thousand lovers have
done the like before him, and never once asked themselves what
brought them there, or found it dull out on the comfortless flags,
with nothing but sooty brick walls to stare at, except two lighted
windows which, for all he knew, illuminated Mrs. MacAnaspie
at her evening meal of tea and shrimps.   But love, if a hard
taskmaster, can pay his slaves with all sorts of pretty, cheating
fairy gold.   Neville, who was not in ordinary a man of imagination, could see through the thick walls and the dingily-illumined
curtains, as plainly as if he saw with mortal eyes, a rosy vision
of beauty, with unconquered dark-blue eyes, and imperial diadem
of hair, fleeing, fleeing far from him into space, and leaving only
a faint trail of perfumed light in the black world behind her.
Still he did so burn to see her just once more with corporeal eyes
—if even Harry, swaggering home from the Golden Shades music-
hall, would only turn up, what a joy it would be !   Nay, he once
conceived a wild thought of knocking at the door, and then
running to hide, in the belief that merely seeing the door open
could not be without its consolations.   Nobody and nothing
appeared, however, until a policeman as dreamy as himself
knocked up against him with the sensation of having knocked
up against a lamp-post.

Luckier than most lovers in such cases, his devotions were
not, as it happened, directed to the wrong address.   Inside the
pall-like curtains of the lighted windows, the rosy vision was in
very truth glowing by Lord Drumshaughlin's side, or, to be
accurate, was seated on a footstool at his knee, while Reggy
Neville and the policeman were begging one another's pardon.
The roses had, indeed, faded since we last saw Miss Westropp in
that faint pink ball-dress which covered her like a beautiful
blush.   There were dark suggestions under her eyes, and white
suggestions about her cheeks, of anxious unrestful nights ; her
hair tumbled in shining cascades around her shoulders, and her
little hand was laid pleadingly upon her father's.   She was justifying, as she had been justifying, oh ! so many weary times
during the last three days, to him and to herself, the determination which had caused Mr. Mortlake's cancerous tongue to wag.
She pleaded under the disadvantage that the very looks and
caresses, which, upon any other point, would have had an easy
victory, did but aggravate intolerably the anguish, the incredi-

H

bility of her present caprice. Briefly, she had come to the de termination that, as Harry could remain no longer in London, and had lost all hope of employment through the medium of Mr. Jelliland, she would herself go back with him to Drum-shaughlin, and try what she could do to save him. The monks all tell us that the postulant's first day of loneliness in his narrow cell is one of miserable doubts whether he altogether knew his own mind when he fled the gladsome world. Such had been Mabel Westropp's lonely conflict during these last bitter nights and days in the torture-chamber in which her own resolution had immured her. Did she really know what she was doing in turning her back on London ? There were a dozen young girls of her season who outshone her in classic perfection of form and distinction of manner ; but there was not one on whom Society was readier to lavish the adoration reserved for the chosen ones to whom, like the Mexicans of old, it offers a year or two of divine honours before immolating them. She was too young to understand that it was the faint sensuous fumes of worship which made the air of ball-rooms so subtly sweet ; she enjoyed it all as naturally as a sensitive flower opens its petals to the sunshine. But she did enjoy it with the simple ardour of a girl for whom the bright paradise of youth was opening in all its freshness and springtime revelry, and who had boundless store of health and joyousness and honesty of heart to find in waltzes, operas, and pretty frocks the materials of immeasurable interest, glory, and delight. She had sipped these pleasures with a freeborn heartiness which had sometimes caused the double-barrelled eye-glasses of the Lady Dankroses to tremble with horror ; in mere wilfulness and caprice, it seemed ; and now, to indulge what seemed no better than caprice, of a newer and more out-rageous fashion, she, who had denied herself nothing, was about to deny herself everything. Was the step she was about to take likely to be of service to anybody ? What real hope could there be for a young gentleman who made a confidant of Quish, the bailiff ? Would he not rather drag her down with him into the abysmal meanness and stagnation of life in an Irish country town ?—into the mosquito-spites of Miss Harman's archery club, or into Miss Deborah Harman's plans for arguing hungry little Papists out of their dogmatic errors with a soup-ladle ? Was even her motive an unmixedly good one ? Was she not—some mocking spirit kept asking her tortured soul—was she not ad-hering to her resolution mainly because in a Quixotic moment she had formed it, and because she found more pleasure in being wilful than in being right ? Had not the very storm, which her determination brought about her, a considerable influence in making that determination unshakable?

There was ever so much truth in these self-reproaches; for, like most young ladies who have enjoyed a father's idolatry without a mother's counsel, she was not always quite sure where duty ended and caprice began. But clear amidst all these swamps and shifting mists of doubt there stood out ineffaceably that lonely figure of her neglected brother, with the vacant eyes and dishevelled hair, moping away his friendless youth in that gloomy sepulchre of a Castle;—picking up the poorest crumbs of human friendship in the stables and the public-house, while she was basking in the glow of London drawing-rooms, sipping the honey of men's vows. Whenever his image came back upon her mind: —Harry, with whom she had first dared the ghost of mad Dick Warbro in the Castle cellars, with whom she had first climbed the breezy heights of Hungry for the white heather, and heard the waterfall dash down to its grave in the Wolves' Glen—she had no more doubt what was her duty than if she saw a child on the edge of the waterfall in Coomnaguira, walking blindfolded. Mabel, though she was two years younger than Harry, and though he had borne her in his strong arms for a considerable portion of that first ascent of Hungry Mountain, regarded him irresistibly in the light of a child; and who could doubt that he stood on the brink of the terrible white abyss—if, haply, he was not already over it? But there was more than that. Plynlymmon was not wholly astray in his cynical surmise of 'a bruise somewhere.' Harry's appearance in London, and the awful gulf it had revealed in the household, had set Mabel's thoughts travelling in regions of vague, feverish terror, in which she cried and strained for a mother's strengthening arm with the longing of a sick child. Some gossamer, chilly shadow began to float between her and all this ball-room radiance; some impalpable, oppressive sense of discomfort which manifested itself in a certain awe of those cold, stately, perfect dames, beside whom she began to feel something of the shrinking of an overrated country coquette. Poor Reggy Neville's luckless declaration of love somehow augmented her unintelligible and unconquerable self-distrust—augmented, above all, her wild lonely aching for a mother's sheltering arm and divining soul. Her feeling upon this score 'was not so much thought as shadowy, formless impression; but it was an impression strong enough to bring back the breath of the pure free hills of Beara, smelling sweeter than all the delicate pastilles and essences of Mayfair. Also, her want of a motherly confidante had given to her sympathies a freer range

than is usual with young beauties whose first Court cóstume was
hardly yet tost. Her highest dream of happiness was making
others happy ; and in the limitless sun-heat of her own bright
nature she could not see why all the world might not be steeped
in the same joyous, tender, hopeful sun-bath, and sing from soul
to soul, and from creature to Creator, like the morning stars.
Perhaps, it was visiting that one lowly spot in her own heart
that gave her so keen a perception of how much loveableness and
how little love the great, dark, suffering, indelibly angelic human
heart was composed. With a vague, girlish zeal, she stormed
against the heartless, self-glorifying league of two against the
world, which cheats the world of woman's unsunned treasures of
human sympathy in the name of Love ; she felt a certain guilty
tremor run through all her ball-room joys whenever she thought
' what was this among so many '—what a speck of costly, selfish
brightness was this amidst the glooms and despairs of London ;
and I am afraid Lady Dankrose would give up all lingering hope
of regeneration for a young lady who would dream now and again
of some new miracle of the loaves and fishes which would make
the ball-room walls expand, until all the sons and daughters of
men were gathered into its golden glow, where there should be
ices, and waltzes, and love-whispers, and divine music for all,
and pinched cheeks and lacerated hearts no more under the sun.
Such was the tangle of half-formed thoughts out of which poor
Mabel's throbbing little heart had to evolve some plan for beginning her regeneration of the world by leaving father and
mother to their own devices in the very crisis of a triumphant
London season. The old man at first stormed and raged like a
maniac when his daughter broke the news to him.

'You shan't! by God, you shan't!' he roared in his rage.
'You are mad. I forbid it. Not another word!' The excitement plunged him into a genuine nervous fever, which left nothing
behind the next day except depression. 'You want to kill me,'
he cried complainingly. 'I'm an old man, Mabel. Don't go and
take the light of my life away with you.' There was a tear in his
eye. The blow had actually struck water from a heart which
self-indulgence had all but turned to stone.

'But, papa, why should you not come with us?'

'I!—leave London!' He started back under a new terror—
his every tendril and tentacle had got gripped into the easy, lazy,
luxuriant life of an elderly London club-beau, like some ancient
mossy parasite clinging around a deciduous tree, and sucking its
juices ; and here was a hatchet lifted to strike away his tenacious
hold of the associations which furnished him with the sap of life,
and fling him, a hacked and withered old creeper, on the ground to

go in search of. something new to cling to. He could scarcely believe his ears.

'Drumshaughlin can be made a jolly place enough for the autumn, I am sure. We should get you up your billiard-room in the Warbro Tower—you should have your sessions and your grand jury—why not a harvest-home ? The grouse-mountains are the best in the county, and then there would be the fox-hunting. It is so long since you had a real gallop, papa. One goes in the Park as the circus horses do.'

'I do not want a gallop, child,' cried Lord Drumshaughlin snappishly. He was alarmed beyond measure to find himself suddenly put upon the defensive by this savage proposal to tear him from his rooted London ties and cast him shuddering into an Irish bog. To be deprived of Mabel was a terrific blow, but to be cast out of London was quite a new fiendish jest of fate which almost took his breath away. 'There are—ahem!—various reasons—decisive reasons—why I cannot live in Ireland.'

'Mr. Harman's ghost stories. Papa, you are not afraid of ghosts—not afraid of anything,' she said proudly.

Lord Drumshaughlin frowned. 'Don't be ridiculous, child. Hans Harman is one of the most cool-headed men in the country, and he has warned me repeatedly that my life would not be worth twenty-four hours' purchase in Drumshaughlin without police protection.'

'Then I really think they ought to shoot himself, for, if any one deserves it, I am sure it is not my dear old pappy.'

Lord Drumshaughlin felt perplexed and angry. He was really an unpopular landlord, as men who stand between hungry people and a full meal will be ; and, besides the chance that his presence in Ireland might charge a blunderbuss against his life, there was the still more formidable certainty that it would stir a battalion of sleeping Irish creditors into activity. He was no more afraid of a bullet now than he was when he saw the flash of Antonaccio's pistol that night in the hotel in the Rue de la Paix. What he shrank from was not the danger, but the discomfort of being paragraphed in the newspapers, of having armed policemen about him instead of his soft-footed valet, of being obliged to keep an eye to his revolver instead of sunning himself in peace at his club windows. This was, however, the least element in his repugnance to quitting London. He had put it forward with emphasis in the belief that murder was of all things the topic most likely to scare a woman, and, behold ! here was his bogey laughed out of countenance, and nothing better left for him to say than, 'I request you will not talk in that manner, Mabel. You do not understand.'

'I do not understand why anybody in the world should want
to hurt a hair of your head, papa—and nobody shall!' she cried
clasping the head referred to in the shelter of her beautiful arms;
and, indeed, any further protection in the way of police escort
seemed a ridiculous impertinence. 'The old people will be only
delighted to have you back once more—I am sure they will. I
have heard them say a thousand times nothing would ever go
wrong if the master was at home to keep an eye to things.
Unless, of course,' she added with a sudden spasm of doubt,
'unless mamma has any objection to your coming.'

'But mamma does object. She would most properly object,'
cried Lord Drumshaughlin, grasping at the suggestion like a
drowning man. 'Your mother cannot be left alone in London.
There really ought to be some consideration for *her*,' he said with
the air of a man who had cheerfully effaced *himself* from the cal-
culation. The last virtue of the egoist, who is not altogether
petrified, is the necessity for weaving some ray of altruism, however flimsy, to cover his selfishness.

'I am afraid mamma would be still less pleased if Harry was
to remain in London,' said Mabel quietly.

'Yes, yes, but Harry does not want to remain in London—I
am sure he does not think of such a thing,' said Lord Drumshaughlin testily. The girl's self-sacrifice stirred up many a bitter
pool of remorse in his own memory, and he tried desperately hard
to think that it was Harry who was a ne'er-do-weel and Mabel an
unfeeling child, and not he himself who was drugged to the lips
in self-indulgence from the guilty days in the Vallinzona down
to this moment when he was letting the son of his impassioned
youth sink back without a struggle into a life of dreary vacancy
and blight. Lord Drumshaughlin had a bad memory, which was
one of his luxuries; he hated anything that jogged it.

'No, dear papa, you will find there is nothing for it but my
own plan.'

'Which is, to rob me of my comfort in my declining days, to
worry your mother, to ruin whatever prospects we ever had in
society—prospects which, you cannot but feel, were dear to me
only as they affected your future and your settlement in life——'

'Papa!'

'But yes, child. You are old enough to know that I am poor,
and that in London you have your choice of scores of young men
who would be able to make a suitable provision for the happiness of
my darling. And you must turn your back upon this—you must
break your mother's heart and mine—all in order that a grown
young man may not feel lonesome in Drumshaughlin Castle, with
two horses to ride and twenty miles of mountain to shoot over.

he cried hotly. It was such a relief to be able to be indignant with somebody besides himself.

The thought that the grown young man was her brother and his son struggled almost to her lips, and that two horses and twenty miles of shooting did not, possibly, mean bliss enough to reconcile him to a tainted name, a mother's repugnance, a father's neglect, and a stunted youth passed far from the splendours which ought to have been his—without one elevating association, one ray of generous ambition, one throb of human sympathy. But she was perfectly aware that when her father spoke hotly it was not because he believed he was right, but because he knew he was wrong ; and she was too well satisfied that she was winning to make a cruel use of her victory.

'I suppose women are always wrong in an argument, papa— that is a good woman's reason why you should let me have my way all the same,' she said laughingly. 'If you are right, Harry will soon enough get tired of me, or I will get tired of him, and abandon him to his dogs and gun. Then you'll have a Prodigal Child returning to beg you not to cast her off just yet to one of those incomparable young gentlemen who, I must say, papa, appear to have been more confidential with you than they have been with me,'—she could not help saying with a touch of her old irrepressible hardihood. 'But just wait until I've had fair play as housekeeper at Drumshaughlin. Give me only four months to try what I can do, and if I cannot tempt you over to my cosy little chimney-corner at Drumshaughlin for the winter, in spite of all Mr. Harman's drawings of death's-heads and cross-bones, I here bind myself to surrender at discretion in the spring, and come back to be disposed of, like the body of a decapitated traitor, at your majesty's pleasure. What could be fairer ?'

The old lord felt a sneaking sense of relief. The ground of debate had been skilfully shifted. He who had, as it were, entered into court in the dread ermine of justice to arraign his daughter for going to Drumshaughlin, shambled out of the dock, glad to escape being sentenced to accompany her. If he were forced to the choice:—his daughter's society, idolatrously as he loved her, in the one scale ; and, in the opposite scale, his club, his haunts, his habits, his dinners, his—other ties which he would have cut out his tongue rather than whisper a hint of in the same room in which his daughter was breathing—his conscience reproached him darkly as to which side his election might incline to. But there was now no need of a vexatious examination of conscience of that sort. A sacrifice, indeed, had to be made for the sake of his children—a sacrifice that he could take some personal credit for ; he even felt some of the pure pleasure of

immolation, for in his heart of hearts he rejoiced that the wealth
of love which he was surrendering was going to enrich his poor
half-witted and slighted son   Distinctly, therefore, he was doing
a meritorious thing ; and now did not Mabel herself tell him that
his severance from London was no part of the plot at all, and
even hint that his presence in Drumshaughlin just yet would only
spoil it ?   To give him his due, he was much too poor a hypocrite
to make any great disguise about his relief.

'Very well, Mabel,' he growled, 'as you have not asked for
my advice, I suppose I ought not to give it' (which sentence was
abruptly closed by two bright red lips). 'All I can say is,' he
added, judicially, sorely at a loss for anything particular to say
at the moment, 'I hope it may do some good to somebody.   Of
course, I shall have to take you across myself.'

'If Mr. Harman will let you,' she said, laughingly.

'Oh, Harman's an ass—confound him !'

'But, indeed, papa, I feel I don't in the least deserve it ; and,
besides, I shall not be dull.   I shall have Harry—and Quish, too,
you know,' she added, merrily.

'Mabel, I insist,' cried Lord Drumshaughlin ; it was the far-
thing in the pound which his conscience wouldn't rest easy until
he had paid by way of composition. 'At least, I shall put you in
the train in Dublin, and see everything right ; and then'—in a
burst of guileless egoism—'there will be just time to catch the
Holyhead boat the same night.   Certainly, Mab !—that's what
we'll do ; I won't hear of your objections, child,' he cried, as if
his catching the returning mail-boat had given him the paramount
and unanswerable triumph in the debate.

Either Lady Drumshaughlin was less tractable, or Mabel used
less pains to win her.   Her ladyship had kept her room ever since
her rencounter with Harry upon the landing-place.   She sent for
him, indeed, the next day, and had a dutiful little interview with
him, and asked him when did he come, and when was he going,
and hoped he would not be such a foolish boy, or let her be hearing unpleasant stories of him ; all of which Harry bore as stolidly
as if his neighbour in a railway carriage had been asking him
wasn't it wretched weather ? and weren't the papers dull ? and
would this train meet the Clapham train at Willesden Junction ?
Everybody understood that her ladyship's nerves were not to be
put to such a test again by Harry's remaining in London ; but
the announcement of the terms on which she was about to get rid
of him perfectly enraged her.   Mabel's beauty was the talisman
that unlocked to her dozens of houses at whose doors she had
spent weary, wistful years of waiting ; and now, in the moment
of victory, her talisman was to be snatched out of her hand ; she

was to be left wandering as of old outside the golden caverns crying : 'Open, millet ! Open, barley !' Her life-struggle for recognition, her hopes of an English peerage and of a noble son-in-law who would make that recognition complete, were to be as good as frustrated— all to indulge a girlish whim which still cut her to the quick while she sneered at it.

'Remember !' she cried, all fury and gesture, her eyes glittering like points of fire. 'Remember you embark upon this folly without my consent and against my most positive desire. You are compromising my prospects and your own, and you know that. I should not be surprised if it was to spite me !' she cried, giving full rein to her passion.

Miss Westropp was as white and almost as much horrified as if her mother had stabbed her. Without once having thought of her as the dream-mother in whose bosom she could cry happy tears, she had always taken it for granted that Lady Drumshaughlin was a handsome woman, sometimes imperious in her temper, always unjust to Harry, but in every other sense soft, caressing, and attractive ; what was her horror now to find a perfect fury glaring at her through her mother's eyes, and threatening her with clenched hands and ground teeth.

'I will come back when you feel better, mother,' Mabel faltered, and almost swooned when she had closed the door. That same night Lady Drumshaughlin, lying on the bed racked with a dreadful headache, sent for her daughter to beg her pardon, and dismissed her with a kiss and a few hoarse, stifled words.

Some singular proceedings of young Neville at this juncture have to be recorded. Harry Westropp rebelled silently against being kidnapped out of London without seeing the City and Suburban run. Mabel, however, dreaded to submit her firmness to any further trial. The way once clear for her to go, go she did ; and, though Harry had conceived some undefined plan of making his escape from the carriage while on the way to Euston, he did not, in fact, find so daring an act of insurrection more feasible than insurrections usually turn out to be at the moment for action. Neville saw them off. Upon some absurd excuse of giving Harry a cigar-case which he had (not) left behind him at the Club, he turned up upon the Euston platform three-quarters of an hour before the departure of the 7.45 A.M. Irish Mail. He was in exultant spirits, notwithstanding Harry's point-blank declaration that the cigar-case wasn't his, and that Neville ought to have known very well he smoked pipes on principle. He bade them all good-bye with strange motions and chuckles of satisfaction, which caused Lord Drumshaughlin inwardly to conclude that young Neville must have been drinking. When the train was gone, he went to the Club for breakfast. Instead of the morning paper he called for a map of Ireland, and spread it out before him, and spent an hour of deep geographical research into the whereabouts of Drumshaughlin. Having swallowed his breakfast, he walked abruptly out of the room, without the smallest heed to the salutations of men to right and left of him. He hailed a cab, and consulted a card which he took out of his pocket-book before giving the direction : ' Messrs. Firman, Dodds, and Slungshot, 24 Gray's Inn Lane.' During three hours he remained closeted with the Real Estate Partner of that eminent firm, who were also his late mother's solicitors. It was pretty late in the afternoon when he strolled back westwards, apparently in excellent humour with himself. The footpath was blocked in front of him in Fleet Street. He looked up, and saw a crowd about the office of one of the sporting newspapers. He started violently, and plunged through the crowd towards a window upon which a page of flimsy had just been pasted up. There was upon it in carbon the announcement :

CITY AND SUBURBAN.

This Day.

Devilshoof .	.	.	.	.	.	.	.	.	1
Carabiche .	.	.	.	.	.	.	.	.	2
Daughter of Thunderer	.	.	.	.	.	.	.	.	3

' By Jove ! how ever could I have forgotten the day ! ' cried Neville to himself, tugging at his yellow moustache. ' I think she'd have done it, if I had been by. I am sure of it. I suppose that scoundrel must have pulled the mare. He always does when he thinks there is nobody looking. What a cursed idiot I am ! Poor old Horace, all that he must have been let in for !—Nothing for it but to see Tinclar, his commission agent, and plot with him how I am to do the settling. Glengariff, of course, is sure to turn out another City and Suburban—I wonder if there is a more unlucky dog in all the world than I ! '

In the smoking-room of the Chrysanthemum that night all the talk of the young men was what had become of Neville ?—did anybody see him ?—what a pot of money all the fellows dropped on Carabiche !—wasn't it a most barefaced piece of business on the turn coming home ?—was there going to be a meeting of the Stewards ?—of course, poor Neville himself was treated as shockingly as anybody, but what the double dash had come over him to leave his mare at the mercy of a scoundrel like that ?

Mortlake took Lord Amaranth into a corner, and took out of

his pocket with much solemnity the unfinished scrawl which Neville had left behind him a few nights ago, giving his stud-groom, Chuddley, that mysterious hint about the substitute for the steel balls. Mortlake waited in meek triumph for the tribute to his omniscience.

'Nonsense!' cried the young lord, tearing the crumpled scrap of paper to fragments and stamping on them scornfully with his foot. 'Neville is a gentleman. Mortlake, you're not fit to black his boots.'

CHAPTER THE ELEVENTH

IN THE CONVENT GARDEN

'OH! Lily, such a man! I wonder where do novelists find their young men!' said a black-eyed young lady, with a saucy, curly head to match. It was one of her few meditative moments. One little hand was pressed against the curls; the other held, half-open in her lap, a yellow-bound novel. 'I wonder where do novel-writers find their young men!'

'What questions you do ask, Georgey!' murmured her companion, who was knitting a blue rose in berlin wool.

'Dear, how I should like to know! The only young man I know is Tom '—Tom was Georgey's brother and a medical student —'and you could never put him into a book. He keeps a pipe, and likes rat-hunting of all things. Besides, he has not the face of a Greek god at all—at least I hope the Greek gods were not gawky boys with freckles.'

'Little boys are never well-looking after three years of age. They are all the same.'

'I don't know. Here is a man with eyes like the sunrise.'

'Nonsense, Georgey, sunrise is yellow; that is not a nice colour for eyes, is it?'

'What do you know of sunrise?' asked Georgey, rudely.

'I have been up to see the sun dance on Easter Sunday morning. It was very cold and quite yellow.'

'But an Italian sunrise, darling! Listen to the description of it: "That sort of dawn in which the light bursts like a luminous soul through the endless blue depths of heaven." Think of a man with eyes like that, speaking like a poet, singing like a nightingale, roaming for ever through sunny vineyards, and think of him breaking his heart because he could not teach a sunburnt peasant girl in the Valdarno how to spell! No wonder all the women in Europe pelted him with flowers. I'm sure *I* should!' said Georgey, with a defiant toss of her little head.

'Georgey!' The blue rose fell from the hands of her companion, and a flush of indignation came over her beautiful face. 'How dare you!'

The girls formed a pretty picture as they confronted one another across the table in the soft lamplight. Georgey O'Meagher was not a beauty; there were certain suggestions of a boy in her way of swinging her limbs, in her rich fleece of curls, and the resolute set of her features. In the Calvary Convent there was much respect for her prowess. She was known to be a dangerous person among the nuns' apple-trees. But she had pretty little ears, pretty little hands, a well-bred little head, a tempting little mouth, and such a glow of life and spirit in her bright eyes— especially when kindled, as they were now, with rebellion—that your first impulse would be to kiss her, and your second impulse not to dare. As for your final opinion, we shall see. With the prettiest expression of wilful naughtiness, she met boldly the indignant gaze of her beautiful friend, in whose scandalised blue eyes, mantling brow, and lips parted in amazement, you might not all at once recognise the original of Jack Harold's St. Cecilia. Her hair flowed down about her shoulders in a pale golden cloud, out of which a delicate face—a little small and round for her great blue eyes, but moulded with such purity and softness that the first breath of emotion sent a divine flush of colour from brow to throat—shone like a saint's out of an Oriental picture. Ivory skin, cheeks with the faint pink blush of an apple-blossom, eyes as pure as a child's, and as rich as a starlit sky—a catalogue of features is as poor a portrait of Lily Dargan as a catalogue of pictures is of Fra Angelico's yellow-haired angels. But if one were painting her, he would choose just this moment when, with rosy lips apart, and cheeks tingling with timid red, she fixed her reproachful and wondering eyes upon the audacious girl who spoke of loving a man as she would of eating sugar-candy. 'Georgey, how dare you!'

'Well!' cried the little rebel, 'I suppose a girl may love a man and say so. I would sooner do that than marry him without loving him and say I do.'

'For shame! to talk of a MAN like that!' The beautiful face was nearly crimson with transparent pain and annoyance.

It was one of Georgey O'Meagher's most dangerous foibles to like to look wicked. 'And why not? A man does not bite because he is a man. Old Murt, the gardener, is a man. What are we learning French or the piano for, I would like to know, if it is not to be sold to a man some day—if he has a prosperous

public-house, well and good ; if he has a profession and keeps a
pony-chaise, so much the better ? Don't look so shocked. It is
true. We have to cringe, and manœuvre, and grimace for a
husband—a husband who may be deaf or have a hump if he is
rich—a husband that may attack you in *delirium tremens* to-day
if he makes a devout act of contrition for it to-morrow. If we
must cringe at all, give me a beautiful being with a soul in him,
and I will cringe to him—ay, and fling myself under his feet,
rather than lay traps for the sort of husband you can catch
among the Drumshaughlin shopkeepers.'

'Georgey, I request you will stop—stop at once !' Diana at
a Paphian festival—the Lady at the revels of Comus and his
crew—could not have been more shamed and distressed than Lily
Dargan. It was only with a violent effort she could articulate :
'All this comes from reading those horrid novels. You know
you ought not ! I will tell Mother Rosalie. It is a dreadful
sin,' and she burst out crying.

In her vehemence, Georgey had not noticed how the brows
contracted and the tears struggled into the big blue eyes. In a
moment she was by her friend's side, kissing the tears off the
peachy cheeks and caressing the golden head as though it was a
beautiful child she was fondling.

'Why, what a fool you are, darling,' she cried. 'Novels
are all stuff and nonsense. Of course they are—at least this
one is.'

'It is more than that—it is wicked—I am sure it is.'

'Very well, dear, that is because they will not let us read
better ones. Mother Rosalie will slap a girl if she talks of love,
but she is the most dreadful matchmaker. She thinks " Martha,
or the Hospital Sister," the best story ever written. We get
hold of one of ——'s and think it better—or at least more real,
for the world is not a hospital, and we, that is I, am not going
to take the veil. There, now !—I won't, dear !' and she
smothered the reproach on Lily Dargan's lips with a kiss. 'You
know what a giddy goose I am. I was only having my laugh.
I know the difference between —— and Thackeray, though
Mother Rosalie would have us to confound them. Of course
there are no young men with endless depths of heaven in their
eyes, and as for their singing like nightingales, they would go
on the stage at so much a night, if they did. I wish you heard
Tom howling " We six magnificent bricks !" No, darling,
" Martha " was right, and I hope she is in heaven.'

'I am sure she is,' said Lily Dargan, earnestly.

'Amen !' responded Georgey. 'I do believe you'll be a saint
yourself. How pretty it would be—" St. Lily of Drumshaughlin "!

I don't see why the Italians should have the whole litany of saints
to themselves.'

'Oh ! hush, dear Georgey ; how can you say such things ?'
and a little shudder passed through her slight frame, while the
delicate colour came and went on her cheek, like the shadows on
a summer lake.

'Because I am bold, and thoughtless, and flippant, and because I cannot help it, dear,' said Georgey, with another kiss ;
kisses being to young ladies' friendships what a grasp of the hand
is to men's. 'There, I shall burn that nasty book to-morrow at
the kitchen-fire like the common hangman, and I'll be a good
girl, and marry a fat grocer, if he gives me the chance. It is as
bright as day,' she cried, parting the curtains before the open
window. 'Come out in the garden, and we'll never talk of love
again, nor of the impudent little Frenchman that makes faces at
us from the college tower—nor of Ken Rohan.' The girls were
sauntering towards the window with their arms round one
another. A faint blush—not in the least like the red outbreak
of a few moments before—stole into Lily Dargan's face. Georgey
saw it, and suddenly, as they were passing the looking-glass that
served the girls for their toilette, cried : 'Why, I declare I am
all stained with jam !' and she almost screamed with laughter.
'Fancy me philosophising about love and marriage, with a streak
of raspberry jam across my cheek ! You are the most innocent
thing in the world not to have seen it.'

'Raspberry jam is no harm,' said Lily Dargan, quite seriously.

'No, dear, nor—come along ! Let's talk of your papa being
made a magistrate, or I shall get wicked again. Hush ! is that
a light in Mother Rosalie's cell ? No, it is only a gleam of moonlight. The dear soul is dreaming of the choirs of heaven these
two hours.'

The two girls were parlour-boarders in the French Convent
of the Order of Calvary—the twin limestone parallelogram
which stood close up to the grounds of the College of St. Fergal
—the two buildings somewhat resembling architecturally a dia-
gram in the Second Book of Euclid's Elements for the use of
Giants. Parlour-boarders meant that, in place of sleeping under
a little blue-and-white counterpane in an avenue of boxed-up
timbered 'cells,' and having the lights put out at nine o'clock
every night, they occupied a small snuggery of their own, with
a patch of carpet in the centre of the shining beeswaxed
floor, and flowered curtains, and a looking-glass of sufficiently
respectable dimensions to frame Lily Dargan's beautiful head
and throat whenever she and her friend were engaged in 'doing'

one another's hair. Parlour-boarders meant also that, although there was a superstition that the young ladies in the snuggery were subject to the same rigid code which regulated the hours, and the slices of mutton, and the reading, and the frocks of the young ladies in the dormitory, that superstition was not more reliable than the superstition that everybody on the Paris boulevards would wear the same hats and dine off the same *menu* as soon as 'Liberté, Égalité, Fraternité' should be chalked up upon the public buildings. Parlour-boarders furthermore (but this is an unimportant detail) meant some trifling inflammation of the quarter's pension. Miss Dargan's papa was looked upon as one of the rising men of Drumshaughlin; and Miss O'Meagher's papa had a brother who was a parish priest and canon of the diocese; and these two young ladies were not only seniors, and seniors in comfortable circumstances, but they were pretty and accomplished seniors, calculated to be ornaments of the convent school and patterns to the little red-legged darlings, who came to the Calvary as to the portals of high society. I hope the reader will think none the worse of Mother Rosalie if she now and again shut her honest old eyes to the privileges of the parlour-boarders *in dubiis*, though *in essentialibus*, or what Mother Rosalie considered *essentialia*, she would as soon have had her honest old eyes torn out with hot irons as that they should wink at the presence, even in the parlour-boarders' snuggery, of a book like that in which Georgey O'Meagher found the young man with eyes like the dawn and the nightingale in his throat. It is certain that, after the gas was put out at nine o'clock, the young ladies sometimes lit a lamp, and it is certain that sometimes, when Mother Rosalie was taking her first nap, the young ladies were walking in the garden in the moonlight. It was a favourite diversion of the romantic Georgey, and Lily liked it because there was a certain mystery which half-frightened, half-soothed her in the dark places under the sycamores when the wind stirred the leaves. The mixture of gloom and of serene brightness in the moonlit garden—of a something that stands clearly revealed in the cold white light, and a something which is only darkly intimated—filled her with a sort of tender awe, as it, I am afraid, suggested to Georgey O'Meagher vague memories of Prince Florizel's palace of silver in the pantomime. The convent parallelogram, like the college parallelogram, stood facing the town of Clonard, dominating the great woodland valley of the Ard like fortresses that held the place for the Church. The residence of the nuns themselves, in which the parlour-boarders had their quarters, was an older building at the rear of the new parallelogram; it had been, with its grounds, the seat of a decayed squire of the most lawless taste in architecture, and, being more comfortable and secluded than presentable, was, by a violent operation, spliced on behind to the parallelogram, or rather the parallelogram clapped on in front, as in those same elements of Euclid you see some overgrown member of the parallel family holding on by the base of a little acute-angled triangle.

, A window opening in the middle (a relic of the days of the squire) enabled the young girls to step out upon the little esplanade which ran along the garden face of the convent. The 'garden' itself was too crowded with foliage to be much of a garden. A few rather neglected plots and borders of common flowers, dappling the green sward, seemed to be there for the sake of appearances. The place was studded thickly with clumps of rhododendrons and umbrageous trees which seemed to be its rightful tenants, and which gave it the sequestered air appropriate for the recreation-ground of the nuns. It was screened from the high-road behind by a lofty wall, which was a continuation of the back-boundary wall of the adjacent college—the junction being at an angle of the garden. Its privacy was further guarded by a row of ancient elms, which had sent out their moss-grown and leafy arms over the roadway, and by a chevaux-de-frise of gnarled ivy along the top of the wall—other title-deeds of the decayed squire's antiquity. The road at the other side, we know already, was that which, winding up the hill from Clonard, and skirting the back boundary-walls, first of the college and then of the convent, took a sudden bend and clomb almost straight up the acclivity behind, until it was lost in the moor upon the summit.

The moon was freshly risen, and had not yet potency enough to extinguish the frostwork of stars which encrusted the heavens. A tranquil, spiritual brightness enwrapped the convent grounds in a beautiful sleep. Mother Rosalie's window was a scroll of shining whiteness like her soul. The avenue of old sycamores in which the girls walked traced patterns of silver embroidery under their feet. The heavy dew of a July night made the arcade of tremulous leaves glisten like a cathedral roofed with gems. The perfume from a tangled border of mignonette supplied a delicious incense, and the lamps were lighted from God's own fulness. I know there are those—even schoolgirls of seventeen—who do not regard moonlight as meaning gems or silver embroidery, but only moonlight; but we are just now seeing it with the eyes of Georgey O'Meagher, who took several turns up and down the sycamore alley without being able to make up her mind to break the stillness, and found her eyes wandering instinctively to the hearse-like plumes of the dwarf firs in the little convent cemetery, under which two old nuns whom she had known, and a novice, a little playmate of hers, were taking their ghostly rest for ever.

'There is a chill in the air ; do you find it, dear ?' she said at last, almost in a whisper, glancing at her companion. To her surprise, Lily's eyes, too, were fixed in reverie upon the fir plumes. 'Poor Mary !' fell from both of the girls' lips together, and tears stood in their eyes. Mary was their little schoolfellow, the novice. They had seen her blue eyes close to open in heaven, and their hands had planted the tufts of violets at the foot of the small white wooden cross which marked her unnamed grave underneath the unraised grass. The girls stole nearer and nearer, they did not know why. They stood quite close to the rustic wicket of the little cemetery ; a shroud of dark foliage concealed the graves like the mystery of death, through which they could see silver sparkles where the moon caught the dew upon the tentacles of a weeping willow. It was so silent, they could hear the leaves trembling ; the coo of the wood-pigeon in a plantation higher up the hill sounded as loud and lonesome as a cry from the Banshee-world. A great sullen cloud, which had been moving up from the horizon, suddenly buried the moon, which nevertheless penetrated her shroud with a murky brightness, as certain saints are said to illuminate their tombs.

'How cold it has grown, and—and—dark !'

It was Lily Dargan who spoke ; her eyes were upon the little graveyard as though she expected a spirit to arise there.

Georgey O'Meagher (and she was reckoned an intrepid girl) found herself trembling violently, too ; her voice sounded as if it were not her own ; she felt the effort in her throat, but the sound seemed to proceed from hollow darkness.

'It *is* cold, dear. I was wrong to bring you out at all—out here. Let us go in.'

The window of their room was only one hundred yards away, the lamp still burning there snugly ; but it seemed miles away. It was only when the girls wound their arms round one another's waists that they recognised how thoroughly frightened they were. They looked at one another in a panic-stricken way. I think they were on the point of flying wildly for their room when Georgey suddenly stood transfixed, with her head bent forward, and said : 'H'sh !' in a long, low whisper.

'D-did—you—hear—any—thing ?'

'Listen—there it is again !'

'Oh, Georgey, I will die of fright ! Why did we come ?'

'Nonsense, darling, it is only some noise in the wood beyond.' Georgey O'Meagher was more afraid of imaginary than of real dangers ; and, only for the silence and the hour, there was nothing supernatural in the distant, dull sounds that struck her ear. But she grew very pale when she found that the sounds were coming nearer ; that they were, in fact, the quick trampling of feet and the crackling of branches through the plantation at the other side of the roadway. The stillness of the night acted like a microphone ; the hurry and the loudness of the sounds became frightful.

Lily Dargan, finding her friend's arm tighten firmly around her, began to feel stronger. 'What can it be?' she whispered, looking into her friend's face for strength.

'Some tramps in the wood, very likely,' said Georgey ; but she stood rooted to the spot. Though her heart was beating as loudly, it seemed, as the scuffling of feet and the crash of the underwood, there was something in that feverous rush of sound that fascinated her ; it would not have been so intolerable if there had even been a cry. Anyone who in a fever has seen a great Something coming silently to crush him will tell you that. She stood and listened, Lily nestling close to her like a frightened bird. There was no doubt about the character of the sounds. A man had leaped out of the wood upon the road heavily ; it was as if he had fallen ; Georgey thought she could hear his very breathing.

'What is that?—the wall!—Oh ! Georgey, come, or I shall die.' But Georgey could not stir, and her stubbornness had something encouraging. She was, nevertheless, horribly alarmed ; she could now hear the creaking of one of the great elm-branches, almost beside her, which depended over the road ; she could hear the scraping and slipping against stones, a something at once stealthy and desperate. Somebody was climbing the wall. For her life she could not move an inch ; her head was swimming ; the beating of her heart and the grinding against the wall, and a renewed trampling through the plantation, were mixed up in a whirl of intolerable noise. A film came over her eyes, as if she were going to swoon ; it was a shudder from the shrinking being who was clinging to her that saved her. When the mist was gone from her eyes, she saw a dark form in the ivy upon the top of the wall. Before she could cry out, a harsh voice roared from the darkness :

'In the Queen's name—stop!' There was one moment's frightful pause. The dark form seemed to crouch down upon the wall ; there was a crash amidst the ivy ; at the same moment a rifle-shot rang through the air with a noise like thunder ; a shriek was heard ; and a body rolled off the wall, and fell with a heavy thud in the convent garden, a few yards from where Georgey O'Meagher stood.

Lily Dargan was insensible in her arms.

CHAPTER THE TWELFTH

SERGEANT SWEENY'S SHOT

'CH-CHUT! Don't scream, please! I'm only come to say good-bye!'

A figure darkened the window of Ken Rohan's little sleeping compartment, where that young gentleman was lying the next morning with a painful sense that his right arm had suddenly declared war against the rest of his body. He was on that haunted road to fever, where the things of the world we leave behind still mingle with the goblins on before us—where we slip into the supernatural with as little surprise as a passenger by the Dover packet slips into sea-sickness. It would not have surprised him a bit if the dark thing in the window turned out to be a winged dragon arriving to bear him off in its claws. What did surprise him was to see Jack Harold ingeniously undo the upper portion of the window-sash and spring to his bedside as softly as a cat.

'Good-bye!' echoed the sick lad, staring wildly. That word had fascinated back his wandering thoughts.

'Yes, I'm off—chased, expelled, sent packing—the devil to pay!'

'Who?—you? I?—tell me, Jack!'

'There now, don't!' As young Rohan fell back with a groan of agony, Jack took the wounded limb into his charge with the confidence of a President of a College of Surgeons and composed it to rest. 'You know I dabble a little in these things—it is not a bad fracture, but you are excited. I ought not to have jumped in upon you like a harlequin; but what would you have? The Doctor was impitiable. He has my trunk ready strapped on an ass's cart this moment, and all his plans laid to smuggle me away by the back-kitchen like a sack of decayed vegetable matter. He dare not let me bid good-bye to the boys'—this with a gleam of triumphant vanity in his eyes. 'I do believe he is afraid they would cry—"Up with the barricades!" in the Examination Hall—who knows? bind their Cornelius Neposes with his own skin! "Above all, don't for your life go near young Rohan—you are that boy's evil genius!" That droll Doctor! But he is not all adamant. He agreed to write to Father Phil to put the best face on things and explain that his reprobate nephew may even yet, by the aid of pious supplications, be snatched from the burning. While he was writing his letter I charmed him with a proposal to go and take a dutiful farewell of Father Mulpetre—

that adorable Father Mulpetre! I did not go to imprint the
kiss of peace upon his damask cheek, but I had the inspiration
to turn the key in the lock of the Doctor's study and drop the
same into the breast-pocket of Father Mulpetre's overcoat which
depended from the hat-rack. Figure to yourself the Doctor at
this moment tranquilly pursuing his exercise in English prose
composition, while your evil genius plants him the ass's cart and
trunk under your window, clambers up the water-spout and—*me
voici!* You see, Ken,' he said, with a sudden tremble in his
voice, while his hand stole tenderly to the sick lad's forehead,
'I could not go away without seeing you—without—without asking you to forgive me'—this, it must be owned, rather in the tone
of gracious penitence with which St. Louis' courtiers purchased
themselves coquettish silver whips—disciplines they used to be
called—and neglected to use them.

But poor Ken was enraptured with his hero's toy penitence.
'Forgive you, Jack! was there ever such a fellow?'

'Ken, you are a grand believer!' his hero used to say, playfully, when he saw that flame in his face, 'you would have been
burned or hanged in the Middle Ages. You may be yet.' But
now the glow and the start ended in another agonised displace-
ment of the broken arm. 'My poor boy!' This time the elder
re-soothed the sufferer with deep concern and with skill. 'I was
wrong to have come—very wrong. I am only injuring you—
good-bye.'

'No, no—don't go yet; you have not told me—I want to know
it all—what has been happening you—me—everybody? What
ails my arm? Is it a bullet?'

'Not a bit of it. Old Assa Fœtida—old Harbottle—says the
fracture is a neat one, but you will have some fever—those demons
of policemen only escape hell by being such bad shots. It must
have been the fall when you stumbled off the ivy into the nuns'
garden.'

'Into the nuns' garden?

'Yes, you see you swung yourself up by the wrong tree—it
was within a few feet of the college boundary, but not quite; and
so you tumbled into the nuns' flower garden—rather into the
arms of two of the young ladies—and, by Jove, of all the young
ladies who eat bread and jam in the world *your* two! There,
there!' noticing a fresh glow of flame kindling. 'Not another
word, if you can't lie still and take down those fiery signals of
yours. See you, it was quite a little poem, and might so very
easily have been epic, if Sergeant Sweeny had been able to shoot
straight.' Jack instantly forgot his solicitude as medical adviser
in the lively self-complacency of the narrator. 'Mother Rosalie

behaved like a brick. It is not the canonical term, but there is
no other word in this swineherd English language of yours. At
first she was disposed to—what you call it ?—cut up rough, thinking that the young ladies had something more to do with it than
screaming. Avow that the circumstances were suspicious—that
dearest old girl called from her dreams of heaven to find a young
man insensible in the convent garden, with two young ladies, one
of them in a dead faint, beside him—yes, sir—you were the young
man. The young lady in the swoon was St. Cecilia—not a stir,
or I am off!—and the young lady who could not afford to faint,
with you two people on her hands, was not the saint but the sinner—her saucy little friend, Georgey—hip, hip, hourra for the
sinners! Mother Rosalie was scandalised and horrified, you may
be sure—in every crease of her cap and every bead of her rosary—
her first expectation was to see fire coming down from heaven on
the spot to consume a sacrilegious generation ;—but when she
learned all about it—that it was a drill-meeting the police came
upon—that there was, or ought to be, an English bullet in your
body—and that it was not an affair of an abduction over the
convent wall, but of a fight for Ireland—the dash of treason instantly captured her old soul—you know Mother Rosalie wrote
Tyrtæan verse in the '48 days, and they say there was a certain
poet with dreamland in his eyes. . . . *N'importe !* Instead
of alarming the town, the dear old Rosalie was chafing your
temples on the parlour sofa, and had old Dr. Harbottle rooting
for bullets, before St. Cecilia's pretty eyes were open, and she
had you smuggled into your bed in college by a conspiracy with
the housekeeper, while Dr. O'Harte was still dreaming of next
quarter's pension——'

'What! He does not know! The Doctor does not know !'

'Bah! so far as Mother Rosalie is concerned—no. So far as
Sergeant Sweeny is concerned—yes, with a thousand thunders !
That assassin was closeted with the Doctor from an early hour this
morning, pouring in red-hot revelations—told him the Government have information that St. Fergal's is honeycombed with
treason—that I—always I !—am the head centre, chief serpent,
and seducer—and that unless St. Fergal's is purged of me at once,
we shall have it all in the newspapers, with arrests, special com-
missions, hangings—devil knows what. The fellow hit better
with his whispers than with his rifle. When Sergeant Sweeny
was gone I had a quarter of an hour with the Doctor in his fiery
furnace. The result was—well, the ass's cart.'

'But, Jack, you are not really going—going for good !'

'For you fellows' good, yes—majorly excommunicated, exorcised, banished—*maledictus ingrediens, maledictus egrediens.* Let

me do the Doctor justice. He did not preach. "There is nothing for it but to pack your trunk, you know, Jack, of course," says the Doctor. "Of course, sir," say I. You see logic always *was* the Doctor's strong point—that and rackets. "I was tempted sorely to kick Sergeant Sweeny down two flights of stairs and out through the scullery," says my brave Doctor. "Boys will be boys. I hid a pikehead once myself—I hope if you rascals are going to face the British army and navy, it will be with something less ridiculous than pikeheads "—word of honour, he did!—"But that's your affair. Mine is to see that the College is not turned into a Guy Fawkes' cellar, while I am responsible for the keys. Fathers don't pay me their nine guineas a quarter to turn out their boys to penal servitude or the gallows. Ah! Jack, it is how it always ends!" and I do assure you this unaccountable Doctor nearly burst out crying. "What is all Irish history but a pile of coffins of the young and brave!" There the Doctor was quite wrong—the English Government buries in quicklime. But that is a parenthesis. He went on : "Well, well—you must not be allowed to infect my boys." There he was now addressing me as if I was the small-pox. "I am not going to have young Rohan shipwrecked, if it is not too late to save him. Molloy will be round for your trunk in ten minutes. You will have plenty of time to catch the mail. I am sorry for your uncle—poor Father Phil. Good-bye, Jack. We will miss you on Examination Day. I don't know what we'll do for a Julius Cæsar. Good-bye—I hope you'll never do any worse than incur the disapproval of Sergeant Sweeny." Great old Doctor!—it went through my heart to turn the key on him in that frivolous manner, but he would insist upon forbidding me to see you under pain of the most awful imprecations, and accordingly—I am here. You know we might not meet again, Ken.'

'Then I—I am not going too?'

'My dear boy, no ; you are but a suckling in the ways of iniquity. You are to be left to your spiritual director and old Harbottle's splints. Hist!' with a sudden pricking of the ears. 'By all the divinities of the Folies-Bergères, that's the Doctor's fist on the panel of the door! He is shouting too! Good-bye.'

'Oh! but, Jack—tell me—about yourself—what—where——'

There was a moment's stop in the champagny prattle. A dash of white that we have seen before came and went in the pretty colour of Jack Harold's cheeks. 'Pouf! who knows! Things happen. First, to my uncle's—after that, *je n'en sais rien*—life, death, love, battle, gallows, Irish Republic—yip, yip, yip, tra, lalla, la, la! Your evil genius is off. Bless you, old boy.' (Taking his hand.) 'Pulse a hundred and twenty. But don't be

afraid—old Assa Fœtida himself could not kill you. Holà ! the
Doctor is kicking ! Another like that, and we'll have the door
down ! There it goes ! Not a moment to spare. Ho, for my
ass's cart !'

The agile body was already half through the window. Ken
Rohan's evil genius was gone. An hour afterwards Ken Rohan's
self was rushing on wings of the winds through a fever-land,
where demon Sergeant Sweenys were firing impossible great guns
at Promethean young rebels, and angels in preposterously large
starched coifs were flying to the rescue. Dr. Harbottle, with an
air of the profoundest wisdom, announced that the pulse was
a hundred and twenty.

CHAPTER THE THIRTEENTH

LES JEUNES MOUSTACHES

BY the superhuman exertions of old Dr. Harbottle (or otherwise), Ken Rohan's fever departed in due season, and, as the
summer wore on, there was little left of the fracture except a
coquettish silk handkerchief, which Ken's sister, Katie, would
insist upon keeping wound around his neck, as a rest for the
wounded limb. Ken had noticed in the looking-glass that a
bright-coloured silk kerchief made a not unbecoming adjunct to
a disabled sword-arm and a pallid cheek. He had noticed, also,
with a certain startled pang of pleasure (if I may so say) that
an aureole of moustache was dawning softly over his upper lip.
Such discoveries are in boyish philosophy events as momentous
as the fall of Sir Isaac Newton's apple. The summer vacation
months lolled away like sultans on their cushions for the invalid
at the Mill. It was worth having a fever for the pleasure of
recovering from it. The ogres of his delirious nights he remembered not at all; but his palate never lost the celestial flavour of
the first cup of creamy tea which his mother put to his lips after
his illness—and sweeter even than the penetrating aroma of that
delicious draught was the beaming joy with which his mother's
eyes followed his raptures.

An evening or two before the vacation-time expired, the Rev.
Dr. O'Harte's stalwart frame loomed up in best holiday form at the
Mill. 'I am on the cruise, Myles,' he explained as the miller
shook him in his honest hug. His cruise was an annual affair
with the Doctor: the chief towns of the Clonard diocese con-
stituting his Spanish Main, and his treasure-ships being the little

pupils whom he convoyed away as prizes to St. Fergal's. That
eventful evening at the Mill always exercised a fascination over
Kon Rohan's memory.   It was one of those dreamy evenings in
September which in Ireland have something of the luxurious
golden quietude of the Yankees' Indian summer, with a tenderness and mobility all their own.   Mrs. Rohan made them tea
in the little rustic summer-house, around whose rude fretwork
seats and open canopy a gay yellow-blossomed creeper flung its
arms in laughing caresses.   Myles Rohan had a secret masculine
aversion to tea.   He usually sat it out manfully, as he plodded
through the five decades of the Rosary, as a matter of stern
family duty.   But on festive summer-house occasions of this sort
he assisted at his wife's tea-making with the sombre enthusiasm
of a Chinee; and though Mrs. Rohan had often sternly warned
him that he could never cut bread-and-butter, he would carve up
the loaf into cyclopean chunks, which he handed around with the
proud air of an artist.   He understood as little of the merits of
cream-cakes or raspberry jam as of that unlucky Greek diph-
thong over which the Eastern and Western Churches parted for
ever; but he understood thoroughly that, whatever absurd charm
attached to these things, his wife's cream-cakes and raspberry
jam realised it in unrivalled perfection; he felt it a proud and
solemn act of homage to her celebrity, and through hers to his
own, gravely to make an appearance of consuming these delicacies
himself.   Indeed, these sweet autumn evening meals in the
summer-house always seemed to him to have something of the
subdued spell of a religious function — what with the subtle
perfume from the tea-urn, that incense of the household altar;
the hush of the sweet-pea laden air, and the choir of little red-
breasted seraphim singing their vespers from their fairy cloisters
in the great elm-tree overhead.   It was ever such a happy little
party.   Dr. O'Harte had a relish for all wholesome things.   He
stalked around the orchard garden with the utmost satisfaction,
while Myles in his garden straw-hat, and with his pruning-hook
in his hand by way of walking-stick, pointed out to him his
celery trenches and brocoli beds, and trees of Holland pippins,
gleaming with golden fruitage worthy of the gardener of the
Hesperides.   Myles was his own gardener — so at least he obstinately believed.   But one of his crosses in life was that quite an
opposite opinion was held by his lame man-of-all-work Danny
—Danny Delea was his full family title on the few occasions
when anybody thought it necessary to go into absurd particulars.
Little old Danny, in addition to tending the Mill, and officiating
as painter, carpenter, and coachman to the household, was particularly proud of his quality as gardener, and upon this subject, as

well as upon politics, held long and aggravated controversies with his master, being always ready to insist *mit Gut und Blut* that in the matter of politics a Fenian fleet would presently come over and sweep the British navy from the seas, and that in the matter of horticulture, the master (God between him and all harm!) would of his own unassisted knowledge 'hardly know a bed of Wellingtons from early Yorks,' while Myles held a confidential opinion that Danny's principal function in the garden was to botch, blight, and thwart every effort of Myles Rohan's own horticultural genius. Dr. O'Harte presided with high delight over the evening's duel between master and man, which, on the present occasion, turned upon the question whether raspberry bushes need sunshine—Danny believing, as vehemently as in the Fenian fleet, that the best thing to do with raspberry bushes was to 'let them grow wild to the divel.' The Doctor's appetite for Mrs. Rohan's delicate cream-cakes was no less keen; nor was his enthusiasm diminished when he found that Mrs. Rohan had eked out these aerial dainties with a cold partridge and a ham, frosted with a peculiar glory composed of powdered eggs and bread-crumbs, and what-not, warmed into a brown, golden glow fit for the gods. His mother's recipe for frosting hams was one of those things in which Ken Rohan believed (and believes) that kingdoms and powers, and all the cookery thereof, could not match the Mill at Greenane. Ken himself enjoyed the scene, the evening, the company, the feast, with all a youthful convalescent's appetite.

'You like the raspberry jam, Ken, don't you?' whispered Katie.

'Like it!' cried Ken, whose ineffable satisfaction he thought he might safely leave to be explained by the vast bites with which he conveyed that condiment to his plentifully engaged mouth. Though he smoked a pipe, with little more than decent show of concealment from his elders, Ken still owned to an unmanly hankering for jam. 'Katie, it's—it's fine!'

A flush of delight broke over Katie's pale cheeks. 'I am so glad,' she whispered softly. 'It is my own. It was I made it—*I*.' Horace was not half so proud and happy over his monument more lasting than brass.

'You, Katie, you! Was it, mother? Why, Katie, you're—you're a genius!' And the enthusiast administered an excruciating hug to his little fair-haired sister, who quietly wiped the jam-stains from her lips, and felt that there was really nothing more in the way of fame to live for—not even the making of mother's cream-cakes themselves. Katie was not a glutton in the matter of happiness.

They were all in a happy humour. The evening scents of the garden-orchard, the ecstasies of the song-birds, Myles Rohan's and the Doctor's exhilarating laughter were pleasant surroundings enough, even without the glory of sea and mountain spread out afar before them. But it was a scene of august beauty The glen in which the Mill nestled opened out into a sumptuous picture of Bantry Bay, with the delicately carved peaks of the Glengariff hills behind; the huge brown silhouette of Hungry Mountain crouching like a leviathan to the right, the Muin-teravara Mountains touched with pale evening gold on the far side of the Bay, and right in front, raised high above its majestic bath of golden waters, Bere Island, reclining like a dark monarch of the east on the resplendent throne which the setting sun behind him gilt with a thousand lavish rays and gems of light.

How soon, alas! amidst such scenes as this the song-birds' vespers are over, and the night comes, and the chills! But the very mutability of the Irish climate has its consolations. Where, except in Ireland (and, perhaps, Scotland), could you enjoy upon one and the same evening the warm sunset colours of that view across Bantry Bay, and the rich fireside glow of comfort in which Dr. O'Harte was snuggling himself half an hour afterwards in the quaint little parlour at the Mill? A nipping breeze had sprung up, and was murmuring with a comfortable sense of helplessness outside the thick-drawn curtains. A breeze always *is* springing up or dying off in that beauteously rugged Glengariff country. Life there is set to a perpetual accompaniment of the winds, now whispering like lovers in your ear, anon thundering through the pine woods with the voice of a Jehovah. The tea-things had given place to a tray of stout-bellied punch tumblers springing from solid stems and unshakable pedestals—'rummers' Ken's grandfathers had called them before him—and with the 'rummers' appeared also what Myles Rohan used to describe unctuously as 'the materials'—to wit, a squat, solid-looking decanter of ancient whisky, a divided lemon, a capacious old-fashioned cut-glass sugar-bowl, and a portly hot-water jug bursting with hospitable intent. Myles set almost as much store by his punch-service as by the age of his malt. The glassware came from sire to son out of a Cork glass factory which was closed half a century before. He took charge of the brewing of 'the materials' by a right as divine as Mrs. Rohan had ruled the tea-table. Dr. O'Harte, who knew an artistic rummer of punch with any man in Munster, sipped the product of Myles' manufacture with a rapturous roll of the eye, which the miller modestly lay in wait for, and which gave him a more intoxicating pleasure than his own fragrant tumblerful of the liquid. Myles had a little time before gone out to open the sluice-gate at the upper end of the glen, and under the influence of the gushing mill-stream, the old wheel was now whirring away outside as busily as its lazy old limbs would carry it. The fire, which was a mixture of peat and coal, leaped and flashed in a hundred pleasant antics amidst the aged solid mahogany furniture, and in the quaint corner where, just over Katie's heavy square piano, there bulged out the stairway between the dwelling-house and the Mill.

'Do you know, Myles,' remarked the Doctor, 'whenever I look at your fire I never despair of a union between Ireland and England! The coal has the staying-power, the body; give me the turf for the poetry, the glow, and the soul of the thing; but the two make a capital blend.'

Then the backgammon-board made its appearance, and while the Doctor and Myles set to like ancient and implacable antagonists upon that somewhat sleepy field of slaughter, Katie opened the enormous black piano—not because anybody asked her, or as if anybody was expected to take any notice of her, but as naturally as the linnets trilled in the snowdrop hedge outside her window in the springtime—and sang Charles Kickham's little ballad 'She lived beside the Anner'—one of those limpid little Irish maiden confidences which refresh the senses like a woodland brook plaintively whispering its way through a bank of violets. Katie's voice was as low and pure and unpretentious as the brook's could have been. Then mamma (which was Myles's name for his wife) glided away from the backgammon-players with Katie to see whether the fire in the Doctor's bedroom was doing cheerily, and to formally instal upon his bed the eider-down quilt, which was Mrs. Rohan's supreme rite of hospitality to a distinguished stranger. The severest trial to which Myles Rohan's religious faith was ever subjected was allowing the Doctor to win at backgammon, but he did it with the courage of an early martyr, and yet with an air of genuineness which left the Doctor in the nighest state of human vanity over his victory.

Then the two men drew their chairs closer to the fire, and the Doctor, patting Ken Rohan's tumbled curls in the old familiar way, said : 'Well, Ken, you will be ready for the road with me to-morrow ?'

'Where, sir ?' Ken asked, with a troubled start.

'Where on earth would it be but to St. Fergal's ?'

'I am not going back, sir,' said Ken, with a composure that astounded himself.

'Not—going—back ?' echoed both the men in chorus, throwing back their chairs, and looking at the stripling as though he had suddenly taken up a carving-knife to kill somebody. **Dr.** O'Harte was the first to recover himself.

'What! you have still Sergeant Sweeny on the brain,' he cried pleasantly. 'My dear boy, all that is forgiven and forgotten.'

'It is not that, sir,' said Ken, still with a calmness that amazed himself even more than it amazed his elders. 'I am not good enough to be a priest, and I am not bad enough to conceal it any longer. I am very, very sorry.'

His father listened with speechless horror. The boy's self-possession goaded him beyond all endurance. He seized one of the heavy tumblers threateningly, spluttering out in a perfect apoplexy of scornful wrath :

'You—you *brat*!'

'Leave this to me, Myles,' said the President in decisive tones, still quite good-humouredly. 'You don't understand these things. The boy is right to speak out. My dear Ken, I know all about it,' he said, putting his large hand kindly on the young fellow's shoulder. 'You have a pipe in your breast-pocket—you have got over the boundary-wall after dark—that young rascal, Jack Harold, was up to everything—perhaps you have been writing love-letters to some of Mother Rosalie's schoolgirls—and you think nothing can wash away your guilt. Nonsense—we have all been boys, and I hope we are not the worse priests for it.'

Ken shook his head. 'Yes, sir,' he said, 'I have done these things ; but—it is not that. It is true that I have a very awful feeling of what a priest ought to be——'

'And isn't, you mean. That is just like you youngsters' impudence. Half your time your thoughts run on clay pipes and bottled stout, and the rest of the time you are raving like German mystics and pitching into us old fellows because we have not sanctity enough to go out into the desert with St. Anthony, or at least as far as Gougaun Barra with St. Finn Barr.'

Ken blushed and started guiltily. Did those keen eyes of the President see into his soul ? He had, indeed, been steeping himself in the sublime love of those very mystics of the Rhineland. In a neglected corner of the college library he had lighted upon Henry Susa's curiously entrancing book, 'The Nine Rocks,' which nobody besides him at St. Fergal's had ever discovered, except a pale-faced young priest, Father William, who died off like one of Susa's own illuminated dreams. This led him on to Ruysbroch's ecstasies, and the sweet unworldly science taught by the Dominican mystic, Tauler ; until his whole ideas of life and religion took their tinge from that mysterious shining brotherhood of the friends of God, who brought down heaven into their monasteries in the midst of a world fœtid with moral and political corruption.

Was the Doctor a wizard to have divined all this ? Nay, had he
not even found out the secret of Ken's musings in St. Finn Barr's
lone retreat at the other side of the mountains in Gougaun Barra,
where the boy would often throw aside his gun, under the influence
of some divinely poetic thought of Susa's, and people again the
Irish saints' stonebox-like little cells amidst the dark wind-scourged
lake in the wild hills, and think, with a sigh, what a change from
these emaciated, transparent figures of the barefooted monks to
the aggressive purple face and gold spectacles of Monsignor
McGrudder, the parish priest of Drumshaughlin !

'No,' pursued the Doctor ; 'every Irish young fellow who feels
a soul stirring within him feels that he wants more haircloth and
ashes in his religion.'

'Infernal impudence ! ' growled Myles Rohan.

'Nay, it is a finer failing than wanting to strike religion out
of the curriculum altogether, as you drop vulgar fractions—a
finer and a more uncommon failing in our currish century ; but I
tell you with all your piety you cannot do it. Sanctity is like
genius : two very glorious, shining things. But the saints and
sages will always be a mere handful. What are you to do with
the Toms, Jacks, and Harrys, who to the end of the chapter will
have homely wits and homely virtues—who, whether the heights
be Mount Sinai or Mount Parnassus, are doomed to stand afar
off in their millions and touch not the borders of the mount ?
The Toms, Jacks, and Harrys are our look-out. We, journeymen
priests, pretend to be a little better than they, but not so much
better that they need despair of being as good, without living on
the top of a pillar, or bewailing the healthiness of their appetite
every time they sit down to a boiled leg of mutton and turnips.
That is not mysticism, but, believe me, it turns out a good average
all-round Christian man—without cant and without vice—sound
in wind and limb, as I may say ;—and as long as human nature
is human nature, that is about as good a working average as you
will produce, either as a comrade for this world, or a candidate
for the next. Take my word for it, Ken, the Irish priesthood is
good enough for you.'

'For me, sir ! good enough ! ' faltered poor Ken, blushing
violently, and not quite sure that this great, carnal, jolly, whole-
some-hearted man was not laughing at his transcendentalism.
'Indeed, indeed, sir, you wrong me. I was never base enough to
think that priests of your pattern could be anything but good and
brave. I *have* sometimes dreamed of an Ireland governed as in
the old days by the harp and the Angelus bell ; but it is just
because my own stormy heart made me so unworthy to dream of
the golden age, much less to bring it back—— '

'Tut, tut! I have no patience with all this blasted Greek and humbug! Be off to bed, sir, and tell your mother to have your packing done in time to catch the nine o'clock.' The sturdy miller had been working all the while like a volcano in labour; and there burst forth at last this rush of lava, piping hot.

'Father, I cannot go back to St. Fergal's,' said Ken, very white, but very calmly. 'I have taken a step that I cannot recall. I have pledged myself to a fight for Ireland—I have sworn it—it may come any day—and, come what may, I will see it through. Father, you know it—you would disown me if I could do otherwise.'

'Oh! so it's that!' cried the President, his heavy brows suddenly darkening, as Ken had often seen the black frown of a storm-cloud all in a moment gather on the steep brows of Hungry. 'You have got entangled in a secret society which is under the curse of your Church—which is organised by heaven knows what lunatic or Government spy—which has not one chance in ten thousand to recommend it to any sane human being—which will explode some night or other in a fiasco that will give the enemy a laugh over their morning newspaper, but will leave many a lonesome home and broken heart in Ireland. And it is because you have not the courage to break from the toils of a squalid enchantress of this sort, that you are going to wreck your life, wreck this home, and bear about with you a legacy of self-reproach that will cling to you here and hereafter.'

'Nearly all that, sir, could have been said against every fight for freedom,' remarked Ken, quietly. 'Hearts break and homes crumble any way in Ireland. Two millions of hearts were broken in this small island since you were of my age—broken miserably of sheer hunger without a blow. The redcoats might have been shooting them in platoons every day since the Famine-time, and they would not have made as many corpses. Enough Irish lives have been thrown away in this generation to have purchased us a hundred Marathons or Bannockburns—something that would have lit up our history for centuries—and we have nothing to show for it but the famine-pits of Skibbereen. These are the trophies of our inglorious wars—the famine-pits, and a few judgeships and places in the Excise for the gentlemen who preached patience and resignation to the will of God, and Parliamentary agitation. We cannot do worse than that, anyhow,' cried Ken, with his eyes kindling; 'believe me, sir, we will do better, and—God will provide!' He was gone before the two elders could move hand or tongue to stop him.

Myles stood rooted to his place, with the heavy tumbler still irresolutely grasped in his hand.

'This is a bad business, Myles; but we mustn't make it worse,' said the Doctor, pushing him kindly back into his seat. 'After all, aren't we a pair of frauds—you and I—in the character of preachers of the Divine Right of Dublin Castle to keep this unfortunate country of ours a slave plantation upon one meal a day! Myles, you and I learned the goose-step by moonlight together once upon a time, and it wasn't such a bad time either.'

'A parcel of beardless boys and drunken cobblers,' muttered the miller, buried in his own thoughts.

'Precisely what my poor father used to say of the '48 men. He was a '98 man himself in his day, and was denounced by the Bishop for supplying a boat-load of provisions to Grouchy when the French were in the Bay yonder. We have grown old and of the peace, Myles—you because of the children and the Mill, I because the Papal Legate in Dublin is an Italian monk in the garb of an Irish Bishop—but if the French were in the Bay again to-night, with those fifteen thousand troops and the hundred thousand stand of arms, do you think Master Ken's heart would beat a little more wildly than yours or mine, in spite of Mills or Cardinals?'

'You always had the cheering word, Doctor,' said the miller, rising slowly and taking his hand. 'Doctor, I will never be the same man again. God bless you! Good-night!' For the first time in his life Myles Rohan forgot to see a guest to his bedroom.

'Oh! Ken, Ken, what is it?' cried Katie, bursting into his room an hour later, with a frightened face, her fair hair streaming about her shoulders.

Ken started as if he had been stung. He had been smoking at the open window in the moonlight—thinking as boys will think—not of the tender hearts he had set aching, but of a gay gold-braided green uniform upon a flashing field. 'How—how are they bearing it?' he faltered.

'Mother is better—she is offering up a novena at the Virgin's altar; but father looks so pale and solemn. I never saw him look like that before. Ken, what have you done? You won't be afraid to tell *me*?'

'I can't be a priest, Katie, and I can't go back to St. Fergal's, and I have told them everything!'

'And is that all? Why, Ken, I knew it all along.'

'Knew it, sis?'

'Well, you see,' said Katie, somewhat nonplussed, 'those hideous clerical coats never did become you, and—and—you know, you have a moustache now. Aren't there enough to be priests without you?'

'It must be a cruel blow,' muttered Ken, as in soliloquy.

'All will be for the best, Ken. I know it will. I don't think you could ever be in the wrong in anything.'

'Nonsense, Katie, I am worse than in the wrong; I have been horribly selfish,' said Ken, brushing past her, and knocking softly at his father's bedroom door. His mother was prostrate before the statue of the Blessed Virgin sobbing or praying, or both. This little altar was her sanctuary from all the world's slings and arrows. The statue was draped with gold-spangled gauze; a vase of flowers, rich or poor, according to the season, was never missing; and there was a little lamp of red glass, in which the float was lighted at emergencies requiring special intercession. The little red lamp was now burning. Myles Rohan was striding up and down the room, with his shirt-collar thrown open at the throat. Before he was conscious that the door had opened, his son was at his feet in a passion of tears. 'Father,' he stammered, 'don't think too hard of me; I am so, so sorry for you both!'

The miller hesitated an instant; then took his son with rough kindness by the shoulder and lifted him to his feet. 'That is right, boy,' he said simply. 'Let there be no more about it. It was the first time you ever cut me to the heart.'

'Thanks be to the Blessed Mother, my prayer is heard!' cried Mrs. Rohan, passionately folding her son in her arms.

'Humph!' said the miller, with something that sounded like a heavy sigh in spite of his effort to muffle it. 'Ken, it is time to get to bed, boy.'

CHAPTER THE FOURTEENTH

FATHER PHIL, BOW-WOW, AND CO.

MRS. ROHAN and Mrs. Harold found much comfort in one another's tea and in the common perversity of their respective boys. Mrs. Harold was a thin, sharp, rheumatic little woman, whose life was one long martyrdom, tempered in a tolerable degree by strong tea and a vigorous tongue. 'Faith, it's quite true, Maria,' said her brother, Father Phil O'Sullivan, in almost the only daring moment of his life, 'you're not only a martyr yourself, but you'd make an army of martyrs.' Father Phil did ample penance for that profane jest in the course of the martyr's despotic reign as his housekeeper. Father Phil himself was only one item in the catalogue of her crosses in life, which she was accustomed to intone from time to time in Mrs. Rohan's sym-

pathetic ear with the gentle resignation proper to the recitation
of the Litany for a Soul Departing. 'That poor foolish husband
of mine—the Lord forgive him!'—'My unfortunate *omadhawn*
of a brother—God pardon me for speaking ill of His clergy!'—
'That poor misguided child of mine!'—were the ordinary terms
in which she recalled the chief personages in her forlorn family
annals. 'But, sure, Kate, it's a world of troubles,' she would
always conclude, applying her lips to the meek 'dandy' of punch,
which wound up their modest revels, as if that, too, were one of
the troubles which had to be resignedly 'offered up.'

In very truth, the good old curate was a trying man to a
matron who had ciphered out, even to the farthings, how far an
income will go, which even in 'a good Shrove' (as a prosperous
marrying season was called) scarcely exceeded ninety pounds a
year, besides a variable tribute of turf, turkeys, and the like.
Her wars with the beggar tribe who swarmed around Father
Phil, by some such instinct as flies do round a sugar-barrel,
though it be empty—are they not written in the annals of every
Drumshaughlin fireside? 'I do assure you, Kate, they poison
the poor man's victuals with their eyes through the window,' she
used to declare. 'This house is really the poorhouse without the
poor-rates——' 'Well, and sure that's what it ought to be, Maria,
after all,' Father Phil used to plead mildly. 'That's what it will be
soon,' used to flash back the answer, with scorn in every scintilla-
tion, from behind the spectacles perched on the tip of Mrs. Harold's
meagre nose, 'if it's any consolation to you to think of your own
flesh and blood ending their days in the infirm ward; but what
are we, to be sure,' and the little nose and spectacles went high
in the air, 'that we should grudge the bit out of our mouths to
the mob of blackguards that have their noses pasted against that
window since early dawn to-day?' 'Well, Maria, it is not much
that the creatures have got for their waiting,' murmured incorrigible Father Phil. 'Much that they have got!' was the
fierce response. 'They'll get a jug of scalding water from me if
they don't clear out of that while the kettle is boiling,' and a
sudden activity of movement among the wistful group outside
the window gave token that Mrs. Harold's rush towards the door
was a not unfamiliar strategic move in their ragamuffin Thirty
Years' Wars.

'Why, then, what do you want *now*?' she demanded from the
door-step, as though the appearance of the ragged, shoeless, wan-
looking, vagabond mob, who were as indispensable a part of
Father Phil's daily life as his snuff-box, were a phenomenon so
unusual that Mrs. Harold expected some first citizen to favour
her with some brief observations for self and fellows, setting forth

K

their wishes in a preamble and resolutions. 'Why don't ye gt over to Monsignor McGrudder's?' she went on, pointing to the handsome new cut-stone glebe-house at the other side of the chapel. This was a home thrust. There was not a beggar in Drumshaughlin who did not wince under the Monsignor's haughty white eyebrows and thick gold-headed stick. 'Ye are all brave enough to rob Father Phil. I declare, I believe ye would have the conscience to eat the flesh off his bones, only ye have not left enough flesh on his bones to tempt ye.'—'Wisha, thin, ma—a—am, not making you a short answer, there won't be many wanting to make a male off o' *you*,' retorted one stout, barelegged virago, with two infants strapped to her back.—Mrs. Harold loftily ignored this Bœotian thrust. 'Why, then, Bow-wow, I'm surprised at you,' she said, turning to a grizzled old cripple, without any arms or legs to speak of, who was borne in a rude box on wheels drawn by the smallest and shaggiest of donkeys. Bow-wow was a nickname which he had accepted so long that he had probably even himself forgotten whatever more ceremonious baptismal description he had ever received, if any. Bow-wow had halted his equipage right across the little wicket outside Father Phil's house, barring all access thereto, and was utilising the interval until Father Phil should appear by imploring alms of the passers-by in the street, as though his donkey-cart formed part of the establishment, and he himself was simply the working partner in the firm of Father Phil, Bow-wow, and Co., General Mendicants. 'I am amazed at you, Bow-wow,' said Mrs. Harold, severely. 'You know very well Father Phil would want to go round for alms in a donkey-cart himself worse than you do, and he'll have to do it before very long, if there'll be anyone left in the parish that won't be beggars themselves.' Bow-wow meekly urged on his hirsute little steed, which always moved away with the melancholy gait of an animal that was cursing the day nature had ever provided it with more serviceable legs than its master; but Bow-wow abandoned the field with the triumphant confidence that, in some clandestine manner too sly for all Mrs. Harold's vigilance, many hours would not pass without Father Phil presenting his guilty visage and furtive four-penny-bit at the hut on the extreme confines of the town, where the cripple maintained a family of blooming urchins for the State. I am not at all defending Father Phil's system of alms-giving, or rather his defiance of all the known laws of Poor Relief. His evidence before a Royal Commission on the Poor Laws would have been absolutely valueless. He would rather have satisfied one little hungry stomach, or dissolved one haggard face into smiles, than have been the author of a whole Blue-book,

Monsignor McGrudder, who was a scholar and a stern political economist, used to say that Father Phil had created half the pauperism in the parish. To which the old curate would good-humouredly reply : 'There's a good deal of truth in that, my dear ; but sure it must be a poor country enough where Bow-wow's is the best trade going.'

Nor was his abuse of fourpenny-bits the only danger from which Father Phil's foolish steps had to be saved by the Angel Guardianship of Mrs. Harold's sharp spectacles and dauntless tongue. His truckling to the beggars was nothing to his softness for sinners. His confessional was even more thronged than his door-step. The average able-bodied sinner would as soon think of confessing his sins at the police-barrack as at Monsignor McGrudder's dread tribunal. The result was that Monsignor McGrudder was usually able to stalk grimly away to his Breviary or his *Freeman* hours before Father Phil had made much headway with the long line of penitents who sat outside his confession-box like a string of anxious authors correcting the proof-sheets of their autobiographies for his sympathetic ear. Upon this hushed and solemn scene, broken only by the occasional murmurs of absolution, or the emergence of some pardoned sinner with a flushed but happy face, there would sometimes burst in the active little housekeeper, and by main force bear him off from the con-fessional with her shrill : ' Why, then, are you ever going to come to your chop ?' and then, in an allocution addressed to the dis-comfited penitents in general : 'Ye'll never stop till ye'll put that poor man in his grave, and add his murder to the rest of your story.' Then there was the legend of the Dead Mass, which you would hear at any chimney-corner in the glens of a winter's night. Whoever spends a night alone in the chapel, you may, perhaps, be aware already, sees a dead priest come up to the altar at the stroke of midnight, in black vestments, and celebrate Mass for a ghostly congregation from the neighbouring churchyard to the tinkle of an unearthly bell. The story went that Mrs. Harold had once surprised Father Phil at one of these spectral midnight celebrations, and had routed the whole sepulchral company bag and baggage—bell, book, and corpse-light—at the sound of her indignant eloquence. The facts were more prosaic. One sum-mer's evening after Vespers Father Phil did not return to tea. Hours passed, and no Father Phil. · The cuckoo over the mantel-piece whispered twelve through the silent house. Mrs. Harold got really alarmed. She bethought herself of the keys which the chapel woman had duly deposited with her hours before for the night. She unlocked the chapel door, which communicated through the sacristy with the priest's cottage. All was dark save where the glimmering lamp before the tabernacle shed an eerie glow that might easily enough have formed part of the super-natural apparatus of the Dead Mass, and there, prostrate before the altar, the light falling with the strangest radiance upon his bright, silvery head, lay the old curate, sleeping as placidly as a child. He had lingered in prayer as usual long after the footfalls of the last worshipper in the darkened chapel had departed, and the prayers or the fatigues of the day proving too much for him, he had glided into his peaceful slumber and been forgotten. 'What are you to do with a man like that?' indignantly asked Mrs. Harold, con-fiding the facts at the time to Mrs. Rohan. 'Would you believe it, the only remark he made was, "Upon my word, Maria, it was very disrespectful to the Blessed Sacrament, and—I really don't believe I've finished my Office."'

It to some extent lightened the blow of her son Jack's ex-pulsion from St. Fergal's that this new misfortune completed her title to be regarded as the most miserable woman in Europe. 'His father got up that French Revolution for no other reason in life that I could ever see except to scald his unfortunate wife's heart,' she declared to Mrs. Rohan in the course of a good cry, 'and now nothing will do his son but to bring another Revolution down upon my head in the end of my days.' The worthy soul spoke of European cataclysms as of a plague of bloodier Bow-wows coming to her door to demand lives in place of fourpenny-bits. For Jack himself she had nothing but maudlin tears and all sorts of culinary comforts and surprises. By a chain of logic which Father Phil found it easier to distrust than answer, she fixed the whole responsibility for Jack's mishap upon the be-wildered head of his uncle. 'You kept the child idling there for years in that college—you know you did, Philip—you and your designing friend, Dr. O'Harte—because my poor Jack was an ornament and an advertisement for your establishment—*your* establishment,' she said with severe emphasis, as if St. Fergal's were a bogus silver-mine, with whose stock Father Phil was 'bearing' the market—'when he might have been earning his bread and on the road to be a Lord Chancellor, if not a Bishop—don't be rude, please, Philip—with all his talents, I don't see why not!—but you and your crafty friend must keep my poor boy there wasting his genius in concealing from innocent fathers and mothers the inferior character of the education and mutton supplied at St. Fergal's; and now, when he has answered your turn, you cast him adrift on the waves of the world on some idiotic excuse or another to please some preposterous Sergeant Sweeny. What are you going to do with the boy, I want to know?' she de-manded almost fiercely; 'what are you going to do with the boy?'

This was an aspect of the case which had not at all occurred to Father Phil, and he felt sorely puzzled how to evade the criminality thus unexpectedly brought home to him. He did not see how matters were to be mended by explaining that he had no more to do with the worldly interests of St. Fergal's than with the treasures in the gold-room of the Bank of England; and what precisely he was expected to do with a fashionable young gentleman with a full-grown appetite and moustache, he could not really undertake, at a moment's notice, even to speculate.

'Well, well, Maria,' he said humbly, 'Jack is a clever fellow, and there are a thousand things that turn up, and in the meantime there is the spare bedroom and Jack will take pot-luck with ourselves. God is good!'—which was Father Phil's amulet against all human perplexities and tempests.

And so Jack Harold, who had come home with certain uneasy presentiments of reproachful looks from his uncle, and scenes of eloquence certainly, and possibly hysterics, with his mother, found himself leagued in a comfortable conspiracy with his mother, on the one hand, to fondle himself into the belief that Father Phil was the author of his ruin, and with Father Phil, on the other hand, to abstract as much small silver as possible from the power and custody of Mrs. Harold. He came as a Prodigal. He remained as a Sultan. Whenever his mother's rueful looks and deep-drawn sighs presented themselves at all uncomfortably to his thoughts, the philosopher dismissed them gaily with the reflection, 'Psha! mother is never happy without her groan. It is her way of enjoying herself. She prefers her share of the milk of human kindness in the form of curds and whey.'

Cynics may smile to learn that Mrs. Rohan was largely consoled for her own son's revolutionary behaviour by the knowledge that so pretty a young gentleman as Jack Harold was rowing in the same boat with him. Somehow Myles Rohan did not relish the prettiness which won his wife's heart to the young Frenchman.

'I don't like them dancing-master ways of his,' the blunt miller used to say in his positive way. But mamma, like mammas in general, if she treasured 'a good boy' in her own family, preferred 'a nice boy' in her neighbour's, and Jack was, by universal female suffrage, the very mould of form for the ambitious youth of Drumshaughlin, wore gloves that were never deformed by a crease, was never long without something new in the cut of his collar or the shade of his necktie, and, in Mrs. Rohan's admiring language, 'if he only wore a glass bead could make it look like a diamond.' Mrs. Rohan's politics, it must be owned, were largely tinctured by the fact that Dawley, the noisy little family tailor, was generally reputed to be a leading personage in the revolutionary organisation. The notion of her darling marching to death or ruin under the command of Dawley was insupportable, but it was quite another thing if youths like Jack Harold were going to ennoble the line of battle with their gay plumes and romantic faces. In her own bright, beautiful girlhood, she had heard the music of battle for Ireland from Thomas Francis Meagher's impassioned lips and read its poetry in the depths of John Blake Dillon's soft dark eyes. Time and worldly interests had caused Myles and herself long ago to put up the warrior politics of their courtship days with their faded love-letters; but it is to just such secret fragrant drawers in the memory that women of the people have recourse in trying hours as women of the drawing-rooms have recourse to *sal volatile*. She felt as only a tender mother's heart can feel the laceration inflicted by Ken's determination to disappoint her cherished dreams. She felt how deeply Myles Rohan's stout flesh had been cut into nearest his very heart of hearts. How much she felt it I am afraid to tell. In a land bright enough to be a showery Heaven, Irish life is a woful circle of Malebolge, each with its tale of sorrows graved in fire. How is the stranger ever to be tempted through the *città dolente* by anybody less potent than a Dante if the gracious shades of the Francescas cannot be got to attend us more and the skulls of Ugone's little people to haunt us less? Mrs. Rohan knew as well as if she had heard the cry of the Banshee that Ken had brought trouble about the Mill; but it was some comfort that, if there was to be suffering, it was to be in the cause which had made her own heart throb in happy days of youth and love; and it was an immeasurable comfort that her boy's fate, whatever it might be, was to be associated with Jack Harold's dashing figure, rather than with Dawley's ridiculous lapboard and pugnacious red nose. Nor let us rail at poor human nature, if Mrs. Rohan felt it a luxury to listen to Mrs. Harold's prolonged family lamentations by the hour, and think that there was one heart as anxious and bruised as her own; for by an ingenious dispensation of Providence, Mrs. Rohan's comfort in inspecting her friend's endless diorama of miseries was surpassed by Mrs. Harold's comfort in painting them.

And, now, how did Ken himself enjoy his emancipation from the Roman collar? At first with all the ecstasy of a mind crowded with images of an ideal world, and with none but the most meagre experiences of the actual world to jostle them. Youth, strength, friendship, love, country, adventure, glory, heaven, were all realities in the rosy lands through which the tide of his young blood was bearing him. They were the only realities that he could see. Care, sin, the ravenous scramble of life, the leaden materialism, the envies, failures, disenchantments, broken hearts—what were they to him but as the surly clouds which one burst of the strong sun tossed from the gay crests of the Glengariff hills? To be sure there were vague spectres of doom lurking far on the horizon; but what adolescent Sir William Wallace was ever checked in his dash upon Stirling Castle by the vision of a headless trunk upon Tyburn Hill! *Monuar!* that our one crowded hour of glorious life should be over so soon, and the world's inexorable steam-engine scream in amidst our fairy glens and mountains! He had a feverish longing for the hills in these days, and the higher the better. The live-green larch groves which skirted the hills stretched down into the very glen from which the mill-stream drew its waters. He would plunge into the wood as into a cool bath of greenery, crunching through the brambles with youth's insolent regret that they were not as strong and matted as the cordage of an American forest, disdaining devious paths over waterfalls which were never half steep or noisy enough, drinking in with a passionate thirst the fragrance of the pine-trees, the lapping of falling waters, and the cool breath of the wind on his temples as the lacework fan of the luminous foliage toyed with the rays of the sun. When he emerged from the trees far up the mountain, amidst the wild crags and their ragged purple banners of waving heather, he seemed to have left all the squalid things of earth behind him. His spirit swelled with something of that exultation which his favourite ascetics of the Rhine experienced as the trammels of the senses fell away. The town, with its sordid architectural rags and smoky fumes, was gone. It was concealed from view by one of those shapely ridges lower down which seemed to flow about the feet of the kingly Caha like the majestic folds of its purple drapery. The scene that was left was vast enough to fill even the imagination of eighteen—thirty miles of broad, placid, glittering waters, between banks which were massy ramparts of mountains, broken into every variety of Titanic sculpture, and coloured with royal dies; immediately underneath the Caha range the glossy green woods and dazzling verdant knolls of Glengariff swelling and heaving amidst ever-rushing waters and classic rocky scaurs worthy of Parthenope, until the trees bend over to see their coquettish images in the fairy mirror of Glengariff Bay. The mimic Bay itself, seen from the height, with its glowing lawns, tasselled islets, and flashing waters, looked like the spoiled darling of the great family of lesser bays and creeks which nestled under the broad wings of the mother bay itself. On the land side, the strength of mountain upon mountain; towards the west, the might of ocean for ever gathering and for ever repulsed—it was a picture large and generous as Ken Rohan's dream of life, and none the less inspiring for floating like it in an illuminated haze.

'Down there,' he would say to Jack Harold, who lay on the heather beside him, waving his hand towards the majestic expanse of water underneath, 'poor Wolfe Tone was tossing for three nights in a French frigate, with an army around him that could have taken Dublin at a hop-step-and-jump, and the cursed Fates would not have it. Just imagine his feelings the night the storm blew him out to sea with all his argosy! The most wonderful thing about Wolfe Tone is not that he should have brought about the expedition to Bantry Bay, but that he should have ever raised his head again to plan another. See that little creek behind Whiddy, where the hooker is creeping in? That is where a party of Frenchmen landed, and Lord Drumshaughlin's grandfather earned his title by getting the natives to pelt stones at them—think of that!—the Revolution knocked at the poor wretches' huts and they stoned her!'

'Naturally,' said Jack, 'when their good Bishop told them that the Revolution was not the prophet but the devil! I am told Monsignor McGrudder is going to tell the faithful the same next Sunday about our noble selves. I wonder, when our own little flotilla comes into Bantry Bay one of those days, shall we have another shower of holy paving-stones?'

'If the flotilla would only come!' muttered Ken, in one of those almost inaudible bursts of emotion which in an ardent nature are more startling than a shout. 'No, the danger is not that Monsignor McGrudder's anathemas will chase us this time. The danger is all the other way.'

'Yes. I guess our Yankee boys are as little disposed to stand nonsense from the Monsignori as the boys of the Boulevard Saint-Michel.'

'Yes, but that's just it. Woe's one day this high-strung Irish race of ours gives up its faith! It is to us what purity is to a woman. Without mystery, without the supernatural, both in religion and in politics, every fruit we care for turns to ashes upon Irish lips. The two things are as inseparable as the songs of David from the stones of Jerusalem. Show me an Irishman whose eye has forgotten to moisten at the memory of his First Communion or of a bar from "The Wearing of the Green," and I will show you a clod as different from his Irish mother-earth as a Houndsditch Jew is from the Machabees. Ours is not only the religion of the Cross—it is the politics of the Cross. Why will Rome goad and force us to rend the Celtic character asunder? Irish youth is the only youth in Christendom that does not want

to pick a quarrel with Rome, and Rome will insist upon picking
a quarrel with us.   Why, look down at that gleaming picture of
verdure, sea, and mountain—the old principality of O'Sullivan
Beara.   More than two hundred and fifty years ago O'Sullivan stood
perhaps on this very spot looking out over Bantry Bay as we are
doing for just such another expedition as we hope to see streaming
up that bay before long.   And whose were the ships upon whom
O'Sullivan Beara's hopes rested ?   They were ships commissioned
with the Pope's money ; they were stored with 'wine from the
royal Pope;' but stored also with arquebuses and bullets from
his Holiness's arsenal.   Why must Rome turn her men now into
a brigade of armed constabulary against us ?   It is Roman policy
that has changed—not we.   Ours is precisely the same imperishable cause, the same unconquerable hope that throbbed in O'Sullivan's heart two hundred and fifty years ago, and this marvellous
old race of ours is not tired yet of its weary watch over Bantry
Bay—no, not though all the legions in English red were to be
reinforced by all the legions in Roman purple !   Show me any
human cause that is such a mystic poem as that !'
    'Hang it, Ken, let's not talk shop,' said Jack Harold,
yawning.
    Ken turned with a strange pang, and looked into his com-
panion's face.   He was lazily embalming a brown butterfly in his
note-book.   It was Ken's first flash of suspicion that in thinking
aloud he was not thinking also the fondest thoughts of his friend.
The lightning lasted for a moment only, but he was horrified to
find what a gulf it showed to be fixed between them.   Then he
felt angry with himself, and exclaimed :
    'You are right, Jack !   I have been ranting, and you have
been taking Luther's advice, "Always rap those visionaries on
the snout."   I suppose it is only between lovers that what is most
dear to us is not ridiculous.   Come, the rooks are flying home to
the Castle—mother's roast goose will be clamouring for us to come
and eat it.'
    'Now *that* is something to go into raptures about !   There
Ken,' said the elder, for the first time noticing a blank something
in his friend's face, and laying both hands on his shoulders in his
endearing way, 'you mustn't mind levity in poor me.   It is my
way—I sometimes think a very cursed way.   My head as well as
my heels seem to have been made for dancing.   You have such
grand vital heats in you—I sometimes wonder your clothes don't
take fire with enthusiasm.   Be content, and don't be too hard
upon giddy insects of the hour like myself, if I can see nothing
in the scenery of the Caha Mountains so fine as the goat's milk
and whisky in the cabin at their foot.   *Allons !*'

Ken Rohan felt penitent and affectionate, but somehow he thought aloud no more with that happy abandonment with which lad and lass pour out their souls under the milk-white thorn. Jack still accompanied him betimes in his mountain rambles; but Ken, for the first time, commenced to find a luxury in being alone in his glens. These vast solitudes had for him something of the sanctity of a cathedral with storied windows, and something of the mystery, beauty, and inspiration of the Future. Jack, for his part, manifested a growing conviction that his corns and tiny patent-leather boots were not constructed for mountain climbing, and divided his time in an increasing degree between easy flirtations with the young lady in towzled hair behind the bar at the billiard-room and superintending the rehearsals of a Christy-minstrel club which had grown up under the influence of his genius.

CHAPTER THE FIFTEENTH

MABEL'S MISSION TO THE HEATHEN

MABEL WESTROPP sat musing discontentedly on a mossy rock at the head of the great waterfall which gleams like a broad band of silver from top to bottom of Hungry Mountain. She was somewhat disappointed with herself and with the world. It was one thing to feel the luxury of a great act of self-renunciation in turning her back on London and all the witchery of its admiring eyes and subtle. incense. It was quite another thing to ask herself, now that she had departed into the wilderness to reclaim Harry, how she was to begin. What practical hope was there that her mission to the heathen would eventuate in the regeneration of Harry, and not in the remorse of a self-willed girl's whim? It is the first torturing temptation that waits him or her who has resolutely turned from the flesh-pots and faced for the wilderness. All the world has faith enough to set forth out of the land of Egypt laden with vessels of silver and gold. It is in the dreary desert marches that the murmurings of the faint or rebellious heart begin. Mabel had plenty of the true 'thirst for immolation.' She missed scarcely at all the homage of young men's eye-glasses, or that glance of concerned criticism from behind women's fans which is to young beauties what mention in the *Gazette* is to the young soldier She would willingly have tattooed her peach-blossom cheeks, and cut off her pale gold hair to the roots, if it could have increased

her slighted brother's cerebral power or kindled his ambition.
The depressing thing was to find that giving up London to bury
herself in Drumshaughlin for his sake promised to be almost as
silly and barren a sacrifice. She found herself drifting to the
conclusion that Quish was a more beneficent influence in Harry's
life than she could hope to be. Quish knew every salmon that
came up and went down under the bridge of Glengariff almost as
a personal friend for whose life and adventures he was collecting
materials ; he could tell the fly for every mountain tarn ; he
could steal with the tread of a Red Indian into the cave where
the seals held their weird parliament ; he was unrivalled in the
uses of the ferret ; he could find a hare at home with nearly as
much certainty as if the address was in the Directory and he
had only to go around and knock ; he was worth a brigade of
beaters on a grouse-mountain ; such is the humility of genius,
he was not above devoting himself to the humble rat of commerce upon a dull day if the kingly otter failed. What chance
had a pink-and-white chit of a girl against dazzling attainments
like these ? Girls were so plentiful, but where would you find
another with all the knowledge concentrated under Quish's hairy
cap ? And what would Harry's life be without its rats, guns,
and fishing-hooks ? Mabel rode with him, fed the dogs for him,
crossed the mountains to the grouse-drive with him as blithely as
a fawn, and even took a gun herself and made a by no means
ignominious bag, and managed all sorts of pretty surprises for
him in the way of luncheons on the hills. She suspected before
long that she only bored him. She was unprepared, however, to
find him one day burst out angrily :
　'Hang it, Mab, you're not going to play the spy on me like
that fellow Harman ?' Strong a vessel as she thought herself,
this reproach brought tears into her woman's eyes. Those tears
did more for the conversion of the heathen than all her elaborate
plots. The kindliest, sheepish expression came into the dull face.
' Don't cry, Mabel,' he said, gently.
　' Harry, you're a darling !' she cried, flinging her arms about
his neck, with a thrill of joy such as was never distilled from a
year of London drawing-rooms.
　' No, I'm not. I'm a fool, and you'll never make anything
else of me, Mab. There—don't—the gun is at full cock. See
here, like a good sis, you're not going to follow a fellow about, are
you ? I don't want luncheons—I hate luncheons. Quish and I
would prefer a pewter at Moll Carty's down in the glen below—
wouldn't we, Quish ?'
　Quish directed one eye to the east and another due west,
and smilingly wagged the hairy cap as a dog would wag his tail.

Whereupon poor Mabel gathered up the little dainties of her lunch-basket as cheerfully as she could, and henceforth definitely surrendered to the superior charms of Quish in the department of outdoor amusements. But if she failed to become Harry's comrade on the hills, how was she to chain a hulking young man in the mouldy drawing-room of Drumshaughlin Castle in the glowing autumn evenings? She early decided to wrap up the drawing-room again in its brown holland winding-sheets, and concentrate her forces in a little snuggery of her own in the angle of a tower, where they had the cosiest little dinners, and where Harry was free to light his pipe and converse with his wolf-hound, Bran, if, as was generally the case, he found more entertainment in that sort of discourse than in the ballads and romances with which, as with the morsels of pigeon-pie in the lunch-baskets, his sister strove to awaken his higher tastes. Certain 'Adventures of Hudden and Dudden and Donald O'Neary' in an old chapbook aroused his enthusiasm to its highest literary pitch. These, with the accounts of the local petty sessions and the betting in the Cork papers, he would listen to with much complacency, but as soon as Mabel attempted a digression into 'The Newcomes' or into 'Lalla Rookh,' he would break away with an aggrieved: 'Don't, Mabel, don't—how you will tease a fellow! Them poetry and things give me a headache. They are too hard' (from which it may be judged that Harry's grammar was not much better than his taste). In music his fancy ranged from a piece of music-hall clatter at that time in the zenith of its fame—'Slap bang, here we are again!'—to the most moonstruck sentimental ditty of the day—in celebration of the virtues of a certain 'Rosalie, the Prairie Flower,' whose thin tinkle of melody and bleating twaddle made Miss Mabel loathe her hypocrisy in making believe to throw her soul into the song. One evening he astounded her by asking:

'Do you know "The Wearing of the Green," Mabel?'

'Good gracious, no! whatever could make you ask?' she cried; but the next day she hunted up the music, and when she seated herself at the piano the same night and her fingers wandered off into the soft thrilling pathos of the rebel tune, Harry suddenly started from his easy chair, and pulling the pipe out of his mouth, cried in his abrupt, vehement way:

'That's right, Mab. By God, there's nobody like you in the world!'

He little suspected how easy a sacrifice it was for the singer to escape from the mawkish praises of 'Rosalie, the Prairie Flower,' to the ringing cadences of the patriotic anthem, which sets to music all the wild sweetness of a losing cause, without any of the deadly depression of a lost one. Besides, much though she marvelled what interest the tune could have for Harry, the touch of higher capabilities which his preference seemed to evince was so delightful a refreshment to poor Mabel's hopes that she threw her whole heart into the task of attracting him to the passion and inspiration of the air. Alas! before three nights were over, he demanded 'Rosalie' again.

.Society there was none in which either Harry or she could find refuge. 'Society' revolved around 'the Club'—so styled *par excellence*, like 'the Tower' or 'the Monument'—as though no well-regulated mind could possibly mistake the institution referred to. 'The Club' was a seedy Holy of Holies of gentility, where retired captains of unidentified fields of fame, a scarlet-faced country squire or two, the fashionable attorney, and the young police-officer in mufti yawned away the days over brandies-and-soda and the stale 'realisms' of the previous year's London smoke-room wit, and passed a large part of the night in the more engrossing cares of poker. Harry, finding brandies-and-soda to be an absurdly overrated tipple at the price, and having no head for poker, and being, moreover, addicted to low company, instinctively shrank away from the halls of dazzling light in which little Flibbert, the sub-inspector of police, improved his accent and nourished his moustache. Except on the rare occasions when Lord Clanlaurance's daughter would drive over for an archery tournament, Mabel's female circle was restricted to the Rector's wife and the Harman women. With the former Mabel could have foregathered famously, only that good, easy-going Mrs. Motherwell seemed to be always foreshadowing the arrival of fresh babies, whenever she was not engaged with the mumps or the croups of those already installed in noisy garrison at the Rectory. The ladies of Mr. Hans Harman's household consisted mainly of his two spinster sisters. There was also his wife—an ailing insignificant creature, suffering from a pinched condition of the facial muscles, which might have been set down either to ill-nature or to hunger; but Mrs. Harman was a person seldom seen and still more rarely noticed in comparison with her vigorous and stylish sisters-in-law. The elder of the sisters barely missed being called a fine woman by exciting an unconquerable temptation to think of her as a fine man. Far from resenting the set of her shoulders or her weight of bone, however, 'Frank' Harman, as she was popularly called, rejoiced in the stride, and the erect air, and the all but six feet of a guardsman, and completed her soldierly character by carrying an immense crossbow sturdily grasped in her right hand in her movements to and from the archery-field, over whose wars and tourneys she presided like a Black Prince in petticoats on the field of Poictiers. 'Frank,' though stern and peremptory in manner, had the reputation of being 'rather a good sort:' was the principal saviour of 'society' in Drumshaughlin from stagnating in its little mean and chilly pools; rallied the bachelors with the unsparing vigour which thoroughly established old maidenhood alone can employ with effect; and once a year routed the surly half-pay captains from their card-tables and grog at the Club to shuffle and splutter about beeswaxed floors among skinny old women in low bodices and half-formed girls savouring of bread-and-butter and the nursery at a Bachelors' Ball. It was only at quite recent country balls that Deborah, the younger sister, passed from the stage of surprise at not being in a waltz, to the stage in which the surprise would be if anybody were to ask her up. She suddenly put off smirks and fashionable gowns, and assumed the dowdy garments and severe concentration of features towards the tip of the nose, which are as the blood on the door-posts by which the serious person establishes her own security against the sword of the Lord. She received a call for the conversion of the hungry little Papists of the Ranties—a nest of incredible human styes perched amidst the naked rocks down by the sea—and during seasons of special starvation moved the rage of Monsignor McGrudder and thrilled the breasts of one of the May meetings in Exeter Hall by particulars of the infant phenomena rescued from the thraldom of the Beast by the operation of Bibles in the Gaelic tongue, with a sort of running commentary of English subscriptions. Miss Deborah was scarcely a more terrible trial to the Monsignor than to the Rector. Poor Mr. Motherwell was a good-natured Englishman, in prime muscular condition, who lived in high good humour with himself and all the Lord's anointed—or unanointed for that matter. He raised for himself a serious storm amongst Miss Deborah's faction in the congregation, by hazarding a hint that he would himself have been better pleased to treat the Ranties to the subscriptions without the theology. 'Edward never will mind what a woman says;—he is sometimes very provoking, I must say—but really, my dear, that young woman's tongue is beyond anything,' said Mrs. Motherwell, pleasantly relating the parish gossip to Mabel from behind a fleecy cloud of baby-linen. 'She told the Sunday-school teacher she believed Mr. Motherwell would turn Jesuit only they would not take over his ridiculous houseful of children. She did, indeed!—as if the poor children could help that naval officer going off without marrying Deborah Harman! Edward would say I am just as bad as she, of course;—but really, my dear, I had to tell her that, if there is anybody to go over to

Rome, she would be better qualified herself for a post on the Inquisition, for there is not a house in the parish that is free from her sharp little eyes, and her tongue is as bad as the faggots.' In virtue of Mr. Hans Harman's agency, of course, the two sisters were assiduous and obsequious callers at the Castle; but though Mabel did her very best to cultivate an interest in archery and Gaelic Bibles, the two Miss Harmans did not take long to conclude, in the sacredness of sisterly confidences—Miss Harman that Mabel was 'cracked,' and Miss Deborah that she was a 'minx;' while as to Harry, upon whom the memory of his residence under the Harman roof weighed like a chronic nightmare with which he might at any time be seized again, he viewed the visits of the sisters as a man who has had apoplectic seizure regards a confusion in the head. When they were on the premises he stole away to the public-house and drank porter.

Look where she would, Miss Westropp could not find that this life-mission of hers, which seemed such a miracle of substantial architecture, with its radiant towers and minarets in the distance, was anything but a damp and chilling cloud, now that she had got into the midst of it. She had tattooed her cheeks—she had sacrificed the bloom and gaiety of her life—and lo! there was nobody a whit the better of it. She would have willingly expended the wealth of her love on those around her. Her eyes ached with the sight of the wretchedness of human life in the glens. It was as visible as smudges of black paint upon a beautiful picture. Miss Deborah, hearing her praise the children's soft Spanish eyes and liquid speech, once suggested a visit to the Ranties and attributed to the heartlessness of a fine lady the shudder with which she pictured herself filling these pinched little stomachs with Miss Deborah's sour texts, and blocking out the only ray from heaven that ever illuminated their hovels. Yet how otherwise was she to make acquaintance with the Ranties? She knew that her father was an unpopular landlord, and dimly recognised that it was not without reason. The country people looked submissive enough—pathetically so, it seemed to her;—but Mr. Hans Harman, who had read them deeply, could tell her what a demon lurked behind those shy, soft eyes. 'They are born actors,' Mr. Harman would say—himself the most ingenuous of men. 'You'll find nothing genuine if you search their romantic rags, except a powder-horn and a charge of slugs.' They might fire at her. Such things had happened to women in Ireland. Here she was, panting with sympathy, driven irresistibly to seek relief outside the stifling little mouldy cupboard of Drumshaughlin society, surrounded on all sides with dumb, pathetic misery which she longed to know how to alleviate; and yet she felt that the mid-African blacks could not be farther from her than the people outside the park wall. She seemed divided from them by endless, invisible differences of birth, race, and creed, which tortured her eyes like fine sand. The Ranties was as unpromising a problem as Miss Deborah's religious enthusiasms, or Harry's lack of intercerebral fibre.

What was a poor little head revolving all these contradictions to conclude but that her mission to the heathen was a folly for which there was no one to blame but her own ill-regulated mind, and her own ineffectual sex ? 'Oh dear, what good are girls at all ?' she cried, beating a little foot fretfully upon the rock at the thought that by divine right of masculinity Quish himself was immeasurably beyond her. 'Why should he not ! Quish knows what he is about and does it. If his thoughts do run on rats and blue worms, nobody can beat him at *that* anyhow. I have dreams that are beyond Quish's comprehension—dreams that life can be made warmer and nobler by high purposes and love ;— but the moment I try to work it out the figures spin in my woman's brain like a sum in trigonometry, and all my gorgeous spirit-world ends like my poor sketch of the glen here— a vague daub of colour, and nothing more !' She took up the sketch-book which had fallen to her feet during her reverie. Drawing she disliked as she did Euclid. Her intended sketch of Eily's Glen had only got as far as a few suggestive dashes in water-colour, which might develop into a mountain cataract or a monster. 'I have made as sad a failure with my poor Harry as with my waterfall,' she sighed, resting her flower-like head against her shapely arm like a tired child for whom the great water- fall was singing its hoarse lullaby. From time to time she could hear Harry's gun popping around the mountain. She had courted him to bring her with him. He had insisted that he, not Quish, should bring her little painting equipage and camp- stool, while Quish carried the gun. The only thing he resented was being kissed for it. In a dim way Harry felt that her resi- dence at the Castle must be dull for her, as well as embarrassing for himself and Quish. It was not exactly the service he would have demanded of his family. He did not see what girls wanted meddling, but he felt, ever so little consciously, it is true, that her presence somehow perfumed his life, as he felt that hawthorn sweetened the meadows, though hawthorn was the last thing in the world he would have gone mooning about. But, when they came to Eily's Rock and the paints were mixed, his eye turned restively from the picture-like glen to the gun on Quish's shoulder.

'I'll just have a shot or two, Mab—not to be in the way, you

know.' But Harry was so far from a hypocrite that he immediately added : 'The fact of it is I can't stand waterfalls and
things. It gives me a headache.'

'Dear, dear; and I wanted you to tell me all about
Eily's Glen, and why this is called Eily's Rock, and who is
Eily.'

'Eily! how on earth should I know? I dare say some nonsense about some girl who made a fool of herself. What questions you do ask, Mab, to be sure. I'll be back before you're
half through with the waterfall.'

'Poor Eily,' sighed Mabel, making a determined effort to
apply herself to her paints. Eily's Rock was a little plateau high
on the mountain breast, which was the favourite point of view
for seeing the Falls. It was in a nook carpeted by lichens and
heather, with a screen of wild ash-trees and an embroidery of
starry canavauns in the crevices to break the savagery of the
threatening mass of rock overhead. The plateau afforded a vast
prospect through a deeply cloven glen over the mouth of the Bay,
with Bere Island set like a huge dark emerald in its waters. It
jutted out almost into the jaws of the great waterfall, which,
after tearing a jagged way down from the higher levels, seemed
to be nursing its resolve for a mightier leap in the dark pool
that circled like an unquiet soul around Eily's Rock, and then
suddenly dashed over the brink in a swift, sheer desperation that
was more terrible in its silence than the deep roar that came back
from the abyss three hundred feet below, where the torrent was
dashed to atoms, as it were, with a yell of pain. It was a scene
of surpassing grandeur ; but in a very few moments she could
only see one figure in mountain, bay, or waterfall. Who
was Eily? and what was it that had consecrated this wild
defile with its thunderous torrent to her gentle name? Something terrible, she felt sure ; that sombre chant of the crushed
torrent was never tuned to the lascivious pleasing of a lute. 'I
am shut out even from the people's legends,' she said, sadly.
'They will not even admit me to the company of their dead. I
don't want to paint any more. If I did, I should have to paint
Eily. I wonder was she such another failure as myself?—I wonder
did she ever sit here as I am doing and think how like our impetuous Irish hearts is that waterfall—so full of brightness and
hope at its first bounds, then doubts, irresolution, dark tumult
just here, where the first check comes—then that grand passionate
leap over the brink, and all is over in a winding-sheet of spray
and a despairful dirge from below! Well, well, there are worse
things than flashing waterfalls losing their lives in the brave
mountains. It is better than going to the great sea like a

L

haughty river Thames with all the foul secrets of London in its bosom——'

She started with a scream, as bang! went a shot quite close to her. A wounded bird fell almost at her feet, and a man and dog sprang out of the underwood.

'Oh! Harry, how you have frightened me! What a clumsy fellow you are——'

She stopped with a fresh cry of alarm, to find that it was not Harry but a stranger, who coloured deeply as he took off his hat, and stammered incoherently: 'Good heavens!—you are not hurt? —thank God! I—I am the miller's son,' said Ken Rohan, still in the deepest confusion. 'My father and I have leave to shoot over Hungry when the family are not at home, and I did not see the flag up at the Castle.'

'Hallo, Ken, so it's you are the poacher!' cried the Lord Harry, leaping out of the brushwood, gun in hand. 'We heard the shot down in the furry glen, and, of course, you've brought down your bird, you lucky beggar. Quish says if you would attend to your gun and leave off star-gazing you wouldn't leave a bird on the mountain.' By some unaccountable accident Harry perceived that the object of his compliments was still standing with his cap off in a state of scarlet abashment. 'Hallo! you don't know my friend, Ken Rohan, Mabel? I do so want you to know him. Ken always stands up for me.'

'Anyone who befriends my brother cannot possibly have a better title to my friendship,' said Miss Westropp, putting out her hand with simple kindness. Her only distinct feeling about the matter at the moment was one of relief that there was anybody who was not Quish in whom Harry manifested an interest, and who returned his passion. Her new acquaintance was simply an algebraic sign standing for the dividend of Quish.

'You are very good,' said Ken Rohan. Her openness severed at one light touch the subtle network of conventional bands and ligaments which impeded the freedom of his limbs. Although a hot Democrat over his pipe, he had the decent Drumshaughlin sense of the pathless jungles that lay between the Mill and the Blue Drawing-room at the Castle; but this maiden, it was plain, was as fearless in the jungle as Una with the lion, and Ken began to feel something of the wild animal's simple allegiance to her. 'I hope,' he said, shyly, 'you will forgive my unlucky shot. It has brought me very undeserved good fortune.' Ken had the weakness to imagine that that sort of thing was, as he had read in story-books, the proper language of the Blue Drawing-room.

'Oh,' she said, without noticing the compliment, 'I am too much used to the sound of my brother's gun to mind. I am not surprised at anything. He will do all sorts of things except stay with his sister while she is sketching Eily's Glen,' she added with a smile.

'Why,' said Harry, with an uncomfortable feeling that he was standing at the bar of justice, 'what could I do for you except upset the paints? I could not even tell you who was Eily. Oh, I say,' he cried, as if a sudden flash of genius lighted his brain, 'here's Ken Rohan knows all the poetry that ever was thought of. If there's any fellow alive who knows all about Eily, here's your man.'

'Miss Westropp's mind has brighter tasks than listening to old women's tales, I am sure,' said unfortunate Ken, who had not yet detached his thoughts from the heroines of the cheap novel series.

'On the contrary, I think there is nothing more horrible than to live in a country without associations. It is like clearing a country of its singing-birds. I have always thought that the only history worth knowing is what they preserve at the fireside, or what the winds and the waterfalls tell you. But to me they will tell nothing,' she said, sadly. 'I am an alien, and am not in the secret.'

'The secret of Eily's Glen is soon told. I am only too glad to find anyone who cares to learn it,' said Ken, whose cheeks had been tingling a little uncomfortably. 'You can barely see the promontory where Dunboy Castle once stood on the island below— it has hardly left ruins enough to make its gravestone—but of course you have heard all about Dunboy——'

'Indeed, no. I have heard Mr. Harman talk of starting a barytes mine there, and that is all. I know scarcely anything famous round the Bay that I could show a stranger, except famine-pits. But I am sure it is too beautiful not to have a history.'

'It has,' said Ken, with kindling eyes. 'There is not a glen or mountain round about you that has not the story of O'Sullivan's last stand for Beara in Elizabeth's wars written on its heart. If there was only somebody to sing it, it would do more to drape Bantry Bay with romance than all the purple-and-gold haze in Glengariff. Why, take that march of his to Fermanagh, when all was lost—his castles in ruins—nine out of every ten of his soldiers dead—the chieftain gathers the remains of his clan around him one night, there in that glen beyond, men, women, and children, and sets out to fight his way from end to end of Ireland—one continuous battle-field two hundred miles long, one line of graves, one red track of blood from Bantry Bay to far Lough Erne—and he did it! They were a lonely and attenuated clan who saw the hills of

Fermanagh—but they did it. It was as brave a deed as Thermopylæ's, upon an immeasurably lovelier scene ; but I should like to know how many cultivated people could keep from laughing if I were to mention Leonidas in the same breath with a creature of the singular name of O'Sullivan Beara !'

'Yes,' she said, meditatively. ' O'Sullivan, pronounced as the country people pronounce it, is ever so much more musical a name than—say Westropp, for example. But,' with an arch smile, ' don't you think we are sometimes not altogether free from blame ourselves if people don't know more about these things ?'

'Yes, indeed,' said Ken, with frank cordiality. 'I only wish we often had as gentle censors to rebuke us for our meanness in thinking that heroes with an O to their name cannot possibly have an interest for persons without holes in their shoes. It is quite true—our conquerors have managed to make us a little bit ashamed of our fathers. They did the Irish a worse injury than stealing their lands and their lives—they wrote lampoons on their tombstones.'

'Let me see, the first Westropp in Drumshaughlin was a captain of horse in these wars. I wonder did he ever charge that little footsore phalanx on its way ? I hope not, even if he stole the land.'

'Nay, but the English captains of horse must not absorb all our maledictions. Nine-tenths of the men who thinned O'Sullivan's clan on the march were his own countrymen. English bribes have done more to wound our self-esteem than English swords. You see it is so much harder for a nation to be obliged to blush than to mourn—especially if you have got to do the two together—Well, but Eily ! Eily was O'Sullivan's daughter, as beautiful, they say, as a Glengariff dawn——'

'Don't you think, if people are really beautiful, the beauty sufficiently comes out in whatever they do ?'

'Beauty is not always wise.'

'Then it is not beauty.'

'I am afraid most people would call our Eily a very foolish person——'

'All that depends upon what you mean by foolishness. Most people thought the Cross foolishness that day on Calvary. I have given you an example of what is really foolish myself,' she added, with a merry smile, ' for I have tried to skip to the end of your story without hearing the beginning.'

'So I was thinking,' put in Harry, boastfully. 'It is always the way with girls. Can't you give Eily a chance ?'

'There is not much of a story,' said Ken. ' Poor Eily's history is not much longer than Viola's. She had told her love,

however : her lover was a young prince named Fergus, to whom
O'Sullivan committed the defence of Dunboy Castle when he
himself joined the Northern Earls in their march to the relief of
Kinsale. It was as stubborn a fight as ever young blood blazed to
hear of ; but it was a fight on the usual conditions on which we
compose Irish history—numbers, discipline, provisions, culverins,
musket-balls, and the historians on one side ; wild hearts, naked
breasts, and empty stomachs on the other ; and the result as
easily seen as a plot in the *Halfpenny Journal.* The siege had
gone on a weary while when word came to Eily O'Sullivan that
Fergus would meet her, dead or alive, here on this very rock
where we stand when the moon came out above the woods over
Coomhōla. She was here the moment the shadows fell, though
there were still three hours before there was any use in casting
her eyes towards Coomhōla. Down there below her poor wistful
eyes could see the flashes of cannon on the promontory, and her
trembling heart sank with every horrible thud, as the detonations
went smashing and rumbling from mountain to mountain over the
waters. She knew there was something more than usual astir—
some desperate fighting going on—perhaps the crisis, perhaps the
end—she could only sink on her knees and pray to Him who
watched so calmly amongst the stars while these poor mortals
were playing out their noisy tragedy below. All she knew was
that Fergus would come. He had once before in the early days
of the siege swum the ditch to meet her in this same spot, and,
now that he promised he would be with her, dead or alive, she
knew that Fergus would not fail.'

'Yes,' said Mabel, solemnly.

'It was a long wait—it must have seemed eternities :—but
at last her eyes caught sight of a faint silver glow over the dark
crest of Cobdhuv. The moon was rising. Eily looked reproachfully
towards Dunboy. As she did so a sheet of wild flame shot up into
the air from the Castle, its fiendish glare flapped its wings like a
spirit of hell over the Bay and was gone. The next instant there
came a shock that seemed to rock the very mountains, and the
whole Castle—the whole promontory it seemed—was hurled into the
air in one red horror, with explosions that thundered from height
to height, until the whole Bay seemed to be rent asunder with
agony, and its fragments flung towards the stars with vomitings
of smoke and flame. That was the funeral pyre of the Castle of
Dunboy. The breach—it was all one vast breach—was carried
earlier in the evening. The fight went on from room to room,
from tower to tower, to the battlements and over the battlements. Fergus made his last stand at the door of a vault which
he had stored with casks of gunpowder to the lips——'

'Yes, yes, I know,' said Mabel faintly.

'Yes, he had barely time to do it. They knew what the vault meant. He was bleeding frightfully, and they snatched the lighting brand out of his hand, but it was too late ; the pall of smoke and flame that Eily saw enwrap the Castle was his winding-sheet and theirs. When the pall lifted, Dunboy was a little heap of blackened stones. Well, it is not history but the old people who tell the rest. They say Eily O'Sullivan was very calm, and turned from that horror towards Coomhōla. The moon was shining over the wood, and she saw Fergus rising from the spray underneath that waterfall beside you—it is not hard to imagine spirits shaping themselves out of it even this moment at high noon—with a great shining wound on his breast, very pale, but with the sweetest smile and open arms, looking his very self. At least all kind hearts will hope that the chieftain was sufficiently life-like to have beguiled a fond maiden, for Eily threw herself into her lover's arms, and O'Sullivan's daughter, like the Castle of Dunboy, was seen no more. When O'Sullivan Beara gathered his clan for that last march to Fermanagh, his daughter and his bravest captain were too far away to hear the bugle-call.'

'She jumped in—there !' said Harry, standing, with a curious mixture of the man's courage and the child's awesomeness on the very brink of the precipice, down which the swift torrent was rushing into its grave of mist far below. 'But why didn't they drag the river away down towards the bridge ? Wasn't there anything more ?' His recollections of 'Hudden and Dudden and Donald O'Neary,' in the crisis involving the last-named gentleman's immersion in deep water in a sack, somehow led Harry to anticipate a more spirited *dénouement.*

'No,' said Ken ; 'there was nothing more—in this world, except that ever since the name of Eily's Glen has given the lovers a more beautiful monument than ever was shaped by the hands of men, and whenever an August moon is rising over the Coomhōla woods you can still see a mystic illuminated rainbow—bright as in the broad daylight—spanning the soft spray under the Falls which was poor Eily's tomb—the country people call it " Eily's wedding-wreath "—but the maiden who has ever laid eyes on Eily O'Sullivan's Rainbow after sunset will never live to be embraced by her lover at an earthly bridal.'

Mabel was looking away into the soft feathery mist with the deep eternal croon of the broken waters in its bosom. Silently she let her unfinished sketch slide down lazily into the abyss. 'I think,' she said, 'I could paint Eily.'

'Why, Mab,' cried Harry, with his loud laugh of discovery, 'you are crying !'

CHAPTER THE SIXTEENTH

THE AMERICAN CAPTAIN

WHEN Ken Rohan was invited by his lively friend, Jack, to make the acquaintance of the American Captain who had arrived to take the district under his charge, it was rather a shock to him to be ushered into the little bar-parlour of the Drumshaughlin Arms Hotel, among a knot of men enveloped in no further mystery than a cloud of tobacco-smoke, and garnished with no more theatrical appearance of conspiracy than pipes and grog. Don't think him too silly a revolutionist if he found this a disappointment. His imagination was apt to do for his mental landscapes what the play of the sunlight did for the fair Glengariff hills. Our lives pass in stumbling over the stocks and stones of the prosaic mountains, which glowed in the distance like mines of amethysts. If our young friend did not actually expect to find revolutionary conspiracy conducted to mysterious music, he had surrounded it in his mind's eye with a sufficiently romantic scenery of midnight glens and shrouded figures speaking a subdued but thrilling language of their own. Here was his romance thrust into a stuffy bar-parlour, with Dawley's little fiery nose shining through the tobacco clouds; and the American Captain, whom he approached with awesome recollections of how heroes with a price upon their heads behaved upon romantic occasions, addressed to him only the cabalistic remark :

'Glad to shake your paw, stranger. Yes, SIR !' (with immense emphasis on the last word, as though it were the official scream of the American eagle). 'Missie'—this to the pretty befringed barmaid—'just fetch us along another whisky-skin, there's a seraph ; and—listen, my dear—if any of them blamed peelers calls to say he has a par-tickler appintment with me, just mention that I have walked round the block to enjoy the scenery.'

'If he insists, Mike,' said Jack Harold, with the appreciative air of a manager who was running a star actor—'if he forces his way in——'

'Wal,' said the Captain, gazing affectionately at his Derringer, 'I guess I can show him a little bit of scenery that will absorb his attention all his mortal days. It's not much of a view,' he said, tapping the diminutive muzzle ; 'but once you've been there you wants to see sights no more.'

'What !—you here !' exclaimed Ken, discovering Harry

Westropp amidst a smoky nimbus blown by a long clay pipe. 'Is it possible ?—you don't mean to say——'

'Why not ?' said the Lord Harry, whose face was flushed. 'Wherever there is any divelment going, I'm your man.' He had picked up certain peculiarities of pronunciation as well as of opinion in the stables. 'I suppose I'm as well able to shoot or be shot as another, and I don't care a damn which it is going to be.'

'Bully for you, lord !' said the Captain ; 'but you just study Clause One of the State Constitution of Kentucky, which provides—whenever there is to be shooting, get your own Derringer in first. As a humane white man, I object to place on a fellow-creature's soul the guilt of shooting *me*.'

How came it that, as Jack Harold's smart gloves had their effect in reconciling illogical Mrs. Rohan to the Revolution, her son now experienced a sense of relief in finding the Lord Harry looming up out of the unromantic fog in which the fumes of grog and tobacco encased the burly figure of the American Captain ? 'Shall I tell you frankly ?' he said to Jack Harold later on. 'Your American Captain jarred upon me most horribly at first. It was all so unlike what I had been dreaming of Lord Edward's gentle chivalry and Emmet's divine enthusiasm —the grace of an ancient cause was so blemished by his roughness—it seemed like putting a frieze coat upon a Greek Apollo. You may laugh at my snobbery when I tell you that the whole thing seemed somehow *vulgar*—psha ! it is sad snobbery in a miller's son.'—'Not at all,' laughed the other, 'we're all aristocrats in our Irish huts. We are all born with royal blood in our veins, and our heads in the clouds. Fifty years ago the Irish people would have worshipped the Lord Harry's foolish head, and turned up their noses at Abe Lincoln as a rail-splitter if he proposed to lead them to liberty. Now it is different. Do you demand a proof of the imbecility of our rulers ? I give you not their confiscations, not their Penal Code, but the fact that they have turned us into Democrats. I point not to Cromwell, but to Captain Mike MacCarthy. It was all but as hard to convert the Irish nation into Democrats as into Protestants. But they have done it—Captain Mike is only the advance-guard of an American invasion that will leave more permanent imprints here than the Norman. Yes, sir,' added Jack, in gay mimicry of the Captain's eagle-cry, 'Mike may be lacking in Grecian lightsomeness, but if you want to carry Cork of a dark night, my faith, Mike is the boy to do it while your heroes in gold-lace and feathers would be bombarding it with ballad-poetry——'

'Yes,' assented Ken, 'we have had too much of the lace and

feathers, and perhaps of the ballad-poetry. My first prejudice *was* a prejudice, and it is gone. Captain Mike is a fine fellow.' If Ken's purple mountains were not of gems, he was of the age that finds it very tolerable to bound over the crags of real life with the free air of the heights blowing around his temples. Still he was unquestionably guilty of the snobbery of being pleased to find the Lord Harry a fellow-conspirator, although, manifestly, poor Harry had been drinking—so difficult was it, in those days, even for the masculine Irish mind to dissociate the ideas of Dawley and Democracy.

'Somebody's got left, eh ?' said the American Captain, imbibing what appeared to be a tumblerful of orange-peel through two straws. 'Somebody's missing ?'

'It's only Mat Murrin—the edithor,' said Dawley, who, being 5ft. 6in. in his vamps, would hear of nothing but physical force, and had a profound disdain for the pen as a weapon for heroes.

'Gen'lemen, I know him from a boy—I was raised on the far side of Cobdhuv beyond,' remarked Captain Mike, whose dialect was the strangest New English hash served up in a rich Munster sauce—'and Mat Murrin has spent all his life in getting left. It is my opinion he will get left at his own funeral. That is what's the matter with you people all the time. If this British Empire was advertised to burst up spontaneous at an hour and place named in the bills, provided the Irish people was punctual on time just for that one auspicious occasion, darned but you'd have Mick and Paddy mouching along half an hour too late hoping they hadn't kep' anybody waiting. Yes, sir—there's a very superior laygend I heard from my poor ould mother—that there's a band of warriors lying asleep somewhere in the Caha Mountains for I disremember how many hundreds of years, and whenever they wake at a certain signal Ireland will be free. That's so ; but they never do wake, and what's more, they never will. Gen'lemen, it is my confidential opinion if they heard the blast of the Last Trumpet, them sleepy warriors of yours would turn in and wait for a second call. That's just the Irish question slick through—plenty of sleep and poverty, and no coming to business.'

'Yeh, wisha, don't be too hard on the ould neighbours, Captain,' said Mat Murrin, putting in his round, beaming face in time to hear the denunciation of his nation's laziness. 'The Lord knows they wake early enough to the kind of life they're provided with. The only wonder is that a great many of them think it worth their while to wake at all.'

'That's so, boss. If the gen'lemen of this 'ere island would only lay on as much horse-power in keeping their appointments

as they do in turning out embroidered excuses for breaking
them, we'd be the most ornamental nation that ever sot up in
business.'

'Upon my conscience, Captain, if you had to bring out the
Banner and forage through the town for a subscriber to pay the
staff, you'd require all your embroidery to face Mrs. Murrin at
the end of the week. I've just been explaining to her that the
emoluments of literature in Drumshaughlin were not calculated
on the basis of the Muse having a houseful of babies. Master
Jack —the Lord love you !— reach us over the decanter.'

'Perfectly, my dear Mat—if we cannot feed the Irish Muse
upon Ambrosia, she need never be short of whisky-punch, and we
have it from our old friend Horace that the Camenæ know a
good drop.'

'Horace! Ah, yes ; great old boy, Quintus !—*Ars Poetica*,
old Falernian and the rest of it—*Dulce est desipere in loco*—that
is, it's sweet to enjoy a glass of grog with Dawley,' said Mat,
with all the pride of a Latinist, letting his eye-glass roll roguishly
from the tumbler to the tailor. Mat had been educated for the
priesthood, and still proudly proclaimed his acquaintance with
Balbus, the wall-builder, and other classical personages.

'I never knew much good to come of leading articles,' snarled
Dawley, who was always detecting scurrilous allusions to his
own red nose in the *Banner*. ''Twas your fine talk and fine
writing that ruined us in 'Forty-eight. I know nothing of your
Latin or trash. I'm a Dimocrat—I don't care who hears it—I'm
a plain working man. I believe in physical force and not in
paper men. Give me men of action !'

'Faith, I will—if you'll give me eight like yourself I'll construct one to begin with,' retorted Mat.

'The gen'leman who calls Latin quotations to order has the
floor,' the Captain interposed, rapping the table peremptorily.
'I don't go much on Latin myself. They didn't give much for
them Latin eppylettes in the Ninth Massachusetts, and I guess
they know'd how to scrooge through the Shenandoah Valley
purty handy without asking their way in seven languages.'

'Ah, but your soldiers have one language that's worth seven
—bad language !' put in Jack.

'Yes, sir—a few,' said the American Captain. 'But the
bottom fact of the small gen'leman's observations is correct—
we've had too much sunburstery and Brian Boru-kery in this
Irish cause. Sentiment in Ireland is as plentiful as ruins and
a'most as onserviceable in a campaign. Round Towers is fine,
but, gen'lemen, you can't get Round Towers to stand agen modern
artillery.'

'There, surely, you are a little unjust to the Round Towers and sentiment,' said Ken, who was by no means at ease seeing his idols bowled over by this rough-riding American soldier. 'They have stood a good deal of artillery. Sentiment and the Round Towers have outlived twenty generations of Strongbows and Cromwells. What brings us here but sentiment?—what else brings you here from the other side of the globe, perhaps to be killed or hanged in an obscure Irish quarrel?'

For the first time the American Captain stared straight into Ken Rohan's eyes. 'I like you, youngster,' he muttered, as if to himself, with a rapid nod; 'yes, there you've got my range—there I climb down.' A wondrous change had come over the face of the swarthy soldier. It was like one of those Canadian landscapes which you see one day in hard-bound snow, and within a week it has burst out into apple-blossoms. He had thrown off the high-pressure American citizen, slang and all, as he might throw off an overcoat, and, for all his thick, black moustache and square shoulders, was an Irish child again. 'I mind, as if it was yesterday, the morning we were put out of the cabin at Coomhōla Bridge. Such a morning, I think, never came out of the sky. It was the first sight of a soldier's coat I ever got in the glens. And sure they need not have brought the redcoats to us —the poor ould man could hardly drag his legs after him with the hunger, and my little sister, Mary—Mat Murrin, you may remember little Mary—it was the famine fever, I believe. I remember a couple of soldiers lifted her on the cart for the workhouse in the sheet, but the poor *girsha* never got there. I went out the first thing this morning to the ould quarryhole where they buried her—there was forty more put in the same morning by the relieving-officer without coffin or sheet, the Lord be kind to them!'

'Forgive me—indeed, indeed, I did not know what I was saying,' said Ken Rohan, pressing the soldier's hand. There was a tear glittering on his own hand when he withdrew it.

'That's what comes of lords and aristocrats,' said Dawley, with a spiteful glance at the Lord Harry.

'Yes,' said Harry, simply. 'I suppose it was the governor—or rather Harman. But Harman's just as hard on me.'

'It's a long while ago,' proceeded the Captain, 'but I can tell you I never slept the night before a battle that I did not dream of little Mary and wish we had the Ninth Massachusetts coming up the glen at the double that morning in Coomhōla. We soon may!' he added, with sudden vehemence, in a low tone.

'Glory!' said a stalwart young fellow, who had not hitherto said a word. He was a stone mason—Con Lehane by name—six

feet high, with shoulders as solidly built as one of his own walls
Con, in his own phrase, 'had no language,' but listened with that
curious, concentrated smile, which in a Celtic face is the signal
of an emotion as impetuous as a charge of cavalry. 'Glory!'
was all that Con said; but it was the sort of speech with which
battles are won.

'Wal, I guess this is foolishness,' said the Captain, suddenly,
as it were, skipping back from Coomhōla to the Shenandoah
Valley; 'but I'm not agen sentiment—the human quartz-rock
was never growed in Ireland that won't show *that* streak of gold
somewhere—all I want to state is that the man who goes after
the British lion for scalps would want something grittier than
poems in his cartouche-belt.'

'You're for a policy of ballads *plus* bullets, hein?' put in Jack.

'Yes, sir—bullets mostly. And I've got to make this further
observation, that there's no use mooning any more after ancient
chieftains for our leaders—the only fight worth a cent you'll ever
make for Ireland again will be made by men in the plain clothes
of the American Constitooshun—men without any genealogy to
signify. There's myself; I'm as average a citizen as a street car
will roll over—nothing ornamental about *me*. There are fools
that'll laugh at your calling me "captain," because I'm not like
them little toy soldiers that's tricked out in scarlet, like cockatoos,
and because I'm only the son of ould Jack Carthy, that kep' the
forge at Coomhōla Bridge long ago—just one of themselves, and
that's what I am, divel a more. But I've got the air of American
freedom in my lungs—I know a thing or two that's useful where
there's bullets flying—and—bet your pile!—if ever you see them
cockatoos in scarlet showing a pair of heels, it won't be the Brian
Borus but the Mike MacCarthys that'll send them flying. Yes,
SIR!'

'Do you hear that! What did I tell you?' cried Dawley,
in a state of high triumph. 'It won't be the Brian Borus that'll
do it.'

'No,' said Mat Murrin, focussing his eye-glass with terrific
deliberation, 'but he didn't say it would be the Dinnisheen
Dawleys that would do it.'

'There's too much cleverness going,' exclaimed Dawley,
fiercely. 'I want something that is not going to end with pen-
and-ink and talk. I want no Parliamentary agitation. I want
work. I want blood. Young lords may laugh——'

'Upon my word I wasn't laughing,' pleaded Harry, who felt
himself fixed by Dawley's fiery little red eyes. 'I assure you no.
And I'm not a lord at all. It's only a nickname they give me—
the Lord Harry.'

'Put the paw there, young one—you're a better man than if you were a duke,' said Captain Mike heartily.

'There's no use buttering him like that. That isn't dimocracy. I saw him laughing. I know I'm only an humble working-man ——'

'Hould your prate!' remarked Con Lehane with the good humour with which a mastiff might address a saucy terrier.

'If the gen'leman who wants blood will only cool his noble thirst with cock-tails for a short time longer I guess he'll find enough of that ruby wine on tap,' said the American Captain, speaking now rapidly and in a thrilling whisper. 'That's the frozen fact. That is what I brought you here to-night to tell you. We are getting near the hour. The boys are coming home. Half the barracks in the country are ours. The militia regiments are with us. By the time the harvest is ripe there'll be an improved American reaper on hand to fix it. *Thiggin-thu!*'

'Grand!' says Con Lehane, the charge-of-cavalry smile about the eyes grimmer than ever.

'That's the talk *I* want to hear!' screamed the little tailor, who, to do him justice, feared nothing in human shape except Mrs. Dawley—a woman of large proportions, who was accustomed to display a rolling-pin and a contempt for democracy.

'And now,' pursued the Captain, 'what I want to know is, supposing our boys keep their appointment, what sort of reception will they have from the people—supposing they land here in Bantry Bay, now, for argument's sake?'

There was an awkward pause. Pulling the British Empire to pieces looks the simplest thing in the world till you come to particulars. Our fervid Celtic faith believes in moving mountains, and hates being teased with petty difficulties about pulleys and means of transport.

'Begor,' says Mat Murrin, not being prepared with any other strategical suggestion, 'we'll drink their health in the biggest bumpers that ever blazed with Irish whisky.'

'I con-clude you'd do that much violence to your feelings without bringing shiploads of people across a hemisphere or two to assist at the de-monstration,' said the Captain drily. 'No, boss—I don't allude to the toast-list, nor the torchlight procession, nor the 'luminated address from the citizens.'

'Give us the guns!' said the stone-mason, in a low, deep voice.

'There goes the Ninth Massachusetts!' said the Captain, fixing his dark eyes upon the speaker's brawny limbs with a critical approval that made Con blush like a rosy russet. 'What I want to know is, can you multiply Con Lehane by fifty

thousand ?   How many more lineal yards of that material have
you got in stock round here ? '

'You'll find too many like me—just as poor and just as
ready,' said Con, sheepishly.

'In the towns, yes,' said Jack Harold. 'But we must not
deceive ourselves. It is different with the country people. There
are good prices for springers. That is their literature, their
history, their heaven. The only cause in which they are willing to
die is filching their neighbour's spot of land. Don't count upon
the farmers. *Parbleu !* They are such miserable creatures that
they have not even found it out. The Society for the Prevention
of Cruelty to Animals might as well expect donkeys to call in the
police to the brutes that flog them. If those charming peasants
ever heard tell of us, we are wild young men—who knows ?—
instigated by the devil.'

'It's the priests that does it,' said Dawley. 'There's Monsignor McGrudder. He tells the ould women we're bringing
over the French Revolution to abolish God and the altar.'

'When our boys go for bear I'd advise the reverend man
not to pan out on that text to any great extent within my lines,'
said the Captain, 'if he don't desire a short road to heaven bored
through his body.'

'That's what I tell 'em,' exclaimed Dawley, triumphantly.
'The French Revolution's too good for them sky-pilots. They're
too purple and fat, and wants bloodletting.'

'That's atrocious ! ' cried Ken Rohan, hotly. 'If we are to
judge three thousand Irish priests by Monsignor McGrudder,
how can you blame Monsignor McGrudder if he judges *us* by
sanguinary balderdash like that ?'

'Balderdash ! ' exclaimed the little tailor, his nose tilted into
the air, like a flash-light on a dangerous coast. 'Listen to that
—balderdash ! '

'Yes, stranger, it was nonsense—bloody nonsense,' said the
American Captain, coolly. 'Shoot your man if he blocks the road,
whoever he is ; but don't go blazing away at the Short Catechism
—you may as well be firing at the moon. It's kind of wrong,
and it wastes cartridges.'

'I for one,' said Ken, whose heat was not altogether allayed
by the Captain's rough-and-ready summary of the theological
tenets of the Ninth Massachusetts—I for one will be no party to
pulling down the Church to stop Monsignor McGrudder's chatter.
It's the one possession the Irish people have got in perpetuity,
except the graveyards. There is one Irish province that was
never confiscated—their hope in a boundless heaven for eternities.
The man would be more accursed than Cromwell who would bar

them out of that bright country for the sake of a few fretful hours on a mere speck of earth in a world which is itself a shadow.'

Dawley listened, open-mouthed; his wrath fortunately tempered by wonder what could all this possibly be about.

'No,' Ken Rohan dashed along. • 'You'll get the Irish people to write, "Liberty, Equality, and Fraternity" in plain letters over the church doors, but you'll never get them to dance carmagnoles on the altars. God forbid you ever should be able! If there is a more detestable thing on earth than an Irish priest without a country, it is an Irish patriot without a God.'

'Do you mean me?' shrieked Dawley, who had seized a tumbler, having, worse still, emptied its contents.

'Don't make a bosthoon of yourself!' said Con Lehane, smilingly, replacing him in his seat.

'*Allons*, my dear Ken, you are as fond of making a preach as the Monsignor himself,' said Jack Harold. 'Dawley can have a horrible revenge by making your new coat a misfit. It would serve you right to prepare you for heaven in garments cut for a mendicant friar. *Eh, gai!* we are perfectly agreed. Brother Dawley has no more notion than you or we have of going to hell to spite Monsignor McGrudder.'

'I hope Dawley and the rest of you will forgive me, I am sure. It's an infernal way I've got,' said Ken, blushing. 'When the Monsignor proceeds from the pulpit into the street and picks up stones against the Irish cause, our friend Dawley may trust me he will not find me making genuflections. The greater the Irish reverence for our faith, the better we are entitled to resent Maynooth College being converted into a sort of auxiliary Constabulary Depôt in which the people's priests are drilled by an Italian Cardinal and turned out for patrol duty in the service of the people's oppressors.'

'I am glad to hear that explanation,' remarked Dawley, with dignity.

'And what is more, I am convinced that the bulk of the young priests resent it more sorely than we can. They have Irish hearts that will never mark time to those Italian drill-masters. Captain MacCarthy need not fear either for priests or people. I know hardly anything about the country except what I have read, or what I hear in the cabins when I drop in to light my pipe; but, so far as I can judge, what you lack is not young fellows to take up arms, but arms for them to take up. The old fellows are still living in the famine-time, many of them with one leg in the famine grave. My own governor's faith in pike-heads is in the grave with Smith O'Brien—he denounces us as furiously as the Monsignor. Age is a time-server all the world over—

Leonidas had more trouble with middle-aged Bœotians than with the Persians; but give the young fellows a chance; let them see your ships here in Bantry Bay, and they will rush to you as the young waterfalls do from the mountains.'

'Glory!' observed Con Lehane.

'Correct,' said the American Captain, with much satisfaction. 'Wal, children, I ain't powerful on Fourth of July work; but just you take home this sentiment, and frame it over your chimney-piece in the most slap-up style this respectable but backward island can pro-duce. If Mike MacCarthy knows a clam-bake from a Confederate shell, your young waterfalls will have the chance before long. Yes, SIR!'

'What do you think of that, Misther Editor?' asked Dawley, with fine scorn for one weaponed with a goose-quill in such an hour.

'Well, then,' said Mat, 'I was just thinking that if you hang up that sentiment anywhere within reach of Mrs. Dawley, I hope you'll give the *Banner* notice, so that a shorthand man may call around and take a note of her remarks. There, now, don't be cross—sure we all have our Mrs. Dawleys—the Five Great Powers of Europe aren't such great fellows when their five wives are anywhere on the premises. This wrangling is dry work. Jack Harold, if you were the decent man a misguided public take you for, you'd be after ordering in another drop of nourishment.'

'The chair recognises Editor Murrin. Another drop of nourishment is in order!' said Captain Mike.

'In the meantime, Mr. Chairman and gentlemen,' said Mat, improving the hint, and solemnly rising, fixing his eye-glass with a majestic sweep of one arm, while the right hand was spread into a statuesque fan-like development springing from a concealed thumb in the arm-hole of his expansive waistcoat—'in the meantime, perhaps, I may be allowed, with the permission of the chair, to embody in the trivial form of a vote of thanks the feelings that are struggling for utterance in every patriotic bosom I behold around me—with the exception of Brother Dawley, whose massive brow, I observe, is corrugated with that severe superiority to the ordinary emotions of our nature which we honour in the tailor even more than we bow the knee to in the man——'

'The usual rot,' remarked the disgusted Dawley, 'you ought to be in Parliament.'

'Mr. Chairman,' said Mat, gorgonising the interruptor through his eye-glass, and then dropping that appendage with a supreme rhetorical grace, 'I might have been tempted to reply in the language of an outraged Parnassus to the impotent interruptions of Blackamoor Lane ' (which was Mr. Dawley's private address), ' only that the drop of nourishment (which I would respectfully invite our honoured friend, Jack Harold, to mix)— only that the drop of nourishment has, I say, opportunely arrived to elevate us above the mental plane of Blackamoor Lane, and, as I may say, to flood the daisy-spangled meadows of patriotism with the sunshine of the human soul.'

' It would carry the Sixth Ward—the whole darned ticket ! ' Captain Mike observed, meditatively.

' But, sir,' proceeded Mat, ' it requires no eloquence, nor indeed whisky-punch, to recommend to this assembly the vote of thanks which swells the heart of Ireland with the force of a volcano of delight when she beholds Captain Mike MacCarthy and the scattered children of her race breasting three thousand miles of billows, with arms in their hands to strike the chains off the limbs of their poor, but universally respected, mother, Ireland.'

' Strikes me this is kind of pre-mature, editor,' said the Captain. ' Wouldn't it be well to wait till the gen'lemen in the billows are signalled off the Fastnet anyhow ? '

' No, sir, the mind's eye sees them already crowding all sail for Bantry Bay, their eyes straining for the land, their hands upon their manly weapons, their hearts panting for the hour when they will cross swords with the red-liveried minions of England——'

' Fine, Mat,' cried Jack Harold, ' but couldn't you manage to sing it ? '

' Ay, ay, a song ! ' shouted everybody.

' No, sir, sing it yourself ! ' thundered Mat Murrin, who, to tell the truth, had forgotten the exact purpose for which he rose, and was beginning to feel lost in three thousand miles of billows of his own rhetoric. ' No, sir, sing it yourself,' cried Mat, suddenly and determinedly sitting down.

' Jack Harold's song ! ' rose in a chorus of relief from a company cloyed with the orator's rich abundance, and Jack, being quick at improvisation and not at all deaf to the seductions of his own pretty baritone, after a brief interval, which he pretended to devote to chaffing the editor and filling his own tumbler, broke into the following brisk verses, which he sang to the swinging air of 'The Low-backed Car' :—

'THE BOYS ARE COMING HOME.'

' Ho ! Con, light up your fires to-night
  On Hungry's tow'ring crest ;
For ships will come, ere morning's light,
  With brave news from the West.

M

And pass the word through all the glens,
To-morrow's signal drum
Will welcome wide o'er Bantry's tide
The Boys who're coming home.
   They're coming, coming home—
   The Boys who've sworn to come—
God light their way to Bantry's Bay
The Boys who're coming home!'

'Their cheeks are brown'd by many a sun,
And plough'd by many a scar;
Their flags are dim with the blood-prints grim,
Of many a foreign war.
But their hearts are Irish as the streams
Glengariff's dells that roam;
Their stoutest blow they swore should go
To the fight for the land at home—
   The small green isle at home,
   The brave old land at home—
My soul! a slashing, smashing blow
Have the Boys who're coming home!'

'Now, Con, away to Hungry's heights!
Haste, Meehul, wake the Glen;
Their ships bring gear worth soldiers' wear
For thrice ten thousand men.
Then, boys, farewell the dance, the fair,
Your Mary's cheeks of bloom,
Till freedom shines o'er the conquering lines
Of the Boys who're coming home.
   They're sailing, thronging home—
   In bold brigades they come—
Old Erin's veins run fire to-night—
Her Boys are coming home!'

Rude as the lines were, they struck sparks from the soul
of Dawley himself. When the last tuneful refrain was ending
the entire party were on their feet, with glowing eyes and
heaving breasts, chorusing as passionately as though they were
wrapped in some wild religious rite. Nowhere in the world is
the science of music so little understood, and nowhere is its
tumultuary empire over the feelings so sovereign, as in Ireland.
It is the only country I know of which records that the Order
of Bards there was powerful enough to inspire kings with as
much uneasiness for their thrones as the Order of Nobles did in
Burgundy and upon the Rhine. Even in godlike Greece Orpheus
did not found an Orpheonic aristocracy. Fancy, in sober-sided
England, a twangling choir from Grub Street marching on White-
hall and bewitching the guns out of the hands of the guards.
Even in quite recent experience, the most formidable part of
Irish rebellions has been done in rhymes to insurrectionary music.

'I could not have expressed it better myself,' said Mat Murrin, whc had joined in the chorus. 'Eloquence does homage to melody. The soaring eagle takes off his hat to the singing-bird. But, Mr. Chairman,' proceeded Mat, rising again, arrayed in all the stately dignity of his eye-glass, 'there is one toast, Mr. Chairman, which no assembly of Irishmen can separate without honouring——'

Until Mat Murrin's soul 'separated' from his body, there was always 'one toast' which demanded a brief tribute of his oratory. They say it was in the course of some observations in recommendation of 'one toast more' that the Angel of Death interrupted him with a summons to a higher—I hope brighter—board.

It was late when Ken Rohan and the Lord Harry found themselves in the street under the cool stars. Harry had been drinking recklessly. He looked tossed and excited. Ken willingly took his arm up the cathedral-like aisle of elm-trees that shaded the avenue to the Castle.

'Ken,' said he, caressing the friendly arm with an affectionate tug. 'You wouldn't see a fellow going to the dogs—going to the devil if you could, would you?'

'No, certainly not—though I am afraid, under certain circumstances, I am capable of going to the devil with him. Why do you ask?'

'Because—because that's where I'm going, and you can pull me up. You can save me.'

'I!'

'If you would only—don't laugh at me!—if you would only say a word for me with your sister, Katie.'

Ken drew away his arm as if an adder had bitten it.

'Damn you! how dare you mention my sister's name?' he cried, in a voice of frenzy.

'I'm as fond of her as you are—fonder,' said Harry, boldly.

'You are drunk. You have never spoken a word to her in all your life. You know you have not!' cried the other, seizing him roughly by the shoulders.

'Don't hold me, Ken! Of course I have not. But I have wished to, ten thousand times. I was watching her—I was worshipping her—many a time when she little knew it. She is the only one in the world that could get any good of me. I would slave in the mines for her. I would be as faithful to her as—as a bulldog.'

'This is nonsense,' said Ken more gently. 'We have both been taking too much. You will forget it all in the morning. Let me request you will never mention my sister's name again,' he added determinedly. He could not exactly analyse his feeling of indignation at Harry's avowal ; but there was something to him insufferable in hearing his gentle, fair-haired little Katie's name made the subject of the maudlin raptures of this tipsy, half-witted young lordling. It angered him, as it would to see the statue of a saint set up for worship in a tap-room.

'I wish those chaps of Mike MacCarthy's would come and give a fellow a chance of getting decently shot or hanged,' said the Lord Harry doggedly. They exchanged not another word—Ken buried in his own sullen thoughts, Harry's weak wits relapsing from their unaccustomed spasm of energy—until Ken, suddenly looking up, found himself at the heavy stone doorway of the Castle. Harry's uncertain pull at the bell seemed to send it pealing through endless stone chambers, dark, silent, and empty. There seemed to be nobody alive in the great house. Before the peal had died away, however, a light flittered into the hall, the heavy chain was half drawn, and a female form appeared at the opening.

'This was mean of you, Mabel,' Harry suddenly cried, in his sulkiest tones. 'I told Quish to wait up. You sent him to bed and waited up to watch me—to see if I had drink taken. I have drink taken. There, that's what you get for playing the spy upon me !' he cried angrily.

The door was now wide open, and Miss Westropp stood facing the two young men by the light of the taper which she carried in her hand, her hair falling in a soft shower about her shoulders. She looked quite white as she said gently : 'Come in, Harry—do please, come in.' Ken Rohan wished he could sink into the centre of the earth out of sight when she turned her eyes upon himself with a placidity worse than the bitterest reproach, and said : 'I am obliged to you, sir, for bringing my brother home. I did not think that he was with you.'

Ken Rohan could not utter a syllable. He only knew that the door closed, and that when he turned to go the stars seemed to have dropped into a fit of blackness. Please don't run away with the belief that the miller's son was in love with Miss Westropp. He would have shrunk from the collocation of their names, even in thought, as he did from the association of Harry's name with his sister's. He would have thought it grotesque, impertinent, inconceivable. He was as faithful an idolator as ever of Miss Lily Dargan's rose-leaf cheeks and great blue eyes— perhaps all the more faithful an idolator. But Miss Westropp's apparition had brought an influence of gracious divinity into his life ; to have forfeited her good opinion was to feel like a reprobate ; and here was his angel, like the Hermit's in Parnell's poem, taking to flight just as she had revealed her silver wings, leaving him in a mood of darkness, very unlike the Hermit's.

CHAPTER THE SEVENTEENTH

THE chapel at Drumshaughlin—(we were still in the days when five-sixths of the Irish people durst not call any place of worship a church except that which they had to pay tithes for not believing in)—the chapel at Drumshaughlin at last Mass on a fine Sunday presented, as it were, the whole face of the community in repose—its piety, and gentility, and beggary, and splendour—its hopes, struggles, and pretensions here below shaded off and harmonised by a certain luminous glow of the hereafter. The men lingered in the chapel-yard as in a sylvan club-room, with the grave-stones under the trees for their arm-chairs, discussing the news in a subdued Sabbath tone (I have never heard a laugh or loud word on such occasions) until the last stroke of the last bell left them not a moment longer to dally. How we all do love to procrastinate to that last stroke of the last bell! Even after the bulk of the congregation were bowed around the lighted altar, there straggled out from the open church-door into the grave-yard a long line of semi-detached worshippers, bare-headed, indeed, and with one knee bent to the earth, but with the other planted at right angles in an erect free-thinking manner, so as to act as a rest for the body. It was one of the most constant topics of Monsignor McGrudder's eloquence and one of the most frequent employments of his gold-headed stick to flog these truants out of their one-foot-on-sea-and-one-foot-on-shore style of devotion. He used to demand of them witheringly whether, when they went to pay their vows at the public-house, they were content to inhale the whiff of alcohol that came through the street-door. They bowed under the reproof, and even under the stick, but still continued to mix the fresh air with their devotions, and to give one knee to God and the other to the world, like more pretentious philosophers; and—oh! the sameness of poor human nature from Drumshaughlin to Bagdad!—only flocked in round the altar when the moment came for announcing which of the neighbours was dead or about to be married, or for which of them an American letter had been received in care of the parish priest.

Say what modern sanitary authorities may against it, there was something exquisitely appropriate in the old fondness for building the church in the midst of the graveyard, or rather clustering the graves around the church, like so many vassals

nestling under the fortress of their lord. The living congregation cannot be in the company of so many dead congregations
without a good many solemn intimations of the supernatural.
The mysteries of the altar acquire a deeper emphasis from the
mysteries of the surrounding tombs. The dead are sometimes
by no means uncheerful company. Years enough had passed to
make it a sort of holy luxury for Mrs. Rohan to sit in the gallery
of a sunny Sunday and think of her lost baby-girl being so near
her—only just underneath the window at which she sat, in that
little mite of a grave, which scarcely any but a mother's eyes
could distinguish in a tiny undulation on the longer grave, where
her stalwart old grandfather lay mouldering. Whenever the wind
whispered in the elm-tree which tapped at the window-panes, it
scarcely required an Irish mother's imagination to hear her little
one's angel voice in the rustle of the leaves ; and the shaft of sunshine which sometimes flashed in beside her, and stretched its
bright wand down to the altar, did surely seem to bear a golden
message from on high. But Mrs. Rohan, like her neighbours,
did not always occupy her leisure moments at chapel in listening
for little Ellie's voice among the elm-leaves. There was Mrs.
Dargan's new bonnet to be studied with a certain gentle envious-
ness ; there was the new development in chignons which the
milliner's young lady visitor, all the way from Cork, sprang upon
an astonished world; Mrs. Deloohery's wonderful taste in flounces
and colours, and Mr. Deloohery's fat pink hands bulging out of
his lavender gloves, like powerful fungi forcing their way out of
a glass-case, were a joy for ever to their town critics, who, if the
truth must be told, resented the intrusion of the ·rich land-
grabber and his wife into their own immemorial gallery with as
fine scorn as Grosvenor Square could defend its drawing-rooms
against Bloomsbury ; innumerable, in fact, were the topics with
which a contemplative mind might not unpleasantly cheat away
the moments while Father Phil was robing for last Mass—if it
were only tracing Maria O'Meagher's last gown through its
transmigrations to the backs of various little Miss O'Meagher's,
observing Mr. Deloohery sit on his hat, or accidentally noticing
that Captain Grogan, an ancient of the Peninsular wars, read his
prayer-book upside down—Captain Grogan, who, being an old
bachelor, always observed in the hunting field, and seldom observed at Mass, was an object of legitimate suspicion around
female tea-tables in Drumshaughlin.

All this little silent comedy vanished, however, with the first
tinkle of the altar-bell. It is wonderful how much awful mystery
can be stored in one plain-featured, old-fashioned little Irish
chapel. One of Ken Rohan's earliest recollections was of being

brought to hear Vespers sung, and coming to the conclusion that the red curtain which covered the choir was placed there to conceal the portals of heaven through which the angels' songs were coming. He grew up to learn that the chief of the angelic singers was a shoemaker's daughter, with a damaged soprano; yet he had only to turn his back on the red curtain still to forget all about the shoemaker and the tonic sol-fa system, and to hear the music of the spheres once more. The Virgin's altar was as humble a little structure as you could find, a meek statue of the Blessed Virgin draped in spangled gauze, a few vases of simple flowers on either side, and a triplet window of common red and blue glass behind. In his acolyte days he used to renew the flowers in the vases and light the clusters of coloured tapers for the May devotions, and used to be as proud of his scarlet soutane and embroidered surplice as we can imagine one of Raphael's cherubs being of his wings. All that you will think passed away when the moustache and pipe came. Not a bit of it. This very Sunday, as his eye wanders to the shady corner where the coloured window casts its rude lancets of red and blue sunlight to right and left of the gentle-faced Virgin, the tapers light up again, and the smell of the May flowers comes to his nostrils, and Father Phil's litany and the chant-like response of the worshippers rise up to the glowing altar like a deep song of the human heart; and he can see almost as vividly as of old the statue smiling back the answer to the delicious prayer, 'O clement, O loving, O sweet Virgin Mary!' and dismissing good boys to the earthly paradise of the scented May evening outside where the thrush is singing. There are few unspoiled Irish souls that cannot have their visions of Mirza in the rudest whitewashed chapel. That, you will say, argues an absurdly emotional way of seeing things as they are not; and the reproach would be quite just if we could be certain that the optic nerve-fibres are the only vehicle of seeing things as they really are; but be this as it may, you will never understand the Irish nature until you come to see how subtly the light of other days and other spheres colours the common sunlight in our prospects.

Whenever Monsignor McGrudder stepped up to the altar at the time usually devoted to Father Phil's sermon, the congregation closed up around the rails with that bustle of interest and general outbreak of coughs and wheezes which is the grace before meat of a crowded assembly that expecteth good things. The laggards all slouched in from the chapel-yard. The Monsignor had never anything pleasant to say. His appearance at sermon-time was usually the signal for the excision of some parish scandal or for some withering observations on the stinginess of the

Easter dues. But we are all more attentive to the Monsignor's scarifying knife than to Father Phil when he promises us the joys of heaven. Monsignor McGrudder belonged to an order of clerical noblesse, in whose cardinal's hat there resided more power than in the Queen's crown within the Irish seas. The Irish-American revolution has extinguished them in a quarter of a century. If you can still find specimens of the breed, they are as the strange fish of the old red sandstone period, which are dug out of the lower coal measures of a subsequent age. But a quarter of a century ago those great ganoids and placoids were still swimming about in all their glory. They were a stiff-necked, and in their way memorable, race, the haughty old Roman Legion by whom the famous Cardinal held Ireland as a conquered province. They had ecclesiastical privilege in their blood. It made them haughtier than a dozen quarterings and a gallery of ancestors make earthly nobles. The sudden efflorescence of their power was one of the first consequences of Catholic emancipation. From the bosom of darkness of the Penal days the Church seemed to have stepped into the dazzle of mediæval Italy. To the guileless confidence which the people gave them without reserve during the ages when they were persecuted together, the clergy now found added the pomp which the people delighted to bestow upon their re-arisen Church, and the homage which the civil authority hastened to pay to a power more popular than the *Nation* newspaper, and more conservative than the police. English policy in Ireland has always proceeded upon the principle of governing by bribing somebody—anybody except the people to be governed. At one time it was the landed men who were maintained as a foreign garrison ; at another time, the people's representatives who were corrupted ; and now it was the people's clergy who were to be tricked out in Government purple and fine linen. Seeing how effectually one bishop had suppressed the sale of the *Nation* within his diocese, and how triumphantly another bishop had defended the place-man who betrayed the Tenant-right Party for certain pieces of Government silver, Dublin Castle conceived the brilliant idea of ruling Ireland henceforth by canon law instead of martial law. The Cardinal's red stockings were welcomed in the throne-room ; the bishops' palaces became fountains of honour where men knelt for judgeships and seats in Parliament, and grovelled on their stomachs for magistracies, poor-law guardian-ships, and all the other little glass beads and bits of ribbon which had so irresistible a glitter in the eyes of a race scorched for cen-turies with the sight of their own abject condition of dishonour. Don't imagine for a moment that a man of the stamp of Monsig-nor McGrudder was conscious to himself of arrogance, much less

of self-seeking. He was as honest as Hildebrand. He had an
unflinching faith in the Church, and that her grandeur was the
one sovereign secret of happiness in this world and in all others.
If he aimed at grandeur himself, it was as he read his Latin Office.
It was in the rubric. He stopped his subscription to the *Banner*
because his name was printed with the mere canon's description
of ' Very Rev.' instead of the ' Right Rev.' of a Domestic Prelate
to the Pope ; but in this he was avenging the dignity of the
Sovereign Pontiff, who bestowed the title, not of plain Daniel
McGrudder, who unworthily held it. Was Mat Murrin to be
allowed to print the name of the Almighty with a small a ? He
was particular to the edging of a button in displaying every scrap
of purple in stock, rochet or soutane, which distinguished the
Monsignor even among the Cathedral Chapter, and would entertain you (if you were a person of eminence) with the minute
details of sacred millinery which differentiated his own costume
from that of the Bishop. As Prior would tell of the nights when
he ' drank champagne with the wits,' the Monsignor would incidentally mention his rubbers of whist for gold points at Cardinal
Rimbomba's tables, or describe some dish of beccafichi or a zam-
baglione invented by Prince Frangipani's cook, on an occasion
that he could mention, and never produced in perfection before or
since.

     Nobody who knew him well—least of all himself—could
easily separate what was merely vain in all this from what he
honestly esteemed to be the decent appurtenances of his dignity.
He had an undeniable appreciation of princes and good dinners.
So had he also a fine taste in old silver for the altar vessels, and
(not so fine a taste) for slabs of lapis lazuli about the tabernacle.
Both were sets of tastes which did not misbeseem his station.
When that which flatters your palate flatters also your pride
as a churchman, who is to say where in this subtle ideo-motor
apparatus of ours the exalted ecclesiastic's sense of ceremonious
fitness ends and the mere titillation of the gustatory nerve
begins ? The Monsignor would acknowledge at the proper tribunal with unaffected humility that he was the most miserable
of sinners ; but he would be a bold man who, without due credentials from Rome, should break in upon his cosy slumbers with
reproachful suggestions of poor old Father Phil's thin figure
braving the midnight storms with the sacraments for the dying,
or who should venture to interrupt one of his arguments on the
improvidence of the poor over his port wine, with a hint that his
port wine were better bestowed than his strictures in Blackamoor
Lane. Not that he was at all a heartless man. The poor were
God's poor, and consequently His humble pastor's. It was only

that his care of the poor took the form of the benevolence of a
Board of Poor Law Commissioners. Bow-wow was to him not
so much an individual as a statistic to be relieved according to
tables of averages. He would indite powerful memorials for the
construction of a fishery pier. He would head influential deputa-
tions to the Chief Secretary in favour of extending the railway
from Garindinny, and even, if speeches and confidential correspondence through the member for the county were of no avail,
would threaten a narrow-minded Treasury with the terrors of a
patriotic public opinion. He would call into the bank-manager's
parlour in a deserving case. He interfered constantly, and with
effect, between a landlord and a body of suppliant tenantry ; but
he interfered as Pope Innocent the Third would interfere between
two Powers that solicited his mediation, so as to make the landlord beholden to him for his rents, and the tenants for continuance in their cabins. He was learned. He had a lofty piety.
Much though he sought from landlords, county members, and
eminent personages of state, he sought nothing for himself. He
had no nephews or nieces. It was his duty as Monsignor and
Vicar-General to be respected, and he was respected—to be
dreaded, and the very stones of Drumshaughlin shook under his
tread. If he had been told that this was not his entire duty as
an Irish priest, he would have been as much astounded as if a
parishioner whom he knocked over the sconce with his gold-
headed stick had summoned him to the police-office for a common
assault, or as if a candidate for the county had passed his door
without anxiously sending in his card. Though he was the son
of an evicted tenant himself, it was often the appointed duty of
tenants to be evicted, as it was of Monsignori to know a good
picture or a good wine. Poverty was one of the divinely insti-
tuted toll-bars on the road to heaven. You might entreat the
turnpike-keeper to reduce his charges in pity for your rags and
bleeding feet ; but the man who talked of tumbling the barrier
and letting the world pass toll-free was—in one word, the French
Revolution. Monsignor McGrudder would not have shirked
poverty himself. In the Penal days he would have said Mass
in a mountain cave, or slept on the heather, or swung from a
gallows, for that matter. Religion would have demanded it, and
religion was the great concern. But religion was now coming
out of the catacombs and marching on the seat of Empire.
After the Fathers of the Desert, the founders of the Basilicas.
Great churches were arising, like aspirations long crushed under
the earth. The fumes of frankincense filled the land. The
despised Popish priest was not only able to swing his Mass-bell
without fear—he was able to appoint Popish judges, to return

Popish members of Parliament, to nominate Popish magistrates.
The electro-plated Catholic upper-class thus manufactured repaid
in sycophancy the ecclesiastical dignitaries to whom they owed
their patents.   The Government, lost in admiration of the discipline with which the Roman Legion moved like one man over
the country, were well content to grant to the Church those little
subsidies of privilege and patronage which promised to get their
fighting done for them against Irish disaffection as effectually as
their subsidies of bullion had kept the allies in the field against
Napoleon.

The ecclesiastical legionaries, on their part, might be excused for seeing their successes in a different light.   The Cardinal
was the most powerful man in Ireland.   The Protestant Church
Establishment was visibly tottering.   Who could tell what might
not arise upon its ruins?   Nay, was not England herself beginning to stir with uneasy longings for the old faith of which
her beautiful minsters were still the sermons, rather than the
tombs?   Was it altogether impossible that that Irish race
which once gave apostles to half Europe, and which has within
the present century utilised its exile for the conquest of two
continents for the faith, should achieve vengeance upon England
in the most glorious of all forms by restoring the gentle power of
the Mass-bell in the greatest of the world's cities over the most
stiff-necked of the world's races?   Here were dreams worthy of
patriotism, indeed !   What, in comparison with splendid destinies
like these, were the squalid ecstasies over a lost provincial
Parliament, or all the pother about Tenant-right and the better
housing of Bow-wow?

'My people,' Monsignor McGrudder began, gracefully replacing the square, tasselled biretta upon his cliff-like brow, and
looking straight before him with a gaze which somehow seemed
to each individual present to be fixed upon him or herself alone,
although a casual observer would have noticed little but a mountainous foam of white eyebrows breaking over the bar of his
thick gold spectacles.   Whenever he began by calling them ' My
people' everybody knew that something spicy and, so to say,
ex-cathedral was coming, and a violent anticipatory catarrh
seized the congregation. 'You may stop your coughing and listen
—I am not going to ask you for subscriptions,' he said harshly.
'No,' he proceeded, amidst the silence into which he had awed
the most phthisicy sufferers in the parish, ' I want to speak
some plain words to you on a matter that affects the liberties of
your children, and perhaps the very existence of this Church of
God in the midst of you.'   A groan of deep interest passed
through the women's side of the chapel, and the men crowded

closer. 'There are wolves going around, and it is my duty as your pastor to warn you. It may be my duty to do more than warn the wicked and designing men who are endeavouring to inoculate my people with the poison of continental atheism. I will not permit—I will not to-le-rate,' he said, raising his voice, 'interlopers coming into my parish to seduce young fools into a secret society condemned by the Church and by the law—a secret society which has not courage enough to capture a police-barrack, but has wickedness enough in its heart to confiscate the property of every man with a decent rag on his back—ay, and to strip the priest of God of his sacred cloth at the very altar. I know these men ; don't let them imagine they can escape my eye. There are some of them listening to me.' Dawley could have sworn that the awful white eyebrows and all the eyebrows in the chapel were bent upon himself. 'I will not name them now ; but I know them, and they know I know them. They are Garibaldians. They are infidels. They are Reds ! ' and there was an awesome vibration in his voice, as if the last word of horror were now spoken. 'I challenge them to deny it. They come here with the bloody teachings of the French Revolution on their lips—perhaps, if the truth were known, with Government gold in their pockets.'

'It's a lie ! ' The cry rang through the chapel like a report of firearms. There was a fearful silence as if everybody expected to see somebody fall. The man who had spoken did not conceal himself. He stood out in the central passage to the altar as if to make himself the more visible—the strangest little crooked figure, bent as to the body, but perfectly erect as to the flashing eye, which he turned fearlessly on the threatening figure at the altar. Ken Rohan, to his horror, recognised little Danny Delea. Danny glanced defiantly over the batteries of eyes turned upon him, grasping his stick the while, and, finding nobody to offer him battle, directed another rebellious look full in Monsignor's face. 'You challenged us for a denial,' he said sharply. 'There it is for you. It's a lie,' he repeated, 'and a *dom* lie ; and I don't care who it is that hears me tell you so to your cheek.' Whereupon Danny put down the lame leg stoutly, and marched straight out of the chapel.

The Monsignor never moved a muscle. A more astounding thing had happened to him than if he had been suddenly seized and stretched on the rack ; but he bore the one shock as he would have borne the other, with a dignity as calm as if he were raking in a gold pool at Cardinal Rimbomba's card-table. Standing there, erect and terrible, he reminded one of his own gold-knobbed stick—as stately about the head and equally sturdy about the body.

'You see!' he said calmly, in the fearful stillness that
followed Danny's last footfall. 'Was I mistaken in telling you
of the spirit that is abroad ? You have heard him yourselves—
you have heard the blasphemer tempting God here to my face—
here in the very presence of Him before whom hosts of adoring
angels are at this moment trembling around your altar.' He
looked terrible as a mediæval exorcist, standing there between
the living and the dead, clad around as it were with the mysteries
of the altar and the graveyard. 'I wonder that he stopped at
giving the lie to the priest of God before His altar. He ought
to have struck me—perhaps murdered me. His French friends
have drunk the blood of priests like water before now. I suppose
that will come next. But that—that *thing*' (with a gesture of
grinding scorn directed towards the door through which little
Danny had disappeared) 'is only the dupe of more dangerous
men. They keep in the background. They mock at the decrees
of the Church. They think they have got hold of the pillars of
the universe with their cobweb philosophies and humbug about
liberty. Let them beware! Four thousand years ago more
powerful men than they formed a secret society, and answered
Moses as you heard me answered here to-day, and every man in
all the tents of Dathan and Abiron was swallowed down alive
into hell. I judge no man—God forbid!—but He to whom
vengeance belongs still walks the earth, and—mark my words!—
His eye is not dimmed nor his arm shortened!'

A woman's scream was heard faintly, and then a shuffling of
feet in the gallery. Mrs. Rohan had fainted in the arms of her
husband and son. 'How shocking!' exclaimed Mrs. Dargan,
with a comfortable shudder. 'I suppose it's Ken, my dear,' she
whispered to the apothecary's lady. 'I heard something about
it. Who would have thought of a genteel boy connecting himself
with such low people ? I am so glad we have removed Lionel
from that odious college. Poor, dear Mrs. Rohan,' she said, in a
tone of deeper concern, joining the circle that had formed around the
fainting figure. 'What a trial! She requires all the sympathy her
friends can give her, and I assure you she will have it, Mr. Rohan.'

'Yes, ma'am, she requires fresh air—please stand out of the
passage,' said the blunt miller, scattering the gaping circle unceremoniously to right and left, and then carrying off his wife as
if she had been an infant in his great arms.

'Hoity-toity!' exclaimed Mrs. Dargan, with a noble effort to
convince herself that she was more indignant than pleased. 'The
boorishness of that man is really unbearable ; but, of course, it
is a terrible blow to them all—we must not be too hard on them.
I dare say the poor thing will have to resign the presidency of the

St. Vincent de Paul Society' (Mrs. Dargan, it was understood,
had been more than once willing to serve the poor in that
capacity) ; 'she could scarcely hold it after this. Humphrey,
my dear, you will have to caution Lily very strictly to have no
more to do with that boy.'

'It's really most unfortunate—most unfortunate,' piped Mr.
Dargan in his thin, apologetic voice. Everything about the little
money-lender was apologetic—his whine, his skip, his attorney's
letters ; his very beard appeared to be always apologising for
being in the way. Feeling bound to do a neighbourly part by
Mrs. Rohan in her mishap, he could think of nothing more immediately useful than nervously pulling on and off his canary-
coloured kid gloves, until he had them transpierced in all directions
by his long, sharp fingers. 'Myles Rohan was always a headstrong man, and rough—very rough. You never know how
things will turn out—no, really.'

'You heard what I said about Lily, my dear ? The child
mustn't get talked about. How very well Monsignor McGrudder
bore it all ! He is such a distinguished-looking man !' And
Mrs. Dargan reopened her prayer-book for the purpose of con-
cluding her devotions.

'I have come round to tell you, sir, that you have behaved
like a brute,' said Myles Rohan, entering the vestry, where the
Monsignor was striding up and down to work off the agitation of
the scene. 'It is the first evil word I have ever said of a priest.
Only that you are a priest and cannot strike me, I would say
more—and worse.'

'You are a worthy man, Myles Rohan, and I am sorry for
you ; but I have a duty to God and to His Church,' said Monsignor McGrudder solemnly, 'and I will do it.'

'Your duty is not to revile my child as if he were a forked
devil or a Government spy,' retorted the miller in his stormy
way. 'I hate this secret society business as much as you do. It
has the heart scalded within me. But when you call upon hell
to open and swallow a parcel of foolish boys—as good boys as
ever your mother reared—because they are silly enough to think
they can free Ireland with pop-guns—why, then, to the dickens
I pitch your loud talk about Atheists and Garibaldians. It is
detestable. It is not true. Don't tell me that the landlords and
the peelers have all the religion that's going to themselves. It
was not to landlords or peelers you ran when there was a better
price for a priest's head than a wolf's. You might leave that sort
of talk to the Crown Prosecutors. The Catholic religion is ours
as well as yours. We don't pay our priests to curse our own
children as reprobates to our faces, and I tell you what, your

reverence,' Myles concluded, all but breathless, from the red-hot whirl of words, 'you'll get a one-pound note from me next Christmas instead of five, and I hope the landlords and the peelers will make good the balance.'

'This is worse than I thought,' said Monsignor McGrudder, when the door banged behind Myles Rohan. He put on his hat with the enormous brim, and by some unaccountable fancy looked into the little mirror hanging by the wall, as if to see whether it still fitted him—whether the grim square face underneath the brim had lost any of its strength or ruddiness. He did not seem over-pleased with the survey. He took up his stick as if he half expected to find it not so stout as usual. He really felt faint and ill. 'I think I will go in by the garden wicket,' he murmured to himself abstractedly. 'I should have as soon expected the stones in the chapel walls to fly out in rebellion.'

Groups still lingered in the chapel-yard discussing the events of the day. The country folk—great, dark-skinned, black-haired fellows, with faces swarthy enough for Spaniards, and dark eyes soft and melancholy enough for Egyptians—moved about as heavily and almost as silently as oxen chewing the cud. 'Bad work !'—'Begor so it appears !' was about the most definite exchange of opinion you could gather among those secretive peasants, over whose hide caution and dissimulation had grown encrusted like the cuirass on the backs of pàlæozoic animals accustomed to be preyed upon. The peasants were still standing irresolute on the isthmus between the old passions of land-grabbing and the new country of Irish-American Democracy. Dawley was the centre of a less reticent knot of artisans and town labourers from whom the rustics kept uneasily aloof. His beady red eyes danced with joy as he beheld Monsignor McGrudder making his way home by the garden entrance, instead of striding through the chapel-yard as usual like a burly hunter among his dogs. 'The Big Man is looking sick,' he exclaimed, with much relish. ' Be the mortial ! little Danny has downed him ! '

'I hope the fright was nothing serious,' said Father Phil, whose old apple-blossom face, in its silver mist of hair, was shining like a sun in a frosty sky at Mrs. Rohan's side at the Mill, almost sooner than it seemed possible for his old legs to carry him from the chapel after Mass. 'You know I had as good reason to be frightened as you. I am sure it was that rascal Jack and his French ways he was speaking of all the time. I am afraid we are all reprobates except the head-constable of police. Well, well,' he added, merrily, 'God is good, and heaven is wide. There will be room enough for more than Head-Constable Muldudden, Mrs. Rohan.'

'It is ten minutes to two o'clock in the day,' cried Myles Rohan, 'and you have run up from the chapel all the way without your breakfast. Don't deny it – don't attempt to conceal your roguery from me. Katie, get a rasher down —run, child. Is the kettle boiling ?'

CHAPTER THE EIGHTEENTH

MR. HANS HARMAN DISSIPATES

'THAT is all you have learned. Why I knew this all along. There are not many things that happen here unknown to me. But, my dear sir, things are not so serious as you imagine,' said Mr. Hans Harman, pleasantly cracking his egg-shell.

'Not serious !' exclaimed young Mr. Flibbert, the officer of police. The bearer of the first tidings of the battle of Waterloo could not have felt more disgusted if he had been told at the Horse Guards that it was really of no consequence and not to make a fuss. 'Not serious ! drilling going on every other night in the mountains—Lord Drumshaughlin's son in it – soldiers singing rebel songs—there are some of the police even that we've got to keep an eye upon——'

'Bah ! all our Irish tragedies end with the first act—the fellows are born actors—any amount of rant, spangles, limelight, and that sort of thing ; but you never get to the killing— at least to any great extent.'

'They've cast lots for Lord Drumshaughlin's property. Dawley, the tailor, has won your place,' said Mr. Flibbert, a little maliciously.

'I am exceedingly glad to hear it. That will keep Dawley in good humour. He will be in no hurry to take up possession, and he will see that nobody shoots me for fear of his putting in a prior claim.'

'I'm afraid you scarcely appreciate the serious character of our information,' said Mr. Flibbert, who was considerably nettled, and tugged at his smear of moustache, as if in some desperate hope of drawing it out to the ferocious proportions which the occasion demanded. 'We have positive information that they not only mean general confiscation but massacre. There is one of those Irish-American fellows knocking about here—you evicted his father, I understand– a fellow as free with his revolver as with his pocket-handkerchief—freer. I am reluctant to say anything to alarm you, Mr. Harman, but I am bound to let you

know my men tell me you are the most unpopular man in the
county.'

The agent pulled a revolver out of his breast-pocket and
levelled it at a robin-redbreast which was bobbing about on
the sill of the open window. Mr. Flibbert jumped and the bird
dropped. 'Let your American fellows beat that,' said Mr. Harman, knocking out the discharged cartridge-case and replacing the
weapon in his pocket. 'I have a stronger objection to shooting
redbreasts than assassins—they say it is unlucky, you know—
but robin-redbreasts have no business coming in my way. My
dear Flibbert, you don't perceive it's *you*, not *me*, this business of
insurrections and Irish Republics is aimed at. And that's why
I am so glad to hear it. It changes the venue from the infernal
land question to Nationality, high falutin and fiddlesticks. What
is a poor devil of a land-agent to people raving about a Republic ?
Nobody is going to lie in a damp ditch to shoot me when he has
the whole British army to blaze away at. I am but small beer
in a matter of *haute politique*. It's *you're* the big game now.
Flibbert, I am sorry for you, but you have the army and the navy
and the volunteers.'

This turn of affairs put Mr. Flibbert in tolerably good humour
with the world and his moustache. 'I dare say we'll be able to
take care of ourselves,' he said, with a modest smile.

'The men who come over to this country to govern us are
idiots at their business, or, instead of losing their heads over every
trumpery drill-meeting, they would keep a rebellion always on
the stocks. There is no better way of keeping the peace. A
national insurrection is really much more easily dealt with than a
dispute about turbary. Even if the thing comes to a head, so
much the better—you have not a mouse stirring for the next
quarter of a century. Besides, it cuts your enemy in two. Do
you think a strong farmer up in Ardigoole will shed his blood to
hand over his farm to a Cabinet of Dawleys ? Do you think
Dawley is going to stump the country with blatherskite about
unexhausted improvements ? No, if your Irishmen must have a
cockshot, put it as high in the sky as possible—he may hit me,
but he never will bring down the moon, nor the British Empire.
The worst of all these miserable governments is, they meanly
leave us, loyal citizens, to stand target when they have an army
with nothing else to do—all to save a few miserable pence in
transport, and pretend it is all our fault. The devil mend the
British Empire, say I, and long live the Irish Republic !'

'Ah ! here comes Miss Harman ! I am so glad !' said young
Mr. Flibbert, who had stolen into society under Miss Harman's
ample shadow, and repaid her patronage by a canine devotion to

N

archery and all other pursuits or persons honoured with his mistress's smile. 'I hope Mrs. Harman is well?'

'She does not feel quite well to-day,' said Miss Harman. The day when Mrs. Harman *did* feel quite well was rather a matter of tradition than of observation, like the blossoming of the century plant. Nobody but a goose would have asked such a question, as Mr. Flibbert perceived plainly enough the moment after he had asked it. But Miss Harman did not dislike little Flibbert, with all his gosling ways. He was as absolutely at her mercy as her parrot was ; and what unmarried woman objects to having a young man trotting at her heels, whom she can honestly despise, and who desires nothing better than to fetch and carry for her? So her eye brightened as she cried : 'Oh, Mr. Flibbert, you are the very one we all wanted to see. Are we going to be piked or have our throats cut in bed, or what? Do tell me. Can this possibly be true about Harry?'

'I am afraid these are official secrets,' said the police-officer with a smile, swelling with gratification, 'though I am not sure that I would not rather incur the censures of Dublin Castle than Miss Harman's.'

'That is so nice,' said Miss Harman, graciously.

'Very well, then, let you people go and betray your country elsewhere—out in the conservatory, for instance—for, to tell you the truth, I'm wretchedly behind with business this morning,' said the agent, with a frank selfishness which half the world mistook for a virtue. 'Is Quish below? Call him up.' The bailiff shuffled into the room, with one eye roving as if in search of a way of escape through the window. 'Quish, you know every turn of Master Harry's?'

'Who, zurr?—I zurr?' croaked Quish, with the voice of a frog suffering from virulent sore throat.

'Yes, you. You know that he is a Fenian and drinks with that American fellow. Yes, you do,' said Mr. Harman sharply, perceiving that the bullet head was wobbling in a strange manner. 'And if you don't, you're not fit for your place, and you can have your wages on Saturday evening, and go. You understand? Very well,' said Mr. Harman, resuming his genial air. 'I have always found you an intelligent fellow, Quish, and though the blackguards abuse you and me, that is no reason why we should not be useful to one another. That is a half-sovereign.'

'Never more welcome, zurr,' gurgled the sore throat, and for the first time in his life it seemed as if Quish's two eyes met upon the coin, which he pounced upon with a demoniacal grin.

'That is a trifle to what may follow, if you keep a sensible head on your shoulders. I want you to tell me all that Master

Harry does, where he goes, whom he meets, and, generally speaking, what's in the wind—you understand ?'

'I understand well enough, zurr,' said the bailiff.

'Not as if you were watching, you perceive—just keep your eyes and ears open, that's all ; and, if you do, I tell you, you may find that I've put you in the way of a gold mine, that's all. Get the trap round.' 'Ireland,' he soliloquised, as he drew on his driving gloves, 'is a country where you will always have the ground mined under your feet. But life is always tolerable if you know the lie of the mines, and have got hold of the fuse. You may even have a counter blow-up, if you feel dull.'

Though it was a morning soaked and soddened with rain, Mr. Hans Harman was in indomitable spirits. He always was, outside the hall-door of Stone Hall. There, if he did not take off his hilarity with his wraps, the servants knew there was somebody to dinner. But it was remarked that nobody could find a satisfactory cause of quarrel with Hans Harman, even when he was executing a writ of ejectment. It is one of the queer points in human nature that he took more pains to do disagreeable things agreeably than most good men take in doing good. It seems probable that there are persons now in hell who might have been in heaven for half the trouble.

'I am not coming to dun you about that trifle of rent, Myles,' he said, as he threw the reins to the boy, and joined Myles Rohan, who was standing at the door of the mill-house with his hands in the pocket of his blousy white breeches, and a less aggressively open look than usual upon his broad ruddy face. 'I always say you are as safe as Threadneedle Street. But the fact of it is, Lord Drumshaughlin is always tight for money —he is a most unreasonable man—it is so long since he saw his property, he forgets that we can't quarry gold out of the Coomhóla grits. And such a temper as he has ! Speaking between you and me, I sometimes think of flying to a ranche in the Rocky Mountains, or mid-Africa, or somewhere. Well, but what can we do to stop his mouth ? It is only a matter of—let me see—yes, by Jove, there are four gales—256l. 14s., besides that little balance for the stable.'

'I am sorry to say I cannot do much at the present moment,' said the miller. 'The milling business is not what it used to be. The Americans are running us off our legs. We are no match for them in this unfortunate country. They have the capital and the new machinery. You can get American flour in Cork market this moment for a song. There will soon be nothing but Indian corn left for us to grind—or to eat, either, I'm thinking.'

'I am sorry to hear that, Myles—you millers used to hold

your heads so high, you know. Those Americans are playing the devil with everything. I would not have an American article enter the country, except American letters. There's an infernal lot of treason in them, but there's money, too. Keep the money, say I, and hang the treason. Well, but we'll have to manage something, you know—a bill at three months, now, would do nicely, and you'll have the harvest-work coming in.'

'There are bills of mine out in both the banks,' said the miller, shaking his head, 'and until I can make a lodgment or so——'

'Pooh! Dargan will discount one for 250*l*. at all events.'

'Dargan and I are not on very good terms. I should not like to ask him.'

'Then *I* will, and I should like to see him refuse *me*! A hundred and fifty will keep his lordship's gout in good humour. I dare say the odd hundred will turn in handy enough for yourself.'

'This is very kind of you, sir,' said the miller, with downcast eyes, colouring.

'Not at all. I'm a skinflint and a heartless tyrant, you know. Or was it a black-livered exterminator you called me that day you ran against me for the chairmanship of the Board, and raked up that old business of the Coomhŏla clearances against me?'

'Well, and I was right about the Coomhŏla clearances, if it comes to that,' cried Myles, bridling up.

'There you go—I knew I would draw the badger,' laughed Mr. Harman, gaily. 'My dear Myles, I would let a fellow heave every adjective in the dictionary at me at a shilling a gross. Besides, I beat you for that chairmanship, you know, so I had the best of the argument. A man must live, even if he is an agent, till you've got an act to hang him. I have to do some grinding, like yourself, only in a different way—worse luck mine. Trade is hard for both of us. Why shouldn't we be good neighbours? By the way, I am sorry to hear of your trouble with your boy, Myles.'

'Well, sir, we can't put old heads on young shoulders, can we?' said the miller, fidgeting a little uneasily.

'Certainly not. I suppose we all had a dash of the devil in us in our time. And after all the devil is not so black as he is painted. Why shouldn't we be able to get the youngster out of harm's way? They'd probably transport him, and it's such utter rubbish, you know. A post in the Four Courts, now—there are so many of those things going that keep a young fellow loyal to his cigars and clean collars. If the Government want the county for their Attorney-General at the election, I really don't see why we of the Drumshaughlin interest should not claim our bunch out of the basket of grapes. You always voted Whig, Myles, in spite of his lordship and myself being on the same side—which was very creditable to your principles. Think it over, and if a note from me to Glascock can put the boy in the way of a good thing— There, I'll say no more. If you've filled the bit of paper, I'll make it all right with old Dargan myself, and send you down the balance in bullion.'

'I wonder is he laughing at me?' mused the miller, scratching his poll, as he saw the agent's tall figure swinging off through the Mill-gate. 'He's a man, somehow, that it's a greater comfort to be pitching into than to be taking a hundred sovereigns from. Sure enough, he caught it hot that day at the Board. Well, well, maybe it's too much of what we call spirit and strong language we have in this country for our means. That hundred comes in the nick of time, whatever.'

'I want you to do a bill of Myles Rohan's for two hundred and fifty,' said Mr. Harman, dangling his long legs unceremoniously from the counter of Mr. Dargan's private money office.

'Hum, Mr. Harman, sir, don't you think now, reely, sir—you see, the milling trade—and, don't you persave, Rohan has been dipping a little lately?' Mr. Dargan piped in his plaintive voice, stroking his starved white beard deprecatingly the while—'I would say dipping, don't you persave?'

'Yes, Rohan has got a bad shake—all round,' said the agent. 'But this is to oblige me, and there is his note of hand.'

Mr. Dargan took the stamped paper in his thin hands, and examined it with the martyr air of an editor who is required by an influential subscriber to insert bad poetry.

'Well, well, Mr. Harman, we have done a goodish bit in this line —you and I have—a goodish bit, I may preshume to say, sir, for a small country practitioner, sir, so to say——'

'And made a devilish pretty thing out of it,' said the agent. 'You might let me have three Bank of England fifties. I don't want to appear in this thing at the bank.'

Mr. Dargan skipped to his safe in a series of mild electric shocks. 'No news yet, sir, about—ahem!—that small affair of mine, sir?' he asked timidly, as he fumbled for his keys.

'About the magistracy?. No, certainly not. These things are not done in a day.'

'Just what I observed to my wife, sir; but you know what leedies are, sir. Lord Drumshaughlin is Lord-Lieutenant of the county—that's what these foolish wimmen do be saying, sir—and his lawrship could arrange it with a scratch of the pen, sir—yes, reelly.'

'You don't imagine Lord Drumshaughlin keeps a staff of clerks to answer all the begging-letters in the county?'

'Indeed, no, sir, it did not strike me that way—that's very clever, sir,' said Mr. Dargan, half closing the safe again, and turning round to face the agent, 'though there be those that would tell you—I don't cleem it myself, sir, but there will be those that will talk and will say—that I have resaved more begging-letters than ever I wrote, and have the signatures at the bottom to show for them, too, sir.'

'Nonsense, Dargan, don't be so hard on my little jokes. The thing will be done, of course, but you know what Lord Drumshaughlin is when he has the gout on him, and you know what a snuffy lot those local magistrates here are, and how they have to be humoured and squared—confound them!—before making you free of the craft. But it's as good as done—take my word for it.'

'That's very eemiable of you, sir,' said the money-lender, dipping the beard until it seemed low enough to sweep the floor. 'Very eemiable, I'm sure, sir; and will be very consoling to Mrs. D.— coming from headquarters. How will you take the balance, sir—notes or gold?'

'That is young Harold—the young Frenchman—Father Phil's scapegrace—crossing the street from the hotel, isn't it? That's all right. Bye-bye, Dargan,' cried the agent, arriving at the door in time to come plump against the cigar smoke of the young gentleman in question. He hailed him with a cheery 'How do you do? I got that application for the Town Hall for your Christy Minstrels. Of course, you must have it. I don't know anything a country town wants more than a good laugh. I wish we could instal your nigger minstrels in the Town Hall permanently in place of the Board of Town Commissioners. Your stump speeches would be just as sensible, and more amusing.'

'I hardly hoped our darkies would earn the civic crown, sir,' laughed Jack, a little embarrassed by the agent's cordiality. 'We owe you a thousand thanks.'

'Not a bit—only the gaslight, which won't be much. Put me down for three front seats.'

'It is very good of you to occupy yourself with such trifles—a man of affairs, who must be so pressed as you.'

'That is the way with all you youngsters—you want to squeeze all the fragrant essences of life into your own scent-bottles, and leave us old fellows nothing but our ledgers and our Bibles. You would never suspect me of a taste for Chopin, now, I dare swear! Come up to Stone Hall some evening and see. I suppose you regard me as the enemy, and will hold no parley with the Philistine?'

'I—I don't understand, sir.'

'Nonsense; you understand very well, and so does all the world. You don't suppose you can conspire with a man like Dawley, now, for instance, without every bird on the hedgerows knowing that you are preparing to blow us all sky-high one of these nights. Don't be a bit alarmed, my dear fellow, and don't in the least apologise. I believe the British Empire will blow you sky-high instead, and therefore I stick by the British Empire; but in the meantime I am very glad indeed to see the British Empire getting a dose of the terrors it thinks so lightly of, when it is we small fry that are being flogged for its sins. Them's my politics. If you think a barefooted Irish Republic, or the county gaol, preferable, that is your affair. I dare say we'll exchange a shot or two some day on the subject—if we let you get hold of revolvers; but *en attendant*, as the French say, I shall be glad if you will drop up to Stone Hall and hear me strum a fugue or two.'

And before a week was over Jack Harold found himself actually in the drawing-room at Stone Hall, lolling over the music-book, while Lord Drumshaughlin's agent was—playing the piano. Mr. Harman's taste for Chopin was no joke. The pianoforte was one of his few dissipations in life. His long white fingers had recourse to the piano after dinner, as other men have recourse to wine. Abbé Liszt's recitals were the one form of London entertainment that attracted him. He himself played with excellent technical skill—some judges thought like a musician, as some judges thought Hans Harman a remarkably handsome man of his years. Others (among whom Jack) remarked that Harman came very near being a great musician, as he came very near being a handsome man; but that there was something just a shade too hard in his touch, as his face was just a shade too thin, and his eyes a shade too bulgy, and his teeth a shade too sharp looking for the best models. But where will you find perfection outside Books of Beauty? How many young girls of Cortone did Zeuxis take as models for his Helen? Young Harold was musician enough to feel a good deal of interest in Mr. Harman's performance, and hypocrite enough to feign a great deal more. He was thoroughly glad to have advanced from the bar-parlour at the Drumshaughlin Arms to the drawing-room at Stone Hall, cheerless and drab though it looked; and I cannot conceal the fact that when Miss Deborah made her appearance with tea our friend courted her and deferred to her with the enthusiasm of a finished young toady. Even gay young revolutionists are not perfect.

'My sister and you ought to be sworn allies, now that you are at war with Monsignor McGrudder,' said the land-agent, who really liked young men's ways, as he liked young monkeys. He spent one whole wet Sunday afternoon in the Regent's Park about the monkey-houses, and expended a large sum in copper on nuts. 'I hear he thundered against you finely.'

'I missed it. I was in bed,' said Jack with a flavour of insolence. 'It is a hint I learned in Paris—tell your *concierge* never to be in a hurry to wake you until the revolution is quite over for the day.'

Miss Deborah, who had only consented to meet the priest's nephew under her brother's orders, and expected to find a bumpkin with an Indian-meal complexion, was greatly edified to find a Papist who was not afraid to talk of his priest with this cheerful impertinence—a young Papist, too, with an uncommonly-turned foreign moustache and a dash of delicate colour in his cheeks. She had remarked his smart dolman with its pretty capuchon as he came up the lawn, and thought it picturesque and *chic*.

'I should hope there are a good many Roman Catholics who are not much frightened by incantations nowadays,' she remarked graciously, 'though it is really distressing the number of poor people who still believe in Mr. McGrudder. We have only to trust to the influence of enlightening zeal and loving counsel to dispel the shades of ignorance which still haunt the darkened souls of our humbler brethren,' said Miss Deborah, falling into a quotation from the last annual report of her society. 'At the same time I feel bound to tell you, Mr. Harold, that I cannot approve of young men lying in bed upon the Sabbath. That is a matter I should like to discuss with you. It is not enough to have lost the relish for the debasing doctrines of Mr. McGrudder. That is something, but it is not all. That is only the first sprinkle of the waters of regeneration——'

'Hang it all, Deborah, you're not going to regenerate the young man with tracts and blankets, I hope,' said Harman.

'Upon my word, I was never half so happy under a pulpit,' said our democratic rascal, more than half persuading himself that the younger Miss Harman had a bright pair of eyes, and a not irresponsive pair when you looked into them, which he did, saucily.

'Your compliments are as inexcusable as brother's levity,' she murmured, dropping her eyes with a guarded sort of austerity.

'Especially as he will have nothing pretty left to say to Miss Westropp, whom I see on the terrace,' said the agent, rising in time to extend his hand to a young girl, who pulled off her straw-hat as she came into the room, with a wolf-hound at her heels, and cried : ' I have come to ask Deborah for a cup of tea. I felt so lonesome—not a soul to talk to except Bran.' Then she stopped, with a startled look, seeing a stranger.

Jack Harold felt as if he would reel and fall. It was the first time in his life he had ever felt faint in presence of a woman. This beautiful apparition had bewitched him. The exquisite curves of the tall slender figure, arrested in that pretty frightened attitude ; the straw-hat with its simple blue ribbon in her hand ; the eager health-flushed face ; the high, shapely neck and masses of shining hair, that threw it all out like the gold ground of a Byzantine picture—all caught his artistic eye ; but it was something more than his eye, it seemed his whole body and soul that was penetrated by this adorable presence.

' Then you have come to the right spot for amusement for this once,' said Mr. Harman. ' Here is the Captain of a Christy Minstrel Club who is undertaking to entertain the whole public next week—one of Harry's friends, too, I understand—Mr. Harold. Come, sir, give us a taste of your quality. See if you can't beat Deborah's green tea with black melody.'

' It will be a sacrilege to put the piano to such uses after Chopin, but if Miss Westropp will in the smallest degree care to listen '—stammered Jack, somewhat mortified to find himself figuring in burnt cork before his goddess.

' I love the slave songs,' said Miss Westropp, cordially.

Jack Harold seated himself at the piano, and floated off into a plaintive Southern plantation song called ' Radoo,' which had a dying fall like the sigh of a love-lorn wind through some lonesome Louisiana creek. The melody was as simple as a child's prayer, and there was something equally touching and seemingly artless in the singing.

' I don't think I ever heard anything prettier in my life,' said Miss Westropp. ' I do wish you would let me take the privilege of your audience and cry " Encore ! " '

Jack Harold's head was swimming in delight. He broke into a passionate little French love-song, with a pretty machinery *larirettes* and *lariras*. He would infuse his whole soul into it, and for the first time found a mincing French chanson not large enough to contain it.

' How good of you ! ' said Miss Westropp ; ' but do you know I liked the negro melody better ? '

' Yes,' he said, ' French is a vile language when you are in earnest. You can't get violets to blow in the asphalte of the Boulevards.'

' No, indeed, you can get very little that is wholesome to grow there,' put in Miss Deborah, sharply. She was beginning to dislike heartily the proceedings of this pert young adventurer. Jack's boasted knowledge of women was but shallow, or he would not have so lightly forgotten the elementary warning of the danger of offending an old woman in trying to please a young one.

But at this moment he had forgotten Miss Deborah's very existence, bright eyes and all. 'The poor minstrel is entitled to send round the hat for the price of his entertainment,' he said to Miss Westropp, reverentially. 'May he beg something in return from you?'

'Did anyone ever hear?' exclaimed Miss Harman, as the two young people went to the piano.

'The young Frenchman is getting on,' said her brother, with much amusement. 'He is a cool young cub.'

'This is an air that my brother took some extraordinary fancy to, and, do you know, I cannot get it out of my head,' said Miss Westropp, and immediately the keys were thrilling with the haunting numbers of 'The Wearing of the Green.' Jack could not believe his ears.

'Mabel, dear, I am surprised,' said Miss Deborah. 'You ought to think of the bad example, if low people hear that you can tolerate a song like that.'

She was interrupted by a peal of silvery laughter. 'Goodness gracious! the notion of people taking their politics from me!' Miss Westropp exclaimed, laughing again with the rippling softness of a little cascade sparkling in the sun.

'This is a very serious matter, dear. Our property and our lives are in danger. Persons who have the responsibilities of rank and birth ought to beware of giving countenance, even in small things, to the designs of the wicked and the vulgar.'

'Hullo, Deborah, Mr. Harold is a rebel of the most emerald dye,' said the agent.

'I was not thinking of Mr. Harold,' replied Miss Harman with the utmost civility and the keenest edge. 'I was thinking of Miss Westropp's position. That is a different thing.'

'Miss Harman is quite right about the danger. That song would make a hundred thousand rebels,' said Jack, fervently.

'If you forbid me to sing it under penalties, you will drive me to sing it from door to door,' said Miss Westropp, in her wilful mood. 'I wonder what there is in this country that it is *not* wrong for me to do except detest the people—and – and'—she had to rise and trip over to the window to prevent herself from finishing—'and preach at them.' She could not forgive Miss Deborah's cruelty to this engaging young plebeian. It was as if Miss Deborah had taken to worrying her fine hound, Bran, with needles. 'Oh, how lovely!' she suddenly exclaimed, signalling joyously to somebody on the lawn. 'Here is Harry come to look for me. It was for me, now, wasn't it, Harry?—and not for Bran?' she asked a little falteringly, as she ushered the Lord Harry into the room.

'Yes, Mabel, I have such news for you—such news!' cried Harry, revelling in the unwonted luxury of self-importance. 'You remember Neville—Reggy Neville!'

'Yes!—has Carabîche been winning something?'

'Carabîche! you stupid! Carabîche has been sold for a hack these three months—sold for a song too, deuce take it!' cried Harry, still on triumphant ground. 'No, he's here, or he'll be here one of those days.'

'He? who? where?'

'Why Neville—all the Nevilles. They have taken Lord Clanlaurance's place. Quish heard it all down at the Post Office. The first load of furniture and things came over this evening from Garrindinny. He is such a devilish good fellow, I ran—I thought you'd like to hear.'

'I am glad!' she cried; then with a comically thoughtful air, 'I do hope he is not coming to make love to anybody.'

'That girl is mad,' said Miss Deborah Harman, when the drawing-room at Stone Hall was once more reduced to decorous gloom. 'There is an unlucky strain in all the family. But what on earth, brother, induced you to admit that singular young French person to this house?'

'My dear Deb,' said the agent, playfully pinching her ear (Miss Deborah was his favourite sister), 'you are a clever woman, but I am not quite a fool. If there is madness in the Drumshaughlin family there is none in ours.'

CHAPTER THE NINETEENTH

L'ANGE AUX GRANDS YEUX BLEUS, ET—L'ANGE AUX GRANDES AILES NOIRES

THERE is a crag of not very difficult ascent near Glengariff, the crown of which is known as the Lady's Seat. It gives you the exhilaration of being on a mountain top, with the refinement of surroundings fit for a lady's bower. The bosses of smooth rock underneath and immediately round you are scored with quaint geological writing, and shaded off into all sorts of beautiful softness by the lichens and fungi which have been for ages creeping into their stony hearts and enamelling them with

flowers and verdure—like vast stone monsters which Queen
Titania's sprites had been decorating with their fairy favours in
their sleep.   So that it was not at all a savage crag, but a mossy
playground, on which the little white-chaliced fungi blossomed
and the heather danced to the music of the rills that for ever
leaped and trickled down the rocks.   Below these gleamed a
stretch of bright green lawn, shaded by ancient oak groves,
through the midst of which there flowed a broad, still river, no
longer agitated by the tributes of its noisy children from the
hills, but gliding on like a monastic life in the maturity of its
vocation, darkly contemplative as it paced along in the solemn
cloisters formed by the oak-trees towards the eternal sea which
was so close at hand.   At a little distance the river washed past
the ruin which the country people called Cromwell's Bridge.
Cromwell's Bridge juts out boldly upon two solid arches into the
middle, and there it stops and holds out an ineffectual arm in the
air—the river only half spanned.   What a type of Cromwell's
work in Ireland is this bridge -- so seemingly irresistible in its
beginnings, so disreputable an old ruin in its results—the impetuous Celtic current still flowing by untamably, and the
bridge-builders pausing helplessly half-way in their work !   But
is there not also a cheery hint in the peaceful charm with which
these rude grey arches melt in with the soft Glengariff landscape ?
The material as well as historic Irish landscape will be all the
more picturesque for its ancient scars and ruins, when they shall
have passed into old bits of scenery—when the rest of Cromwell's
rough achievements shall have been given over as a bad job as
frankly as the Glengariff bridge, and buried like it in kindly
Irish mosses and wild flowers.   Beyond the bridge the river
swoons away into the bay, like a wood-nymph that has finished
her course ; and fairy-bright is her death-bed amidst graceful
wood shadows and smooth shelves of rock, over which the shrubs
dip their pretty fronds in the cool night-green water.   The whole
scene—river, lawn, woods, crags and all—was clasped in the
rugged embrace of the Caha ridge, which seemed to have put on
purple-splashed garments to please the coquettish beauty in its
arms.   The gracefullest point of the range - the slender pyramid
which Celtic fancy called the ' Witches' Hill,' and some latterday
Batavian, ' The Sugarloaf '—rose quite close to the Lady's Crag —
only the river and its verdant marges, it seemed, between—and
the sun's glitter on its bright gauzy purple coat was like the
smile of a strong man-at-arms looking down protectingly on his
gentle sister hight and all her tender greenery.
    Ken Rohan sprawled in the heather in this luxurious spot,
looking out intently over all the intervening rock-work and

glossy verdure towards the sea. He had come to feel a painful longing in this direction. The miracles of beauty all around were very well, but *there* his hope lay ; a path of boundless promise was open over the waves to what he began to find his somewhat land-locked life ; and as the days passed he began to lust more and more fretfully to see the nozzles of the American ships coming round the point and hear the booming of the guns. He was aroused by a merry crinkle of girlish laughter on the acclivity just underneath him. Looking round, he caught flashes of feminine drapery among the bushes that grew over and around its path to the Lady's Seat. Not being in the mood to encounter tourists, who were accustomed to profane this spot with sand-wich-baskets, he was about to slide down the rock into the under-wood, when Georgey O'Meagher, being the winner in a race to the top, arrived, breathless, and accosted him with the most joyous surprise.

'What good luck !—I mean good luck for you, you surly fellow,' she cried—the latter member of the sentence with a pretty pout.

'By Jove, Georgey, it *is* good luck to meet you ; you look as beautiful as a Glengariff fairy queen with that grand glow you have.'

'You wretched hypocrite, 'twasn't myself I was thinking about—'twas of somebody I've been running races with—some-body who'll be here this moment——'

'You don't mean——'

'Of course I do. Somebody, for you, could mean nobody but one body. I've beaten Lily hollow up the rocks, but *here* she carries all before her. Here you are, lazy bones,' she cried to Lily Dargan, who now struggled up faintly, 'and here's Ken Rohan to see you beaten all to fits.' Miss O'Meagher was a somewhat slangy person, as we know. 'See what a vengeful thing I am ! There, now, you're exhausted. I wonder if you could manage to rest yourself on that seat without feeling lone-some, while I go in search of that precious little coral *clathrus* with the hard name. It's a thing one of Mother Rosalie's girls—an English girl—used to brag about,' she explained to Ken. 'I don't know whether it's worth the search, I'm sure ; but she says they find it around Torquay, and I should like to know what they grow at Torquay that we can't do at least as well in Glengariff I'm off.'

'Georgey ! Georgey !' exclaimed Miss Dargan in very genuine distress, but the curly head was gone. The two young people, to their mutual alarm, found themselves alone. What with the fright and the race uphill, Lily's little panting heart was glad to

seek rest by sinking on the rustic seat. 'What a silly, provoking
girl she is!' she murmured, with as near an approach to vexation
as features used to a lifelong sweet composure could express.

'I—I hope you are not afraid of me,' stammered Ken, feeling,
if the truth must be told, stupid to distraction. He felt a guilty
shock, in the presence of his love, to remember how little love had
been in his thoughts of late. I tremble for the opinion young
ladies of sixteen and thereabouts will hold of him ; but the fact
is, Lily's fairy form and blameless blue eyes had got a good deal
jostled out of sight, like a baby in a crowd, by the burly figures
of Captain Mike MacCarthy and Monsignor McGrudder. It is a
way with those young Hotspurs. When they take to 'dreams of
iron wars' their bonny Kates have often enough to put up with
the rude hint that 'this is no world to tilt with lips in.' Kate,
however, has a knack of recovering her empire. Our Hotspur
was at her feet already—I don't mean in the literal sense—
thoroughly ashamed of himself for ever having forgotten the
potency of his lady's fan. This is, perhaps, a high-flown way of
putting his halting observation. 'I hope you are not afraid of
me, Lily.'

'No, indeed, Ken. Why should I ?' she said, looking at him
with those clear blue eyes, which shone with the simplicity of
two violets on a dewy bank. To which his ungrateful response
was a desperate stare, and an almost inaudible passionate cry :
'You have eyes out of heaven !' He sat down beside her at the
usual unnegotiable distance at which love's engineers open their
parallels, and captured one little outpost hand with the most delicate blue tracery wandering over its soft snow. A pretty pair of
creatures enough they looked amidst the picture-scenery to the
music of the waterfalls—she with the mild lightnings in her large
blue eyes, he flushed with the passion which would have made a
much more ill-cut profile than his look luminous—as promising a
pair of pretty ones as ever softened the Arcadian hills with their
melodious sighing. Alas ! how the prettiest of these pastoral reeds
get out of tune, even in Arcadia !

She drew away her hand determinedly.

'Ken, you mustn't ! It is wicked I must tell you. You
won't be angry with me, will you ? I am not to speak to you
any more'—faltering just a little at the last.

Here was an heroic situation for a young gentleman who had
just been reproaching himself—perhaps with some little *soupçon*
of vain-gloriousness, as men will—with having been neglectful of
his goddess under the stress of weighty cares of state ; and now
the goddess tells him with the calmest celestial expression of
countenance that, so far from her having languished for his devo

tion, he must please to give her shrine a wide berth for the future, if he does not want celestial bull-dogs set at him. Is Ken Rohan the only member of the base masculine fraternity whose fidelity is all the more ardent for a snubbing?

'You are joking,' he said, in the trepidatory tone of one who had just heard that the Last Trumpet was about to sound, and, incredible though it seemed, had it on authority which he did not dare to doubt. 'You don't usually tease a fellow, Lily.'

'No, indeed, I am quite in earnest. Mamma says you have set yourself against the Church and connected yourself with low people, and that a curse follows such things, and I don't know what else.'

Ken burst out laughing—not a gay laugh. 'And is that all?' he asked, almost rudely.

'Well, papa and mamma say it is very terrible and will end badly.'

'No doubt it will not end in the Commission of the Peace,' cried Ken, stung and daunted in an intolerable way by her tranquillity. 'But, good heavens! Lily, do you know what it is that we are going to fight for? Why, it will be a whole nation in arms! It will be battle, glory, freedom! I am nobody yet, but I am young and have my chance, and, when all is over, I will either have died as enviably as ever the heart of a soldier panted to die, or I will be one of the heroes of a war of independence, and the men who look askance at us and curse to-day will grovel at our feet and chant *Te Deums*!'

'I am sure I hope you will be great and happy, Ken——'

'Happy, and you beat me from you like a dog!'

'How can you say such a thing?' said Lily, a tear trembling now in the big blue eye. 'I will miss you ever so much. But papa and mamma are positive that we mustn't meet any more, and, you know, I could not do what would be wrong.'

'Say that you think of me as they do, and I am done. You always tell the truth, Lily. Tell me that there is somebody else that you are fonder of, and I will go and find Georgey for you.'

She blushed violently, 'Well, Ken, I must say mamma mentioned that she had other views for me——'

'Thank you, Lily; you are a brave girl. I hope you will be as happy as a queen,' said Ken, not very bravely.

'But I don't think there is anybody that I will ever care for as much as I did for you, Ken,' she said, artlessly. 'I mean that we were always such sweethearts, you know, and you were always so brave and tender to me. I am sure I wish these dreadful things would not be always happening when nobody wants them.'

Her last words were smothered with a kiss—this time an en-

tirely successful one – and her fragile daintily-moulded waist was
in the grasp of a violent man. 'Lily,' he said, in low, rapid tones,
'if we like one another like that—if we love one another—who
has the right to part us? Why should your father and mother
make us two miserable for life? What are money and the wretched
little rags of distinction that people scramble for in country villages? I am unknown and poor; but we can wait, Lily, and we
have the wealth of the Indies, in the meantime, in one another's
love. If we fail—well, any tears you ever drop on my grave will
not be tears of shame. But we won't fail, darling—we will
win—we will clothe this old land with sunshine from sea to sea—
and we will have a nation of soldiers with their victorious banners
to attend your wedding and to worship your blue eyes.'

'Let me go, Ken—please, let me go,' cried Lily, struggling,
with an energy marvellous in so small a person, to release herself.
'Somebody will come. I will hate myself if you do not go at
once. It is unkind of you—it is wrong—it is a sin!'

'A sin to love you and ask you not to make both of us
wretched for life, darling!'

'A sin for me—yes, certainly— to be here kissed by a young
man whom my parents have forbidden me ever to speak to again.'
This she said with a decisiveness the most astonishing ever recorded of a young lady of her years and amiability, and then she
burst into a flood of tears. 'I did not think you would stay
arguing with me,' she cried, passionately. 'Call Georgey to me—
call Georgey, please, instantly, or I shall cry out!'

'And the horrible thing,' remarked Georgey O'Meagher, confiding some vague guesses at what had happened, to her friend,
Katie Rohan, that evening, in the seclusion of the latter's tiny
blue-and-white papered bedroom, 'the horrible thing is that it all
comes of that wretched midget, Mr. Flibbert, fluttering about for
old Dargan's money.'

'You don't mean to say that it is he who has made this
change in Lily?' asked Katie indignantly.

'I don't know that anything will ever make a change in Lily.
She is a petrified lump of perfection,' said Georgey, in a not very
sisterly tone, 'but I mean that that conceited little creature has
been to tea with the Dargans more than once, and that Mrs.
Dargan is mean enough to set her cap at him because he is a sort
of an officer and in the Club. Poor Ken! Poor boy!'

The two girls looked at one another, the colour flying to and
from their cheeks.

'Oh! dear Georgey, I wish—I do wish ——' Katie flung her
arms around her friend, and whatever she wished was buried

between a pair of soft white necks where the girls hid their telltale faces.

It was anything but exhilarating to Ken Rohan, in his present mood, to hear the lark-like voice of Jack Harold as he mounted the heights chirping the gay carillon of some *café chantant* love ditty, with an airy dash of *zim v'lan, la's* through it. They had not been much together of late. The one was too busy with his Christy Minstrels and the other with his dreams. A Christy Minstrel is not the very gentlest physician for a wounded heart. Ken glanced around nervously for some way of escape; but it was too late. Jack's confounded bavarding Closerie-de-Lilas voice hailed him.

'Hillo, ho, ho, boy! I have searched the Glen, there are I don't know how many hours for you. I have seen the vision of your *ange aux grands yeux bleus*. Then I knew you could not be far. Ken, she looked divine—her hat alone was an apotheosis.'

'I hate small talk on serious subjects,' said the other impatiently. 'Let's talk of something else, Jack.'

'Nay, but by Saint Patrick, we will talk of nothing else, while there is a Philomel in all these woods to sigh with us—and, indeed, whether there is or not. That is what I have come to talk to you about. I can talk of nothing else. I can think of nothing else. Ken, on the subject of woman you will never hear my mocking voice again. I will listen to you by the hour pouring out the perfections of your loved one. I will give you verse for verse and rapture for rapture. Don't spare your poetry—pile it on heavens high. I will agree with you in every syllable of worship of our divinity except her name. There you will be mistaken; but that is a detail. Now, seriously—most seriously—I am in love!'

'I have no doubt about the love, and I am sure you are serious in thinking yourself serious.'

'Listen, Ken—I have come to you as the fellow of all the world to bring a wildly-throbbing heart to. Do not revenge yourself for my infernal flippancy by making fun of me like that. I know my faults. I am only a poor devil who twangs a guitar. Nobody will ever believe I have a deeper note in me. I sometimes hardly believe it myself,' he said, in a strangely downcast way.

'Why, old fellow, what could put such things into your head?' said Ken, his own haggard face lighting up with kindness. 'I think you could do anything and win anybody.'

'We shall see! *Quoi qu'il en soit*, this time it will be all deadly earnest. I have found at last that life may have a purpose which is no joke. I am tired of trifling. Polly Atkins, at the

o

Drum, is a good girl, but I could not stand her small beer to-day. I had to come to find you. You are such a grand audience! I wish I could drop that cursed Christy concert. It's so idiotic— though she *did* so like that little slave-song. Oh! Ken, she is the most glorious creature that ever made a man feel as if he could climb to the stars to win her!'

'I *am* glad, Jack. Tell us all about it,' said Ken Rohan, who, although not in the humour to respond to raptures about woman's love just then, was relieved to find that Cupid's new victim was entirely too much occupied with his own delightful pains to pay much attention to the bloodless cheek and lack-lustre eye of his companion. He had found 'an audience,' and that was a true, as well as a frank, statement of what he had come in search of.

The story of his meeting with Mabel Westropp was narrated with such touches of colour as Jack Harold's nimble fancy knew excellently well how to wash in. The artist co-operated with the devotee in painting the willowy figure, the showery yellow hair, the sweet sincerity of his goddess; and he would not have been a vocalist if he had omitted her artless compliment to his singing, nor a lover if he had not constructed out of this and several other the like fairy filaments, quite a glistening fabric of hopes for his wooing.

'Yes, she is very lovely, and, I think, better even than she is beautiful,' said Ken Rohan fervently.

'What! Do you know her?' asked the other, with a sudden pang.

'By Jove, old fellow, you *are* in love! There are a thousand jealous devils in that look of yours. You may disband your devils. I am the most harmless of mankind to you. I only met Miss Westropp accidentally with Harry, and I am not likely to meet her again. But I say, Jack,' he continued, not exactly discerning in what direction he could suggest hopes that would feed his friend's daring ambition to Lord Drumshaughlin's daughter's hand, and quite alive to the folly of disheartening him, 'how the deuce did you pick up with that fellow Harman?'

The other coloured slightly. He had passed over this part of the narrative in a sketchy manner. With any other censor he would have sported his acquaintances at Stone Hall as a feather in his cap; but Ken's glum stoicism made him uncomfortable about his innocent little vanities. Still he made a gallant rally to carry it off impudently.

'Oh,' he said, 'Harman and I pound the piano together a little sometimes. You see we may have differences enough in Ireland without differing as to musical notation. A man may deserve to be shot as an agent and play a very passable thing from Bach *en attendant.*'

'These are dangerous times,' said the other gravely. 'Harman is a cunning fellow, and would not be half so dangerous only for his candour.'

'I believe well! But I humbly pretend to the talent to *ménager* my acquaintance as well as choose them,' replied Jack, a little nettled. 'Besides,' he proceeded more placably, 'a footing in the enemy's camp is ever useful. Harman is up to everything that the police think is worth knowing. *Par exemple,* he dropped me a hint about that fellow Dawley—you would hardly believe it—of course, it was only a hint. But damn Harman and Dawley to the lowest cellar! What brings their infernal names into the same world with Mabel Westropp? Ken, she is the loveliest—the most adorable——'

'God prosper you, Jack!' said his friend, pressing his hand. 'I envy you—your hope!' He had almost to choke himself to swallow down a moan that came from his own lacerated heart. 'Come,' said he, with a good-humoured smile, 'it is my turn to tell you it is growing late. You find something better than goat's milk and whisky on the Glengariff Hills, after all?'

'Ah!' cried Jack Harold with a happy laugh, 'because those heather hills of yours now have the grace to blush and acknowledge their goddess.'

Three or four nights afterwards Myles Rohan fell off his office-stool in a fit. It happened in this wise. Danny had several hours before shut down the sluice-gate and stopped the water-wheel, the drought having reduced the millstream to a rill, and had locked up the premises for the night; Myles, as had happened several times after tea, had quitted the parlour, taking the key with him, and unlocked the office and lighted the gas. He had spent many absorbed hours of late over his accounts and bundle of freight-notes. It so chanced that, some loads of corn having arrived unexpectedly from the Garrindinny railway station, Danny was called up to the windlass to hoist in the sacks, and, having come into the office for the carter's docket, found his master's body lying beside the overturned stool in a great blotch of blood, which was still oozing from a wound in the head; the teeth were locked tightly together, and the breathing that of a man almost strangled.

Though Mrs. Rohan was a delicate woman, who indulged in her full share of woman's luxury—complaining—she took the command in this emergency by as divine a right as Israel Putnam in his shirt-sleeves, fresh from the plough, went to the front at

Bunker's Hill. She had the wound in the head bandaged, and the blood sponged away, and the throat freed, while the carters were standing glued to the ground in stupefied horror. She had, with Ken's and Danny's help, a comfortable bed made up in the office, and a fire sparkling in the grate. By the time the old doctor came, blinking profoundly through his round spectacles, and administering his sparse medical knowledge with an abundance of stock consolations, Mrs. Rohan's decisive measures had already tided over the worst of the fit, and the excellent doctor gradually came to see that his directions were as superfluous as his condolences. 'He is at present, madam, exhibiting favourable symptoms of a somnolent condition, with still some stertorous indications as to breathing,' he observed, with much impressiveness.——'Yes, doctor, he is getting into a beautiful sleep, thank God!' said Mrs. Rohan. Another wonderful thing was to see how coolly little Katie bore herself amidst the horrors which paralysed the rough carters—Katie, who would almost swoon with terror every time the blood even of a chicken came to be shed on the premises. She was as white as her own little counterpane, indeed, but there was not a tear or a cry; and she moved about with the mysterious instinct of those gracious presences which are missing nowhere and are noticed nowhere, and which are as welcome in a sick room as lint.

The wound in the head had saved Myles Rohan. He fell into a heavy sleep. Towards three o'clock in the morning, when the dawn began to struggle with the night-lights, Mrs. Rohan, watching by the bedside, felt an outstretched arm laid upon her hand, and in a mute transport of joy saw Myles sitting up in the bed. He could not speak, however. Several gallant efforts, which I shrink from describing, made that plain. He motioned convulsively towards the high desk at which he had been writing when he fell. She thought she understood. In an instant she had writing materials at his hand. He scrawled, very eagerly and rudely :

'Documents on desk. Don't want the children know,' and then signalled for them violently. There was a letter advising him of the failure of a Cork corn merchant with whom he had considerable transactions; there was an account with a stinging word or two written across it in red ink; and there was a cheque of his own, with two still more intolerable words on the face of it. He pounced on them like a wild animal, and stuffed them under his pillow, and then calmly lay back with something like a smile on his face, as though the bad news were now effectually placed beyond discovery by the children.

Poor Myles's plan for keeping the children in the dark was

not, however, destined to be successful. Ken Rohan was at his
father's business at the mill by cock-crow the next morning, after
a night of torturing self-reproaches upon his own selfish idleness
and unprofitableness. He would begin at the very beginning
and aid Danny (to that stiff-necked and ungrateful person's deep-
mouthed indignation) by setting the wheel in motion before there
was water to turn it, and the hoppers before they had anything
but one another to grind. When the post arrived, he could not
go far through his father's letters without receiving dismal intimations that his son's wayward course was not the only cloud
that had been daunting the miller's sturdy heart of late. One
letter he had torn open amidst the heap of invoices, business
notes, and accounts, without noticing Mr. Hans Harman's cognisance, a boar's head, stamped on sealing-wax on the cover. The
letter fascinated him as though the Harman family boar's head
were the head of a Gorgon :—

Confidential.   Stone Hall, 8th Sept., 186-.

'DEAR ROHAN,—You will see by enclosed note from the
Attorney-General (which I must ask you to return) that I have
been as good as my word. You will see also that there is no time
to be lost to save our young friend from mischief.—Yours, &c.
                                            'HANS HARMAN.'

The enclosure from the Attorney-General, the Right Hon.
Tobias Glascock, contained these words on the second leaf of a
letter, the first of which had been detached :

'Your young *protégé* bears a bad reputation with the police ;
but if you really want him transferred from the gallows to the
Civil Service, there is a Second Clerkship in the Pipe-Roll Office
which you can have for him on the understanding that you will
answer with your head for his loyalty and (what is of more
consequence) for the county.—T. G.'

Ken read this over and over till his eyelids grew hot and his
brain was on fire. His cheeks could scarcely have tingled more
if they had been cut across with a riding-whip.
'Great God !' he cried, in an agony, 'have I sunk into such
a pit of infamy as this ?—made a subject of bargain and sale in
some wretched market of corruption, for God knows what base
considerations—pitched into some scullion's office by the Government I have dared to dream of overturning—nay, indebted for it,
as for a favour—bound in eternal gratitude for it to the man who
is probably a personal enemy and certainly a pestilent villain.

Gracious heaven! what is to be done? I feel as if I were in a bath of boiling pitch.'

And Mrs. Rohan and Katie, seeing him stride about all day in a raging fever, marvelled that the poor boy took on so at his father's condition, and thought they had found an antidote for the whole trouble when they were able to report that the sufferer was beginning to articulate faintly again. What was actually passing through Ken's mind at the moment was a fancied scene in which he was flinging the fragments of Mr. Hans Harman's letter in his teeth in his own office with words that would bite like vitriol. Such, alas! is youth's selfishness that, when he espied Dr. O'Harte's massive figure arriving at the Mill (the great-hearted Doctor having caught the very first train to his old friend's bedside, the moment the tidings reached him, notwithstanding his unconquerable terror of death scenes), his first thought of joy was not so much that his father had found a friend as that he himself had found a counsellor, whose broad shoulders were enormously comforting in an emergency of this kind.

'This seems to be a good post enough,' was the Doctor's first remark, after he had read the letters a couple of times leisurely. 'There are a great many people who are neither knaves nor lickspittles who would jump at it.' He turned his keen eyes full on the young man, as if in search of some carefully concealed flaw in his bold purpose. A less practised eye than his would have given up the search at sight of that transparent face with the indignant blood manning its battlements. 'Very well, Ken, I understand you,' he said, in an altered key, 'and you are right. You ought not in your position to close with Harman's offer. But recollect, sir,' he suddenly said, with sternness, 'your poor father's feelings ought to be considered as well as your own in this matter.' The deep flush of shame that suddenly mantled Ken's cheeks and forehead told how keenly the reproach had gone home. 'Before you indulge in any expensive luxury of indignation, recollect that your poor father has had trials, and must have had sore ones before he would ask or receive favours from Hans Harman. It would be murder to involve your father in any further worry in his present state. It looks like a merciful arrangement of Providence that he should know nothing about it. Besides, the note looks like a civil one; and why answer it with insult? Upon the whole, I can see nothing better to do with this offer for the present than to put it here,' he said, putting the letter with its enclosure into the fire; 'and let it rest there,' he added, as the nomination to the Second Clerkship in the Pipe-Roll Office turned into a little heap of white ashes.

Myles Rohan's power of speech returned, and Dr. O'Harte, immensely relieved to find that it was not to be a death-bed scene after all, blossomed into the sunniest spirits, and, like a triumphant surgeon after an operation, roared out : 'I knew I'd do it, Myles. I knew my old bark would bring your view-halloo back, if there was a shout in the country.' Myles shifted his position so as to cover one of the documents which was escaping from under his pillow, and with his hospitable smile, though the old hearty voice was feeble, responded : 'You always had the cheerful word, Doctor ! You're as welcome as the flowers of May.'

'It has caused a great shock in town, and I am really distressed,' said Monsignor McGrudder, with whom Dr. O'Harte was dining that evening, 'for I always will say that Myles Rohan is an upright man. I am not sure that I ought not to call to see him myself,' said the Monsignor, with a graciousness worthy of Cardinal Rimbomba's reception-room on an Ambassadors' Night, 'only that his son is one of those rash young men that make scenes—you understand ?'

'I understand perfectly,' said the Doctor, with a roll of the eye which made a young priest sitting opposite him choke and redden in a remarkable manner. 'Besides, I don't think it is necessary.'

'Unless,' said Monsignor McGrudder, 'unless that, of course, it is a singular and shocking event – I go no further than that—and for Myles Rohan's sake I should not like my people to consider it a judgment from Providence for the language he unhappily did use to me.'

'Your people are more likely to consider it an invitation from Providence to break your windows,' said Dr. O'Harte, dryly.

CHAPTER THE TWENTIETH

MABEL OPENS A MENAGERIE

THERE was a letter from Lord Drumshaughlin lying on the breakfast-table, which Mabel immediately pounced upon, and kissed. 'Dear, old papa ! so the gout has given him permission to write at last,' she cried, opening it as she might a jewel-box, and lingering fondly, as girls are apt to do, to observe the look of it. The writing was quaint and crooked, but refined, as became handwriting subject to fits of the gout. It was upon thick club notepaper, and faintly scented, Mabel thought. The old lord began in an elevated strain of moral reflection, with a touching reference to filial insensibility to the tribulations of desolate old age. 'For myself, my dear Mabel,' he wrote, 'I do not complain. I have been too long inured to suffering and neglect. You will be sorry to hear, by the way, that the gout has advanced to the knee-joint, and your mother has not been much asked to the country since your departure—which has not improved the temper of either of us. As I have said, however, I should be disposed to waive my own claim to a daughter's duty and affection towards a father who has always idolised her if I could persuade myself that the extraordinary resolution you have taken of burying yourself from the world was attended with any compensating advantage, either to your own happiness or the reformation of the foolish boy to whom you are inconsiderately sacrificing so precious a portion of your youth and of your father's comfort. I am not surprised, however, to learn that you have consigned yourself to a hopeless and ungrateful task, and that you have not only failed to influence him for the better, but that he has of late fallen more and more into courses which young ladies of your age, brought up as you have been, cannot be expected to understand, much less to correct him in. You will sufficiently appreciate his position when I tell you that there is serious danger of his entangling himself in an alliance that would be disgraceful to our family, and that he is, I learn on the surest authority, involved deeply in an atrocious communistic conspiracy for an armed insurrection against the forces of the Crown and the abolition of property and religion.'

Miss Westropp paused, and looked very grave and thoughtful.

'Well, what is it ?' said the Lord Harry, swallowing down a vast mouthful of game-pie, in order to be in a position to look aggressive. 'Pitching into me, of course?'

'I know now what keeps you out of bed o' nights,' said his sister calmly.

As various causes, all of a more or less questionable character, combined to keep him out of bed onights', Harry coloured guiltily, and could think of nothing better to do than to look sulky.

'You are engaged in a conspiracy—you are getting up a rising—don't deny it.'

'Well !' he said, doggedly, much relieved that this was the worst discovery he had to encounter.

'And that is the meaning of your asking me for "The Wearing of the Green"; and the young fellow at the Mill, and that young fellow who sang at Mr. Harman's, are in it, too, and are your brother-conspirators !'

'And if they are,' cried Harry, bracing himself for an encounter which he had long foreseen with trepidation. 'Mabel, I must ask you once for all what business it is of yours? Am I or am I not in your custody? If I am, hadn't you better commit me to the asylum at once as a hopeless idiot, and get rid of me?'

'Oh, Harry——'

'Listen to me, now; we'll have this out,' he went on, with the impetuosity of a mountain torrent. 'Sermons will do no good to me nor to yourself; you may as well go back and enjoy yourself and let me go my ways. I 'listed twice, and they would not let me alone. They would buy me out—buy me out and fling me here like a weed to rot. Very well, I've 'listed now where they can't buy me out. I suppose my father has found out all about it, and has written to you abusing me. Let him blaze away! I *am* in a conspiracy—up to the neck in it. I *am* booked for a fight—I hope a bloody fight—and the sooner the better. I suppose it is not loyal nor respectable—so much the better. It's respectable for Harman to beat his wife and hunt poor devils into the workhouse. What is loyalty to me? An Irish Republic can't make me a more miserable failure than I am—and can't make anybody else more miserable than they are, either, so far as I can see hereabouts. Ken Rohan *is* in it and Jack Harold *is* in it, and they're two finer fellows than any two I know of the groggy aristocrats that you'll find painting their red noses at the club below. There, now, you know it all; and you can blab if you like, and you can inform Harman from me that he may go tell the police, or may go to the devil!'

'Well, but I'm not so sorry to hear it, dear,' said his sister, rising and winding her arms around the neck of the infuriated boy.

He started back, upsetting a plate into fragments, and looked sternly at her with half-angry incredulity, as if he was not quite sure that she was not laughing at him, and was perfectly sure she was proposing conundrums to him. 'You do say such things, and surprise one so. I can't make you out,' he said.

'My dear Harry, I'm not quite sure that I can make out myself,' she answered, with a smile; 'but I know that whatever good thing interests you interests me—I don't understand these things much of course; but if this fight that you young men are dreaming of be a fight in which you will deserve the people's prayers and their love—if it be a fight to make them happy and free, instead of looking down on them and grinding them—why then, I don't know how a man could live or die for a more noble object, and, if you have thrown your heart into a cause like that, you can have me, if you like, as a co-conspirator.'

Harry was puzzled much by Mabel's way of putting it, but
he understood swiftly enough that, instead of giving him the
expected blowing up, Mabel was going to behave the pal ; and
he was immensely elated, and even began to assert the superior
privileges of his sex in the partnership.

'You know, I don't think girls are of much use in things of
this kind,' he said. 'They're such cowards, and then they get
chattering. It's like a girl carrying a gun on a mountain. The
girl carries the gun, but you have to carry the girl,' said Harry,
with high delight in his own wit.

'Yes,' said Mabel, smiling, 'we are useless creatures ; that
is, if there was nothing to be done in the world but shooting
grouse.'

'Exactly,' said Harry, with great satisfaction. 'There are
such lots of other things to be done. By Jove, yes ! ' he exclaimed,
as some particularly brilliant idea flashed upon him—'You must
know Mike MacCarthy—the American Captain, as we call him
—you will like him immensely, Mabel ! He's not exactly like
one of the captains at the club, you know, but there is more
gold in Mike MacCarthy than there is in a regiment of such
fellows.'

'Very well ; I am getting on in conspiracy,' said Mabel, with
a merry laugh. 'And now, Harry, as you have told me one
thing, you may as well tell me all. We have heard the worst of
the conspirator. I want to know something now of you in another
character—something in which you were so deep a conspirator,
sir, that I never even suspected.' The hint about that 'entangling alliance' in Lord Drumshaughlin's letter had piqued her
woman's curiosity more intensely than all his lordship's grave
forebodings of the 'abolition of property and religion.' She
longed to know all about it ; and yet it was not without a
cowardly sinking of the heart she approached a knowledge of the
particulars.

'Well, what is it now, Mabel ? Will you never let a fellow
alone ? ' said Harry petulantly.

'Not till you beat me,' she laughed.

'Like Harman,' he interjected malevolently.

'Come, sir, it is your sins that are in question and not Mr.
Harman's. Harry, you are in love ! There now, don't strike
me, and you needn't answer. I have got the answer already.
Your cheeks are as red as a rose, Harry. Do tell me all.'

'Oh, bother ! It's nothing ; and, of course, I'm as unlucky
a devil as usual—and, besides, you wouldn't care to hear,
Mabel.'

'Wouldn't care to hear ! I don't understand, Harry. There

can be nothing that you need not be ashamed to tell that I shall not be eager to hear.'

'I mean that people talk such fudge about low associations, you know, as if Kate Rohan weren't half a dozen heavens too high for me.'

'What, that pretty, fair-haired little girl at the Mill ?'

'Yes,' said Harry defiantly. 'If you ever saw her—there can be no mistake, for there isn't another like her in the world.'

'Why, Harry, who would ever have supposed you were such a romantic darling !'

'I don't know what you call romantic ; but I mean it. But where's the good of anything with an unlucky dog like me ?'

'And has this affair—gone very far ?'

'I have never exchanged a word with her in my life. I don't suppose she's aware of my existence, and I believe I am to fight a duel with her brother Ken if I ever mention her name again.'

'My poor Harry,' she exclaimed, flinging her arms round him, 'and this is the dishonour and crime they make such an outcry about ! Why, I was never so proud of you in all my life ! Don't lose heart a bit ; we're sworn comrades in this conspiracy as well as in the other ! One more question, and I will never tease you again,' she said, after a moment's pause. 'Tell me truly was it your friend Mr. Rohan who set you drinking that night he came to the Castle with you !'

'Great heavens, no ! It was he that picked me up, or I should have drunk a great deal more. Ken Rohan set a fellow tippling ! Why, he is a bit of a preacher !'

'Very well, get out the pony-chaise, and we'll come along and find the Nevilles.'

The Nevilles, who had rented Clanlaurance Castle (old Lord Clanlaurance having taken his large family of girls, maladies, and debts to some undiscoverable Saxon village whose postal address was Dresden) were a race singularly compounded of iron and aristocracy. Joshua Neville was a successful ironmaster, whose name, printed on the mineral wagons of the firm, was to be seen rushing or shunting about every railway siding in Yorkshire. Joshua Neville was, like his superscription on the mineral wagons, a plain, strong-looking, unadorned man. There was an unverified impression that he had been brought up as a Quaker. He retained something of that character in his dress ; but had long been the most considerable man in the chapel of a strong-headed Congregationalist minister in Sheffield, and, in the local council, and subsequently in the Imperial Parliament, acquired the reputation of a despiser of rank and humbug, and a man who believed that empurpled kings and generals in gold lace were a tawdry pack of rascals who were cheating the people out of the two greatest of human blessings, cheap food and peace. He used to make it a boast that the only heraldic cognisance he knew in his family was a flat iron. When he married the daughter of one of the oldest-blooded noblemen in the Riding, it was largely (so, at least, he persuaded himself) as a blow against aristocratic pretension—to show that the gouty joints of the double-distilled Earl of Winspurleigh and De Grosse himself were obliged to bend the knee to iron. The match between Lady Margery and Joshua Neville, unpropitious though it looked, turned out indifferently well after all, but it was the iron that gave way in the combination, strong as it looked. Joshua Neville was not at all daunted, and not overmuch dazzled, by Lady Margery's fine friends and their fine houses ; but he did not find it so easy to put the pageant of aristocracy to flight by merely showing his own shaggy figure. He found that there was more strength in the soft beautiful limbs of society than he had given it credit for. He had iron enough in him to assert himself ; but Joshua Neville was possessed of that first treasure of happiness and fatal disqualification for successful ambition—an easy temper. Lady Margery had her way, as delicately but effectively as a fine perfume. He allowed his boy to be called by the outlandish name of Reginald (the name of Winspurleighs and De Grosses ancient enough to have been brothers-in-arms of Tasso's crusading hero of that name) ; and in due time he allowed him to be sent to Oxford, instead of being packed off at six o'clock in the morning to a desk at the works, like his fathers (I mean his iron fathers) before him. Joshua even permitted himself to be attached to the house at Buckingham Gate for the London season as a decorous sort of Iron Stick-in-Waiting, and moved through his wife's rooms of a night with a certain grave interest, and without attracting the comments of the old women.

'I don't love this kind of thing, my dear,' he used to say. 'I don't see any way in which I can be of much use to you, except to pay the bills. But I will do that, Margery, and I hope you won't find me too much in the way.'

For the which compliant temper, I suspect, the rogue felt himself secretly rewarded by the vicarious dissipation that the austerest of men enjoys from his wife's social distinction, and still more by the honest wifely tenderness with which Lady Margery in a certain reserved but grateful way repaid him until the day when she joined the ancestral Winspurleighs and De Grosses with as much pompous funeral furniture and genteel company as the most high-flying of those crusading grandees had gone to his shelf in the family vault withal. From the day of her death Joshua Neville's ambition (a simple, yet very uncommon one) became to be on as good terms with his children as he had been with his wife. The children having been brought up wholly on Winspurleigh lines, and the ironmaster's lighter tastes in life being comprised in a fishing-rod, an occasional scramble into the German language, and a devotion to geology and one or two of its kindred sciences, he did not at first see what function he was to fulfil with that object, except the old one of paying the bills— a post which Reggy's life and adventures at Brazenose rendered no sinecure. To his intense astonishment and delight, however, he found that his children did not at all look down upon him, but on the contrary petted him and deferred to him as to an elderly, plain-featured brother. The truth is that they inherited more of the Sheffield iron than of the Winspurleigh ichor. Not that the girls, at least, at all suspected that. They were finished on the best lines, so to say ; and their tastes, words, and ways were those of any other three young women in the boudoirs between the Park and Eaton Square. But they were girls who had more good sense than wit or pretension, and they had an abundance of wholesome red English blood which made the ironmaster feel very much at home with them. Reginald was a more incompre- hensible creature, at once the most expensive of plebeians and the most plebeian of aristocrats. He had imbibed at the University all the fashionable neutrality as to reading and erudition in the stables and on the river, without betraying the least conscious- ness either that he had the Crusader blood to boast of among the young Tories or the no less insolent pride in his father's stithies to parade among the rising Radicals. He came back from Brazenose a fine healthy animal, deeply in debt, knowing much about horses, and nothing about Shakespeare except the name and that he was probably a poet. Joshua Neville had some anxious self-questionings as to whether his son was not a mere fool ; but he soon found that stupidity was only the outer (though a pretty thick) rind of a character the kernel of which was sincerity and a certain blunt cast-iron Quixotism—a character in which (including the stupidity) he took an indulgent paternal interest, as inherited chiefly from the Nevilles. When he learned that Reggy desired him to rent Clanlaurance Castle for the autumn, and that he had sold Carabîche and his share in the establishment at Newmarket, he was surprised, but not at all thunderstruck. He would not have been thunderstruck if Reggy had enlisted as a common soldier or become a Jesuit. When the girls dropped him a hint that the Wild Irish Girl was the attrac- tion at Glengariff, he was very glad to hear that the young fellow was after a pretty girl. The only thing that perturbed him was a certain unpleasant impression of Lord Drumshaughlin's reputation as an old reprobate ; for Joshua Neville had an old-fashioned fanaticism about his Bible ; but Reggy's friend, Horace Westropp, seemed to him an honest fellow, and the Wild Irish Girl a beautiful lass, whom it was quite natural for a young man to rave about ; and so he at once accepted the Glengariff situation, and bowled up to Clanlaurance Castle with his caravan of girls and trunks with a cheerful conviction that Reggy's affair was as good as settled, now that he was himself a consenting party.

'I am afraid you will find this a very stupid place after London,' said Miss Westropp, as they sat at lunch.

'Oh, no ; I hear there is archery, and a dance now and then when a frigate comes,' said one of the girls.

'Dull ? Quite the contrary,' said Mr. Neville, anxious to put in an encouraging word for the country. 'Glengariff has no end of interest for me. My father came over here as a member of the Friends' Committee in the Famine. I remember the first sovereign I ever had I subscribed it to our little family fund for the poor Irish.

'Yes,' Miss Westropp remarked quietly. 'We are rich enough in Famine memories.'

'But that's not all. Come, you mustn't run down your country like that,' he said good-humouredly. 'If you had nothing to show but the Coomhōla grits, Glengariff would always be a place of interest and renown—in the eye of the geologist at any rate. Girls, we must take the first opportunity of making out the Coomhōla grits. I believe you won't get many fossils, but the formation gives us one of the most curious links in palæozoic history— this whole neighbourhood is singularly rich in the fish-life of the Devonian period.'

'I can give you as gamey a fish as ever you hooked any day you like,' said Harry, who did not see why the Devonian period (whatever it might be) should not extend to the nineteenth century. 'And there's no end of carp and perch in the loughs.'

'That is very interesting,' said Mr. Neville, who was consoled for this alarming contempt of the charms of geology by the promised feast to his other *belle passion* of rod-fishing. 'I will certainly do myself the pleasure of placing myself under your direction. I mean to see and do everything. I have a theory that whatever country a man owes hospitality to, it is his duty to learn all about it and do the best he can for it.'

'Our fashion here is just the other way,' said Miss Westropp. 'It is supposed to be vulgar for a man who lives by the country to do anything but abuse it.'

'Yes, and I think that is one of the very points to which attention ought to be directed,' said Mr. Neville, preparing with much animation to mount one of his hobby-horses. 'That's just what leaves you with no other industries but agitation and the begging-box.'

'You'll have the governor in a few days producing a plan for the pacification of Ireland, and making the whole thing as clear as daylight,' broke in Reggy, who had been twirling his moustache in some alarm.

'Well,' rejoined his father, placidly, 'it is true I have a few ideas upon the subject, and if I should happen to put them in ship-shape some day——'

'They'll set us all to sleep, governor,' said his undutiful son.

'Your father's plan will have one great advantage,' said Miss Westropp, coming to the rescue. 'It cannot possibly be worse than the plans they've been trying up to the present. Here have we, Westropps, been on the shores of Bantry Bay ever since the sixteenth century, and a man or woman of our house never knew a soul among the people that pay us rent—I mean, knew in any real sense—until Harry here broke the ice.'

'I, Mabel! Nonsense!' said Harry, blushing. The affability with which he drank pewters at Moll Carty's with the boys had never occurred to him in that dignified light before, and he was never sure that compliments to him were not sarcasms.

'I believe you are fond of the Germans, Mr. Neville. I think it is Schiller who gives us a test of what real nobles ought to be——'

'Ah! yes, Schiller,' observed Mr. Neville, smiling and stroking his beard profoundly.

'Their names ought to have a good ring in the country——'

'"*Ein guter Klang im Lande!*"' said Mr. Neville, in higher delight with the quotation than he had ever been with the poetry.

'How many of our nobles would pass the mint if they were assayed in that way? Why, they rather pique themselves on being detested.'

'That is a just observation, Miss Westropp,' said the iron-master. 'I have often remarked it myself—my poor wife used to have a good many of these people about the house—an Irish land-lord would have nothing to talk about if he was not bragging about being shot at or deserving to be.'

'Oh, come, hang it, there are no better judges of a horse,' said his son, who thought it a duty to stand up for Horace's Irish friends.

'And no worse judges of a human being,' said Miss Westropp; 'at least a human being in frieze and with a Kerry accent. Here they are, for centuries, with millions of the kindest hearts in the world around them pining for somebody to idolise, and they have never yet been able to see that there was anything but a crew of beggars and assassins on their estates or any cure for them except to clear them out.'

'And are you really interested in—in—that sort of thing?' asked Reggy, with an earnest astonishment that made Miss Westropp smile. He would as soon have expected to hear that her bright eyes were secretly addicted to logarithms, or that she had fallen in love with one of his father's forges.

'I am only a woman, and a very helpless one,' said Mabel, 'but I should like very much to interest people—important people — in doing something to brighten the world around them a bit.'

Young Neville's eyes said what his English tongue refused to say for him, 'You brighten the world every moment of your existence. You have nothing to do but to live to brighten it. But what sort of brightness do you expect from a poor devil like me?'

'But politics is such a dull subject, and so—so argumentative,' said one of the Misses Neville (people were never quite sure who was who among the Neville girls). 'You can't get people to talk politics—can you, dear?'

'Why not? What better do they talk about?' said Mabel warmly. 'The weather?'

'The weather, very largely,' assented Joshua Neville.

'Or the betting, or some French milliner's new way of twisting a hat out of shape. Three-fourths of what people say in society bores the person who says and the person who hears it. Yet how many hard and cheerless lives are sacrificed to bring those two people together in a London drawing room to bore one another! How much less dull the thousands might be if they would only give themselves a little trouble to make the millions happier! And yet society will admit any well-dressed crime except enthusiasm. You may talk for hours and hours about all that is worst in your neighbours; you will hear a roomful of young women pretend to know all about the odds that a parcel of rascally bookmakers have settled in some public-house; but the moment you start any topic in the least generous or noble —if it be the freedom or happiness of millions of people here in the world, and for endless ages—you are denounced as a prig, if a man; and, if a woman—I really don't know what name they would find for a monster like myself.'

'I should like to catch them!' muttered young Neville between his teeth.

'They would have you up for seditious language, Mabel,' said Harry with a laugh, 'and they will if you don't mind.'

'Then I won't mind, for I am a born rebel against a great deal
that passes for law in England and against almost everything that
is called law in Ireland. In England you at all events regard the
people as part of your establishment, like your dogs—you feed
them and fondle them. In Ireland we treat them as beggars at
the gate, and send for the police for them—nay, it is still worse,
for we first knock the people down and empty their wallets, and
then we call on the constable, and abuse them to the world for
mendicants.'

'These are very remarkable observations—"first knock the
people down and rob them, and then abuse them as beggars." I
must really take a note of it,' said Joshua Neville, whose face
during Mabel's tirade was a curious study—the Wild Irish Girl
held something so like his own rugged sentiments, yet so transformed with Irish poetry, that he was puzzled to recognise them.
Joshua Neville had poetry in his own texture, but it was of the
fossiliferous order—embedded in rocks—rather than of the subtle
Ariel sort which lights up the hills and whispers through the
woodlands. Miss Westropp impressed him like the Glengariff
landscape—his Cromhöla grits were the only parts of it he understood ; the rest was unintelligible but wondrous fair—though, of
course, shadowy and impracticable, as became Irish views either
in politics or scenery. 'Who would have expected to hear all
this from a person in your class ? '

'No, indeed ; and in me it is extremely vulgar. But, do you
know, it seems to me vulgarity is just what we want—if vulgarity
means being a little like our neighbours and feeling like them.
The most vulgar—and the most blessed—system I know was the
Irish clan system, in which the chief was everybody's cousin.
Our system is to keep the chief everybody's enemy. People are
more in dread of being thought vulgar than of being wicked. But
to my mind, so far as there is any reproach in the word, there is
no vulgarity like the vulgarity of the man who will run down his
countrymen as beggars over champagne bought with the beggars'
pence, and give himself the airs of a god because some ancestor of
his was successful in a highway robbery—or, as he would call it,
won a battle—three or four hundred years ago. The worst vulgarians you will meet in Ireland are those who have titles or are
hunting for titles. There was only one Irish nobleman for the
past century that anybody remembers, and in speaking of him, as
of the Kings of England, people do not even mention his family
name. It is enough to say "Lord Edward."'

'Yes, I remember,' said the ironmaster, who had conscientiously read a History of Ireland, as a qualification for his Irish
trip. He was not the man to be content with the guide-book.

'He was a fine fellow ; but don't you think he rather—threw himself away, if I may say so—speaking as a practical man, you know, Miss Westropp ? '

'I dare say every man has to throw himself away on something, or on nothing. Men throw themselves away on studying the habits of frogs—and great men. Men throw themselves away on brandy-and-soda at the Club below. How many Irish peers have gone to their graves since Lord Edward's time ; and who loves them ! who, even, remembers their names ? All the gazettes of Europe could not give a man more enviable fame than to be mentioned in Irish peasants' cabins in their evening prayers. I am afraid you will find most of us ambitious rather to be mentioned in their curses. You happy-tempered English folk don't curse, or I should have deserved to be mentioned in *your* curses for making disagreeable speeches to you, instead of doing what I came to do—asking you all over to our old den—Harry's and mine. You will let me drive the girls over this afternoon for a cup of tea, won't you ? But you will find this Irish question haunting your window, whether you will or no, like the face of a hungry child ; and believe me, when you hear people say they detest politics, that only means that they have sent for a policeman and removed the pale cheeks and the hungry eyes to prison. The rest you will have to find out for yourself, but I wanted you to know, when you hear people rating Harry with low tastes and agitation, and rebellion, and the rest of it, it is all my fault. Harry fights under my flag, and his enemies are my enemies.'

'Happy Harry ! I only wish the Guards were in such luck !' said young Neville, in a low tone.

'Mabel always takes my part,' said the Lord Harry, proudly. He was astounded to find himself gradually rising from a position in which he had honestly regarded Quish the bailiff as a more gifted being into heroic proportions which enabled him to look down upon Guardsmen.

The girls floated away to discuss what could be done with Lord Clanlaurance's starved greenhouses.

'I wonder could a fellow—an outsider, I mean—ever understand Ireland !' said Reggy, actively applying for information to his moustache.

'Come along, and show me the stables, and give me a cigar, and I'll tell you all about it,' said Harry. 'I know so devilish little, 'twon't take long. We're going to fight you, whenever we get the chance. That's all. Girls will always talk such poetry about things !'

'I wish *I* could fall into the habit,' said the Guardsman, with a groan, as he lit his cigar. 'If it were only as easy as the fighting !'

Miss Westropp was not a person to do things by halves. She had received the strangest exhilaration from circumstances that would have repelled and horrified any young lady of well-regulated mind with whom she was acquainted. But the discerning reader will have seen long ago that Miss Mabel's was by no means a well-regulated mind. She would never have carried off the premium for ladylike deportment at a young ladies' finishing academy. I am free to confess that the influence which had led Harry to prefer the stables to the club as a social resort had, in a very different order, imparted an element of wilfulness and neglect to the character of his beautiful sister. Her mind was not at all a Dutch flower-garden cut to pattern. It was as fair as Glengariff, but had something also of Glengariff's wildness and unaccountable shadows. So far from being shocked to find her brother leagued with low people for some madcap feat of arms, it gave new fuel to her belief in Harry's reclamation. She felt to some extent the intoxication of the explorer who has rushed on undauntedly against all warnings, and has found a North-West passage where all the world prophesied eternal ice. She now knew the worst ; and what had all the dark hints of shameful passion and unspeakable conspiracy come to but a boy's unspoken love and a soldier's fight for freedom? Why should he not fall in love with the miller's daughter? Her gentle eyes could never lead him into perdition. Was he to fall in love with Miss Deborah Harman? Rebellion might or might not be a rash thing – even a deadly thing—but could it possibly be worse than a life spent at Moll Carty's in a soulless bondage to Quish ?— nay, could it possibly be more ignoble than the vacuous lives of the pimply young squires who dawdled at the Club in the cast-off fashions and vices of last year's London season? Her life at the Castle, which seemed so bleak and sterile, had all of a sudden flowered into interest. Her sympathies ran like a wild vine in search of things to cling around ; and, lo ! not only was Harry submitting to her graceful chains, but there was not a cabin far or near to which her wild festoons were not extending. She no longer felt herself under the chilling suspicion of coming as one of Miss Deborah's missionaries to the Ranties. She had got a key that opened every cabin and every heart in it, and she felt a new entrancing spirit expanding within her as her eye ranged over the royal picture spread under the Castle windows, to think that she could now understand not only its mountains, woods, and waters, but its past and future—that the mission of the Westropp race for the future was to brighten the hearths and not quench them—that the curls of smoke along the hillsides rose like maledictions no longer, but like blessings from the

simple glowing hearts within. In addition to the divine necessity of the perfume-laden rose which she felt to spread herself
abroad, she was indulging the wilful blood of the Westropps in
doing as she pleased, and gratifying a feminine foible also in doing
as the spiteful little coteries of Drumshaughlin society did not
please. She sent presents of grapes and peaches to Myles
Rohan's sick-bed, and placed at his disposal the old bath-chair
to which her father had once been reduced by violent access of
the gout—which, however, the sturdy miller resisted as a well-
intended but intolerable imputation of effeminacy. When the
alarm at the Mill was over, she availed herself of Mrs. Rohan's
circle of introductions to the pinched and aching clients of her
Society of St. Vincent de Paul. Life was not worth living, in
Mrs. Dargan's eyes, for quite half a day after they beheld so
astounding a freak on the part of the great lady at the Castle.
The presidency of the St. Vincent de Paul Society had never
before struck her as at once so offensive a work of holiness and
yet so legitimate an object of pious ambition in the right hands.
Katie Rohan Miss Westropp could not make much of. The shy
creature shrank from notice like a frightened fawn. Though she
was almost her own age, Mabel felt strong enough to take her in
her arms as she would a timid child. Captain Mike MacCarthy
she met early, and liked cordially.

'Ma'am, your most obedient,' said the American Captain,
with a bow oddly suggestive at one and the same time of a
Versailles salon of the last century and of a contemporary log-
hut ; for Captain Mike, albeit his heavy black moustache and
bomb-shell talk, was the courtliest of backwoodsmen. 'Ours is
about as big a continent as there's on show ; but it don't grow
anything of your par-ticular complexion, Miss. This little playground of a country pro-duces uncommon purty playthings, I
must, as a candid Amurrican citizen, certify.'

'You are very flattering,' said Miss Westropp, smilingly,
' and very forgiving,' she added in a gentle tone. 'Harry told
me something of what happened long ago. Well, you have your
revenge. We thought we were disposing of you for ever by
driving you across the Atlantic, and you are coming back our
master.'

' No, ma'am, there's one species of slavery the Amurrican constitooshun ain't never abolished and never wants to. Its name
is woman. You, and the likes of you, will have your slave planta-
tions all the time, and Mike MacCarthy will be the darndest
quiet nigger that ever hoed corn as long as *you* hold the whip.
But I'm not going for to deny,' said the Captain, ' that the
people who went in emigrant ships are coming back in Amurrican

bottoms and with Amurrican principles. Human natur is going to kick up purty lively in this oppressed country before very long. I guess we're going to pass this wrinkled old hag of a system of government of yours through our patent Columbian mangle and bring her out as young as – as you, Miss. We've got your range already. Every Amurrican letter read in an Irish cabin is the reading of a Declaration of Independence. You'd have to stop the ocean postage before you could stop our invasion—and it's too late now—we're here!'

'I'm beginning to be a little afraid of you invaders,' laughed Mabel, with a little shudder which was not all jocose; 'but you won't be too hard on sinners who do penance, will you?'

'Miss,' said the American Captain, 'the Ninth Massachusetts would feed you with rose leaves. And it ain't clear to me,' he added, staring reverentially at her faintly-blushing cheek, 'it ain't clear to me, on the look of you, that that has not been your or'nery diet.'

'Captain Mike is rather down on his luck,' said the Lord Harry some days afterwards. 'Isn't it funny? The poor beggar has had to pawn his revolver. I caught him at it. He has not got his remittances, and they're pestering him about his bill at the hotel, and the police are beginning to hover about unpleasantly. Mabel, I wish you would let me bring him to dinner. I rather suspect he has had no breakfast.'

'And it was only yesterday I saw in the newspapers that these American filibusters are wallowing in the gold of their unfortunate dupes,' said Miss Westropp, meditatively.

'Oh, you know, there's plenty of money,' said Harry, fearing that he had been an unskilful diplomatist. 'They have no end of guns and money. There may be a fleet of them in the Bay any morning. But it's deuced awkward for a fellow in the meantime to be reminded of his bill and to feel hungry.'

'Why should not Captain MacCarthy have a room here?' said Miss Westropp, suddenly. 'There's plenty of house-room, goodness knows; and he's such fun! And wouldn't it be poetic justice—isn't it perhaps a small history of our time—that we, who evicted him from his cabin twenty years ago, should instal him in the Castle now?'

'The very thing that struck myself, but I was afraid to ask. By Jove, Mabel, you are a witch—or an angel. You are making a new man of me,' cried Harry, who had several times lately become dimly unconscious with what floods of radiance this bright spirit was suffusing his withered life. 'Why do you do it, Mab? What do you expect from *me?* I can never do anything to make you happy—no more than a big dog—can I?'

'You have done it already, dear,' said Mabel, with a mother's fond look of pride, 'for you *are* a new man!'

No wonder that Miss Deborah Harman, retailing rumours of these doings to the Neville girls, should hint at the gravest fears that affection could suggest as to the mental and moral condition of the Hon. Miss Westropp. 'Frank' Harman, being content with equipping the three Miss Nevilles with bows and arrows, and getting the young Guardsman to allow himself to be put up for the Club, and hinting what an adorable place Lord Clanlaurance's lawn would make for a garden party, was not inclined to be too hard upon the Wild Irish Girl whose eyes had attracted the Nevilles to a dull neighbourhood; but Miss Deborah, in whose mind the acidity of personal rivalry was now added to the promptings of apostolic zeal, was less disposed to spare the sisterly rod.

'There are really limits to everything, and only that Hans is so provokingly easygoing with women, he would let Lord Drumshaughlin know what people are saying. Mr. Harman, you know, is not in the least afraid to say what he thinks,' she said, proudly. 'He would throw up the agency altogether only that the Drumshaughlins are so wretchedly poor, and he is anxious to keep things together as long as he can. But really it is time for some friend of the family to speak. Mabel is turning the place into a perfect menagerie. One does not know what strange-looking people one may meet, if one visits there—Fenians, or French monkeys, or Americans with bowie-knives. Fancy, the police are actually watching the place!'

'We dine with the Westropps this evening,' said Miss Neville, in some alarm. 'I like Mabel ever so much—she is so engaging, and so uncommon, you know—but I do hope there will be nothing uncomfortable.'

'You are to be envied, my dear Miss Neville,' said Miss Deborah, sweetly. 'You will, perhaps, be taken down to dinner by Dawley, the tailor.'

CHAPTER THE TWENTY-FIRST

LOTOS-EATER VERSUS IRONMASTER

'You will bore yourself to death in this infernal hole,' said young Mr. Flibbert, flogging his trousers with his riding switch, as the Guardsman and he stood on the steps of the Club, with minds as vacant as the sleepy square in front of them, which

was large enough for the Life Guards Grey themselves to
manœuvre in, and at this moment contained no sign of life
except a hen or two clucking tunefully in the lazy sunshine.

'Oh, no, if I don't bore other people to death,' said Neville.
'I like the place. Don't you ?'

As a matter of fact little Flibbert had never felt happier in
his life. Here he was patronising a Life Guardsman as rich as a
silver mine on the father's side, and inheriting the tip-top blood
of the Winspurleighs. (He had been following it back to the
Middle Ages in the Club copy of Debrett.) A small audience,
just to see with what ease he bore himself, would have completed
the Sub-Inspector's self-satisfaction. But it would never do to
let the world know this. He shrugged his shoulders with the air
of one for whom a stirring world of wits and bright eyes was
languishing, while duty condemned him to listen to the morning
song of the poultry of Drumshaughlin.

'One Irish village is as good as another,' he remarked, resignedly, 'and as cursedly bad.'

'Then why do people come so long a way to see Glengariff ?

'They come because they have not got to stay,' said Flibbert,
laughing gaily at his own paradox, and making a note of it for
further circulation. 'The people who are admiring the rocks to-
day will be trying one another's temper to-morrow, and will hail
the long car as a deliverer the day after for taking them away to
Kenmare or to Old Harry. Surely *you* don't go in for scenery
and that kind of thing ?'

'No, no,' said Neville, somewhat nettled to find himself
obliged to account for his presence in Glengariff, 'but I like to
have beautiful and simple things around me, and I think there is
plenty here to interest a fellow if he looks about.'

'Yes,' said little Flibbert, who was apt to let his wit run
away with him when he felt himself in the satiric vein. 'There
is one of our most eminent citizens—old Cambie, the linen-
draper, opposite—you see the bill for sale under the Bankruptcy
Court on the shutters. The old gentleman is in the horrors. That
is his little girl going for the doctor.'

'Then he is only imitating his betters,' said Neville, with some
disgust. 'The steward told me just now he spent the night holding
down some young squire from near Bantry who's in the horrors, too.'

'Yes, young Bloodstone, of Broadlands—there's an impression
that he and the scullery-maid are married. The Bloodstones are
broken, horse, foot, and artillery.'

'It seems to me everybody in this country is bankrupt or
going to be, except you gentlemen who have the governing of
it. *You*, at all events, ought to see some good in it.'

'Oh, of course, it has its amusing side,' laughed the little police officer, mistaking the young Englishman's disgust for a compliment, which enabled him to forget the tangle of debts which was secretly wound round his own legs and arms, 'only for the horrible sameness of the thing. Here's old Captain Grogan now, toddling across the square at precisely the same hour as he has come for twenty years past, and he will make precisely the same joke that he has made for twenty years, seize the same chair and the same paper, and maunder over the same measure of brandy-and-water till old Captain Grumpus is wheeled in at one o'clock in his bath-chair to resume the same battle over the campaign in China. You see, it becomes rather slow,' sneered Flibbert, who, having found it heaven to get into the Club, was now beginning to find a higher heaven in despising it.

'I should think all that was comfortable enough,' said Neville, simply. 'I don't find life very brilliant anywhere. Don't you often find crowded London rooms every bit as dull as that square?'

'Ah, the Harmans!' cried young Mr. Flibbert, hailing the Harman family trap, with an enthusiasm, perhaps, heightened by the sense of escape from the appeal to his own experiences of London drawing-rooms. 'We are going to invoke your sisters' aid for a flower-show—may we count upon you?'

'I'm of no use at that kind of thing,' said Neville, 'but if anybody thinks I am, I always go upon the principle of not objecting.'

In truth, young Neville was beginning to feel amazingly at home amidst his new surroundings. When he looked out on the map for Glengariff, it was with no more thought of the place or the people than one who buys a pearl necklace has of the country of the pearl-divers. He considered it solely as a portion of land and water which had the happiness to be in the immediate neighbourhood of Miss Westropp. If Lord Clanlaurance's Castle were as distant as the Sahara Desert, and as ugly, he would have rented it all the same. His one vague notion of what brought him to Glengariff was that of lying like a big dog at his mistress's feet, blinking faithfully at her in the sun. He had not imagination enough, or selfishness enough, to think what he was to do with himself in the necessary intervals. He would not have repined in the least if he had found himself a thousand miles away from billiard balls and betting tapes. What he was not in the least prepared for was to find that he had stumbled into the oddest new world, which was as unlike the world seen from the Chrysanthemum Club windows as a wild rose was unlike an orchid, and—more surprising still—that it was interesting him a great deal more. Doubtless, if Miss Westropp had not shown that wild interest of hers in the natives, he would have come and gone without observing particularly whether the people were black, white, or yellow; whether they spoke Gaelic or Cherokee; but now that his attention was directed to the subject, he began to find a certain opiate charm in the lazy Spanish melancholy of the place. The men seemed to puff away their sorrows in their tobacco-smoke. It seemed to him that the children were more at ease in their rags than the young gentlemen in the bow window of the Chrysanthemum were in their high collars. Irish poverty has the picturesque advantage of having smiles more easily at command than tears. We easily forgive the misery that a small coin or even a kind word from us can dissolve into happy dimples and rude sonnets of liquid gratitude. Charity in this form becomes a heady dissipation. Young Neville indulged in it as lawlessly as Father Phil, and became almost as popular. He forgot all about the smokiness of the cabins in the rich caressing word of welcome. Even those Irish peasants who have forgotten all else of their own ancient tongue, still go to the old Gaelic fount for their language of endearment—their *magragals* and *mavourneens*, which are no more to be done into English than the Mass; and there is a quaint religious spell of its own in this heart-worship in the lost tongue. Then Neville, who, because he was the shyest, was supposed to be the stiffest of mankind in his relations with the softer sex, was immeasurably pleased to find that the peasant girls had an instinctive confidence in his honest blue eyes. Their open, fearless faces and merry eyes were as ready to sparkle and laugh under his glance as mountain brooks in the sunshine. Those who have endured the miseries of a shy man will not need to be told that, to such unwieldy creatures no womanly flattery can be so sweet as a look of confidence from an untutored girl. Any man may have flattery who can pay for it, but it is only a good face that an innocent girl will look straight at without confusion, though it is, oftener than not, a plain face. Finally, having been stunned all his life in the domestic circle with the praises of industry and iron, he found a relief in the dreamy, out-at-elbows, half-happy, half-despairing apathy of life in and about Drumshaughlin; and having been drilled in a regiment of young men, who all dressed, lived, and thought alike, according to a stern creed which cripples young souls more remorselessly than the Chinese do their children's toes, it was quite a novel, and, after the first start or two, not unpleasant sensation to find himself plunging into wild, free, barbaric latitudes, where young men still talked of dying for a sentiment, and were actually preparing to do it. So far as I have observed,

Englishmen have their doubts about their own national stiffness of tongue and joints, as they, once in a way, have even about the Christian Revelation. They have not the least notion of forsaking the one or the other, but they have a weakness for things as different as possible from their own received beliefs, if only because they are different. Neville did not mean to have his own clothes cut by Dawley, nor himself to engage in treasonable practices; but outlandish garments and treason were like potheen whisky among the illicit pleasures of the country, and, right or wrong, the whole life of the place was so much more piquant than two rows of perfectly dressed people in carriages going up the Row, to yawn in the faces of other two rows of ditto ditto coming down.

Perhaps the hardest of Miss Westropp's pets to understand was the American Captain. Englishmen love to think that all their actions are determined by the rules of pure prose, merciless logic, and hard sense. They are, on the contrary, the most whimsical and sentimental of men. They are only in dread of being thought so. What possible process of logic could account for the fact that Neville's notion of the cause of law and order in Ireland was decided by the offensive twist of Sub-Inspector Flibbert's moustache, and that he only came to like Captain Mike MacCarthy by disliking Flibbert? So it was, at all events. He could not help thinking what a figure burly Captain Mike, with his antic dialect, devil-may-care felt hat, and square-cut clothes of dingy black, would cut among the young men of the Knightsbridge mess, with whom an ill-chosen word was as painful a disfigurement as a crease in their morning coats; but then he thought how little Flibbert's irritating strut and Drumshaughlin fashions would fare in the same company; and the next time he met the American Captain, he astonished that grizzly warrior by saying, 'I've been reading up your war a bit. There was never anything like it—such dogged hard work, I mean.'

'Just so. There wasn't much of a show—no return tickets at excursion rates—no programme of dance music on the grounds. No, sir, 'twas all con-ducted on strict business principles. When you've got to kill a million and a half of your fellow-men in a limited time, where's the use of dressing them up in osprey feathers and them kind of fixings? I don't deny there's pluck behind your fine coats, you Britishers—not by no means,' said the Captain, determined to be generous. 'Your boys have done some rale purty things from time to time, in a small way. All I want entered on the minutes is that an army don't miss pipeclay when it's short of boots. When we started out after Joe Johnson, the Union supplied us with a gun and cartridge-belt, and I guess that was about all—except fellows to fire at. We wrastled Joe's hash purty powerful all the same for plain citizens. You think that's bragging?' An unconquerably candid increase of colour in Neville's fresh face betrayed him. He had indeed been thinking vaguely that this was not Knightsbridge form. It seemed an additional rudeness to force him to confess or deny it. But he did not yet know Captain Mike. 'So it is bragging,' said the American Captain, knocking away a pyramid of ashes from the end of his cigar with leisurely gravity. 'Rather 'taint bragging—it's advertising. What's a new country like ours to do but advertise? She's bet out of the market unless she advertises. It's all well for your crowd to hold your tongues about your battles, an' look modest—silence comes easier to you than descriptive particulars—I don't say nothing agen it—but your advertising's done for you—you've had your historians booming along ever so many centuries now—had a'most all the lying to yourselves. Consequence is you're a great nation—you've only got to hold your tongue for people to believe Battles of Waterloo about you. We're only beginners—we're not above writin' our own puffs and stickin' our own bills—else I'd like to know who's goin' to hear that Gettysburg was a bigger day's work than Waterloo! No, sir, we ain't ashamed of advertising honest goods. And our work on the Potomac was real honest. I can tell you them that came out alive deserved the remarks of the *Gettysburg Evening Telegram.* Yes, sir.'

'I can easily believe it,' said the young Life Guardsman fervently. 'Won't you have another cigar?'

Joshua Neville was attracted by his new Irish surroundings from a totally opposite standpoint to his son's. Reggy liked them because they were so utterly un-English ; his father because he felt stirred by a mission to make them as English as his own flesh and blood. The young Guardsman was of the type of Norman invaders who had to be restrained by statute from adopting the wild Irish dress and marrying an Irish wife. The native faults of character which inspired the father with the ambition of reforming them, rather disposed the son to imitate them. He fretted under the sense of his own taciturnity and poverty of mental landscape. He envied this people, their imaginativeness, their recklessness, their elegant laziness, their power of dining on National aspirations and supping divinely on an evening prayer. He only wished he could be as nimble of wit and lazy of limb as the most incorrigible of them. His father, on the other hand, could not see why they might not become as methodical and practical and as much attached to the grindstone for the grindstone's sake as he was himself. The two impressions

only differed from the point of view. The Englishman, as a
social animal, is the most diffident of men; the Englishman
of Commerce the most indomitable. The young Guardsman, it
must be confessed, only saw the outer rind of things. Joshua
Neville could not in the least understand why Glengariff should
not be in its kind as thriving a place as the Black Country;
scenery, of course, had no chance in the market against coal and
iron; but he had known no end of good strokes made in scenery,
and with an inferior article, too, to that which a Glengariff
prospectus could put on the market. What gold diggings
that ugly blotch of mud which the Liverpudlians take for the
seashore had been turned into! And there were lots of things
to be done with Glengariff besides floating a Casino. He had
satisfied himself by personal investigation (as well as out of the
pages of Thom's Almanac) that the district was singularly rich in
mineral wealth, and that the coast was teeming with fishes running about in vain importuning the natives to catch them. It
gave Joshua Neville genuine personal pain that this should be
so. Curiously enough, it was not without a certain subtle sense
of national self-satisfaction as well that he devoted himself to
noting down the hundred-and-one things which might be done
with the Glengariff country, and were not. He developed as
keen a relish for investigating the economic eccentricities of the
place day by day as his son did for shooting over the mountains.
And what bags the father as well as the son made! Everything
wanted mending everywhere. The house drains of Clanlaurance
Castle were of as archaic a type as the arrangement for emit-
ting smoke through the thatch of the huts at the Ranties. One
day he sighed over a pitful of fish laid out for manure for want
of a market. Another, he noted with horror that the fishery
pier, which it had taken a quarter of a century of agitation to
erect, had been erected at the only spot on that part of the coast
where the hungry sea could burst in (as, of course, it duly did,
and scooped away the foundations like so much piecrust at a
bite). It was, in its way, a still more trying thing to a man of
business to find that even the town clock was of the most un-
steady and dissipated habits as a time-keeper, being sometimes
too fast, often too slow, and still oftener altogether asleep at its
post. It was one of Joshua Neville's boasts to possess a chro-
nometer which showed Greenwich as well as Irish time without
a variation of twenty seconds in as many months. Precision in
such matters he regarded as of the essence of English greatness;
fancy, then, this shameless clock coolly lying to the extent of
twenty minutes at a time, and a morning or two after declining
point blank to give any information whatever on the subject.

'Now, what have you got to say to that?' he demanded in a tone in which sincere annoyance was blended with no less sincere complacency. 'English rule does not set the works of a clock astray. As a strong well-wisher of Ireland, I want to know why you won't keep the correct time?'

'Because, like the Atlantic ocean, we've got so much of it on our hands that it is not worth measuring to a nicety,' said the Rector, good-humouredly.

'Well, indeed, now that you mention it,' said Father Phil, 'a queer thing happened myself the other morning through the vagaries of that same town clock—bad cess to it for a town clock! I —I hadn't my own watch convenient,' stammered the old priest, with a suspicion of deeper red on his weather-beaten apple cheeks, 'and when I jumped out of bed to look at the town clock, I found to my horror that it was within a minute of the hour for eight o'clock Mass, and the bell not rung nor the chapel opened. There was no sign of the chapel-woman. I rushed out and rang the bell myself—not very artistically, I am afraid, but I suppose I put my heart in it, for before I had given the last tug at the bell I had the whole town, men, women, and children, rushing out half-dressed to know what was the matter. What do you think? The town clock was not going at all that night—it was only four o'clock in the morning; and, of course, when the people heard the bell banging away at that unearthly hour they thought it must be a fire or the Fenians that were after coming. I am told that Patsy Kent, who has the winding of the town clock, was on a slight bit of a caper at the time. He is one of the most harmless creatures you would meet in a day's walk only for an occasional drop too much. But, upon my word, they are the kindest people in the world, or they would have thought it was not Patsy Kent but I that was on the caper that morning.'

Joshua Neville felt in the depths of his logical soul that this was not a relevant answer to his remark on the disregard of precision in native time-keeping; but he felt some difficulty in resuming the theme in view of a droll little drama, which seemed to impart a certain halo to Patsy Kent's reprehensible part in the town clock's aberrations. His heart warmed to the American Captain when that grizzled warrior broke out—

'That's my native land down to the bed-rock! and I'll venture a small pile you didn't bring Patsy fooling out of his bed that morning—he was too drunk for that. I reckon he thought himself the most sensible man in the town in that transaction. Most probable, if Editor Murrin called around for his views for the *Banner*, Patsy would maintain in big type that 'twas all the fault of his reverence in bein' up so early.'

'Maybe there's some sense in that same,' said Father Phil, judicially shaking his head.

'No, sir—nary bit—not as much sense as would keep a mosquito from buzzing when he means business. No, sir, the gen'leman from Sheffield's quite right—I expect I have located you correctly, boss?'

'I do come from that part of the country,' said Neville, gravely.

'That's so. The Hon. Joshua Neville's ideas are the ideas of a brainy man, if he will allow a plain Amurrican citizen to say so. It's what I've been saying all over the camp since I came hereabouts—what you want is to keep tugging at that bell all the time till you wake Patsy Kent, and wake the town, and wake the whole blessed poppy-headed country. This, sir, would be a great country if the people only knew what o'clock it is.'

'It's all very well for you to taunt Patsy with not knowing what o'clock it is—you haven't stolen his watch. We have—Mr. Neville and I,' said the Rector.

'That, of course, is a joke,' said Neville, who was always uneasy in metaphorical discourse.

'It's no joke for the creatures in those cabins yonder. Our great nation has been picking their tattered pockets ever since the Crusades or so. It's no joke for me either. If everybody had his own, my gold repeater would be in Father Phil's pocket and not in mine.'

'Why, then, my dear, I'm not so well able to keep a silver one when I've got it,' said Father Phil, with a smile.

'No. Somebody else would rob you if I didn't; so I hold on to the gold repeater and to the Church Establishment; but I don't feel at all commissioned from on high to lecture you on the faults of this Papistical watch of yours. No, Mr. Neville; you'll find a thousand things wrong in this country, but nothing so wrong as ourselves—I with my 600l. a year of Irish money for cursing the Irish people, and you, who pay an army (God forgive you!) to collect my ill-gotten goods for me.'

'My dear Mr. Motherwell, you mistake me, I assure you,' pleaded Neville, earnestly. 'Nothing could be further from my thoughts than to wound the susceptibilities of our Irish brethren. They are most estimable people—forgive me for saying it in your presence, Father O'Sullivan—charming people, positively charming! I only want to know how to serve them—I do, indeed. I quite agree with our good friend the Rector that the Church Establishment is an anachronism, and I am prepared to co-operate in any properly matured scheme of disestablishment and disendowment.'

'Just so; and rob Mrs. Motherwell and the babies by way of appeasing your conscience for robbing the Irish nation at large,' said the Rector, his big brown eyes glistening good-humouredly under the soft felt hat from amidst billows of silky brown hair and beard. 'But I can tell you, you won't find Mrs. Motherwell submitting to your penal laws as meekly as the conquered Jacobites did.'

'Bully for Mrs. M. !' observed the American Captain.

They were bowling along merrily through the Pass of Keiman-Eigh on their way to a picnic of Miss Westropp's devising. The chatter and laughter of the younger folk in the waggonette in front came back in melodious echoes from crag to crag, to the amazement of the mountain goats, who shook their scandalised beards gravely from their heights at the disturbers of the lonely pass.

'We have behaved cruelly—infamously, to the Irish people in the past,' pursued the ironmaster.

'That's right; pitch into your grandfather !' said the Rector.

'No, it's yours I am pitching into,' said Neville, much gratified with his retort. 'My grandfather was a Horne Tooke man. He might as well have been a Council of Trent man so far as the loaves and fishes were concerned. He was a stubborn kind of man—as stubborn as if he was an Irish Papist. By his will he directed that he should be buried in his own back garden, as the law would not allow him to be buried to his liking. But I don't damp down my furnaces because my grandfather was put into York Jail for his opinions.'

'It must be a fine thing to have the furnaces, anyway,' remarked Father Phil, offering his snuffbox all round.

'Yes, but that is just it. Why don't you have the furnaces ?'

'Wisha, my dear, a morsel of live turf is good enough for poor people.'

'But there is no penal law now against furnaces. There is no penal law against the Irish acquiring property, education, and industry. You have our law ; you have the British Constitution.'

'Well, then, so I am told,' said the old Curate, musingly. 'We are never transported now for looking for education, if we only knew where to look for it. There is nothing to prevent every gorsoon in the country aspiring to be a judge or a deputy lieutenant—not a ha'porth in life, except, maybe, the want of a pair of shoes to the poor gorsoon's feet or so.'

'God bless my soul ! You don't mean to argue that Catholic Emancipation itself is a failure ?' asked the ironmaster, in deep perplexity.

'Eh ! I didn't say that, did I ?' cried Father Phil, in alarm.

'It's just like my sense to go knocking my old muddled head against Catholic Emancipation ; God forgive me my sins ! No, indeed, Mr. Neville, Catholic Emancipation is a grand mouthful of a word, and thankful we are to the kind gentlemen that sent it to us ; but—but—well, it's a foolish old man that says it—but I wonder some one don't bring in a law to leave the people a meal of potatoes in peace and the cabin to cover them. That don't sound a very unreasonable programme, does it, sir ? As far as I can make out, our unfortunate race has spent seven hundred years looking for that much, and we haven't got it yet.'

'Quite right,' exclaimed the Rector. 'And if you'll only pass that little Bill of Father Phil's, you'll have the Glensmen the happiest dogs alive, without blast-furnaces and steam-ploughs and all the rest of the modern apparatus for blinding and deafening people. My dear Mr. Neville, when I came to Ireland first I could teach every peasant around here how to grow three times the amount of his crops and live in a rose-trellised cottage, but I soon found that the simplest way to teach Darby how to manage his farm would be to put myself in Darby's shoes and show what a sumptuous livelihood for Mrs. Motherwell and the little Motherwells I could knock out of Darby's few acres of rocks with Hans Harman's whip over my back. Mrs. Motherwell had not sufficient confidence in my superior economic theories to give up the Rectory and try the experiment, and she showed her customary good sense, for I have long ago discovered that I had more to learn from Darby than Darby had from me. He's the only person in these parts who is not a humbug or a plunderer. Every ear of corn that grows it's he that raises it and it's we who blast it. We build a pier in the spot where it's most convenient for the sea to come and swallow it, and we taunt him with his genius for bungling. We run up ridiculous chimney-shafts where there is no ore, and we have the impudence to twit him with his lack of enterprise in mining.'

'You surely do not deny that copper is to be found, or that the people would be the better for working it ?' said Mr. Neville.

'Talk of your trumpery copper-mine ! Why these peasants have created a gold-mine where nature never intended one. They have beaten the alchemists. With their bare hands they have scraped gold out of the granite rocks, and the moment we could catch a few glistening grains with them, we, superior people, knocked them down and robbed them. They have just three little possessions that they value in life — their cabins, their faith, and their day-dreams about an impossible Ireland. What visible function does English rule perform in their eyes, except subsidising Hans Harman to hover at their door, his excellent sister to poison their faith, and the police to send their boys into penal servitude for being boys? Why, the principal fault of the Irish as a nation is that they have not cut our throats many a day ago. I don't know what saved us, except their superior sense of humour—they hate us less because they very properly laugh at us more—at our airs and our ignorance, and our cant and our hectoring; our broken-backed piers and our copper-mines that won't work! Father Phil, give me a pinch of your snuff if you can't give me a pinch of your patience.'

'Rector, let me have the privilege, sir, of dipping in that snuff-box after you on behalf of the Irish race at home and abroad,' said the American Captain, with majestic grace.

'My dear sir,' said Joshua Neville, 'I trust you will permit me to make a short memorandum of your views. I am only anxious for light. I should much rather be shown to be in the wrong than that the Irish people should suffer by my being in the right. But do I understand you to hold—really, you know—that charges of indolence and improvidence now, for example, are purely the creation of ignorance or malice?'

'Not a bit of it. Hans Harman quite properly calls them indolent. Their rent is three times Griffith's valuation—"three Griffiths," as they call it. They could increase it to four Griffiths if they were more industrious. They're not such fools. Indolence is one of the best products of this country. Irish indolence is Nature's anæsthetic for Irish misery. Only for the comfortable feeling it diffuses through the bones, they would have died long ago under the knife of operators like our friend Harman. You think an Irish peasant is wasting his time when you see him lolling in the sun, sucking a black pipe? My dear sir, you never made a greater mistake. He is a Bank of England Director, counting his treasures. He is a ragged philosopher up among his stars. He is a barefooted anchoret of the desert beholding visions. When you think he is idling, he is really quitting the rocks and the "three Griffiths" of his miserable present, for the boundless estates which he holds, rent free, in the past and in the future. Ask Father Phil!—is there a hut amongst these hills where you won't find a family who can look back upon a genealogy of kings and saints, and forward to the joys of heaven with a firmer faith than they can count upon their breakfast? Believe me, a people who can get that much bliss out of a black pipe are more sensibly employed than in getting up an additional pound of flesh for us, landlords and parsons, to slice away at.'

'Oh come, that would be an argument for the lotos-eater,' said the ironmaster, gravely shaking his head.

'There is a great deal to be said for the lotos-eater. I could

Q

never understand what was wrong with lotos-eating What more blessed esculent than lotos does your nineteenth century produce for you, with all its thundering steam-ploughs and puffing and blowing ? That gospel of work for work sake, and noise for noise sake, is the greatest superstition of an age that turns up its impudent little nose at the Pentateuch. I can understand St. Peter of Alcantara preferring to walk bare-footed on sharp thorns, during a life which he regarded as a mere hop-skip-and-a-jump to an eternity of joy unutterable ; but here is an age of fanatics, whose highest heaven it is to live in the boiler of a steam-engine, and go shrieking about the world, tearing through everything sacred and peaceable, and scorching up every bright green thing in nature, for no earthly object that I could ever see, except to make all the world as uncomfortable, hot, and mad as themselves. I do verily believe men and women endure as many torments in the course of a London season in out-manœuvring, out-shining, and out-boring each other as would have entitled them to canonization in the ages of faith, if their penances had been offered up with the proper dispositions. So it is with your Parliament men, so it is with the whole pushing, brawling, pack of reformers, scientists, and hydra-headed quacks, who are the boast of their age.

> Let us alone !
> Time driveth onward fast,
> And in a little time our lips are mute.
> Let us alone !

With all my heart I echo that immortal song of the lotos-eaters —for I am a bit of a lotos-eater myself—(a tobacco pipe and fishing rod happen to be my own particular vehicle for imbibing the aroma). If Hans Harman could find out where the Irish peasant grows his lotos crop, he would rack-rent it most unmercifully. But that is where Paddy has the advantage over his oppressors—that within that smoky cabin of his and within those lean four bones of his he possesses a gleaming paradise of hope and memory, and his high and mighty lord away in London, who abuses Paddy as a lazy-bones, in reality envies him his knack of lying on his back in fields of asphodel, dreaming of past glories and future heavens, and only wishes that yawning in the bow-windows of a club in St. James's Street were as delicious a way of idling.'

'I hope you will not publish a volume of sermons in praise of idling,' laughed Mr. Neville.

'I am too idle to do anything of the sort ; but, my dear sir, idling is one of the lost arts. It is almost as extinct in Western Europe as the Greek and Roman classics were in the days of Attila and Genseric. Christendom flocked to Ireland as to a

University in those days to learn the alphabet and the Apostles Creed. Take care the nineteenth century may not have to resort to Ireland again to dip its fevered brow in our cool mountain streams, and relearn the ancient art of idling like a gentleman and dreaming like an angel on a regimen of potatoes in a palace of thatch.'

'Hands up, there, Rector; you are laughing at us now,' observed the American Captain, reproachfully.

'At least I practise what I preach. Ask Deborah Harman if I am not the most abandoned lotos-eater—ask that excellent creature how I have neglected a divine call for the purchase of little Papists !'

'Our boys can starve or lounge agen any born nation that ever *I* bored for ile in,' said Captain Mike; 'but bust me if I ever ondherstood before that slow starvation was such a rosy means of livelihood. Likely that's why they all died in the famine times as tame as a Dakotah flat, when they could have gorged themselves with rations of prime pork and hot corn if they took half the trouble in fighting that they did in dying. I see it all now— 'twas only their way of enjoying life, and I'm bound to say the British Constitooshun provided on the most liberal terms for that peculiar species of national recreation. I never see'd the fun of it before !'

'It was horrible,' said Neville, in a deep voice.

'No, no, Rector. Our crowd starve pretty considerable— they idle all they can—they have no more energy than the smoke of their pipes; but don't you domesticate the hallucination that it's because their catechism sets down laziness as one of the theological virtues. It's not because they finds it uncommon ex-hilaratin' to be buried up to the chin in a pit of eternal stagnation. No, sir, their limbs are idle just for the same reason that their jaws were idle in the famine—because there's nothin' much to keep them exercised. Just you drop Paddy down upon any plank road in our Re-public, and observe how he'll skip ! Meet him loafin' around any Irish town you please to nominate, he'll tell you: "Ballyforlornmore may have the light coming through the roof of its hat, but this is the God-forsakenest hole the sky ever drizzled on !" Meet him in a timber city three weeks old, up Minnesota way—if 'twas the darnedest insane settlement that ever frisked in a swamp—he'll tell you in an accent entered according to Act of Congress: "This, sir, is going to be the queen city of this hull God-dam section, and don't you forget it !" And, sir, the Queen City that black-avised swamp will be, bet your choicest book of sermons ! and 'twill have its tour daily journals, with staff correspondence from Washington, an' its baseball team, and its hydralic elevators in the hotels; and the next time you pass the de-pot goin' West you'll likely hear the conductor informing the citizens in the cars that this is Garryowen-na-Gloria City.'

'And is it so hopeless to look for a spirit like that at home ?'

'You see, you've changed the name of our old Isle of Saints into Leper Island, and your Pharisees and Sadducee chaps are scandalised that them lazy lepers don't hurry up, and make their doomed quarantine station of a country hop around in polkas of civilisation. No, sir, I guess—subject to the correction of reverend practitioners present—it don't transpire from the sacred volume that these lepers were ever par-ticularly lively locomotors except about advancin' in force on the Pool of Bethsaida. The Atlantic Ocean is our Irish Pool of Bethsaida. Sir, the angel of Amurrican freedom agitates these three thousand miles of salt water every voyage for all the wounded critters of the airth. Your Irish emigrant, when he leaves the Cove of Cork, may be the wofullest churchyard phe-nomenon whose burial was ever neglected. By the time he passes Fire Island, he's got the Declaration of Independence hummin' through his blood, and as he absorbs his first measure of Bourbon whiskey in the saloon of a free country he is fit to run an elevated railroad over the Rockies. Yes, sir-r-r !'

'Now you're talking in parables,' said the ironmaster, with a smile. 'There you Irish gentlemen have got the advantage of us. Allegorical language is like one of your luminous mountain mists —uncommonly beautiful ; but, rather, don't you think, confuses the landscape a bit ? We, matter-of-fact Englishmen, like to look at things as they really are.'

'Some of us,' said the Rector, who was engaged in charging his great meerschaum pipe. 'You will find that the mists are just as real as the mountains—as if the whole world were not groping in mists and confusion ! as if your Sheffield, under its hideous black canopy of steel filings and soot, saw things clearer than St. Finn Barr did here long ago amidst the storms and rainbows ! My dear sir, don't let us run away with the idea that we have got the exclusive patent for human happiness in that ugly apparatus of steel rails, telegraph wires, gaspipes, and main drains which we call civilisation. Of course, I know we to a great extent run the show, and are bound to advertise, but don't let us burn as heretics every man who won't aspire to our Anglo-Saxon heaven, with its choirs of stokers, plumbers, and political economists. Upon my conscience, I could construct a prettier heaven out of the materials lying around St. Finn Barr's cell here than out of all the steel in Sheffield.'

'Authorities about Ireland are a little conflicting,' said Mr.

Neville. 'I am afraid I will have to let you settle with our good friend the Captain, if his countrymen can see heaven in their mists at home, why they should go building elevated railroads over the Rocky Mountains.'

'No bad blood whatever between the Rector's mists and my Rockies,' said the Captain. 'Both corrugated facts. They only show that a man's got nothing more sensible to do in Ireland under present circumstances than moon around, and that the Rector, bein' a man of sense, does it—only shows that if you plant the robust Englishman of commerce in Glengariff, you'll have him stargazing. Plant the average Glengariff deadbeat under the Starry Flag, and your Manchester bagman ain't in it with him in the wholesale civilisation line. It's not the man that's dozin'—it's the in-stitooshuns. In Amurricker, boss, the in-stitooshuns says "Look alive !" an' Paddy starts out and jest paints that Continent red ! In Ireland the in-stitooshuns says, "Where's the use ?" an' Paddy makes answer "Divil a bit, that I can see," and, like a sensible citizen, curls himself up in his old rags and his ruins, and dreams of his great grandfather, who was King of Eevelaura or of a throne in heaven with St. Finn Barr and Father Phil.'

'Don't, Mike !' said the old priest, gently ; 'St. Finn Barr may be listening to you.'

'Troth, then, he'll never hear my mother's son say anything that an honest Irish saint need feel unaisy about. St. Finn Barr was the first saint she ever taught me to call down out of heaven—St. Barry we used to call him, as friendly as if he was one of ourselves—and indeed many a time I could all but see his wings flashing down through the thatch, though it was only a weeshy gorsoon that called him, and nothin' but a smoky ould cabin to welcome him to. God be with them times, and with her that was the light of that cabin !' His voice sank into the soft caressing Irish accents of his Coomhōla days.

Joshua Neville unconsciously lifted his hat in sympathy with the Irish-American's wideawake.

'No,' said the American Captain, more briskly, " Mike Mac-Carthy ain't the man to say agen givin' our ould saints a good show, or, for the matter of that, our new ones—you may look as wicked as you like, Father Phil—if it was Councillor Trent himself that was here I'd say to your face—there ain't a saint in the calendar that need feel himself demeaned by being named in your company.' (How far the Captain's unidentified 'Councillor Trent' may have had to do with the authors of the Tridentine Decrees I must leave the theologians to speculate.) 'What I objects to is you ain't got energy enough even to run your

ruins in a business-like way—you've got a streak of luck in the
way of eminent bones and antiquities fit to beat the Tomb of
the Apostles, and darn'd if you know how to work it for half
its worth. I was just explainin' the difference oetween Mike
MacCarthy, of Coomhōla, and the same as he is to be observed
in the plug hat of a naturalised Amurrican citizen at 385 East
Thirty-Third Street, Worcester, Mass. Why, if our city could
only turn up a saint with a record like St. Finn Barr—if we
had only that unrivalled stock of carved and painted mountains
for a background, and an ode only half as good as poor Callanan's
to boom the concern—why, sir, we should have a St. Finn Barr
Centennial; with complimentary tickets to the press of the
civilised world; and the massed choirs of Europe and America
for a mammoth Gregorian chant, with, perhaps, some slight
accompaniment of artillery or so; whenever the centennial gave
out, we should have our poet to exhume away out Lisbon way,
and bring the dead singer home in state, and bring out a funeral
edition of his works for sale in the procession—we should have
our crypt for any bones of undoubted respectability that might
be lying around—we should have our white marble shrines
and our silver bells, like the best of them—we should have *ex-
votos* of gold bracelets and diamonds hung over the Holy Well,
instead of them miserable rags fluttering on the bush yonder—
we should have hotel proprietors clawing each other's eyes out
for building lots—we should have——'

'Mike, Mike, I'm afraid you'd have everything except the
blessing of God and of St. Finn Barr,' said the old curate, gravely.
'I don't know that the blessings always go with the big hotels.
I'm sure St. Finn Barr is as thankful for the poor little rags as
he would be for diamond earrings.'

'There it is again! Crash goes Amurrican enterprise, and
Father Phil's picturesque beggarmen pro-ceed to stand at ease and
light their pipes, and make themselves comfortable on the ruins,'
sighed Captain Mike.

'Just what I should like to do myself,' observed the Rector,
'if there was nobody looking.'

'I say nothing of the particular form of h'm—industrial
development just sketched out in the original if somewhat—h'm
— enterprising colours, peculiar to the imagination of the
New World; but what a site for a Hydropathic Establishment now, for example! What a lake! And just look at the
colour of that stream—why, it has travelled over copper all the
way! Surely, *surely*, my dear Father O'Sullivan,' urged Joshua
Neville, whose eyes were filled with the beautiful mountain shapes
now unfolding their secrets, dark and bright, around him, 'surely

St. Finn Barr could never wish that his lovely solitude should remain a solitude always !'

'It's not Father Phil's saint that warns off trespassers ; it's Hans Harman, that keeps the place for his private devotions—at least for the shooting season,' said the Rector. 'Gougaun Barra is sacred not to poor St. Finn Barr's cell, but to Lord Drum shaughlin's shooting box.'

'But is there no cure for this Irish paralysis ?' asked the iron-master, with just a trace of impatience in his tone. Here were three men, all for different, and, as it seemed to him, contradictory reason, barring every avenue of energy with deadening forebodings and an almost contented despair. To the Englishman's first buoyant persuasion that he understands all about the Irish mystery was succeeding the Englishman's second sickening suspicion that nobody of British blood could ever possibly understand it. But he was not going to give it up like that. His national pride chafed under the notion that the stubborn British vigour which had met Napoleon in arms and ruled the empire of Aurungzebe as easily as the parish of St. Pancras, should recoil before this tatterdemalion Sphinx in the western seas. 'Our excellent friend from the New World knows what I mean. He has seen what human energy can do to move mountains. He agrees with me that it is shameful to leave a nation plunged in this unnatural stupor. He is himself a living argument how easily we might have a startling awakening. Can nothing be done ? If advice won't do, will capital ?'

'Not any goods comin' with the chalk-mark of your British Custom House—neither your advice nor your bullion—nary cent !' said the American Captain, shaking his head. 'Your observations upon the beauties of enterprise and the drawbacks of hunger and ease as a profession is sound·doctrine—sound as Sinai thunder, sir—but as long as your observations are discharged from a British pulpit, our boys will no more listen than they read the eloquent tracts agen Popery you used to ship over some years ago. They'll eye your volume of sermons on energy as they did your Bibles in the Gaelic tongue, and they'll regard your British capital as they regarded the soup and blankets with which you used to enforce Protestant theology—they'll think you've some new patent on hand for advertising your superior virtue, likely by a dip in their ragged pockets, and sure as thunder by mortifying their national pride.'

'Still fretting over the Penal Laws and the Norman Conquest ! My dear sir, the Normans conquered us, Browns, Jones, and Robinsons, as well as they did you—appropriated our Saxon lands, outlawed our Saxon tongue, made swineherds of our Saxon fathers, and have kept us Saxon commonalty the under dog pretty much to this day.   Do you suppose you could rouse Hodge to fight out the battles of Hereward, the Saxon ?   Do you think I am going to neglect an order for steel rails because we live under a German Sovereign and a French aristocracy ?   My dear sir, a man's duty is to live his life in the nineteenth century, not to go back patching together the old skeletons of the twelfth. Why should you even stop at the twelfth ? 'Ireland's first grievance against England—the greatest of all—dates from the Glacial Period.   You know the whole central plateau of Ireland was a priceless coal bed until a glacier came and whisked it clean off to Northumberland, and left you a shuddering bog in its place.   We are willing to do what we can to make restitution for the past ; but are we to begin by sending back your coal-beds ?'

'No, sir—among other reasons, because I guess you've about raised all the boodle that was in them mines out of them before exposing the early delinquencies of that glacier.   No, sir, we give up your ill-gotten coals ; but that is not the only big steal your thieving glaciers have scooped out of this crucified country. Every year that passes there's a thick crust of gold deposited over the Irish bogs by the industry of Mick and Paddy, like reefs raised by the coral insects — " rent" your gold-bugs call it : — and every year, as sure as the " blight," one of your blamed glaciers comes hulking along, and shovels Mick's gold-fields across to London as clean as the coal-beds.   Sir, 'taint one ancient glacier that's the matter — your British system acts as a patent double-action glacier all the time — chucking the gold-fields out into England on its yearly trip, and chucking the people back into the Atlantic Ocean on its return journey. Your Government-by-Glacier has chilled the marrow in the people's bones—it has froze the blood in their hearts agen you.   They regard John Bull as a huge, hectoring, plundering old iceberg.   If the Archangel Gabriel were to preach industry with a British accent—if the whole heavenly choir were to chant it to the tune of " Rule Britannia," they would have no show with an Irish audience.   Sir, they would hiss the heavenly host, if they had to frizzle for it in the 'tarnal penitentiary.'

'Well, but what if you set it to the music of "Hail Columbia"?' suggested Neville, with a smile.

'Ah ! there you've got right down to the nub of this question. Sir, if you want to wake the dead in Ireland, you jest try a blast on the Amurrican horn.   They don't suspect *us* of bringin' powder and shot agen Popery in our carpet-bags.   They have no con-scientious squirms about *our* bank drafts bein' the price of their immortal souls. No, boss—if ever again the benumbed bones of Ireland are to hop under the influence of the sparkling wine-cup of civilisation, that new corpse-reviver will have to be mixed by an Amurrican barman and tossed off with a squeeze of the Declaration of Independence. The trouble is, I guess, the first Amurrican lesson in the alphabet of hope and manhood will have to be, "Sling down your rifles, you boys, and jest make them Britishers git" !'

'*Nec sat rationis in armis*—put not your trust in blackthorn sticks as against the new breechloaders. You'll make as bad a job of your rebellion as they do of their chimney-shafts and fishery piers,' says the Rector. 'But I dare say you will have it. An Irish lad of spirit looks forward to his going out in a rising, as an English lad does to going up for the mathematical tripos. I thank God I was never born with a mission to set things right. Here we are, and here come Miss Westropp and luncheon. Who could ever have thought a discourse on Irish politics would end in anything so practical and delightful ?'

'My dear sir, you are not going to make me despair of a country, where we, Irish, American, and English—Catholic, Protestant, and Dissenter—have had such an amicable morning,' said Joshua Neville, cheerily. He had been bred up to a set of opinions as rigid and plain-featured as a Sheffield Sunday, and he found himself enjoying a short holiday from his ancestral prejudices, as a jaded Briton, escaping for the first time from the boredom of his irreproachable country, enjoys the red-breeched soldiers and the muslin halos of the *matelottes*, and the fearful and wonderful jabber of the pier at Boulogne. Popish idolatry and Irish rebellion were, to the writers and readers of his early lesson books, what the abominations of the groves were to King Amasias, in the days of his innocence ; and, here he was, like that latitudinarian young monarch, contracting a dangerous familiarity with the gods of the Edomite. How, indeed, was the sturdiest old English Protestant fervour to work itself into alarm by picturing to himself Father Phil setting a match to the fires of Smithfield, or Captain Mike spitting babies on his honest clumsy pike-head, after the manner of the favourite rebel pastimes depicted in Cruikshank's engravings ? 'Tut, tut, the problem cannot be such a desperate one. If three races and three religions can mingle so pleasantly here and now, why should it be impossible to extend the harmony from a waggonette to a nation ?'

'On one condition, perhaps,' said the American Captain, in the low, deep tones which he somehow made better heard than his bravura notes—'If you could strike an international Miss

Mabel—if statesmen could only learn Miss Westropp's angel knack of making people love one another—and if you, gen'lemen pulpiters, would help teach 'em !'

CHAPTER THE TWENTY-SECOND

IN LONE GOUGAUN BARRA

Miss Westropp's little party at Gougaun Barra was one of the most daring social adventures since Florizel, Prince of Bohemia, danced at the sheep-shearing with his shepherd lass.   Even Prince Florizel, it will be remembered, though it was a gallant child, had not much to say for himself when angry old Bohemia burst in upon the festivities.   There was no danger of any similar visitation on the part of Miss Westropp's respectable father.   Lord Drumshaughlin never ruled his family, except in the sense in which a volcano might be said to rule the surrounding country by an occasional terrifying explosion.   At present the volcano was occupied wholly with its selfish internal affairs—such dark flaming tumult of feelings as many an elderly epicurean in a club reading-room bears about with him, in whom habits of self-indulgence and pecuniary embarrassments make a pretty Gehenna between them.   But Miss Deborah Harman felt herself coerced, as a person more or less *in loco parentis* to a friendless girl, as well as in the imperative interest of scandalised society, to acquaint Lady Drumshaughlin with the facts of the Gougaun Barra expedition, in a despatch, every letter of which was formed with a point like a needle, and underlined like a deep bass musical score.

' When the Hon. Miss Westropp's strange acquaintances have become the subject of *police-barrack gossip*, my dear Lady Drumshaughlin,' she wrote, ' it would be a crime against a family which has always held its head high in the county, as well as a *cruelty* to the young lady herself, who is *animated by the very best principles*, but whose impulsive good nature and inexperience expose her to the influence of *designing persons*, if I were to hesitate any longer to place you in possession of certain recent and *most painful* proceedings at Drumshaughlin, lest they should have to reach your ears when too late in some less friendly and *more distressing* manner.   You can imagine, my dear Lady Drumshaughlin, with what grief and horror my brother has learned on the very highest official authority that an American Fenian (a man of the lowest and *most vulgar* manners), who is engaged in organising a conspiracy for the overthrow of the authority of *our Most Gracious Sovereign* and the massacre of the Protestant population, is actually received and lodged in Drumshaughlin Castle ; where he is the *inseparable companion* of young Mr. Westropp, and is allowed to smoke the vilest cigars in the yellow drawing-room and expectorates upon the carpet.' Nor was this the worst which affrighted maiden modesty had to report of its erring sister at the Castle. The affection which Miss Harman had ' always borne your *sweet child* no less than my duty to that society to which we both belong, not to speak of interests *still more sacred* which a Christian mother will not need to be reminded of '—in short compelled her, in deep anguish and italics, to pass from the minor delinquencies of the yellow drawing-room to the *scandalum magnatum* of the pilgrimage to Gougaun Barra— a place notorious for a holy well dedicated to one of *those dreadful local saints*, who is worshipped once a year at a disgraceful orgie called a " pattern " by a peasantry steeped in *incredible superstition and whiskey*. I myself utterly reject the inferences, which, nevertheless, I am aware some excellent *and truly evangelical souls* have been led to deduce from the fact that Miss Westropp's principal associate in this unhappy affair at Gougaun Barra is *the Romish priest* of this place—an artful man who, under *the disguise of white hairs and seeming simplicity* of life, doth most grievously obstruct the work of the Gospel in this darkened portion of God's vineyard. I shrink from lacerating *a mother's heart* by attaching the slightest credence to rumours that Priest Sullivan has been suffered to convert *your ladyship's own boudoir* into an oratory for the purposes of Romish idolatry (the blue and silver hangings, it would seem, are to be spared, *these being the colours of the Virgin*). Such rumours are, of course, absurd, and only show what people will say when their faith *and their lives* are trembling in the balance. And, after all, my dear Lady Drumshaughlin, what can the best friends of the family find it in our hearts to reply when people point to the fact that not only does Miss Westropp patronise *Romish superstition* by a pilgrimage to a holy well under the guidance of the local priest, but entertains afterwards *with partridge and champagne* an assemblage of extraordinary persons, of whom it will be sufficient for me to say the odious American was not the most undesirable companion for a young lady of your daughter's age and rank ? God forbid that I should convey the impression that persons like the miller's son and daughter may *not be quite respectable* people in their way (the daughter, you may remember, is the young person for whom Mr. Harry conceived *that ridiculous attachment*). But you can imagine the humiliation, the agony,

with which those who would be Miss Westropp's safest and most
natural friends—those of her own station and traditions—see her
gliding into the companionship of young men (and young women)
who ought to be inside their father's counters, dubious French
adventurers, and discharged soldiers—persons whose *ill-breeding*
may easily lead them to misconceive *the too confiding* character of
one so much above them, for in these days the humblest origin is
no guarantee against *the most outrageous pretensions.* Unreflecting
persons may say—Oh, but the rector, Mr. Motherwell, and his
wife actively participated in these painful occurrences. So they
did. It was *an additional affront* to decent Protestant feeling.
We are no longer surprised, however we may be grieved, by *the
eccentricities* of a clergyman whose spirituality has withered under
the upas tree of grossly material *domestic* influences—who makes
a profane jest of the motives of his more-zealous co-labourers in
the field of Protestant truth, and openly attacks the dear Established Church from which he derives six hundred pounds a year
with the parsonage house and *an excellent fruit garden* (the peaches
were really famous until Mr. Motherwell's *dreadful children* were
sufficiently grown to put their father's doctrine of spoliation into
practice). The young ladies of the Neville family deserve more
commiseration in the circumstances which force them into associations which must be repugnant to their tastes and to the proper
pride of the Winspurleighs. Their brother is *a fool* (I write with
the more freedom, my dear Lady Drumshaughlin, because it is
notorious that Miss Westropp *constantly snubs him*), though I
cannot believe the prevalent rumour that there have been words between him and the young French student, in which the latter had
the insolence to mix up your daughter's name—(the insolence of
those French creatures is sometimes beyond belief). Mr. Neville
himself is *a Radical,* who will not stop at subjecting his dear girls
to any humiliation for the sake of his tedious theories and popularity-hunting—he has already incited *the ignorant peasantry* to
put *the most audacious price on fish* and poultry by some trash he
has published in a vile local print about plans for developing the
resources of Glengariff and nonsense of that kind. My dear Lady
Drumshaughlin, I really think *the police* ought to protect us from
vulgar and inquisitive Englishmen as well as from the bowie-
knife of that *monster* at the Castle. If they are going to suspend
the Habeas Corpus Act, I do wish Lord Drumshaughlin would get
them to insert a provision for stopping the tourists' long car. The *low
people* who use that mode of conveyance demoralise an unsophisti-
cated population *with silver coins,* and put into their heads *the most
pernicious* Radical claptrap as to their own misery and the tyranny
of their superiors. My brother is beginning to notice that men pass

him on the road now sometimes *without even raising their hands to their hats!* It is all very well for Mr. Neville to amuse himself (as *he does not shoot or yacht*) by scattering sixpenny bits and keeping the company of *traitors and conspirators.* He will be safe in his warm English home when some dark night next winter *his present friends* will be *blackening their faces* for the work of murdering helpless women in their beds—if that should be, indeed, *the worst* that is reserved for us. But to you, my dear Lady Drumshaughlin, whose castle is being made the headquarters of traitors—whose *drawing-room carpet* is soiled with their disgusting smoking habits—whose foolish son is already *entangled* in the *snares* of *an impudent village hussy*—whose daughter's reputation may be at this hour, for aught I know, the sport of *Yankee assassins* and *Popish priests* in their *midnight cabals'*— and so on, and so on, until Miss Harman the elder, to whom her sister declaimed the letter in one of those gushes of confidence which sisters discussing the foibles of their friend over their bed-room fire at bed-time find so irresistible, called out, 'My dear Deb, now that you have relieved your feelings by writing it, put it into the fire and come to bed.'

'Don't be provoking, dear,' said the authoress, with some asperity.

'Are you mad? You don't mean to say you are really going to call in Lady Drum to lecture Mabel on morals and Popery?'

'I mean to say that there are scandals going on here, under our eyes, which it would be sinful to conceal fron that girl's mother——'

'Who from the riches of her own early experience——'

'Will be all the better able to appreciate the danger, my dear,' said Miss Deborah, with that sort of 'smile which is noticeable chiefly for a show of teeth.

'She may take offence. She is suspected of being a Romanist herself. All these yellow-skinned foreign women are. They don't like being preached at. She may find an agent whose sister will not think she has a mission to count the family's champagne bottles and inquire what becomes of the cold partridges. She may send Hans packing, and where should we, patterns of perfection, be then?'

'Sister, it is evident that our brother has not seen fit to take you into his confidence as to the relations between the Drumshaughlins and their agent,' with a still broader display of smiling teeth. 'The people are paupers, dear. I don't know that the time may not have come for curing some people of their airs——'

'I really don't know what harm Mabel does, Deborah. She can't help being so good-looking, can she?'

'Sister !'

'Well, but after all, why shouldn't she choose her guests without consulting us ? Goodness knows she might easily find livelier company than your Dorcas Society, Deb. May Neville tells me the American Captain is great fun -- says such droll things, and wants to teach her ladies' base-ball as 'tis played in Saratoga. You know you were a little gone about that young French fellow yourself, Deb—you needn't blush, child—girls will be girls.'

'Sister ! this vulgurity is unpardonable. It seems to be epidemic since that shameless girl set the fashion,' cried Miss Deborah, flinging down the pen wrathfully, and pacing the room in an austere fury. 'Your language could not be coarser if you had been of the Gougaun Barra party yourself ——'

'I was not asked, dear—worse luck mine,' said Frank Harman, leisurely tying an article of headdress which, in that privileged apartment and at that confidential hour, shall be sacred from more particular description.

Miss Deborah stopped and looked at her with a flash of scorn in her eyes that seemed to have scorched up the tears that had begun to glitter there.

'Property, society, religion, our very lives are in danger,' she almost screamed ; 'and you talk like that of the miscreants who, perhaps, this very night may burst into this chamber to murder us. You are prepared to take sides against your own sister with the wicked, headstrong girl who takes these odious traitors to her bosom.'

'That "sweet child" of whom you write so handsomely to Lady Drum ? Fiddlesticks ! Deborah, you know very well the police are there to look after treason and nonsense of that kind. The question is, are we to make life in this dull place unbearable because Mabel Westropp has taken to slumming and democracy, and that kind of thing ? Is she to form one party in the parish and we another ? Are we to wile people away from her picnics and little dinners to slices of pound-cake in this dismal house, and entertain them with Hans's symphonies and Mrs. Harman's cough ? I tell you she'd beat us out of the field in a week's campaign. I don't know a companionable young man worth his salt. who would not follow her to the Holy Well, or to the Pope's toe, for that matter, if she lifted her little finger. Thanks, I don't want to be left to the company of young Mr. Primshanks, your prodigy of the Church Missions' work, who likes to sing hymns because he can do nothing in the world that is more amusing.'

'I do believe you have set your heart on learning baseball from the American Captain, Frances,' said Miss Deborah fiercely.

'I suppose an American Captain may be as good as a naval Captain, dear—and, perhaps, more faithful.'

'Insolent!' cried the younger sister, flinging her head back out of the firelight with something like a snort of pain. She still opened with as much rage as more submissive maidens in her case would open with deep-drawn sighs the secret drawer of her mother's little ebony work-box, where she preserved certain wretched yellow scrawls on the ship's note-paper of her Majesty's sloop of war *Inconstant*—preserved them, goodness knows why, for the commander of the *Inconstant* was now the father of a blooming flotilla of young Inconstants, and one of the trashy ancient manuscripts bore in a corner the endorsement ' No case,' with the initials of the eminent counsel to whom they had been submitted for advice on proofs in a certain contemplated action for damages.

' Come, come, Deb ; nobody ever minds what I say, child. I have had my own Captains of the *Inconstant*—half-a-dozen of them, the unfeeling brutes—and I never dreamt of paying them the compliment of breaking my heart about the best of them,' said Frank Harman, putting her arm not ungracefully around her sister's neck, with a kiss. ' You and I must not quarrel, dear. We can't afford to make Stone Hall a less cheerful place of residence than it is,' she said with a slight shudder.

' Why, sister, how—how old you look in that—in that—' said the other, suddenly starting back with a look of pain—I don't think there was any look of triumph there.

' Yes, dear, I look, and am, an old campaigner—as old as Catholic Emancipation. I have no more chance of a husband than of bringing back the Penal Laws,' said the elder pleasantly, scanning Miss Deborah's fresher face with a certain motherly fondness, ' but I declare *you* are quite a girl yet, Debby. If you would only give up those tedious tracts and things, I declare I don't see why—— Well, well, you shall post your letter to Lady Drum, and you must let me keep that wicked Mabel on my hands. You know Hans has a maxim that it is less important to stand well with your friends than with your enemies. Put out the light, dear. I don't want to have enemies ; but, if you do, I dare say that letter will bring you some pretty entertainment ; and in the meantime I'll run over to-morrow to tell Mabel that some strait-laced persons have been writing to her mother, and to get an introduction to her American Captain.'

' Sister, I am afraid you are very worldly,' murmured Miss Deborah, softly, as she blew out the light.

Little did the guilty company at the Holy Well anticipate what an all-searching eye was upon their evil doings. Miss

Westropp saw one thing clear enough—that the misery of Irish society was that its elements obstinately declined to fuse. The two races were two excellent metals brayed together for ages in the same crucible, and still there is no more sign of their running into combination than if they had been cold iron and cold stone. Was she the first childish philosopher who dreamed of seeing yellow gold gleaming at the bottom of the melting-pot some morning under the spell of some yet to be discovered alchemy of the heart? And how was she to know that those innocent-looking precipitates she was bringing together would cause such a terrific blow-up in her little laboratory? For the moment her pretty sorcery worked famously. Artful Old Jesuit and recreant Parson—the young Guardsman with the subtle perfume of the Chrysanthemum Club, and Ken Rohan with the dust of his meal bags—the miller's little shrinking wild rose, and the rich blossoms from the Winspurleigh conservatories—iron Englishman, mercurial Frenchman, and fuliginous American, made as harmonious a picture under her smile as the gay kiss of the sun made of the old saint's crumbling cloister and Mr. Hans Harman's shooting box—of the fresh green islet in the lake and the darkling clefts in which the eagles nested. The Artful Old Jesuit was master of all the guileless lore of the hermitage—where the saint's knees had left their print in the rock—where the eagles from Mullagh used to hide his dinner—where his penitential tears one morning suddenly gathered into a holy well, whose limpid waters were fed ever since, no man knew whence—perhaps by angels in the night-time—who knew?

'You know we don't want the Rector to believe all these things,' said Father Phil, smilingly.

'He'd better not,' said Mrs. Motherwell, tapping her husband pleasantly with an ancient sunshade of shot silk.

'Upon my word, Jane, it puts me to the pin of my collar to believe all I've got to believe as an honest Protestant Clerk without adding St. Finn Barr's eagles to the Thirty-nine Articles,' said the Rector. 'At the same time I think the angels are just as likely to come down and fill the peasants' Holy Well as they are to fill the philosophers' inkbottles. Our saucy century might do worse than cool its brows by a dip in the Holy Wells.'

'Do you think the angels do really sometimes come here still, sir?' seriously asked Mabel, gently laying a hand on the old priest's arm.

'If she asked me I should say they do—decidedly,' blurted out the Rector in an enthusiastic aside, which brought him another rap from the shot-silk sunshade.

Father Phil's faded old eyes filled with wondrous merry kindness as they rested on the bright face so earnestly upheld to his. 'How should I know, my dear young lady? It would take wiser heads than mine to tell. Maybe the angels are sometimes nearer to us than we think.'

'I wonder are they all as kind to silly girls as you are, sir—it was so good of you to come to-day!' she murmured fervently, her tiny gloved hand still resting on the old man's rusty, shrunken sleeve, where they stood on the lonely islet in the lake amidst the storm-scourged hills. 'Heigho! a girl can never be a saint, nor anything else that is great or brave. Fancy one of us women shivering alone here of a winter's night, like St. Finn Barr, when all these black hills were moaning under the storms and lightning! What a coward I should be!'

'I don't see any harm in seeing the place by daylight, with a fresh young face or two round, and a little luncheon,' said Mrs. Motherwell. 'We're not all made for saints. Somebody must be left to look after the hampers. Don't you think it is about time to be unpacking them, dear?'

'What should I ever have done without you, my dear Mrs. Motherwell?' cried Mabel, imprinting a sunny little kiss on that lady's pleasant matronly cheek.

'Nonsense, child!' The Rector's wife *did* feel that she had risked something for her young friend in braving Miss Deborah Harman's celestial vengeance to render this little Gougaun Barra party possible. As a matter of fact that exemplary young lady organised a demonstration of the Church Mission people and dependents at Stone Hall to bustle out of church the following Sunday when the Rector was beginning his sermon, and stopped a week's wages from the old man at the lodge gate because the withered little lady, his wife, did not gather up her old legs fast enough to join in the manifestation. Mrs. Motherwell's bosom *did* gently swell with the dignity of being the most important member of the party—the oxygen of the Gougaun Barra air for the occasion—the salt which lent to the contents of the hampers their irreproachable matronly savour. 'Nonsense, child! what would you do without me? Rather tell me what Tom, and Bob, and Emma, and that awful little urchin Wopsy, are doing without me at the Rectory! Falling into the fire, or stealing the jam, or skating down the banisters as usual, I'll be bound.'

'Just as sensibly employed as if they were a synod of scientists. Jane, thou carnally-minded woman, get thee to the hampers,' sang out the Rector.

'That,' said Ken Rohan to a pretty semicircle of the Neville girls, 'that is the oldest stone monastery in Western Europe.'

'What! these funny little things!' observed N. G. No. 1,

R

poking her parasol at the cramped, lichen-eaten stone niches on whose hard pillows St. Finn Barr's monks expiated the sins of their days of nature. 'How uncomfortable! Just think how tiny they would look in the middle of that awful place we saw in Rome. Don't you remember that night by moonlight, Carrie? It was all so vast, and I think they told us it was ever so much older than this.'

'The Coliseum is not the same thing, dear,' said N. G. No. 2, severely.

'No, of course, it is not the same thing,' assented No. 1, cheerfully.

'The men who built these cells sang matins in Gougaun Barra when Charlemagne was a little barbarian. Young King Alfred came here to them to learn his alphabet,' said the young miller rudely. In his present heart-sore condition he exulted in showing what mindless gadding fireflies women were—all except his mother and little sister Katie. He had joined this party of pleasure specially to show how lightly their stings and arrows glanced off his armour. He rejoiced that Miss Neville the First mistook the Coliseum for a Christian monastery. Would Miss Neville the Second be able to tell who her King Arthur was?

'So King Arthur came here to school? Well, I hope they taught him not to be too hard upon ignorant strangers,' said No. 2, placidly stooping to secure a maidenhair fern. If the truth must be told, the young ladies were not at all preoccupied with the young man's pallid looks or the circles round his eyes. They accepted his companionship with the same easy courtesy with which they might reply to the person sitting next them at an Interlaken table d'hôte if he inquired whether they had yet been to Lauterbrunnen, and had they heard old Mère de Glace, as they called her, who lived in ice at Meiringen, twangling her unearthly dulcimer?

'Strangers have generally fared better at our hands than we at theirs,' retorted young Rohan, sullenly.

'So I have heard papa say. I am so sorry,' said Miss Neville the Second, in the same tranquil way. Rudeness of speech she presumed to be, like the accent, a rustic peculiarity.

'Monks are delightful creatures. Don't you remember that dear, droll little man, who used to take us little things for a ride on old Beppo, that great St. Bernard of his?' said Miss Neville the younger, who had been searching all the memories of her life for something pleasant to say. 'But don't you think the Italians rather spoil their pictures—their Assumptions and things—by putting so very many monks in heaven? You know the habit is not one that you would care to be looking at always, is it?'

'The monk's habit is the grandest human dress ever invented;

what ages of hussars' jackets and Paris fashions it has seen come
and go! And it comes in picturesquely anywhere—in a picture,
on the stage, in a cloister, at a coronation, on a battle-field, in
a Day of Judgment,' cried Ken Rohan, who was always ready
to sail off into 'clouds of divine obscurity' with his mystics of
the Rhine, whenever the divinities of this nether world were not
behaving satisfactorily. 'What is there in the life of soldier,
poet, politician, man of pleasure, or man of science, to compare
with the life of St. Finn Barr here among his mountains? What
has your greatest general done but set women and children crying?
Make a man prime minister to-day, and he'll be fuming over
what the papers are saying of his speech to-morrow morning.
The poet has a nagging wife, perhaps—or, if not, nags at his
daughter on his own account—Milton did it, with all the lustrous
shapes of Paradise floating round him. Science! there are a
million millions of starry worlds beckoning down at us every
night, and Goldschmidt or Chacornac thinks it glory enough for
the watchings of a lifetime if he discovers half a dozen trumpery
little asteroids, and if he does not get abused as a·thief in the
astronomical journals. Pleasure!—which produces no classic,
except the cookery book, and pays its worshippers with yawns
and headaches! Immortality! Your human great ones enjoy
it just as much as they enjoy silver breast-plates on their coffins.
And, indeed, the best thing about the human chatter which we
call immortality is that the immortals are not alive to listen to
it. Do you suppose Shakespeare would accept immortality if it
condemned him to listen to bores droning into his ear for all
eternity how very clever that Hamlet, Prince of Denmark is?
But our brave St. Finn Barr—how different an immortality his
is! even as the world goes. People say—I sometimes believe
myself—he walks these hills to this hour; and if he does it is
not to see his name pecked at by sour-lipped critics, but to find
a loving shrine glowing for him in every peasant's cabin, in
women's hearts, and children's evening prayers. Nay, what a
mortal life he lived!—what battles with the most puissant foe
that ever encountered human valour! What shocks with the
legions of the Lost Archangel, and what triumphs! Did he
speak? He had the Court of Heaven for an audience. Was he
dreamy? He had the sun to paint the hills for him, the waterfalls to be his sparkling silver, the sunsets to give him gold and
gems, the wild birds to chirp his operas, the wailing winds and
the thunder crashes to illustrate his sombre midnight imaginings.
He could not flourish his measuring-tape at the bright stars, nor
blink at them through an eye-glass, forsooth—no, but he could
mount among the stars; he could mount universe upon universe

beyond them. The heavens were open to him as a pleasure-gar
den, angels to spread his feasts, and an endless eternity to enjoy
them.'

'I should say it must have been rather lonesome sometimes,'
said N. G. No. 2 ; ' and don't you think a little selfish ?'

Ken started and coloured. His fit had carried him clean away.
He had forgotten the three bright, healthy girls beside him as
utterly as St. Finn Barr could have forgotten the trammels of
the flesh in one of his ecstasies. The thought crossed him (the
sinner, not the saint) that these rosy-cheeked damsels in their
graceful silver grey frocks and broad straw hats would fill a
prettier corner of a picture than the strapping monks from Fra
Angelico's convent. But St. Finn Barr's deep burning eyes and
cavernous cheeks instantly rose up to him as a type of man—
great man, and as the type of woman—soft, waxen, infantile, ineffectual woman, a certain peach-blossom baby face in a frame-
work of pale yellow hair—so fair, but so unapprehensive, so
faithless, so inane; and he bit his lip to think he could have
been even for a moment shaken in his creed that the poor Miss
Nevilles, with all their innocent bloom and finery, were an impertinence in this solemn place.

'Selfish ? No, I don't think so,' he said dogmatically. ' A
noble life does a good deal to ennoble others, however hidden it
may be. Do you see the little pool in front of us ? That is the
source of the River Lee. Do you see what a poor little trickling
thing it looks stumbling and coaxing its way among those savage
rocks ? That brook becomes a river, and fertilises many a mile
of cornfields, and flows out of Cork Harbour with argosies on its
broad bosom. St. Finn Barr's influence was like his own River
Lee. It began unknown among the clouds and in the mountains ;
the wee mountain streamlet forced its brave way through a rocky
wilderness as obstinate as the heart of this nineteenth century ;
and from that day to this it blesses the fields and the cities of
men on its bright way to the eternal ocean.'

' It must be very nice to be a great river—I mean a great man,
and do—all sorts of fine things,' said the youngest Miss Neville,
a little absently ; then with a joyous start, 'I see Mabel sig-
nailing She wants us to come to her. It must be luncheon.'

Katie Rohan did not make a brilliant figure in society. The
only reason why she had come at all was that she had not the
courage to deny a wish which so dazzling a creature as Miss
Westropp preferred to her. The only genuine pleasure she experienced was the sense of having her brother's strong arm behind
her. She hung about him timidly, and, when Miss Westropp
handed him over to the Neville girls, she thought of asking

desperately if she might go with him. When she became aware that Harry Westropp's eyes were fixed on her, and that young gentleman, to relieve the situation, asked her wouldn't she like a ride on a mountain pony, she felt a sudden struggling about the eyelids, and would have given worlds to find some place where she might cry. How she wondered—how she shuddered at the boldness of her high-spirited friend, Georgey O'Meagher, who declared that a pony ride was the very thing, and before many minutes was dashing gaily around the margin of the lake on a shaggy little mountain brute, running a handicap with the captain of the Life Guards Grey mounted on a donkey! Nor did our poor Katie feel very much more at home when Miss Westropp, seeing her embarrassment, slipped her own arm in hers, and drew her along like a little sister. Somehow, of all the strangers, she gravitated most towards Mrs. Motherwell; and when, there being question of unlimbering the hampers, Katie petitioned softly— 'May I help you, Mrs. Motherwell?' and the Rector's wife, looking kindly down upon the blushing, frightened face, said, 'Indeed, you may, child, and you must,' the girl tripped away among the plates, and pies, and tablecloths as though the only possible bit of happiness in connection with these proceedings had befallen her. The young Guardsman, for his part, submitted with great solemnity to the inglorious contest to which he was challenged, enjoyed immensely Georgey O'Meagher's glowing cheeks and silvery laughter as she turned round with flying hat-strings to wave him a taunting adieu, and laboured conscientiously to arouse some spark of ambition in his own unemotional steed; but he soon tired of inciting a donkey to practise standing on his head—tired even somewhat of Miss Georgey's exuberant spirits.

Young Neville had reasons of his own for being out of sorts; the principal one, I am ashamed to say, being that Jack Harold's rattling tongue had been livelier and saucier than ever on the road from Glengariff, and that Miss Westropp's eyes had sparkled and laughed all the time. No man could have been less vain than he of the Winspurleigh quarterings, much less of the Neville bank account; but the Crusader blood would sometimes stir in him. Quite right that Mabel should sun these good people with her beams; the proper business of suns and other beauteous bodies in high stations was to overleap society's petty park-walls and fling their kindly radiance far and wide; but wasn't it overdoing the thing for Mabel to behave as if her bright orbs were not bestowing but receiving brilliancy from a pert French tallow candle? Nor was his dissatisfaction with Mabel the less because he felt still more dissatisfied with himself for being dissatisfied.

He found himself drifting gloomily about the edge of the lake with Harry, who sought an outlet for his own bruised feelings by telling his friend of a notable pike which inhabited the lake, and detailing the various cunning traps of spoon-bait, sprat-bait, worms, and nightlines he had laid in vain for the creature's destruction; when he was amazed to hear Neville grind out under his moustache, ' I should like to wring his neck——'

' What a funny way of killing pike ! But you'd first have to catch him,' said Harry, who had not an exalted idea of the sportsmanly capacities of the English nation.

Jack Harold, in the meantime, was at the highest top sparkle of self-contentment, which he was too apt (as who is not ?) to take for granted means general contentment as well. He rippled over with mocking little stories upon all sorts of droll topics, from imaginary saints' sweethearts to Mr. Hans Harman's secret attachment to the pianoforte ; he won Mrs. Motherwell's heart by fishing up her cameo brooch from the bottom of the waggonette, when everybody else was in despair of recovering that priceless family heirloom ; he set the champagne bottles standing up to their necks in an ice-cool mountain spring ; and gave profound instructions as to the seasoning of the mayonnaise ; he displayed a rarer gift than any of these, by giving up metal more attractive in order to exchange ideas with Mr. Neville on the geological features of Gougaun Barra. What Mr. Neville saw in the lonely glen was not the shining footprints of the saint, but the track of a glacier scored as plain as print upon the naked mountain-sides and in the great boulders which lay scattered like capital letters in the geological narrative. Mr. Neville was not a sanguine man, except in the iron market and in the science of geology. Those were firm ground. His feet could not have stumbled less there if he had had an Œcumenical Council to guide them. But all beyond was more or less empirical and unsure. He envied sanguine men their faiths and enthusiasms—sometimes bitterly envied them— but he could not see with their eyes, and he was too bluntly veracious a man to pretend he could. What he saw were clouds, doubts, qualifications, a sad tangle of illusions and possibilities, a woful deal to be said on both sides. An humble soul withal, he did penance for his own scepticism about most of the things of which men raved by a haunting suspicion that it was his own defect of sensibility, his own bareness of imagination, that was at fault. Fancy, then, his relief to find a youth of Jack Harold's abounding belief in all the lighter and brighter creeds of life, doing homage to his own homely geological gods as of a sublimer order than all the dreams of fancy and all the pictured drama of history !

' My faith ! What is the Bodleian Library in face of your

Bibliothèque, of which the volumes are mountains, and the shelves extend themselves to the centre of the earth? What is the history of the historians? In time, a wink of eye; in matter, the Thousand and One Nights reduced to legal affidavit, and attested by a thousand and one perjuries. The world's hair has dressed itself—has, what you call it? stood on end—one, two, three thousand years in horror of that monster of a Minotaur—half-bull, half-man—which our brave Theseus slew us. Bah! The monster was a simple father of family of the most respectable; a certain General Taurus, whose King named himself Minos, and our brave Theseus amused himself by inventing a *conte drolatique* for that Grand Bébé, posterity. History sings alleluiahs of the most piercing over the tomb of Curtius, who jumped his horse into the gulf and saved Rome. What hecatombs, what myriads of schoolboy victims have smoked upon the altars of that devil of a Curtius! Bah for History! The outraged pantaloons of our schoolboys are avenged. Curtius has gone down like the Bastille. Without doubt he sacrificed his horse like a brave man, but himself!—My faith, when his horse signalised itself by floundering into the mud, Curtius made vain efforts to compel the mad quadruped to return on its steps—after which Curtius abandoned the horse without ceremony, and went home to receive the felicitations of his excellent mother and the garlands of an idiotic posterity.'

'These are singularly interesting circumstances,' observed Joshua Neville.

'These are but a brick from the building—from that triste Asile des Aliénés which pleases itself to be called History—in whose chambers they profess to show you the little generations of men in their little fits of *delirium tremens*. But *your* History!—what epochs upon epochs!—what events! The march of glaciers—the subsidence of continents—the reconstruction of kingdoms that have perished—there are millions of years to the last bone in their living things, to the least twig in their forests! And is all that written by a patriot historian lying for the honour of his flag?—by a critic, perhaps, in a state of indigestion?—by a poor devil of a journalist (who knows?) inventing for his little supper? Parbleu, no! There are your volumes piled æon after æon, stereotyped in imperishable stone, in a language that cannot err, by an author that has no prejudices, no gastric follicles to get deranged, and no eye to the verdict of the Boulevards and the libraries which circulate! I don't wonder, Mr. Neville, that you find there a science which resumes history, poetry, romance, religion. I have lightly dipped into Murchison on the Silurian system, and do I find there less

than the charm of your romancing Herodotus ? For example,
you find the diary of your glacier printed across the rocks in
the Pass of Keim-a-Eigh in plainer characters than Xenophon
records the parasangs traversed by his ridiculous Ten Thousand
—not so ? Without doubt the alluvial deposits of Bantry Bay
open to you a more glorious procession of past ages and races
than the richest page of Thucydides ? hein ?'

When Mr. Neville came to discuss the evidence for the
footprints of his glacier in more detail, he found his lively companion less communicative ; but a man once put in good humour
with his own knowledge seldom objects to. imparting more than
he receives. Jack Harold knew enough about geology, as about
many other things, to be able to throw a certain lambent brightness over what he could not understand ; and Mr. Neville
informed Miss Westropp that they had had a most interesting
chat, and that he found Gougaun Barra charming ; upon which
Mabel shot a glance of gratitude to our young geologist.

'But what on earth has become of our American Captain ? I
thought he was with you,' exclaimed Miss Westropp, in some alarm.

The Rector put his finger to his lips, and pointed to a figure
half concealed by the ruined wall that overhung the Holy Well.
They stole over on tiptoe and looked in. Captain Mike was on his
knees bareheaded under the wild ash tree which shaded the Holy
Well, and whose branches were drooping under the poor tags of
coloured cloth which were hung there by grateful pilgrims. There
was something in the spectacle of the bronzed soldier, kneeling
there under the open sky, his hands clasped, and his great chest
shaken with strong emotion, which caused the lookers-on to hold
their breath, and the men unconsciously to doff their hats. The
soldier rose, his bosom still heaving. He pulled out a large blue
silk handkerchief, and drew it across his eyes ; and then, as if a
sudden thought had struck him, knotted the handkerchief to one
of the boughs of the ash tree among the peasants' humble tributes
of their faith. He knelt down again at the foot of the ash tree
and pulled out his clasp-knife. The lookers-on watched him
with painful intentness. He scooped out carefully with his knife
a tiny green sod at the root of the wild ash, placed it tenderly
in his hat, which he put on his head, and then rose to go. As he
did so, and before they could retreat, his eye caught the guilty
faces of the eaves-droppers. He was not in the least disconcerted.

'So, I guess you people seen the whole show ?' he said, good-
humouredly. 'Wal, it does a man good to make a real stark
blithering moon-calf of hisself once in a life or so, anyway.
There is nothin' in our Re-publican Constooshun agen it.. No,
sir ! 'Tis three-and-twenty year last Lady Day in Harvest since

I paid my rounds before at St. Finn Barr's Well. There were them with me then that are not here now—that never'll be here again. God rest you, little Mauryeen, an' the poor ould father, Jack !'

'Amen,' said Father Phil, reverently. 'He was a decent man !'

'I guess a petrified old Grand Army man's got things to sink Artesian wells in him when he looks back to his boyhood a few, and I just struck water there a moment ago, that's all. Don't you be skeered, Rector, at my hangin' up the han'kecher on that ould bush. When a man sheds a tear or two on bottom principles, over all that's past an' gone, I kind o' think an honest Irish saint will be as glad to get 'em as if they was di'monds the size of a Wall Street speculator's.'

Miss Westropp looked as if she could have kissed Captain Mike's gunpowder-stained yellow cheek.

'And the green sod you cut ?' she whispered softly.

'Oh !' laughed Captain Mike, taking off his hat, and surveying its verdant contents complacently. 'Wal, you see, Missie, I couldn't get the saint's autograph lyin' around nohow, so I thought the next best thing would be a sprig of shamrock that was wathered with his blessin'. I've got an ould mother out yonder in East Thirty-second Street, Worcester, Mass, corner Kalabash Avenue, and won't her ould eyes jest skip when she sees that or'nery lookin' sod of Irish airth ! Guess she'll go prayin' around a darn'd sight holier than if 'twar a block of real estate willed to the family—'twill fit where the real estate won't, in her coffin. An' you go Nap ! she'll bring it along where she's goin' ; and if I don't see them shamrocks shinin' in Heaven yet —wal, 'twill be because even the ould mother's prayers can't smuggle a perditioned old grizzly from the Ninth Massachusetts inside the line.'

Miss Westropp's lions and fatlings lay down together with much content in the summer shade, though only a little child was leading them. The picnic party was going gaily. Mabel would not hear of defiling the sacred isle itself with chicken-bones and wine-corks. It was holy ground. ('And besides, my dear,' remarked Mrs. Motherwell, 'I see Bow-wow making for the Holy Well to perform his ablutions.') The tablecloth was spread on a patch of vivid green lawn sloping down from the shooting-lodge to the verge of the lake. The whole wild scene lay below them enclosed as in a gigantic bowl ; the great brown scarred mountains hemming in the lake on all sides bore some fantastic resemblance to a circle of Titanic monks kneeling around the mystic waters in their rugged brown cowls, their crouching backs scored deep with penances, no sound breaking the eternal stillness but the mysterious whispered litanies of the waterfalls. In the centre of this sombre company gleamed the gem-like islet, whose rich greenery and worn grey ruins the sun seemed to take a special delight in picking out and fondling. The waters immediately around it were also wrought by the sun into a halo of shimmering glory ; but the rest of the lake cowered under the black shadows of the mountains in austere boding depths of gloom, which seemed to have bidden farewell for ever to the sun. The almost intolerable loneliness of the place was relieved by a few ragged yellow sheaves of corn in a reclaimed patch of ground on the sunny shoulder of one of the hills. The old farmer himself, in his patched flannel jacket, standing pensively over his sorry harvest, with his tottering cabin and barefooted urchins for a background, seemed to be pointing the half-gay, half-pathetic moral, that a man need not be one of St. Finn Barr's monks to find life sufficiently full of penitential exercises in Gougaun Barra, and that upon the whole perhaps Mr. Hans Harman was as hard an antagonist for a poor man to wrestle for life with in a dark hour as—more pretentious powers of darkness.

All creeds, races, and castes agree once a day—at dinner-hour. Men may differ as to the form of grace before meat, but all the family of Adam acknowledge a common parentage as to what follows. The keen mountain air, and perhaps a certain platonic recollection of the old monk's bleak penances and meagre larder, diffused a general feeling of present comfort at sight of Mrs. Motherwell assuming the command of the game-pie, and Father Phil carving the ham with an expression of face as cheerily frosted as that decorated joint itself. Even disinterested readers sometimes linger to take in the savour of such toothsome human festivities —to receive one of Mrs. Motherwell's plentiful helpings from the grouse pie ; to see the Rector cut up the partridge, with dashing digressions into the neat's tongue ; to hear the American Captain demanding the pleasure of wine all round, even to the youngest Miss Neville, who had never before seen such a droll man, and nearly spilled her wineglass with laughing ; to behold Katie Rohan trotting up triumphantly with a dish of bursting potatoes smoking hot, which that wonderful Mrs. Motherwell and she had cooked over a fire which these conspirators had set going somehow in the cobwebbed kitchen grate at the Lodge ; to see the great Guardsman nervously escorting dishes of trembling jelly from the hampers and escorting back precarious pyramids of plates ; to hear the clink and the gaiety and prattle —the hundred pretty idiotic tricks and innocent nothings, which on these occasions light up young hearts (and, if the truth were told, may·

hap, old ones too) with more genuine joy than half a dozen Dr.
Johnsons flashing and blazing around Sir Joshua's table. Most
of the business that makes life pleasantest is transacted in exceedingly small coin, luckily for those who are but scantily furnished with Bank of England notes, in wit or in stamped paper.

Of course the American Captain felt obliged under the influence of emotions to which the young Republican heart of Great
America was as susceptible as the more historic but played-out
shrines of European chivalry and romance—emotions which he
hoped were not altogether dead even in the extinct volcano which
once kicked up shines at the head of C company, Ninth
Massachusetts Volunteers—felt coerced by every sentiment of
homage to youth and beauty joined with goodness which he need
not apologise to St. Finn Barr for describing as unsurpassable,
and a sumptuous hospitality which would not discredit the First
Floor Room at Delmonico's—felt coerced, in short, to get on his
legs and propose the health of Miss Westropp in a speech which
would have made her sink into the earth if she had not so thoroughly
enjoyed it from beginning to end.

The Rector, entering into the humour of the moment, took it
upon himself to respond in the name of the young lady, explaining,
with a quizzical look around to see whether Mrs. Motherwell, who
was stowing away the dessert-plates, was out of hearing, that he
had by no means resigned his own interest in youth and beauty,
although circumstances over which he had no control might
possibly render it dangerous for him to proclaim that sentiment
in too high a key at the present moment, whereat good Mrs.
Motherwell smiled and said : ' Fie, Edward ; I heard you ! I'll
tell Miss Deborah !' The Rector concluded by, to his horror,
proposing Father Phil, in glowing and generous terms, which
grew terribly in earnest as he proceeded. The old priest fidgeted
and blushed, and smiled all the while, with exclamations of ' Oh,
dear me !' ' Did you ever hear such a thing ?' ' Listen to that
now !' ' Mrs. Motherwell ! who'd ever have thought he was such
a play-boy !'—and when the Rector wound up the ' three cheers
more' by calling for ' a Protestant one,' which he gave as lustily
as Luther's Latin, Father Phil could be by no means tempted on
his legs, but kept murmuring, in a state of amused indignation—
' I'm sure it was all that rascal Jack's doing.'

Everybody looked happy, Mabel silently noted with joy—even
to Bow-wow, who after invoking saintly assistance at the Holy
Well, steered his withered limbs and his tiny donkey-cart within
respectful hail of the picnic party, and experienced substantial
proof of the efficacy of his pilgrimage, in the shape of a piled
plateful of cold fowl and ham, which Katie Rohan tripped down

to present to him with Mrs. Motherwell's compliments. Presently
that rascal Jack himself was on his feet, to observe that 'there
was one present here amongst them whom it would be a stain on
national hospitality, a libel on national gratitude—why should
he not say it, parbleu?—a blot on the national escutcheon if
they were to separate without honouring;' and he proceeded to
propose Mr. Neville's health as a man, as an Englishman, as a
philanthropist, as a geologist, in language which he considered
highly felicitous, and which he by no means intended to exceed
the limits of good-natured pleasantry proper to such occasions.
The toast was a great success in all quarters except that where
young Neville sat communing with his moustache and looking
excessively sulky.

Mr. Neville himself rose to reply with as much modest diffidence and painful distillation of words as distinguished him on the
few occasions when he ventured to catch Mr. Speaker's eye during
the dinner-hour, when Mr. Speaker's was almost the only eye open
of the half a dozen or so pairs of eyes present. He declared that
he did not at all take the perfervid eulogies of his vivacious
young friend *au sérieux*; but for all that he was frankly obliged
to them all. And then, finding the words flow more readily
when he had not to describe his feelings, the honest gentleman
launched out into a short summary of his own observations, social,
statistical, mineralogical, on the condition of Ireland, with an
earnest promise of his own humble co operation in any efforts for
the amelioration of that beautiful country and its gifted race.
Nothing attested Mr. Neville's real popularity all round better
than the fact that his excellent but slightly dry observations were
received with every demonstration of enthusiasm, Jack's voice and
glass sounding loudest in the chorus. The young Guardsman alone
preserved a gloomy demeanour, and held even darker consultations
with his moustache in reference to the applause than while his
father's eloquence was in progress.

Mrs. Motherwell and her happy little aide-de-camp Katie arrived with tea, which was hailed with great applause, and of which
thereupon Mrs. Motherwell declared that Katie had had the brewing all to herself—a statement which instantly dashed poor
Katie's happiness to the earth, and very nearly dashed the teapot
which she was carrying to the earth also. Nor were her nerves
quieted when Harry Westropp developed a sudden and inordinate
passion for tea-drinking. The poor lad, whose thirst had been
allayed with copious draughts of other liquids during the speech-
making, carried his cup again and again to be filled out of Katie's
teapot, remarking each time 'Never drank such a thing!' 'It's
delicious!' 'It's divine!' until Mabel seized a favourable

moment to snatch the cup out of his hand with a frown, and released poor Katie, who ran in a state of horrible confusion to Mrs. Motherwell's side and snuggled there.

The party broke into groups. The old fellows lighted their cigars (the Rector would not surrender his own trusty and well-beloved meerschaum). They enlisted Katie's services for a supply of hot water and lemons, with an ultimate view to whiskey-punch. The girls had brought their croquet balls and mallets, and Jack Harold was looking up an eligible piece of sward. 'You meant to be insulting just now, did you?' he heard, in a harsh voice at his ear, and looking around saw young Neville black as thunder. 'You wanted to try your damned French jackanape's jokes with my father?'

Harold's cheeks paled slightly before this angry apparition, but he answered in his usual airy way : 'How, my friend? Is it that the wine of Champagne has conquered the Life Guards Grey and avenged Waterloo? Or is it thy insuccess in Miss Georgey's donkey race that has shaded thy young days? The donkey is one of the least considerate of animals.'

'The donkeys are less objectionable animals to me than curs,' hissed Neville furiously. 'I wish you would come aside and speak plain English, confound you.'

Miss Westropp was standing beside them and had overheard the last words, having already noted Reggy Neville's frowning looks. She looked him now steadily in the face with an expression of angry reproach that he shrank under.

'You are engaged, Mr. Neville, as Miss O'Meagher's partner. They are beginning. Mr. Harold has promised to take me to hear the echoes at Mullagh. It is time for us to be off, Mr. Harold. You must make the echoes sing to me.' And to his unutterable joy and amazement Jack Harold marched off with Miss Westropp by his side.

Young Neville stood looking after them as rigid as if he were looking at Medea's head, until a gay, silvery voice carolled in his ear : 'Upon my word, Captain Neville, you are a most valuable partner—when one finds you. Even if you are a big Englishman, you needn't drive a poor Irish girl to hunt the mountain for your highness to beseech you to accept—your mallet.' He turned abruptly and met Georgey O'Meagher's laughing dark eyes.

'Thanks!' he said simply. 'I am a donkey.'

'Goodness gracious!' cried the owner of the dark eyes, opening them wide in wonder and alarm. 'No, indeed, you're not!—you're—you're—oh! there, you're an Englishman!—and I wish they were all as good as you! Come along, and help me to beat your sister,' said this most audacious girl. He came along.

CHAPTER THE TWENTY-THIRD

WHAT THE ECHOES HEARD

THE moment after proposing to walk to Mullagh Miss Westropp repented it. She desired to punish that sulky Reggy, who ought to have known better, and this occurred to her as a sharp and ready form of correction ; but, like most young ladies of her age who will have their way, she did not find her way such a primrose path when she had it. She was not, however, the girl to turn back merely because there were difficulties about going forward. Jack Harold, for his part, was walking in a dream of bliss. He could not feel that his feet were touching the earth. If the beautiful, lightsome creature by his side had suddenly developed wings it would only have seemed the due completion of his experiences. He had fallen wildly, madly in love with a star millions of millions of miles away, and, lo ! the star had stepped down and was at this moment enveloping him in its rapturous ethereal flame. If one's longing for the stars were to be gratified, the first sensation of mixing with the celestial rays would most likely be one of considerable confusion. Jack Harold was a pretty bold aerial navigator ; but his first rush of whirling emotions—surprise, gratitude, and love—rendered him merely stupid and speechless. He replied to Miss Westropp's remarks in a constrained and incoherent way. Having to paint her as no better and no worse than she is, I am afraid it must be hinted that she experienced a glow, possibly ever so faint, of triumph to find this bright child of the people—this hardy young condottiere, with the confident tongue and the glittering sword of fancy—so manifestly subdued by her presence. Like the knowing young person she was, she did her girlish best to rally him out of his embarrassment. There can be no better proof how completely Jack's conflagration of heart had mastered him than that she should have found any necessity for doing so ; but she did.

'I do believe we have missed the path,' she had to say at last, catching a glimpse of the water almost beneath them.

' Delicious ! ' he cried, looking at her fixedly as if to make sure she had not vanished in a train of light.

'Good heavens, stop ! It is a precipice ! ' exclaimed the girl, pulling him back just as he had stepped on a ledge of rock which fell sheer down into the lake.

'Comme ça ! It was a trance. If one could only make it eternal by stepping over ! '

'It would not be fair to pull me over with you, instead of bringing me to Mullagh, would it?'

'No, it would be fairer for you to pitch me over all by myself, for an imbecile,' he exclaimed, now thoroughly awake and brisk. 'But they are quite near, our echoes, you are going to see. It is necessary to descend. There is no danger. But then you are brave as——'

'As a goat. Yes; I was brought up in the same manner,' laughed Mabel, bounding gaily down from one rocky foothold or clump of broom to another into the woody ravine below, and maliciously baffling every plot of her young guide to lend her manual assistance in the descent.

'They are heavenly!' she cried, as she stood with her hands clasped, listening to the ravishing orchestra of silver trumpets that was set pealing in the deep purple heart of Mullagh by Jack Harold's performance on the key-bugle (which he had snatched out of the trembling hands of the old man whose trade it was to entertain rare visitors with the echoes). The story went that the secret musicians were a band of sorcerers from the far East who had once alighted in Gougaun Barra in the guise of angels to bewitch the old monks with their eyes of unholy blue. The stern saint banished them to a prison in the unsunned centre of the mountain, where they have ever since been purging their offence with penitential song, and where of a stormy winter night you can hear the imprisoned damsels loading the night wind with the mysterious wail of the *Miserere*.

'Many's the time I heard it myself, sure enough,' said the old owner of the key-bugle. 'But sure the ould strain must be in 'em yet, afther all their pinances, for troth they're as fond of a twist of a love-song as ever to this day. It seems the saint don't be always listenin', an' whinever they gets his back turned, they'll give you out praise of a purty lady sweeter and readier, I'll warrant you, than ever they chants the Seven Penitential Psalms.'

'I go to try whether the saint is listening now,' said Jack, throwing aside the old bugle and preparing to sing.

'Begor, the saint himself wouldn't say agin praising Miss Mabel. The birds on the bushes do that,' said the old fellow in his soft dulcet patois, with the homage of an ancient cavalier beaming out of every old wrinkle of his worn hungry face.

'Pray don't!' cried Mabel, laying a hand earnestly on Jack's arm. 'Why spoil the delicious calm of the place? Don't be wicked!'

'If I were to be banished into the heart of Mullagh myself for it, I must!' was the reply, and the next instant he broke into the rich cooing notes of a Provençal serenade, in which the quaint conceit was that of a nightingale who grows intoxicated with love for a fair lady, outside whose window he used to sing, and, after pouring out his soul in ecstasies of hopeless passion, beats himself to death against the barred casement of his mistress. The melody was warm with the voluptuous breath of almond-blossoms and violet-fields, and giddy with the wine and sunbrightness and passion of the south; and every verse died away in long low flute-like sighings, as if the overwrought bird would expire of delicious pain. Either the saint was dozing or he relented; for the silvery choir inside the caverns of Mullagh took up the notes as though they found in the love song the passionate compensation for many a dreary night of penance; and as the singer paused after every bar, the tremendous sounding-board of the precipitous heights in front of him caught up the burden, and back in a very ecstasy of ethereal music warbled the notes, dying, rallying, swooning—dying until the very heart of the great mountain seemed to be sick with love. When all was over, truth to tell, the singer was almost as faint as the nightingale. He had never before found the process of singing a French love song so enthralling, so agonising.

Miss Westropp sat silent quite a long while after the last of the echoes had expired in a silvery sigh far away. Music affected her with an intensity of pleasure so keen that it was almost pain. Every nerve and fibre of her body were strings of a mysterious lute which thrilled at the touch of delicate sound-waves, even as the dainty echoes seemed to thrill the adamant nerve-centres of the mountain. There was a soul, as well as a brilliant art, about the song; and the uncommon accompaniment had awakened the still subtler supernatural chords within her. She suddenly started, as if from a trance. 'How clever you are!' she cried fervently.

'Clever! So are ten thousand chorus singers of whom the hire is thirty shillings by the week,' said Jack Harold bitterly. The unusual emotional strain had left him strangely dejected.

'No, no—chorus-singers do not sing like that. And you can do so many things!'

'All as substantial as the echoes and as hopeful as the sighs of that little beast of a rossignol.' They were sitting under a thorn-tree beside a whispering little brook that lived in a grassy dingle at the feet of the great mountain. He was flinging pebbles fretfully into the little chirping brook as if its joy offended him. He was surprised and angered to find himself in an unaccustomed mood of self-deprecation, almost self-hatred.

'Nightingales, too, have their part in life—a very beautiful part,' she said, with a gentle smile. 'The world is happier for its nightingales than for its renowned generals. I should say the nightingales are pretty happy, too.'

'My faith, yes, when they have not the impertinence to fall in love with a lady,' he said, still more petulantly.

'Nonsense, the nightingales know better than that, and you have a hundred gifts beside the nightingale's, and I do want the world to hear something better from you than a foolish serenade.'

'*You* want!' he cried, searching her face with a startled, hungry look; then again dejectedly. 'Do not waste enchantments upon a poor wretch. Why should *you* care ?'

'Because I like you,' she replied, fixing her clear eyes on him. 'Because the world might be so much brighter a place if we would help one another—because I am sure you could do things that would make us all so proud of you—because—oh dear ! because I am a woman and cannot even tell !'

'You are a woman and can do things more marvellous. One word from you means heaven, and another despair.'

'Now, your nightingale is warbling again,' she said with a smile. 'Provençal romancists exaggerate sadly.'

'There is but a moment you have said I might do something better than twitter in the hedges—something high—who knows? —something great. Believe it ?' he cried earnestly. 'I have laughed, danced, chattered, trifled—turned life into a café chantant. Assuredly, but what would you have ? Life in Ireland is one long funeral procession. Hopes, projects, movements, industries, villages, cities are going to the grave all the time. One has only to laugh or die. But I have had my dreams. I have breathed the air of the heights. I have felt the intoxication of the blue ether. What do I say ? I have dared to fly into the very blaze of the sun—I quiver with ecstasy there at this moment—but with terror, also, helas ! lest my poor Dædalus' wings should melt and the rash mortal fall from that furnace of bliss through I know not what worlds of ruin and despair. Do not imagine that this is Provençal poetry. It is not. It means life. I may mean death.· It is Love !'

There was a hectic glow in his face, and a husky undertone in his voice, which alarmed Miss Westropp a little in such a trifler—interested her, too, in this bright climber soaring at such venturesome heights in his pretty French plumage. She smiled to think of poor Reggy Neville spreading his great goose wings for such a flight. 'I suppose I ought to be glad to hear you are in love, but do you know I am not ?' she said. 'It only suggests to me that we have heard the echoes, and that we ought to be going back. It seems as if young people cannot entertain one

another for ten minutes without bringing in that tiresome word
"love," and then steps in Propriety and reads the Riot Act.'

'Is it so tiresome for a goddess to see her worshippers kneel
for mercy?'

'I am not entitled to answer for the goddesses,' she answered
with a smile. 'But if by worship you mean the things young
men think it necessary to say during quadrilles or going down to
supper, I am not surprised to hear that there used to be a good
deal of yawning among the heathen divinities. If the newspapers
could report a single ball as they report the House of Commons it
would be the break-up of Society.'

'You jest. You would not have Love talk like a blue-book?
What would have all the poets, wits, musicians, painters, sculp-
tors, achieved beyond uttering that one little word, Love, in colour,
book, or marble? It has been their masterpiece, their dream,
their heaven. Utter that talismanic word, and the dullest room
becomes an Ali Baba's cave, the fiddlers change into angelic choirs,
remarks about the weather wreathe themselves into sonnets of
Petrarch, going down to supper becomes a promenade amidst the
thymy plots of Paradise. I doubted it once. I even mocked. I
doubt it no more. Assuredly, it is not you who doubt it?'

'I do not doubt that there are always half a dozen persons in
a ball-room who are perfectly content, either with themselves, or
with other people's disappointment. There are fifty weary old
mammas crossed and wretched. There are a thousand tender
souls shut out in the cold street without as much as a gleam of
love. Don't you think the pleasures of your half a dozen Queens
of Love are purchased a little too dearly? I declare I think Love
is the most selfish monopolist, the most cruel and heartless tyrant
in the world. Men make revolutions to upset monarchs. I
really think they would act more sensibly to conspire against those
Queens of Fashion on their insolent thrones. What king exacts
such capricious taxes, or wastes the youth of a country in such silly
wars, or claims such a monopoly of that first necessary of life—
human affection?'

'And when you had your Marie Antoinettes' heads in a basket,
what then?' he asked, chafing to find what he mistook for his
own strains of persiflage retorted upon him, but uncertain how
to bring matters back to his now passionate mood. 'Whom will
you give to the Ephesians in place of their Diana? Is there
another word worth naming in the same breath with Love?'

'There is a better word—Kindness. Love is the miser that
hoards up treasures of human kindness that were meant to gladden
the world. Kindness is a beautiful princess, born to bless and
be blest by millions. Love is an ogre that carries her off to his

enchanted castle and devours her bones at an unholy feast of his own. Oh! dear me, there might be so much happiness in the world, and there is so little! There are so many tender hearts hungering and thirsting for affection, and Love flashes by in his gay chariot and bruises them under his wheels!'

'Yes, without doubt, Love is sufficiently cruel,' groaned young Harold, as if he already felt the first crunch of the chariot-wheels, 'and sufficiently blind,' he added bitterly. 'Would you, then, make Love a Department of State, like the Poor Law, *par exemple* ?'

'Well, sir, why should killing be the only virtue which the State undertakes to provide, with *Gazettes* for its glorification and ambulances for its wounds? I am very sure that youth's generous years would be more nobly, even more happily, spent in offices of human kindness than either in the barrack-rooms of armies or in the tinsel courts of Love. Every other form of human affection, friendship, patriotism, religion, adventure, ambition, have inspired great and beneficial deeds for mankind. What has the world to thank Love for but its wars, its follies, its crimes, and its minor poets? Oh! to think what blessings women might have filled the world with, if they had taken half the pains to urge men to great deeds that they took to seduce them into disgrace or folly! What tasks for human happiness Love might have exacted from Hercules, if that wretched woman had not preferred to flatter her vanity by keeping him dangling at her distaff! How many a Samson who might have turned humanity's mills, and won its battles, some vile traitress has driven to pull down temples on his own head and on society's in his madness! What feats of war against poverty, misery, and oppression, women might have commanded in the Ages of Chivalry, if all the troubadours chanted about the power of ladies' eyes was not as false as fairy gold! And what is the fact - the Ages of Chivalry were ages of darkness and bloodshed. They burned poor old wrinkled women as witches, and lived and died under the spell of witches with fair faces, and their dainty Queens of Love could think of nothing better to decorate their cavaliers for than some bloody piece of entertainment in the lists or some tawdry copy of adoring verses to their own charms. Perhaps it was not all the fault of the poor Queens of Love. I suppose they suspected the value of the vows of those Knights of Chivalry as well as of their sonnets, and dared not put their love to the test of any real deed of beneficence or self-denial They knew that the women men raved about were the Helens and the Cleopatras, or at least the Queen Guineveres--women who ought to have been whipped. They never heard of Monica.

They burned Joan of Arc as a witch.   Don Quixote was the only
real Knight of Chivalry, and he shamed his order, not by doing
ridiculous things, but by aiming at anything really good with
anything like sincerity and self-denial.   And so it goes on to
this day, this glittering, false-hearted, cruel court of Love, except
that the jousts are now usually fought with bags of gold in place
of Toledo steel or canzoneros, and men and women talk an unreal language, and exchange perjured vows, or vows that at the
very best consecrate two people to life-long selfishness—and poor,
wistful, suffering, loveless humanity crouches outside the cloth-of-
gold pavilion, with envy and anger in eyes that might be so easily
brightened, and a thousand dark cares eating at hearts that God
formed brimming over with kindly human affections.   Oh, it is
terrible ! it is terrible !'   And the delicate head dropped upon a
delicate pedestal of arm, and a mist of tears rose between her
eyes and the laughing brook.

Was ever lover palpitating with a tale of love in so provoking
a situation ?   For the first time in his life a hardened scoffer had
prostrated himself at the shrine of love with a heart genuinely on
fire, racked with sighs, panting for self-immolation, flaming with
the most praiseworthy emotions—not a wholly uninteresting
object, he humbly conceived, in the sight of God or woman.   What
was his amazement, his mortification, to find the door of the temple
slammed in his face, and to be told by the very divinity herself
that his new faith was a wicked heathen humbug, and that all the
pairs of pretty ones who ever swore by the silver moon or by the
roses of spring, were so many young spendthrift clerks, who had
robbed the bank—so many traitorous conspiracies of two against
human happiness—so many double-barrelled blunderbusses aimed
from behind a hedge at the greatest happiness of the greatest
number ?   If, indeed, he could ever flatter himself that the divinity
was addressing her observations to her lovelorn worshipper at all—
for Mabel fixed her eyes on the gossiping brook as though she had
no other listener.   What ill logicians lovers be !   A moment ago he
was plunged in an abject sense of his own worthlessness.   No
sooner did anyone else seem to be of the same opinion than Master
Jack's self-esteem sprang indignantly to arms.   One of the evil
turns it did him was to convince him that both her heretical
revolt from the creed of Cupid and her fit of abstraction were
simply sallies of coquettish cruelty ; and nobody resents more
virtuously than your chartered trifler any unbecoming levity in
serious matters.   It was quite morosely he said : ' Have you so
many tears for the victims of Love in the middle ages that you
have no pity left for your own ?'

There was that in his tone which startled her like the thrill of a sudden wound. 'My own!' she cried, facing full around, her lips parted, her eyes opening wide, and their blue depths deepening with wonderment. 'My victims!—mine!' she repeated in a voice almost of terror.

'Your victims, yes! Do you doubt that you behold one of them?—But, good God, who would not feel it ecstasy to be your victim? who would not think it heaven to die at your feet—to be stretched on the rack for you?' he exclaimed, drunk with the beauty of those wide wondering eyes. 'If a thunderbolt should come to crush me I must say it—you are my love, my life, my heaven, my hope here and hereafter! Oh, Mabel!' and with the rapturous terror of one stealing fire from heaven he touched the trembling little hand beside him.

Her frightened questioning look was gone. As if an adder had bitten her hand, she started to her feet, her limbs trembling violently, but her face terrible with anger and bitter shame—so terrible that he quailed into the very earth, it seemed to him, under the power of that fragile creature of cowardly pink and white tissue. She seemed to notice his subjugated look; the armed pride of nostrils, lips, and eyes passed away; she looked very faint and tremulous. 'I am afraid, sir, it is no longer possible for me to think that this is a pleasantry,' she said, in a gentle, uncertain tone. 'I have been very stupid, and, I am afraid, very wrong. May I ask you to return with me at once? I need hardly suggest to you not to let my guests suspect anything of this.'

He felt himself being driven down into the bowels of the earth, and yet there was no depth deep enough to hide him, no mountain compassionate enough to cover him. He could not for all the world have articulated that little word 'Mabel' again, nor lay hold of that small hand. Her calmness stunned him like one of those softly-moving silent somethings that descend upon us in a nightmare. I wish for poor Jack's sake he aroused himself from his nightmare in a worthier temper; but he, in fact, awoke to the keen smart of his own injuries. The only relief he could find from the thought of the worlds of bliss that had escaped him was in the cankering thought of his personal grievances.

'I do not comprehend,' he said, doggedly. 'Is it then a crime to love you to madness? Is your name a blasphemy, perhaps, on peasant lips? Is it not permitted even to the heart you break to expire under your eyes? Is it not worth one regard of pity even, this rude heart of a plebeian, which dares to die at your feet?'

'Pray, pray, do not speak like that!' she said, still gentle and like one in pain.

'Why not? you have made me feel it. Is not the despair to

which you dismiss me black enough without contempt?' he cried furiously. 'Would you have stepped aside from my love as if it were a taint, ma foi!—if I had knelt en aristocrate—in the uniform of the Life Guards, par exemple?'

The proud blood flamed into her face again, but she subdued it with something like a sob of pain, and said humbly: 'I dare say I have done something to deserve this. I thought that people might meet, and like, and help one another, and be all the happier for it. There seemed to be so much to be fond of all around, and so little harm in being happy and trying to make others so! I did think we could all have been so kind and sunny here to-day without—without talking of things—O, so sacred, so solemn, so worthy of years upon years of noble and unselfish lives! Forgive me if I dare not answer—if I would give worlds to forget I ever heard—words such as you have uttered to-day, upon a subject on which years of intimate communion, not to speak of an acquaintance such as ours, might have led me to expect reserve. I am myself to blame. I thought young people might laugh in the innocent sun a while without that venomous Love lurking in the grass. I—I did not understand these things. I —I think I understand them now,' she added, with a shudder. 'If my thoughtlessness causes you an hour of wretchedness, believe me you will be avenged by heavy retribution upon me, who will have more vacant and inglorious hours to suffer in. Come, we have delayed such a dreadful time. And see what a storm has been gathering. There goes the thunder. Listen!'

'Naturally. You have blotted the sun out of the sky for me in every case,' he cried, with a countenance as gloomy as the clammy rain-clouds that were creeping down the sides of the Mullagh.

'Come,' she said, 'we must not let a thunder-cloud conquer us in this hard world. You will forgive me and be forgiven, will you not?' and she put out her hand with a smile which might have chased thunder, if Olympus were still swayed by the susceptible Thunderer of old. Large raindrops were falling on her gauzy frock and in her bright hair. Against the lowering background and amidst the thunder-claps her light girlish figure actually shone. Young Harold was seized with an impulse to fling himself on the wet grass and kiss the ground under her feet. He did not do that; but he bent down and kissed, as reverently as if it were an angel's, the little hand he had a few minutes before profaned with a very different touch.

'You are as far from me as the seraphim, C'est fini!' he said quietly. 'My argosy is shipwrecked. My hope is drowned leagues deep. But you have given me the only noble moment of my life in suffering for your sake.'

Without another word he took off his overcoat and wrapped it with almost reverent solicitude around the frail summer drapery which was already cowering under the rough rain-drops. She did not resist at all, but thanked him with a grateful smile, and whispered softly : 'You will see the sun again after this gloom, and you will be as sparkling as the sunshine.' He made no reply. The deadening rain-drifts swishing down the ravine were not more comfortless than the face they beat upon—the thunder-claps now vibrating in heartbreaking *miserere* notes through the mysterious flinty cloisters of Mullagh were not more woful than the echoes in his own heart—as he stalked along in silence by her side.

Mabel's Hy Brasil—the little isle of bliss she was building herself 'midmost the beating of a stormy sea'—had dipped under the waves as suddenly as St. Finn Barr's green sun-gilt isle had disappeared in the shuddering embraces of the mists. Her faith in the resources of her own small head received a rude shake. Her reconstructed social system seemed to have as poor a look-out as the damp-looking party in great coats and wraps whom she found huddled in the kitchen of the shooting-lodge awaiting her. But it is wonderful what courage women will show amidst the wreck of worlds. The Guardsman, who was looking out for her, and whose eyes jealously pounced on the happy over-coat that enveloped her, could not have guessed anything unusual from her face if he had been put to the torture for it (as, indeed, he was). He had taken his stand in the portico with the young men, cloud-compelling vigorously from three blazing cigars and drinking brandy and water from Harry's flask ; and a green school-girl could have read his own face as he stared out into the blinding rain, and fidgeted for some pretext to go out at all events and enjoy a drenching to the skin. 'I should say to get a sound wetting must be the best thing to do in weather like this,' he observed, with a terrific eruption of fiery smoke.

'A fine rattling rainstorm is often as good company on the mountain as a flask,' said Ken Rohan ; 'but,' he added, with a meaning smile, 'it is not often a fellow is in such luck with his rainstorm as that confounded Harold is. I really think it's almost time to organise a search party—Deuce take the fellow ! here they come !'

'You see you wanted to see Ireland, Mr. Neville, and we have managed to let you see Gougaun Barra in tears as well as in its coat of many colours. You won't judge us too harshly—will you ?—when you think how soon the storm and weeping follow the sunshiny laughter in this poor wayward Irish life of ours ?' said Miss Westropp, as she shook the rain out of her sunny hair, while Mrs. Motherwell roused the fire into a furnace.

'My dear young lady, I don't know that I'm not in love with the mists even more than with the splendours,' said Joshua Neville, his grey face bent towards her in a dim quakerly glow of enthusiasm.

'Distinct development of Celtic exaggeration. Falling into lotos-eating habits already,' remarked the Rector.

'Exaggeration! Rector, no man ever runn'd down exaggeration that know'd how to exaggerate himself—don't you b'lieve it,' said the American Captain. 'I'd like to know what Raphael and them boys had their paints for but to exaggerate. I guess them Arabian Nights' Entertainments wor about as tall a thing in the line of exaggeration as you'll find on the market; an' what was the boss observation of the greatest Englishman you've growed since we left you? Why, sir, he said he only wished them Arabian Nights was true. Wal, the next best thing to their being true is not to go buzzin' round wantin' to argue from all the Evangelists whether they are or not, anyhow; an', sir, that's where our national genius comes in. May Hans Harman fly away with the thatch if there's a cabin 'round here where they couldn't light you up the lamps of Bagdad readier than they could pro-duce the common paraffin of commerce. Yes, sir!'

'Fie, Captain MacCarthy. I hope my Prince is not out of your Arabian Nights,' laughed the youngest of the Miss Nevilles, whose fortunes the American Captain had been telling, on the most lavish scale, from their palms after a dark method into which he was initiated by an ancient Indian squaw in the Sioux War (Captain Mike pronounced it 'Soo').

'No, missie; if your Prince ain't an honest article—if your Prince ain't a daisy—let that respectable old Soo female rise up from her grave down McGahan's Gulch way and sneck up the scalp of the pale face now addressing the Convention!' said the Captain. 'As an Amurrican Republican, princes offends my principles; but in justice to the memory of old Roaring Firewater (that was her maiden name, missie), truth compels me to certify that your Prince will turn up on time as punctual as a Presidential 'lection, and as elegantly fixed up as Solomon in all his glory.'

'And if he don't, he ought to, which is the next best thing,' put in the Rector.

'Clear out of this, the whole pack of you good-for-nothing men, if ever we are to get the child's clothes dry,' said Mrs. Motherwell.

They were all comfortably tucked into the waggonettes in snug casemates of umbrellas, furs, rugs, and friezes—listening to the rain as a philosophic rifleman, safe in his sheltered pit, might to the whistling of the bullets—when a wild figure started out of the mist with frantic shouts to the drivers to stop. 'It's a sick-call,' said Father Phil, indulging in a suspiration which sounded like a sigh in reduced circumstances—a sigh that seemed to say : 'I—hope—I—don't—intrude—I—beg—nobody—will—pay—the—smallest—attention—to—*me*.' The poor old man was beginning to feel some guilty glow of comfort in his cosy corner, where Mabel was nestling like a golden fairy under his old green coat. 'Well, Meehul, is it the old woman that's taking it into her head to die again?'

'Shure enough, thin, sir,' said the old messenger, with a certain quizzical gleam on his queer old puckered face. 'But she's going entirely this time.'

'Don't you think, now, she might put it off for a fine evening, Meehul?' asked the priest in a vein of gentle drollery, for the old woman was an ancient client, who resorted to the last offices of religion as regularly as more fashionable old dames do to the Homburg spas.

'Oh, begor, I darn't face home without you, Father Phil. She'd live a purpose to roast the four bones o' me.'

'There won't be much on them four bones of yours worth roasting after this journey, my poor man,' said the priest, surveying the odd gaunt figure in the rain-soaked flannel waistcoat, with shoes like enormous blisters of yellow mud, and a lock of draggled grey hair floating in the wind through a rent in his hat, but a jewel of unconquerable good-humour lurking under his shaggy eyebrows. 'It's my belief that old woman of yours will introduce you and me to the Last Sacraments of the Church before she'll want them herself, Meehul. Well, well, I suppose the old women have as good a right to their little enjoyments as the rest of us,' said Father Phil, extricating himself from his warm shelter-trench, and shaking himself cheerily like a wiry old withered water-dog.

'And you are going in this cutting storm!' cried Mabel, imprisoning his great bare palm with two caressing little hands, while her eyes travelled lovingly from the old priest's mouldy overcoat to the time-worn, broad-brimmed hat, down whose cracks the unmannerly rain was now channelling out watercourses, while the wind blew about the silver-bright scattered hairs underneath. 'If I could only go instead of you——!'

'It's nothing at all—only up the hill a piece, my dear,' said Father Phil gaily. 'An umbrella! my dear child, 'twould not live on the mountain in a storm like that, no more than your pretty sunshade. Send round the carriage for me? Listen to that, Meehul! Nothing less than a carriage road would do you up to the top of Cnocaunacurraghcooish for grandeur! Troth, I'm thinking, Meehul, they'd have evicted you out of that many's the day ago only they'd have to cut a road to get at you. No, no—tell one of the boys of the Learys in the Pass to catch a pony and send him round for me. Meehul and I will take a skirt across the hill. Come, 'tis time for us to be trudging, honest man, if you and I are to escape that roasting.'

'Don't tell me St. Finn Barr don't still walk them hills!' roared the American Captain, as the driver cracked his whip, and the old battered hat and the blowing silver hair disappeared in the blinding raindrifts up the mountain. 'Don't tell me. That's all I want to observe. No, by God—don't! That's all! Missie, be good enough to batter me about the head with that knobstick,' he said suddenly. 'Or mebbe you'd ask the Rector to oblige by crunching my toe with the heel of his boot a few; but it took all the grit in that oath to do justice to the occasion—or'nery able-bodied blasphemy ain't equal to it.'

'Up the hill a piece' was only Father Phil's sketchy way of describing a couple of hours' climbing, groping, and jumping up and around and into the black quagmires, and over the gigantic boulders that compose the bleak hill country which extends from the romantic Pass of Keim-an-Eigh until its brown wastes melt into the soft tincture of the Kerry hills towards Glenflesk. An inhospitable wild at the best, any less infallible guide than Meehul must have lost all trace of his whereabouts in the whirling and all but solid white vapour that swathed them round and round like a winding-sheet, and any less experienced mountaineer than Father Phil must have found a grave in some inky bog-hole or at the bottom of some smooth-faced precipice in endeavouring to follow. The horrors of darkness were beginning to be added to the rest, when their eyes caught the glimmer from Meehul's hut amongst the rocks of Cnocaunacurraghcooish in an eyrie almost as inapproachable as its name.

'O wisha, I declare to the saints above, if she isn't sittin' by the hob with her tay-pot, as grawver as a judge, afther all our dhrowndin and clamper,' cried Meehul, so disgusted with the sight that met his eyes when he lifted the latch that he still stood out under the swirling downpour with his hand on the latch. 'Why, thin, Maurya, 'tis a wondher 'tisnt taking a shaugh of the pipe, you are, or out enjoyin' a mouthful of fresh air, 'tis such an illigant fine evenin' for walkin'.'

'Oh, thin! Oh, thin! I suppose I ought to pass an apology for not bein' dead in the bed before you, you unfeeling ould cawbogue, an' to fling your jokes like a play-boy at one that won't long be a trouble to you,' said a sharp voice from amidst the deep glow of the peat fire ; then more shrilly as the wind and rain came whisking in at the open door and mixed furniture, showers of red sparks, and human figures in a demoniacal dance in the chimney-corner : ' Glory be to them that's on high, will you shut the doore, you angish of a man ? Don't you think you'll be rid of me soon enough without sending in a black hurleycane on my back, or do you want to sind the childhers' supper up the chimley ? '

' There's a good deal of sense in that, Maurya, indeed, I must allow,' said Father Phil, coming forward into the blaze, and directing the stream from his dripping hat into an unobtrusive corner.

' O, wisha, wisha, Father Phil, but you're dhrownded intirely ! ' cried the old woman, now rising with sudden energy and curtseying profoundly, as she tenderly pushed the old priest into her own warm corner beside the blaze. ' Humbly axin' your pardon, your reverence, and sorry I am that I'm not in a dyin' state to receive you this night, afther all your throuble in climbin' up to this misfortunate place. Sure I believe it was the scent of your reverence on the mountain that brought me around ; there's luck and grace wherever you go ; but, see now, what should come into my mind all of a sudden, whin I ought to be thinkin' o' my last end, but that I'd like to get up an' mix a small little grain of tay, with a fresh egg baten down in it ; and shure enough, there it was simmerin' be the fire, whin your reverence condescinded to the ould doore.'

' No harm in life done, Maurya,' said the priest, with the sweetest droll expression. ' Sure, it's no sin to say I'd rather be drinking a cup of tea with an old neighbour any night than administering Extreme Unction to her ; and upon my word, Maurya, I mean to try if there isn't some good in the pot, like yourself, this chilly night, if you have no objection to share with a benighted traveller.'

' Shure ! O, thin, it's you that's as welcome to it as the angels, if every dhrop in the pot was a jewel out of the Injies ! ' cried the old dame, her faded eyes glowing, a quite beautiful smile on her pinched, cadaverous cheeks, and her limbs bustling about, as though she had just drunk a potion of youth like Dr. Faustus. ' O, but you're perish'd, Father Phil—the coat is wringin'. Here, gorsoon, run out for a brusna of turf—run, I say !—and show his reverence's coat to the fire ! And listen, your reverence,' the poor old creature whispered, with a gracious delicacy that mortal language will never paint, in a voice not meant for the children to hear, 'there's a weeshy dhrop of nourishment there in the bottle that the ould man is ordhered to take when the rheumatic pains is bad, an' might it be pleasing to your reverence to put it to your lips, just to take the cowld o' the mountain out o' you?'

'Indeed, then, I will, Maurya, with a heart and a half—the drop of nourishment, by all means!' said Father Phil, in high good humour. 'Well, well, and how are all the boys and girls?' he cried, seating himself comfortably on the one straw-bottomed chair of the establishment within the ruddy glare of the firelight, and taking in the whole contents of the cabin in one smiling survey; whereupon the young ones, who had respectfully shrunk away from the fire, the girls with the corners of their bibs coquettishly inserted between their red lips, and the boys wearing an air of preternatural solemnity, found it necessary to retreat a little further out of the firelight to conceal the smiling and blushing signals they threw out to the old priest; while the little heifer, which inhabited the far corner of the cabin (in exchange for whose warmth Drimin returned her own quota of animal heat and her own sweet, wholesome breath), seemed to have caught Father Phil's eye with much content, on her own account, and murmured a gentle domestic mwaw! of welcome as the spokesman of her own department of the family.

'Well, thin, indeed, I'd like you'd spake to that foolish boy of mine, Father Phil, and glad I am that you're here to do it,' said Meehul, pointing the finger of public opinion in the shape of his caubeen in the direction of a tall, clean-limbed youth, who had quitted the fire on the priest's entrance, and now stood shyly in an attitude of lounging strength by the wall behind the smaller youngsters.

'O dear! and what has Owen been doing? I hope it wasn't card-playing, now? or, maybe, down at the dance-house?' said Father Phil, directing a not very menacing scrutiny upon the young fellow, who only coloured and turned his head shyly aside a little into the shade.

'Worse than that, your reverence, worse than that—out of his bed, night-walkin', whin it's nothin' but mischief he and the likes of him can be brewin',' said Meehul, in a grave voice. 'I'm towlt it's down in the Glen he do be with the boys, dhrilling, and I don't know what—dhrilling with the Fee-neens, your reverence, and casting bullets in the ould forge beyant—God give 'em sinse, the poor foolish gorsoons!—as if it woren't hard enough for a poor man to knock out the praties for the childher,' he said, with a heavy sigh, 'without bringing the Fee-neens, and maybe the army, down upon our backs!'

'O my goodness, you're a terrible boy!' said Father Phil, in his severest manner. 'Didn't you hear what Monsignor McGrudder said to you the other Sunday! Didn't you hear him telling you that you are flying in the face of God and His Church, and that you're bound to obey the law at the peril of your life and your liberty here, and your eternal damnation hereafter?'

'What have you to say to that?' urged the old farmer, encouraged by the lad's embarrassed silence.

A curious shy smile crept over Owen's handsome face, as he said in a modest undertone : 'Troth, Father Phil, not making your reverence a short answer, it's not everything that Monsignor McGrudder do be saying that people would swear by—we can't be much worse than we are, anyway.'

'O holy Lord!—did you hear that!' cried old Meehul, in horror. 'Now, who's right? That's what comes of your Feeneens and your night-walking and your stravaguing about the forge—he turns upon God's own blessed priest!'

'Yerra, you're always goin' on at that boy!' sharply interposed the old woman, who was now decanting a fragrant blend of the tea and the drop of nourishment into her one cracked teacup for his reverence. 'Sure it's thrue enough for him, since Father McGrudder got that furrin' name of his, he's more like a lord than a soggarth. I don't know what he wants o' them hard names for at all among poor people.'

'Maurya, Maurya, 'tis lucky for you you're not going in for the Last Sacraments to-night,' said the gentle pulpiter, with a face of smiling reproof. 'Well, but you know, Owen, my lad, no young fellow was ever good for either God or country, if he falls into bad ways and neglects his religion. If Monsignor McGrudder refuses you the Sacraments, unless you give up the secret society, what will you do then? You won't defy the wrath of God, boy, will you?'

The lad drew himself up in an attitude of quiet strength that showed that the midnight drillings had not been altogether thrown away upon his supple frame. He blushed again, as if the words did not come to him too easily ; then with a half-sheepish, whole-affectionate smile, he murmured, 'Well, your reverence, if it comes to that—if we never do any worse than strike an honest blow for the poor ould counthry, I don't think, Father Phil, you'll ever see us short yourself.'

'Well, well—maybe not, maybe not—God direct you, boy! God direct you!' cried the old priest, as if he were half inclined to laugh, and still more inclined to sigh. 'After all, Meehul,' he said, turning to the old man, 'after all, we mustn't be too hard on Owen—the poor boys will have enemies enough against them without you and me joining the Peelers.'

And he changed the subject by subjecting the little ones to a Holy Inquisition as to their proficiency in their prayers. This was a subject which gave the little people more confidence to advance out of their blushing retirement; and the old priest soon had one pair of wondering blue eyes looking up at him from his knee, and his hand on the yellow curls that crowned another pair, while the whole family knelt in the flickering turf-glow to repeat the heavenly-human invocation : ' O clement, O loving, O sweet, Virgin Mary ! ' until the tottering cabin, in its weird colouring, looked like a picture after the Florentine school of Cherubim at Home, and the tempest outside, now subsiding into moans, might have been the cry of the demons in outer darkness.

Then Father Phil entertained the young folk with a story of the priest-hunters long ago on the mountains around Gougaun, and how they were foiled by a supernatural mist which St. Finn Barr raised before their eyes, and under whose spell those wicked hunters with their horses stepped into the depths of the lake ; and just as the little romance had arrived at that happy stage, Owen put in his head to say :

' The pony is here, Father Phil, and the storm is gone, and the moon is shinin' splendid, glory be to God ! '

Is it so very horrible if old Meehul's little flock went to their not too unkind bed of heather with a suspicion that St. Finn Barr had more than need be told to do with providing Father Phil with his supply of silver moonlight, as well as with the mist that buried the priest-hunters at the bottom of the lake ?

' Good-night ! ' sang out the old priest, as he sank down placidly on the cushion-like back of his hairy pony. ' Don't be in too great a hurry dying again for the winter, Maurya—though, upon my conscience,' he said to himself, like a prayer, ' that " Hail Holy Queen ! " was as good as a picnic.'

Certainly the folk in the waggonettes were not so merry, as they bored their way through the tunnel of dense gray moisture which overhung the road. The state of the weather luckily offered them a plausible explanation of their dulness ; but it was painfully clear to Mabel that it was the silence which had fallen upon Jack Harold's gay carillon of song and laughter, so incessantly rippling on the way to the picnic, that really made the difference. After the first thrill of unselfish adoration as he kissed his lost divinity's hand, the sense of hopeless loss, of disappointment, chagrin, despair, had rushed upon him in a resistless tide and ' spoiled the sweet world's taste.' The master of many legions of airy quips and graces had allowed his mishap quite to

·pluck him down. It was not comforting to masculine vanity to contrast his face of helpless woe with the brave fight Mabel herself made to divert attention from his large-writ wretchedness, by arousing her own bright spirits and witching voice to double duty. She succeeded so well that Captain Mike—who, even he! had so far yielded to the influence of the hour as to lapse into a gruesome and somewhat prolix ghost-story of a certain blood-boulter'd runaway nigger, who blew out the Confederate camp-fires through his grinning teeth the night before Grant crossed the Rappahannock (which was the more singular that, in a reply to a query of Mr. Neville, it would seem that the spectre appeared in fiery flames, since it was not easy for a ghost of the coloured race to make his own complexion effective in the dark)—gradually rose to such a pitch of high spirits that he insisted on outbawling the storm with the rollicking Federal chorus, ' 'Twas by mistake we lost Bull Run '; after which he treated the storm to the stirring American marching-song, ' Tramp, tramp, tramp, the boys are marching !' which was new at this side of the Atlantic at the time, and has since, by one of the extraordinary freaks of history, remained to give an air to the Irish national anthem. Nobody would have guessed that the bright figure that tripped up the Castle steps was not every whit as lightsome-hearted as she who tripped down in the rosy morning. But, if Miss Deborah Harman could have had a peep at the poor, little, sobbing, wretched, broken thing that flung itself on a certain daintily-valanced bed the moment the sound of the wheels was gone, even that stern brow might have framed a less virtuous frown for the Hon. Miss Westropp's guilty dissipations at Gougaun Barra, and her treasons against her Sovereign and against society, in consideration of the swiftness with which their punishment overtook them. She did not dare to question herself why Jack Harold's declaration of love had so shocked, so almost horrified her. I think she was in dread that pride of blood and a haughty, sensitive self-respect, barely, if at all, distinguishable from self-consciousness and self-will, would have rushed with an answer. What she felt was a vague horror lest all her dreams of beneficence and usefulness might be but the crude follies of an ignorant girl, and might expose her to other misunderstandings— other wounds—other insults, a rebellious voice within her whispered—like that dreadful murmur of her name, and that touching of her hand, which even now caused her to draw up the offended hand with a start, as if it had been bitten. Was she even sure that it was going to end there ? If one of Harry's democratic friends (with the very sincerest motives, too, the unhappy young man ! and with probably horrible pain to himself as the issue) dared to make love to her because she had treated him as an equal in two or three casual rencounters, what dangers, what terrors, in another order, might not be brewing even at this very moment in the library under her own roof, where another of Harry's friends—the American Captain—had just sat himself down to write despatches, probably to some occult band of conspirators, possibly to give the signal for some bloody insurrection! The poor child cowered and moaned with terror before the dreadful apparitions that her own imperious self-indulgence seemed to be calling up around her, and it would have gratified the virtuous zeal of all moralists like Miss Deborah Harman, who desired nothing but to see vice temperately chastised and virtue modestly rewarded, to observe how our poor little reconstructor of society put her helpless little hands to her bursting little head, and in a passion of tears cried out, 'Oh, mother!—why have I not a mother? Oh, father, dear old father!—I am so wretched!—why don't you come?'

CHAPTER THE TWENTY-FOURTH

LITERATURE'S 'FIRST KISS'

'Eh? A cheque! Blood alive, boy, you don't say so!' exclaimed Myles Rohan in the breakfast-room at the Mill, holding the slip of paper between his fingers, as if he were not quite sure it might not come to pieces with rough handling, and lifting it up to the light as if there was bound to be some hallucination to be seen through, and bringing his spectacles to bear on the signature with the stern determination to unmask the forgery. 'Faith, it looks all right, and you'll get real money for it, boy, eh?'

'I should rather think so, sir,' said his son, trying to conceal his delight by displaying the placid air of one who was accustomed to having shovelfuls of gold weighed out to him across bank counters without counting.

'No chance of a mistake—"no funds," or something of that sort, I mean, eh?'

Ken and his mother and sister all looked at the unnatural miller as though he had run down the credit of the Bank of England just when his own son had got charge of the gold-room.

'Begor, that's one of the quarest things I ever saw! Four pounds for a screed of poetry—it was poetry, Ken, wasn't it?' chuckled the miller, regardless of the eyes of wrath that were directed on him. 'Well, now, I never thought them newspapers did more than keep Mat Murrin and the likes of him in grog—and, indeed, 'twould be fitter for him to keep them little brats of

his in boots, by the same token. Faith, Ken, 'twouldn't take
you long to grind out the value of a cart load of flour at that
rate, boy, eh ? I wonder could Danny lend a hand now—he had
a power of poetry in his head always ?'

Ken's proud bearing gave place to an angry scarlet flush ;
but Myles Rohan had not been in good humour so often of late
that any of the kind hearts around the breakfast-table could
afford to resent his little indulgence. Only Katie, who had
been standing with her hand on the young author's shoulders,
prouder even than he, stole over and let her hand play with the
miller's hairs, now sparse and greyish-looking enough, and said,
with a reproachful kiss : 'Oh, pa, dear! how can you ? All the
world is talking of it, and you know you are prouder of Ken this
moment than any of us—you know you are !'

'Of course I am, you little puss. Isn't he a poet, and didn't
I always tell him he never would make a miller ? But he
wouldn't take my advice—he wouldn't take my advice !' said the
miller crustily. He had lately contracted the very unusual
habit of repeating his words, and his head fell a little forward
when he was puzzled.

'Well, well, sir, four pounds isn't too bad for eighty lines of
poetry, is it ?' said Ken, whom Katie's comprehensive compliment
from 'all the world' had reduced to a state of blushing humility
about his performance. 'And I can grind out lots more like that,
and I may be able to lend a hand at the Mill, too, if Danny and
you won't make any crushing observations on my stupidity—if it
was only to shoulder a sack—I'm more than a match for Danny
there, as big as he talks.'

'You're a good boy, Ken,' said the miller, and, as he lifted
his eye, something glittered in the corner of it. 'At least, you'd
be a good boy if you weren't a fool, but I suppose that's the way
with all of ye young fellows—ye wait to get sense till the sense
isn't worth carrying—except to the grave.'

'Well, but honestly now, Myles dear,' said Mrs. Rohan,
'honestly, didn't the four pounds give you a surprise ? Isn't it—
isn't it—splendid ?—besides the fame !'

'Honestly, I'll have more respect for Mat Murrin all the days
of my life, old woman,' said Myles, in the old boisterous humour.
''Twas the first time I ever suspected there was money enough in
them wet rags of newspapers to give them a heat to the fire.
But, sure, why not ? The milling hasn't been so thriving a trade
of late,' he said gloomily, 'that newspapers and poetry mightn't
be easily better. There's your cheque, boy, and God bless you !
And I *am* proud of you, and I know that, whatever you do, you'll
do honestly and well, like a man.'

T

'Father, there's only one thing in all the world that could make me prouder!' said Ken, with a swelling heart, 'and that's that you'll keep the cheque, and that you'll believe it's but the beginning of many and many a cheque that will gladden your heart, and—who knows?—help to tide over our little troubles, and keep us together in happiness many a day at the Mill. I do think I can see my way to being of some practical use to you.'

'You remember me reading last winter, Myles,' said Mrs. Rohan, 'about Sir Walter Scott—that he wiped off a debt of 90,000*l.*—I think it was—by writing books alone in a few years. I'm sure I don't see why, Ken——'but Mrs. Rohan's golden plans for opening a Waverley novel mine amidst the Drumshaughlin rocks were extinguished by an indignant, 'Oh, bother!—don't, mother!' from the prospective king of that bonanza.

'Well, but, Ken, you know, authors *do* rise to—to anything, nowadays,' said Katie. 'Didn't the Queen send a telegram the other day to inquire for Mr. Dickens's health?'

'She did, indeed, and even paid a shilling for it,' laughed Ken. 'I hope her Majesty won't come inquiring about me,' he added, coughing violently to prevent anybody noticing what he felt to be a cruel *mauvaise plaisanterie* the moment he had uttered it.

'Yes, yes,' said Myles Rohan, whom even the four sovereigns of solid bullion had not converted into any great opinion of the new gold diggings, and who, after consigning the cheque to his pocket-book, had lapsed into the morning paper. 'But talk of your fame and your poets—if you want to know what fame is, listen to this! O, blood alive, it's better than the cheque!' and he spread out the paper before him at arm's length, like a gourmand contemplating some succulent dish, while he read out:

'The Lord Chancellor, on the recommendation of the Right Hon. Lord Drumshaughlin, Lord Lieutenant of the County, has been pleased to appoint Humphrey Dargan, Esquire, of The Bank, Drumshaughlin, and The Roses, Glengariff, to the Commission of the Peace for the county of Cork.'

'That's what *I* call fame for you!—and public virtue—and glory alleluiah—all at a moderate interest of ten per cent., compound!' cried Myles Rohan, choking with laughter. 'The Lord Chancellor and the Right Hon. Lord Drumshaughlin have been pleased to step into the Bank, a-mossa!—the Bank, I declare by all the golden balls in Lombardy!—maybe to do a little bit of their own, begor!—why not?—by all accounts some of them want it, as badly as another. The Roses, too! As sure as you live, The Roses is the poetry for poor Nat Harris's cottage down in the Glen that honest Humphrey law'd the widow and her three helpless daughters out of, the poor little Roses! The Roses—divel a finer! Now, I'll warrant you, Ken, Matt Murrin must have got more than your four pounds for putting in that bit of poetry, though it only comes to three lines! And they tell us all the corruption in this country was done at the time of the Union!—as if an honest 15,000*l.* for a borough to an owld family weren't a decenter transaction for the country anyway than the Lord Chancellor's crown of glory for the gombeen man at The Roses! Ho, ho! by the powers of war, 'tis no wonder this is a prosperous country—'tis no wonder we glory in our immortal Constitution!'

'About time to smash it and trample it,' muttered Ken, between his teeth.

'No, boy—it's more likely to smash and trample you and me—the British Constitution, and its distinguished pillar at The Roses—smash and trample you and me, boy!' repeated the miller, and the head fell forward again musingly. It may be that the date (a very near one) of a certain acceptance under lock and key in the dingy parlour of the Bank had supplanted in Myles Rohan's mind's eye the grotesque image of the new-blown justice strutting as Armiger with his dozen white luces in his coat. They were all silent. For various reasons the Bank seemed to exercise an uncanny influence over the Mill. That newspaper paragraph was not good fun. Mrs. Rohan could have sentenced herself to penal servitude for life for her neglect of duty in not knowing that there would be something disagreeable in that paper, and cutting it out with a scissors, as though the gift of prophecy and the scissors-work of a sub-editor formed part of her ordinary housewifely daily life. Katie could think of nothing deeper to do than slipping an arm around Myles Rohan's neck, and with a kindly face inquiring: 'I wonder what title they could give you that would make me one little bit prouder than I am of calling you my own dear, dear Pappy—if they were to make you King!'

Myles Rohan was less ashamed of caresses since his illness than he used to be. 'By George, Katie,' he cried gaily, 'when they make me King, I'll make you First Flatterer in Ordinary—there's my royal seal upon it,' as he kissed the two sweet blush-rose cheeks. 'Yes, thank God, other people have their Roses, too—Roses that they would not exchange for all the Lord Chancellor's sealing-wax and all the wealth of the Indies.' He returned in high good humour to his breakfast and his newspaper.

'Hum! "The Fenian Conspiracy—More Arrests—Rumoured American Invasion"—Damn their rumours!—all stuff and foolishness! "Another Landlord Shot in Tipperary"—as if *that* was

T 2

any news to ask a penny for! Eh! what? By all the Latin-speaking cows in Kerry! the Dargans have the whole newspaper to themselves! Listen to this, old woman, and young woman, too :—"Marriages—On the 23rd inst., at Cork, privately, by special license——"'

'Oh, papa, how could you?' cried Katie, deadly pale, suddenly snatching the newspaper from his hand; then, colouring confusedly : 'I mean, why won't you finish your bit of grilled chicken instead of poking through that nasty paper?'

'Eh? bless my soul! what's the matter with *you*, little puss?' said the miller. 'You are the first woman that ever thought the marriages the worst part of a paper.'

'Let's see, Katie—give it to me,' cried Ken, securing the newspaper at one swift dart. Mother and sister almost swooned with terror as they watched him. He was almost as white as themselves, but smiled bravely. 'Why,' he said, as his eye darted at the announcement, 'it's only what everyone anticipated. I don't see why you shouldn't have let the governor finish, Katie' —and without a quiver he read out himself :

'FLIBBERT—DARGAN.—On the 23rd inst., at Cork, privately, by special license, Augustus George Flibbert, Sub-Inspector, Irish Constabulary, second cousin of Major the Hon. George Flitingly Flibbert, of Flibbertigibbert Castle, N.B., and formerly of the 1st Princess Charlotte's Own Hussars, to Lilian (Lily), daughter of Humphrey Dargan, Esquire, Justice of the Peace, of The Bank, Drumshaughlin, and The Roses, Glengariff. No cards.'

'That's all,' said Ken, the brave smile never flinching.

'The Roses again, and of course the judicial ermine dangling between Humphrey's legs already! Devil a fear but the two paragraphs were concocted by the one hand; the title must have been whisked off to the wedding the moment it arrived, like a pair of lavender kids sent home barely in time. Upon my conscience as a miller, the pretty letters J.P. look very like a present from the bridegroom. Who could dispense honours in Ireland if not the Chief of Police? And, by all accounts, little Flibbert had nothing more valuable to make a present of—except of course his name—the proud name of the nephew of Major the Hon. Whatdoyoucallim of Castle Balderdash.' He did not in the least understand that there was a tenderer stab in the announcement. 'And so that pink little chit of a thing has married a Peeler?' he went on. 'What the dickens did *she* want getting married for?'

'She didn't want to get married at all—she *couldn't* want to get married at all—not to a ridiculous creature like that!' broke in Mrs. Rohan, partly to relieve her own indignant feelings, but chiefly to cut short the miller's blundering badinage. ''Twas her wretched mother that wanted to make a match above the pawn-office—'twas her crawling father that wanted it to cringe his way into the club—'twas little Flibbert that wanted to fill his empty pockets out of Humphrey Dargan's strong box—and a pretty mess they've made of it for the miserable little girl between them.'

'Order, order, old woman! Father Phil will give you a month of rosaries for all that cataract of uncharity,' laughed the miller.

'I see the carts from Grallagh are waiting to be loaded,' said Ken, looking out at the window. 'I'd better look sharp about the invoices, if I don't want to bring Danny's thunders on my head.'

'Oh, Myles, Myles, how could you have sported with the poor boy's feelings like that?' cried Mrs. Rohan, as the door closed behind him.

'Eh? What the divel—I ask God's pardon!—what the potentate—we—mustn't—name have I done *now*? or what the ditto, ditto, ails you, woman, at all, at all, this morning?'

'My dear Myles, you cannot but have suspected something of the relations between Lily and Ken——'

Myles burst into a laugh. 'Oh, come, that bangs Banagher, and Banagher bangs the—same gentleman just referred to. Their relations!—taking a wife, I suppose, all to himself!—it was to have been a small villa residence, of course, and maybe Mr. and Mrs. Ken would have put up with a pony chaise for the present, just to show that they had no mean pride. Have you got any more to tell me about that wonderful boy of yours? Perhaps he wants to rob the mail-car. Maybe he'd like to introduce a rhinoceros or two into this establishment. And you talk of things of that kind—Kate, relations with young women and the rest of it—you talk of it as if he wasn't a brat of a boy who ought to be thrashed for his nonsense—you talk of it,' he said, with kindling passion, 'as if—as if I was the man I once was— as if Humphrey Dargan may not as likely as not evict me out of the Mill as he writted poor Nat Harris out of The Roses! Kate, the lad's a fine lad; but I don't know what's over him, some-thing that isn't lucky, I am sure. He turns his back on the Priesthood and he pitches head foremost into some infernal secret society; he receives the curse of the Church; he is subject to God knows what penalties from the law; he is drilling by night; he is writing poetry by day; and now it seems he is in love, and

we have had a narrow escape of a wedding in the family. Kate,
it's not that he's in love with that little girl of Dargan's. That's
not what's the matter. It's worse than that. Mark my words
for it ! That boy is IN LOVE WITH A BANSHEE !'

'He is your son and mine, Myles, and a better son father or
mother never reared !' cried Mrs. Rohan, with one of those gushes
of tender tears which are the end of controversy.

Katie had followed this paragon out and slipped her arm
through his, and murmured : 'Dear, dear Ken.' They were
standing in the little glass-framed portico ; a teeming fuchsia tree
shaking its prodigal blossom at the doorway, and a Holland pippin
tree presenting its golden fruit on bended knees, or at least with
bended back, a few yards away.

'Why, Katie, what's up ?' he said, looking down at her
smilingly. 'Did you think that—that paragraph—had knocked
me out of time ? Well, so it did—it was a bit sudden, somehow
—I—I didn't think it would be quite so soon,' at which point a
gulp in the throat went within an ace of spoiling his whole speech,
but it was only an instant's work when down went the lump in
the throat and back came the smile to the clear eye. 'But don't
be a bit afraid, sis—do I look as if this thing had crushed me ?'
It was a face of clear health and brightness she looked up to, and
none the less interesting to young ladies of Katie's age for the
traces of pallor in the cheeks and sadness in the smile. She
pressed his arm fondly, and said nothing. 'It hasn't crushed me,
and it won't, Katie ! Lily acted like a good girl—I mean good
to her parents. Flibbert cannot but be fond of her. But I've
thought it all, all out, Katie—it won't beat me down. There's
braver work than that to do in the world, and we'll do it, sis—at
least, we'll have a good try !'

'My heart of hearts ! my own brave boy !' cried Mrs. Rohan,
who came behind him in time to hear his last words and fold him
passionately in her arms. How wearisome, alas! are those precious embraces enjoyed in print ! Didn't even Ken Rohan, in
the very radiance of love that shone through and through him
from these two women's hearts, feel some lurking sense of satiety ?
And did not the feeling mingle—ever, ever so fugitively and unconsciously it is true—with the deeper and better emotions which
caused him to say, looking proudly from one glowing face to the
other : 'I know now why God permits so much wickedness in
the world. It is to prevent mothers and sisters from turning a
fellow's head ?' O thoughtless, thoughtless youth, and self-suffi-
cient sex that remembered not at all that the mothers, and sisters,
too, have to endure their share of the unkindness—nay that. for
all he knew, pink little Lily Dargan may have been at that

very moment sitting silent in a dreary Dublin hotel, opposite a husband absorbed in the newspaper on the third day of their honeymoon, and suspecting ever so dimly, and so resignedly, that unkindness may have its icy fangs also for 'fellows' of the feminine gender.

Old Danny was leaning contemplatively against one of the loaded sacks, with his hand on his infirm knee. Ken was slipping into the office like a laggard schoolboy under the withering eye of the master. To his surprise the old fellow plucked him humbly by the coat, and said : 'Whisper, Master Ken—is it true what I hear?' 'What is it now, Danny? In the devil's name, what?' cried Ken, with some horrible suspicion that he was to be treated to more condolences on the happiness of Mr. Augustus George Flibbert. 'That poem sir—is it yours?—out of your own head now, raally?' cried Danny, producing a well-thumbed old newspaper from inside his waistcoat, as tenderly as if it were a baby he were interrupting in sleep. 'It is! I see it in your eyes. Wisha! give me the hand, my darling child! I'll never say a word to you again, if you were to take the lynch-pin out of the ould mill-wheel. By the mortial, there's a regiment of sogers charging for Ireland in them verses!' I wonder if a great poet ever reads the cold judgment of a great review with anything like the divine glory of joy with which Ken Rohan read the critique in lame old Danny's eyes! For the happiness of great and small who labour up those chilly Parnassus sides let us hope so.

Let us hope, also, for the sake of the rules of book-keeping, that the figures in the Grallagh carter's weigh-notes were duly entered according to Cocker ; for they were entered by one whose thoughts were soaring as far as the new asteroid above the office ceiling, and the Grallagh carter's lazy 'hee ups!' and whip-cracks were no sooner heard outside the door than the unprofitable accountant was away through the Glen—he did not know or care whither, so it was only higher in the air—to find space and review-ground enough for the tumultuous army of emotions that were shouting within him. I don't know what young ladies (who perhaps will toss their pretty heads at the notion of there being such a thing as first love for a miserable damp provincial newspaper) will think of Ken Rohan when the fact comes out that he felt his step on the mountain positively lighter than usual, and the air about his temples more buoyant. But it was even so. The announcement of the marriage had actually benefited him—had almost pleasured him. It was the drop-scene of a drama that was over—one in which he had not been cast for an agreeable part. The marriage to the scion of the illustrious house of Flibberti-gibbet had ended the unreal phantom-play. For the Sub-

Inspector's wife, he knew her not. There was no such person that he could remember to have met. Lily Dargan's peach-blossom face and seraph's eyes had passed away into a spirit-form that floated in the air on the heights above him—or, rather, now that he looked closer, it was *not* quite the same tranquil, seraphic child-face ; but blood of a more rushing red, and eyes of a more kindling blue, that waved him upwards with the sight of flashing banners and the sound of beating drums. Until this transmigration he had wrestled miserably with his love—cursed all woman-kind, and found that blue eyes outlive curses ; yoked himself from daybreak to the mill-wheel and its desk, and could hear but the name mumbled at every revolution of the wheel and written across every page of the ledger ; recurred to the sweet mystic peace of the cloisters of the Rhineland, only to be haunted by his Lorelei with mocking whispers that the world was fair ; took his gun over leagues of moor without firing a shot ; scanned the bay even for the coming fleet and coming clash of action, and turned away with the sick feeling that he could see nothing but his own loveless skiff adrift on the blank darkling seas. When all of a sudden, one night, there came a rush of something – he knew not what nor whence—something hot, bright, strenuous – over his brain ; and he jumped from his bed of fever, and struck a light, and with the stump of a pencil, on the blank fly-leaf of a book of devotion which lay on his table, scrawled that Something down in a spasm of exquisite pain. He returned to bed for the first deep happy sleep that visited his pillow since the day Lily's eyeballs flashed fire on him at the Lady's Crag. It is possible the judicious would smile if I were to transcribe the something as it was extant the next morning in the uncouth pencil scrawl, which Ken ran to his dressing-table to inspect, as a young mother might run to a cradle only just inhabited. Which, indeed, of our souls' most precious possessions, in either verse or cradle, wears the same con-secrated light in the eyes of a General Public, however indulgent, as in our own fond parental dreams ? Yet what hopes, what joys, what passions may be born into the world in one of those insignificant (and possibly squalling) mites ? 'All I can tell in-credulous young ladies is that, if the editor of a certain Dublin weekly journal had been a beauty of 'rose-misted marble,' at whose feet he was laying the fortunes of a life, Ken Rohan could not have put his manuscript into the Post-office with more deli-cious tremblings, with darker forebodings, or more glorious glints of hope ; and when in a stealthy place he opened the paper, and saw his verses there before him, alive and imperishable, if the limp, ink-smeared sheet had been the rose-misted beauty, with smiling lustrous harebell eyes, presenting her ripe lips to him, he could scarcely have been more strongly tempted to bend down and kiss them. It may mollify legitimate feminine indignation to know that there the similarity of charms between the cherry lips and the damp newspaper ends; and that seldom, indeed, do the raptures of literary *belles passions* extend far beyond the first kiss. But with that first kiss Ken Rohan was still palpitating. He had found another spirit-Lily, whose match-making mother would not throw eyes at sub-inspectors. Or, rather, it was the same spirit—his own unchangeable dream and love—that had passed from the gross body of The Bank, Drumshaughlin, to beckon him in clouds of glorious purpose towards the Heights. He had found a mistress, who lighted up all together every power and aspiration of his soul—Patriotism, Romance, Daring, Action, Hope—all the bright signal-fires of flaming youth. All these were burning and leaping within him, and he had discovered a way of spreading the sacred fire to other hearts. He had put his mouth to a magic bugle, which might raise millions of souls in arms beside old Danny's. And as he bounded up the hills to-day, with his eyes full of the rushing Vision above him and before him, it seemed to him—kind hearts, pray remember he was barely eighteen—as if he could imagine a whole world-spread race trooping across oceans and continents to the valley below, to listen for his message and carry the heights at his word of command. No, thou surly, common-sensical, old unbelieving millions —Ken's radiant mistress does not in the least look like a Banshee this morning!

CHAPTER THE TWENTY-FIFTH

TWO YOUNG MEN

'IT was a good inspiration! I swore to myself that I should find you here!' said Jack Harold, capturing his friend affectionately by the arm. ' Ken, you are the Pope of father confessors, where it is an affair of the heart.'

Ken Rohan started uneasily. By some extraordinary process of illogic, the subject of Jack's love-affairs somehow worried him since that ramble to Mullagh to hear the echoes in a solitude of two. I hear the novel-reading sleuth-hound proclaiming already that Ken's spirit-mistress is undergoing another transfiguration— the hair to a fairer gold, the eyes to a more living blue. 'Come, not so much to beat your breast as to sing *Gloria in excelsis*, Jacko, I suspect?' said Ken Rohan not too graciously.

'Look here !　Have I the air of a conqueror ?' said the other ; and Ken looking, staggered back from the picture of crushed and torn misery before him. 'Good God ! Jack, my poor fellow ! ' was all he could stammer.

'You see !　Let us sit down.　I am tired, sick, damned,' said young Harold, sinking on the heather. 'But you will not close the confessional even to damned souls, you ! Ken, I feel the need of speaking or—yes, killing myself.　You are the only man in the world who would even understand.　The table of sins does not aid.'

'You have at least one unusual advantage, old boy ; you have a confessor in the same case as his penitent,' said Ken, with a sad little laugh.　'I am just after reading in the paper that St. Cecilia—you remember St. Cecilia, Jack !—is at present on her honeymoon—married to a policeman.'

'Yes, Ken, I have heard — I had forgotten,' said Jack, guiltily.　'You see I am not going to attenuate my little feeble-nesses—my crimes.　I forget your misery in my own.　But I for-get for the same reason that I make you my confessor—because I knew—I thought—you would not sink to your knees under a blow as I—you would not throw up your hands.　You have not thrown up your hands, Ken ?'

'No,' said the other, scarcely conscious that he spoke, looking up as if he saw something on the crest of the mountain.

'Let us see.　How old are you ?'

'The great interest Snap-apple Night has for me is that it will make me eighteen.'

'*Croix Dieu !* And I—I am twenty.　Let us be exact.　I am three months more.　Your eyes ask what that wishes to say ? I will tell you.　It wishes to say that I am ages older than you, and you have reached manhood before me—it wishes to say that, we being struck by the same thunderbolt—we two—it is I who kneel, and it is you who listen to my whine—it wishes to say that you have courage, faith, youth, innocence, and that I am weak, hackneyed, heartless, disenchanted, a shallow persifleur, and—and—a coward !　There.　You have heard my confession now. Great God !' He dashed his hands against his face, as if to hide some horrible sin there, and his chest and knees were pressed together in an agony of convulsive sobs.　Ken's old brindled terrier, Snipe, who had been skirmishing after grouse, stopped and looked at him with the oddest sympathetic eyes of wonder.

Ken Rohan was dazed.　His friend had been to him always a superior being, a gifted creature born to shine and soar ; one whom he should no more have suspected of being weighed down with human woe than a lark ; and, nevertheless, one of those

dainty, cunningly-tempered blades that are none the less puissant
in the brave squares of war for their jewelled hafts and silken
baldrics—a gay, dazzling Alcibiades, who, if he would march on
the field of Mantinea with painted cupids on his shield, could bite
like a lion in the thick of the battle. To see this superb creature
wounding himself with hideous self-reproaches, and writhing in
self-abasement at *his* feet, seemed a subversion of all natural laws
to the younger man. It was as if the stars cast themselves on
the earth and declared that there was no use in shining. ' My
poor Jack,' he said gently, ' the very violence of this agony tells
how you libel yourself. I knew always what an unapproachable
fellow you are. What charms, what gifts—nonsense, man !
I'm not to be deceived by your nightmares ! What genius !
But I never gave you credit for this. My dear boy, you rise
heavens high in the estimation of your father confessor, when he
sees you shaken by these transports of generous passion simply
because a pretty girl—yes, a beautiful one—I understand your
gesture—— '

' You understand nothing except your own incuraole optimism,
your own invincible innocence ! ' exclaimed Harold, bounding
like a wounded stag in whom the offending arrow was turned.
' Sacré ! is it necessary to tear off the bandage before you will
believe the sores ? It is not because she has rejected me—if that
is not a phrase too grandiose for a light frissonnement of the hem
of her robe at contact with a mendicant. I have not so much
désintéressement.'

' It is not that ! '

' Not that alone. That was the last double-or-quits stake in
a desperate game. That was the vision they say a drowning man
sees, which showed me all that I might have been, and what a
suffocating wretch I am. It has set me redacting my life, and
what do I see ? A youth dedicated to playing advertisement-
from-the-life to a miserable country school—a genius, *le joli mot!*
which consumed itself in dazzling the school-boy's mammas ! I
return home—what a moqueur word ! what an advantage to the
Frenchman who lodges *à la belle étoile* that his language spares
him that stab !—I return here—what do I say ?—I am chased
here like a houseless animal !—to find myself a tax upon a poor
old man, to find that every lump of sugar placed in my cup is a
lump taken out of his, not to be able, my faith, to examine my
own hat in the mirror without seeing his poor old hat in ruins
there instead, reproaching me. One object presented itself to my
hungry heart which might have redressed all—which might have
lifted me above these squalid cares, these dwarfish associations,
this pit of egotism without even ambition, of niaiseries which

have not even the distinction of being crimes. My love for her was the one ray of heaven left in my soul. It was as white as my rosette of First Communion. Could I have won her, I might have scaled heights, scaled heaven—so I thought. It was only to add a touch of insanity to the follies of a Pape des Fous. She did not even refuse. A thousand devils! No!—she only shuddered; and then worse—she made me adore the ground under her feet because she threw me one glance of pity. And, last of all humiliations, of all horrors—she was right! My egotism vociferates No! but my love for her condemns me to bear a louder voice which says: "Thou liest to thy nose! She is as far above thee as the moon is above the wretch who toddles out of a wine shop by her light. Thy very love for her is only an ambuscade which has failed, an impertinence which has been chastised, a vanity which has suicided. itself. Va-t-en! bury thyself at a cross-roads, if thou hast the courage to recognise thyself a corpse!" And I have not the courage! My farceur genius conducts me to a climax *pour rire*, and leaves me without home, without love, without career, a creature as dreary as an empty sepulchre, in a country where I cannot even speak English without provoking a smile, where I have no business except a ragamuffin brainless conspiracy, which cannot afford its Generals of Division their dinner— which will never arrive at offering its abonnés even a respectable occasion of suicide—and in which, *pour comble de bonheur*, I have had the belle idée of entangling the only friend I have in the world. Do you comprehend, now?'

'I comprehend that we are both in the same boat, and that a dangerous sea is running; but I comprehend also that youth without danger would be youth in a Quaker's hat. I don't say, "*Vive l'orage!*" but I say, "*A bas l'orage!*" We'll breast the waves, old boy—we'll top them! How often I have heard you sing, with your own Béranger, that in a garret one is in heaven at twenty-one. And you have not come to the garret, nor even to twenty-one!'

There was an unconscious retorting of his own philosophy upon himself in the words, which depressed the young Parisian wretchedly. He would sooner have heard the Scriptures cited than Béranger.

'Yes,' he said bitterly; 'but Drumshaughlin is not the Quartier. It is Bœotia. It is Sahara. This country has no horizon but sand. It stifles me! There are only two careers in Ireland for a young fellow of spirit—he must go into penal servitude or into *delirium tremens*. I would choose the latter, naturally, but for two reasons —whisky is too brutal for my palate, and I cannot afford to go into *delirium* on the wines of Bourgogne or Cham-

pagne; for the other—b-r-r-r ! I doubt whether, if they had com-
muted the lion-eatings of the Christian martyrs to penal servitude,
they would have held out ; and '—with one of his satirical shrugs,
for the satirical devil was coming back into him—'I am not a
Christian martyr; besides, à quoi bon !'

Ken Rohan's fresh voice broke out, like a mountain cascade,
into the inspiriting chorus—

> 'They're coming, thronging home;
> In bold brigades they come !
> Old Erin's veins
> Run fire to night—
> Her boys are coming home !'

until the mountain and bay seemed to be ringing with the gladsome promise.

The sound of his own chorus smote upon Jack's nerves unpleasantly, like a reproachful face looking in at the window.

'Bah !' said he savagely, 'the song lies ! Believe its author.
The boys are *not* coming home—have no means of coming; and if
they come would be without bed or supper, unless the Queen
lodged and fed them.'

'Do you know anything ?—have you heard anything ?' asked
the other, growing a little pale.

'Yes, there is bad news—arrests—quarrels—informers—all
sorts of coups de foudre. What are you to think of imbeciles
who let Captain Mike pawn his revolver by way of commissariat ?
But it is not that,' he burst out, the throes of agony suddenly coming
back. 'To you all, that is a tocsin of battle—the summons to do and
suffer for the Right, for an enchanted Cause, for a fated Race—at
worst, the refrain of a consecrated *Marseillaise* on the march to
the guillotine. Will you never see what my confession means—
that you are a Believer, a Galahad, a Crusader with the Holy
Grail glittering before your eyes, while I—a thousand devils !—I
doubt everything, even myself—a vagabond troubadour, to whom
his verses are no more than his ribbons—a sceptic, to whom principle is only the prate of a dull pedant—an egotist, to whom self-
sacrifice is a mere sottise—a lâche, I tell you ! to whom the vision
of a gallows simply gives the indigestion.'

'Jack, Jack, the indigestion comes from other things than
staring at a gallows, which is not even visible. You don't mean
all this,' said the younger man cheerily. 'We all have our
miserable moments of doubt and cowardice. Did you ever hear
the advice a deep thinker once gave ? "Always do what you are
afraid to do ?" All men have their fears. All men grumble.
So does the soldier lying out in the trenches up to his knees in
water. But he does not desert because he has his doubts of the

plan of campaign--not, at all events, while the bullets are flying Neither, old man, will you.'

'I am not sure of that. I am not sure of anything,' said his friend, pulling plumes of heather-bells to pieces. 'There is the gulf between you and me—a gulf of twelve centuries or so, as wide as from a Mass of St. Finn Barr to Cham's latest caricature on a Boulevard kiosque. Listen! I do not believe in Patriotism. I am a cosmopolitan, and think countries all a mere arrangement of railways and paquebots—diablement clumsy, it is true. I do not believe in St. Finn Barr to any great extent. You may well start—I wish I could. I believe in one God, *ego*, and now his statues are thrown down and their noses broken. Can you suggest to me any more sensible prayer in such circumstances than that the sky should fall and bury me, or, at least (since that would not be worth the trouble), that a tile should fall on my head with exactitude!'

'Good heavens!'

'Now you commence to perceive. After all, what would you have? I was not brought up in the cloisters of Clairvaux, but in the back parlour of a café—La Mère Médecine, Rue St.-Sévérin —with the Jardin Bullier en face,' he cried, with a little shrug and the *rire diabolique* which distinguish philosophers of his corps like a sardonic uniform.

'For shame, Jack! If you had La Mère Médecine for a nurse, you have glorious old Father Phil for an uncle; and there is more wisdom, more truth, more honour, more inspiration, more know-ledge and manhood and glory here and hereafter under his battered old hat——'

'Than would equip his nephew and a whole caféful of his early perceptors—perfectly! But, you see, these droll little marmosets of students did not study the Fathers—they rather studied the Sons—and the Daughters, my faith—enormously the Daughters! They puffed away all gods, ancient and modern, impartially with their tobacco-smoke. They abolished the Decalogue, and sub-stituted one simple rubric: "Thou shalt do what thou pleaseth except believe in God." Goddesses they admitted—from the Odéon, chiefly—and their reign was not for all eternity, these poor devils of goddesses. Their Revolutions even were the amuse-ments of a Fête Diable—a new piece in an open-air theatre, entrée libre—a stimulant more intoxicating than blue wine, and less expensive than the jeunes dernières from the Odéon.'

'At least you Parisians captured the Bastille, as well as danced on the ruins.'

'Without doubt; but, you conceive, I was only born in time for the latter part of the performance.' After the bitter smile again came the pang and dejected look. 'Bah! you are right. They knew how to die. I only don't know how to live. I am only a plated Parisian—a rustic imitation daubed over spurious metal. I lost our simple Irish faiths without acquiring theirs. They had their fine fanaticisms of Comtism, science, human solidarity, heaven upon earth, even hell upon earth—for they had their true church, too, those drolls of anarchists! If they were not to let me have my worship of the Creator, I compromised by refusing divine honours also to their demi-mondaine Goddess of Liberty, or to an Orsini bomb, or even to a bust of Voltaire. Effectively, all I learned from them was that the great duty of life was to make it amusing, and that all unpleasant questions of Duty, Faith, *Undé? Indé?* and the like, were the conundrums of bores, if not the abracadabra of hypocrites and humbugs. Have you heard the credo of our sect?

> J'ajourne le problème insondable,
> J'ajourne Meduse et Satan,
> Et je dis au Sphinx formidable:
> Je parle à la rose, va-t-en!

When *my* rose answered "*Va-t-en!* thyself, thou slug, thy very touch infects my petals!" what ought the logical slug to do, who has abolished heaven and earth for itself, and country, and home, and love, but crawl to your feet and pray you to set your heel upon it, since under this triste sky, under the oppressive solemnities of your insular virtue, it can no longer hope even to flutter as a butterfly amidst the green acacias of the Boulevards and their witty sunshine. You don't comprehend all this—perhaps you are as shocked as Monsignor McGrudder at this world without a God, this restless crater heart of the nineteeth century vomiting blasphemy at your heaven, and scorching up your every green thing. Naturally! Happily you know nothing of the caverns in which I have heard those fierce central fires boil and roar—May the devil flay me, but you are laughing! I have said things that from serious lips I know would be poison and daggers to you, and you find me even more amusing than blasphemous. And that is my shame, my curse, my death—that you are right in laughing at my history, as she was right in not deigning even to reject my love; and, like Rigoletto, I will have to die before anybody will believe that I am not joking!'

'Come, Jack, if you will believe in nothing else in the world, believe that I am not such a brute as that—nay, as a beginning of a better faith, believe that, without your knowing it, I have been your companion down among those internal, or infernal, furnaces of our age—and have, perhaps, got singed there. Who

that was ever young has not ?—unless, indeed, Monsignor McGrudder, if *he* was ever young—at least in the present century. No,
I was only smiling at your opinion of my innocence. My dear
boy, I have heard the volcanoes bubble. If I have not heard
your philosophies of La Mère Médecine, I have heard their
masters, and in a more formidable mood than over their cups—
in their books. And what does it all come to? The buzz of a
swarm of fireflies who think the world was never illuminated
before until their own dazzling generation—the burrowings in the
stones of St. Peter's of minute insects who flatter themselves
they are making unparalleled progress in the demolition of the
edifice. The only thing new about your modern thaumaturgus
is that, in place of an alchemist wrapped in his fine dream of
turning all our dross into gold, he has given us an analytical
chemist bent upon resolving all our gold into dross—into doubts,
self-introspections, individualisms, all sorts of purblind little
peerings and pryings, till he has analysed a human soul out of
every phase of consciousness except dyspepsia ; for what, after
all, is doubt but a dyspepsia of the soul? There, now, don't be
afraid I am going to preach you out of your own little attack of
the malady by readings from black-letter volumes in folio. But,
whenever I hear the Pistols and Bardolphs of this nineteenth
century chanting their tipsy canticle :

> Glory to Man in the highest !
> For Man is the Master of Things !—

I think of the poor little Master of Things stretching out his
atomy sceptre towards the million billions of worlds glowing
above him (from some of which, they tell us, a ray of light
travelling ever since the Creation Day has not yet had time to
arrive on earth)—I think of all the generations of Pythagoreans,
Mambres with their enchanting rods, Demetriuses and their
mobs of silversmiths, Rosencrantzes with their crucibles, Vol-
taires with their grin, physicists with their jelly-specks that have
undertaken from time to time to command the morning star and
have vanished themselves into the shadow of a name, leaving the
world more puzzled than ever by the mystery of Life and Love
in a child's cradle, by the mystery of Death in a child's coffin—
I think of all this, and your young Master of Things in the Rue
St. Sévérin must excuse me if I cannot be very apprehensive that
they are going to blow away the Throne of the Universe with
the smoke of their cigarettes.'

'Neither, my friend, will you blow away the Nineteenth Century—devil take it !—with a devout *Apage Sathanas !*'

'Goodness gracious ! Do you suppose I would be much a

matricide, if I could ?--the glorious benignant mother-age that
nursed us—that has settled upon us such an inheritance of knowledge, and Freedom, and strength for the weak, and love for all
the children of men ! Not a bit of it—let us spin on through as
many Reform tempests, Anti-Slave wars, or, for the matter of
that, as many Days of July as you please, until human life shall
be no more subject to the tortures of human disease than to be
broken on the wheel—until every desolate human heart shall feel
the rustle of Love's zephyr-wings—until standing armies of men-
shooters shall seem as loathsome a sight as standing armies of
cannibals, and all the energies, the emulations, the genius, the
heroism, the treasures now lavished in bedrenching our brothers'
homes with blood and pain shall be turned to the service of human
happiness. Hurrah for it all !—and what is it all but Applied
Christianity ?—the development into franchises, State-Socialism,
and a thousand groping, darkly-striving International Congresses
of that law of human existence in which a greater than philosopher nineteen centuries ago summed up Christianity and all that
has followed, or ever will follow : " Three things remain : Faith,
Hope, and Charity ; but the greatest of these is Charity." But
I am absurd enough not to see any conflict at all, but rather the
eternal complement of one another, between the Faith of the
Seventh Century and the Humanity of the Nineteenth. When
the Nineteenth Century shall have done all that science, legisla-
tion, and brotherly loving-kindness can do for man's human part,
then will remain the infinite depths and longings of his Divine
part all the more quickened, all the more unsatisfied, oppressed
with a mystery to which there can be but one key, palpitating
with a worship of which there can be but one object ; and in
that day don't be surprised if you should see your proud Nineteenth Century, or your prouder Twentieth Century, going back
to my bare-footed Seventh Century for the secret of its desert
cells -- presenting its happy Brotherhood of Humanity for initiation into a happier Brotherhood of Divinity—and extinguishing,
without either the fires of Smithfield or the fires of Geneva, the
innumerable army of Bigots of Irreligion, Quackery, and Selfishness who trade on the glory, darken the conscience, stun the ears,
and drain the spiritual nature of this great, half-instructed,
human-hearted giant of an age of ours.'

' In effect, my friend, since you took the liberty to smile, I go
to claim the privilege to yawn. Advertisement Numéro Un !'
cried the incorrigible child of La Mère Médecine, who, to say the
truth, had lost sight of his own interesting figure wholly in this
high Drama of the Centuries.

The flush of passionate rhetoric and the laugh of good-

humoured guilt and high spirits were perpetually chasing one
another on Ken Rohan's face. 'I suppose that is what you call
penitence in the Latin Quarter—first kneel to your Father-con-
fessor, and then block his birretta,' he said, blushing and laughing.
'Well, I *have* taken a long-winded way of saying that Religion
may be trusted to take care of itself—almost as long-winded as
if it were an attack on Christianity. Let us have plenty of air
and sunlight and all that will come right, without our shutting
ourselves up in that torture-chamber of self-consciousness which
our modern enlightenment has invented for itself in place of the
mediæval rack—and which may be just as stifling as the Leads of
Venice, and break every bone in one's body every bit as mad-
deningly as the Parisian Bed of Leather. Let that pass ; but '—
and here the hot, eager look again flashed back into power—' our
poor old land is not so well able to take care of herself—Jack, you
don't mean, you can't mean, that you are going to make one other
deserter from her thin battalions—just, too, when young blood is
panting for the first rush of the battle ! '
  'Suppose I demand to be disbanded with your standing armies
of cannibals ? '
  'No, no—you wrong your birth—you wrong your manhood—
with quibbles—with—with treason—like that ! You can't mean
to suggest that desertion of our own poor old stricken and sorrowful mother at home is the first step to drying the tears of
mothers in Arabia or Peru ; you don't mean to say that these
hills, where our fathers fought that long losing fight for faith and
home, where the very air thrills with their stories, where every
glen is strewn with their ruined shrines and fortresses and their
graveyards ; you don't mean—you daren't say !—all this represents to you nothing but so much land surrounded by water, like
an island in the South Pacific ; you know, you feel as well as I,
that all these delicate threads of association, these acquired subtle
tendrils of kinship and of common sufferings and common hopes,
twined round every joint and power of our being in a sacred
nerve-system of their own, to which we owe some of the most
aerial music, some of the divinest intimations of human nature,
and that a true heart, like a stone cast into a pond, has to begin
at the centre of duty, home, and love, and as sure as it begins
there will go on in expanding circles from its own hearth, over its
own town, its own country, its own human kind, until its influence
at the last widens into the ocean of Eternal Love. Psha ! of
course, you have been only teasing me with one of your confounded
paradoxes, and I see "Numéro Deux" this moment forming on
your irreverent lips.'
  'Ken, I feel like one of those mediæval rakes who, when

diablement ruined, were always despatched to fight for the Holy
Sepulchre.   Hearing you talk is like going out to the Crusades.
But it's no use.   It's all very well for you strong hulking unshakable Tancreds—apropos, Ken,' he demanded with a start,
'where have you been hiding those broad shoulders of yours and
that biceps ?   I never remarked before what a very monster you
grow !—*you* will never sheath sword till you burst in over the
walls of Jerusalem among the Saracens ; but for nous autres,
we feather-handed Rinaldos—bah ! I'd go a thousand miles to
hear the "*Ecco il fonte del riso*" of the Sirens, and I should be
only enormously obliged to that witch of a woman—what's her
name ?—to show me the way.'

The other, as if a thought struck him, suddenly faced his
friend and stared at him.   'Come,' he said, 'it was not to tell
me things of that sort that you came here.   Tell me frankly :
why did you open your heart to me as you have done to-day ?'

'Je n'en sais rien !   Because I felt the necessity for confessing, as a gipsy might for stealing.'   Again the light tone all
in an instant grew tremulous, and his face succumbed as under
the talons of a bird of prey to the deforming work of wrinkles
and livid hues.   'Ah, yes !—it was because I felt as if it were
going to be the last reputable act of my life.   Because—you may
well think the irreligion of La Mère Médecine has its comic
side !--because I have some presentiment --some witch's shibbo-
leth cry—some haunting devil-knows-what within me – that
seems to say we will never greet again, we two, quite like this.'

He looked so broken that Ken Rohan felt strong enough
to take him in his arms like a sick child.   'Tush !' he cried ;
'Let me kick over that witch's cauldron right away.   Listen
to me for ten seconds, and see if I don't confute that bit of
prophecy and send your midnight hags to their broomsticks!
My dear boy, I suffered just like you under the torturing
irons of the same three cruel devils—disappointed love, hungry
energies, and empty pockets.   I roamed the blasted heaths like
you, with just such another mess of hell-broth seething in my
heart.   Did you ever notice with what agonies and fevers an
angry fistula gathers, and how, at one small prick of the lancet,
out flies the fever like an exorcised devil, and the healthy blood
bounds through your veins again for joy ?   Jack, old man, my
devil's gone—by the simplest of all possible pricks—and so
shall we send your's shrieking after him.   Read that letter '

He took out of its envelope in his breast-pocket a letter
stamped with the florid green crest and daring motto, 'To
Arms !' of the revolutionary organ in Dublin, and set Jack
deciphering the following note in the weird hermetic characters

U 2

which are as sacred to critics as the symbols of their prescriptions are to doctors:

                        ' Office of the X——: Y—— Z—— St.
' *Confidential.*   ' Dublin, October 4, 186—,

'DEAR SIR :—Your ballad 'has made a stir. It evinces qualities so uncommon that I am tempted to write in the hope of stimulating you to other and systematic work in the same direction. For one reason or another, our movement has sadly lacked literary inspiration. The base Parliamentary agitators have made men sick of the very names of eloquence and poetry, and have set them busy forging firebrands and looking up rifles instead. Besides, ours is so rudely democratic an uprising, that the cultured class shrink from soiling their silks and velvets in such rough company, and our stormy young democrats, in revenge, rage against mere intellectual graces as foppery and carpet-ware. I so strongly feel that no movement of national proportions can subsist long upon no better intellectual problem than the pass-words and gabble of secret lodges, that I have time and again revolved plans for lighting a more generous flame in the youth of the country, and giving our movement an outward and visible form, which would appeal to the pride of our race and the respect of nations. If you can see your way to rendering me regular assistance to that end, in whatever literary form you may cast your thoughts, and whether here in Dublin or through the post, I hope to be able to suggest financial arrangements which will be satisfactory ; and if you should chance to know of any others whose literary gifts would be likely to further my views, I shall take it as an additional favour if you will kindly place me in communication with them. I have directed our cashier to remit for the ballad, and beg you to believe me

                        'Yours very faithfully,
                        '_____ _____.'

'Our disease is the same—suppressed fever; the remedy is action—action, with a dash of inspiration in it; and there goes the tucket of drums !' said Ken Rohan, while the other toiled through the editor's gnarled pen-work. 'It's the very thing for you as well as me. You can turn off these things as fast as a smith can make sparks fly. You can wrap our struggle in glittering robes of wit and fancy enough to dazzle Bagdad. Sir, we shall scatter brightness like a pair of sun-gods, and make an unsuspecting world gape, too, I warrant you. We shall touch an electric button here, and millions of our kin, from pole to pole, will answer with the sweetest music of their hearts. We will have a little

Grassmere of our own—why not "The Glen Poets," as well as "The Lake Poets"? Who knows? Fellows may talk of our lying day-dreaming here to-day in the heather, as they tell of poor Davis and Dillon under their oak-tree that day in the Phœnix Park. And, then, I can tell you that cashier is by no means the shabbiest person in the partnership—by Jove, sir! didn't my grumbling old dad look queer when I shied a cheque for four pounds at his head, the old Goth!'

Jack Harold had mastered the contents of the letter. He folded it irresolutely, and for a moment sat listening to his friend's boyish clatter with a mournful smile. 'My poor Ken!' he said at last, returning the letter. 'Then you have not seen the Stop Press edition of the Cork papers?'

Ken looked at him. 'No,' he said, tightening the muscles of his mouth involuntarily.

'That journal of yours was suppressed last night, and the types carted away to Dublin Castle. The editor is in Richmond jail, charged with treason-felony.'

Ken Rohan said nothing. There was a singing in his ears, as if some heavy body were squeezing the lobes of his brain down flat. When his thought-mechanism began to work again, the first idea it importuned him with was—terror of his father's triumphant eye—horror, lest the cheque should have been presented and dishonoured. This happy irrelevancy broke the force of the blow, as a bullet will sometimes glance off a button or a coin over the heart, and leave only a hot smart, when it might have left a death-wound. He sprang to his feet.

'By Jove!' he cried, 'I musn't give the governor that crow. I will have to lay hold of that cheque, by hook or crook. Come!'

'Willingly, if you will only tell me whither,' said the other, bewildered and haggard. 'To the devil, if one could get there without so many disgusting formalities. I wonder what better could two fellows like you and me do than walk into old Dargan's back parlour, clap him our revolvers to the head, and help ourselves to his gold and notes. What else is that little policeman doing? What else has the old harpy himself been doing all his life? Patzy Driscoll's lugger would put us across to France in a clin d'œil,' he added, with a harsh, bantering laugh.

'The Glen school of poetry is getting on—the Glen singers in a new sphere of imagination as Jail-Birds,' laughed Ken Rohan, who, soothly, was too much rapt in his own thoughts to pay the smallest attention to his friend's banter, and answered him by a process of what the physiologists call unconscious cerebration.

'En tout cas, jail-birds,' said the other, doggedly. 'The arrests in Dublin are en masse. There is to be a Special Commission.'

'It looks like business,' exclaimed Ken, with sudden animation. 'Depend upon it, the Government would not have struck only that we're on the eve of stirring days. It was perhaps a race who should strike first, and now comes the striking back.'

'Our hearts are mighty, our skins are whole, and burnt sack will be the issue, my friend—it is always the conclusion of "Freedom's Battle" in your Ireland. We lack the Queen's English most puissantly—you others as well as I.'

'That's ridiculous, and it's unjust,' cried Ken, hotly. 'You don't, seriously, dream that all this fermentation of a race—these young peasant armies that spring up every moonlight night—the militia regiments—ay, even the regulars that we hear yelling our choruses—the American flotilla—the war-worn Captain Mike MacCarthys that are swarming over in every American steamer—that all this is going to vanish as softly as a mountain mist, merely because the Government has made a descent on a newspaper-office and laid the editor by the heels ?'

'No—not if the rest of your calculations are as substantial as that Elysium which you have planted for the Glen Poets with the munificence of a Bon Dieu.'

'By George, was there ever such an earthquake-shock for our poor paradise of pleasure ! Well, sir, we've only got to turn out like Adam and make the best of it. Or rather, why should we give up our paradise at all without a tussle for it ? No doubt the flowers will get a bit bruised if we've got to plough our Elysian Fields with cavalry-charges and cannon-wheels; but it is not at our age that fellows object to a burst of rifle-music in their heaven by way of psalmody. The case is just this. If this swoop in Dublin means immediate action—why, then, we're saved the trouble of thinking—it's "Up, and away, my merry, merry men ! Roderick vich Alpine Dhu, ho, iero !" If the time is not yet ripe, and if the movement has still to be kept in high heat—why, then, it's a louder call than ever to use our pens while the swords are fashioning. But come along, and I'll tell you what I mean. Why, what the deuce is the matter with you, Jack ?'

The elder youth stood surveying him in a mood of curious melancholy. He looked around as if making a mental sketch of the curves and shadows of the mountain glens and the indentations of the great Bay. 'Dame !' he cried, shrugging his shoulders, 'Monsignor M'Grudder would feel himself diablement flattered if he knew how I am haunted. Wouldn't it be curious if—— Give me your hand, Ken. Allons !'

'Still under the charm of the Weird Sisters!' laughed Ken, receiving his volatile friend's unaccustomed embrace with wonder, but overmastered by his own clamorous thought. 'We'll scarcely be in time to collar that infernal cheque. By the way, why shouldn't the governor have his laugh?' he suddenly fell communing with himself. 'Poor old dad hasn't had too many jolly moments lately. The triumph of his prophecies about poetry and rebellion will perhaps save him from realising other aspects of the news. Why, of course he shall have his crow! I'm not the first great poet whose drafts on a perverse public have been delayed in payment. And it's only delayed. Won't I have the last of the laugh against the governor by-and-by, that's all, when my cheque takes rank as a Treasury Bill, as soon as the Irish Republic gets into working order! Come, and I'll tell you all my plans. Let's be off and find the Captain.'

'Par hasard, you will find him in the county jail.'

'Then we *will* find him there!' laughed Ken, and he dashed down the mountain, taking boulders and quagmires steeplechase-fashion, in a way that caused Snipe's black muzzle and short tail to prick up as at sight of a paradise of rats while he bounded after him.

They found the American Captain without going so far afield (or shall we say a-dungeon?) as the county jail. He was studying the Stop Press edition with the aid of an enormous black cigar in the dingy back shop in which Mat Murrin, like a Jupiter in his shirt-sleeves, was hammering out his thunders for that night's *Banner*. 'Just dropped in to tap the Editor's wires,' said Captain Mike. 'News purty niftey, hey, sonnies? Straight without sugar, hey, boys?' It was the first time Ken Rohan had ever penetrated the recesses of Mat's cloudy Olympus; and his wonder and awe in these mysterious regions acted, as the thought of the cheque had done, as a fresh bullet-conductor to render him insensible for the moment to any deadlier impressions. In those days, at all events, the operations by which a newspaper came into being and was sped upon its wondrous work was sufficiently enveloped in mystery to render the floor of a newspaper-office holy ground to an imaginative country schoolboy. His eye rested with an entirely new degree of reverence upon Jupiter Tonans determinedly squared out before a great blotched 'slip' of printing-paper and a half-finished tumbler of whisky-and-water, while a youthful scion of the editorial family squatting on the floor beside his chair was in vain endeavouring, by pinching his trousers and monotonous vocal performances of a funereal character, to awaken its stern parent to a petition for 'a penny for bull's-eyes.' He took in with much respect the cloud-capt window-panes, crippled furniture, and *débris* of ragged ledgers, hieroglyphic 'proofs,' job-printing bills, tobacco-pipes, newspaper exchanges, and household odds-and-ends (including Mrs. Murrin's walking-bonnet) which adorned the sanctuary, and sniffed up the vague mouldy smell of paste, printing-inks, and rotting newspaper files, as a sweet incense peculiarly acceptable to the nostrils of the masses. It was impossible to resist the temptation to skip into the printing-office, which was as visible as anything could be through the nebulous window of Mat's throne-room ; and here our young friend gazed in silent awe at the boxes of types at rest in their various compartments like an innumerable army asleep in their encampments—so still, and yet with such a wonder-working potency to arise and conquer the world ; and he listened intently while Noble Nolan, the foreman, explained to him how the tiny metal soldiers were put together and went forth to the machine-room in all their panoply ; and he heard the snort of Mat Murrin's small donkey-engine, as if it were a wild spirit getting up steam to fly through the roof and through the civilised world presently on those ' wings of the Press.'

His state of wonderment was not lost upon the editor, who threw down his pen as if there was really nothing more for the pen of man or angel to add on the subject, and, fixing his eye-glass with majesty, said : 'Singular the power of the Press, isn't it ? By the way, that was a very creditable thing of yours in the *X——*, young Rohan—I should say, devilish creditable. Shouldn't be surprised if 'twas that brought the Government down on them. Why not try a little thing, an occasional scintilla or so, for the *Banner* ? We are always anxious to encourage local talent in the *Banner*. *I* don't mind if they suppress me, not a blasted bit.'

' By George, that was the very thing I came here to propose ! ' said young Rohan, whom Mat's jolly carnal voice at once recalled from cloudland. ' And if Captain Mike only agrees with me, sir, we'll make the *Banner* flap its old wings in a way that will astonish Drumshaughlin.'

' Aloysia, darling,' said Mat to the grimy little cherub at his side, 'tell your ma—tumblers, lovey, tumblers,'—a commission which the g. l. c. rushed to execute with all the more expedition that, as the next best thing to bull's-eyes, she had just succeeded in upsetting the contents of the ink-bottle over Mat's leading article. ' Here, Noble Nolan,' he thundered out into the print-ing-office. ' Bless my soul ! ' observing the black cloud over-spreading his manuscript like the Eastern Question, of which his readers received so many inky bodements, ' that child's passion for literary work is—really unnatural ! I am afraid you won't be able to read it, Noble Nolan.'

'It don't matter, sir,' said Noble Nolan, meekly draining off the superfluous fluid, and disappearing with a sigh which seemed to indicate that reading Mat's MS. under an eclipse was but a slight additional item in the extraordinary duties of Mat Murrin's foreman, compositor, machine-boy, jcb-printer, accountant, advertising agent, bill-diplomatist, and (in general) Cabinet Minister in-waiting.

'Now, young Rohan!' said Mat, readjusting the eye-glass and the editorial chair in a more affable manner, and proceeding to charge a clay pipe and pass a depleted tobacco-pouch around. Thus encouraged, Ken Rohan unfolded his scheme, having first elicited Captain Mike's opinion that the Dublin arrests would not be allowed to force the leaders into immediate or premature action. 'I don't know a darned bit myself,' he said. 'I only know my orders is to freeze on right here till further orders, and I'll freeze. There are fools at head-quarters fit for anything,' he groaned, with recollections of his pawned revolver and unpaid hotel-bill, 'but I guess they ain't such goslings as not to be prepared for a blizzard of this sort. No sir, we ain't going to get rushed, I reckon, till the boys from the other side are signalled.' In that case, young Rohan's plan was, briefly, that the work of the suppressed newspaper should be taken up, and the confidence of the organisation maintained, by a journal of which he was ready to assume the risky honours of director. One openly printed within reach of the Castle would not survive a second issue. His notion was that Mat Murrin's printing office should be availed of for the purpose. A district so sequestered would be the last in the island suspected of being the fountain of a revolutionary newspaper propaganda. The carters from the Cork breweries could convey the edition in barrels, that would pass as returned empties; and from Cork the railways would send the paper flying like the fiery cross from shore to shore of Ireland. The *Banner* would continue to wave on its own account over the local battlements; but Mat would, of course, be still worshipped with divine honours as the one undivided and indivisible Cloud-Compeller of the firm, while young Harold and young Rohan were to pour out the treasures of their capacious intellects weekly, in coruscations of patriotic passion, song, wit, and story, in the secret press. 'Yes, but, by all the boodlers in the Sixth Ward, I'm going to chip in too, young fellars!' sang out the Captain, in high glee. 'I kin turn a rale tony yarn with any of the boys on this bar. Jest send round your shorthand man to take me on. Why I wasn't scalped at M'Gahan's Gulch by them red Soo divvils, or by the Nigger Ghost of the Rappahannock—guess you don't come on a strike like that this side. No, sir.'

While these plans were in course of development, **Mat Mur-rin** had vanished incontinently at certain rumblings of female thunder (so to speak) on the kitchen staircase ; and the plotters could hear, amidst their own eager colloquy, fragments of another stifled exchange of views from the depths:—*e.g.* (in damaged but high soprano) 'An unpardonable old fool'—(in *tenore* the least in the world *robusto*) 'Eliza, my love, reelly'—(sop. con spirito) 'gadding about with the young spree-boys in place of putting a decent stitch of clothes on the backs of your children' —. (ten.-rall.) 'there now—thank you, my heart's jewel—the decanter:'—after which, preceded by a light oscillatory echo, Jupiter emerged from his cloud, serenely bearing a little tray of glasses with a flat-jowled decanter of spirits.

'The resources of this establishment are at your service, gentlemen, as long as there's a tatter of the old *Banner* flying,' said the Editor, as he distributed the 'spirits' in a series of large-hearted, or, as he would himself say, *flauhoolach* spills. 'But you see it's all a question of ha'pence—damn them same ha'pence! Swift was right—this would be the happiest little country in the world if such things were never invented. But there they are—the mean little copper sprissauns—or rather, faith, there they aren't, for I may impart to you, gentlemen, in confidence, that I'm no more in a position to start a newspaper, privately or publicly, big or little, at this moment than to launch a fleet of ironclads into Bantry Bay to sweep British commerce from the seas, however excellent both consummations would be. What is it now, Noble Nolan?' he demanded, with dignity, as the foreman reappeared at the glass door of the print-ing-office with a *Miserere* expression of countenance.

'The staff won't set it, sir—they refuse to set it,' he said, agitating gently the MS. of Mat's black-avised leading article.

'What, can't make me out in the dark, eh?—turn up their noses at a blotch of ink, the rascals, do they? Well, I suppose we must re-indite the legend for the rogues.'

'It isn't that, sir. The staff say they won't bring out the *Banner* unless they get their wages down.'

'The staff say that, do they?' thundered Jupiter, arising in his wrath. 'The staff say they won't bring out the *Banner*—they l let it drop in the face of the enemy—they'll let it drop, and be damned to them! Noble Nolan, this is rebellion foul and unnatural—all-abhorred rebellion, sir. Tell the staff on barren mountains shall we starve ere we redeem the traitors from our coffers. Tell the staff to get them to their cases or to get them to the devil.'

The foreman stood scratching his head in a mildly suggestive manner. ' 'Tis coming on five o'clock, sir, and I'm afraid we may lose the post,' he said, gently.

'Upon my soul, we just may, most Noble Nolan—we just may, as you remark,' said Jupiter, laying down the sceptre of the skies and imbibing a mouthful of the whisky-and-water. 'What's to be done, ancient comrade, eh? You might drop round and collect that little thing of old Dargan's for the magistracy and the wedding—charge him election rates, a shilling a line, the thundering old thief.'

'I collected that early this morning, sir, for the missus. I believe the butcher wouldn't send the chops,' he added in a confidential undertone.

'Ha, domestic treason, too! Well, let us inspect the books,' said Mat, running his finger down the well-thumbed pages of an anarchical old ledger. ' Now, there's that double-ad. of The Drumshaughlin Crystal Palace—thirty shillings an insertion. Oh! I forgot—the Crystal Palace is in the Court. Why the devil weren't we in the Court ourselves long ago, Noble Nolan, and why didn't we come out of it as rich as Begums?—that's what I want to know. You couldn't manage to get the Town Clerk to back a little bill on the security of the next quarter's account for the Commissioners' ad.—no?'

'Tried him last week, sir—said the Commissioners mightn't like it, if it oozed out.'

'Never much good in that same Town Clerk since he took the pledge—the *Banner* will have to flap a protecting wing or so over our corporate institutions, I'm thinking. K.L.M.—"M'Grudder—stop"—ay, the gold-spectacled Italian old son of a Sabine, "stop," as I hope whenever he gets a distant view of Heaven he'll stop there! N.O.P.—running perilously low in the alphabet, as I'm a Gentleman of the Press. Stay—that damned auctioneer hasn't stumped up yet—a low fellow, with two public-houses, and a sketch of a farm, besides the auctioneering. Not a sixpence, and two months overdue.'

'I called to him three times last pay-day, sir, and got nothing but the heighth of im-*pidd*-ence from him, with respects, to you,' said the meek foreman, showing that even meek foremen have their feelings, like the gods and rich auctioneers with two public-houses and a sketch of a farm.

'The heighth of im-*pidd*-ence, you did—did you? Noble Nolan, we'll roast that auctioneer—we'll baste him finely in his own gravy—and we'll distribute the joint among the Staff, sir, in platefuls, or what's better still, in bottlefuls. Just attend to me. This is an order from me on the auctioneer's pub. for whisky and porter to the value of one pound sterling, which, according to my reckoning, comes to sixty glasses best John Jameson, or one hundred and twenty pints J. J. Murphy & Co's porter, to be charged against my account. Give the blackguard one more chance, and, if he won't pay up, send down the Staff on him, as soon as they've got out the *Banner*—let them call for liquor *galore* and make a night of it, and present this note of mine in payment for it all ; and if he objects, you may mention to the Staff that I won't deduct anything from their wages if they leave that slug of a fellow an eye or two as black as my MS. in a mild way ; and I shouldn't object if a few of the decent neighbours were called in just to take pot luck in the entertainment, do you mind ? There, now, my delicate Ariel, my tricky spirit, go charge my goblins that they grind his joints—the heighth of im-*pidd*-ence, did he, the subternatural bosthoon ?—we'll hunt him soundly. Depart, Noble Nolan, and tell the boys for Heaven's sake to hurry up with that article—this really wouldn't be a country worth living in if the Government hadn't an opportunity of perusing our views on their iniquitous proceedings in the morning. Prithee, despatch !'

The familiar spirit vanished with Mat's sign-manual, as though all this were not altogether a phenomenal episode in transactions with the Staff.

' I hope we weren't in the way, mate ? Leastways, my heavy curse on fortune that our purses weren't in the way to go on active service,' said the American Captain, who had been a highly edified and sympathetic student of the *Banner's* commercial system.

' Oh, they'll fetch that stingy old curmudgeon right enough, you'll find—either that, or we'll have fireworks and torchlight processions when the Staff get out,' said Mat, resuming the eyeglass and his place in the councils of the nation. ' No, gentlemen, this slight interruption wasn't at all irrelevant, because it explained exactly what I was trying to convey. We couldn't clean out an auctioneer's pub. every week on a national scale, could we ?' said the Editor, unbending at last into a sly chuckle and another deep 'mouthful' out of his tumbler.

Young Rohan was prepared, of course, with a suggestion for the financial part of the difficulty. The secret Press would be an indispensable part of the organisation. The organisation must be prepared to undertake the preliminary expense. How could one small thousand dollars of the tens of thousands weekly subscribed in America be more faithfully invested for the advantage of the cause ? He proposed that, fortified with credentials from Captain Mike, Jack Harold should undertake a mission to Dublin to communicate with the chief of the Secret Council with a view to obtain the necessary funds, and acquire possession of the agents' book of the suppressed journal, which would enable the new organ to start upon its work immediately at ridiculously small cost to begin with ; and, once launched on its career, the returns would not merely recoup the initial expenditure, but bring in an amply sufficient revenue to remunerate the publisher and the contributors. The scheme, advocated with all Ken's sanguine and impetuous rhetoric, carried all before it, and the friends thrashed it out affectionately in all its possible and impossible bearings, until the golden contents of the flat-jowled decanter had given place to cold white vacancy—(like a bright soul emptied of its rich life, a process with which decanters are familiar)—and until certain fioriture of the damaged soprano on the staircase again made Jupiter Tonans paler than he had grown in presence of the ultimatum of the Staff. (The Staff, for their part, were all this time setting away like men whose every stickful of the *Banner's* views in solid type brought them a hundred yards nearer to the bung of the auctioneer's whisky-casks.)

'I think, Captain, you'd betther remain where you are till I skirmish up the street a bit. I don't like the way thim Bobbies are hoverin',' said Con Lehane, the stone-mason, putting in his honest mug and massive shoulders from the shop with the air of a mastiff on duty.

Ken Rohan strolled back to the Mill, in a state of exultation, in which he was prepared to welcome his father's banter about the profession of poetry with the most filial indulgence, and was astounded to find that unaccountable old miller take him brusquely by the hand, as a rough dog might take a child's, and never make the smallest reference to the cheque or to the fate of the revolutionary organ ; on the contrary, after dinner, for the first time since the ominous word 'Fenianism' was breathed in the household, he related how he had once made a journey to Dublin to see John Mitchel about a consignment of pikeheads, and how grandly Mitchel's dark hair clustered over his forehead. The two young men had parted with the understanding that Jack Harold was to start on his Dublin embassy by the morning mail-car, fortified with ten sovereigns and some shillings, which Ken Rohan had banked with his mother, since his early child days, as a fortune for little Katie, and to which that reckless young lady proposed secretly to add two sovereigns of her own, the proceeds of two consecutive years' prizes for 'best general conduct' while under the wing of darling old Mother Rosalie. The prospect of a journey to Dublin, rather than any other aspect of the undertaking, had put the ambassador in high good-humour, and he grasped Ken Rohan's hand buoyantly, whispering—

'The foul midnight hags have sung their chant du départ.
They are gone ! You are a greater enchanter than they.'

As he walked away, he met Mr. Hans Harman.

CHAPTER THE TWENTY-SIXTH

HARMANIANA

'I'M the enemy, you know, Dawley. Beware of me ! It's only
fair to tell you that,' said Mr. Hans Harman, with his back to
the scant fire in his bleak study at Stone Hall. He seemed to
have found a saving in coals by this system of heating. He
absorbed sufficient caloric himself with a trifling consumption of
coals, and his visitors were dependent upon him for their heat
supply. If he wanted to freeze, he need only look it—there was
nothing else in the room to counteract the impression. If he
beamed and glowed, the visitor might still feel chilly enough,
animally speaking, but Hans Harman's geniality only sparkled
the more for the surrounding polar region. His large handsome
eyes at present shone with mischief-loving warmth, like a frisky
sea-coal fire. Dawley, the tailor, looked as though he were
enjoying the privilege of warming his hands at them. It being a
cold autumn-deathbed day, warmth in some form was opportune,
and it never struck Dawley that the glow in Hans Harman's face
would have been as well if it proceeded from the grate. 'You're
a famous rebel, all the world knows—something high up, now,
I'd swear—a Brigadier-General with a cocked-hat, very likely ?
I hear the most desperate stories about the marching and the
square-forming of your midnight battalions in the Glen. Well,
well,' he rattled along, noting pleasantly that the Brigadier-
General's cocked-hat was already dancing proudly in Dawley's
beady little eyes and on the tip of his cocked-nose, 'we'll have
to be shooting and charging one another one of those days, I
presume—and, mind, you must expect no quarter from me !—but
in the meantime, Dawley, I hope you won't disappoint me about
that knickerbocker suit this week. I may have to wear it
against you in the campaign hereafter ; but that's no reason why
it shouldn't be honourably paid for and a good fit—a credit to
both of us.'

'You'll have it by Saturday, sir, as neat as a glove, if I have
to sit up all night for it on well-water,' said Dawley.

'It's no business of mine, of course ; but really one does
sometimes scruple to see a smart fellow like you, with your inte

resting little family—the fourth or the fifth, that last little event, which, Dawley ? '

' I thank God I'm not afflicted with them kind of things, sir,' said the Brigadier-General, with a somewhat stiff toss of the cocked-hat and feathers.

' True, by Jove ! I had forgotten that there was somebody as lucky as myself in this baby-squalling country,' laughed Mr. Harman, imperturbably. ' But it is all the more painful to see a man, who hasn't a houseful of brats to drag him down, and who might make his way in the world, made the dupe of men without a grain of his own honesty or capacity—men that are, perhaps, feeding on the fat of the land while he is squatted all night with his lapboard stitching a knickerbocker suit. Not but what I should be the last in the world to object to hard industry on a knickerbocker suit,' he added, with a genial laugh.

' Indeed, it's de quare set of Democrats dat's going—dat's true enough,' mused Dawley, as if to himself. ' Making an Irish Republic be gallivanting in a Castle, and shaping up to de aris-tocracy. As if dat was what de people subscribed dere hard-earned money for ! '

' Between ourselves, Dawley, I think your Democrats show their very good sense in not residing in Blackamoor Lane as long as they can enjoy high life in a Castle,' laughed the agent. ' Well, I don't want to worm myself into your confidence in matters of that sort ; though, perhaps, it would be easy enough for me to make a good fellow of myself by pretending that I'm not against you—resolutely and mercilessly against you. I will only say that it's a pity, that's all ; and if you only knew the kind of men you are trusting to—how they are trafficking on you and selling you in droves, by Jove ! and not for a hatful of sove-reigns even, but for a night's rations of whisky. Stay, Dawley, I know you won't abuse my confidence any more than make my coat a misfit, though we *are* enemies—open, honourable enemies There is one of these rascals below. Just step behind that screen, and you will hear for yourself.'

Mr. Harman rang the bell, and Quish plantigraded into the room like an elephant that had playfully deprived one of the public of a hairy cap. ' Well, fellow,' said the agent, severely, ' you've spent that last half-sovereign—gone into Moll Carty's till—poured down your own thirsty gullet, eh ? '

The elephant intimated by a heavy double-shuffle of its hind hooves, and certain vague noises in the gullet in question, that the agent was impregnable in his facts.

' Precious bad value you gave the Government for its money —for you know well, sir, it's the money of the public and not

mine that you are soaking yourself in whisky with. You'll
have to look sharp, sir, and let us know more of this infernal
conspiracy, or I'll hand you over to public justice and make an
example of you—do you hear?'

'I'll do my best, zurr,' said Quish, who essayed the smallest
effort of eloquence with as painful a wrestling of the spirit as the
orator Flood when he used to rise for one of his great efforts.

'Well, what have been the American Captain's movements
since you last reported?'

'Twenty-three brace on Thursday, and two blackcock.' This
was the one topic in the world on which his tongue was not
clogged with triple chains. 'Friday, a parcel of boys scared the
birds, drat 'em!—only a few brace and an odd snipe.'

The agent frowned angrily. 'Don't put me off with your
infernal dogboy humbug,' he said, menacingly. 'You know very
well what I mean—any drilling?—any strangers in square-toed
boots?—any meeting of Centres at the Castle, eh?'

'Lots, zurr,' said the monster, looking roguishly with one
eye and truculently with the other. 'Hid in the 'servathry an'
hurd it all. Seems there's a change from the Bay—ships are to
come round to Kenmare—some big fellow 'spected next week
that'll settle it all. Quish will keep an eye. Half a sov, zurr,'
belched the animal, panting after so much violent word-vomiting.

'Vague and incoherent, as usual. I wish your ear was more
serviceable than your mouth, or, better still, if you'd brush the
mud out of whatever answers you for a noddle,' said the agent
contemptuously. 'Well, there's the money, and mind you report
the instant this stranger sets foot in the district; or—listen!—
so sure as you'll never look your hangman straight in the face,
you'll make that hangman's acquaintance—either that, or I'll
denounce you to the vengeance of the men you are betraying—
perhaps to Dawley, the tailor, who, I hear, is a desperate fellow
with the revolver. Go!'

'Oyeh, the little *keolawn*!' snorted Quish, with the contempt
of an elephant for a gad-fly. 'More power to your honour!'
and, burying the piece of gold in his paw, with the clutch of a
fasting wild animal, the great slouching mass fumbled out of the
room, hairy cap and all.

'Oh the villainy!' exclaimed little Dawley, stalking out of
his ambush with a brow of darkness. '"*A little keolawn*" from
dat cross-eyed abortion!—de bloody misbegotten caricature of
ould Nick! "*Keolawn*" from Quish de bailiff! Oh den, oh
den, wasn't I de Job of a man to listen dere foreninst him, an'
not try whedder a bullet wouldn't be ashamed of lodgin' in his
ugly carcase!'

'But you mustn't, you know—honour bright !—in justice to *me*,' said Mr. Hans Harman, affably. 'I hope the rascal hasn't ruffled your feelings—Quish is not altogether the worst of them. I was only just anxious to let you know, in a friendly sort of way, what mines are opening under honest fellows' feet—because after all, you know, it's not because men are political opponents that they may not give some credit for honesty where it's due. There now—I'll shoot you down like a dog all the same when you take the field, Dawley. Saturday, then, be it ; and for your life none of your atrocious velvet collars on a shooting-coat.' Whereupon Mr. Hans Harman's eyes opened the door for Dawley and—

> Kicked him downstairs with such a good grace,
> That D. thought he was kicking him up.

Perhaps it was the draughty, stony-faced staircase that did it, but the supplies of cheerful warmth the agent took in at the study-grate were exhausted before he had mounted to his wife's room ; for it seemed to be a gust of cold air that entered the darkened sick-room with him and blew into the drawn, livid, peevish face fastened, as in some slow torturing apparatus, upon the pillows of the vast gloomy bed. Hans Harman, however, regaled the invalid with a cheerful smile and a hand that, so to say, presented the smile on a silver salver, as he said : 'And how are you to-day, my dear ?'—looking then for an answer to Miss Deborah, as if the sufferer had nothing further to do with it, but had bequeathed her views on such matters to her sister-in-law, as sole depository and Authorised Version thereof. 'No worse,' was the laconic reply of Miss Deborah, who was standing sturdily over the pinched white face, with the open Bible on the one hand, and a bowl of some nauseous homœopathic mess, which she prided herself on brewing herself, on the other—a sainted she-dragon flapping darkly around the dismal bed—a Holy Inquisitor demanding incessantly of a patient 'put to the question' what further the most unreasonable of sufferers could desire than a dark chamber, a bed as pompous as a hearse, medicinal draughts of choicest colocynth, the Holy Scriptures, and a woman of inflexible virtue to administer these good things in their wholesome season. Mr. Harman was a dutiful husband ; but, having cheered his wife with his customary dutiful visit, and, being a man who lived laborious days, public duty compelled him and the gust of cold air to take their departure, carrying with them Miss Deborah's consoling bulletin ; they, in fact, as the French say, took note of the minister's assurance, and passed to the order of the day.

The next order of the day was the Mill at Greenane, where the indefatigable agent descended as from a chariot of the sun half an hour afterwards, having, in the meantime, accumulated stores of warmth that ordinary terrestrial grates are inadequate to account for, even if a bitter October blast had not been blowing all the way. 'Only pulled up to see how you are, Rohan ; glad to see you so sturdy on your pins again,' he said. 'This is bad news in the paper—suppression of this Fenian newspaper, and the rest of it ; hope it isn't true that your son wrote some dreadful thing or other that got it suppressed.' This last thrust was not so artistic but that the point of steel was visible, for the contemptuous disregard of his offer of the clerkship in the Pipe Roll Office rankled in the agent's recollection sorely.

He had made the one thrust that could stir the miller's slumbering independence. 'Thank you, sahr ! I suppose my son will be able to take care of himself,' he said, with a touch of the iron virility before which the agent had so often quaked in the Board-room and at town's meetings.

'Faith, I hope so for his sake, and for yours. Young gentlemen that turn up their noses at a snug berth in the Four Courts, and won't even be commonly civil to those that offer it, don't easily learn that when they dash their heads against stone walls it's not the stone walls that get hurt. But what the deuce has come over *you*, Rohan, that you should copy the boy's manner as well as his objections to a Government situation ?'

The miller did not know in the least what he was driving at. But he supposed the reference was to something that might have happened about the time of his illness, and, as he did not choose to let the world know the gaps and fogs that still infested his memory of that period, he found it easier to resent the almost undisguised malice of the agent's observation. 'Whatever I have to say to a man, I say it to his face aboveboard. You must excuse me if I'm too old to take lessons in your model-school, Mr. Harman,' he said hotly. 'And as for Government situations, 'tis nothing so wonderful if a boy of mine does not ambition blacking the boots of them that made Humphrey Dargan a magistrate.' At which rough hug Myles chuckled like a lusty wrestler.

'Come, Rohan, confound it, you must not let Humphrey hear that,' laughed the agent, jumping into the trap, and bending down cheerfully to whisper the remainder. 'At all events unless you're prepared to take up that little bill of his for 300*l.* on the 24th. He's such an infernal old screw he wouldn't do it for me, unless I handed over to him that old decree for possession, you remember, as security. Of course, that does not matter to a man of your means. But that's old Humphrey's way, and that's what has brought him to be a Justice of the Peace—that and civility. I'm just driving up to see him take his seat—just to give him a neighbourly leg-up, you know. Good-day, Rohan. I'm sorry I don't find you in such good health this morning.'

'Handed over the decree for possession to old Dargan!' repeated the miller, stopping to watch the agent's half-blood mare cavorting and her master distributing salutes up the street. 'They're up to mischief. They're infernal scoundrels, both!' said Myles Rohan, as he turned to his books and freight-notes with a heavy heart.

Mr. Hans Harman descended from his chariot of the sun at the side-door of the dog-hole called the magistrates' room, from which, through another door, the magisterial deities were wont to rise upon the Bench of the Petty Sessions Chamber, like rododaktulous morning. 'Admiral, I'm so glad!' cried Mr. Harman, greeting with respectful enthusiasm a noble-looking, silvery-frosted old gentleman, who had not yet taken off his old-fashioned cloak and gloves.

'I hope that this isn't true, Harman?—at all events that we're not to expect his company here to-day?' said the Admiral, tranquilly.

The agent laughed, and shrugged his shoulders. 'It's rather a trial, of course; but you won't be too hard on the old ass, Admiral—I don't think you could be hard upon anybody.'

Admiral Ffrench was a gentleman of ancient stock and of an ancient school. As a curly-headed boy, he volunteered from the British Navy to accompany Canaris in the almost incredible adventures of his fireships, and with his own hand tore down the ensign of the Turkish Vice-Admiral at Navarino. The last chapter of his youthful book of Greek romance was a marriage with a beautiful princess of the house of Ypsilanti, whom he brought home and worshipped with simple rapture for twenty years at Castle Ffrench, and at whose grave he continued to worship with a gentle resignation ever since. In the simple-hearted old gentleman who lived like an easy father among his tenants, presided over the bench of magistrates with the sweet stateliness of an Eastern Haroun, and warmed the community generally like an unobtrusive old sun beaming out of a silvery mist, it required some effort of imagination to remember the bright reckless curls and fiery eyes of the British boy who bounded up the rigging of the Turkish frigate 'Amurath the Second' to the music of the guns at Navarino. It was indeed difficult to figure to oneself Admiral Ffrench being hard upon anybody. Nevertheless, there was some faint flush of Navarino under his brows this morning that rather discomposed the agent as he said : 'I do think Lord Drumshaughlin might have spared us this. If he will not remain here himself to do his duty by his people, at least he might have some consideration for those who do not desert their post. Either that, or he might be a little more candid, and appoint his estate bailiff to the Commission of the Peace at once——'

'Well, well, my dear Admiral, you know what Lord Drumshaughlin is,' began the agent, humbly.

'I knew what he was—a gentleman, and a not unworthy one,' said the old Admiral, with something like a sigh.

'Of course, old Dargan is rather a trial to one in your position,' pursued the agent, passing over the interruption ; 'but, you see, the old donkey kept pestering ; he has got a good bit of land in one way or another—extensive ratepayer, and all to that—and there was such a row, you know, about the Roman Catholics not being represented on the Bench ; and he has a ridiculous wife, who would sell herself to the devil to be called a Justice of the Peace's lady—absurd creatures ! But I do assure you, my dear Admiral, old Dargan is quite harmless, and understands, you know—he will make no mistakes as between him and you, depend on it ; and, after all, a local man like that may be useful. The Sub-Inspector has married that little girl of his—a very presentable little girl, and a tidy thing, you may be sure,' rattled along the agent, who saw nothing better for it than to rattle along. 'He's up for the Club—I do hope you won't say anything against it—your voice would be decisive, Admiral Ffrench; but you're too good-natured to do anything of the sort. He has promised a subscription of 50l. a year to the Hunt, and, between ourselves, unless somebody like that comes to the rescue, I don't see how we're to avoid selling the dogs.'

'Sell them, and be hanged, sir !—or, better still, shoot them, if our sport is to depend upon the alms or the bribes of a gombeen-man !' the old Admiral at last burst out, with a flash and shock as if every gun in Navarino's Bay was in action ; but the smoke and thunder instantly died away. 'I don't presume to understand how the world goes now,' he proceeded, calmly. 'In my day we used to think that a man wanted some better credentials than his bank-book to be called a gentleman. But I dare say, so many things are changing, we old fogeys may as well reconcile ourselves to Lord Drumshaughlin's latest appointment as well as to the rest.'

'Just like your kind heart, my dear Admiral,' cried the agent. 'How lucky ! here Dargan just comes. How do, Mr. Dargan ! Wish you joy ! Admiral, will you kindly let me introduce——'

'Will you kindly let me tell a constable to call my coachman ?'

said the old Admiral, statelily moving towards the door, hat in hand.

'The Petty Sessions' Book is all ready, sir. You are not going ?' exclaimed the Petty Sessions Clerk, staring with all his eyes. For nearly twenty years there had not been a Drum-shaughlin Petty Sessions without that kindly old magistrate beaming down from the chair like an Angel of Justice grown soft-hearted and ancient.

'Thanks, Sibwight, you may go on. I don't feel well to-day,' said Admiral Ffrench, as his carriage came to the door. Sibwight never saw the Admiral's face again at that same door.

'The old Admiral's looking shaky—shouldn't be surprised if 'twas a fit, poor old boy,' observed Mr. Hans Harman, turning undauntedly to the new magistrate, who was at the moment too much engaged in deliberating whether he should keep on his canary-coloured gloves on the bench or no, to concern himself with minor troubles. 'The old order changeth, Humphrey, my good friend; these old buffers would leave the business of the country in a pretty way without an infusion of vigorous new blood like yours and mine. The devil drown them black!' he added, in confidential soliloquy. Then he turned to Lord Dunmanus' agent—bald, bland, and comfortable-looking. 'Pilkington, I move you take the chair. I know no man so worthy of being the poor old Admiral's successor. You don't know our new colleague, Mr. Dargan ?' And Pilkington's smooth face, lighted with joy by his new distinction, graciously extended the illumination to Hans Harman's *protégé* in the canary-coloured gloves.

Alas! how the day-dreams cozen us the moment they cease to be dreams! Did ever new member, waiting for the Speaker's command to advance to the table, find the indifferent yawning House around him quite the glory he had paid for ? Did ever world-enthralling orator await his turn to rise without thinking how much better it would be to go home and get to bed ? Did ever even lover (for no novelist of discretion is likely to place a mere listening senate on a level with his incomparable audience of one)—did ever even lover (of twenty or upwards) languish over the roseate cheek of beauty at any great length without finding the language of the affections a little tedious ? Humphrey Dargan, even in the first bliss of his arm-chair on the judicial heights to Mr. Pilkington's left, was reflecting that he had passed happier moments in his own little fly-blown parlour behind the pawn-shop.

Women are sturdier idol-worshippers. Mrs. Dargan was all that day floating in a very heaven. All her heart could desire further would be that the president of the Ladies' St. Vincent de

Paul Society and other ladies of her acquaintance should be admitted to a distant view of her beatitude. She learned with some
indignation that it was only ladies with black eyes and in a more
or less paulo-post state of intoxication that were wont to mingle
with the audience in the Sessions' Court, even upon occasions of
magnitude. She dressed Humphrey for the ceremony and combed
his muddy grey locks, as she had combed Lionel's curls for his first
children's tea party (how she now hugged herself, by the way, on
her courage in calling him Lionel, instead of branding the boy
for life with some odious nickname like Kennedy or Paddy!)
The old fellow assured her, almost with tears in his eyes, that there
was no special costume as a magistrate prescribed in his commission ; but fire could not melt out of her the opinion that something on a super-Sunday scale of splendour was called for, and a
light blue tie, the languishing yellow gloves, and a blazing
diamond-ring, specially selected from the jewel-box in the pawn-
office, were the least that would satisfy her stern conceptions of
duty to society. She flattened her face against the window pane
to observe the impression made upon the public by the new justice
on his way up the street, and pranced with indignation when a
raw young policeman let him pass, like any civic varlet, without
raising his hand to his helmet in salute. She rang the bell, and
said to her husband's confidential man, who answered the summons : ' I think, Sweeny, you might walk over and incidentally
remind Sub-constable Doody who Himself is. The young man
may not be able to read the paper, but I think you might hint
to him that his officer is,' said the magistrate's wife, grandly casting her eyes upon a cabinet photo of Mr. Augustus George Flibbert, which illustrified the mantelpiece. Sweeny, hastening upon
the heels of the ill-starred policeman, was properly indignant to
find the passage between the pawn-office and the dwelling house
blocked by the ragged figure of our friend Meehul, from Cnockawnacurraghkooish, got up on a humble scale of Sunday magnificence of his own, with his best shirt trying to frown the tattered
ends of the flannel waistcoat out of view, and his old locks ruth-
lessly debarred from their privilege of taking the air through the
roof of his hat. ' Is *he* within?' whispered Meehul the Magnificent, with a jerk of his thumb towards the back parlour.

' His wurdship is gone to the coort,' said Sweeny, with a
gesture scarcely less grand than his mistress's apostrophe of Sub-
constable Doody.

' *Ké hú shin?* (who's that?)' asked Meehul, scratching his
poll, ''tisn't his wurdship I want, but ould Humphrey—about
the little bill,' he added, in a tremulous whisper.

' Misther Dargan is a ma-*jest*-rate,' quoth Sweeny. ' Stand out of the way, and don't make so free with your betthers,' flinging the old fellow rudely against the doorpost, and hieing after the policeman, while poor Meehul meekly pursued his old hat into the gutter, where his little contrivance for improving the appearance of his headgear by stuffing a red handkerchief between his hair and the open sky stood pitilessly exposed to the public.

Old Humphrey, in the meanwhile, not being composed of the undaunted mettle of his wife, did not find it too gay to feel the eyes of the world fixed upon him. Truly, he had solved the glove enigma by the expedient of pulling one glove off, and leaving the other on, but he was oppressed with a horrid suspicion that the eyes of the world were fixed on the one staring yellow glove that remained, and the finger of the world pointing with scorn and derision to his miserable compromise; and the feeling grew so intolerable that he nervously jerked the yellow hand off the desk and plunged it in his small-clothes, as if the limb, like that of Mutius Scaevola, had been roasting in a slow yellow flame, and he had just ducked it in a pool of water to ease the pain. His one judicial action was not of propitious omen. 'Speek up to the gentlemen, mem; give us your neem!' he said to a virago, who was endeavouring to defend the poker as an implement in neighbourly controversy.

'Me name, is it?' cried the amazon, who thought she scented a foe in his worship. 'It's an honester name than your own, you ould common extortioner! And if you haven't my name, you have many's the good pound of my value in your pop-shop, you hoary ould catamountain!—"Gintlemin," av ye plaze! Troth, the gintlemin would want to have an eye to their watches while they're keeping *your* company, Humphrey, me honey.' At which Mr. Pilkington's round face rippled with fat merriment, while he offered a decorous appeal for 'silence' to the roar from the gallery.

Mr. Dargan could not help thinking that justice was much better vindicated by Head-Constable Muldudden, who shook the woman with the grip of a brown bear, and said: 'How daar you talk like that—to his worship? Do you know you've just been guilt of a contimpt punishable by seven days summarily under the 29th Section of the Petty Sessions Act? Do you know *that*?' —and his worship followed with much respect the legal opinions with which Head-Constable Muldudden (a potentate of might in Drumshaughlin) from time to time favoured the magistrates during the sitting. He was not at all sorry when public justice was satisfied for the day, and Mr. Hans Harman and he strolled back to the Bank together.

'I see you're knocking away the shop from your own diggings. Quite right,' said the agent, pleasantly, nodding to where Con Lehane was at work on the partition wall. 'And, of course, you'll arrange to give up the retail licence?'

'Well, sir, the sperrits line brings in a pretty penny. Don't you think, now, it's rather a sheeme, now, speeking as a sinsible man who knows what treede is, sir?' said Dargan, discontentedly.

'The Chancellor's got some nonsense in his head about it— he won't have whisky,' said the agent. 'Hullo, Meehul, so you're not out of Cnockaawn yet? you have more lives than a cat, you old slyboots!'—this to the old Cnockawnacurraghkooish mountainy-man, who was in waiting around the door, his hand raised to his hat in an enchanted attitude, as if waiting to have some spell taken off before it could be lowered, and his knees also cringing dutifully in a position of submissive discomfort.

'There's no use in your coming about this door, my good man,' said the new magistrate, haughtily. 'I'll seize, or give you twenty pounds to clear out? I never'll make my own of the land.'

'Shure, 'twas only tin pound your honour lint me two years ago, when the owld cow got the red wather. I paid you back five an' twenty pounds honest one time with another since, and afther all that you bring out forty pound agin me. Begor, it's the quarest 'rithmetic ever *I* seen!' said the old peasant, growing bolder in his perplexity and desperation.

'You forget the account for the Indian meal, my man,' said the new J.P.

'The account for Injia male! That manes the two shillins a bag more than I could get it in any house in the town for,' said Meehul.

'And be the same token, Meehul,' struck in the sinister factotum Sweeny, 'your wife is daling in the shop over the bridge for tay an' yellow male, my fine fellow.'

'I can't stop talking to you here,' said Mr. Dargan. 'You can take twenty pounds or the Sheriff,' and he entered the hall with the agent.

'Twenty pound! 'Tis hardly 'twould bring the childher as far as the workhouse!' groaned Meehul, his eyes following in a stupid despair.

'Don't go for a bit, Meehul, and I'll see what I can do for you—but he's a devilish hard nut, Meehul, between ourselves—a devilish hard nut,' said Mr. Hans Harman, who had dropped behind for a moment to whisper this in the ear of the old peasant, with a knowing wink.

The old mountainy-man scratched his head, in a curious puzzle of gratitude, suspicion, and grinding misery. 'Begor, they may all say what they like of him,' he muttered to himself as the door closed, 'but there are worse divels than Hans Harman going.'

'Of course, you might throw that fellow's land in with your mountain,' said the agent, when they were ensconced in the shadows of the back parlour, and the blind pulled down, 'but the place wouldn't fatten snipe, and he has a dangerous son. If you'd just seize the heifer of a morning, he'd probably raise a fiver in one way or another and buy her out, and you'd make a better thing of it. I suppose that was your son in the passage?' he said, referring to Master Lionel, who had made a descent from Trinity College for the wedding, and was at present engaged in overcrowding Drumshaughlin with the most *chic* Dublin fashions in Tyrolese hats, prodigious stand-up collars, and magenta neckties (it was in the brief reign of that lackadaisical shade). 'By the way,' he continued, as a happy thought struck him, 'you'll be wanting to settle him down to something. The Attorney-General, Glascock, has given me the nomination to a handsome little thing in the Pipe Roll Office—nothing to do, ninety pounds a year to begin, and quite the right kind of thing, you know, though it's called a clerkship. What if I present you with the nomination for your lad as a sort of birthday present to you on this your magisterial natal-day—eh, Dargan?'

'A clerkship at ninety pounds a year,' repeated the magisterial baby, stroking his puddled grey beard reflectively. 'Thank you, sir—you're very obliging, I'm sure—most eemiable of you, Mr. Harman; but his mother has, ahem! other views for Lionel. Lord Dunbrody's son and he are College chums—a bit of a scapegrace, no doubt—it runs in them genteel families—but he talks of getting Lionel into the—ahem!—Diplomatic Service through the influence of his respected father.'

'The devil he does!' cried Hans Harman, walking towards the window to discharge an oath into the street in safety. (The respectable father happened to be in the respectable Bankruptcy Court.) 'Very well, Dargan, to business. First, you've got the decree for possession of the Mill. Very well, if he doesn't stump up on the 24th, I don't care how soon you execute it. My bailiff will have to take the possession formally; but it will have to be known that it is you are working—you understand?'

'I understand, sir,' said old Humphrey, licking one hand unctuously with the other. (The gloves were now gone, and he felt at home with his hands once more.) 'Though, indeed, I'm really sorry for Myles Rohan—an old neebour, sir, though a little im-*pate*-yus.'

'Now, to talk of more important matters. The time of redemption for the mortgage for 45,000*l.* is more than a year expired—three half-years' interest overdue? Very well, the Court cannot possibly resist an application for sale. A judge will be sitting on Tuesday. You must have notice of application lodged at once. A conditional order will go as a matter of course. The second mortgagee, you know, Hugg, I can make all right, and then if you get the carriage of sale, and if I can get appointed Receiver to watch you—as, of course, I must, on the part of the owner—well, well, my good friend, you and I will manage to console ourselves on the ruin of Carthage, eh ?'

'No fear of that ironmaster up at Lord Dunmanus' place bidding, sir ?' asked Dargan, his velvety eyes blinking like those of an ancient cat in their ambush of eyebrow. 'He's rich, and I hear he likes the place.'

'Pooh ! he's an Englishman and an ass. Wait till we have a parcel of arrests or a bit of a rising somewhere in his neighbourhood. My dear Dargan, there could not possibly be a more opportune moment for a sale—country in a disturbed state, smouldering volcano, pending insurrection, threat-talking of the Protestant inhabitants (I forgot you're not a Protestant, Humphrey—but these Fenian fellows are no bigots—they'll make a bonfire of your Bishops, as well as ours, quite impartially—Monsignor M'Grudder will tell you that)—in short, if we get queasy old Grimshaw, the Land Judge, on a good morning for the liver, you and I, sir, will be a pair of kings making a partition of a kingdom.'

'We'll have to dip very deep to get at so much money, Mr. Harman, sir,' squeaked the money-lender, shaking his head. 'I can tell you that the loan for that Hugg mortgage pushed me tight—painfully tight, I do assure you, sir.'

'If it did, you held it pretty tight—insisted on having the deed lodged with you as security, as if you were dealing with a sharper, confound you ! You've got it in that safe behind you, this moment, I'd wager my neck, if you haven't set it to breed more gold elsewhere.'

Old Dargan made a nervous backward movement towards the safe, as if at some vague thought of its being threatened. 'Besides that 12,000*l.* I've advanced in your own name,' he proceeded, ignoring Mr. Harman's levity, 'a trifle, sir, but you can't conceive, Mr. Harman, how it strained my little manes.'

'Oh, come, *that* I could have had in the open market at your rate—six per cent.'

'No doubt, sir—for the matter of that, so could his lordship himself, perhaps—he, he!' said old Humphrey, with a grin which seemed to be devoted chiefly to apologising for itself; 'and I'm sure his lordship ought to be a greeteful man if *he* is only charged six per cent. for it—truly greeteful, sir.'

'You won't make as big a fortune as a wit as you have done on stamped paper, Humphrey—take my advice,' said the agent, showing two ranks of teeth as sharp-looking as fixed bayonets, as well as equally shining. 'It just comes to this—those three mortgages in your safe are as good security as bank-notes, and 120,000*l*. or 140,000*l*. would cover the whole purchase. Why, you'd have fellows tumbling over one another to advance it. I'm not sure that Hugg himself couldn't manage to raise it, if he was driven to it'—and the fixed bayonets again glittered significantly in the sun.

The money-lender started, and placed one palm of his long skinny hands against the other—a favourite deprecatory gesture of his. 'Of course, sir,' we could make a push—a push, Mr. Harman, don't you observe?—but, indeed, and in double deed, I've dipped more deeply than I'd like Mrs. D. to know at the present, sir; and, after all, Irish land may not be always, you know—in the disturbed state of the country, now, for example——.'

'A disturbed pot of stirabout! Tush, Humphrey, my good friend; we'll be indebted to the disturbers in the purchase-money for five years off—maybe ten, if the fellows give us a respectable rising, but they won't. Then, don't you see, it is I who will have to return the rent-roll—you don't understand—and it is not necessary that you should,' he went on, rapidly. 'I tell you we've got but to stretch out our hands to make the greatest *coup* of the century, and with as little risk of any sort or kind as you would run in sweeping that spider off your window-pane—which, between ourselves, Humphrey, if I were you, I should have removed from the Bank window as a personal insult. If you move next Tuesday, there need be no opposition to the order being made absolute, and if there is proper diligence used about the proof of title, we may have the Ordnance Survey fellows on the lands before Christmas.'

'I will post over to 'Torney Wrixon directly I'm done ainner, sir,' said the money-lender; and then, with his hands working in a new fit of emotion, he mumbled: 'There's one trifling matter, sir, if I'm not too persumshus, sir——'

'Well?' said the agent, turning sharply.

'It's Mrs. D., sir—wimmen are such fidgets—so onraysonable,

I do assure you, sir—about the Club, sir—she wants to know—
ah—hum—how the little affair is going on, in short!'

'Oh, the ballot! In short, it's going on like a house afire—
like hell's blazes!' laughed the agent, boisterously. 'We'll pull
you through, Humphrey, my old friend—always, with that
cheque for the Hunt, mind! I don't see why you shouldn't turn
out in scarlet yourself, and take the value of your money. I
don't see why Mrs. D. shouldn't turn out herself, for that matter
—and Flibbert's wife, and the young gentleman who won't take
that thing in the Pipe Roll Office—I don't see why the Dargan
family should not have lands, castle, title, mingle in the gilded
saloons of the aristocracy, out-dazzle the biggest nobs in the
country—if the head of the house will only keep that venerable
noddle of his well screwed on to his shoulders and—have just the
least bit in life of patience.'

It was after delivering himself of this outburst (in which
Humphrey Dargan in vain puzzled himself to separate the irony
from the high spirits) that Mr. Hans Harman stumbled upon
Jack Harold on his way from the conference at the *Banner* office,
and ejaculated : 'Good heavens! what a relief to meet somebody
whose brain is not a petty cash-box!' as he walked up to the
young man, and, a thought suddenly striking him, said, 'Come,
and oblige a lonesome man by having a bit of dinner with him.
I have something to say to you—not a warrant for your body,'
he added, smilingly ; for, apart from the circumstance that
Dawley happened to be at this moment a scowling witness of the
cordialities of the agent and the young rebel, Hans Harman felt
a powerful personal attraction towards this bright French streak
of colour in the drab life of Drumshaughlin.

Jack Harold changed colour ; perhaps the bodements of the
weird sisters were audible for a faint moment or two again ; but
the two besetting weaknesses of his character were—first, the
impulse to flee from trouble as the swallows flee from winter,
and, secondly, a craving for the society of a station above his
own. Humphrey Dargan and he sought the society of their
social superior for curiously opposite reasons—the young man
because he felt he was fitted for it, the money-lender because he
felt that he was not. Miss Deborah looked sourly enough upon
her brother's guest, chiefly because she remembered the scene
when Mabel sang 'The Wearing of the Green,' and, among other
reasons, because the 'bit of dinner' consisted of a small dish of
beefsteak, weakly reinforced by a much cut-up cold leg of
mutton ; but the agent's jollity, and a bottle of dry Pommery,
of which, to Miss Deborah's consternation, he himself wrung the
gold head off—both coinciding with the reaction from Jack's

recent penitential mood—soon made the cold mutton, and the cold room, and Miss Deborah's cold smile, warm into a banquet for the gods in the young Sybarite's eyes. Hans Harman himself, though he was in all but form a teetotaller (Miss Deborah was one with the fierceness of a Captain Hew-Agag-to-pieces-before-the-Lord of the old Puritan days), genially fiddled with the champagne bottle in the neighbourhood of his own glass every time that he refilled his guest's; and Jack, who was on the full tide of wit and spirits, did not at all notice, when the last gush of creamy gold sparkled into his glass, that it was he himself who had finished it unaided !

Frank Harman (who had no prejudices against champagne) had vanished before there was any question of uncorking the bottle of Pommery. She was not in a particularly good humour. The announcement of little Flibbert's marriage had filled her with the desire of birching her audacious little *élève* within an inch of his life. 'The puppy ! the wretched, sordid little beggar !—to use the footing she had given him in society for the purpose of driving a bargain for that creepy old fellow's money and his pink doll of a daughter, and to do all this without even asking her leave !' Further, she did not like Jack Harold. He was too clever to be a Flibbert, and too mincing to be a man ; and perhaps the circumstance that Miss Deborah was of a different opinion had also something to say to it. Frank, at all events, fled on the pretext of scouring the country on her canvass for old Dargan's name for the Club (personally, she would have preferred ducking old Dargan's beard in the water-butt; but Frank was too loyal a party-man, so to say, not to see that this was the battle of the Harman interest ; and so she grudged not flying over hill and dale to do her duty by the flag). 'It will be a tough matter,' she remarked, as she drew on her gauntlets on the steps at Stone Hall before departing. 'Hans, I hope you won't be doing those things any more. But I dare say we'll pull it off all right, if Admiral Ffrench will only keep those transcendental airs of his at Castle Ffrench—as if it were so much worse to introduce an Irish gombeen-man into society than a Greek dancing girl !'

'You'll do it, Frank—curse the pompous old humbug ! ... you know what he said to me to-day ?—that we might as well make Quish a magistrate next ! By Jove ! it would serve him right to have Quish put up for the Club—and carry him !'

'He wouldn't be a much uglier dose,' laughed Frank, as she gathered up the reins and gave the air a flick with her driving-whip.

'I don't see why I shouldn't,' mused Hans Harman, as he sat sipping his coffee after dinner, while Jack smoked a thick cigar

and dived into a bottle of claret. Mr. Harman had no views
himself, but had a humane toleration of them in others. 'By
George ! if I meet a third beardless brat who flings an appointment at the Four Courts in my face, this is no longer a country
worth living in——. I like you,' he said, abruptly, 'and I do
not like to see you running to rust in this hole—perhaps running
your neck into a halter. Read that.' He shoved across a scrawl
under an official stamp from Glascock : 'I understand your fellow
has not come to the scratch at the Pipe Roll Office. The appointment will have to be filled at once unless you bring up your man.'
—'It's one of the prettiest posts that ever a young gentleman
drew caricatures in,' the agent proceeded. 'I mean to bring up
my man, and my man is—yourself, if your highness should be
pleased not to snub me for my impertinence.'

The Pommery and St. Estèphe lifted from Jack's brain, like
a gas held in suspension by some strong agency. Wonder, shame,
delight, remorse, coursed after one another, like wild animals, in
his thoughts. Recollections of the day's scene amidst the heather,
of his presentiment, of his mission to Dublin—curiously enough,
even of Father Phil's not very dreadful-looking countenance—
tormented him ; but they angered more than softened him. He
felt a grievance against them for haunting him with looks so
green and pale—these he could dismiss as envious creatures
flocking to imprison his good fortune. What alarmed him more
was—what could be the object of this man's bounty ? What
could be the consideration to be exacted in return ? Hot and
uncomfortable apprehensions besieged him upon this point.

The agent's keen, careless-looking eyes seemed to divine the
explanation of his half-rapturous, half-shamefaced look. 'Don't
suppose I want to swear you to loyalty over a bowl of blood,' he
said, laughingly. 'If, upon fair trial, you prefer a cell on Spike
Island to a desk at the Four Courts, don't limit your ambition on
my account. I should like to serve you—it's a whim of mine—
and as soon as my whim is gratified, we're quits—if you don't
choose still to look in on me once in a way and hear me pound
out a sonata or so.'

'Agreed, sir. I thank you, and—and *I* like *you*, also '—
which was quite true, a *risqué* acquaintance of this kind, among
such unexpected surroundings, and cemented on such whimsical
principle, having all the fascination of a romance of the Latin
Quarter for young Harold's Bohemian soul. And Hans Harman
could really be one of the most enchanting of men, with his frank,
handsome eyes and audacious wit. So, of course, could one
Mephistopheles, famed in German story ; and, as he clasped
Harman's hand to clinch the bargain, our poor Jack could not

help thinking of that other bargain in Dr. Faustus' chamber.
But Master Jack was not the one to draw back from quaffing a
cup of pleasure once at his lips in order to analyse its supernatural or subternatural ingredients. Was it his fault that
Harman should take a liking to him? Was it a bit stranger than
his taking a liking to the pianoforte? Was he to repulse the
pretty vixen, Fortune, like another Joseph, when she rushed into
his arms, without any solicitation of his, and offered him safety,
a career, a future, just when his future promised to be inclosed
in a burglar's stone cage, and when he was cursing his pusil-
lanimity in the department of suicide? He had never set up for
a Joseph—the young cynic chuckled to himself, shrugging his
shoulders; and though, of course, those ninety pounds a year
would come out of the enemy's treasury, might not there per-
adventure be even some patriotic advantage in getting a footing
in the enemy's camp? For example, could he possibly have a
better cover for his embassy to Dublin? and that service once
creditably performed for his friends, people would get accustomed
to his continued absence in Dublin, and a hundred things might
happen that would give people other things to think of, or cause
them to think that he had behaved like a sensible son, who had
bethought him at last of his duty to his mother's rheumatics and
his uncle's well-worn hat. 'I am ready, sir—I can start in the
morning!' he cried, in the jubilant manner in which he always
came to the end of his thinking; and he poured out a jorum of
claret, which once more brought down the influence of the claret
and champagne that went before it tingling and rioting in his
blood.

'That's right; I like a fellow who can make up his mind,'
said Hans Harman, going to the piano; and presently a grey-faced
woman in a plumed bed in her hearse of a room upstairs could
hear the sonorous chords of one of Mendelssohn's Lieder faintly
throbbing through the stony-hearted house, and, later on, Jack
Harold's gay voice and funny French *Zim v'lan la!* mocking the
dreariness of the sick-room like impish laughter. Considering for
what a weary length of time, however, Mrs. Harman had chosen
to be an invalid, she would have been a most unreasonable
woman to expect her hard-working husband permanently to nail
up the pianoforte, the only dissipation of his life, the only joyous
whisper in the house; and, to give poor ailing, trivial, ineffectual
Mrs. Harman her due, she never thought of doing anything so
unreasonable, and requiring such a wild pitch of energy, as
complaining.

Just as Miss Deborah and the tea-service had arrived, a telegram was put into Mr. Harman's hand, with which the messenger

had just posted over from Garrindinny. He left the room with some mumbled excuse about business, and the new clerk in the Pipe Roll Office, with some dismay, found himself *tête-à-tête* with the youthful Rock of Ages.

'I shall not incommode you soon again, Miss Harman—I am going away,' was the pleasantest remark he could find to make.

'Indeed!' she said, sharply. 'I dare say it is only others who have a right to be concerned about that.'

There was something in her face, and in the sudden inundation of the cup of tea she was pouring out, which caused him to start violently.

'By heavens! there is not a woman in the whole world, except my foolish old mother, who will give me a tear with her adieu,' he cried, eagerly.

'I do wish you would not swear,' she said, in a gentle voice.

'Even if I swore that I would go to the ends of the earth to win your love!' said the unconscionable scamp, drawing his chair nearer, and capturing one of her hands. Pity 'tis, 'tis true; but stranger even than the fact that the young adventurer, who, ten minutes before, had no more notion of making love to Miss Deborah Harman than of marrying a stone figure on a monument, was now ready to drop at her feet, with a whole hive of honey vows if needful; stranger still is the fact that so shrewd a young woman as Miss Deborah never once thought of casting up her keen eyes to see if the young rascal was humbugging her. And, strangest of all, when she pushed him away in a flurry and said, 'You really mustn't,' he found that the freak which he began in mere wantonness was fastened upon him in deadly earnest.

'I should have thought you preferred duets at the Castle,' she said, rallying her bitterness, when the rest of her grim, heavy-armed virtues seemed to fly to her.

I really cannot report what the bottle of Pommery sec and the bottle of St. Estèphe dictated to him to say in way of reply. The imprisoned damsels who echoed his furnace-vows of love at the foot of Mullagh would have submitted to an additional century of penances in the interest of their sex for having given currency to divers oaths so perfidious. But Jack was now fully, recklessly, under the influence of the potion. Miss Westropp he still saw shining as an angel, as a star, worlds above the level at which he was at present grovelling; but the empyrean heavens had given him up, and he had given up the empyrean heavens. The tag of French philosophy which says, 'When one cannot have what one loves, it is necessary to love what one has,' occurred to him as suiting his own case ex

cellently well ; and if Miss Deborah was to be had, he began
to see a hundred excellent philosophic reasons for loving her.
Even in the matter of personal attractions, her bright eyes, and
face reblossoming under his gaze like a rose that was but lightly
visited by an untimely frost, showed wonderfully fair, especially
in the glowing medium which French wines diffuse about our
visions. He recaptured the hand, he advanced with a dash
to the waist, he sighed, and whispered, and glowed, and ' in
short ' (as old Humphrey Dargan would say), he conquered the
simple lady's heart, beyond the power of all the eloquence of the
Church Mission pulpits, and all the irrefragable logic of their
tracts to ransom it.

'And do you—really—really'—she cried, almost sobbing with
joy and fear—shrinking even from completing the sentence. But
he, of course, completed it for her by taking her in his arms un-
resistingly and kissing her. Every woman is beautiful when she
avows her love ; and, when he saw this stray spirit so helplessly
under his spell, and saw her face raised to his own, swimming, as it
were, in a golden sea of joyous wonder, he might very easily have
persuaded himself that it was not vanity, but genuine love ; not
love of the lost empyrean sort, of course, but still of a highly
respectable and interesting character—that shone in his returning
gaze, and burned in his answering kisses. The plain English of
all which is—that he took Miss Deborah's heart, as he took the
ninety pounds a year in the Pipe Roll Office, as the best price he
could get for tarnished affections and unprincipled wits.

'But you are going :—is it possible you are going—and to-
morrow ?' she cried in a sudden spasm of terror.

'To-morrow—but I will return—when you will—at your
summons,' he said. 'And I will get the summons, n'est ce pas ?'

'Hush, it is Hans !' she whispered ; and the agent returned
into the room, with the telegram still in his hand, looking so
worried, for all his jaunty attempts to hide it, that young Hare d
at once saw the desirability of securing his letter of introduction
to the Attorney-General and making his adieux.

When he got into the outer air, it was with a stifling sensation that the whole drama of Hans Harman's singular offer
and his sister's more singular surrender, must have been a
drunken dream, the work of the bright treacherous spirits he
had taken in, of which nothing now remained except the headache which was beginning to rack his brain. But the letter of
introduction in his breast pocket was there to assure him that it
was all as real as anything in this spectral and absurd world
could be ; and the more he thought of it, the more gaily he
hummed to himself, in a sort of impromptu operatic recitative

that, if he had sold himself (as what man must not in the inevitable hour when *il faut se ranger ?*) at least there might be
worse bargains for a little frivolous marmoset like himself than
a cosy official career in the metropolis and the sister of the most
influential agent in the county for a partner. Nevertheless, he
crept upstairs without the least crinkle of his usual boisterous
comings and goings, passing Father Phil's door on tiptoe, as if
he had just been picking his purse and was afraid he might
awake and raise the cry of 'Stop thief!' and when two hours
afterwards his poor old mother, under the influence of one
of those mysterious monitors which seem to be vouchsafed to
mothers' hearts alone, came into his room wrapt in an old shawl,
to imprint a kiss upon her darling's forehead, thinking he was
asleep and dreaming sweetly, he felt that kiss burn into his very
brain, as if nothing beautiful and pure could touch him for the
future without turning to torture ; and the hours chimed one
after the other till the ghostly dawn crept in without his being
able to satisfy himself, out of all the brilliant saws of all the
rollicking philosophers of La Mère Médecine, that this feeling
was altogether due to the headache and the last of Hans Harman's St. Estèphe not being up to the mark.

'What is it, Hans?' said Miss Deborah, more softly than
usual, when her brother and she were left alone.

'It's the devil,' said he, striding up and down the room. 'It's
a telegram from Lord Drumshaughlin to say he's coming home.
It's an upset to all our arrangements. And when I send for
that old idiot, Dargan, to countermand his visit to Wrixon, I
find that he's gone and the harm's done. Damn Drumshaughlin
for coming! Damn old Dargan for going! Damn most people
I know in this infernal world!'

'Lord Drumshaughlin coming home!' cried Miss Deborah,
with a burst of delight. 'Then my letter to Lady Drumshaughlin
telling her of Mabel's doings, has had its effect.'

'*Your* letter!' he cried, stopping in his stride. 'Then it's
you that have brought him over?'

'Well, you know, brother, that girl's conduct was becoming
really unbearable, and I thought a slight hint to her mother——'

'Hell's fire and demons! woman, what business had you
thinking anything?' he screamed, turning upon her as if the
spirits he had just invoked were leaping in forked flames from
his eyes and mouth. 'Get out of this, to bed, or to the devil!'
and, as if his hand itched to deface something, he flung a sugar-
bowl furiously at a console-glass over her head, and brought the
fragments crashing about her.

For the first time in the sombre records of domestic encounters

at Stone Hall, that strong-willed woman answered only with
tears ; which unlooked-for event so soften ed the agent that he
laid his hand penitently on he) shoulder and said : 'Don't. I
was damnably annoyed—damnably. But you and I mustn't
fall out, Debby.' Astute a man as Hans Harman was, he little
suspected the real secret of the warm, forgiving pressure of the
hand, with which she answered him, or that the tears she shed
then and for hours after she found herself safe in her bedroom
were tears of ecstasy and wonderment, which had no more
relation to Lord Drumshaughlin's coming home or the broken
console-glass than the song of the lark has to the price of
turkeys. Miss Deborah did feel as light as Shelley's lark—such
is the power of love, even in Stone Hall !

CHAPTER THE TWENTY-SEVENTH

LORD DRUMSHAUGHLIN MAKES A RESOLUTION

MISS DEBORAH HARMAN'S epistle on the enormities of the picnic
at Gougaun Barra followed Lady Drumshaughlin to a country
house of the Marchioness of Asphodel at The Meads, in Primroseshire, where she was one of a large house-party assembled for
the slaughter of the Marquis's pheasants. How Lady Drum came
to be opening her letters in a pretty Louis Quinze room at the
Meads, with the pink-like wolds and copses of a rural English shire
unrolled like an ancient patent of nobility before her windows, is
one of those mysteries of the great world which outsiders can
only vaguely guess at. It is cer'ain that Lady Asphodel, at this
moment exchanging corfidences with her husband in her boudoir,
would have rung the bel! and ordered Lady Drumshaughlin's
carriage for the twelve o'clock train to King's Cross, and changed
the most objectionable guest in the house into the Louis Quinze
room in way of feminine irony, if she was at liberty to consult
her own feelings. But what black slave seven hundred feet down
in a coal mine is less at liberty than a great lady ? and where is
a great lady so little at liberty as in her own house ? For some
obscure reason, she invited the dark-skinned, dark-eyed woman
to the house, and caressed her sufficiently in company. The
chances are that young Lord Amaranth, who had taken to
patronising Lady Drum, had given his mother to understand that
he would not be of the Meads party if Lady Drum was ruled
out ; and the Marchioness, having reasons of her own for desiring

to enchain her son in the quiet charms of Primroseshire, instead of seeing him entangling himself matrimonially with music-hall artistes, prize-fighting at Mile End, or gambling at Monte Carlo, had capitulated to his terms.   Young Amaranth was a sad scamp; and all his mother's thoughts, and many of his father's, were devoted to reclaiming him.   A fancy he had expressed for one of the American beauties of the season had offered the unfortunate Marchioness the first reasonable hope of res- cuing him from the lake of fire and pitch which he was pleased to call life.   Miss Ruysdael's satiny olive skin, blushing with modest self-satisfaction at its own loveliness—her soft dark eyes, tiny hands and feet, and lissom figure—her sincerity and fearlessness of speech, and withal the diamond neatness and sparkle of everything that rippled through the ivory and vermilion portals of her pretty mouth—carried all before them in the London drawing-rooms since that other *avis insolita*, the Wild Irish Girl, had flashed through them into space ; and even Lord Amaranth, who was credibly informed that American women were creatures who lectured you by the hour through the nose on Woman's Rights, and probably spat on the carpet, was graciously pleased to pronounce the Knickerbocker Girl stunning.   To his unhappy mother's dismay, however, Lord Amaranth having, under threat to take the next tidal train for Paris, obtained the addition of Lady Drumshaughlin to the shooting-party at The Meads, would insist on devoting himself to that lady, who was old enough to be his mother, while he allowed the young men to flutter about the beautiful American with no more concern than if she were a hag of seventy and had a hump.

This little comedy, played on the poor Marchioness's own boards, she herself supplying all the appointments, did not, of course, escape the observation of the guests.   The women would not be women, if they did not temper their disgust of Lord Amaranth's infatuated flirtation with that old woman with a certain degree of indulgence in view of his neglect of the American heiress.   High-born English women are wondrous fair.   Who has ever seen the House of Lords on a great night without turning from the rickety mob of old fellows on the crimson cushions, to marvel at the beauty that rays down from the Peeresses' Galleries overhead, more gracious than the *frou-frou* of their silks, and more splendid than the dazzle of their diamonds ?   The real power of the Second Estate of the British Realm lies not in one House of Peers, but in five hundred houses of Peeresses.   Nevertheless, Lady Asphodel's women guests were given to confess to their own hearts that, for all their own brilliant loveliness—the perfection of delicacy with the perfection of health—they were outshone in one of their own shires by this fragile-looking American girl ; not merely in piquancy of wit or style, for that they could easily have forgiven, but in that inborn repose of manner, which is supposed to run in the blood like prerogative. The elegance of a king-dom, where women are only pets, found itself overmatched by the unconscious reposefulness of a republic, where women are queens ; and Miss Ruysdael was as much at home as a sun-beam, neither more or less. As the clever minx must, of course, be setting her cap at the young heir of Asphodelland all the more resolutely, that she affected to be as insensible to his exist-ence as if he were one of the Cupids figured on the delicate porce-lain tray which brought her afternoon tea ; the general feminine circle marked, therefore, with a callous feline interest the neglect with which Lord Amaranth repaid her ; and to her own amazement, Lady Drumshaughlin (who had never been able to make much progress among English women) found herself not only the object of the young moon-calf's idiotic attentions, but, to some extent, the suc-cessful champion of European womanhood against the invasions of an upstart New World. The last thing that occurred to Lady Drumshaughlin, was that she was paying any dangerous price for her singular success. She was even foolish enough to feel flattered.

Miss Deborah's angular note came as a most unwelcome in-trusion. At first it so upset her temper that she made as if she would tear it to flitters ; then she paused, and laid it down, and struck at it with her clenched fist ; and then she began a quick, nervous pacing up and down the room, with an expression of face which she did not care to stop to contemplate in the mirror. It was, of course, worrying beyond conception that that girl should be losing herself among those horrid creatures when she might be shaming Miss Ruysdael's waxen cheeks with her own dazzling beauty of morning-rose-colour. The insolence of the agent's sister in intruding her intolerable condolences was still worse. But this was a hard, selfish woman, whom the news af-flicted chiefly because of its bearing on her own fortunes. Some-thing must be done promptly, it was clear. But her invitation to the Meads covered three weeks, only one of which had expired. If she went up to London to seek her husband, upon what pretext was she to get back ? Mabel had unfeelingly deserted her just as her aid seemed indispensable to her mother's safe establishment in society ; had preferred to follow her own whimsical and irritating worship of that boy ; and left her mother to struggle as best she might up that awful gilded staircase where so many a stout-hearted aspirant faints under the silent stare of the Medusa-heads of feminine cruelty and insular prejudice which mount guard there. She *had* got the better of the Medusæ. She had her foot planted on the highest stair—installed in one of the haughtiest houses in England, and no inconsiderable personage in the little drama there enacting. It was all too novel in her shaded life not to be intoxicating, dangerously intoxicating.

She was not going to leave her ground of vantage. She resolved to send Miss Harman's letter to her husband by post. She inclosed it with a few trebly underlined words of her own, saying: 'This is dreadful. Something ought to be done at once. You know Mabel and Ireland, and can best decide what.'

The letter found Lord Drumshaughlin the following morning in his apartments in a demure bachelor's club in Sackville Street, Piccadilly. Towzled, unshaved, in an untidy dressing-gown, and presenting altogether the male counterfeit presentment of an elderly lady with her hair in curl-papers, he was stamping up and down in a state of great perturbation. His mail had been particularly disagreeable. One letter in especial, which lay among the breakfast things, with a clumsily scribbled cheque, seemed to worry him. We have only to turn over the letter to sympathise with the unfortunate peer's perturbation. It bore the address, 'The Roses, Glengarriff,' embossed in a staring carmine-coloured plaster overhead, and was intended to be a handsome expression of gratitude from the new Justice of the Peace ; but, alas for his intentions! if Humphrey Dargan had been a mediæval torturer working the iron boot, he could not have given Lord Drumshaughlin's gouty toes a more excruciating twist in every sentence. 'I am sure,' he added, after many profuse expressions of eternal indebtedness, recorded in a hand that could scarcely have been less impressive if it had been the work of an inky caterpillar raised to the judicial bench, 'I am sure your lordship will not think it too presumptious in an humble man like yours to command, if I venture to offer some substantial proof of my undying appreciation of your lordship's kindness, in the shape of the enclosed small cheque for 500l. (five hundred pounds), knowing, as circumstances of a business character have confidenshally brought to my knowlidge, that your lordship's private manes are not at all times commenshurate with the requirements of your noble station and of your own generous heart.' Then, as if all the flowery resources of the Roses were exhausted in this burst of high-flown eloquence, the new Justice of the Peace added in a P.S.—'Nobody is any the wiser of this except Mrs. D., whose idea it was. If your lordship was raally pressed, I would not mind making it a thousand as a little matter strictly between your lordship and myself. P.P.S.—I am open to any reasonable offer as to interest on the morgidge.—H. D.'

'Heaven, and earth, and hell, have I come to that !' roared Ralph Westropp, assaulting his two sidelocks together with a

wrench that threatened to be their last. ' 'Twasn't enough to
have to raise this—thing to the commission—to defile the name
of gentleman by giving him the right to it—but he must actually
take to patronise me—subsidise me—pity me, by God !—And
isn't he quite right !   Would it be so much worse, if I slipped
that cheque into my pocket !—if I sent him a hint to "make it a
thousand " ?   Would I have been so sure of myself if he had done
the thing with less clumsy brutality—with less vile spelling ?
And I was once Ralph Westropp.   This broken, abandoned, disreputable old man, whom this creepy beetle of a money-lender
tips as he might tip the housekeeper at my castle !   O my God !
—if there is such a being as the God of my young days still left
in this infernal upstart world !'

He strode up and down again—in a less savage temper now—
in a more whipt and conscience-stricken one—haggard wrinkles
ploughing up his face to the eyes—his handsome form bent and
twisted as in an ague—the whole man so dethroned and ruinous-
looking, it seemed as if you could see the grey of the undyed
roots of his hair visibly spreading and freezing up the dye before
it.   They say a drowning man sees his whole life pass in procession before him in one suffocating instant.   Humphrey Dargan's well-intended communication brought a perfect ocean of
degradation tumbling and surging in Ralph Westropp's ears, and
with the suffocating feeling came the awful flash light over his
selfish, worthless, bankrupt life :—a great station in his own
country shamefully deserted—a vast estate dissipated—a youth
of wit and beauty withered into unlovely, dyed, and patched old
age—a home crammed with skeletons and besieged with duns—a
life whose public aspect was summarised in the gombeen-man's
bribe, and its private aspect in the gossamer three-cornered note
which was breathing out its perfume alongside the money-lender's
letter on the breakfast table.   A bitter, bitter retrospect it was
of a proud, bright, wilful spirit for ever on the wing from the cold
native climes of duty to the tropic lands of indolence and pleasure, without country, without object, without inspiring love to
direct its flight—a life spent in evading moral and financial
creditors alike—a life opening in broad, generous, sun-gilt sweeps
of landscape, and closing in inglorious foetid quagmires of self-
indulgence.   It was while this dark company of spectres, all
claiming to be his own property, were gibbering past him, a sort
of field-day of a reviewing general in the infernal shades, that
Lady Drumshaughlin's note with Deborah Harman's letter was
delivered to him.   He read the note and the epistle it contained
with singular calmness. There was even a tranquil nobility about
his air that impressed his servant Mundle more than a volley of

oaths. Deborah's news completed his decision. When he had finished the reading he rose, took Dargan's letter and cheque between his fingers, as if the touch of them burnt into his blood, and put them in the fire, where he watched them blacken and crumple like damned souls in the heart of it. Then he gave one indecisive glance at the pretty three-cornered missive, and flung that into the blaze, too. The flimsy little note fluttered like a frightened dainty thing towards the flame, but evaded it and effected a trembling escape into the fender. Lord Drumshaughlin dragged it pitilessly forth, and cast it back into the jaws of the fire, and this time with his boot pressed it to its fate until the poor little pink wings were ashes. Then he strode to his dressing-room. He reappeared after an incredibly brief interval neatly dressed, but for the first time his grey hairs were left to proclaim themselves in all their greyness; there was not even any suggestion of mysterious pomades about the yellow furrowed cheeks; and from loose appearances about the chest it was plain that the arrangements, whatever they were, that made Ralph Westropp's juvenile figure the wonder of old clubmen had been discarded.

Lord Drumshaughlin had been all his life a lazy, but never a cowardly man. The second blow, instead of dejecting him still further, only steadied him. Duty, which he had spent his feeble years in dodging, has come upon him at last like an armed man, and Ralph Westropp turned to face the enemy as unflinchingly as he had long ago faced Antonaccio's pistol in the hotel of the Rue de la Paix. That intolerable sting Humphrey Dargan had inserted in his easy-chair had cured him of his weakness for cushions. He had behaved like an idiot, like a coward, like a reprobate. Quite true. He almost felt the sanguine blood fly to his yellow cheeks as he thought of it all—how he had ceased to be an Irish gentleman, without becoming more than an English club Bohemian—how he had cringed to money-lenders instead of mastering his affairs like a man—how he had allowed his wretched Harry to drift from him into vacancy, and his beautiful Mabel into God only knew what fantastic follies of an innocent childish heart—and how for all these treasures wasted, and abdicated duties, he had substituted the dreary joys of that dreariest of egoists, the elderly-juvenile man of pleasure—the sodden club enjoyments of the table, the unwholesome appetite for late hours and gaslight and green tables and smoking-room banalities, and the rest of the feverish follies which make young cheeks pale and old ones shameless—these, and the little three-cornered note, whose scent had just died away in ashes. But it was not too late.

at least, to die with harness on his back—who knew ? Perhaps not too late to retrieve the fortunes of the day ? Imprimis, these troubles must be faced on the spot—in Ireland. The first thing was to rescue Mabel from this monstrous rabble Harry's low associations had brought about the poor child ; this much was so clear to him that he performed the whole journey to Drumshaughlin in imagination without a stop, even to telegraphing Mick Brine to have his chaise-and-pair in waiting at the night mail train in Garrindinny the night before, so as to press on without the intermission of an hour. So much accomplished, a resolute attempt must be made to grapple with the financial condition of the estate ; and, above all, and at any cost, to shake off Humphrey Dargan's unbearable clutches. After all the Dargan mortgage was only for 55,000l. and upon not too advantageous terms in the present prospects of Irish landed security—six per cent. There could be no insuperable difficulty about contracting a fresh loan—at two per cent. additional, perhaps, but even so—that would beat the gombeen-man's insolent claws off the estate, and place Lord Drumshaughlin in a position to give the answer for which the creature's letter cried to Heaven. And in casting about for a financial Machine-god, Lord Drumshaughlin's thoughts recurred to Hugg, the second mortgagee, whose present lien was only for 30,000l. and who might be willing enough to consolidate the whole loan upon the estate at his own figure of eight per cent. Hugg, it seemed, was some city notable who, for reasons of his own, did not choose to be known as the money-lending Petite Bourse, and Hans Harman, who was in the secret (as he was in all others), had observed the obligations of confidence so rigorously that he had himself, with Mundle, witnessed the signature to the mortgage-deed.; but Hugg was beyond question some Jewish Crœsus, doubtless in the House —possibly on the Treasury Bench, as Harman once more than half hinted—and the thought had struck Lord Drumshaughlin that, if he could only get into communication with Hugg himself, who would scarcely fear to entrust his secret to the honour of a Westropp, it might be possible to strike up an understanding more satisfactory than could be obtained on pedantic lines of business. It seemed to him he could face the rearrangement of his affairs with a lighter heart, if he was in a position to approach Hans Harman with some bold and fruitful suggestion of his own, instead of turning to his agent helplessly for baby-feeding, as he had always hitherto done in every whining, sickish moment. And it was to the Hugg address in South Audley Street, Grosvenor Square, his cab was now speeding with a celerity which, yet, was not half impetuous enough for the eager,

fretting fire within.   For—who will sound that fathomless
ocean of mystery, the ordinary human aorta ?—he who had
stepped into the cab a chastened penitent, had already grown
so rebellious-proud of his own virtuous resolutions that he
burst into imprecations on the slowness of those infernal jades
of cab-horses, and on stepping out felt coerced to present the
cabby with an additional half-crown as a propitiatory sacrifice
to his own conscience and cabby's outraged pride in his steed.

'Eh ? 'Pon my soul, 27A is a dancing-master !' cried Lord
Drumshaughlin, bounding up the steps, only to find the brass plate
on the ground-floor suite sacred to M. Passeul et Filles, professors
of the new waltzes.   The first-floor afforded no better light.   It
was the dingy domain of a corsetière of the same grand nation.
'M. Ougg ? mais non, monsieur,' said the civil little corset-maker,
shaking her head.   'M. Ougg ?   Ah, my God, I recollect myself.
A letter to that address entremêled itself with my letters one
morning, there are some months, and the Madame d'en-bas—
Madame la propriétaire—Madame Callaghan, charged herself
with it.   Sonnette de rez de chaussée, Monsieur—en bas,' twittered
the little staymaker ; and Lord Drumshaughlin applied himself
to the area-bell.   The lady of the house, Madame Callaghan, a
slatternly, bony woman, with a soft Munster accent disguised in
a harsh voice, and in those tags of Cockney speech which the
humbler Irish in England sometimes assume, as, in a way, taking
out naturalisation papers, answered him at the area gate.

'No,' said the Madame d'en-bas. 'Mr. Hugg didn't live here,
and she didn't know where he lived ; but if there was any com-
mands for Mr. Hugg she would take charge of them.'——'Perhaps she would be good enough to say how soon she could
convey a communication to Mr. Hugg ?'——'Didn't know from
Adam—maybe a week, maybe a month—a gentleman called and
tuk away letters—didn't know how soon he'd call again, and didn't
care.'——'A gentleman called ! Indeed ! And pray might he
inquire what sort of gentleman ?'——'That he might find from
them whose business it was to tell him,' snapped the suspicious
dame, banging the area-gate in his face.

'Yes, hang it ! always failed in diplomacy—as what did I
not fail in ?' reflected his lordship, as he walked away towards
the Chief Secretary's house in the adjoining square—'Shall have
to fall back upon Hans Harman, as usual, _he_ won't fail ! _He'd_
find Hugg.   _He'd_ tear all about him out of that damned surly
old shrew faster than Torquemada would with his pincers.
Hugg !—what a deucedly uncomfortable name—Bug, Mug, Lug,
Tug, Dug, Jug, Drug, Slug, Thug—why, you might set a whole
Chamber of Horrors to rhyme with it ! But Harman'll be a

match for 'em all. He'll get Hugg to extinguish Dargan, and then you'll have Harman coming down to extinguish Hugg, or trumping him with some other mysterious old financier—an astonishing fellow !—an invaluable fellow !—and, by Jove ! he *did* warn me what would come of this madcap adventure of Mabel's —just as it turned out—Hah ! glad to see I'm not wholly out of luck to-day. Chief Secretary in town, and I've run him down, too !' he cried, as he stopped opposite a mansion in the Square. The blinds were all close-drawn, and muffled in proper autumnal weeds of widowhood for a family out of town ; but Lord Drumshaughlin espied two men of drilled backs, loafing in elaborate idleness about the railings, their real calling about as well disguised in civilian dress as the frog who would a-wooing go must have looked in morning costume.

'Would you kindly present this card to Mr. Jelliland, and say the matter is urgent?' he said boldly to the servant who opened the door, and who, with a glance at the card, said hesitatingly : 'Not altogether certain whether 'ee's returned from the Hahirish Hoffice, m' lawd—p'raps your lawdsh'p would please to hentaw.'——'Thanks ; make your mind easy about that; his detectives are at the door,' replied his lordship, resolutely pushing his way into the dining-room.'

In a moment, the servant returned and ushered him upstairs into a snuggery, where John Jelliland sat cowering over his desk by the fire amidst mountains of official documents, reports, and warrants, amidst which he appeared to be burrowing for the bare life like a dormouse in a particularly hard winter. The Secretary was woefully changed since we last saw him in the fresh gloss of his office. The little bald head that bobbed up to welcome Lord Drumshaughlin did so much less stiffly, and more amicably. The sparse hairs that peered about the edges of the bald wastes of his scalp on either side, like sad veterans inspecting the graves of their old comrades, had grown ever so much sparser and greyer within these few Irish months ; and the keen little bird's eye with which John Jelliland took in the whole Irish situation at a glance had grown strangely dim and suggested spectacles. The fact of it was things had not turned out precisely as any reasoning being who was not an Irishman would have expected them to turn out in that provoking country. The army of projects with which he went to the country had not quite, as the French say, marched. It was not that he was beaten in fair fight ; but, like the Earl of Essex's splendid cohorts, had got lost in the bogs. Most excellent and painstaking of men, he pegged away like a Titan at his *magnum opus*, or scheme for the reclamation of Slob Lands and the drainage of the Suck— a meandering, ne'er-do-weel river in Connaught, which spreads its lazy limbs over miles of country in the best months of the year for no other object in life than to suck haystacks, cornstooks, and weak-minded live stock into its worthless gullet—for, as the member for the county observed, 'the blackguard river wasn't even fit to make whisky-and-water.' John Jelliland had taken this common disturber of Irish peace and happiness by the throat. He set a Parliamentary Committee and a Hybrid Committee at the monster. He ran down himself to take personal cognisance of the river at its unholy work. He subsequently brought the House of Commons boating gently down the sluggish mazes of that incorrigible stream, in a speech of two hours' duration, in which he was accompanied by a beautiful serenade of ' hear, hears,' from the Member for the County, and at the termination of which a frivolous Member of the Opposition suggested that, if it was a Bill for the drainage of old Jelliland, as well as the Suck, the House would vote it *nemine contradicente*. It never for one instant struck the honest gentleman that all that was sound in Ireland was not watching with breathless interest his encounter with that Connaught river-demon ; and, the devil once victoriously cast out of the Suck, and the river put peacefully to sleep in its bed, John Jelliland could see further conquests ahead in the way of cutting off a few more Bishoprics from the Establishment, and even rejoicing the soul of the Irish tenant with some modest legal *viaticum*, some slight testimony of natural regard, on eviction— the background always gleaming with an eventually happy, loyal and contented Ireland, lapt in universal law, and having nothing further for the heart of man to desire except some state courtesies to the Cardinal's red stockings and charitable institutions, an occasional magistracy for a devout Catholic, or a Governorship of the Loochoo Islands for some Parliamentary Patriot of more than usually ardent spirit (or spirits).

Immersed in such flattering visions—floating gently along one evening upon one of those dreamy boating excursions on the broad bosom of the Suck—he suddenly met a man who said : 'Jelliland, are you mad or dreaming ? Don't you see that the people you suppose are watching you with admiring eyes from the banks are getting guns and pikes upon their shoulders ? Have you eyes, that you don't perceive that it's not a question of the overflow of the Suck, but of the outburst of an insurrection ? For heaven's sake, dock up your ridiculous boating apparatus — send it adrift to the deep sea or to the devil—ring the alarum-bell, and draft your Insurrection Act, or it's yourself and your empire that'll soon be drifting to the deep sea or— further ! ' It was upon that night many of John Jelliland's remaining hair sickened and died, or survived as sadder and greyer monitors. That night also there was born into his brain an infant suspicion that that bird's-eye view of his had possibly overlooked some important elements of the Irish problem—that the policy of Blue-book Jelly must be postponed for a policy of Red-coat Steel —and that, in fact, Ireland was a country intended by an all-chastising Providence for the sole purpose of plaguing that England and those Englishmen whom Providence most loved. Ever since, it was rivers of blood and not of muddy Suck-water that overflowed the poor gentleman's vision, until now, when Mrs. Jelliland and the girls were away basking in the after-season on the golden sands of Ostend, the unfortunate Secretary was still chained to his kennel in Grosvenor Square, absorbing the horrors of police reports, signing warrants of arrest, and listening to all the maddening Dutch chorus of panic, advice, information, and abjuration that reached him from a country from which the next telegram might bring news of the first shot of an insurrection.

If Ireland's mission in the universe was to chasten John Jelliland's good soul, the Green Isle had not lived in vain. The Secretary was as humble, cordial, and amenable to reason as could be. 'My dear lord,' he cried, shaking himself up out of his papers, like a genial rat popping out of his hole, 'I'm so glad—so pleased to have the benefit of your counsel at such a crisis for your unfortunate country.'

'To tell the truth, Mr. Jelliland, my advice about Ireland is not worth three straws—not worth more than my advice how to get at King Theodore of Abyssinia,' said his visitor.

The Secretary's lower lip fell. He did not like levity in such matters. These Irish lords were as bad as the rebels and the rivers. It wouldn't be such a bad thing to make absenteeism a treason-felony as well as burying an old pikehead. But the old Adam was not yet dead in John Jelliland. He at once concluded that he could see through this visit of Lord Drumshaughlin. He remembered their former interview, and his instinct as a politician smote him that he had never since done anything to propitiate a man who would almost certainly be elected for the vacant Irish Representative Peerage, and whose important County might at any moment fall vacant whenever a place sufficiently shady could be got for old O'Shaughnessy. Besides, at the remembrance of that odd stripling, Harry, a curiously humbling thought struck the Secretary.

'How is your son?' he said. 'What a sharp fellow! I remember very well he was the first who told me all about this conspiracy—one of the best informed young persons I have ever met on the subject of Ireland. I have been casting about to see

what we could do for him.' He had been casting about for just
three minutes on the subject; but John Jelliland, who, in the
ordinary concerns of life, was stern Truth itself, admitted in
politics a certain degree of what the theologians call 'economy'—
Political Economy, in the casuist's sense, not in Adam Smith's or
Ricardo's. 'You know a young fellow like that generally does
best in the Colonies.' There was some vague association in his
mind between Harry and Botany Bay, which he could not for
the life of him account for.

'The Colonies—a capital place for a young fellow,' said Lord
Drumshaughlin, with surprise.

'Well, they're raising a Cape Mounted Force, and I should
say a commission there would suit your young fellow down to
the ground. I'll write to Sir Frederick Flamwell, the Colonial
Secretary, this afternoon, if you have no objection. It's a curious
thing how my little dachshund Halmar took to your son,' observed
Mr. Jelliland, with a deep sigh. 'Do you know I've lost Halmar
since? As your boy said, I would give almost anything for a
pup out of that bitch. Singular how capitally Halmar and your
boy understood one another,'—and the whimsical thought flashed
across his mind that upon the whole Pepper would have made a
better Chief Secretary for Ireland than his master—a thought
which, grotesque as it was, somehow saddened him. 'Well, well,
I suppose we cannot do better than put up Flamwell for that
commission.'

'I am very heartily obliged to you,' exclaimed Lord Drumshaughlin, in much surprise and glee, 'but—ah—to be frank with
you, it was not about that I called.'

'Oh!' said the Chief Secretary.

'No. The truth is, I suppose you're aware that my boy,
Harry, is as wild as a young colt, and has drawn all sorts of
loiterers and queer characters—Fenians and all that—about
my place, Drumshaughlin Castle.'

Ha! *Now* John Jelliland could read him through and
through. So then this extraordinary business of the American
Captain, and the strange doings reported by the police from
Drumshaughlin Castle, were part of a plan to bring pressure to
bear on the Government to make provision for this young scapegrace, Westropp; and now that the plot had been successful,
and the young fellow handsomely transported to the colonies,
Lord Drumshaughlin wanted to save the retreat of his minor
accomplices. There was nothing too deep or base for those
Irish place-hunters. But even maimed as he was by the cata-
strophe on the Suck, John Jelliland was, at least, not to be de
ceived by their knavery.

'I understand, my lord, perfectly,' he said, with an icy smile of self-satisfaction.

'In particular, I am informed that there is an American emissary——'

'Quite so, my dear lord—the name is, I am confident, M'Carthy, and, I rather think, Michael,' said the secretary, proudly.

'According to the information that reached me, the fellow has actually taken up his quarters in my Castle.'

'Precisely ; and, of course, you want us not to execute the warrant—to let the fellow slip through to America—no fuss or annoyance about the thing. Well, I dare say, if you really desire it—if you insist——'

'Heaven and earth, no, my dear sir,' thundered Lord Drumshaughlin. 'Do you think I am stark mad, or perhaps a Fenian myself ? I am going home to Drumshaughlin to-night, and do you think I want an American filibusterer to meet me in my own arm-chair with a bowie knife ? Good heavens, no ! Pardon my heat, my dear sir. But what I came to ask you to do was to have the fellow's arrest effected before I reach there—this very night, if possible—so that there may be no possible room for doubt as to the attitude of the Government, or as to my own, with regard to fellows of that kind. And the only other favour I should entreat is that the affair may be conducted with as little alarm or annoyance as possible to my daughter, who, for her foolish brother's sake, appears to have tolerated this man's presence under my roof.'

John Jelliland sank back in his chair, as if another wideweltering river Suck had overflowed and overwhelmed him. The rod of an all-chastening Providence had been used once more upon his unoffending shoulders. But he was now getting rather broken to the discipline. In a moment or two, he meekly kissed the rod, and once and for ever dismissed Ireland and Irishmen as the Sphinxes of the nations—the teasing, shifting, rebellious, fascinating, ragged Unknown and Unknowable.

'So that was what you desired, Lord Drumshaughlin,' said the Chief Secretary, with a sigh of resignation. 'Certainly. The warrant for that man's arrest—a most dangerous man—went over several days ago. It shall be executed to-night, and, of course, as you suggest, with every possible consideration for Miss Westropp's feelings.'

As Lord Drumshaughlin drove back to the club to dine, and set Mundle at the work of packing, he somehow felt that he, who had set out as a bare-footed penitent, was returning as a victorious general ; for he had not only crushed treason's head, but he, of course, debited himself with the piece of luck that had befallen Harry, as though it had been the result of deep forethought and diplomacy of his own.   He pulled up outside a telegraph station in Piccadilly, and despatched the following telegram to Garrin-dinny, prepaying postage to Stone Hall, Drumshaughlin :—

'Am returning to Ireland by night-mail from Euston.— DRUMSHAUGHLIN.'

CHAPTER THE TWENTY-EIGHTH

A FIGURE IN THE DARK

THE Hon. Miss Westropp was relieved from an unexpected quar-ter of the miserable doubts which haunted her ever since young Harold burst into her poor little fairyland like a Black Knight with his declaration of love.   It was Frank Harman who effected her deliverance.   That good-natured grenadier thought the genial off-hand way was the best way of reassuring Mabel that her offences had not put her outside the pale of society.

'Deborah is such an absurd creature.'   Miss Harman rattled along, as if crossing a stonewall country at an easy gallop.   'She'd really leave one no society but Mr. Primshanks, and no literature except his hymn-book.   I am positively in dread she will forbid the Two-Shilling Novel Series the house next.   As for you, my dear child, the naughtiest heroine in the Series is not a more dreadful young person in her eyes.'

'Indeed ?' said Mabel.

'Yes.   You know what Deborah is—thinks there ought to be a law to oblige young men to go about logged and muzzled, and that a young lady who marries out of the county families might almost as well have forgotten to be married at all.'

'I don't think these are matters for coarse jests,' said Miss Westropp, repressing herself with some difficulty.

'Nor I ; but, I assure you, Deborah doesn't at all regard it as a jest.   She is quite seriously shocked by your wicked Gun-powder Plot against the foundations of society, dear.   As for me, I am never done telling her that the time for those ridiculous old strait-laced frumps and social distinctions of hers is gone with Noah's Flood.   We're all changing and turning the old order topsy-turvy ; and why not ?   There's my brother Hans moving heaven and earth to carry that old gombeen-man, Dargan, for the Club.   I'm canvassing for him myself.   What do I care whether a man had a grandfather, or is a grandfather unto himself ?   In a progressive age he may be just as useful, if he only keeps a loan-bank, or just as good a soldier if he's only an American. *Apropos*, my dear Mabel, I must know your American Captain; I hear such funny stories of him. Do trot him out. I am dying to meet him. I am positively determined to meet him.'

Frank Harman had galloped breezily along without in the least noticing the colour mounting in Miss Westropp's cheek. The latter could bear it no longer.

'I am afraid,' she said, touching the bell, 'I shall have to leave my guest, Captain MacCarthy, some liberty in the selection of his acquaintances, and for the future I shall have to claim some voice also in choosing my own. Order Miss Harman's pony-chaise to the door, please Mary.'

Miss Harman's candid impertinences and her sister's poisonous tattle completely reassured Miss Westrópp that she could not be so far wrong in breaking from the traditions of a society such as theirs to brighten and be brightened by the lives of the simple, kindly, honest-hearted folk, who gathered around her as around a glowing fire that had suddenly leaped forth in their chill world. After all, was young Harold's hysterical love-fit so unpardonable a piece of silliness compared with Miss Deborah's infamous hints and envious green-glasses? Which was the more truly vulgar figure--that of the bony female grenadier, just gone—herself the daughter of a successful tithe-proctor—affecting to make and unmake social laws like an Eastern Sultana? or Captain Mike's rugged form, strong as a mountain pine, with a voice that could be gentle as a zephyr whispering among the pine-tops? Were the young fellows who raved of rushing steeds and clashing swords in an open field for Ireland so much worse company for Harry than the young squireens who only raved of the ambitions of a horse-jockey in the tipple of a groom? Was it really so very degrading, in the midst of the beauteous glens, to feel the quickening glow of friends, home, and country, instead of regarding them all as a turnkey's daughter might regard her father's prisoners—as an Hyrcanean tiger's daughter might regard her father's prey? And, when she flitted among the mountain cabins, welcomed to the warmest corner, romping with the children, listening to the old man's tales, soothing a heathery sick-bed with her bright eyes (and, perhaps, now and again, with some less potent cordials)—was she in very truth betraying the cause of society, morality, and religion, because she did not use their hospitality as a sanitary detective, spoil their Heaven to give their cabins a coat of whitewash, and force them to swallow down one of the Thirty-nine Articles with every mouthful of port-wine? She could not think so; and as a matter of fact, she did not

Z

reason the matter out with any such particularity. A German poet once said that the Rose is without a Wherefore : ' *Sie blühet weil sie blühet.*' Mabel Westropp blossomed and gave forth perfume because it was her nature to ; and the sweet scent flowed over the mountain sides all the more deliciously after the Harman rain-storm had beaten upon the tender petals.

Her life passed in a whirl of simple delights those days : trotting through the woods with the little Motherwells; watching her chrysanthemums come out in their battalions of pink and white ; organising apple-feasts and kiss-in-the-ring for the urchins of the Ranties ; plotting mysterious loans and packages of tea for some of the most desolate creatures on Mrs. Rohan's lists ; amusing Harry's ambition in the parting of his hair ; working a Grand Army badge for Captain Mike ; reading the German poets with Joshua Neville (who, it must be owned, admired the German poesy chiefly for the rugged, old-red-sand-stone look of it in print, and who every day with new wonder beheld these uncouth, wrought-iron words dissolve in honey music on Mabel's lips and shape themselves in airy visions under her spells). With Georgey O'Meagher she became fast friends, and early elicited from that frank young party the open secret of her unrequited passion for Ken Rohan.

'Oh, yes,' Georgey would say, in one of their schoolgirl cœnacula, 'I love him oceans wide and mountains high, and I would tell him so, too, only he wouldn't in the least believe me. I do believe he's nearly as fond of me as he is of his dog Snipe ; but that's just it—he's fond of me in precisely the same manner, and how *could* he ever suspect that Snipe should have matrimonial designs on him ? '

'If he is conceited enough to be capable of making such a comparison, I want to hear no more of him,' said Miss Westropp energetically.

'*He* compare a woman with a terrier ! Why, the truth is, he will insist on thinking all women are angels, or ought to be. And, indeed, they're not—at least, I know *I'm* not ; and,' with a saucy pout, 'I'm not so much worse than that provoking little vessel of perfection, Lily Dargan, whom he used to adore under the name of St. Cecilia, and who has got married to little Mr. Flibbert, the policeman.'

'Dear, dear, what a misery it must be for you, child ! '

'Oh, no, it isn't. I don't at all mean to die of love—especially as long as you lend me Captain Neville to flirt with,' laughed Miss Georgey. 'I have no more notion of crying my eyes out for Ken Rohan than for a Prince of the blood royal—though, indeed, I'd die for him ten times over if 'twould be of any use to

him,' she burst out impetuously. 'I'd be with him in this conspiracy or rebellion, or whatever it's going to be, only they object
to our petticoats and are afraid we'd faint. And as I'm no use
myself, I've given him Tom.'

'And who is Tom?' asked Miss Westropp, with much
interest.

'Tom is my brother—we call him the Doctor, because he has
no more chance of becoming a Doctor than I have of becoming
Brigadier-General. I told him the other day, "Tom, you must
be sworn in a Fenian." "And what is that?" said he, for the
boy thinks of nothing but his tobacco-pipe and bottled stout, and
he does ask such puzzling questions. "Oh, bother," I said, "ask
Ken Rohan, and, wherever he goes, follow him." "All right,
Georgey," said Tom—and, though he's not much at his books,
Tom will follow, you may be sure, if it was to death, or to the
gates of—the English headquarters, you know.'

'But do you think there is really, *really* any danger of—of
things of that sort?' asked Mabel, shuddering.

'I have no head for politics—not much head for anything
else, either; but I don't see why Irish boys should not try a
change under their own flag as well as Captain Neville would go
out to-morrow and risk his life against some miserable swarm of
Abyssinians or Ashantees. I like men to risk their lives. It is
the only proof of sincerity you can get from them. And then it
is a woman's duty to weep as she can't fight, and there must be
such a pride in weeping for the brave.'

Mabel looked very white, and trembled. 'I'm such a
coward,' she said, faintly. 'Don't, dear!—I know I should
die of terror to think of—poor Harry, now, for instance.—It
is too horrible! And, ah! what a different thing for *our* poor
boys from going out clad with all the glory of an irresistible
Empire!'

'Upon my word, Miss Westropp, you have only yourself to
blame if *I* count Captain Neville among *our* poor boys, and
object wholly to his being eaten by African cannibals for the
glory of the Empire,' said irrepressible Georgey.

And Miss Westropp was unquestionably responsible for throwing Georgey O'Meagher and the young Guardsman a good deal
together; and could not altogether shut her eyes to the result of
rides, croquet-matches, and parlour games (Georgey, like the in-
experienced, buoyant-hearted country girl she was, once actually
proposed bandaging Reggy Neville for blind-man's-buff) in which
the great, shy, faithful soldier found himself warming and sparkling in the sunbeams of the young Irish girl's ruisselant wit and
artless ways. Miss Westropp was not sure that Reggy Neville

was not falling in love with Georgey O'Meagher. She was not
even sure that she regretted it. Neville himself was almost the
only person who did not suspect his danger. He was a poor hand
at psychic analysis; but if he were asked off-hand why he found
Glengariff so pleasant he would probably have thought of Harry's
otter-hunting as readily as of Georgey O'Meagher's croquet-mallet.
Pleasant he unmistakably found it. 'What on earth is this the
fellows are saying of you, old Reggy?' wrote his friend, Horace
Westropp, from Birdcage Walk. 'The very least I hear of you
is that you have turned Rebel Chief, and are drilling and
arming your outlaws by the thousand in the fastnesses of Glengariff. In solemn earnest, dear old man, there are all sorts of
stories about the disaffection of the troops of Bantry, and it
seems some of the soldiers in their cups have actually named you
as designated to head the mutiny. Pray, don't laugh. Also,
pray don't send me a second to arrange a duel in your bloodthirsty name. Of course it is all some ridiculous blunder; but
I assure you solemnly there has been some portentous communication from the Horse Guards, and you mustn't be thunderstruck
if you receive a missive one of these mornings from old Thirlwall
cancelling your leave. It would be the best joke of the century,
only you are such a muddling old good-natured Don Quixote, one
can never be quite sure there may not be some grain of truth in
it. For Heaven's sake run across and join me at the Liverpool
Cup, and you and I will dress the whole thing into a practical
joke that will drive old Thirlwall out of the service.'

Reggy did not run over for the Liverpool Cup. He took the
affair in deadly earnest, and by the next post addressed to Lord
Thirlwall, who was commanding the Life Guards Grey, a communication as stiff as that grumpy veteran's rheumatic knee-
joints: to wit: 'My Lord,—I am informed that some insulting
nonsense as to the object of my visit here has been whispered to
you, and that, so far from kicking the person who brought you
the report, your lordship is actually about to address a serious
communication to me upon the subject. If the report is groundless, I have to entreat your lordship's forgiveness. If my information is accurate, I may, perhaps, save you and myself any
further annoyance upon the subject, by begging you to accept my
resignation of a commission in a corps whose commander is
capable of such an affront to the honour of one of his officers. I
have the honour,' &c.

Nor was the young Guardsman's temper mollified by what
happened between Mr. Hans Harman and himself in the hunting
field a morning or two after. 'Will you allow one of the ab-
origines and an old fellow to make a suggestion to the unsuspect-

ing stranger, Captain Neville?' said the agent, while the dogs were fumbling about the gorse of the cover.

'Willingly; only I warn you I'm the most mulish of men.'

'It is,' said Harman, speaking more seriously than usual, 'that you will not increase the difficulties of men in our own rank in Ireland by giving to our enemies—low and dangerous enemies—the countenance of a name like yours.'

'Oh! I thought you were going to ask me not to give a black bean against your friend Mr. Dargan,' said Neville, brusquely.

'Well, we're not running Dargan on the score of his ancestry, of course; but Dargan is a loyal man--Dargan is not under the observation of the police,' said the agent in low, significant tones.

'If half they say of him be true, I'd think more of the police if he was.'

'Eh?' stammered the agent, growing pale with anger or with doubt or with both.

'I'm not going to discuss Mr. Dargan's virtues,' said the Guardsman, haughtily. 'But you force me to tell you this much, Mr. Harman—that, so far as my experience goes, I am prouder of my own friends in Drumshaughlin than I should be of yours.'

There was something about this blunt, downright young Englishman which cowed Hans Harman grievously. 'That's right; pitch into us,' he said, with an affectation of good-humoured banter. 'We're doing England's business, and meet the usual fate of men on foreign service—get criticised and thrown over at home. But it is not for the sake of us poor devils of loyalists alone I spoke to you -it was for your own sake, too, as well. You, I dare say, have not heard how these people abuse your confidence—how were you to know that there is serious disaffection in the Bantry barracks—that drunken soldiers have been actually making free with your name?'

'So this is where the stories that reached the Horse Guards came from!' was the thought that flashed on Neville's angry brain. He looked straight into the agent's eyes, as he said deliberately: 'If you can find me anybody making free with my name who is not disposed to shelter himself behind drunken soldiers, I will be thankful to you if you will let me know his address; and, in the meantime, Mr. Harman, being a mere Englishman, I intend to treat all the rest of your reports about Ireland as of equal authority with this,' and he jerked his horse's head aside with a gesture of open disgust and contempt. Horace Westropp and the Horse Guards and Mr. Hans Harman had, in fact, all unconsciously conspired to complete the charm which Reggy's residence in the Glen had been weaving around him by such divers aids as grouse moors, otter streams, bright eyes, and the indefinable sense of expanding beyond his own stifling shell.

His sisters, it must be admitted, by no means shared his fanaticism. They were growing dreadfully tired of Clanlaurance Castle. They might have made the round of a dozen of the best houses in Britain, while they were incarcerated in this dreary, draughty old barrack of a castle, oscillating uncomfortably between Mabel's little society and a little society in which they were forced to hear Mabel venomously spoken of, and not very much more enamoured of Frank Harman's bows and arrows than of the American Captain's gift of fortune-telling and outlandish metaphors. They were thoroughly good girls—as blooming and natural as if they had not all the effulgence of seven centuries of Winspurleighs to turn their heads on one side of the house, and all Joshua Neville's forges roaring in full blast around them on the other. It was no fault of theirs if they were bred to tastes which did not find satisfaction among the simple scenes and strange people around them. It was only what all girls in all ages would have done in the like circumstances, if they frequently put their heads together at bed-time to moan over an affectionate little note from Lady Asphodel pressing them to be of the party in Primroseshire—if they devoutly recited the litany of all the pleasant people that were staying at Aunt Asphodel's—(I dare say I have mentioned that the Marchioness was a younger sister of Lady Margery)—and if they timidly questioned one another why, if Reggy wanted Mabel, he did not ask her, and get done with it ? Besides their preoccupation about losing the party at the Meads, the girls were also vaguely conscious of apprehensions which they rather looked than spoke on a subject into which Georgey O'Meagher's bright black eyes and saucy curls largely entered. The Neville girls were as kind to Georgey as they were to everybody else ; but it is perhaps needless to say that the innocent rompish ways of the Irish rustic beauty did not impress Aunt Asphodel's nieces with the same unmingled delight wherewith they too plainly impressed their brother. The elder girl, especially, noticed so many indescribable nothings that, in urging upon papa the desirability of making a movement towards England before the Primroseshire party should break up, she thought it her duty delicately to shadow forth her apprehensions of a possible O'Meagher quartering on the Winspurleigh shield.

'Nonsense, my dear child !' exclaimed Joshua Neville, who, if he knew anything, claimed to know men and women. 'That's an uncommonly pretty little girl ; but the notion of a man with eyes in his head thinking of anybody else in the presence of

Mabel !—I say you have no right to think your brother a born idiot, child.' And he selfishly stifled discussion as to flitting into Primroseshire, by intimating that Aunt Asphodel always made his head ache, whereas he had never once felt his temples throb in the bracing air of Glengariff. Papa's health and happiness were the last words with Joshua Neville's daughters. Ida and her sisters, like the dear girls that they were, dismissed Primrose-shire with a sigh (and possibly with a little cry), and set them-selves resolutely to like Lord Clanlaurance's rookery. Wicked, wicked Joshua Neville ! and all-too-confiding Ida ! I do verily believe that what the ironmaster was thinking of above all else was his own delicious readings from the German poets, and his own conviction, rapturously whispered to himself a hundred times a day in the inmost, inmost shrine of his simple, rugged hidden heart, that he would be the happiest ironmaster who ever lit a furnace if he had Mabel Westropp for his daughter-in-law.

And this young lady was all the time an observer how Reggy Neville was beginning to lie in wait for the comings and goings of Miss Georgey, and never once frowned—if she did not actually smile. She found herself degenerating into a shameless match-maker also in the matter of poor Harry's unspoken love. With Harry unrequited love at the Mill meant prolonged visits to Moll Carthy's. Whisky was the only mistress to whom he could declare his passion without the terror of making a speech or getting laughed at. Mabel saw with misery that poor little Katie Rohan's too evident terror of his attentions was driving him more and more to the feet of his more compliant goddess. She courted little Katie so assiduously for Harry's sake that she ended by doating on her for her own sake; for, once the timid shrinking from a great lady evaporated under Mabel's soft sun-shiny smiles, Katie put forth all the pure sweetness of her nature as confidingly as a violet in a safe woodland nook, and the elder girl wound her arms round her with the fondness of a mother thrilling under the artless caresses of a winsome baby. Katie was a curious study to her. In household matters she left Mabel a thousand miles behind. In the making of a lemon-pudding, or in prescribing for a sore throat, or managing the pillows of a sick bed, she was as practical as a certificated nurse, and as confident of her own strength as a navvy. But of the great world beyond the Mill at Greenane, she knew no more than the robin-redbreast knows of the atmosphere of the sun. All she was aware of was that Myles Rohan was the wisest of men, her mother the noblest of women, and Ken the bravest of heroes ; and, for the rest, the great universe an enlarged chapel with the gold-fretted firmament for a roof, and the everlasting angels for a choir ; with wicked

spirits, also, doubtless hovering somewhere in exterior darkness
but kept in subjection by Mother Rosalie's prayers, and fleeing in
terror under the all-subduing eye of Father Phil.　If it ever
occurred to her to think what could be her own part among the
rolling world, it was doubtless in the spirit in which the mouse of
the fable might have dreamed the night the lion did it the honour
of allowing the creature to nibble his high and mighty chains
away.　, Miss Westropp, looking down from the heights of her
own wide experience of half a London season and (in very truth)
much anxious thought and reading of her own, watched this
miracle of simplicity with the protecting tenderness with which a
Guardian Angel overshadows a child on its knees at evening
prayer.　In the beautiful book of Tobias, the Guardian Angel
helps the young Tobias to a wife ; but when the Guardian Angel
commenced to hint never so dimly of Harry as a husband, Katie's
little soul shrank and trembled with pain as though it was one of
the wicked spirits that had evaded Father Phil's vigilance and
was whispering to her.

'Oh, don't ! don't ! never—never again !' she cried, in an
agony of tears ; and Mabel, who was scarcely less frightened than
Katie herself, took her in her arms, and, though she did not in
the least comprehend, assured her never, never, never !—'I thought
you knew,' she murmured, when at last a reassured smile began to
dawn through her blinding tears.—'Knew, dear ?' exclaimed
Mabel, in bewilderment.—'I mean that I am going to be a nun,'
she said, in a joyous whisper, such as might ripple from the lips
of a West-End beauty confiding to her sister the first news that
the young Duke had proposed and been accepted.　Then, as if
eager to atone for her passing association of Mabel with the
spirits of darkness, she murmured : 'You won't tell if I show
you something, will you ?' to which the answer was of the sort
which enables young ladies to dispense with speeches in schoolgirl
conferences.　They were in Katie's own little snowy room with
the tender blue forget-me-not papering.　She unlocked her work-
box, and, after taking out a movable crimson nest of compartments for thimbles, needles, and what not, produced a packet of
letters tied with white satin ribbon from the cavity underneath,
and proceeded to unfold the love-letters which had been passing
between Mother Rosalie and her little pupil ever since Katie had
quitted the convent at Clonard.　Such a seraphic smile as Katie
kissed them with ! and how those fading puce pages from poor
old Mother Rosalie's cramped knuckles glowed and shone with a
light of affection such as never yet beamed on a court of justice
out of the correspondence in a breach of promise case ! and how
Mabel Westropp longed to take off her shoes while treading in

that pure virginal shrine where the old nun trembling on the threshold of heaven, and the child who seemed to have but lately left it, whispered to one another the beautiful secrets of their souls. One thing was clear to Mabel. It was all over with un. lucky Harry. This child was engaged in a love-match in which the mere thought of poor Harry was grotesque and blasphemous— a love-match as inexorable and as enduring as eternity.

'You understand now!' said Katie, watching with flushing check the effect of Mother Rosalie's artless heaven-thoughts.

'Yes, dear,' said Miss Westropp, almost in a whisper, with a deep sigh, re-tying the packet with the white satin string; and by an impulse she could not control, she took Katie's hand in her own, and bent down and kissed it, in token that the subject of poor Harry's ill-starred love was over between them for ever.

This terror once removed, however, Katie's discomfort at sight of Harry completely disappeared, and the poor lad began to find himself as much at home in the family circle at the Mill as Snipe curled up on the hearthrug. Having no higher an opinion of himself than he had of Snipe, he was quite content like him to lie dumb in the firelight and blink his eyes respectfully at his mistress, and lie in wait for the slightest hint to fetch and carry for her; while Katie, for her part, began to entertain towards him very much the same sort of fondness that children commonly feel for a big dog. Mabel, only too happy to see him devouring tea out of Katie's dainty flowered evening-cups, instead of dipping in Moll Carthy's pewter measures, had not the heart to tell poor Harry that the secret of his present contentment was the certainty of his future disappointment. It must be stated, also, that Miss Mabel felt a growing vague necessity for assuring some mysterious accusing spirit within her that it was her interest in Harry's love affair which made her so frequent a figure in the chimney-corner at the Mill; she felt reluctant to cut off so capital a plea of self-justification. She did not dare to ask herself why young Rohan's name so incessantly crossed and recrossed her daily life, without her ever summoning it up, and yet without her ever feeling provoked to hear it. But when a young person, who has been listening to Georgey O'Meagher crowning a young man's brows with roses during the day, has sufficient patience left to watch new crowns of roses being plaited for him all the evening by an idolatrous mother and fanatical sister, the argus-eyed reader will know how to discount the firmness of soul of the haughty patrician who only a few days ago so chafed under the scene at Mullagh and railed at lovers as the cutpurses and assassins of human happiness! I offer no opinion myself. I am perfectly sure that Mabel would have torn her flesh with whips

if anybody had suggested to her that she was falling in love
with Ken Rohan. Such a thought would have been to her
simply horrible—inconceivable. But I am sure also that it was
not Mrs. Rohan's cream-cakes alone that caused her to spend so
many joyous October evenings in the ruddy parlour firelight at
the Mill, trolling glees and duets with Katie, plotting future little
raids of benevolence with the President of the Ladies' St. Vincent
de Paul Society, and throwing Myles Rohan into ecstasies of
perplexity between regard for his fame as an invincible back-
gammon-player and incapacity to hurt, even on a backgammon-
board, an opponent so divinely fair.

'What *can* have delayed Harry?' asked Miss Westropp for
the second or third time on one of those occasions. Harry had
been falling into the habit of dropping in at or after tea-time at
the Mill to pick up his sister and see her home. It gave him an
excuse for coming, and it gave her an excuse for staying. It was
growing late now, and Myles Rohan, who was forbidden late
hours, had pushed away the backgammon-board and was looking
sleepy.

'Ken, put on your hat, and see Miss Westropp safe to the
Castle,' said Mrs. Rohan, to whom the order seemed as natural
as it would seem to a London middle-class mother to despatch her
son for a cab. Nor did it seem a very much graver matter to the
young people.

'All right, mother—Snipe and myself,' said Ken, gaily.

'And won't Master Harry catch it!' said the young lady, half-
laughingly, half-assuredly, tying on her hat.

When they got out of the homely warmth of the parlour into
the open air not a word passed between them. Not that there
was embarrassment on either side. She had no more apprehension of a renewal of the Mullagh nightingale song than of the
sullen wintry sky falling. As for him, he was undoubtedly ill at
ease whenever Miss Westropp was in the Mill parlour. She
appeared to him to be as beautiful as the sun. When a luminary
of the sun's size compresses itself into a room twenty-six feet by
eighteen, sunworshippers naturally feel it hot and blinding and
do not breathe comfortably. But he had a fanciful notion that,
once out in the expansive air, this bright being's brightness was
not so oppressive—that she had more room to shine without overwhelming—and so he marched along filling himself gratefully
with her sunshine, entirely oblivious of the fact that, to the eye
of the general public, it was not sunlight but darkly-drifting
clouds and death-dealing October winds that were in possession
of the horizon. All happy moments are moments of silence.
Words are but the strugglings through which they come or the

sighs with which they go. This short, silent walk was a moment of beautiful felicity for young Rohan—felicity so reverent, so unearthly, it reminded him (be it without impiety said) of his feelings as an altar-boy when changing the flowers or lights about the Blessed Sacrament during the Forty Hours' Adoration.

As they passed the lodge-gate, with the stone catomountains grinning from the pillars overhead, the winds were prowling murderously among the branches of the great elm-tree avenue, and the killed and wounded autumn leaves were falling around them at every blast. Now and again, the moon managed to tear its way out of the clouds as if to detect the night-winds at their deadly work; but the moment after it was thrust back behind the hurrying black clouds, as if by a brutal cordon of policemen in their dark great-coats. As they passed a point where the umbrageous shadows of the avenue were thickest, just where it opened into the wide sweep of lawn and gravel before the Castle steps, Snipe, who had been caraçolling nimbly after the shadows raised by the occasional bursts of moonlight, suddenly barked violently, and then fell back with a yell of pain. The two young people started. At the same moment a torn streak of moonlight shot across the avenue, and they saw a dark figure springing over the wire paling from the angry dog. It was the work of an instant. The figure was buried in a dense shrubbery, and all was still. It might have been some optical fancy, only that Snipe's deep growl was still breaking the silence.

'Who—what could it be?' she said in a tremulous whisper, catching him irresolutely by the arm.

'I suppose somebody about the Castle—perhaps some fellow with an eye upon the pheasants,' he replied, not knowing particularly what he said. 'Nobody that will harm *you*, Miss Westropp, anyway.'

'I am such a wretched coward,' she said, letting go his arm and walking steadily forward to the door. 'Thank you, Mr. Rohan. Mrs. Keyes will teach me courage until Harry comes,' she said, extending her hand, as he pulled at the housekeeper's bell. 'I wonder *has* he come?' she added, almost to herself, looking round with a shudder at the mournful night and the dark screen of foliage in which the figure had disappeared; and she somehow slightly drew in her hand.

'Bless my soul, Miss, and isn't Master Harry with you?' exclaimed the old prim-capped housekeeper, who herself stood in the doorway.

'Then he is not in?—nor Captain MacCarthy?'

'The Captain, you know, Miss, has his latch-key; but he hasn't been in to dinner—has not been in since morning.'

'Is—is there anything to fear? *Can* anything have happened? Tell me—do!—do not be afraid to trust me!' she said, turning to her companion with a white, grave face.

'Not that I know, Miss Westropp—certainly not,' he replied; but the news in the morning papers flashed back upon his mind, and now that he thought of it, the man who clambered over the fence was dragging something like a rifle with him. She noticed by the lamplight the spasm of doubt crossing his face, and he saw her own face grow whiter. 'I will try if I can't beat up Harry and the Captain, or'—a thought suddenly struck him—'maybe Mrs. Keyes and yourself will allow me to stay with you till they come—it cannot be very long.'

'God bless us! my darling child—how frightened you look! —as if you had seen something!' cried the old housekeeper, drawing the shrinking figure within her arms. 'Yes, Mr. Rohan, certainly, you will stay,' she said, decisively. 'Something has frightened her.'

'Only a man that the dog barked at in the plantation beyond —some poacher, I dare say, or somebody making a short cut home through the Park,' said Ken Rohan, following the housekeeper through a shadowy, gaping corridor to the little snuggery Mabel had fitted up for her guests among the vast solitudes of the dreary mansion—like one of the little Arab cooking-fires you see nestling among the colossal pink-granite ruins of Memphis. Miss Westropp would have it that she was now all right; but the housekeeper would insist on dragging her off to her own little room to take off her things and douche her wrists and temples with eau-de-cologne. Ken took a turn or two up and down opposite the glowing hearth, on which a fire of pine-logs and peat was frisking and crackling merrily. Then something seemed to draw him towards the quaint trifoliated window, and he found himself again surveying the spot where the figure had started out of the darkness and as quickly returned to it. The moon had again obtained a momentary ascendency over the rebellious clouds, and was flashing out and back with the warring fortunes of the moment. His eye suddenly rested on the penumbra of a man cast by the moonlight beyond the fringe of the deeper mass of shade made by the trees. The shadow paced up and down measuredly. It stopped, and a second shadow crept up from the gloom of the avenue, and the two seemed to hold ghostly communion together, after which both shadows shrank back into the mass of gloom. Again the moon got the worst of it in the elemental war, and all was darkness.

'I am afraid I have not distinguished myself,' said a voice behind, and turning with a start he saw that Miss Westropp had

re-entered the room. 'I have made, oh! so many valiant resolutions, and then at the first shadow of danger—oh, that shadow!'
she again broke down into a shuddering whisper, and sank into
a chair. 'I do wish that Harry would come!'

'Of course he will come. If you had seen as many shadows
as Harry and I have seen together by moonlight lately, one way-
farer more or less after dark would not strike you as very odd,'
he replied with a cheery smile.

'You have not told me—I do want you to tell me—truly—is
there trouble coming? and do you really, really think it is not
madness for our poor unarmed peasant lads to think of coping
with British regiments and artillery—heavy guns that would
smash through this house as easily as if it were cardboard?' she
asked, looking him earnestly in the face.

He started. It was the first time the question had ever presented itself to his own mind so pointedly. 'It would be indeed
impossible not to answer such a question as that truly,' he said,
his head involuntarily bending in homage to the sweet, searching
face that was fixed upon him. 'My answer is that I do not
know, and I have no right to ask. There are soldiers at the
head of this movement—veterans of the greatest war of the
century. Captain Mike is but one of thousands—one of tens of
thousands who are dispersed through every parish in the country,
or awaiting the signal to embark on ships that will bring them
to this very Bay. The men who carried the Cemetery Heights
at Gettysburg may be trusted to know their business. It is
theirs to decide what is to be done. We of the rank-and-file
have only to wait till the word is passed and do it. I have told
you all I know, Miss Westropp, except this—that, upon my
honour, I am not aware of any immediate peril pending in this
locality.'

'My poor Harry!' she said, bursting into tears.

How he seemed to envy Harry the danger, the death, that
would make such tears flow for *him*! How reverently he would
kiss the bullet that would entitle him to them! And oh! to
think of kissing those tears away on a field of victory. He sat
silent, as though a word would be sacrilegious.

'How you must despise me?' she said, looking up all at once
with a sad smile breaking through glassy barriers. 'Do you
know, I have been schooling myself to this ever so long—persuading myself that, when the time comes, I should surrender Harry
to his country like a heroine—and you see the result, the moment
even a shadow seems to cross me!'

'I fancy,' said Ken Rohan, 'women bear the apprehension of
danger worse than men, but meet the reality more bravely.'

'Some women do,' she said, with a sigh. 'There is that Italian girl in Mrs. Browning's glorious poem. Do you know I have been reading it over and over again these days to gain courage?—as one reads the Bible for courage of another kind. See!' and the book opened where a marker had been inserted at the famous lines :

> Heroic males the country bears—
> But daughters give up more than sons:
> Flags wave, drums beat, and unawares
> You flash your souls out with the guns,
> And take your Heaven at once.
> But we!—we empty heart and home
> Of life's life, love! We bear to think
> You're gone—to feel you may not come—
> To hear the door-latch stir and clink,
> Yet no more you ! . . . nor sink.
> Dear God! when Italy is one,
> Complete, content from bound to bound,
> Suppose, for my share, earth's undone,
> By one grave in't !—as one small wound
> Will kill a man, 'tis found.
> What then? If love's delight must end,
> At least we'll clear its truth from flaws.
> I love thee, love thee, sweetest friend!
> Now take my sweetest without pause,
> And help the Nation's cause.
> And thus of noble Italy
> We'll both be worthy! Let her show
> The future how we made her free,
> Not sparing life . . . nor Giulio
> Nor this . . . this heart-break. Go!

'It *is* glorious! No wonder Italy is free,' said young Rohan, passionately. ' "Parting Lovers," the poem is called.'

'Poor Harry is my Giulio,' she said, without noticing, 'and oh, dear me, I do so grudge him—I do so shudder!'

Ken Rohan's heart said to him darkly, 'She well may. If it were with us only a matter of "flashing our souls out with the guns" there needn't be much shuddering ; it is different when it is a matter of flashing our souls into a garotter's jacket—into a felon's hell.' But aloud he said gaily, 'Yes, but you'll end by saying "Go!" and go he will, and return, too! Italy is not going to have all the poetry and triumph to herself.'

'But why go at all? Why for ever these miserable flags and drums and the tears that follow them? O there is so much goodness in the world, so much unselfishness, so much affection!—and yet a handful of wicked, selfish, heartless men and women force guns into the hands of the millions who only want to be kind to one another, and bid them slay and mangle or be slain! Who would

be the worse if our poor folk had their little cabins safe over their
heads—had the genius of their indestructible old race restored
again to its kindly throne in Eirinn of the Streams ? Why should
that shadow cross our path to-night ?   Why cannot the two
nations—why cannot all the world—sit as you and I are sitting
here to-night, respecting one another, admiring one another,
liking one another—I only too happy to think that some of your
bright Celtic blood flows in my veins—and you not, I think,
at all disposed to let this foolish blood of mine flow out in order
to analyse how much of it is Protestant and English ?   Oh ! why
cannot people be the same in millions ?'

'Because there are not many like you in the world—if there
is another one,' he said fervently, almost in a whisper.

'I did not mean you to say that, and I did think you would
have known that I did not mean you to say it,' she said, with a
flush of pain.

'I did—I do know it, Miss Westropp ; forgive me,' he cried,
reverently bowing his head.   'After all, what do we all dream
but that there may be—that there are—millions like you in the
most brilliant part of you—a compassionate human soul ?
Heaven grant it if ever this heart-breaking old world is to be
put to rights !'

'Or,' said she, her little head supported thoughtfully between
her hands, 'if the old nun is not wiser than all the philosophers
and statesmen, and if all the pangs and complications of this
shadowy world are not divine messages to remind us of a brighter
——   Didn't you hear some noise ? Listen ! There it is again
—trampling on the gravel. Heavens ! what has happened ?'
and she sprang to the window and tore aside the blind.   'Look !
The place is full of them—of armed men !'

At the same moment the great hall-bell was tugged and sent
its alarum vibrating through the silent caverns of the Castle.

'May I leave you for one moment to see what it is about—one
moment only, and I will be back ?' he said, moving towards the
door.

'No, no !—I must know,' she cried, springing after him.
'Thank you !—I am all right now ;' and when he reached the
heavy oaken portal, she was beside him, white, but calm.

'Who's there ?' he demanded, as the bell went off into new
and more violent convulsions.

'In the Queen's name—open !' answered a deep voice outside.

Young Rohan undid the massive chain fastenings, and the
great door swung slowly back. The light of the hall-lamp fell
upon clumsy dark figures, shrouded in frieze great-coats, and be-

hind them a vague living mass, amidst which the light picked out flashes of scarlet and the tips of bayonets here and there against the shifting black background. The foremost of the great-coats pushed unceremoniously forward. Ken Rohan put him quietly but resolutely back.

'Let me pass,' said the man, gruffly, thrusting forward a rifle.

'Not until you've explained your business,' said Rohan, grasping the rifle with both hands by the barrel.

'You have no right to see the warrant—it is a felony—the 11th and 12th Victoria will tell you that—we've a right to enter, arrest, and search,' said Head-Constable Muldudden, whose pride in the legal reference had checked for the moment his rude onset. 'I bear a warrant for the arrest of Michael MacCarthy, commonly called Captain MacCarthy, on a charge of Trayson-felony—resist me at your perr'l !'

'Captain MacCarthy is not in this house—upon my word !' came the answer, in Miss Westropp's calm, clear tones. She stood forward, facing the lurid circle of arms and rough figures like some statue of a Madonna suddenly gleaming into life.

The policemen on the steps involuntarily stepped back a pace. Muldudden's hand went perforce to his hat as in the old exorcisms the Evil Spirit is compelled to make the sign of the Cross at departing. 'Very sorry, Miss,' he said, with a certain cowed insistence, 'but orders is orders. We'll have to search the Castle.'

'Miss Westropp has pledged her honour that Captain Mac-Carthy is not here,' said Rohan. 'Do you persist in breaking into the house at this time of night, when you know there is nobody but a helpless lady and her servants on the premises ?'

'*You* are there,' said the other, with insolent meaning. 'Stand aside, if you don't want to commit a misdemeanour yourself, my fine fellow, as you've escaped trayson-felony this time.'

The head-constable made a lunge forward again with the muzzle of his rifle. Quick as thought the young man had wrenched it out of his hands, and held the clubbed musket fixed menacingly over his head in the doorway.

'Stop !' cried an authoritative voice, its owner advancing out of the darkness. 'There are express orders not to give Miss Westropp any unnecessary annoyance. If Miss Westropp assures you that the man named in the warrant is not in the house it is sufficient. Head Constable Muldudden, you can fall back.'

'Mr. Hans Harman !' exclaimed Miss Westropp, as the agent, wrapped in a heavy cloak, pushed the policeman on the steps back into the darkness, and doffed his low-crowned hat.

' Pray, am I to count myself indebted to you for terminating or
for initiating this visit ?

' An accident—a mere accident—my being here, I assure you,
my dear young lady. A dreadful duty—but these are dreadful
times. The officer of police, Mr. Flibbert, was away on his
honeymoon—it was a very pressing matter—and as there was no
other magistrate immediately available, Muldudden called upon
me—pressed me into the service by my allegiance, so to say.'

' I have no doubt he called upon the proper person, sir,' she
replied, in a tone that somehow prompted him to put up his
hand to see if anything had cut him across the cheek. ' Am I to
consider myself free to treat this scene as closed, or does your
duty to your Sovereign press you any further ? '

' Young ladies, of course, cannot be expected to understand
the stern duties that times like these impose upon men ; but I
assure you that the instructions were that you should be treated
with every possible consideration.'

And doubtless, sir, so I have been. Is there anything
more ?' she asked, holding the great door half open. His sleek
self-command forsook him under the lash of that girlish voice.
' Nothing more,' he said, as he turned into the darkness, ' except
that your father will be here to-morrow night, and will, no
doubt, take care that there shall be no repetition of the proceedings which caused this visit to Drumshaughlin Castle, and
no continuance of the acquaintances which pain his daughter's
best friends.' The hoarse order—' Fall in—march ! ' and the
heavy trampling on the gravel were the last sounds that came
through as the great iron-clamped door swung back into its
chains.

' My father returning, and not a word to give me notice—not
a message or a hint to *me* ? ' mused Miss Westropp, as she faced
back through the echoing corridor. ' Oh ! I dare say he has
been teased to death with that ill-natured gossip of Harman's,
and is coming back to give me a terrible blazing-up for my
iniquities, dear old pappy ! Only wait till we see whether it's
Mr. Hans Harman or I that will have the worst of his agent's
exploits to-night from him ! Oh ! but Captain MacCarthy—my
poor, poor Captain ! '

' Captain Mike's old luck—but 'twas a close thing this time,'
said Ken Rohan. ' Somebody must have passed the word.'

' Oh ! but if not—if he does not know—go and find him ! go
and warn him ! go ! ' she cried, vehemently. ' I will not feel
lonesome now—and—what a selfish creature I am !—how they
must be waiting and trembling for *you* all this time at the Mill,
while I have been keeping you here to nurse me ! And my own

▲ ▲

poor Harry—God of Sorrows! what a country is this!—what a tangle of hopeless chains around young lives! Where can Harry be? How is the Captain to be warned? What is to be done?'

'Here is somebody who will, perhaps, answer the question for us,' said Rohan, as the hall-bell again sounded.

'Heavens! if it should be the Captain!—He is lost!' she cried, white as death.

'It is Harry—I hear his voice in the corridor,' he answered; and the next moment Harry Westropp staggered into the room, like one drunk or insane, and tumbled into a chair, crying: 'Whisky—for God's sake, Mabel, whisky!' His eyes were staring wildly, his light hair tossing in anarchy, his throat, as Ken Rohan placed the tumbler in his hands, burning like the funnel of a ship's boiler. 'The police were here?' he ejaculated, after a greedy gulp. 'I passed two of them this moment in the avenue. They are outside still. Have they told you?'

'In Heaven's name, what?' cried Miss Westropp, who had sunk on her knees at his feet, with her hands clasped.

The strain appeared to have been too much for his mental faculties. His head fell heavily between his hands, and tears broke from his eyes; and all that was distinguishable from his sobs was 'Quish! poor Quish!'

CHAPTER THE TWENTY-NINTH

QUISH GOES HOME

EARLIER on that night of uneasy moaning winds a man glided into the darkened chapel. Only one half of the door remained open, the keeper having already bolted the other half for the night, as a signal to stray worshippers that the hour of total closing was at hand. Inside all was getting dark, except where a feeble red glow from the lamp before the altar trembled in the deep gloom like the heart of a mystery. The man stumbled against a pillar and fell on his knees. A fugitive gleam of moonlight burst on him as through a bull's-eye, deepening every furrow on his haggard face, and making the statue of a past parish priest fixed against the wall beside him horrible with the bluish-white tinge of a dead man's face. He shrank back blinded. The patch of troubled moonlight disappeared, and seemed to have deprived him of the light of his eyes. There was not a sound in the chapel. The pillars and confessionals loomed darkly like monstrous dead forms. It seemed to him that his own breathing must be heard in the most distant corners, so loud it sounded and so fiercely it tore its way through his chest. He staggered back towards the doorway, and had one hand on the handle of the inner swing-door when the low groan-like cadence of a Latin prayer somewhere in the darkness first startled, and then reassured him. He let go the door-handle and crept again along the wall, groping his way stealthily till he started back again with trembling limbs. His hand had touched the cold white face of the dead parish priest. He gently resumed his way on tip-toe towards the altar-lamp, and presently, just as the red glow died off into deep umbered shadows, he stood beside a prostrate form with something that shone like a silver crown on its head. 'Father Phil,' muttered the man in a hoarse whisper which, nevertheless, he thought sounded like the alarm of a great bell. The silver crown continued to be bent low before the tabernacle, and no sign of life came until again there came that low wailing Latin heart-cry : '*Si iniquitates observaveris, Domine, Domine, quis sustinebit ?*'—that sad-sweet hymn of human weakness in which saint and sinner, great and lowly, have for thousands of years confessed a common kindred before the all-spotless, all-mighty, all-merciful Throne. The man trembled violently, and seemed to hesitate ; then, as if worked to desperation, he plucked the old priest by the soutane, whispering in a thick voice in his ear :

'For God's sake, quick, Father Phil ! A man is dying !'

The old priest started. His first confused impression was that some damned soul had just addressed him. But Father Phil had lived too long in both worlds, and seen too much of their trouble, to be very much perturbed by summonses either from the living or the dead. He groped for his biretta on the altar-step, and silently drew the stranger into the adjoining sacristy, where a taper was lighted. The stranger shrank back as if the sun out of heaven had suddenly flashed in his eyes.

'What ! Owen !' cried the priest. 'Is it the old man ? What has happened, boy ? Why do you look so frightened ?'

'It's Quish —Quish the bailiff !' The words struggled out in a rasping gurgle. The boy's face seemed to have absorbed fifty years of cares and hardness since the night we saw him in his father's cabin at Cnocawn. 'Quick, Father, or you'll hardly ketch him !'

The priest turned his eyes full on the old-young face cowering before him, and all the blood in young Owen's heart seemed to fly to that face under his scrutiny. 'O—oh !' he cried, in a voice that rent his hearer's heartstrings. 'Oh ! you unhappy boy !' Without another word, he flung aside his soutane, and seized his black-green overcoat and hat. In his haste the old hat rolled on the floor. The young lad knelt on the floor to pick it up. He remained on both knees, with a downcast face of misery, holding out the hat in his hand. The old priest looked at him, took the hat with a shudder, and murmured 'God forgive you!' The other rose, and a dark scowl disfigured his young face horribly.

'Amen, Father,' he said, half sullenly, 'but he was an informer!'

The priest turned on him a dreadful look. The young fellow's powerful frame fell in under it as if that Spanish contracting iron cage was crushing his bones. 'Don't tell me!' he cried, with the dread emphasis of an exorcist. Then, seeing him broken: 'Is it at his mother's place he is—the body is?' he asked, more gently.

'It is, your reverence—but he is not dead—you will be in time,' said the other, eagerly.

'Quick, get round my pony,' said Father Phil, placing the viaticum and the oils for the Last Sacrament in his breast.

Five minutes afterwards the old pony and its old rider were plunging away into the night. As Owen slunk away under the cloak made for him by the hurrying clouds, another figure, which had been lurking about the chapel, moved up to him. 'Gimme de tool, now, quick—and get home,' whispered the new comer. 'My God! what is dat patch? It's blood.'

The moon had suddenly shot out upon the two men like a flash of limelight. It revealed a great dark smear upon the white flannel vest which the young man wore over his chest under the outer jacket. 'I suppose it is!' he said in a voice out of a sepulchre. 'I did not notice. It must have been the body— while I was carryin' it.'

'Man, how you are trembling! Are you a coward?' said the other, plucking him roughly by the arm.

'A coward!' was the deep reply. 'I brought the body to his mother's doore—I sent the priest to him myself—how many men would daar do that? Would you do it?' he said, turning on him like a young wild beast, as another flying ray of moonlight fell on the little hellfire-tipped nose of Dawley. There was something in the sight that enraged him. He seized Dawley by the throat with both his hands, and shook him as easily as if he were a small dog in the claws of a young tiger. 'Look!' he cried, in a terrible whisper, 'I hope there is no mistake about this night's work, or——'

'Mistake!' replied the other, wriggling himself free, and gasping for breath. 'Yerra, in de honour o' God, man, do you want de people to tink you escaped from a madhouse? or are you goin' to bring de Bobbies down atop of us admirin' dat shirt o' yours? Gimme de ting you know, I tell you, an' peg away home, an' burn dem bloody rags of yours to blazes.' The other pulled a pistol, whose barrel still smelt of gunpowder from his bosom, and Dawley pounced on it and covered it up. 'You're a brave lad, Owen,' he said, 'an' you've ridded Ireland of a scorpion to-night.'

'God sind Father Phil 'll be in time whatever!' was the young peasant's last husky words, as he stood for a moment gazing down the road by which the priest's pony had disappeared; then plunged into a narrow laneway, and made for the mountains.

Quish, in addition to his nest over the stables at the Castle, possessed a more regular home of his own among the Bauherla Mountains, where they join hands with the wild range over Gougaun Barra. The cabin was pitched under shelter of a black escarpment of rock, down which in wintry weather a savage young yellow cataract smashed its way, and reeled headlong in foaming torrents under, and now and again over, the ruins of the bridge which spanned the public road lower down. Quish's 'stripe' of land consisted of some black potato beds descending steeply from the cabin door, and at present littered with rotten stalks; and outside these some diminutive ragged fields which had once been reclaimed and fenced in with enormous stone fences by some former tenant, but were now re-invaded by gorse and flowering heather, as though it was these Vandal tribes that had broken down the massy stone walls and were reconquering their old territory, blasting and burning up everything on their barbaric line of march. Quish was no farmer. His duties as estate bailiff supplied him with the means of living, and his avocations on the moors and rivers were the only delights, except red-headed whisky, which it ever entered into his overgrown bulbous head to conceive. He cultivated as many black beds of potato-mould as he himself in an industrious mood could plant, and as his old mother at her leisure could dig out; and his only other agricultural appurtenances were a stunted mountain milch-cow, as ill-favoured as himself, and some goats which gave the old lady's legs and voice a wholesome degree of exercise in hunting and cursing them all over the mountain. In the one-windowed hut which dominated this bleak mass of mountain, and which to Father Phil as he caught sight of it on the public road below presented the appearance of a burning eye set in the forehead of a monster, Quish preserved what more pretentious people would call his home; and it was here that at this moment, while the priest's pony was picking its way through the black morasses and rocky watercourses towards the light, the bailiff lay moaning in dull inarticulate agony, like a dumb animal. Bright as the light looked, as seen against the black mountain heights, it was only a miserable smoking paraffin lamp, the upper portion of whose chimney was a mass of stinking soot. The bloodshot-looking rays that issued from the unblackened glass bulb did not do much more than the uncanny flicker of a wet turf fire to throw light into the hideous corners of the cabin, where all sorts of weird things—peering fowls' eyes among the rafters, filthy-looking stone bed-recesses, horse-collars that had a strangling look, the ugly little cow's fixed staring eyeballs—loomed and winked in horrid mystery out of the all-pervading wreaths of turf-smoke. The elfin light, foraging under the deep canopy of a bedstead, apparently built upon a stone shelf, from time to time picked out another luminous pair of eyes:—if one may describe as a pair two so irreconcilably opposed orbs as those of the dwarf, which in his present agony squinted and leered more horribly than ever in a demoniac grin. Sometimes his eyes would close, and the purple weal across his cheek would disappear in a corpse-like pallor; then, with a groan as of a volcano in labour, the dead mass would stir again, the long hairy paws would be flung out in fever, the purple gash would fill again as if a great dab of blood had been dropped upon the face, and those hideous unearthly eyes would go tumbling and flashing in all directions, like ogres searching for their victims. If there was a finishing touch wanting to the horror of the scene, it was supplied by the awful creature wringing her hands by the bedside. Quish's mother was the type of an old woman who would have been burned as a witch three or four centuries ago—bony, crooked, filthy-looking, with protruding yellow tusks, hawk's eyes buried under cavernous grizzly eyebrows, naked bony arms that seemed to reach to her feet, the whole floating against an eerie mist of wild grey hairs that suggested thoughts of their being blown about by the midnight air at some witches' Sabbath. Who Quish was, none but the old creature could tell; and an ancient sepulchre would have been more communicative. It never occurred to Quish himself that his parentage could be a matter of any greater interest than the parentage of his moorhens, seals, or salmon; it did not strike him even that he required any more than these any second descriptive name. Whether Quish was intended to be a christian name or surname was to him as meaningless a point of controversy as that of the Procession of the Holy Ghost; he had probably sprung up as one of the fungi that sprout from the refuse of great houses; and the old woman had been so long without anything either to hope or dread from human interest, except the companionship of her mis-shapen child, that she had possibly lost faith in the real facts of the story herself, so buried had they become amidst the rotting memories of her sepulchral life.

So deadened had she grown to human experiences, that when,

an hour ago, the door of the cabin was roughly kicked in, and she found her son's body laid across the threshold, it took her a considerable time to realise that there was anything more than a fit of drunkenness in question. This was the less surprising that there was no trace of external bleeding. Owen might have spared himself his anxiety about the dark blotches on his flannel vest. They were only the soft mud with which the body got enamelled when it fell upon the roadway. Drunkenness, however, seemed no more terrible to the old woman in her son than his ill-mated eyes or disfigured cheek. She gathered up the body with that superhuman strength which mothers have upon emergency, and trundled it into the bedstead, and listened patiently for the snore that would tell her her boy was enjoying himself after his own peculiar way (God bless him !). Instead of the comfortable snore she heard sounds in the throat that appalled her ; and when, holding the smutty lamp over the bed, she saw that the red blotches on the cheek and lips had grown a ghastly grey, and that the forehead was glistening with beads of cold sweat, and when, bending down, she found that the deep grommelings that came through the teeth were groans of agony, the lamp almost fell out of her hands in terror. 'Mo stóir, mo stóir ! what have they done to my boy, my darling boy ?' she cried, her brain suddenly taking fire with intelligence. She knew enough of the risks and penalties of his calling to be prepared for anything. Instinctively she tore open his clothes and searched for blood. The clothes were not bloody. She snatched at the shirt. Her hawk's eye pounced upon a small round hole burnt through it, the edges slightly singed. She knew now what she would find inside. Over the left lung there was a small blue discoloration that would scarcely have suggested a wound at all only for a tiny smear of blood that had escaped from the blue lips of the bullet-hole. With a wail of lamentation that seemed to pierce the mountain she threw herself on the body. 'Murder!' she screamed, with the wild instinct of one who knew she was miles away from the habitations of men, but was determined that her cry should be heard as plainly as she knew thunderclaps in the Bauherla Mountains were heard in valleys far away. All at once she found her arm clutched, and a hoarse voice liker thunder than her own mumbled :

'Howld yer whisht, woman ; will you howld yer whisht ?'

It was Quish who had recovered consciousness, and was now sinking back into a tortured bellowing rumble after his spring at the arm of the frantic woman. 'Drink !' was all he could articulate, his parched tongue lolling out horribly, 'drink !' She put a black bottle to his lips. He sucked the neck of the bottle

into his throat, as if he were going to bite it off ; then sank back
again without further sound or movement. The old woman set
up her howl anew. ' Whisht, I tell you again !—whisht ! ' roared
the dwarf, his eyes flaring wildly as if in a desperate attempt to
unite in withering her.

'Whisht ? an' my boy murthered before my face !—whisht !
an' his corpse left on the thrashil' of his owld mother's doore ! '
wailed the old creature, her skinny arms and grey hairs waving
as in some eerie midnight storm.

This time the wounded man darted up, and pulled her down
to him in the grasp of a demon. 'If you shout again, I'll—I'll
kill you !' he whispered, in a voice that made her blood freeze
with terror. ' What business is it o' yours ? ' Then he relaxed
his grip of the poor old trembling hag, and in a lower creaking
whisper, and with the most diabolical gambolling expression of
deep cunning in his eyes, he muttered : ' Whisper, mother ! I
suppose 'twas the boys done it,' and lay back, as if the observation were some plaster to the red-hot wound that was boring into
his heart.

The old woman was silent. She beat her old stupid head with
both hands, as though the intelligence so long slumbering within
would only act upon the direst compulsion. She looked earnestly
into his rolling eyes to read the secret that seemed to be starting
out of them. At last she understood. ' I won't cry "murder !"
any more !' she whispered. The trembling eyes closed with
satisfaction. ' Drink !' was all that the blackening lips uttered
forth.

'Oh, but to die without the priest, the docthor ! Wirra,
wirra, an' am I to lave him here alone ? ' cried the old woman,
and wandering from side to side of the cabin like a she-wolf
in a cage, the while the wounded man groaned like one whose
pain was past expressing, and the lonesome winds sang their
horrible *caoine* around the cabin, and the ugly brindled cow from
her own corner contributed an occasional forlorn bellow to the
unearthly noises of the night. At last the mother could stand
the helpless agony no longer. 'I won't say "murder !" acushla,'
she whispered softly over the bed, 'but if I was to be kilt an' was
to burn for ever for it, I'll shout, an' if there's a God in heaven
he'll hear me !' And flinging open the door of the cabin, she
faced the black night, and raised a yell of 'Help, help!' with
such superhuman force that from that height, it seemed to shoot
through the troubled darkness like the cry of a damned soul, and
to echo from mountain to mountain.

'All right, Judy—all right !—I am coming ! It is I—Father
Phil !' answered the priest out of the gloom.

'Thank God, an' the Holy Virgin! My cry is heard! My boy is saved!' exclaimed the old creature, sinking on her knees at the doorstep, and bending wildly down till she seemed to kiss the muddy ground the heaven-sent visitor trod upon.

Father Phil was sufficiently familiar with bodily as well as spiritual ailments to see at a glance that the absence of a doctor was a matter of the very smallest consequence to Quish. Nothing but his herculean bodily strength was keeping him alive. As to Father Phil's own mysterious surgery of the soul, who can tell how fared it? All I know is that, ten minutes afterwards, when the old priest in his violet stole and silvery nimbus, pronounced the august words of the Absolution and bade the Christian soul go forth to meet its Creator under the pitiful wings of escorting angels, the lonesome mountain cabin looked as holy a place as more pretentious temples. What a Leveller the Church is! What a Revolutionist whose barricades are death-beds. What a Socialist whose one ceremony of initiation is to die! How strange it seems, and good—the thought that to the angels hovering in the turf-smoke the soul encased in Quish's gnomelike body, and peeping out from behind Quish's twisted eyes may have looked more beautiful than many a soul that escapes from flesh of rose-tinted satin on a death-bed of rustling laces and in clouds of perfume! The old mother herself, kneeling by the bedside with the lighted taper in her hand, while the dying man was being marked with the sacred chrism, looked no longer like the weird sister caught riding on a broomstick, but rather like some gaunt female eremite of the desert kneeling for her eternal reward. The very night-winds appeared to have changed their dismal chant into a pathetic requiem.

Quish raised himself on his elbow and gazed intently into, or rather around, the priest's face. 'Whisper, Father Phil,' he said, in a voice that seemed to be evolved from the clashing of rusty iron files. 'Do you think there is a chance for an object like me up there—you know where?'—the eyes rolling violently towards the thatch.

'A chance! my poor boy—yes! I wish I had as good a chance as you have this moment, with God's holy help!' said the old priest, laying a soothing hand upon the burning forehead and leaving a tear glittering there, too, like a jewel. 'Quish,' he added solemnly, 'you forgive them that did this night's work?'

'Oyeh, I do an' welcome, Father,' was the reply, with the oddest contorted expression, like a hobgoblin jest, struggling on his features. 'I daar say some o' the boys heerd that Hans Harman gev me a half-sufferin or so once an' away to play the informer for him, an' they didn't ondherstand, the craythurs—

they didn't ondherstand!'—he repeated with something like a ghoulish laugh.

'Then it wasn't true?—they wronged you along with murdering you?' cried the priest.

'True! Sell Masther Harry to Hans Harman for half a sufferin! True!' cried the dwarf, starting up and flinging out his hairy paws in a way that made Father Phil himself recoil in terror; but when the paroxysm was at its worst it broke in hideous laughter like the rattling of rusty iron chains in his chest. 'Why,' he jerked out in spasms of frightful merriment, 'Masther Harry know'd every word—we med it all up together —we turned every pinny of Hans' dirty money into honest pewthers at Moll Carty's. True!' and he was going off into another volcanic eruption of delirious laughter; when, changing his thoughts to some more torturing one, he gripped Father Phil by the coat-sleeve with his burning paw, and whispered feverishly : 'Father, will you do one thing for a dying man?'

'I will,' said the old priest solemnly.

'See him—tell him—don't tell him to come—no, no, don't so much as hint such a thing—let him know ould Quish is goin' home —that's all,' he gasped; and then, falling back with a yell of pain : 'Quick, Father Phil—I'm a'most bet; but I won't give in till—till I know there's no use in waitin'.'

An hour wore away, and another. The old woman, swinging her body to and fro in that rhythmic movement which is to Irish grief what dancing is to French gaiety, accompanied herself with a low crooning orchestra which, mingling with the moaning treble of the winds, had the effect of a lullaby for the dying. The patient doggedly refused to open his lips to give expression to his internal torments. He was waiting like one of those patient-eyed animals that you see tethered uncomfortably in a cart on the way to the shambles. The sense of waiting seemed to have killed the sense of pain. He lay so still that the *calliagh* once or twice ceased her chant to make sure that the eyes turned so intently towards the doorway were not glazed in death.

'It's he! I hear the step down the *borheen*. It's he!' he suddenly shouted, flinging out his arms, and seeming to make the crazy cabin tremble with the wild, shrill halloo he had learned among the beaters on the mountains. After which, he fell back motionless, and his eyes closed.

Quish's keen ear was not at fault; but it took a long while yet before Harry Westropp, toiling up the jagged watercourse by the help of an occasional flash of moonlight, had his hand on the latch of the bailiff's cabin.

A weenuch, a weenuch, it's too late!' wailed the old woman,

dragging him to the bedside, and holding the sooty lamp over the ghastly figure extended there.

'Mother, howld yer whisht!' cried the dwarf opening his eyes with as terrifying an effect as if he had opened them in his coffin. 'Masther Harry,' he whispered hoarsely, 'who are thim with you?'

Harry looked at him bewildered. He supposed his mind must be wandering.

'With me? I came alone.'

The other shook his head. 'I hear em this moment on the stepping-stones across the sthrame. Don't tell me! A hare couldn't run on that mountain unknownst to me.' The deadly doubt which convulsed his face, when he besought Father Phil to communicate with his young master, seemed to have taken possession of him again. 'Whisper, Masther Harry,' he gurgled out, drawing Harry's head down to him in an eager, feverish way. 'The ould 'oman is deaf an' won't hear. It wasn't that *you* had any doubt of Quish? It wasn't to relieve *your* mind the boys put me out of the way?'

Harry started back as if a bullet had gone to his heart. 'God of Heaven!' he cried, "my poor Quish, do you think I'm a murderer? do you think I'm the vilest brute that ever bit the hand of his best friend?'

'Because,' continued the other, confidentially, 'it isn't that 'twould matter a *traneen*; my child, I'd boil every dhrop of my blood for you—I'd grind every bone in my ould carcase, if 'twas plasin' you to accept of it. But if I could make sure it wasn't *you* had any fear Quish would harm you dead or alive—if 'twas only a mistake of the boys——'

Harry could not answer a word. There seemed to be a boulder fixed in his throat. But his tears fell on the dying man's face, and Quish's burning flesh seemed to drink them up like an elixir, and to understand them better than if they were most musical eloquence.

'Thank God!' he muttered, huskily. 'An', Masther Harry,' with a glance in the direction of his mother, 'you won't see the ould woman short of the sup of tay?'

Harry pressed his hand, and Quish reclined back with the comforted air of a man whose will had just been read over and signed. For a few moments nothing was heard but Quish's pained breathing, the old mother's woeful lullaby, and the uneasy voices of the night. A face pressed close outside the window (for Quish's instinct had not deceived him), was pressed closer, as if trying to hear the very silence. Once more the monstrous bullet-head shot upwards, shaking with a preternatural chuckle. 'Well, begor, 'twas a fine sell on ould Harman, any way!' he coughed out, his distorted

mouth, mangled cheek, and bulging eyes tossing as in a whirlpool
of ghastly glee. 'Sell Master Harry for Hans Harman's goold !
Heugh ! heugh ! heugh !' He clutched Harry Westropp's hand
and licked it with parched kisses, like a powerful dog, only so
hungrily it seemed as if he were about to bite the limb into his
jaws.

At the same moment the door was thrown open, and two
policemen burst into the cabin in a gush of icy wind.

'What's this ? What the devil do you mean ?' cried Harry
passionately.

They were daunted by his words and by the glare, and started
back ; but one of them immediately recovered himself. 'Very
sorry, sir,' he said hurriedly, 'but some crime—perhaps a murder
—has been committed. We must hear the statement of the
dying man.'

Quish had fallen back, still clutching Harry Westropp's left
hand, and gluing it to his hungry lips. Harry suddenly felt the
grasp relax and grow cold—a cold that bit into his marrow. He
bent down. Quish's cold fingers still held the hand in a last effort
to keep it pressed to the cold lips. The lips pressed their last.
A mysterious grey beauty glimmered over the face. 'He is dead !'
said Harry Westropp, falling on his knees on the cabin floor.

'How cursed awkwardly these things happen !' exclaimed Mr.
Hans Harman when, some hours after his return from the
abortive expedition to Drumshaughlin Castle, a police orderly
disturbed him in his bedroom (where he was not in bed) with the
intelligence that the bailiff had been fired at and mortally wounded
on the public road outside his own house in the Bauherla
Mountains. 'If this had only come last night, or if Lord Drumshaughlin had not left Euston to-night, a telegram to say the
estate bailiff had been shot dead would have ended this trip which
Deborah has brought upon us with her infernal virtuous starch-
ing and strait-lacing. Now I'm afraid it's too late. He's on the
road, and his blood will be up. He is quite capable of saying I
got it up to frighten him. Well, well, who the devil cares what
he says, if it comes to that ?' muttered the agent, kicking the fire
viciously for not having more heat in it. 'Quish is one precious
rascal gone, and Dawley is another still more precious rascal; who
has obligingly knotted a rope around his neck and presented the
other end to me. For, of course, it was Dawley—that is to say,
it was so promptly and pluckily done, that, of course, it was somebody else he got to do it for him. Well, well, we mustn't neglect
the agrarian bearing of this business on the value of landed property hereabouts for the satisfaction of hanging Dawley—he'll

wait, and can be turned to good account in the meantime. What a cub that young Rohan is ! How I should have liked to lay the cat-o'-nine-tails across his insolent hide, while that madcap girl was girding at me ! By George, there goes three o'clock ! Heigho ! it makes a man feel queer to think of his bailiff lying dead with a bullet in his lungs, and no blood——' He deliberated for a moment. 'I think upon the whole Quish will be worth a wire to the Kingstown boat, who knows ?'

At daybreak that morning Meehul the tenant under sentence of eviction at Cnocaunacurraghcooish, and Owen his son, were arrested on a charge of wilful murder.

CHAPTER THE THIRTIETH

LORD DRUMSHAUGHLIN'S BLOOD UP

As Lord Drumshaughlin stepped off the gangway of the mail-boat at Kingstown Pier, a telegraph messenger put a yellow despatch into his hands. He read : 'Quish, estate bailiff, fired at and murdered last night. Tenant, under notice of eviction, arrested. ' Harman.' The agent was right in anticipating that the news would not deter Lord Drumshaughlin from pursuing his journey. He was right, perhaps, too, in assuming that if the news had come sooner the journey would never have been begun. One of Lord Drumshaughlin's most industrious tasks in life was finding honourable causes of quarrel with his good resolutions. Coming across in the mail-boat, a hundred devils of indolence, selfishness, irresolution, and gout were prompting him to return to London. He examined the chalky deposits around his swollen knuckles with a certain affectionate interest as old friends, who might at any moment supply him with an adequate excuse for giving up his Drumshaughlin expedition ; and I am not sure that he would not have had a bottle of port-wine opened with his supper, with a view to nursing his gout, only that he dreaded ship's port even more than the loss of his club cookery and tricorne notes. The murder of his bailiff was the one spur that could have roused him from his ignoble sluggardice. The pretended fear of a blunderbuss and the real irksomeness of going about with his hand on his revolver had often enough served him as excellent apologies for shirking duty in Ireland ; but now that he was on the road, and that this news savoured of an attempt to intimidate him, the note of danger was to him what the cry of horn and hounds is to an old foxhunter. If every ditch between Kingstown and Drumshaughlin was lined with blunderbusses, he would run the gauntlet all the more gaily. If every knuckle and toe-joint were to swell in rebellion, he would only push on the more doggedly to revenge this barbarous slaughter of his servant—this intolerable insult to his own courage and his pride.

Lord Drumshaughlin's virtue usually took the form of a rage. He became possessed with a fearful fury towards his tenants.

'The curs!—the slaves!—the savages!—I let them alone all these years, and here is my reward! I'll show them! I'll pinch their cowardly bones for them! By God, I'll fire them out like a rabbit-warren!' he cried to himself, while hotel touts were in vain inquiring from him the destination of his luggage. He trampled over railway-porters and cabmen, as if they were so many tedious impediments to his vengeance; soothing them, nevertheless, with liberal plasters of half crowns. He tore through Dublin as if his cab were a car of juggernaut crunching over a prostrate city of assassins. He threatened to withdraw his name from the directorate of the West Cork Railway Company because their time-table imposed upon him a delay of three hours in Cork. To a fat city knight, an apothecary, who sidled up to him in the coffee-room of the County Club, with his condolences and the latest particulars of the murder from the evening editions, and who, with the most obsequious intentions possible, ventured to hint that such a thing could not possibly have happened if his lordship had gladdened the eyes of his respectful adorers with an occasional glimpse of his person in the country, his lordship replied, brutally: 'No doubt, sir—I have been so long away that I have really forgotten that I had the honour of your acquaintance.' And then remarked to a bald-headed old deputy lieutenant who was dining off a mutton-chop at the same table, 'How can you blame men for keeping away from Ireland when they can't even enter the County Club without rubbing skirts with a fellow of that kind?' When he was disgorged on the Garrindinny railway station towards three o'clock in the morning, and Head Constable Muldudden met him with a polite suggestion of a police escort, he replied, summarily, 'Nonsense! Certainly not!' To the amicable overtures of the driver, who told him the road was bad and the storm rising, and that Mick Brine's best bedroom was at his lordship's service for the night, he responded by jumping into the chaise and observing, 'Drive on, damn you!' paying half a sovereign for his oath as an extra at the end of his journey.

It was a night of miserable discomfort; and as he drove past the stone catamountains over the lodge-gate, his own hair bristled up catamountain-like with the prospect of the cheerless reception that awaited him and the fine store of grievances he would thereby accumulate.   He had omitted to advise his daughter of his coming, lest he should baulk the ends of justice by putting the American Captain on his guard ; and now he hugged himself upon the rich materials that a man in a towering rage would find ready to be sworn at in a cold and sleepy Castle at the end of a dismal journey in the grey winter dawn.   It was downright provoking to him to find a light beckoning to him cheerily from the hall ; as who should say, 'Don't expect to catch us napping, you dear old Lord Catamountain ; we shan't let you have so much as a growl or a profane adjective in comfort after your journey ; you will find everything as snug as if you had sent on a regiment of flunkeys—your breakfast-kettle simmering on the hob, a fire roaring in your bedroom, your slippers lying in wait on the hearthrug to welcome your gouty old toes in their soft embraces.'   Nay, the driver had barely tugged at the bell, when Lord Drumshaughlin found Mabel's clinging arms round his neck and her bright hair wooing him in a shower of gold.   Which made him a sulkier Roman Father than ever.

'Why, Mabel, how is this ? You have not been in bed, child ?' he cried, when he had leisure to examine her pale face in the cheerful light of the breakfast-room. 'It was high time to put an end to this kind of thing,' he growled, with knit brows, as though Mabel were a young spendthrift whose nights were habitually passed in the dissipations of the gaming-table and he had just arrived as a grey-haired angel-guardian in the nick of time to avert her ruin.   She saw that he was too well contented with his own virtue to be reminded that he had forgotten to take her into his confidence as to his movements, and had obliged her to remain up all night in miserable uncertainty as to the hour or method of his coming.   He took the offensive from the beginning.   Poor Mabel's anticipation of an easy victory over Mr. Hans Harman was utterly dispelled in presence of her father's angry and louring face.   She trembled like a peculiarly depraved schoolboy under the master's uplifted rod.   All her poor little plots for his comfort were sternly stamped under foot.   He insisted that the bedroom fire smoked abominably.   He threatened to stamp the breakfast things under foot in a realistic sense.   'Nonsense, child—you ought to know it's not slops of that kind, but a glass of grog, a man wants after such a journey.'   He expressed a preference for whisky, in the hope that none might be at the moment procurable ; and when the whisky appeared, he muttered : 'Hum, I daresay that boy has been drinking—or perhaps that American fellow.   Mabel,' he cried, turning on her his fiercest scrutiny, 'I understand that the police have failed to apprehend that man.   I trust I may take it for granted that my house is no longer a sanctuary for rebels and assassins—I hope I may conclude that the man is not concealed anywhere on my premises—in any of those old turrets, for instance, or in the stables ?'

'Papa !' she cried, with a proud flash of indignation, 'I have pledged my word !' Then she broke down and cried like the most commonplace young lady going.

'Come, come, Mabel, I beg there shall be no scenes—I am not equal to it,' he exclaimed, playing the martyr for one pathetic moment in order to heighten the effect of his iron determination. 'You see what your folly has brought us to—my house watched by the police like a coiner's, my family made the subject of gossip, my bailiff murdered, and, perhaps, for all I know, the murderer entertained in my own house by my own daughter.'

'Father !' she cried, her eyes positively blazing through her tears, 'you are the only person living who dare say that to me. Captain MacCarthy is as incapable of that horrid deed as—as you are !'

'Yes, yes, I am not going to enter into arguments with school-girls. It is not with you I am angry, Mabel,' he said, magnanimously. 'You meant it all for the best, and that kind of thing, and what was a child like you to know of the world ? It was my fault, my crime, not to have guided you—not to have enforced my authority and restrained you. I confess my weakness, and I shall not be guilty of it again. I have come to take up possession of my own house—to rule in my own family—and to do what I like with my own property ; and I tell you once for all that it will be my first duty to deliver you from the associations into which your ignorance of the world has betrayed you, and my second duty to purge my estate of this bloodguiltiness, if I have to clear it of its savages as bare as the day it was created. Now, child, remember I require some sleep—let Harman be informed that he will find me breakfasting at two.' And he swept off in a blaze of stern resolution and self-sacrifice.

Harman found him expanding in all the vainglory of an indolent man who has suddenly asserted his mastery over his own affairs. He had taken the reins of a restive team at a dangerous pass, and he felt all the old teamster's exhilaration in testing the strength of his wrist, and observing how his wild team responded to the crack of his whip. 'Things have got into a confoundedly ugly mess all round, Harman,' he said, with the air of a Sultan who had taken a sudden fit of industry with his Grand Vizier. 'It will require prompt and decisive measures to pull them out again, and I've come over in the mood to do something decisive, I can tell you.'

'I should say your lordship, at all times, is nothing, if not decisive,' said the agent, bowing like a handsome cat licking her velvet paws.

'That's what I'm not—never was till now. You think it's an attack of the gout, Harman, and that it's necessary to say some thing pleasant. No, sir; it's necessary to say things unpleasant— damnably unpleasant—and they shall be said. First, as to this murder of unfortunate Quish—Quish was that boy's evil genius, but he was a faithful animal in his way, and I am not going to have a servant of mine butchered at my door by a pack of un grateful barbarians. They shall have to find the murderer—they shall have to give up the murderer and bring him to the gallows, or they shall sweat for it—every rafter in their murderous homes shall shake for it, Harman. Do you understand? If the curs will bite the hand that fondled them—that gave them their own way all these years—why then,' with an oath, 'we'll try a cut of the horsewhip on their cowardly carcasses—we'll tickle them— we'll see if the hounds can't be made to squeal, Harman, you and I.'

'I wouldn't be for doing anything precipitate, my lord,' said the velvety agent, rubbing his whiskers reflectively.

'Yes, but, by God, that's the very thing *I* would do and will do,' roared Lord Drumshaughlin. 'They humbug you, Harman, —this splash of bloodshed has unnerved you—has intimidated you, plainly.'

'At least, I may plead that my nerves have been broken down in your lordship's service—in doing your lordship's work,' said the agent, with downcast eyes.

'You were always a good fellow, Harman—as reliable as the multiplication table, by God,' said his lordship, encouragingly, 'but it always did strike me you trusted too much to the silent operation of a writ served with a good-humoured joke or two in dealing with an imaginative people like the Irish, the grand thing is to do something sudden and striking. Let me see. Did I understand you to mention that this fellow who is arrested is under notice of eviction? Very good, the eviction must be carried out at once—to-morrow morning. Now, I want to know is there anybody except this American fellow—anybody connected with the estate—whom you suspect to be the ringleader, the man in the background, in devilry of this kind?'

'Well,' said the agent, hesitatingly, 'young Rohan, the miller's son, is, I should say, the most pestilent young cub in the parish, and there *is* a writ for possession out against his father, but——'

'Let it be executed without a day's delay. Do you hear? To-morrow, if you have already given notice at the workhouse.'

'I was about to mention to your lordship——'

B B

'Damn it, Harman, none of your lawyer's quibbles and wrig
glings. I insist! I'll superintend the evictions myself, if your
stomach is at all qualmish. Now that I think of it, my presence
would probably have an excellent moral effect. I'll shoulder a
crowbar myself, if you please, but I'm resolved these fellows shall
learn that they are dealing with a man who'll stand no nonsense
until we've washed the stain of blood off this estate—until we've
watered it with the fellow's tears of penance, by Jove!' cried
Lord Drumshaughlin, enamoured of his own Cromwellian thorough-
ness.

Mr. Hans Harman listened in an attitude in which he might
either have seemed tranquilly self-satisfied or overawed by his
principal's imposing cannon smoke and bounce. 'There *is* a difficulty, my lord, although it is one that can be got over,' he said,
quietly, 'and that is that the writs for possession in both these
cases are in the hands of our friend Dargan, as security for advances of rent made by him.'

Lord Drumshaughlin bounded at the name, as if it had been the
point of a javelin piercing his flesh. 'Then,' he cried, furiously,
'they will have to be got out of his hands, and not only these writs
but this estate will have to be got out of his hands – and, to be plain
with you, Harman, it was mainly to shake that fellow's clammy,
thievish hands off my estate that I have come over—much more
than to teach the police how to clear the country of these Irish-
American vermin.'

It was Hans Harman's turn to be startled. His fine eyes
shot out from their ambush as if to discover how much Lord
Drumshaughlin had discovered.

'Yes,' pursued his lordship, fortified by the agent's attitude
of attention. 'It was the bitterest dose that poverty ever shoved
down a man's throat to have to recommend the fellow for the
Commission—you ought never to have let things go so far as that,
Harman. But imagine the creature's effrontery, his cold-blooded,
patronising, inconceivable insolence—would you believe it?—
Pshaw! no matter!' he said, on second thoughts, as if the blood
in his corded veins would have burst, if he were to dwell on the
details of Humphrey Dargan's letter of gratitude and its accompanying cheque. 'It's enough for you to know that life is not
worth living while I feel that fellow's creepy hand upon my
throat, and at any cost I'm determined that we shall shake him
off, pay him, discharge him, kick him out, damn him—you and I,
Harman,' he added, with a sudden show of coaxing tenderness to
the agent, as if conscious that, however proudly he could afford
to stand alone in other respects, Hans Harman was an indispensable *vade mecum* in the details of finance. 'The fact of it is,

Harman, your friend Hugg will have to come to the rescue.
His rate of interest is stiffer, but at least he does not cross and
recross my life every day in the intolerable way in which old
Dargan does. Hugg doesn't pester me for the commission of the
peace—Hugg does not take me by the arm and invite himself to
my dinner-table, and sit on my stomach like a nightmare.
You've saved me from that, Harman. Be my fairy godfather
once more, there's a good chap—consolidate the mortgages at
eight per cent. if necessary—call in Hugg—call in the twelve
tribes of Judea if you will—but for heaven's sake place me in a
position in which I can present my compliments to Humphrey
Dargan in just three unmanacled sentences.'

'This, my lord, is a grave matter,' said the agent, shaking his
head portentously, 'and I am grieved that you have formed so
rooted an ill-opinion of Humphrey Dargan. His incumbrance
tots up to fifty-five thousand, with three gales of interest—the
terms, too, very advantageous, and I need hardly tell you that
the present moment, with the bailiff's corpse still unburied on our
hands, would be an unfortunate one to go into the market for so
enormous an operation.'

Lord Drumshaughlin made a gesture of impatience. 'I beg
you will step down out of the pulpit, Harman,' he said, 'and tell
me how we are to kick the gombeen-man off my premises.'

'For one moment, bear with me,' continued Harman, with
quiet decision. 'I grant your lordship Dargan is a preposterous
animal when he struts in peacock's feathers—though I'm bound
to say it's that ridiculous wife of his who keeps nagging him into
most of his follies; but, admitting that he would melt down a
pretty heap of his sovereigns for a gilt title, or an armchair in
the Club, or a nod from your lordship, is that so unpardonable an
ambition in the eyes of a man—if your lordship seeks my advice,
you must let me give it plainly—of a man who has more cheap
titles and nods to dispose of than sovereigns? Nods are an easier
source of revenue than rents. You will say it is irksome to give
Humphrey Dargan two fingers in public. No doubt; but it is
less irksome than having your bailiffs shot through the lungs.
Both are incidents of Irish landed property. Where's the objection to levying a small rent off a gombeen-man's vanity, if you
see none to levying it off Meehul's reclaimed rocks at Cnocaunacurraghcooish? Both are your rights, your royalties, your flotsam
and jetsam, like the seaweed that drifts in on your foreshore. Perhaps you scruple giving a few snuffy old Grand Llamas like Admiral
Ffrench a gentleman from a pawn-office as a colleague on the
judicial bench? Pshaw! Admiral Ffrench can afford to be
worshipped in his old family coach and fling bribes to his tenants

—there's not an acre of Castle Ffrench under mortgage—simply because his grandfather had the sense to dispose of his borough on first-rate terms to Castlereagh ; while your lordship is struggling in the fetters of three generations of incumbrancers in consequence of *your* grandfather's absurd objections to the Act of Union. Your lordship would be only avenging the honour of your family by reminding men who have the blood-money of an Irish Parliament in their pockets that they'll have to accept a gentry of goombeen-men with their bargain.'

'I presume it is to your acquaintance with Dargan we are indebted for this vulgarity,' said Lord Drumshaughlin, with a slight shudder of disgust.

'An acquaintance formed in negociating matters of more interest to your lordship than to me,' retorted the agent, bowing coolly.

'Eh ! What ! Why this is insolence !' roared his lordship 'Stop!—do you hear me, damn you ?—*Stop !*'

'That is precisely what I can *not* do, my lord, until I have given you the advice and the warning you have yourself invited,' said the agent, whose cheeks were a little paler than usual, but who spoke with the air of authoritative respect of a nurse dealing with a fractious high-born baby. 'If Dargan's birth and manners have become insupportable to you, the first honourable shape criticism ought to take, obviously, would be to pay him his debt. That I take to be the upshot of your lordship's proposal just now, and of your lordship's natural impatience at this moment with my slow-witted method of coming to business. Well, the time has come to tell your lordship candidly—from my knowledge of the estate and of your lordship's affairs (and I am not sure that I know all)—to shake off Dargan at the present stage of affairs would involve an operation which is impracticable—impossible.'

Lord Drumshaughlin, who was drawn up haughtily before the fire in his dressing-gown, and who had taken up a cigar as if to beguile the time until the agent's impertinences should have been fired off, suddenly started, and flung the cigar under the grate.

'Your lordship will do me the justice of admitting that I have frequently warned you that financial projects of yours were injudicious, improvident, hazardous ; but I have never until now felt myself compelled to go further and use the term impossible. I now decisively say—impossible,' proceeded the agent, alive to the effect he was producing. 'Hugg will do no more, and I am not sure that Hugg and Dargan are not acting in concert. I omit that little thing of my own, which, of course, is of small importance to anybody except a pigmy capitalist like myself ; but, putting that aside, it would take a sop of a hundred thousand in round numbers to stuff the mouths of Hugg and Dargan. If anybody can tell me where you're to get such a sum as that in a country about to be delivered of a rebellion—on the security of an estate where rackrenting, I make bold to say, has been developed to the utmost limit of high art, and where the tenants are so expert in the use of firearms—all I can say is I shall be happy to learn the address of so romantic a financier ; but I should myself be inclined to inquire for him at the County Lunatic Asylum. No, my lord,' he continued, elated with the unexpected ease with which he had cowed his irascible tyrant, and putting the finishing touch to his triumph now by showing that he could be as amiable and resourceful as he was firm, ' we cannot afford to demand Dargan's patent of gentility for fear he might play us the ugly trick of producing a parchment deed with your lordship's signature at the bottom of it. These fellows have their own grim sense of humour. No, we must manage Dargan, and thank Providence which has created him with tastes so easily manageable as the taste for a spurious coat of arms. Believe me, nothing is simpler than to keep Dargan on your hands and make him eternally indebted to you. His name is up for the Club at this moment, and there are symptoms of opposition.'

' For the Club ! ' echoed Lord Drumshaughlin.

' For the Club,' repeated Harman. ' Your lordship's influence would be decisive one way or the other. Dargan may not be the partner you would choose for a rubber of whist ; but your lordship won't be there to want partners. Even if you were, you would find Dargan no more in the way than a spittoon, and we should always have his cheque-book writing excuses for his presence. Your lordship has already offended the old hidalgos as much by making him a magistrate as you could do by quartering him on them at the Club. Let me only hint that you mean to carry him—that you have made this journey over specially for the purpose—and I hardly know any proposal you could make to Humphrey Dargan, short of putting his mortgage behind the fire, that he would stickle at. The overdue interest he would throw into capital without a second thought—that I'll answer for—and I'm not at all certain that he could not be induced to consolidate the whole of the incumbrance on terms that would enable you to snap your fingers at Hugg and, for that matter, at myself, if my own little debt in the slightest degree embarrasses you. My lord, may I announce to Humphrey Dargan that you have come across to back him up, and not to throw him over ? '

' Harman, you used to be a teetotaller. You do not look as if you had been drinking,' said Lord Drumshaughlin, with the

unnatural calmness which Hans Harman had mistaken for fear
It was the first time a servant of his had ever braved his wrath,
and the first effect of the phenomenon upon him was one of
bewilderment, as of a monarch whose footstool had risen up and
was flying at his head. He had all his life stinted himself in
temper less even than in money ; and an arrogant temper is the
most exacting of all creditors. 'Let me understand clearly. Are
you my agent for the receipt of rents, or are we partners in some
bankrupt swindling concern which can only keep going by my
making myself the slave of a village money-lender, and betraying
the obligations of rank and honour even more basely than I have
mismanaged my property ? If that is your view, don't you think
it would be a simpler and more straightforward transaction if
you proposed that we should chloroform Humphrey Dargan and
rob his safe, and destroy the mortgage deed ? Or what the devil
is your view, if you're not mad yourself, or if you don't want to
drive me mad ?'

'My view is,' said the agent, unflinchingly, 'that if your lordship is not able to pay three gales of interest in gold, and if
Humphrey Dargan is fool enough to accept them in smiles and
handshakes, he ought to get them. And that your lordship may
be in possession of my entire view, my view is that, unless you
are prepared to pay him in one sort of coin or in the other, Dargan
is the sort of man who is less capable of forgiving an injury than
of forgiving a debt, and is capable of proceeding to any length
when it is a question of satisfying an injury and a debt together.'

'Have you anything else to add in the way of insolence ?'

'I have nothing to add to the candid expression of opinion to
which my duty and your lordship's invitation have driven me
except this—that if Humphrey Dargan is rejected at the Club by
reason of your lordship turning down your thumbs, he is quite
capable of filing a petition for sale of the estate—a petition which
I don't see how we are to resist, if, as I suspect, Hugg and he
understand one another—and I hope it is not necessary to remind
your lordship how many years' purchase an Irish landed property
is likely to fetch at this moment in a district which is a Fenian
hotbed, and with a drawing of Quish's coffin prefixed to the
rental.' Whether it was that his vanity and Lord Drumshaughlin's preternatural stillness for the moment deluded so shrewd a
man as Hans Harman into the belief that he had conquered ;
whether he thought he could see his way to new financial combinations founded upon an accommodation between the money-
lender and Lord Drumshaughlin ; or whether he was of set purpose arousing in the latter a temper which he knew would make
an accommodation impossible—it is certain that he spoke with a

ooldness of glance which astonished Lord Drumshaughlin almost
as much as his hardihood of speech.

Lord Drumshaughlin was silent for an instant. Every sentence of the agent's had wounded him as excruciatingly as a
heavy boot trampling upon his chalky great-toe ; but he felt that
the occasion demanded something worthier than one of his ordinary flights of gouty fury. He took two or three strides up and
down, as if struggling with the choler that was rising in him like
the reek of a limekiln. All at once he faced the agent, and said:
' Harman, you are an old servant, or I dare say you are aware I
should have sent you through the window for half the insolence
you have just uttered.'

' Too old to take your lordship seriously in pleasantries of this
sort,' said the agent, with a bow.

' Yes, but, by God ! not old enough to have learned that I
don't pay an agent to beard me in my own house with his twopenny-ha'penny sarcasms,' roared Lord Drumshaughlin, boiling
over. ' Now listen. I have dealt with this fellow for money,
as I have dealt with him for groceries, paying him the full
market value of his commodities. You tell me that on the
strength of that transaction he has a right to wriggle himself
into this house as a joint master—to assert a co-partnership
with me in my property and rank—to command me body and
soul. You tell me that there is no escape from him—that he
has me tethered with bonds and parchments from which there
is no deliverance. You go further, and suggest that, in order to
make better terms for myself with this Caliban in my own
ignominious bondage, I should enable him to subject every man
of birth and spirit to the same degrading necessity I am under
myself of accepting him as an associate and an equal. Now listen
—I will be driven out of this house by the sheriff first—I will put
a bullet through my head first, if that should be the last luxury I
can allow myself. Things have reached a pretty pass when a
Westropp of Drumshaughlin is obliged to make it clear that he
does not intend to turn pander to the ambitions of a vile gombeen-man and his wife. His letter and your own words here to-
day warn me that I have fallen to that depth of suspicion. I ask
pardon,' he said with some dignity, ' in so far as any ignorance or
folly of mine in money matters may have encouraged the belief
that I had so far forgotten all that makes life endurable to a man
of honour ; but I trust it will never again be necessary to repeat
to Mr. Dargan or to you that the relation between us is one
strictly defined by the deed of mortgage, and that that relation
leaves me for the present, at all events, the master of my own
property and the guardian of my own honour. I will not support

him for the Club—do you hear, Harman? I will throw in a black bean myself. I will canvass against him, if it is possible that so scurvy a creature can have the smallest chance of bribing himself into the society of gentlemen. If you are right in supposing that nothing but a sale can deliver me from this man's claws, there can be little regret about parting with a position which I could only hold as Humphrey Dargan's stipendiary and bear-leader. But I have yet to learn that an Irish landed estate has become so out-at-elbows a property that a man with a rental of seven thousand a year has no alternative but to remain all his lifetime the bond-slave of a damned rustic usurer for a debt of fifty-five thousand; and, Harman, if your experience can give me no better suggestion in that direction than one that might have been offered to a dis-reputable gambler by his disreputable pal, I shall only have to look elsewhere for assistance.' And Lord Drumshaughlin bounced out of the room, banging the door with a violence that seemed to make the very walls of the Castle shake with indignation.

Mr. Hans Harman smiled, and proceeded to make a call in connection with the canvass for his nominee. He knew his principal well enough to make sure that, once his explosion of dignity had come off to his satisfaction, Lord Drumshaughlin would either forget the matter wholly, or soar into some other airy scheme of financial castle-building, and ask Humphrey Dargan to dine with him and discuss it. If this should be the issue, the agent saw his way to a further exploitation of the money-lender's vanities and Lord Drumshaughlin's necessities on his own account, without exposing the affairs of the estate to the prying eyes of the Landed Estates Court. If, on the other hand, Lord Drumshaughlin's pig-headed arrogance should go on gathering to the point of open rupture, he was prepared for that eventuality also. So Frank Harman's pony-chaise continued to circulate from one house of county gentility to another; and various mysterious presents of poultry and preserves (the happy thought of that princess of diplomats, Mrs. Dargan) followed in her wake; and Harman dug every necessitous half-pay office ron the club register under the ribs with confidential geniality; and the general tone of such club conversation as was permitted to interrupt the knocking of billiard-balls and the absorption of whisky-and-water was that, if Lord Drumshaughlin was deter-mined that they should have his company on the Bench whether they liked or no, there could be no great harm in introducing his purse into their society also, as the most tolerable part of him. 'He'll do as well as another to lose to me at half-crown whist,' grinned old Major Grogan, to whose purple nose the ace and knave were understood to contribute more nourishment than her

Majesty's pension list did. 'A fellow who knows he has nothing but his purse to pay his way with is no more embarrassing in society than the waiter who moves about with iced champagne,' was the judicial verdict of a scorbutic young gentleman who, on the strength of having once dined in a cabinet particulier of the Café Royal and finished up after the Alhambra in a Leicester-square oyster-room with a cousin in the Guards who was invited to Marlborough House, passed for a man of fashion among the honest, pudding-headed, golden youth of Drumshaughlin—odd-looking, innocent Minotaurs, with the heads of scarlet-cheeked young bulls and the gaiters of grooms in full-dress.

Another force in Humphrey Dargan's favour was set to work upon the hurried arrival home of Sub-Inspector Flibbert and his bride. His honeymoon was sadly darkened by the news of the tremendous events that were enacting at Drumshaughlin in his absence and without his authority. Upon the first hint of the warrant for the American Captain, he expressed grave fears to his wife that she would have to give up the Castle Drawing-room, as if the prospect of escaping that awful presentation were not the best bit of news the poor child had heard on her honeymoon. When later on in the day he purchased from a bawling news-vendor the intelligence of the assassination of the bailiff, he rushed in to bid her to pack her trunks for the night mail to the South; and the alacrity with which she obeyed his joyous message did not in the least diminish his resentful feeling that it was some-how to his wife's passion for Viceregal festivities he owed his absence from Drumshaughlin when the two greatest opportunities of his life had arrived and caught him napping. 'Indeed, indeed, Augustus, I never wanted to remain at all,' she was experienced enough in the ways of men to plead. 'Of course, dear,' he answered, sweetly, 'only you forgot to mention that in time. Now we have managed matters so that we have not only missed my chances at Drumshaughlin, but we shall miss the Drawing-room here as well.' To which Lily thought it inadvisable to make any remark, even in the shape of a furtive tear; but all the way down in the stifling train had oppressive dreams of putting forward the date of the murder, and putting back the date of the Drawing-room for her own wicked purposes; and towards the end of the journey began to cast timid looks at Augustus George, as if it was really she herself who had committed the murder and was being brought back in custody. It may easily be inferred that poor Lily had found the honeymoon the most trying episode in her life, since a day long ago when a child she had missed her little companions and been delivered to Mother Rosalie at the Convent gate by a strange man who had found her

crying, and who had made faces at her and personated 'The Bo<
Man' for the purpose of illustrating the horrors that awaited bold
little girls who had miched from school. Augustus George had
not at all made faces at her, but, on the contrary, doated very
sufficiently on her blush-rosy cheeks; still she could not help
associating his figure with that of the strange man, and once or
twice, perhaps, she sighed for a dear old Mother Rosalie at the
end of the journey to take her back and slap her. The only real
friend she made on the wedding trip was an ancient sentimental
chambermaid at the dreary hotel, with whom she found shelter
from the eyes of those awful waiters, and who patronised her like
a pretty baby. Mr. Flibbert's friends at the Depôt—the 'County,'
with a fierce moustache which had ceased to be civilian without
having become quite military; the 'County's' lady, a terrific
personage who was to present her at the Drawing-room; the barely
razorable cadets. who were quaffing their first goblet of Dublin
life, and whose talk was of the new regulation in the Code as to
boot-money, and whether young Hankoff found his old station at
Killala or his new station at Killaloe the beastlier hole of the
two—all those great folk, and the more dazzling ordeal they pre-
figured to her of the Throne-Room, simply filled with terror the
shrinking, convent-bred little country girl. Flibbert admired
her so much that he considered it almost a personal affront that
she could not be got to 'come out.' A criticism which he overheard one green cadet confiding to another, 'Devilish pretty, you
know, but such a little ninny!' rankled in his mind to such a
degree that he seriously thought of consulting the 'County's' wife
as to whether a course of lessons in elocution, or at an Academy
of Deportment, or perhaps in a Riding School for Young Ladies,
was usually found to be of most effect in such cases. At home at
The Roses (which Mrs. Dargan had bestowed on the young people
as a temporary residence, old Humphrey having stoutly refused
to quit his old pawn-office parlour) the Sub-Inspector's wife failed
to rise to the height of Mr. Flibbert's ideal as dismally as she had
done in the gilded drawing-rooms of the Depôt. She was like a
seedling of gentility which would not come up, and all her new
friends, and even her own mother, were engaged daily in rooting
up the earth about her to inquire why she was not coming on.
With Frank Harman, singularly enough, alone of her husband's
set, she established some approach to a friendly alliance—such
alliance as a sickly flower in a London back yard may be said to
have struck up with the great blank walls which do not fall and
crush it. She called Miss Harman 'ma'am' with the sweetest
good faith, and seemed to be honestly apologising for being in the
way when she called; and that genial grenadier was so touched

with the poor child's simplicity that she, as it were, took her in
her lap as caressingly as if she was a silky little Blenheim spaniel,
and said she was a great deal too good for that mercenary little
Flibbert, and peremptorily pitched into the fire a packet of
leaflets against Popery which Miss Deborah had prescribed for
Lily as improving literature.

His wife's want of social enterprise was a grievous trial to the
Sub-Inspector, who, however, accepted her shortcomings without
the least intentional unkindness, and set himself to reconquer
Miss Harman's favour with more assiduity than he had ever
dreamt of devoting to the winning of poor Lily's love. He was
much consoled for his absence during the two historic events of
the week by the failure of his subordinate, Head-Constable Muldudden, either to apprehend the American conspirator or to
elicit the smallest scrap of evidence against Quish's murderers.
There were not wanting in the force men who, either toadying
to Mr. Flibbert's greatness, or envious of the well-known legal
attainments of the Head-Constable, were ready with specious
stories of how the American Captain was seen escaping through
the shrubbery owing to Muldudden's neglect to place a policeman
on the postern gate ; and how a police patrol were bound to have
taken Quish's murderers red-handed only that the same jolter-
headed Muldudden had instructed the patrol to take the
Coomhŏla-road instead of that over the Bauherla Mountains on
that particular evening. Flibbert, who naturally regarded the
swoop on the American Captain and the murder as attempts of a
designing subordinate to take a mean advantage of his absence,
was, if possible, even more sarcastic on the arrangements which
Muldudden had made than on those which he had omitted ; and
when that discredited commander ventured to suggest from
certain appearances that the American Captain might possibly be
lying hidden in the belfry, the Sub-Inspector said : 'Don't be a
donkey, Muldudden !' in the hearing of a whole day-room-full of
grinning subordinates.

'Well, sir,' said the unfortunate Head-Constable, making a
last gallant rally of his forces, 'if you'll refer to page 96 of
" Humphrey's Justice of the Peace " you'll find——'

'How to let murderers and conspirators slip through my
fingers, no doubt,' sneered Flibbert, who thought his own remark
so crushing that he determined to mention it incidentally to the
County-Inspector. Mr. Flibbert, in fact, took up charge of the
peace of the community with the air of a Curius Dentatus recalled by his country from his Sabine cottage. Every day that
the American Captain remained uncaught and the Bauherla
Mountain murder untraced he looked a deeper and deeper fellow

for preserving the secret so long ; and now that he had Humphrey
Dargan's iron safe behind him, and a public looking up to him as
its preserver from the horrors of rebellion and assassination, he
had no longer any false modesty about asserting his own importance as one of the Great Powers of Drumshaughlin society.   He
was slightly taken aback when, proposing to himself a cosy, confidential chat with Lord Drumshaughlin touching the peace of
the district and the follies of his son, Harry, his card was answered
with an intimation that, if he had any message for Lord Drumshaughlin, he might send it in by the maid servant ; but Miss
Harman and Mr. Flibbert quite agreed that Lord Drumshaughlin
was an old tyrant who was probably mad and who certainly
drank ; and they agreed still more cheerfully that, between the
Harman influence and the Flibbert influence, Humphrey Dargan's
election was as safe a prediction as the next eclipse of the moon announced in the almanacs.   Young Lionel Dargan, who remained in
Drumshaughlin smoking eightpenny cigars on the Club steps with
the Sub-Inspector, and discovering some object of sudden interest
in the sky when Ken Rohan passed on the other side, was only
tearing himself from the embraces of his college chum, Lord Shinrone's son, for a few days longer to see whether his father's election
to the Club might not be triumphantly followed by his own.

    ' By George, here's Drumshaughlin ! looking as touchy as the
very—gout.   Come to carry our gombeen friend, of course ! '
cried old Grogan, who was one of a group before the reading-room
fire on the evening of the ballot.   There was an unprecedented
muster of members, and the regular set of army men and evergreen old bachelors, who spent their evenings over their spirits-
and-water, card-tables, and Tory papers, were amazed at the
number of unexpected ghosts that arose as on a general resurrection night—those queer anchorets of the desert whom county
society loses sight of from time to time, nobody can tell how :
men who have become so absorbed in the breeding of shorthorns
that they only turn up like the shorthorns on cattle-show days,
with apparently a strong dash of the shorthorn strain in their
own ways, and even countenances ; men who are reputed to have
had attacks only known to the doctor, or to have been married to
their housekeepers, or to have been reduced to living off their
own poultry-yard ; or again, men smitten with some household
grief, some adored daughter cut off in the May-morn of her days,
some son banished in disgrace to the Colonies, and who are seldom seen out of their sepulchres except at some pressing call of
public duty—the Grand Jury, the election of a Chairman of
Board of Guardians, or an insurrection.   ' Harman must have
made a deuce of a whip,' remarked Major Grogan to his friend

Captain Brandeth, as all those unaccustomed spirits of health or
goblins damned glided into the rooms—men pale with the gracious
dignity of grief, men who paid their debts in cruel wrinkles, men
whose eyes and noses were beginning to wear the ignoble purple
livery of Drink, and men who only looked in for the night from
Aix or Egypt as a composition with their consciences for
neglected duty, as a beauty might call into a cottage after a
riotous London season.

'I did think my old friend wou'd not have thrown in his weight
against us on this occasion,' said Admiral Ffrench, with his sad
old courtly smile, as Lord Drumshaughlin made for his corner
with outstretched hand.

'Why? How do you mean?'

'Well, I cannot help thinking that you might have left this
to your agent, Drumshaughlin, and left us old fellows some chance
of a stand in our last ditch.'

'Your last ditch! You don't mean to say the fellow is going
to win?'

'Look around you, and see how Harman has done his whipping-
up. I never mean to be seen in this room again. *Morituri te
salutamus.* If we had not been handicapped by having your
name against us, indeed——'

'My name! Who has dared to use my name? Why, my
dear Admiral, my name and my vote will be for hunting the fellow like a vagabond dog with the most ignominious article you
can find in the kitchen tied to his infernal impudent tail.'

Admiral Ffrench and his sedate group of county magnates
started delightedly, as if a bombshell sailing down upon them had
burst in bonbons instead of splinters of old iron. 'Why, we
have only to send that around, and all is over,' the Admiral exclaimed. 'Ralph, this is more like the old friend I once had :—
do you remember the night some young dare-devils presented the
Lord Chancellor at the Historical with a face as black as a Christy
Minstrel, Ralph?—and the night of the row at the Turkish Embassy—how that fat old Pasha did yell when you knocked him
over into the flower-pots and walked off with the lady in your
arms?- and do you recollect that morning with the French
sergens-de-ville, coming home from—Ah, dear ! ah, dear!' and
the two old fellows fell on one another's shoulders and shook
hands and laughed and (I rather suspect) cried for old times'
sadly-joyous sake. 'Well, well, I am not sure that things have
grown so much better in these wise days. I am told there is not
a single nobleman's son in Trinity College now, except poor old
Shinrone's, who is hired out to a tutor as an advertisement.
They have fallen back on the agents' sons, and the bailiffs'. They

tell me a young fellow of Dargan's is the most fashionable figure in Grafton Street of an afternoon. Ralph, my old friend, that grandfather of mine made a pretty mess of it when he sold Clonakilty to Castlereagh. We, who had this country as our Garden of Paradise, are jostled out of it by the Dargans, if worse still does not happen us—if we're not content to remain and take their pay. Well, it's something if we can remind this man that there is still some savour of prerogative left in us. I confess I was beginning to forget myself that there was anything wanting to the title of gentleman which a fee paid at the office of Ulster King of Arms could not purchase.'

They had chatted together in a confidential corner : it was years since the Admiral's grave sweet face of courtesy had been so disturbed by the old wild blood of Navarino, and a moment afterwards he cast his eyes timidly around to see if anyone was looking ;—but the fact that Lord Drumshaughlin had come to pill Humphrey Dargan could not long remain a secret. The rooms were by this time unusually full of bustle and animation. The Dargan faction was triumphant. Little Flibbert was an Iron Duke on the field of Waterloo. He discussed the prospects of a rising with the sangfroid of an experienced statesman who created apprehensions in order to allay them with a wave of his hand. He was so knowing on the subject of Quish's murderers that it would have seemed a pity to spoil so exquisitely deep a game by catching them.

'Upon my soul, that little man takes the British Empire under his patronage more gracefully than the lady with the trident in the penny pieces,' remarked a plethoric old Major who had smelt gunpowder.

'My dear fellow, why not ?' said the Admiral, with a smile. 'We've set up the policeman as a god over the people, and it's only even-handed justice that he should end by ordering us to our knees ourselves. Here's Mr. Hans Harman, who wants us to add Mr. Flibbert's father-in-law to our family circle, and yet we are surprised that in a country where the magistrates take their law from Head-Constable Muldudden society should begin to revolve around the Sub-Inspector.'

'After all, Admiral,' said Hans Harman, pleasantly, ' so high-born and good-natured a man as you ought to be above objecting to a man's making his money in trade.'

'What I object to is his making his character of gentleman in money,' rejoined the Admiral. 'If there is to be equality—by all means ; but why not try the plan of making all our neighbours—the whole people—our friends and equals, instead of honouring the sordid vulgarians who have successfully plundered them ?'

'Suppose we begin by balloting for the two interesting peasants who shot my bailiff the other night, and who are possibly lying inside the hedge to-night for myself ?' said Hans Harman, with that growing mixture of boldness with his bonhomie which had already perplexed Lord Drumshaughlin. 'But I am not sure that you will get the Club to agree with you, Admiral. Hullo, Deverell ! Didn't let the sciatica frighten you, eh ?' he said, gaily, turning to a dry cheese-paring of a man, who seemed to have invested all the vivacity of his life in a large family of daughters, and who had invested a considerable loan from Humphrey Dargan in the same quarter.

But shortly after Lord Drumshaughlin's arrival in the reading-room there seemed to run around the buzzing groups some strange electric current, the first effect of which was a whispering hush, and the next effect a polyphloisboisterous hum of voices, laughter and excitement. The knowledge that Lord Drumshaughlin had brought not a white but a black bean in his pocket circulated rapidly, and added to the interest of the struggle in the ballot between the old school and the new a fresh excitement as to the result of the inexplicable duel between Lord Drumshaughlin and his agent. Harman's face darkened, but his eye glanced over his own musters with assurance.

'This is deuced bad conduct on Lord Drumshaughlin's part,' said Mr. Flibbert, tugging nervously at his moustache, as if it were the American Captain he were dragging out of his lurking-place. 'I really must get Mr. Dargan to take notice of it.'

'Pooh !' was the agent's whispered reply. 'The notice to take of it is to win without him and in spite of him.' Then undauntedly to his wavering legionaries : 'Of course eveybody understands Drumshaughlin's position is a peculiar one. He is bound to make some show as the haughty Custos Rotulorum and all that you see, but they will be no friends who will do him the ill turn of voting with him.'

The voting went on slowly. Men seemed to have been stricken with a sudden incapacity to make up their minds. Harman flitted more actively than ever through the rooms, without, however, approaching Lord Drumshaughlin's group. Admiral Ffrench, who had come to lead a forlorn hope, was beginning to feel (not now for the first time in his life) that forlorn hopes sometimes in a twinkle turn to glittering victories. The excitement was running higher. So was the betting.

'I'll give you five to one still on the Gombeen-man,' said one of the young gentlemen in white coats, scarlet gills, and horsey continuations, to Reggy Neville.

'No,' said the Guardsman. 'Can't, as a stranger, interfere

very sorry, for I should dearly like to lay something against that
little policeman.'

'I had hardly hoped ever to see a spark of public spirit in the
county again,' said a delicately-featured old Deputy-Lieutenant,
who had hobbled in on a crutch and on the arm of Admiral
Ffrench.

'It was really time for Lord Drumshaughlin to put himself
at the head of the county,' said another.

'The presumption of the fellow!' remarked the landlords
attorney of the district, a loud-lunged, truculent plebeian, who
had only edged his way into the Club himself some six months
before. 'And Harman swears he'll carry him still.'

'No, he won't!' cried one of the younger men, bursting into
the group. 'Harman has thrown up the sponge. The nomination
it withdrawn.'

The news was true. Upon a rapid review of his mutinous
forces, Hans Harman had come to the determination to withdraw
the name and stop the balloting. 'You have won, my lord,'
he said, laughingly, but with something like a faint red glare
louring out of his smiling dark eyes. 'I hope it may turn out
that you have been as wise as you have been brave.'

'Trust me, Harman, as you have failed as a diplomatist, you
will never be a success as a bully,' replied Lord Drumshaughlin,
as he drew his furred overcoat about his ears and passed out on
the arm of Admiral Ffrench.

Two mornings afterwards Lord Drumshaughlin was served
from the Landed Estates Court, in Dublin, with notice of a conditional order of sale, requiring him within twenty-eight days to
show cause why the court should not proceed to a sale of the estate
on foot of a certain mortgage transaction duly set forth in the
matter of Ralph Adalbert Warbro Westropp, Baron Drumshaughlin, Owner; Humphrey Dargan, Petitioner.

CHAPTER THE THIRTY-FIRST

IN THE CHURCHYARD

MONSIGNOR MCGRUDDER was staggered. He could swear he had
heard singular noises in the churchyard outside his window. He
was sitting later than usual, examining the plates attached to
Miss Stokes' edition of the 'Notes on Irish Architecture,' in his
old-fashioned chintz-covered armchair, in the room which was at
once his study and bedroom at the back of the new cut-stone

Presbytery, looking out on the graveyard. The antiquated arm-chair, with arms like lofty fortifications and cushions like fragments of a feather-bed, was the only article of furniture at all old-fashioned in the room. The Monsignor had found himself unable to sacrifice this relic of old simplicity, this ancient seat of homely comfort, to the more ambitious requirements of his new Italian dignities. His old friend in chintz survived amidst the brass-mounted bedstead, mirrored wardrobe, and polished birch appointments of the bedroom in the new Presbytery, even as the worn, plain, old silver chalice, which was handed down from the Penal Days, was still to be seen among the gold and jewelled cups of the Emancipation times in the sacrarium. The rest of the room was equipped in a style of costliness, which wanted nothing but a woman's taste to make it elegant. A black and yellow Japanese folding-screen gracefully marked the transition from the region of the bed to the region of the books. The bookcases were of shiny oak ; the volumes themselves splendid in gold-printed half-calf ; the two regular library-chairs covered with stamped white leather ; the fire was in the custody of brass dogs, in a dainty prison of glossy white and black tiles, and any indiscreet glow that escaped from it fell into the respectable arms of a fluffy white hearthrug which suggested something of the animal life of the North Pole as well as just a suspicion of the want of animal heat appertaining to those latitudes as well. Please don't do the Monsignor the injustice of supposing that he lolled in all this luxury like an Epicurean philosopher. He found the old arm-chair the most luxurious article in the room--that and a few old books hidden in the basement of the bookshelves because of their shabby exteriors. He would have given up the Presbytery for a cabin of thatch in the mountains, cheerfully, if the necessities of the Church had demanded it. But the Church did not demand it. The Church, on the contrary, demanded once more a position of splendour and power in the land, and demanded that he, as one of her empurpled captains, should prove himself equal to her more exalted fortunes by holding his head as high as his predecessors of the Penal Days had held theirs low. He accordingly built the cut-stone Presbytery, as he placed the purple edging round his buttons, because the rubric so ordained ; and he bought the birchwood wardrobe, as he contemplated himself in its glass panel, in his tasselled biretta and soutane, simply as portion of the statelier finery that beseemed the Church's new career.

The Monsignor applied himself again determinedly to the engravings. He examined with the genuine archæological eye, which is, (necessarily) rather that of the stonemason than the enthusiast, the zigzag lacework tracery of a recessed doorway in

King Cormac's Cathedral on the Rock of Cashel; but, before he
had half-mastered the details of the pattern, the sound from the
graveyard again struck his ear. He threw himself back into the
capacious feather-bed bosom of the arm-chair to consider what it
was like. At one moment he thought it resembled a muffled cry,
and at another it seemed to sound more like weird diabolical
laughter. He lifted the green jalousie of the window overlooking
the graveyard and looked out. The night was pitch-dark. A
nipping wind was blowing the few last leaves of the elm-tree
outside against the window panes, and (a thing that struck the
Monsignor more uncomfortably than the ghostly tapping of the
leaves) was beating a sort of chattering tattoo between the ill-
jointed sections of the window-frame. As his eyes came to
forage more expertly in the darkness, the skeleton arms of the
moaning elm-tree, and here and there an indistinct gray blotch
of tombstone with stiff plumes of cypress standing over them like
mourners, began to come out in gloomy silhouette, and then a
bright eye of light which caused him to start back. He had
noticed that mysterious eye in the darkness more than once
before during the last few nights. He pressed his face close to
the glass again in order to fix its exact position. It looked a
mere spot of light; but the surrounding gloom intensified its
thin ray until it extended like a mystic white shining sword
across the graves. He was now certain it proceeded from the
Tower which rose in the graveyard at the rear of the Chapel,
separated only by a stretch of grassy mounds and mouldering
tombstones from the back windows of the Presbytery. Monsignor
McGrudder was an ardent partisan by pen and deed in the never-
ending wars as to the origin of the Irish Round Towers—those
Irish Sphinxes at whose base a thousand devastating invaders
have swept by, with fire and sword, and left them still lifting
their graceful stone fingers silently to the sky, putting to the
puzzled generations the conundrum who built them, how or when,
or why?—a type of the still greater mystery how the Irish race
itself has survived all the salt tides that have ebbed and flowed
over it, miserable age after age, and has kept its well-spring pure
in the deep living heart of it? The Monsignor was of the school
that insists the Round Towers were Christian belfries built with
an eye to serving as the strong box for the valuables of the
adjoining churches in case of a raid by the freebooting Danes.
In testimony of the faith that was in him, and in proof of the
eligibility of such structures as bell-towers, he himself built a
Round Tower at the rear of the chapel, in the upper chamber of
which, pierced by four large opes towards the main points of the
compass, he hung the bell. Opinions differed about Monsignor

McGrudder's Tower almost as much as about the ancient conundrums after which it was modelled—differed as to whether the
architecture of the Round Tower was ever caricatured more
abominably than by this lanky stone beehive ; differed especially
as to whether the structure was not more effectual in smothering
the clangour of the bell than in publishing it. The Monsignor,
however, it is scarcely necessary to add, was as much pleased
with his tower and his bell as with his theory. It was at once
his strength and his weakness that whatever he, in his biretta
and purple-edged buttons, believed to be right was in his eyes a
dogma, wanting only the vote of an Œcumenical Council to be
de fide.

'A light in the Tower at such an hour !—oh, it must be
Mrs. Lehane, the chapel-woman I Somebody's dead, perhaps,
and she's arranging to have the funeral bell tolled to-morrow.'
And he returned to the wavy stone tracery of King Cormac's
recessed doorway. But he could see nothing in the engraving
but his own Tower, with the phosphorescent blade of light, like
Death's sickle, glittering over the shuddering graves. He looked
around the room, and found it chilly. In his zeal for the Church's
speedy rehabilitation in the matter of presbyteries, the Monsignor,
being his own architect, had unfortunately hung the door of his
room on the wrong side, and had, moreover, left the door-handle
open to the seductions of any wanton winter wind that chose to
demoralise it ; in addition to which the fire-grate had to a large
extent lost in warmth what it had gained in elegance ; so that at
this moment almost as icy a blast was moaning about the room
as in the graveyard. He stamped his foot two or three times
with annoyance at finding that he felt nervous and uneasy. His
wrought-iron frame had never been quite the same since the day
his authority had been flouted to his face on his own altar.
Though he followed up his anathemas against the secret society
with unflinching vigour in sermon and confessional, he had an
uneasy consciousness that the young men were not afraid of him—
that his diatribes only made the reckless more reckless, and that
the remainder quietly listened to him within the church doors,
and went their own ways the moment they crossed the threshold.
To a priest conscientiously alive to his responsibility for the eternal
salvation of all these young souls, the failure of his authority was as
saddening as it was astounding to the high-stomached churchman.
He could not in his heart, nor even in his face or frame, conceal
the effects of the blow which he—the haughty purpleman, who
had rolled in Cardinals' carriages to the houses of Roman Princesses—had sustained from little Danny, the miller's lame man.
Even at this moment he felt that it was little Danny, and not the

churchyard sounds and chills, that was unnerving him. While he lay back in his arm-chair irresolute, a continued low, wailing croon was heard from the darkness. This time the sound was unmistakable. It was still going on, in a muffled cadence, and the cry, dirge, diabolical chorus, or whatever it might be, proceeded beyond doubt from the graveyard.

Monsignor McGrudder sprang to his feet. He was not superstitious. Still less was he a coward. He did not believe there was question of anything supernatural, and he was not afraid of anything human. The next minute he was in the open air, un fastening the wicket into the graveyard, his gold-knobbed oak cudgel grasped in his left hand. The graveyard looked deadly dark. For the first few moments he could distinguish nothing but the spectral cypress sentinels over the tombs, and hear nothing but the dismal w—u—u—h of the wind through the trees. His feet stumbled over a mound. He remembered it was the grave where the murdered bailiff, Quish, had been interred less than two weeks before.

As to which, I must break through all the rules of art to narrate *hic et nunc* a circumstance that marked the burial. It was a lonesome affair, poor Quish's last earthly expedition—the most lonesome of all terrestrial sights—an Irish funeral avoided by the people. It was not that anybody specially disliked Quish, or that everybody was not horrified by his fate ; but the mere whisper of his having suffered as an informer made the coffin exhale a certain nameless contagion that made people shrink from it as from the first unburied body in a mediæval plague. Those who kept away from the funeral could not have explained in the least why they did so. Law is so often villainy in Ireland that the presumption is always in favour of a breach of it. When Monsignor McGrudder said the last prayer over the coffin in a strain that made it sound like a stern exorcism of the murderers, the only mourners left were Harry Westropp and Ken Rohan (who took Harry's arm and who noticed Dawley's scowling eyes fixed on him as he walked behind the coffin) and Mr. Hans Harman, who seemed to take a more important part than the corpse in the ceremonial. Mr. Harman was giving the grave-digger some instruction in the use of his mattock, when Harry, who had barely tolerated the agent's proceedings until now, flew at him like a tiger with fiery eyeballs, and snatched the mattock out of his hand. ' Be off out of this ! ' he shouted, furiously. ' You've done enough already to put Quish in his grave. 'Twas you and your infernal attempts to bribe him to spy upon me that brought him where he is. There was better stuff in Quish than in a regiment of fellows like you. It's you, and not he, that 'twould be worth

somebody's while chastising.   Be off !   I'll stand no more of your
hypocritical grief, damn you !   Leave the rest of this to me.   Quish
would sooner have one shovelful of earth thrown on his coffin by
me than if you were to raise a tombstone of gold over him.   Be
off, I tell you—this instant – or——.'   His terrible look and uplifted mattock told Hans Harman for the first time in his life
what terror is.   He grew as ashen pale as a corpse and staggered
out of the graveyard ; and Harry not only dropped shovelfuls of
earth upon his dead friend's coffin, but wetted them with tears
such as a National Funeral Procession does not always draw in
Westminster Abbey. Poor Quish's happy super-earthly face would
have been worth beholding at that moment.

It was not of Quish's ghost, however, that Monsignor
McGrudder was thinking as he fumbled over the new-made grave.
The confused muffled noises had reached his ear again.   They
proceeded as before from the direction of the Tower, which was
at present screened from his view by some thick pyramids of yew-
tree.   He groped towards the path which he knew led directly to
the door of the belfry. Just as he had found the path, a peremptory voice beside him called out :

'Who goes there ?' and at the same moment he saw the figure
of a man emerge from between two yew-trees and stand full in
front of him.

'Who are you, yourself, fellow ? and what are you doing here
at this time of night ?' answered Monsignor, sturdily grasping his
stick.

'Who are you ?—Answer, or I'll fire !' cried the man, and
Monsignor McGrudder heard an ominous click and vaguely distinguished a gleaming barrel almost at his spectacles.

He was now genuinely startled.   The towering impassive
figure, the quick deep words, the click of the hammer, and the
glimmer of nickel were unmistakable.   'For Heaven's sake, stop
—I'm Monsignor McGrudder !' he cried, with a sickening feeling of feebleness.

'Thank God you said it, your Reverence.   Another moment,
and you were a dead man !'   The revolver-barrel disappeared
from before Monsignor McGrudder's spectacles.   At the same
moment he caught an indistinct glimpse of his interlocutor's face.

'Con Lehane !' exclaimed Monsignor McGrudder.   'You
ruffian, is it you that dare stop your priest and threaten tc
murder him ?'   The Monsignor's dread was now changed into a
sacred fury, and he whirled his great stick fiercely over the head
of the man in front of him.

'Take care of your stick, your Reverence,' whispered the huge
fellow, quietly.   'This is no child's play.   Put it down !'

'You miserable man, do you dare to talk to me in language like that?'

'Put it down, I say! There, don't raise your voice again, your Reverence. Now, you will have to go back into your house and give me your word you will never breathe a syllable of this, or'——said Con Lehane, in whose hand the revolver still gleamed, 'I will be obliged to keep your Reverence in custody and ask you to step over to the Tower.'

It was not in the least physical terror that was agitating Monsignor McGrudder. It was the self-same agony of shame and indignation that had convulsed him the day little Danny flung the lie in his teeth on the altar. It was not himself, but the whole power of his order, the whole awful authority and dignity of the Church, that seemed to be thus baited and outraged. A great surge of passion rose to his brain.

'I will not give my word—I'll alarm the town—I will denounce you the world over. Ruffian!—murderer!—fire if you dare!'

'One word more, and, as God is my judge, I *will* fire!'

This time Monsignor McGrudder felt the cold metal of the the muzzle touching his forehead. In one lightning-flash of thought, he compared his own strong frame with the towering but not so burly figure before him, and thought that at the most he would be dying in a sacred cause; then that horror of death, which often haunts those who oftenest weigh the eternal issues that depend on it, came over him, with the thought of the immeasurable calamities for religion that might follow such a tragic scandal—all in one flash of consciousness. The next moment he said meekly, almost entreatingly:

'Con Lehane, you were once a good Catholic boy. Go, in God's name, and do no worse than you have done.'

'I am on duty, your Reverence. There may be life depending on it—more valuable life than mine. Give me your promise, quick.'

'And, if I don't, you will detain me by force—me, your own priest—and you will kill me, if I resist?'

'I will!' said Con Lehane, in a deep, solemn voice. In the darkness the huge globules of icy perspiration tumbling down his forehead were not visible. The grim revolver-barrel was. 'Come, your Reverence—lose no more time. Do you promise, or do you not?'

'I promise,' said Monsignor McGrudder, turning back towards the Presbytery, like an unsubdued prisoner staggering from the hands of the torturer. 'May God forgive you!'

'Amen, your Reverence!—and forgive you!—Ireland has

enemies enough without you,' said Con Lehane, putting the revolver in his breast-pocket, and turning towards the Tower.

I hate mystifying my readers. A man who invites people to dinner might as well begin by ushering them into the coal-cellar. Be it known at once, therefore, that the glint of light across the graveyard came from a chink in the doorway of the lower chamber of the Tower where the American Captain and a party of his friends were assembled in the glow of a fire that had nothing of churchyard gloom around it. There were pistols upon the table, amidst the remains of a supper, with some bottles and tumblers. Upon the day when Con Lehane 'didn't like the way them Bobbies were hovering' around the *Banner* Office while the Captain was enveloped in Olympian clouds of cigar-smoke in the back-shop, a hurried council of war was held, and was barely in session when Mat Murrin was beckoned out into the back-kitchen where some mysterious magnetic familiar spirit from the Telegraph Office whispered that the order for the Captain's immediate arrest had just come off the wires.

'Well,' said Mat, returning to the Council of War, 'what do you say to bolting the front door and summoning the Staff? 'Tis a pity the poor divels hadn't a taste of the auctioneer's John Jameson first to put a soul in them after their day at the case. But Noble Nolan can slip out and get in a jar or two that'll stand a siege. There's an old shot gun over that press there, if you'll find anything in the powder-horn—I never had occasion to use it myself since the night Hans Harman's blackguard election mob tried their tricks on the *Banner* office. And don't you think Mrs. Murrin might as well get down a few pots of boiling water? 'Twould be very effective from the top window—Aloysia, darling, Aloysia!'

But Con Lehane was prepared with a more promising project. His mother, as chapel-woman, had the keys of the Chapel and the Round Tower under her dominion. What more unsuspicious refuge could be found than under the very wing of Monsignor McGrudder and in the midst of a graveyard? The Round Tower too, in obedience to the obliquity of Monsignor McGrudder's architectural genius, seemed to be built with a special view of stifling the voice of the bell before it could reach the ears of the public, for it was completely screened from the view of the street by the Chapel, and could only be subjected to a close inspection by the few who cared to take their walks abroad among dead people whose bones were apt sometimes to come above the ground in a manner not altogether supernatural nor yet at all cheerful.

'I guess that's just where I'm goin' to wade in. Con Lehane
you're a lad of some savvy—powerfully so, sir!' said Captain
Mike. 'As I have got to dust out of the Castle at all, there
ain't nobody's hospitality more to my taste than the gen'leman's
with the Italian nickname. Sir, it'll bust the crust of that
worthy old sacred volcano if ever the public should ascertain that
while he was cursin' me a-hundred-and-forty-pounds-of-steam-
power in the Chapel, he was all the time entertainin' me in ray-
shershay style in the Round Tower.'

'Don't you think 'twill be a little—ahem! depressing to the
spirits?' asked Mat Murrin, with a slight shudder—'or rather
not depressing, so far as spirits of a certain order are concerned,
but perhaps rather calculated to raise them?'

'No, sir. No better company than dead men—I've know'd
'em now this long while—spent an odd night or so with 'em,
thousands of 'em away down the Wilderness way, and with
Meade that night at Gettysburg, an' never know'd a man of 'em
to rise up an' do anything onneighbourly, though they'd got no
coffins to shake themselves out of. God rest 'em, good old boys!
The Tower's the ticket, Con Lehane'——

And hence it came to pass that, to the rest of the maddening
problems to which the Irish Round Towers gave rise in Monsignor
McGrudder's mind, was added now the mystery that his own
Round Tower was giving forth unaccountable lights and sounds
at an advanced hour of the night, and sentinelled by parishioners
with cocked revolvers. With proper adherence to the architectural type, the entrance door was at some height from the ground,
and was approached by a short ladder, which was removable at
will, and which was the abiding terror of the old chapel-woman's
life. The lower chamber was separated from the bell-chamber by
a loft pierced in the centre by a square opening through which a
ladder went up and the bell-chain came down. It was upon this
loft that Captain Mike's mattress was laid. The room below was
heated from a fire-place which Mrs. Lehane had established in
connection with the flue of the adjoining vestry in order to
comfort herself during those icy winter days, when she had sometimes to toll the bell all day for some departed member of the
public. There was thus an unsuspicious exit provided for the
smoke of the fire at which Mrs. Lehane cooked the Captain's
meals, and it was easy to stuff the unglazed apertures by which
daylight entered the lower portion of the Tower, so that no artificial light from within should show itself, unless through some
such accidental slit or chink as emitted the ray of light which
startled Monsignor McGrudder. Here Captain Mike smoked
and snoozed away the days of his captivity, and entertained him-

self in the open air among the tombstones after dark ; and here
he toasted his own bacon rasher with an old campaigner's relish,
whenever the old chapel-woman judged it unsafe to approach the
Tower, and smacked his lips over even prettier dainties, which
Katie Rohan would smuggle in under that pirate little mantelette
of hers when she came to morning Mass or her daily visit to the
Blessed Sacrament, and which, there is some reason to suspect, in
part found their way from a pair of lily hands in the kitchen of
Drumshaughlin Castle.

At this moment, however, he was not trusting to the inhabitants of the cemetery for company. In the richer than Rembrandt
glow of a red-hearted fire of turf and pine logs, a number of young
men sat close together around two travellers who had just arrived,
and who in personal appearance were as distant from one another
as the two shores of the Atlantic Ocean. One, who went by the
name of Mr. Mahon, was devoured with all his eyes by Ken
Rohan, for there sat the poet and principal contributor to the
suppressed revolutionary organ. Ken looked at him with a face
like a verse of Mr. Browning's "Ah! did you Once see Shelley
Plain ?" He might, indeed, have sat for the portrait of a poet,
and to a painter of the seventeenth century rather than of the
nineteenth. His costume when he entered was an old and still
older-fashioned cloth cloak which fell over his broad shoulders in
picturesque folds, and a soft felt hat under whose broad shade
you saw nothing but two luminous eyes burning in the midst of
a gloom of hair. When the Tyrolese hat slid off, all you noticed
still was the thick fall of intensely black hair streaked with grey
which rolled down in a stately broad cascade almost to the
shoulders, and the large lustrous eyes which looked out of their
dusky mist of hair glowingly, and yet not as if they were fixed
upon any particular thing. (The grey-streaked black locks have
since been shorn by a convict's scissors, and while the icy fangs
of six winters were fixing and unfixing themselves on the bleak
Portland quarries, that far-away dreamy look of Mr. Mahon's
was brought back to a blinding world of granite-dressing under
the spell of a turnkey's oath and cutlass.) The features were
white and delicate, as of a man who either thought too much, or
ate too little, or both :—a thin, almost transparent nose, with
nostrils that were apt to quiver as reeds do in the wind ; lips
that seemed to quiver also in their narrow region of colour
within the circumambient waves of grey-black beard and moustache ; a white dome of forehead, looking tapering and not very
broad, perhaps owing to the masses of shadowy hair that en-
croached upon it :—altogether a simple, pathetic, beautiful face,
such as you could imagine lying extended on a crucifix and

smiling. So, at least, Ken Rohan in his enthusiasm thought :—
for, woe is me ! how cruelly our gods sometimes disappoint us in
the flesh !—our patriot has a consumptive cough, our beauty a
temper, our poet a hump, our saint takes snuff, even our general
wears spectacles !—yet here before him was the man whose
poems had given Ken Rohan his first glimpse of uncreated light,
and he was the best poem of the lot himself.   Less youthful and
cooler-headed observers would perhaps make a more contracted
estimate of Mr. Mahon's poems, as well as of his personal attractions ; but it was impossible to know his history of lifelong,
passionate clinging to a losing cause without pity for the hapless
land and wonder for the strange romantic chances which brought
this gentle dreamy creature to be one of the chiefs of a desperate
revolutionary enterprise.   Judge, then, our young friend's ecstasy
when he found that Mr. Mahon had admired his own first wild-
bird singing in the proscribed journal ; and that his great bright
eyes glowed still more brightly when he heard that Ken's was
the pen which was glittering and lightening in the new secret
revolutionary sheet.   Jack Harold's mission to Dublin had
borne immediate fruit, and several numbers of the new journal
had already been spirited away to Cork in the porter-casks,
sending the strangest electric current along the young nerve-
centres of the country, and bringing back an even stranger
interacting spiritual thrill to the young gentleman who worked
the battery.   Mr. Mahon patted his head, smiling with ever so
sweet a pathos ; and the young fellow bent down his head in a
state of sacred happiness which reminded him singularly of his
Confirmation Day when the consecrating chrism touched his
forehead.

Mr. Mahon's companion did not at all share Ken Rohan's
unalloyed enthusiasm on the subject of the poet.   The General,
as he was in respectful whispers called, was a somewhat low-
sized, compactly-built, middle-aged man, with a strong bronzed
face, a quiet manner, and a decisive grey eye—the man of action
in every line of his clean-shaven face, and in every stiff, upright
hair that resisted to the last the embaldening process which was
spreading from the crown of his scalp.   Unlike the poet's dreamy
vagueness of look as was the dart of his quick eye, his soft, low
voice and high-bred repose of manner offered no less striking a
contrast to the hearty boisterous tones and fantastic dialect of
Captain Mike.   It was West Point against the Ninth Massachusetts Volunteers—the cultured, skilled, scientific soldier, and
the reckless, rollicking son of the people, who made for the
Rappahannock with no other education than a brave heart and a
certain knack with his rifle.   The one mysterious communion

cup which united them all was an indescribable feeling of thumping at the heart and tightness in the throat at mention of the name of Ireland; and the sensation was no less masterful, though he was better able to conceal it, in the cool, almost cynical-looking General, who had never before this morning laid his eyes on the Irish hills, but had heard at his father's knee forty years ago the story of his flight from Tipperary as leader of one of the rustic tithe battles in which the troops had been repulsed with slaughter. His first arrival on the Irish shores was of an uncommon character. For a whole day and a whole night, a stout schooner had been lying off Galley Head, hovering in the track of the American liners, its little row-boat ready in the water, and the men on board eagerly scanning every dark object that broke upon the Western horizon. They were waiting by arrangement for the overdue Guion steamer, and Mr. Mahon in his soft hat and flowing cloak was in nominal command of the crew, though there was the strongest reason to think that his thoughts and his gaze were all the time floating millions of miles in the air. Shortly after daybreak the look-out man distinguished the welcome Guion's red funnels, and the schooner bore up right in her path, while two of the men jumped into the row-boat. Ten minutes afterwards the monster steamship came up ploughing and puffing. The men in the row-boat pulled out into the wash of the steamer just at the point where the stern was passing them. As they did so, they saw a man jump over the railing on the poop, and, after pausing an instant to steady himself, take a tremendous leap into the sea. They could see a few excited figures rush to the railings; but the steamer was already flying far from the spot where the body of the man overboard had been engulphed. The boat-men had a few horrible moments of anxiety, while their eyes searched the boiling white waters, their own boat tossing like a cockle-shell in the waves ground into fury by the ship's paddles. Then they saw a dark object emerge at some little distance, and to their joy saw it was the head and shoulders of a man swimming lustily. Twenty strokes pulled in a delirium of delight, and they had the General in the boat, the coolest person of the three after his adventure. As the Government had taken to swooping upon all Irish Americans indiscriminately the moment the tender boarded the Atlantic liners at Queenstown, this risky mode of landing had been prearranged with the Dublin Directory, who had despatched Mr. Mahon to carry out their portion of the plan, while the General had seconded his own nerve and strength as a swimmer by an ingenious swimming apparatus, which would have enabled him to live for a considerable time in the water at need—if, for example, the steamer had passed Galley Head in the dark and if there should be any confusion about the coloured signals prearranged. When the General got on board the lugger, they found Mr. Mahon lying fast asleep in his flowing cloak, with his jetty, white-streaked locks blowing about his face. The vigils of the long, disconsolate night had been too much for him, and from waking dreams he had glided into sleeping ones of a franker character.

'It did not seem to matter much,' said the General afterwards to Captain Mike—'things seemed to go on all the better without him :—but business is business. There was a sharp temptation to begin my acquaintance with Mr. Mahon by shooting him.'

'Revolver only loaded with sea-water, I guess !'

'And, besides, it would have been more satisfactory and more just to shoot those who sent him. I don't like it, MacCarthy. I tell you candidly, I don't like it.'

'Seems more ornamental in a Poet's Corner than at the angle of a trench, I do con-cede, General. But Mahon is a noble piece of statuary all the same—would do immortal credit to the artist as a National Statoo of a Lost Cause.'

'Our business here is not to lose causes but to win them,' remarked the General, decisively, biting the end off a cigar. Nor was he much better satisfied to see how many irresponsible-looking youths were assembled in the Tower to receive him, as leading personages in the district. 'They are fine lads enough,' he said to Captain Mike. 'They will do capitally after a week or two in the field. But surely you don't expect me to tell my business to all these youngsters. I didn't undertake to come to Ireland to address monster meetings.' As a matter of fact, he devoted himself to acquiring information rather than imparting it ; cross-examining the young men keenly as to the state of things in their several charges, and confining his explanations of his own apparition to a general intimation that he had come as the harbinger of an American expedition and of an immediate insurrection. Nor were any further particulars demanded, or even desired. Your true Celt never cares to spoil a good mystery by sniffing about for details. The signal for action was enough to set their young hearts chirping more contentedly than if the whole campaign had been figured out to them in maps and statistics. It was not a Celtic generation that lost faith in the Pillar of Fire that went before the hosts of Israel.

'The sooner they go now the better ; and let us get to business,' whispered the General, as soon as he had learned as much and said as little as he thought judicious. He was a little uneasy at seeing a hot supper and some long-necked bottles introduced into their deliberations.

Captain Mike looked at him half-respectfully, half-reproach-fully. 'General,' he said, ' you may clean out this island of the Britishers, and you will—in genu-ine Sedgwick's New Yorker style—in a word, bully ; but I'm derned if you're goin' for to e-ject Editor Murrin before he's finished his grog. Don't you be too rough on the boys, General, you needn't rar'. It's in their blood—and—darn'd if it ain't in mine, too. Mat Murrin, send on the decanter ! A piece of the breast of that goose for the General, Ken, my lad—not forgetting the concealment.'

And the General's own grave, close-knit face began to smoothe out under the spell of the riant gaiety which breaks from Irish hearts at the approach of danger, as trains of sparks fly from the flintstone with every clash of steel. The boys seemed to be already clustered around their first camp-fire the night before their first battle ; and boys with the heady vapours of young enthusiasm in their brain were not likely to remember that the most important part of a battle consists in the surgical operations and the undress burying-work, and the mourning-gowns and streaming eyes and desolate hearts that make the rear-guard. The plates clashed and the wine glug-gluged, and the glasses rang, and the pine-logs sparkled, and the laughter and the wit outsparkled all. Don't tell me that Irish humour departed just as shoes for Irish feet were coming ! In a night-mail train coming home from the Mallow Election, I have seen friends Healy and Sexton burst into coruscations of wit which lit up the whole one hundred and forty miles of metals, like a fairy torchlight procession. I have seen the dingy Reporters' Room of the *Freeman's Journal* flashing and flashing again with a war of wits that would have made the old rafters of the Mitre Tavern split for joy—wit kindlier, and perhaps not much less keen, than if the tossing curls of the dear old Chief who presided had been the scratchwig of the grim Doctor himself. But who shall repeat the dainty aerial music of such hours ? Who shall bring back the foam that mantled for one evanescent moment upon last year's champagne ? Nothing in nature, we know, is destroyed. Is it too great a stretch of optimism to believe that, like the subtle essence of Attic souls themselves, the bouquet of their wit and the very foam of their champagne only pass into a higher state—are, so to say, stored up in celestial cellars for eternal consumption on a never-ending Attic Night ?

Don t understand me as meaning that the youngsters planted on stools, logs, or improvised stone seats around Captain Mike's board pelted one another with witticisms which would have passed muster with a College of Wits, or which would have kept the incomparable Mr. Boswell up half the night posting his journal, if he had happened to be concealed under the table ; but understand in the fullest possible sense that they were as merry a crew as ever showered the bright grapeshot of the brain in the face of Death and rioted with the best blood chambered in their bosoms as a preliminary to spilling it in the vanguard of a glorious field. Who was to tell them to-night that the flashing field they dreamed of was to contract into a burglar's cell, and that the only uniform they would ever see bedeck the Irish Rebel Army would be the Convict's Grey ?

The moment, of course, arrived when Mat Murrin got on his legs to announce the discovery that 'there is one to-night among us—or, rather, there are two to-night among us.' The latter circumstance obliged him to divide his remarks into two flights :—in one of which he gracefully took Mr. Mahon on his roclike pinions and deposited him upon one of the most purpureal heights of Parnassus among the greatest poets of ancient and modern times—and in the second, taking unto himself the wings of the American bald eagle, he rapidly skimmed the history of the Great War from the day when the fall of Fort Sumter threw a live coal on the heart of the American people, until the day when Sherman completed his programme of 'smashing things to the sea'; wisely considering that the exploits of the General (of which he was as ignorant as of his name) must come in somewhere, and gently insinuating that they came in everywhere, and that the entire war was a drama produced under the sole management of our mysterious and invincible General. Both flights, of course, ended in a clinking of glasses, and a yell of 'Hip, hip, hurrahs !' that must have disturbed the pillow of any dead man whose sleep was not of the most irrevocable character.

Mr. Mahon shambled through a few sentences of blushing acknowledgment ; but was plainly delighted. This scene of the mess-tent on the eve of battle for Ireland was just one of those his imagination had a thousand times pictured ; the adventure, and the contagious gaiety of the youngsters, made his old heart fresh.

Not so the General. What impressed his practical mind most was the amazing indiscretion of this noisy revelry—with lives, perhaps with the fate of the revolution, at stake. Still the situation was somehow too strong for him. 'Gentlemen,' he said, with grave courtesy, when a wild demand for 'the General' forced him to his feet, 'You must allow me to postpone my speech until the night we shall have done something to brag of—if I happen to be in a position to respond. I am not in command as yet ; but, though it may seem a rough answer to your toast, I warn you that if I were this would be an affair for court-martial.'

'The General's right,' said Captain Mike, gravely. 'It's not necessary to raise the dead on the present occasion.'

'Divvel a ha'porth to fear, General, Con Lehane's on guard,' said Mat Murrin, with the assured emphasis with which a German sings 'The Watch on the Rhine;' and, though the voices for a time waxed timid under the General's rebuke, Mat's incorrigible example soon again carried all before it, and he had Ken singing a little rebel war-song wrapped in fire, and he set Captain Mike to follow with the rollicking Federal chorus of—

> In Sixty-one the war began—
> Hurrah! hurrah!
> In Sixty-two we'll pull it through,
> Hurrah!
> In Sixty-three the nigger'll be free,
> In Sixty-four the war'll be o'er,
> And Abe's eyes will gleam with glee,
> When Johnny comes marching home!

This was the chorus which—vastly deadened, no doubt, by the thick walls of the Tower—had startled Monsignor McGrudder in his room. The strains of the last verse were still vibrating, when a low knock on the iron door announced Con Lehane with the report of his encounter with the Monsignor in the grave-yard.

'Blood alive!' exclaimed Mat Murrin, who felt himself to be the guilty author of the mischief.

The General smiled quietly, but only said: 'Gone to alarm the police, I suppose?'

'No, no,' said Con Lehane, earnestly. 'He's not so bad as that. He gave his word. He may curse as a matter of duty; but his word of honour is pledged, and he won't break *that*, my life on it.'

'Hum! I've met some slippery gentlemen of his cloth,' said the General, bringing his revolver to half-cock, and burying it somewhere about his breast. 'I presume, gentlemen, it is only necessary to say good-night,' he added, with a significant glance towards the door. 'I think you might keep young Rohan, on the look of him.' This in an undertone to Captain Mike, as the others filtered out. 'Now that we're alone,' he proceeded rapidly, 'let me say what brought me and what you've got to do. I am nominated to the command of the Southern District, and am on my way to Dublin to receive my instructions from the Directory, and to inquire for myself how matters stand. The expedition from the other side is ready. The first of our cruisers was to start four days after me. Barring accidents of weather, she is timed to be off Cooiloch Bay the eighth night from this.'

'And I guess we're to be thar on time?' asked the Captain.

'You're to direct them which of the creeks it may be safest to run into. The password will be "Celts with a vengeance." You're to be responsible for the arrangements for transporting the arms and ammunition they'll bring secretly to Cork, after which you're to cut the telegraph wires, arrange for the landing of the men, and go for Bantry Barracks in concert with our friends in red. After that—the deluge!'

'General, I chip in,' said the Captain, caressing his moustache with much contentment. 'The first point is not to get jailed meanwhiles. This place ain't safe after to-night, even with Con Lehane on guard. I suspect this grizzly knows his way to a well with any mocassin'd son of a Soo. I have my eye on a spot where I can lie low this moment. And you?'

'I hope to cover half the ground to Cork before daybreak,' said the other, burying himself in the mountainous frieze coat, with which he equipped himself after landing. 'Mr. Mahon is not a riding man, and will travel more slowly. I hope he will forgive me for suggesting that he should throw off that cloak and hat. Nothing could be more picturesque, but that's just it—it's so picturesque there is not a policeman with half an eye that won't fall admiring it.'

'And there is a warrant out against you for high treason?' said Ken Rohan, tenderly. 'I saw that they searched your house.'

'Yes; but you see I am a born conspirator,' replied the poet, who really believed it, and to whom any suggestion to the contrary was as bitter aloes. 'I really am.'

'So is a bed of posies bombshells,' whispered Captain Mike in an aside to the General. 'But that's brother Mahon's way—he'd give up his life before he'd give up that ridiklous poet's uniform of his.'

'If Mr. Mahon will stay here, he will be quite safe, and he will have my bed at the Mill with more welcome than a king,' said Ken Rohan, timidly, as if there were really a crown of gold rounding Mr. Mahon's temples.

The poet put his hand upon his head again, affectionately, but shook his own head with a sad smile. 'I must be going, like the General,' he said.

'Then, I shall get out the pony and trap, and put you as far on your road by daybreak as the General himself,' cried Ken Rohan with delight.

'That being settled, gentlemen—good-night. We'll meet again, I dare say, if there's anything worth meeting for.' And the

General passed out at the iron-door among the graves, where Con Lehane was waiting to pilot him to his horse.

The next morning, while the woods and waters were shivering in cold silence under the bloodshot lights of a wintry dawn, Joshua Neville was taking his usual early walk in the high-terraced gardens behind Clanlaurance Castle, when he saw the American Captain walk out of one of the arbours to meet him.

He could not have been more amazed if the Prince of Darkness had started out of the ground in burning full-dress. 'You here !' he exclaimed, tortured with all sorts of vague visions of celebrated outlaws from Jack Cade to Rob Roy M'Gregor, and unable to settle in the least whether his own duty as an English liegeman required him to deal with the intruder, sword-in-hand, after the manner of 'Alexander Iden, an Esquire of Kent,' upon a like historic occasion—even if there was a sword immediately procurable.

'I guess so,' said the American Captain. 'You once mentioned that you never missed this sunrise walk of yours in the gardens. I've been three frozen hours waitin' for you in yonder bower o' roses by Bendemeer's stream. I went within a stave of getting my ankle cracked in one of them blamed steel-traps under the wall yonder, only, like everythin' belonging to old man Clanlaurance, the thing was slightly out of order.'

'So like Lord Clanlaurance !' exclaimed the ironmaster, whom anything that jarred on his sense of the practical and orderly recalled for the moment from more abstract considerations. 'But —er—ah——'

'What brings me here, you naturally ask ?' said the Captain, charitably glossing over the fact that he had *not* asked. 'Wal, not to burn fireworks over it, fact is there's Injuns around, an I've made tracks to your stockade for shelter.'

'To me ! An Englishman !' cried Joshua Neville, who was making a rapid mental comparison between Captain Mike's brawny frame and his own shrunken Sunday-citizen figure, and darkly considering whether, nevertheless, Duty might not call upon him to disregard the odds.

'I guess I ain't the first hunted refugee from the nigger-drivers that found a friendly lighthouse in an Englishman's eye ! 'Taint the English we're in grips with :—it's with the swell mob that stole your flag an' run this island in the Pirate business. Anyways, Englishman or Choctaw, you seemed to strike me as a kind of whole man, an' I jest said I'd step 'round an' bore.'

'It's High Treason, is it not ?' asked Neville in a miserable state of indecision. The word 'Treason,' which falls on Irish ears like hushed music, laden, as were once the names of Balmerino and Kil-

marnock, with associations which melt the gentle and fire the brave
conjured up in Joshua Neville's well-ordered English mind hateful
notions of traitors taken in some treacherous deed of guilt against
their Queen and country—of subterranean dungeons, and streaming blocks, and ghastly heads held up by the blood-clotted hair.

'High treason—that, I am given to understand, is the legend,'
said Captain Mike.

'And the penalty is—Death !'

'That always *is* about the penalty, unless you get the c'rect
drop on the enemy fust.'

'It would be misprision of treason on my part to harbour you
—involving imprisonment—involving perhaps penal servitude.'

'Seems to me 'most everything in this island is Treason that
is not Robbery,' the Captain remarked, with a sigh. He had
been travelling all night, and looked sufficiently spent and
haggard. 'Wal, I daar say you're right—it's no affair of yours
—it's our business to do our dying and penal-servituding for
ourselves. Good-bye, boss—hope there ain't no offence given or
taken—an' only hope in conclusion old man Clanlaurance ain't
left no more o' them idiotic man-traps foolin' around that wall.'

'Stay—you mistake me,' said the ironmaster, who, having
made up his mind on any subject, did not fear to shock a world
in arms. 'An Englishman finds some difficulty in placing himself at your point of view; but I think I understand. You are
welcome to make my home your own, if you will give your word
to use it only as a sanctuary, and in no other way than for the
purpose of securing your escape from the country. On these
terms you can command my home and me.'

'Wal, boss, this is fair—it's generous—it bears out my ideas
in boring in this gulch. But it won't do. I don't propose—by
no manner of means—to use your house 'cept as reverently as if
'twor a church to cover my head for seven nights from the present; but as to what I may do outside it, after, or meanwhiles—
I can't allow my hands to be tied by your kindness, no more'n by
Queen Victoria's handcuffs—no SIR ! Thankee all the same,
Honourable Joshua Neville, and, as a plain Amurrican citizen—
put the hand there.' Whereupon he crunched the ironmaster's
hand in a grip like that of his own relentless steam hammers, and
turned to go.

'Be it so. You shall stay—and stay on your own terms,'
said Neville, a wondrous beam of deep grey philanthropy playing
over his strong face like a Quakerly nimbus. 'I came to Ireland
determined not to be drawn by a hair's breadth into partisanship
on either side; but I find it's impossible to escape the infection
One has only to choose between the rebel-fever and the cruel

mania for mastering the people, and upon the whole—I've chosen. Come in to breakfast.'

The American Captain stood for a moment on the garden-path, watching the play of the Quakerly nimbus over Joshua Neville's rugged features, and thinking how really beautiful this hardened old Sheffield steel face looked this wintry morning. 'Wal, boss,' he remarked, as he walked on towards the Castle, 'if they sent over a few more Englishmen of your streak, I guess they'd do more execution among our boys than as many regiments of redcoats, in a permanent sort of way.'

CHAPTER THE THIRTY-SECOND

A LYNCH-PIN OUT OF THE MILL-WHEEL

MR. HANS HARMAN stood in the dismal dining-room of Stone Hall, solemnly welcoming the funeral guests. It did not need the dead, heavy, almost solid mist that was descending outside, pressing the spirit of man down and down as though all the bright airs of heaven were coagulating into a jelly of despair—it scarcely needed the dull blood-coloured blinds down and the undertaker's men shuffling about presenting bands of crape as if they were so many wreaths of black immortelles laid on the altar of the god Death—it did not at all require those hundred uncomfortable intimations, which we can all feel and never describe, of the presence of a corpse upstairs, to make the dining-room of Stone Hall look its part on an occasion of this kind. It seemed to have been designed by the architect as a place for funeral festivities. Indeed, the gentlemen sipping port wine and nibbling plum-cake there at this moment scarcely remembered to have seen it used since the last death in the family ; and more than one of them, in a decorous, funereal way, said so to one another between their sips. The fact is, Hans Harman neither cared for wine nor the price of it ; and he could find few of his cattle-show neighbours with a passion for Schubert and Bach and long-haired, sempiternally-twangling gentlemen of their profession. He himself, singularly enough, seemed designed by nature's architect also to play an imposing and irreproachable part on a melancholy occasion. His tall, handsome figure, his face which seemed a little too white for most other purposes of social life, the grave melancholy smile in his fine eyes like mourning on a coquettish beauty, the subdued shake of his large white hands—all impressed the beholders with a sense, so to say. of comfortable

gloom and propriety, and rendered them insensible of the fact
that he kept standing as usual in the immediate front of the fire
absorbing more carbonic comfort than went to all the rest of the
assembled mourners. It can scarcely be necessary to introduce
the córpse upstairs by name, even if the coffin was not long ago
sealed up. Poor Rebecca Harman's unhappy shadow is one of
those that flit across the stage of the great drama of life with no
greater part than 'A Gaoler' or 'A Mariner' in one of Shakespeare's playbills. She was much more at ease in her coffin than
she had been in the more spacious hearse-bed in which she had
been for years, as it were, attending her own funeral. The
gentle reader may at once dismiss any horrible suspicion that it
would be well for the coroner to disturb the poor lady's bones
and inquire more particularly how she came by her death.
There was nothing that the most rigid straining of the laws of
England could impeach—nothing that the most searching analysis
could turn up its nose at. There was not the smallest trace of
arsenic in the bitter-flavoured homœopathic doses with which
Miss Deborah plied her patient. It was only the flavour of
sisterly virtue turned slightly acid. A jury must have found that
during those latter months Hans Harman never omitted his dutiful daily visit, never omitted to smile a cheerful smile or drop an
encouraging word, and that at the last, when he was standing by
the hearse-bed and Miss Deborah softly said : 'You are dying
now, Rebecca, and I ask you, are you not quite happy, and has
not Hans always been an indulgent husband to you !' the person
under cross-examination passed out of the world without the
least attempt to impugn either of these propositions. The truth
is, poor Rebecca was a trying, discontented, out-of-joint creature
—hers was one of those dreary loveless careers (so numerous,
alas !) of which people say with a sigh, as did an ancient little
spinster lady, who was Mrs. Harman's only confidante in life, and
who by some misunderstanding did not reach the death-bed
until there was nothing to be confided unless the funeral arrangements : 'Under other circumstances it might have been so different.'

At all events that poor lonely soul can scarcely have felt lone-
lier at departing from Stone Hall ; and now that her body was on
the point of departing also, Hans Harman not merely feigned
grief, but felt it—recalled with real remorse the misunderstandings, incompatibilities, or what not that had caused their married
life to be lived at opposite ice-bound poles ; recalled with real
softness the few touches of sentiment that he was able to throw
like ever so long faded spring-flowers on the coffin ; and had
almost persuaded himself, among others, that he was a sorrow-

stricken lonely man, who, but for his natural bonhomie and pluck, would break down altogether, when his eye caught sight of Lord Drumshaughlin's figure in the gloom near the doorway, and the shadow of poor Rebecca retreated respectfully into the background. Lord Drumshaughlin had not seen his agent since the night of Mr. Dargan's disaster at the Club ; and Hans Harman, whose temper rather than his policy had goaded him into an open rupture with his principal, had been casting about anxiously for some avenue of reconciliation. The sight of Lord Drumshaughlin sent such a warm thrill through him that he felt himself able to resign his monopoly of the fire and make his way, with a solemn determined enthusiasm, to Lord Drumshaughlin's hand.

'This is kind—it is magnanimous, my lord,' he murmured, enfolding the delicate white hand pretty much as if he were taking the communion-cup.

'Not at all—quite deserve it from me, Harman,' mumbled Lord Drumshaughlin, in his grand manner. He really looked such a patrician figure of gracious dignity and grave sympathy that even Hans Harman's sharp eyes could not have discovered that his lordship had been fidgetting ever since in a confluent fever of gout and incapacity to see daylight through his affairs without the assistance of his agent's keen vision, and that, like himself, he had been praying for some pretext that would enable him to square his pride with his interest. 'This is—er—a sad affair.'

'Makes a man feel a bit solitary on the housetops, I can tell your lordship. You can understand now why I was not in the humour to look you up sooner as to what's to be done about the Conditional Order ; but if it would be convenient to your lordship after ——after this'——

'Shouldn't have dreamt of mentioning it myself, Harman, upon so—in fact, upon such an occasion ; but if, as you say—— ahem——after this'——

Both men broke off in a manner that might either indicate grief too sacred for expression, or might (and probably did) intimate some shadowy unformed feeling in both minds that the worn body upstairs connected by the comprehensive term 'this' was somehow or other standing between these gentlemen and business as well as (a harder thing for a dead body to do) treading upon Lord Drumshaughlin's gouty toes. 'This,' however, was in due order and ceremony thrust down the stone-faced stairs, and hurried away through the mud-jelly at as round a pace as the public convenience demanded to a spot where there was no more hurry, and where there will be no more thrusting out ; and the insignificant little old maid shed the only unhired tears that the occasion produced ; and Miss Deborah had leisure to examine in the mirror how she would look in mourning ; and the man-servant wavered unsteadily in the empty dining-room between an unrivalled opportunity of getting drunk, and the dread knowledge that Mr. Hans Harman's eye had been counting the bottles, and probably measuring the number of glasses unconsumed ; and Hans Harman himself performed the last offices with all the more genuine tenderness and gratitude at the thought that Rebecca had at all events been the means of bringing Lord Drumshaughlin back to Stone Hall — so that, altogether, nothing in poor Mrs. Harman's life was such a success as her funeral.

'I have arranged the business of evicting the people at the Mill,' remarked the widower, later in the day, in the breakfast-room at the Castle. He was anxious to recommence friendly relations by a hint first, that he had been mindful of the wish for a policy of Thorough expressed by his principal, and, secondly, that he still regarded Lord Drumshaughlin as in a position to do what he liked with his own. Thirdly, and of course, chiefly, he was consumed with a hatred of Ken Rohan, which, for a man of Harman's logical and unemotional mental machinery, was most unreasoning ; for the only positive grievances he could recall against young Rohan was that the latter had declined to be served by him, that he had happened to be a silent witness of Miss Westropp's scathing words the night of the attempted arrest at the Castle, and that he had happened to be a silent witness also of Harry's terrific threat over Quish's coffin in the graveyard. For all these reasons he added with unction : 'The eviction will take place to-morrow.'

'I am not sure that—er—there is any particular hurry,' said Lord Drumshaughlin, feeling irritated that his resolution should be so pitilessly remembered, but fearing to appear to snub his agent's zeal, and still more fearing to incur his contempt by avow-ing how brittle had been the tables of his Draconian Code.

'The arrangements are all made, my lord,' said the agent, with some alarm. 'You remember the determination you ex-pressed'——

'Yes, yes—be it so. By Jove, there's a more important question I want to ask you, Harman—when am I to be evicted myself ?' said Lord Drumshaughlin. All his assumed gaiety and real pluck could not conceal the hungry uncertain questioning of his eye, nor conceal the ravages the last few weeks had made in his face, which had bidden farewell to 'make-ups' and dyes for ever.

'Pooh, it's not so bad as that, my lord—yet,' said the agent, who had marked that supplicating look in the inner chambers of Lord Drumshaughlin's eyes, and with a burst of uncanny inward laughter noted how different from the air of haughty triumph with which he had sailed out of the Club on Admiral Ffrench's arm. But, remembering former explosions of Ralph Westropp's pride, he kept his satisfaction entirely for internal consumption. 'I presume,' he said, tentatively, watching the effect of his words with a stealthy cat-like glance out of the corners of his downcast lids, 'I presume that—ahem—your lordship's views about Dargan remain unchanged ? Quite so,' he said, quickly, noticing indica-tions that were not quite supplicatory. 'So I took for granted. Well, my lord, it is as I anticipated—money-lenders always do understand one another—Hugg joins in the petition of sale, and it would be idle for us to resist the order being made absolute. It will be almost a matter of course.'

'A matter of course that my estate which I or mine have held for nearly four hundred years should go for a song to some pelting land-jobber—perhaps to Humphrey Dargan ! A matter of course that I should be swindled and beggared because a few gales of interest to a usurer are overdue !' roared Lord Drum-shaughlin. The hectic spot which was beginning to glow in the middle of his cheek required no touch of rouge to heighten it.

'By no means. Your lordship did not allow me to finish,' said the agent, with scrupulous deference—the deference of a skilled angler who pays out plenty of line to a gamey fish in whose gills he feels that his hook is securely fastened. 'Dargan and Hugg acting together, the Landed Estates Court has almost no option but to order the examination of title and proceed to a sale. But we can invoke the Court of Chancery to intervene and forbid the sacrifice of the property. We can obtain the appoint-ment of a Receiver in Chancery—the incumbrancers could not well object to my being appointed receiver, I being to some small extent—ahem—an incumbrancer myself. I would be still your lordship's agent under the legal fiction of a new title—the rents would flow in as usual, subject to the formality of an account to the Master in Chancery—the court would never allow a sale to the disadvantage of the estate without my report - and the result would be that we would be masters of the situation, and would have time enough either to finance a new loan, or to propose a composition with the incumbrancers, and get the petition dis-charged. You follow me, my lord ?'

'Perfectly,' said Lord Drumshaughlin, in a subdued voice. 'The upshot of it appears to be that I am no longer to be master here, but some Master in the Four Courts.'

'That, my lord, is a *jeu de mots*—nothing more, believe me,' said Harman. 'The upshot is that you play off against Humphrey Dargan's stamped deed the Lord Chancellor's Seal.'

Lord Drumshaughlin remained silent and composed. All the venomous tophus seemed to have fled his joints in presence of the terrible levin flash out of the sky which seemed to have struck and withered him root and branch. Like the stout old oak he was, he presented a more dignified figure under the lightning-stroke than while the miserable parasites were clinging to him with all their family of gnawing fungi. One of the few things he knew, outside the accomplishments of his own butterfly world, was how to die. Hans Harman could have taken much more cheerfully one of his old fiery eruptions than his present calm, pathetic, scarcely reproachful silence. Not that his lordship even remotely suspected the real scope of his agent's projects. Unluckily for himself, he had so accustomed himself to Hans Harman's easy guidance in financial matters that the very thought of figures had become to him as offensive as a chemical analysis of the constituents of his pernicious drug would be to a confirmed opium-eater. All he knew was that he, the lord of a princely extent of country, he who had the portraits of more than twenty ancestors in his dining-room, was invited now to enter villainous-smelling law courts in some dubious bankrupt capacity, and, if ever he was to emerge from that frouzy precinct, would come out a dingy incumbered old wreck, no more like the Ralph Westropp who had once sparkled in the eye of Europe than the decrepid fogey who scrambles for the fire at the Old Man's Hospital in Kilmainham was like the dashing hussar who had once curvetted and kissed hands on his way to fight Napoleon.

'Well, well, Harman—I will think it over—I will think it over,' he said at last, giving Harman his hand with a stately courtesy, as if he were extending it to a vassal to kiss; and when the door closed upon the agent, as if he felt the need of flying from the darkest spot in his mind to the brightest, he rang the bell, and flinging himself wearily in his easy chair, asked: 'Where is Miss Westropp?'

'Here, papa, and so is your lunch,' said a voice of music in his ear; and, a moment afterwards, as his lips touched his daughter's golden-crowned forehead, and he felt her soft arm steal round his neck, Ralph Westropp thought to himself here was a treasure worth all the woods and cornfields of Drumshaughlin—worth all the bosky acres that were ever put up and knocked down in the Landed Estates Court.

'I almost wish,' pondered the agent, as he drove down the avenue, 'we could patch things up again—Dargan is furious, of course, but it would be easy to square *him*—Psha ! you're in a maudlin mood this morning, Hans Harman—it's poor Rebecca ! No, no, we haven't gone thus far prosperously to founder in harbour and in a dead calm.   Drumshaughlin is too weak or too lazy to slave-drive his tenants himself.   He expects that I shall keep his bath of golden waters filled, and then soothes his conscience by abusing me himself as well as inviting the public to fire at me.   There has been quite enough of this sort of cheap virtue—if I've taken the administration and risk, it's about time I reaped some more substantial reward than a stingy commission. At all events the situation is now mine, to be managed to my own liking, as circumstances may determine.   Hallo, you there — Dawley—I want you at Stone Hall, the sooner the better—do you hear ?'

The insolent tone of the request was not lost upon Dawley, who looked after the trap with a curious blending of pugnacity and quailing in his little eyes which, as well as his nose, were unusually fiery from recent potations.   Nevertheless he found himself shuffling along in the direction of Stone Hall, and in due time he found himself slouching about still more uncomfortably in front of Mr. Hans Harman, who was affording his hands the benefit of the fire by playing bopeep with them under his coat-tails while he faced his visitor.

'Now,' said the agent, coolly, ' I have not a policeman concealed behind that screen—I always deal aboveboard with a man —so we can speak freely.   I daresay you scarcely require me to tell you that I know who killed Quish.'

A momentary nervous tremor shot through Dawley's limbs ; then he screwed his lips tightly together.

'I see you're wondering that I have *not* a policeman concealed on the premises,' proceeded Harman, his handsome smiling eyes watching every twitch of a muscle in the other's face like a superb cat, with a small mouse between its paws.   'You know you're sold, eh ?'

Blotches of dirty white overspread Dawley's face, to the lips — almost to the tip of the nose.   By a desperate effort he crushed on his lips the cry : 'Has he split ?' but not before Harman could almost see his bloodless lips form the words.   Dawley's face suddenly collapsed into a more whining aspect ; and he said, with as much simplicity as he could put in the words : 'Me ? yerra, what had I to do wid it, in de honour o' God ?'

'You're a precious rascal !' cried Harman, his smiling eyes filling with threatening light.   'Perhaps, you want me to ring the bell and send for a policeman to explain it to *him* ? Dawley,' he said, suddenly and fiercely, ' you deserve to be hanged, and I'll have you hanged by the neck until you're dead the moment it suits me.'

A look of desperation flamed up red into the other's face and eyes. 'Damn you!' he cried, fumbling in his breast pocket. 'You're a—Devil!'

'No, I'm not a devil, but I'm a devilish good shot,' said the agent, swiftly covering his visitor with a revolver, and advancing a pace nearer to him to be surer of his aim. 'Put down whatever you've in your breast there—put it out on that table – one —two'——

The trembling wretch was fascinated as by the eye of a snake-charmer; he dropped a pinfire revolver on the table, so precipitately that a shot went off, and the bullet passed through a skirt of the agent's coat.

'I never would depend upon those pinfire things if I were you,' said the agent. 'You see? Here is the bullet-hole, there is your empty revolver—I have only to ring, and you're convicted of an attempt to murder me in my own house, after murdering my bailiff.' He saw Dawley stagger up against a book-case to find support against the drab topsy-turvy mist that was dancing before his eyes and the cold sweats that were sapping his limbs. 'Now, Dawley,' resumed Mr. Hans Harman, putting up his revolver, and speaking in an almost genial tone, 'I've always warned you that I am an enemy; but I've told you also that you might find me no worse at a pinch than some of the so-called friends who are duping you into putting your neck where they will never put their own :—now, I don't mean to ring for the policeman. I don't mean to hand you over to the hangman '—he noticed the startled, half-doubting expression of relief that crossed the wretched face—'not if you enable me to let you off with an easy conscience. I cannot be a party to condoning a horrible murder; but I can and will secure you immunity if you will aid me and justice to bring home guilt to those who are behind you—to those who have egged you on to murder and to more important crimes of treason. For instance'—his keen meaningful eyes penetrating him through and through—'if that young Rohan was in any way responsible—I'm not saying that he was, mind'——

'Do you know what Quish was shot for?' said the other, with a snort like a caged beast. 'Shoot me at once and be done wid it—hell to you!'

'I will not shoot you at once, because I can hang you at leisure,' said the agent, coldly—'that is, if you're so ungrateful and so idiotic as to drive me to it. I should think it is not curses I have earned by not only saving you from the gallows, but opening your way to a handsome reward—for you have only to aid me to hunt down treason and murder to be a richer fellow than a century in Blackamoor Lane would make you ; and you must know as well as I do that it's only a question whether your accomplices will hang you, or whether you'll be too quick for them. I don't know that I have anything else to say, and you look as if you thought this interview had lasted sufficiently long. Think it over, and make up your mind. I don't want to take any unfair advantage of you. But beware of attempting to obtain any unfair advantage over *me*. Though my revolver won't follow you, my eye will ; and, if you try it, you're a rat in a trap, and—I'll let in the bulldogs. Turn the handle of the door the other way—that's it. Yes, you may go,' Hans Harman nodded, as the wretched creature paused humbly for the signal. ' I think,' he said, looking at himself in the somewhat dark steely mirror, 'this hasn't been a bad afternoon's work.'

In the meantime all was getting ready for the sheriff at the Mill at Greenane. There was a cargo of Californian wheat on its way, in which Myles Rohan held a third with some Cork merchants, and on which he had relied to satisfy the writ, and, at all events, stave off the evil hour ; but his partners, Messrs. Waffles and Greany, were unwilling to sell at the depressed prices that ruled the market, and he quietly bowed his head before the gathering storm, and said it might as well come soon as late. In Ireland neighbours aid one another against the Sheriff, as white settlers in the western backwoods used to draw together on the first signal of the scalpers. Myles Rohan had only to pass the word to have assembled a trusty garrison with their pitchforks at the Millhouse ; but, Myles being a stern law-and-order man, they did the next best offices of good neighbourhood by helping to remove the furniture and proffering their own houses as an asylum either for the household effects or for their owners. Men who had not spoken to the sturdy miller for years arrived silently with their carts and bore away chairs, tables, and bedsteads with the solemn tenderness of Sisters of Charity binding up a cruel wound. Mrs. Harold, who was one of the most awful of human beings at bewailing her own imaginary woes, was the most helpful and devoted in assuaging the real ones of others. Father Phil used to say with a smile that the happiest moments of his life were when some killed or wounded neighbour needed the sleepless energies of Maria. At this moment she was director-general of operations at the Mill, her wailful voice sounding crisp and clear as a bell, and the bitter eyes behind the spectacles quiet and decisive as those of a general in the thick of a battle. ' Of course, Kate,' she remarked to Mrs. Rohan,

'Myles and the children will not think of going anywhere but to us. You know Jack is away, and there's plenty of room—Ken will have to stow himself away upon the sofa in Father Phil's room—but it does a youngster good to have to rough it.' The only time Maria lost her temper was when Mrs. Rohan timidly broke to her the intelligence that this was impossible—that quiet lodgings had been already secured which they were furnishing from the Mill and striving to make as like the mill-parlour as possible in Myles' eyes. Mrs. Rohan herself bore the blow with a cheerful heroism which never deserted her, unless when her eyes fell upon the miller. Then indeed these eyes filled with tears which she dared not let fall, and the first desolate pang the eviction brought her was to find that the little Oratory of the Blessed Virgin, at which she had so often found her tears turn to golden treasure, had been dismantled of its statue and tapers in the process of removal, and that she had no longer whereto to bring her lacerated soul for balm. Still her greater terror for Myles caused her to aid busily and even smilingly, while the massive old mahogany tables and sideboards—the pride of the family for generations—were borne out like so many coffins with ancient friends inside ; and while the old silver, and the old cut-glass, and all the old sacred vessels of her housekeeping were being ransacked, and pawed and scattered.

The young people (as is young people's way) found a certain assuagement of the sorrow of quitting their old home in the mere movement, variety, and change of the removal operations—in the flitting to and fro of so many friendly faces, in the unusually hearty grip of friendly hands, in the bustle of carts coming and going, and heavy furniture bumping funnily downstairs. Katie, without at all knowing she was making the effort, was shining over the desolate house with softer lustre than ever—as the sun lights the bare mountain side with tenderer colours than ever he expends upon the best pastures. It was only one or two very slight circumstances that unnerved her :—as, for instance, when she found a carter lighting his pipe in her now vacant little room amidst the white and blue forget-me-nots ; and when Georgey O'Meagher and she, making a last visit to see that there was nothing forgotten in the garret (a region which, in their youthful play-hours, had been the dark home of all sorts of mysterious bogies, and which it had been one of Ken's earliest triumphs of manhood to have explored alone in the dark), and saw its timber ribs and mysterious corners now exposed and naked in the rude light which rushed in where a wooden shutter had been torn from the skylight—as if all the romance and wonder of their young lives were being carted away with the furniture.

Ken was escaping most of the worries of the removal by having the more instant terrors of Mat Murrin's printer's devil at his heels; for, although Mat confidentially posed as the principal thunderer in the secret sheet, it was in reality written from opening poem to closing paragraph by his young catechumen. Ken had become absorbed to his heart's core in his work. The mere feeling that every sentence was written with a sword hanging by a hair over his head brought out the best that was in him, and imparted a strange charm to those hot secret hours in which he seemed to be giving out the best blood chambered in his bosom in thoughts that shone and burned. He wrote with his feet in the polar circle and his brain in the tropics. The strange thing was that he so little knew why or where in the mysterious recesses of his being these springs suddenly bubbled forth. He felt only that their bright waters were a-flowing, and that forth they must gush amidst all sorts of enchanted scenery—red battle-fields, or whispering woodland nooks, or the sunlit corn-fielded future. Another source of endless wonder to him was to find that his thoughts affected others as they affected himself—to feel that they made young pulses throb and young veins run fire, and to thrill with the sense of a certain ecstatic sacramental union between him and them. He had become known and strangely beloved by the young men; and the greatest marvel of all to him was to discover that the electricity which supplied his verses seemed to have flowed into the veins and muscles of his hand, so that he shook hands with a strange trembling sense of giving and receiving joy. One wrapt in such a Mahomet-vision, and with the patient face of Noble Nolan plaintively awaiting at his elbow the leaves of his Koran as they were struck off, had not much attention to spare for the packing of chairs and bedsteads at the Mill—especially within a few days of the Revolution which was to right all by upsetting all—though once captured by his mother and chained to the work, nobody was so expert as Ken in picking wooden bedsteads to pieces, and whisking the old mahogany legs with the brass castors from under Katie's coffin-like pianoforte, and coaxing the unwieldy musical coffin itself past sharp edges of the stairs and through impossible doors.

The saddest man at the Mill was Danny Delea. He chafed rebelliously against the notion of surrendering the Mill without a blow. For the first time in his life, he did not return blow for blow when Myles Rohan that morning said to him with a mournful smile: 'What about that Fenian fleet of yours, Danny, that was to have come and freed us all?' Danny looked at him, and there was something in the miller's face that froze the retort upon his lips. 'Thrue for you, sir, begor!—they're not up to time,' he replied, celebrating the miller's little joke with the best laugh he could muster. Then with a touch of the old incorrigible Adam: 'But who knows? It's not too late yet.' He hovered about all day uneasily, as if he had still some haunting feeling that the fleet might be signalled in the Bay in time to avert the eviction. But evening came, and no fleet, and Danny stopped the mill-wheel with the sensation of a man plunging a dagger into an old friend's heart; and then he walked up the glen by the old mill-race for the last time, and he let down the sluice-gates, and it seemed to him the blood in his own veins ceased to flow at the same moment with the mill-stream.

They had left the miller's own little office undisturbed as long as possible, and were glad to see him take refuge there from the sights and sounds attending the disruption of his old home. They had carefully trimmed the fire, and brightened the place more than usual, so as to remove up to the last moment from Myles Rohan's mind every suggestion of his little snuggery being so soon to be broken up; and Myles had sat all day fumbling over his books and arranging his papers in a more cheerful mood than they had seen in him for many a day. The hour came at last, however, for smuggling him away to his new quarters. Mrs. Rohan entered the office. He was finishing the last lines of a large straggling communication on a sheet of foolscap, and leaned back admiring the performance with much apparent satisfaction.

'Time to be off, Kate, eh?' he cried cheerily, as she entered.

'It is, Myles darling. Father Phil insists on having us down to tea.'

'Father Phil would insist on having us up to heaven, and not only us, but every living creature on the earth beside us,' said the miller, adding, with a laugh that nearly forced the tears out of Mrs. Rohan's eyelids, 'I don't believe he'd even shut out Hans Harman! Do you know what I've been at, old woman?' he continued, holding up the sheet of foolscap with an author's fondness; 'guess what I've done there!'

'Something as foolish and as loveable as usual, I'm sure, Myles.'

'It's Katie's little fortune for the convent,' he whispered triumphantly. 'I've made that sure against all storms, anyway. Kate, darling, 'twill be better for you and for the children when I'm dead.'

'Don't! oh, don't! You know I can bear anything but

your saying that,' she cried, breaking down in a passion of sobs on his shoulder.

'Mamma, you're an old fool. I tell you it will—better for the children and better for you. The insurance for fifteen hundred on my life is at the bank, but there's only 250*l*. against it. You'll spend many a happy and prosperous day yet at the Mill, old woman—Ha, who's that? Come in,' he cried, and seeing a telegraph messenger enter, the miller darted upon his message with the eagerness of a bird of prey. 'It's all right, Kate, old woman! The Sheriff needn't call! They've sold the cargo—a glorious bargain—and this is a message from Waffles and Greany that I may draw against them for three hundred.'

'God and His holy angels be praised!' she exclaimed, sinking on her knees. Then, noticing that, as though the excitement had been too much for him, Myles was staggering back with his hand to his forehead, she sprang to his side with a cry of terror: 'Myles, darling!—what is it?—speak to me! O my God!'

He did not speak to her. She laid him back in his easy chair, and the dreadful symptoms she knew so well came back— that horrible twitching of the mouth, as if a strong man were struggling for the power of speech against some demoniac pincers that were dragging it from between his jaws—that awful, awful look of the poor purposeless eye that feels a world in ruins toppling down about it—that convulsive clutch of the hand, with the paper securing Katie's little fortune still grasped between the fingers, like the flag of a brave soldier going down with his face to the foe. The Sheriff need *not* call. The sudden rush of joy had come too late to do aught but devastate the already overwrought and overswollen blood-vessels of the brain. Myles Rohan's second stroke had come; and again, in that same office, the bed had to be improvised; and again the old doctor, standing over the stricken, speechless body, watch in hand, as if appointing the number of minutes there were to live, shook his vacuous old head with the wisdom of one who had just negotiated with Death as long a respite of execution as possible, and announced what uncertificated agonised hearts had divined before him—that there would probably not be a third stroke.

Shortly after the roll of the doctor's gig had died down, with a joyous cry there appeared in the doorway a sylphid figure breathless and rosy with excitement, and, at sight of the group around the bed, started back white with horror. Katie Rohan turned for a moment, and putting her arm round Mabel Westropp's waist, kissed her white cheek silently, and in a moment was wrapt in her patient again. This creature, helpless as a baby, and shyer than a fawn in the great world, moved in a sick room with the strength of a goddess—*incessu patuit Dea*—and oh ! so much more blessed a goddess than she whose team of swans brushed the Paphian air with her wanton perfumes ! Ken Rohan thought Miss Westropp looked like fainting, and without a word placed a chair for her ; but she waved it off with a hand in which he saw she held a document, and silently joined the angel guar dian figures by the bedside. For a while the patient's harsh breathing was the only break in the stillness. Without any authority from the old doctor, Myles Rohan became astonishingly better, the awful strangling contest abated, and Mrs. Rohan thought she could discern some ray of tranquil consciousness with more purposeful concentration of the eyes. 'Thank God and His Blessed Mother !' she cried, sinking to her knees to murmur a prayer, which, to the indomitable faith of an Irish mother, was of more efficacious service to the poor sufferer than the old doctor's prophylactics. The pendulum of the little clock on the mantel-piece tolled out the seconds with the apparent thunder of a great bell, but somehow the strokes seemed less and less like those of a death-bell, and grew less and less noticeable at all— which is always a good sign in such cases. Myles was manifestly recovering consciousness. But the watchers stood there all the time in the same attitude, fascinated, strained, silent.

Possibly a couple of hours—to Mrs. Rohan and Katie they seemed a couple of eternities—had passed in this way, when the working of wheels over the gravel outside was heard, and a great jolly voice that sounded like a peal of joy-bells. The door w: s thrown open, and the same scene was enacted as at M: s Westropp's coming—first, a merry burst of geniality, then a movement of horror, and the jollity all struck of a heap. This time it was the Very Rev. Dr. O'Harte's massive figure that sus- tained the shock, and sustained it infinitely worse than the fragile red-and-white-rosy being who sustained the former one. All men are more or less cowards in presence of distress ; and Dr. O'Harte, who would have died at the stake stoutly himself, or have faced a hell-fire of bullets still more gaily, was the veriest baby by the bedside of a suffering friend—had a very Sybarite's shrink- ing from graves, and worms, and epitaphs at close quarters. Katie Rohan could have at this moment ordered him about like a child.

'Oh, Doctor, look ! He knows you !' exclaimed Mrs. Rohan in an ecstacy of delight. The sick man's retina had, indeed, caught some some vague impression of the great burly figure : or perhaps the peal-of-joy-bells voice had somehow or other rung a responsive peal within that insurrectionary city of poor Myles' brain. There was clearly a look of pleased intelligence in the

eye, and the fact acted as a marvellous restorative to Dr.
O'Harte's spirits, and indeed diffused a glow of confidence and
delight all round. It no longer seemed to be a sacrilege to speak
above one's breath.

'Oh then, oh then,' said the Doctor, after he had laid his
broad palm healingly on the hot corded brow, 'was there ever
such luck ? I missed the midday train fron Clonard by the
twinkling of an eye, or all this would not have occurred.'

'Would not have occurred, Doctor ?' said Mrs. Rohan, with
surprise. 'What could have prevented it ?'

'This,' producing a heavy little white bag—'this bag of dirty
sovereigns would have prevented it ; worse luck that any of
God's creatures should be depending upon the wretched, soulless
dross to save him from death and misery.'

'Sir,' said Ken, with something swelling in his throat, 'you
cannot mean——'

'I mean nothing whatever, except that I'm not such a
monster as to see the dogs rending my old friend limb by limb,
when a little bag of sovereigns flung into Hans Harman's jaws
would save him.' He didn't mention that his own savings for
the next summer's holiday went into the little bag, and that he
had to invoke a friend's name at the bank to add the final
hundred sovereigns. 'But, bother it for a story, I should miss
the train for the first time in my life, and arrive in time to find
that Hans Harman has been too much for us.'

'God bless you, Doctor !—no, the sight of you there by his
side has been better to Myles than your weight in sovereigns !'
Mrs. Rohan said, taking his hand, without increasing his disappointment by letting him know that he had been anticipated
also by the telegram of Messrs. Waffles and Greany. 'Why,
look ! he not only knows you—he hears you !'

'Then he'll hear a bit of news that'll please him better than
even to hear that we've hunted the Sheriff. Myles, old man—
I'm a Bishop, or as good as a Bishop ! Ha ! I knew I'd warm
the cockles of your heart !' cried the Doctor, as he saw the light
of intelligence not merely flicker, but fairly sparkle out amidst
the smothering features.

'You don't say it, Doctor, or—or—what am I to call you,
sir ?' said Mrs. Rohan, reverently.

'Anything you like, so long as you call me old friend,' was
the hearty reply. 'Yes, the poor old Bishop could stand it no
longer.'

'Dead ?'

'No, no—only old, and nearly blind, and wholly deaf. He's
the sweetest and simplest old gentleman that ever lived. He

E E

takes me for an aristocratic Whig, and thinks I'm the deepest fellow in the ministry, because I keep his accounts square and rattle up the builders for him; and so, he has applied for an Assistant Bishop, with right of succession, naming me, and there's news from the Propaganda this morning that my name is approved of and the Brief on its way. So look alive, old man— good people are scarce—we're not going to let old friends die in this diocese without a special licence from the Assistant Bishop. Father Phil may order a new hat and learn to cut up a turkey as soon as he likes, for the first old parish priest full of years and honours that takes his honours and himself off to heaven, we'll run Father Phil in, if it takes wild horses to drag him. And lookee, sirrah,' he said, turning to Ken, and chucking him in the old hearty way under the chin, 'don't you go telling in this new organ of the devil that I hear you're setting fire to the country with—don't you go telling the public that you've heard the new Assistant Bishop sing "Who fears to speak of '98," and that his ex-pelling Jack Harold from St. Fergal's was all rank hypocrisy. You see, Ken,' he added more confidentially, ''twas Jack's expulsion that finished my reputation, and clinched the affair of the Bishopric; and, though I'll have to try still whether I can't preach the madness out of your young brain, you might go further and fare worse. How would you have liked Monsignor McGrudder for a Bishop? Ah! Myles, you old sinner, I observe that you enjoy the villany of us ecclesiastics more than you'd enjoy a dose of divinity or a dose of physic! Well, well, old friend, I forgive you everything except spoiling my fine plot to-day.' And in truth Myles looked so bright at the moment, it looked as if he might spoil the plot of the other Doctor as well.

'If he only knew how *my* little plot has been spoiled!' sighed Miss Westropp, as Katie and she stood whispering apart. 'I had everything so beautifully arranged to play the good fairy, and here I arrive, first to find that I'm too late, and then to find that, even if I were not, a stronger good fairy, and a better good fairy, has cut me out.'

'What can you mean? and what is that paper you have never once dropped from your hand? You *will* tell me, wont you?'

'Oh dear, I had forgotten,' she cried, looking at the document as one looks at a love-letter that has lost its spell; 'what chance has it now against the Doctor's bag of sovereigns? Perhaps it would be resented as a grace coming from an enemy.'

'Oh, Miss Westropp!' exclaimed Katie, completing her speech by taking the other's hand fondly, and kissing it before its owner could know the use it was to be put to.

'Exactly -Miss Westropp, the landlord's daughter – not Mabel, Katie's friend. Yes, yes, dear—it's selfish of me to say so, and it's not true either,' and the two girls exchanged the kiss of peace in true girl fashion ; 'and I'll tell you what 'tis all about, and it is not much of a plot after all. You must know that papa is not a hard, cruel man at all—he is the dearest old pappy in the world—at least, I know he is to me. But he does not know things. He is away so long, and figures so worry his poor head, and he has so much to trouble him—indeed, indeed, he has.'

'Yes, dear,' said Katie, with a sigh. In all departments of truth she could hold her own. 'But isn't it so much the better ? Which of us would be good, if there was not something to suffer ?'

'You little humbug, I do believe you would be good among a legion of evil sprits, and you would be more than a match for them too.'

'Don't ! please, Miss—Mabel,' said Katie, scarlet with the feeling that she had done something to attract notice to herself. ' But about your story ?'

'Well, I found papa in one of his good moments this afternoon, and I explained matters a little to him about the Mill, and about the whole of you, and he despatched a messenger straight to Mr. Hans Harman for the writ that was to be executed to-morrow, and—here it is,' she whispered softly, grasping the official blue document in her hand, this time as though it was a caged wild animal which might escape.

Katie was a person so little learned in the law that she looked as if she did not yet quite understand.

'Well, of course, I flew here with the expectation of giving you all a greater surprise than the Sheriff, but a pleasanter one, and I find that I am late, and that I am useless, and that there is nothing to be done except this '--she tipped the writ quietly into the fire, and stood in front of the blaze until she saw the last shred of Myles Rohan's debt to Lord Drumshaughlin vanish up the chimney.

Katie stood stupefied for a moment. 'Oh, Mabel,' she cried then, 'I must tell ! You have done a thing that will give him more joy than if you had filled the room with gold.'

So that upon the whole, though he never told the secret, one may suspect that Myles Rohan, paralysed and voiceless, and with nothing but a wistful smile to give the key to the depths of his dumb soul, was a happier man on his bed of pain than thousands without bodily ailment who tossed under eiderdown counterpanes in golden palaces that night.

Danny Delea was in the Glen at the first peep of dawn, and

he lifted the sluice-gates once more, as if the current that he
sent gushing through the mill-race were blood transferred into
exhausted veins, and he set the old mill-wheel a-rolling with the
wondering reverence of a man assisting at a resurrection of the
dead. And he humbly took credit to himself for his prescience,
seeing that, if the Fleet had not arrived, something equally
wonderful had.

CHAPTER THE THIRTY-THIRD.

'TRAMP, TRAMP, TRAMP, THE BOYS ARE MARCHING!'

A TAPPING at his window aroused Ken Rohan from sleep. It had
been the eighth night since the General's appearance at the Tower,
and it was not difficult, you may be sure, to awaken our young
friend from dreams of which the scenery was battlefields and the
accompanying music cannon shots. A dark figure loomed up
against the faint pearly light. He recognised Con Lehane, and
instantly threw up the window. It was a November dawn of a
splendour that sometimes in this mild clime seems to be kept in
celestial stock all the year round :—the sun just breaking his
golden way through bars of violet cloud, like a young exiled prince
coming to his throne ; and all his skyey dominions in the east
strown in his bosom with primrose light, whose morning purity
was not yet stained with the garish shameless excess of golden
flattery, which attends suns and monarchs in the noonday of their
reigns. Con, though his tossed air and mud-splashed clothes were
those of a man who had spent the night afoot, nevertheless looked
quite a gay herald of the morning, and his face shone like the sun
as he whispered :
  'She's come !'
  A great throb of joy, such as men only feel at a few rare
moments in life—some at reading a prosy paragraph in the *Gazette,*
some on hearing the first trembling confession of a maiden's love
—passed through young Rohan's body and soul. If 'she' was,
indeed, the Banshee of whom Myles Rohan once said his son was
enamoured, assuredly being in love with a Banshee has its ecstasies
for young hearts just as real as though the heaving white bosom,
and sad, sad eyes of the Irish Rosaleen had a kingdom instead
of a gallows to reward her lovers withal. He darted at the note
which Con Lehane extracted (of all places in the world) from the
muzzle of his revolver and extended to him. The note read as
follows :
  'They are in Cooiloch Bay. Pass the word for to-night at ten

in Coomhóla Glen.   Yourself I want to join us on board as soon
after nightfall as possible.   Con will direct you where and how.
All will be in readiness for landing, and we will be upon them in
Bantry by daybreak.   You know the pass-word : Mike.'

'And so they've really come, Con ?   And you've seen them ?'

'As large as life, and that's large enough—every man of them
as big and as tanned as the Captain.'

'It's grand !' cried Ken Rohan, in a burst of joy.   He could
scarcely realise that he was not dreaming.   That the fleet, or at
least the first flagship of the fleet, of Ireland's deliverers from
across the ocean should be actually at anchor a few miles away—
long as he had dreamed of it and counted on it—seemed as much
too good to be true as that other scarcely wilder dream of O'Don-
nell's magic Horse asleep under Ryal Aileach those three hundred
years back, suddenly starting to life with their armour braced,
and their horses ready-saddled, at the long-awaited signal of
Ireland's deliverance.   'It's simply grand !'

'Grand is no name for it !   There *is* no name for it—its name
is Bullets !' said Con, in a voice of deep content.   'I must be
trudging.'

'But the Captain tells me you are to be my guide.'

'I have arranged it all.   There will be a pony waiting for you
at five o'clock under the trees at the bridge of Trafrask.   Patsy
Driscoll will have the lugger lying under the pier at Ballycrovane,
and will put you on board.   I am on my way to Bantry with
despatches for the General, and to give the sojers the word.
Dawley will be at your service to warn the Glens.'

'I do not like Dawley,' said Ken, with a frown, almost to
himself.   'I don't know how it is.'

'Dawley is a noisy little bantam cock ; but he's Sub-centre.
We cannot pass him over.   That's Democracy, Master Ken,' said
.the brawny stonemason, with a twinkle of drollery in his honest
·grey eye, as he recalled little Dawley's previous insistence on the
Rights of Man.

'I wish Democracy would give us a few more comrades like
you, Con, and a few less like Dawley—Democracy would be a
more comfortable religion.   Good-bye ; when we meet again it
will be for hotter work.'

'Glory !' says Con Lehane, hugging the proffered hand, and
vanishing.

Further sleep was out of the question.   The young man
threw on his clothes, in a state of high exhilaration.   Happening
to glance at himself in the glass, an odd thought struck him.
Where was the gay uniform that had formed so conspicuous a
feature of his dreams of the hour of action !   Such are the

points in which young idealists first recognise the chill of dis-
enchantment. Here was a young fellow, casting his life against
all the gold and steel of England's strength, and counting the
odds not at all, or counting them only to feel a more seductive
thrill of danger, but disappointed and depressed because death
was not to be fronted in the precise tight-fitting tunic and gay braids
which had flashed over his imaginary fields of fame. Not that it
was all a mere tailoring question between a youthful gallant
and his looking-glass. Harold's light prophecy, that the only
uniform the Irish Republic would ever afford its army would be
one of convict's-grey, hovered coldly round him, and set him
pondering gloomily, remorsefully, upon themes that the trumpet's
shrillest note never quite silences, even in youth's whirling heyday—thoughts of opportunities neglected, obligations evaded,
affection unrequited, a vain and headlong past, a future lit by
wild flashes only less perilous than the darksome background. He
found his eyes drawn towards the window, where the night-light
still sicklily inflaming the closed blind told where his father was
lying and his mother watching ; and a sob of penitence shook
him at thought of how he had already lacerated these loving
hearts, and of the more cruel wound that now awaited them. It
was not until a light hand was laid on his shoulder, and a
whisper, 'I am so glad you are up,' reached his ear, that he
turned, and saw Katie, looking very white.

'Why, sis, what's this ? What's up ?'

'You are in danger,' she said, the words coming from her lips
firmly, but with a hollow ring, as from one standing on a scaffold.
'There is not a moment to be lost. At nine o'clock you are to be
arrested.'

'And pray, how did you find out all this, you little wizard ?'

'It is no joke. It is certain. My informant is one who
knows. She risked a good deal this morning to come to warn
you.'

'She ! Then it's a lady ! You little frightened sphinx, don't
be putting those romantic conundrums to me ; tell me, who
is it ?'

'That is her secret.' Katie did not feel herself free to mention
that she also had had her visitor tapping at her chamber window
at the dawn, and she was somehow glad that she had been bound
not to tell Ken that when the hood of her visitor's peasant cloak
was tremblingly thrown back, the face underneath was the face of
Lily Dargan, the blush-rosy cheeks all whited over, the night-
dews clinging to her hair, and her large blue eyes for once filled
with a very decided expression—that of terror. It was the only
feat of daring of her life. She had heard her husband completing

with the Head Constable the arrangements for young Rohan's arrest ; and all the night through (Mr. Flibbert having arranged to sleep at the barracks in Drumshaughlin in order to be early on the spot) she walked up and down her lonesome room at The Roses, her little heart beating against its bars in the throes of a fearful determination, her thoughts flitting all in a tremble from spring-coloured hours in the Glen, long ago, to that fearful night in the Convent garden, and then to half-felt, half-rejected memories of words and looks on a certain recent summer's day at the Lady's Seat, and of certain still more recent hours of aching dreariness. Then she shook those half-formed fancies from her, as though they were serpents trying to sting her, and strove to persuade herself that it was Mrs. Rohan's bursting heart, and Katie's straining eyes, as they gazed on the vacant chair at the fireside, that she was thinking of ; and then those old words and looks came whispering and peeping back, and the poor child, unable any longer to cope with herself or with the world, flung herself on her knees as the most wretched of sinners and the most guilty of womankind. Of the guilt we may have our doubts, but of the womankind there can be none, for, of course, she rose from her knees to throw on the peasant's cloak, and to slip out at the hall-door, amidst the terrors of a burglar with an unmuzzled bulldog at his heels, and to fly over the hills to Katie's bedroom at the mill, in the dark shuddering hours before dawn, all the way glancing to right and left out of her terrified eyes, as if the mountain peaks were about to fall on her, and as if the sun stealthily creeping up behind Cobdhuv were a detective officer about to turn on the glare of his lantern upon her guilty track. For some reason or other, Katie Rohan was hardly more grateful to Mr. Flibbert's wife for her warning than for laying upon her the obligation not to let Ken know where it came from.   'That's her secret,' she said, decisively.

'I think I know !' he cried, his blood seeming to change to a celestial fire and the earth to fly from under his feet as he mounted to the very morning skies for startled joy.   Young persons will, no doubt, conclude that his thoughts reverted to the *ange aux grands yeux bleus* of his College days as his Guardian Angel—that some lingering ray of the old love gave him a glimpse of the slender shrinking figure stumbling over the wild hills in the darkness to save him.   But, as a matter of fact, when the image of the Sub-Inspector's wife occurred to him, it was to be instantly dismissed with impatience.   He could think of but one figure, one pair of angel-blue eyes, one deliverer from whom the warning would be worth having.   It was another fairy-gift of the bright creature who had put the writ for possession of the Mill into the office fire. Lord Drumshaughlin, as Lord Lieutenant of the county, had doubtless been made aware of the Government's plans, and she had charmed him out of his secret as she had charmed him out of his writ. 'Yes, it's she! There can be only one "she" in the world,' he soliloquised, 'millions of miles up among the songs of the morning stars.'

'Do you think so?' said Katie, not knowing well what to make of his raptures. 'Come, that does not matter. What is to be done? Where are you to fly to?'

'Don't trouble about that. It is all settled. I will not have to fly far nor to remain away long, sis.'

'Not remain away long! What *can* you mean?'

'That, sis, is *my* secret,' he said, laughingly.

'You know best, Ken. Whatever you do will be right and brave,' she said, her white lips still as firm as those of true women always are in cases of real emergency. 'Only do make haste. Your breakfast will be ready in five minutes.'

There was but one place where he could pass his last five minutes at home. The night-light was still burning dimly in the darkened room; but the daylight had by this time pierced the blinds, and searched out with its pallid light two faces wan with that unearthly grey lustre which towards morning touches features worn by long sleeplessness. Both his father and mother were asleep: the sturdy miller composed into a deep tranquil slumber, which, but for the laboured breathing, was rigid and waxen enough for death; Mrs. Rohan fallen asleep in the easy chair by the bedside, with one hand still wandering anxiously over the bed, as though reluctant to abandon its watch. Myles Rohan had been several days before moved into his old room, and all its old associations restored, even to the tiny red lamp burning before the spangled statue of the Blessed Virgin. The solemnity of the place, the twilight mystery, the glimmering lamp, the ancient black mahogany bedstead like a catafalque, with the grey body fixedly extended on it, impressed young Rohan at the moment, and for many a subsequent day and year, with the feeling of assisting at a Mass for the Dead in a crypt. It was with an irresistible sensation of awe he bent down and kissed his father's brave honest brow, which to his lips felt like cold yellow marble. It was as if somebody unseen were waiting behind him with the lid of the coffin to close it. He dared not kiss his mother's wasted face for fear of waking her. She had not slept until now since the evening Myles received his stroke, and, besides, he shrank from the agony of a parting scene with her. He pressed his lips reverently, as though he were touching the relics of a Saint, upon the delicate white hand, over whose pure field of snow the blue veins were defined almost too clearly. At the same moment he softly drew from one of her fingers a worn old-fashioned twisted hoop of gold. It was a ring of her own mother's, which she had often told him would be her gift to his bride upon his wedding day. This, somehow, seemed to Ken to be in a manner his wedding day. She quivered at the touch of his lips, and murmured : 'My son !—my heart !' He started back in terror, but she did not move again—the fatigues of the last seven sleepless nights had been too much for her. He sank on his knees by the bedside ; and now again the idea of the Dead Mass came powerfully back upon him, and his breast heaved and shook with sobs which it took him all his strength to keep from adding their passionate *De Profundis* chant to the illusion.

'Come !' whispered a voice behind him. 'It is better as it is ;' and he felt himself drawn with gentle violence out of the room to a room of fragrant tea and glowing ham and eggs ; and that businesslike mite, Katie, directed the eating of the breakfast as well as the preparation of it, and never once gave token of the avalanche of despair and woe that she saw all the time coming down upon her head, until brother and sister were parting in the little glass portico beside the rotting bones of the dead fuchsia-tree. Then, as she clung to his neck tremulously for a moment, she only said : 'Oh, Ken !' and said the rest in her own room in heartcries that it is not well to hear.

He stopped for a short time at the Mill to entrust certain messages touching the gathering in Coomhōla to Danny, who danced around him on the lame leg with incredulous joy at the news, and with every pirouette cried, 'Say it again, my darling child !' until it began to be a question whether he might not go on 'saying it again' until his darling child should be in the hands of the police. Danny Delea could not have been a happier man if the ship in Cooiloch Bay were a treasure-ship laden up to the hatches with gold pieces bequeathed to himself by some trans-atlantic billionaire. Young Rohan looked at his watch. It was already half-past eight o'clock, and nine was the hour named for the arrest. He plunged into the Glen behind the Mill, and his foot was soon crunching the dead leaves and decomposing brambles of the woods upon the mountain slope. The old sense of exhila-ration at getting higher in the pure air filled his lungs and seemed to give wings to his feet. Once he turned at a point where a mossy rock hanging over a torrent gave him a last look at the Mill. There was the thin white smoke of the dwelling-house curling up as peacefully as if the household below had no other care than to breathe out blessings, and there was the tawny water-wheel drowsing along as though the world had no livelier business than to listen to its ancient tale. But he started as his eye travelled farther. The stretch of roadway leading from the furthest outpost of the town to the Mill at Greenane was heavily shaded with trees except at one spot where it crossed a bridge over the millstream. This glaring space of white was now blackened with a long thin moving column, punctuated with points of steel. Then the warning was well founded, and he was not a moment too soon! He disappeared again into the tangle of firs and naked larches—this time with a more inspiriting sense of danger overcome, of glorious adventures opening; above all, with the haunting, intoxicating thought of where the warning came from. He could think of nothing else. All beside he had left behind him, as a commander evacuates a fortress to which he will presently return with gun and trumpet. But that Guardian Angel thought was to accompany him, to inspire him, to be his heavenly food of hope, to be his very star and prize of victory. That old vague vision of a resplendent form of Liberty beckoning him to the heights was more clearly visible than ever to-day, but it had taken definite shape : it shone with wildly tender human eyes ; it seemed to murmur a hope which he did not dare to hear —which gave him the sensation of desiring to throw himself down with his face to the earth in worship. His winged feet sped along. His old passion for meeting obstructions for the pleasure of conquering them was amply gratified to-day. The mountain watercourses were charged with dark-brown waters, hissing and gurgling around every rocky obstacle, tugging viciously at roots of ash-trees and tufts of heather, and then bursting down headlong, panting to engulf something ; the rock lichens were as slippery as ice ; every plateau or hollow was a quaking mass of sodden turf-mould, hardly to be distinguished from the pits of blackish bog-water that yawned here and there. But he sprang over the angry torrents, he clambered from rock to rock, he jumped in and out among the treacherous bog-pits, as lightly as a bee skimming flowers. He was already miles away among the desolate recesses of the hills. For miles on every side tumbled hills and hollows of volcanic rocks of a funereal grey-and-black limestone, fissured and polished by the winds and rains of ages, and clotted with dismal pools like bowls of black blood ; a land of silence whenever the winds were not holding their mournful Witches' Sabbath ; a land of solitude where you would wonder how the heather itself came to dwell there and to expect a living, only that you wondered still more to see a shieling or two, like an eagle's nest, behind some precarious rocky battlement, as though even here the unfortunate wild peasant bird, after finding food for his young ravens, was not sure that he might not have to fight for the home of his nestlings.

There were already many hours to spare before the pony would be waiting beside the bridge below Eily's Glen, but he found himself already drifting in that direction, the stone wastes that stretched between the Hag's Hill and Hungry Mountain being the region where he was most secure from observation. It was one of those intensely still November days which are to the dying year what sleep is to a beautiful creature on her death-bed. The sun's gold track all but showed through as well as on the skirts of the flossy white clouds, which seemed to have the mission of subduing the steel-blue sky to a proper wintry tone without being in a hurry. The horizon on all sides was bounded by a band of thicker and more leaden clouds, which seemed to be just pausing for a heavy nap before proceeding to advance upon the grey-blue sun-suffused territory towards the meridian; and the deep stillness of the heavens communicated itself to the earth, where the hardy mountain cattle stood in a stupor like that of the clouds, and the fields and cabins in the valley below lay in an azure-grey soundless slumber. His aimless steps were beginning to be affected by the all-pervading lethargy when his ears caught the distant roar of the great waterfall. A few minutes after he could see the torrent itself where it dashed to its awful suicide from Eily's Rock. The sight fascinated him. Every line and detail of his first meeting with Miss Westropp at that spot -- every look, every word—flashed back upon his memory with the vividness of delirium. He found himself bounding thither; he was under the necessity of worshipping some visible thing, and what worthier of worship than the rock she had rested on? It was now as clear to himself, as it must be to the reader, that he was in love with Mabel Westropp; but even yet he did not dare, in his most roseate dreams, to picture herself and himself as a pair of mundane lovers, marrying and given in marriage, with mutual hands and lips made for mutual uses. Constantly though her gracious spirit had got interfused with his life of late—irresistibly though every ideal he worshipped—Country, Liberty, Literature, Love—beamed on him with her eyes, and glowed with the glow of her soft cheek—he had never once himself figured in that incomparable procession, but as a vassal worshipping the ground his queen trod on, as a slave repaid with one smile for a life of servitude, as a faithful troubadour destined to publish his mistress's praises to the ends of the earth for the mere joy of singing them. Never till this morning; but the mysterious message to which he owed his liberty had undoubtedly breathed some inexpressible hope, which he was forbidden to listen to, which it was an agony, though a very delicious one, even to think of, but which nevertheless would come whispering its aërial music, and

would set his heart throbbing with its divine smart.   Sometimes,
indeed, the thought that the warning might have been, after all,
only an act of ordinary benevolence, like the cancelling the writ
of eviction—perhaps prompted by no other motive but that of
saving his mother and sister from pain, or, at best, saving Harry's
comrade from destruction—would descend upon his dreams like
an eagle on a nest of doves.   But, if that were so, why should
she not have despatched Harry with the message instead of risking her father's anger by her secret expedition at peep-o'-day ?—
why, for that matter, should she have bound Katie to any secrecy
at all ?   And yet his heart sank as the eternal question loured
down upon him—what was he that heaven should visibly open
and catch him up into its courts of jasper and bright gold !

The hoarse death-groan of the cataract came nearer and louder.
He had to slide down the face of stony escarpments, holding on
by one clump of heather or arbutus branch or another, from the
higher regions of the mountain.   To one less versed in moun-
taineering, or with more leisure for estimating danger, the rate at
which he floundered down this giant's stairs on the brink of the
cataract would have been dizzying.   From where he was gripping
his roots or clefts in the rock the toy-like valley below showed
like a village in Liliput, and the steep mountain might have been
a Brobdingnagian monster, upon whose black bosom the waterfall
was a great gash through which his life-blood was pouring.   Lower
and lower he slided to the woody brink of the great pool in which
the broken waters from the higher reaches gathered for their great
leap.   How he remembered the very mountain ash-tree past which
he had sprung on the plateau, gun in hand, on the former day of
gold !   He grasped its stem again like an old friend.   Then he
staggered back, and put his hands to his eyes to see whether he
was really awake.   Miss Westropp was there before him !   His
eyes were perfectly trustworthy.   She was sitting in the very
same spot where he had first surprised her, and engaged in the
very same operation :—that is to say, she had a sketching-book on
her knees and a pencil in her hand, and her eyes were fixed worlds
away from the sketch-book and pencil.   He could scarcely even
yet believe it—love at nineteen can fling such glittering veils of
romantic mystery around the commonest coincidences.   His eyes
swam, and so did his brain.   He could hear the ticking of his
pulse as loudly as one hears the ticking of a watch in a sick-
chamber.   In starting back a branch of the ash-tree had come
away in his hand with a crash.   The gold lock which escaped
under her little mountain hat of dark green felt whisked suddenly
around, and they were facing one another—she on her feet, with
a white face and a little cry of alarm.

'A thousand pardons,' he said, advancing a step, as if fearing to see her fall ; but a certain look in her eye stopped him —a look rather of annoyance than of faintness. 'I—I seem to be always in need of your forgiveness,' he stammered. 'Who could have expected that I should find you here ?'

Her first look of annoyance passed away at sight of his genuine surprise. 'Oh, it is no harm,' she said, simply. 'I come here often. The glen is so beautiful, and that sad little story of Eily gives the place an interest.'

'I did not hope so soon to have the chance of thanking you — of telling you how proud I am to be your debtor,' he said, by an irresistible impulse.

She was perplexed, almost terrified, by the heat of gratitude that burned in his eyes. Doubtless, he was thinking of the writ of eviction. 'Don't, please !' she said, with a decisive little wave of her hand.

She was offended with his warmth, perhaps, or annoyed at having her secret found out, and desired to banish the subject ; but Ken Rohan was more convinced than ever that he had guessed aright. His eyes fell upon the sketch-book, which had fluttered to the ground in her confusion. 'How stupid of me ! You have been sketching Eily's Glen ?' he said, as he stooped for the open leaves. 'May I look?'

'No—pray, no !' she exclaimed, sharply, with a deep scarlet flush that might have been anger, or anger mixed with something else. She seized the book from his hands almost rudely. 'A mere fancy—and I was attending to it as little as usual.'

He was in a dream again. He could not feel the rock under him. The sketch was on the leaf upturned to him. In stooping for it, he could not help seeing it. That one glance had photographed every line of it in his soul for ever—it was a scarcely half-finished sketch of the scene in the legend. The figure of Eily had not been pencilled in ; it was represented only by a few vague curves ; but that of her lover was distinctly visible rising out of the cloudy spray underneath the rock. The spirit-like lineaments were delicately drawn ; but he could not help seeing that the features bore a resemblance which he could not even think of without fancying himself in a delirium. 'I would give all the world for another look at that sketch,' he said, without knowing what he was saying—almost without knowing that he was saying anything.

Again a proud light flashed from her eyes that made him sick with his audacity. She noted his contrite aspect, and, as if to thank him for it, said with a smile : 'It is the first time anybody has ever set a price upon my idle scrawls. They generally end by going over the brink, like Eily.'

He started, as if somebody had made a thrust to put himself over.

'No,' she said, still smiling, 'this one I will keep—at least till I finish it—if it is ever to be finished.'

It seemed to him as if the mountain was going around—as if the sun was dancing before his eyes. Every struggle of his to seem collected was a woful failure. 'I am glad that little story interested you,' he said, not daring to say anything less commonplace.

'Yes, and yet Eily was so wrong!—there are so many better things to be done in the world than rushing over a precipice into a lover's arms—so many more unselfish things.' She stood facing the ghostly steaming abyss of spray as if she was arguing earnestly against some spirit she saw in it. 'What is this cruel Love that robs the world for the benefit of one? Why should not the love of one human soul be rather a reason for loving all the rest as well?'

'I suppose because life is not long enough to love one soul sufficiently, when people really love,' he said, scarcely knowing whether he was addressed at all—'because the human heart is not capable of containing half the bliss of one such love.'

'Ah!' she said, with a smile, 'I was not thinking of the two who love, but of the millions who have nobody to love or to be loved by. But that is one of the subjects on which they tell me I am a bore. Will you think it very shocking if I tell you that I hate the very name of Love?' This, with a little stamp of the foot, which was all the more emphatic that she had just mentioned the name at least four times with a softness that, to young Rohan's ear, sounded like a note from a Canticle of the Seraphim. 'What is this?' she asked abruptly, pointing downwards over the Bay. 'I did not know that the Fleet was in the Bay. Why, they are only just arriving!'

His eyes followed hers over the waters of Berehaven. There were five or six great war-ships planted, like horrible sores, on the bosom of the great Bay, usually as undisturbed as a lake among the virgin forests of a Red Indian reserve. They had barely arrived, and were still spouting black steam from their funnels, like monsters out of breath. One or two had actually dropped their anchors; the others were drifting slowly to their appointed ground; tiny despatch-boats were shooting in and out among them. England's strength had hitherto been to him a vague bookish abstraction—a tradition of indeed later date than the labyrinth of Minotaur, but of not much more dreadful bearing on his actual life. His estimate of the forces to be counted with had been formed largely from little Mr. Flibbert's slender shanks, and from the infantry detachment at Bantry, who outbawled Captain Mike himself at a rebel chorus. The war-ships, for the first time, terrible as the tremendous shadow of Destiny in a Greek tragedy, overpowered him with the thought—what was a parcel of unarmed Irish peasant lads to do against these iron fortresses, with their mouths of fire—nay, against a power of which these were the mere scouts and outposts? That was only the anxiety of a moment—the keen, resolute eyes of the General, and the bronzed faces of a hundred thousand Irish veterans behind him, blotted out all other visions. But there was a suggestion of betrayal about the arrival of the ironclads in the Bay on this particular day of the Rising which went to his heart like cold lead, and oppressed him with the thought of the American ship in the roadstead at the other side of the promontory, only an hour's steam away, within the very jaws of these iron monsters. It might be too late at nightfall; the strangers must be warned at once.

'Good-day, Miss Westropp,' he said, raising his hat. 'Good-bye!'

She gave a startled look into his face, and instantly read the meaning of the three upright furrows between the eyebrows and the set muscles of the mouth. 'Something is wrong,' she said, very calmly, in an almost caressing voice. 'Tell me—trust me. I will not faint at all. You know I am your fellow-conspirator, and I have a right to know—a right, I mean,' she added, with downcast eyes, 'for Harry's sake.'

He paused a moment. 'Yes,' he said, 'it is better you should hear from me. And it is not your courage I am afraid of testing. I remember the verses about the Italian girl and her soldier of Liberty. Well—marching orders have come for Giulio, that is all,' he whispered, with a tender gaiety, looking down upon her, as if he were not quite sure, nevertheless, that a supporting arm might not be necessary.

She trembled violently, and became very white. She looked away towards the water to steady herself, and the great warships danced in her sight, as if they were demons preparing to spring upon her, breathing fire from their dark nostrils. She turned to young Rohan, and through her mist of tears she seemed to see only his spirit rising out of the deadly white vapour of the water-fall, as in her drawing. She even fancied she felt herself drawn under some compulsive spell to the brink of the fatal rock. But if Mabel Westropp's heart had the softness of a timid child's, the native pride that cuirassed it was of a temper fit for a heroine in one of Tasso's combats. 'Ah!' was all she said, or rather sighed, though she found the air choking her, and the dizzy thunder of the bottom of the cataract might have been rumbling within her own small head. For a moment only she lost self-control when her eyes caught sight again of the black unwieldy men-of-war, and as she murmured, shudderingly, 'Those horrid guns!' all her woman's terrors seemed to vibrate in the words.

Was it her courage or her weakness that most transported him? Transported he was, at all events, beyond anything that I could possibly get a grown public to credit of anybody, except a Professor of Provençal hyperbole, or the young rustic Celt of nineteen whom we are dealing with—so enamoured that he would have worshipped her for the word to cast himself into the vaporous abyss for her sake—so infatuated that he could imagine the officers of the Royal Squadron—if they could have seen and heard her—spiking 'those horrid guns' for fear of hurting her.

'Yes,' he said, for want of something he desired to say, 'they look formidable, don't they? And they are. But that is only one side of the picture. There are other men and other guns in Cooiloch Bay at this moment, with a different mission.'

She shuddered again. Then she said suddenly: 'Did you know that Harry was to leave for London in the morning to take up an appointment at the Cape?'

'Indeed!'

'Yes. The Chief Secretary has kindly procured him a command in a Colonial mounted regiment. He had all his arrangements made. He went down to the Mill last night—as I thought to tell you, and bid you good-bye. I have not spoken with him since. Poor boy, how this changes matters for him! To-morrow he would have been off!'

The anxious furrows came back over young Rohan's brows. 'Let him go,' he said with earnestness. 'Make him go!'

'Just as the men in Cooiloch Bay you have just spoken of are coming! This is your tribute of compassion for a woman. It is not your advice to a man. Oh, no,' she said, proudly, 'Harry will not choose a moment like this for deserting, depend upon it. And now I have one favour to ask of you : if he is to go, let it be with you. Why should I not say that I like to think of you and him and pray for you and him together?'

She extended her hand with the frankest sweet tenderness, and looked into his eyes without a tear in her own. Without in the least knowing what he did—knowing only that heaven was glowing around him—he knelt, and kissed the proffered little hand. He felt it tremble in his grasp, but it was not until he had a second time and a third time touched it with his burning lips that it was withdrawn.

'I did not mean that. But you are a privileged person

to-day—you are in danger,' she said, smiling sadly, as if to disguise the agitated colour with which her cheek was rosed over. 'Oh dear, what a sad country this is! I suppose it is nearly three hundred years now since the night this place became Eily's Rock?'

'Yes, but after all what a glorious old fight it is! These ships below are beginning to-day just where they began the day they opened fire on the Castle of Dunboy.'

'Perhaps to end ——'

'Not with a plunge from Eily's Rock, assuredly,' he said gaily. 'And if it end as Fergus ended,—why, Fergus is about the most enviable fellow in all Irish history, except,'—an uncontrollable impulse wrung it from him—'except myself, if, if—— Oh, Miss Westropp, can you understand how a man would face danger with a joyous heart and a charmed life, if he could only carry in his bosom your slightest token—your least whisper of hope.'

'I have given you my brother,' she said in a low voice, with downcast eyes. And so they parted.

She was spared the agony of devoting Harry to destruction, however—he had devoted himself. Mrs. Keyes put into her trembling hands, when she reached the Castle that afternoon, an ill-spelled pencil writing in a schoolboy scrawl, which she deciphered as follows :—'I have seene Katie. You no the rest. I am going to joyne Ken. Dont be fritened, Mab, you mussent cry. You were the onely one in the wurld that gave me fayre play—Quish and you. Goodby. HARRY.' When he went to the Mill, the previous evening, to bid farewell on his departure for South Africa, Harry happened to meet Katie Rohan feeding her favourite old green-plumed Russian duck outside the portico, and thereupon, in his simple, straightforward way, said :

'Katie—it's no harm my calling you Katie, is it, for this once?—I am going away. Is there any chance?' Then, seeing the poor child totter against the portico in terror : 'I know I frighten you. Why do you hate me, Katie? I love you more than I could tell if I had all my life to tell you. I would live for you, or die a thousand deaths for you. Try me.'

'Oh, hush,' she said, trembling violently all over, and crimson with confusion. 'Somebody will hear you. I don't hate you at all. I like you ever, ever so much—I think you are ever, ever so good, and I am sure you will find somebody good and beautiful that will love you, and love you tenderly. But I—Mr. Westropp, I thought your sister had told you—it is dreadful—it is sin for me to stand here and speak to you on such a subject. I should die if you ever mention it again.' She flew into the house, like a pet fawn that had suddenly seen a kennel of dogs unloosed at her.

F F

He turned away towards the solitude of the Glen without entering the house. 'I suppose,' he said to himself, as he plunged into the deepening shadows, 'a fellow can get killed in South Africa as well as anywhere else, but—it is such a long way off.' And when, after wandering aimlessly about the mountains all the night, he met Con Lehane on his mission to Bantry after daybreak, and heard the announcement of the Rising, he hailed it as a special message from Heaven for his convenience. When Ken Rohan reached Patsy Driscoll's yawl that evening, Harry was already there to welcome him.

In the meantime there hung over Drumshaughlin and the surrounding glens that mysterious silence which, among men, as in inanimate nature, is so often the presage of a storm. A Rising is (I may not yet quite say, used to be) a sort of Silver Jubilee in every generous Irish life. Young men look forward to their own Rising, and old men look back upon theirs ; and the whole population, non-combatant as well as combatant, feel some such tender interest in the event as the whole public, even those least addicted to matrimony, feel in a Breach of Promise of Marriage case. It did not require any official premonition to tell a sleuth-hound of Head-Constable Muldudden's experience that there was something ominous in the very stillness of the people. If the foibles of the great may be faithfully confessed, Head-Constable Muldudden's zeal had been much stimulated, and his spirits much raised, by the breakdown of Mr. Flibbert's Napoleonic strategic arrangements for the capture of Ken Rohan. His eagle eye early darted upon certain whispering conferences at street corners, and certain ponies making for the mountains in different directions, and certain peculiarly fiery appearances about the eyes and nose of Dawley, and a certain filtering procession of young men passing into the chapel throughout the day, and into Father Phil's confession-box and out again with happy lighting faces—from all of which, and many other symptoms, Mul-D., as he was playfully called in the dayroom, concluded, with swelling bosom and snuff taken in handfuls, that the Government's information was correct, and that the opportunity of his, Mul-D.'s, life had arrived.

As the evening wore on, Mat Murrin took furtive opportunities of embracing his various darlings on one lying pretext or another, and had serious thoughts of writing out his last testament and leaving it behind him, until he remarked that that was the only thing he had to leave behind except various bills of sale and paper obligations to the bank. And at last the moment came, in the back shop, for bidding farewell in state to Mrs. Murrin.

'You have always been a good wife to me, Aloysia. God bless you!' he said, in his finest manner, kissing her.

'Is this true, what I hear, Mat Murrin, that it's out in the Rising you're going?' asked Mrs. Murrin, with astonishing composure under the circumstances.

'Well, you know, Aloysia, we're all—in fact, I may say, bound to lend a hand, don't you observe? "England expects every man," etcetera—or, rather, not England—may the devil knock the nose off her! I beg your pardon for indulging in what may seem profane language, Aloysia, on the present occasion; but—ahem!—in point of fact, good-bye, old woman!' he said, bolting for the door.

'Mat,' she said, tenderly, 'I'd like to say a word to you, before you go away from me like that, and we can't speak to our liking here for fear the police would be in on us.'

'Certainly, Aloysia; why not upstairs, darling?' said Mat, who was no more deceived by the sweet tranquillity of the wife of his bosom than Head-Constable Mul-D. by the meek looks of the able-bodied penitents trooping into Father Phil's confessional. 'A blowing-up, of course, but we may as well have it over at once,' he said to himself gaily, mounting the stairs three at a bound. 'Here, Aloysia?' he proposed, pushing in the door of the drawing-room on the first floor.

'Higher,' she said; 'the people could hear us from the street.'

'By George, it's going to be a blizzard!' he cried, as he mounted another flight of stairs more nervously. 'This will do, at all events?' he said, throwing open the door of his bedroom, and walking in.

'That will do,' said sturdy Aloysia, flinging him forward with a force that sent him spinning to the further end of the room, slamming the door after her, and turning the key in the lock outside.

'Hallo! What is this? Aloysia, here, Aloysia, I say,' cried Mat, when his first stupefaction was over. 'What does this outrage mean?'

'It means that you'll stay where you are till 'tis safe to let you out,' was the tranquil response.

'I'll break the door. I'll break the furniture. I'll set fire to the house - as I'm a living man I will,' he said, delivering desperate kicks on the panel of the door.

'If you make any more noise I'll call in the police to you,' cried his wife, sternly. 'I will, as I'm a living woman, and that's as good an oath as your own.'

A cold perspiration broke out all over the editor; but, after a few desperate runs at the door, without succeeding in bringing it down at the critical moment, he laid down his arms at discretion. He applied his mouth cooingly to the empty key-hole. 'Well, but, Aloysia, dear, this is really ridiculous—it is in the highest degree absurd. Just only listen a moment to reason. My precious ——'

'Reason !' retorted the indignant voice outside. 'You propose to go out to fight the British Empire—you that couldn't walk to Mass with your corns—you that have a houseful of hungry children that God sent you to provide for—and *you* have the impudence to talk of reason, you miserable object !'

Mat threw up his hands in despair, and for a short while silently waited developments, like a deep old fox sitting on his tail. As soon as he judged that Mrs. Murrin must have departed he crept to the window. It was a back window, fully forty feet above the level of the ground. Desperate thoughts of tying the bedclothes in a rope occurred to him, but, when he looked into the blank abyss underneath, he dismissed these boy burglar's resources as inventions of the penny novelists. The only gleam of comfort he could see in the darkness came through a skylight in the printing-office, whose glass roof lay slightly to his right in the yard underneath the window. There was light in the printing-office, and the idea of arousing the Staff to the rescue of their Chief began to take possession of him. The situation was an ignominious one ; but a charge of cowardice was more ignominious still. The world knew what an unreasonable woman Mrs. Murrin was, and was not quite so well provided with evidence what a hero her husband was. He dropped a halfpenny quietly in the direction of the skylight. It was never heard of more. It probably found its grave in a cesspool close by. This time he determined to try a heavier and more reliable coin. He aimed a penny viciously at the skylight. It had scarcely left his hand when he heard the crash of glass in the roof of the printing-office, and heard at the same moment Noble Nolan's pious exclamation of astonishment : 'Oh, glory be to God !' He immediately thrust his body half out of the window, and began to shout in a heavy stage whisper, making a trumpet of his hands : 'Noble Nolan—Noble Nolan, I say ! Noble Nolan !' again.

'My God, sir, is it yourself ?' at last came the weak voice from below. 'Where, in the name of God, are you, and what is the matter ?'

'Here, at the second-floor bedroom window, locked in by that ridiculous woman. Come up, and terminate the tension of this intolerable situation,' he said, unconsciously lapsing into one of his own leading articles. 'Come up, and unlock the door, like a Christian man.'

'Hould on for a minute, sir,' said the voice, and for a short while there was a suspenseful silence, after which the voice was heard, more cautiously—'Are you there, sir?'

'I am ; but why the devil are you there and not here ?'

'Oh, begor, sir, I daren't. The missis is on the landing with the fire-shovel.'

'Noble Nolan,' roared Mat, like a general in the field, 'order up the Staff, and let them carry that landing by assault, if necessary ; do you hear—by assault? They have my authority I now issue it as an order to the Staff.'

'Begor, sir,' was the apologetic reply, 'every man and boy on the Staff is on his way to Coombōla this hour back. The whole country is out !'

'Well,' said Mat, after a few moments of wild recurrence to the rope-of-blankets idea, 'I'm pleased to know that the *Banner* is adequately represented, at all events. Noble Nolan, you can be of some slight assistance to me, without encountering Mrs. Murrin or the fire-iron. I have discovered a ball of twine here on the table—a ball of twine. Do you follow me ?'

'Indeed I do, sir,' said the gentle foreman, who had followed his master for many a year through graver intricacies than the ball of twine was likely to produce.

'Well,' proceeded Mat, 'the arrangements up here, if this outrage is to continue, are of a highly inadequate character—in short, I'm devilish thirsty, and I want a drink. Do you follow me ?'

'I think I do, sir,' came the answer, more diffidently than ever.

'Noble Nolan, you were always a decent fellow, though never a good judge of a glass of whisky yourself. Well, now, I want you to go across the street, to Mr Tummulty's public-house, with my compliments, for a bottle of his John Jameson of '38, and when I let fall the slight mode of communication the gods have devised for us in growing the hemp that made this ball of twine, you will, with your accustomed fidelity to the best interests of the *Banner*, affix the bottle securely to the end thereof, and I will myself perform the remainder of the enterprise. Do you observe ?'

'There is only one thing more, Noble Nolan,' he said, ten minutes afterwards, after triumphantly hauling in the refreshment. 'I wish you to convey to the boys my deep indignation that various causes over which I have no control—that, in fact, the conduct of a misguided woman—precludes me from having the pleasure of their society in Coombōla ; and you will, please, convey to the general in command my special wish that, on their capturing the town, their first operation shall be directed to the deliverance of Mat Murrin from this preposterous captivity.'

'Now,' he soliloquised, as he pulled out a pocket corkscrew and proceeded to open the bottle, 'perhaps, after all, trials like Aloysia are sometimes designed by a merciful Providence for a man's good. Next to bearing a hand in whatever is going in Coomhōla, this isn't altogether so bad of a cold night for a gentleman on the freezing side of forty.'

CHAPTER THE THIRTY-FOURTH.

THE AMERICAN SHIP.

MR. FROUDE, who loves Irish scenery with the same intensity with which he misreads Irish character, has lavished some of his finest art in pen-and-ink pictures of the beautiful promontory which divides Bantry Bay from Kenmare Bay. The backbone of twisted mountains lies along the whole length of the peninsula for thirty miles, like the skeleton of a fallen Titan, from which Dursey Island has got separated like a gigantic toe-joint. To the three chief peaks the poetic Irish gave the names of the Hill of Anger, the Hill of Battle, and the Hill of Weeping. Once a soldier of a surveying party benighted on the bleak top of the Hill of Anger (Cnocdhiad) jokingly remarked that it would be better christened the Hill of Hunger; and a prosy posterity has ever since seen on the brow of Cnocdhiad, not the storm-clouds of its Irish title, but the breakfastless private of Engineers, and has agreed to call it Hungry Hill. What a miniature portrait of the two nations! and how like the fate of that other romantic tapering peak over Glengariff, to which the dreamy Celt assigned the name of the Witches' Hill (Cnocnacalliagh) and some tourist in the wholesale grocery line that of the Sugarloaf!

Hastening from the Waterfall through the Wolves' Glen, Ken Rohan found his mountain pony at the appointed trysting-place near the bridge of Trafrask, and, leaving Bantry Bay behind him, faced for the steep mountain road which climbs straight over the shoulders of the Old Cow Mountain into Glanloch. The stillness of the atmosphere gave place to a subtle, chilly tremor, and as the pony dived deeper into the gloom of the mountains strange lurid tints began to shoot through the dense grey clouds. The short twilight had already set in, and if Ken had not traversed every mile of the mountains by night as well as by day on many a daybreak appointment with the grouse and cock, he might have been daunted by the darkening and apparently inextricable maze of heights and glens that was closing around him. The sun, which was going down behind the crooked back of Slieve Miskish, was still shimmering bravely through a tawny gold shower, and lit the strangest shades of peace and lurid red among the storm-clouds in the opposite side of the sky, like the reflection of some dull conflagration among the woody recesses of Glanmore. The beautiful glen could still be seen stretched away to the north-east in soft realms of limpid lake and evergreen woods and tenderly circling mountains, like a beautiful maiden in a camp of rough warrior men. On the horseman's left hand the small sister glen of Glanbeg—a still more charming, shrinking little rustic beauty —was sinking quite away into the gloom of the angry overhanging mountains between it and the dying sun. The suspenseful stillness of the air began to be broken by a low crooning sound, such as might be emitted by great lonesome mountains in pain. Ken knew the sound as familiarly as if it were part of a local code of signals. The road sank deeper into the long, wild ravine of Clugher, bordered on one side by the giant black escarpments of Hungry on its northern face, and on the other by great naked stone-coffin like piles of rocks, littering the whole bleak line of descent towards Cooiloch Bay, like some uncovered cemetery of dead sons of Anak. The sun's brief struggle behind Slieve Miskish was already over. A bright gold scroll of cloud gleamed out for a moment, epitaph-like, over its grave ; and then, like most florid epitaphs, was rubbed out by the heavy blood-shot thunderclouds that now in all directions began to pour in, rending one another for the dead sun's inheritance. Suddenly a short deafening thunder-smash resounded at Ken Rohan's ear, horrible enough, it seemed, to have cracked the gloomy jagged mass of mountain over his head. The crooning winds appeared to pause for a frightened moment or two to listen. Then the clouds burst, and the winds shrieked, and thunder crashed from height to height, and the road was swallowed up in a miserable black abyss, through which the lightning sported like an imp of darkness, and the whirling rain cut with icy whips, and a hundred waterfalls, suddenly swollen, dashed towards the roadway through the darkness with a remorseless hungry roar that was appalling. The ill-defined road-track was not visible for three yards in front ; every moment it seemed as if some ferocious torrent were coming to tear it away. An unaccustomed steed or horseman might well have quailed in the midst of so hopeless-looking and terrible an outlook. But the pony picked his business-like way through the inspissated gloom and storm, as though the winds and thunderclouds were old travelling companions with whom he had a working understanding not to interfere with one another's trade upon the road ; and Ken found in this grand orchestral war of the mountains an almost exhilarating dramatic overture to the great scenes that were beginning to rush red on his sight. The rain grew colder and more bitter until it changed to volleys of fierce hailstones, and then again into driving cataracts of icy liquid snow, when, yet again, the gale would sweep all before it, and so rage and bluster that the snow itself could scarcely find where to fall. And now to the awful diapason of the winds began to be added the deep answering roar of the ocean, where a speck of light from the lighthouse at Inishfarnard, now and again flickering out of the gloom, announced the neighbourhood of Cooiloch Bay. The gnome-like threatening masses of mountain impending over the pass of Clugher began to recede; the noise of breakers and their terrible white light mingled more and more with the shrieks and frozen breath of the storm on the defenceless stretches of the road as it wound down to the shore.

'Ho, there, stranger!—in the name of the Irish Republic, stand!'

Ken Rohan started violently. The challenge rang out a few feet in front of him, where the road doubled around a tremendous cromlech-like table of detached rock; and a thick-set figure loomed up at the pony's bridle.

'It's all right; the very man we were waiting for. Come along, Ken, old boy; all's ready; Patsy Driscoll's yawl is at the pier,' sang out the joyous voice of the Lord Harry. 'You can spare your bullet for birds of another feather; we'll have flocks of them on the wing around us by-and-by,' he said to his burly companion at the pony's head.

'That's so,' said the other, leisurely lowering a rifle which he had at his shoulder. 'Stranger, my respects, sir; allow an old Grand Army man to shake your hand; glad I had not the honour of shooting you. Pass!' Ken Rohan could distinguish dimly a thick horseshoe moustache and swarthy face under a soft slouched hat.

Harry was in riotous spirits, and full of the news, as they floundered along towards the pier through the storm. The coast-guard station was taken. A boat-load of armed men from the ship landed at daybreak, and took back the four coastguards as prisoners. The only wire to the place was cut; and the 'Garryowen,' as the American ship was called, was as secluded from observation in Cooiloch Bay as if enveloped in a coat of darkness. The coastguard station was held by an armed party, of whom he of the slouched hat and ready rifle was one of the outposts. The whole roadway towards the shore was blocked with country carts. These had been pouring in all day to serve for the transport of the arms. The landing was to begin at once, if this unlucky gale did not delay matters.

'They're devilish fine fellows—as hardy as cannon-balls, every man of them !' roared Harry, in high delight, through the grinding music of the storm. 'Such heaps of breechloaders, and a couple of lovely little field-pieces—artillery, fancy ! Captain Mike is in grand fettle. Ken, old boy, we're going to have a glorious ruction of it this time ! Is that Patsy ? All right, boy—bring her head round a bit—nearer to the stairs, confound it!--now for the jump, Ken—hurrah !—let her go, Patsy, and keep her head for Inishfarnard—give me the bow oar—and now, boys, row for it like the devil.'

Off rolled the yawl into darksome, shifting, blinding abysses, where the spray from below and the icy deluge from above mingled in one indistinguishable chaos, rocking with the waves, and blown madly about by the winds. The oars alone were practicable, and Patsy Driscoll's yawl was better accustomed to use its wings than its lumbering oars ; but the gale was blowing off shore, and Patsy Driscoll could almost have trusted his little 'Mary Anne' to find her way if the breakers had rolled clean over Inishfarnard lighthouse and its glimmering beacon, and everybody in the boat knew how to handle an oar, and everybody's veins were so pulsing with high spirits that each roar of the gale and each white monster of a sea that smashed in impotent white rage on their stern was received with a chorus of jubilee in the wild musical Gaelic whoop of the crew of the 'Mary Anne.'

'Here she is!—back there !—ship that confounded oar of yours, Soolivan—now, then, show a light, if you don't want a shower of bullets round our ears. Ahoy, there !—all right, Captain—·it's the "Mary Anne" ! ' It was marvellous to note how the first clash of action and of danger roused the born soldier in Ralph Westropp's son. It was the happiest night of his life.

The 'Garryowen'—a sharp, low-built, workmanlike Yankee vessel, with bare foremast and mizenmast concentrated almost at her middle—was riding with an open hawser towards the wind, under cover of a sweep of headland at the north-east corner of Cooiloch Bay, with a steadiness which she owed to the fact that she was loaded with arms and cartridges up to her floor-heads. A skipper, who might have sat for the portrait of Uncle Sam – slim build, lank cheeks, peaked goatee, laconic speech, leisurely drawl, and all—was standing by the bulwarks as Ken Rohan and Harry clambered on board from the tipsy little yawl.

'Yes, sir, rough –a few,' he said, as Harry shook himself like a blithe water-dog. ' Unless you can slow down that gale purty shortly guess we'll have to jump this town.'

'Nary jump—see you in the huckleberry country fust, Captain Slapper—not till we've made the British lion do some jumping fust, anyhow,' rolled out Captain Mike's melodious voice, as he embraced Ken Rohan like an immense black bear taking him into his hug. 'Gen'lemen, you're welcome; Ken Rohan, sir, this gale is something worth advertising as a world-renowned Face Bleach! Couldn't get up a bigger thing in the States, with all our blizzard-power and extent of territory—no, sir! Come along and know the boys. Accommodation limited, gen'lemen, but welcome more extensive than a Board of Alderman's boodle. Brothers of the Army of the Irish Republic,' said the Captain, with a grandiose sweep of his wideawake hat, 'the first out-post of the Irish fighting line greets the first flight of Amurrican Birds of Freedom.'

Ken was surrounded by groups of bronzed, stalwart figures; his hands grasped with a magnetic silent clutch; fiery, dark eyes flashing out on all sides of him from the dusky faces of armed men in heavy military cloaks. His heart bounded with delight. If iron men with glowing hearts like these were to be his comrades in the fight for Ireland, who could help feeling the wine of battle mount to his head? and what young head effervescing with such a vintage could pause to count the chances? The strangers were most of them officers of some rank; most of them also taciturn men, who spoke chiefly with their eyes—deep, kindly Irish eyes, however, in which passionate feeling was only subdued by discipline, as men obey the whisper: 'Silence in the ranks.' The cabin was an indescribable litter of supper, bottles, arms, and accountrements; some men were cutting up the last slices of fresh mountain mutton and fowls and hams obtained from the shore during the day, and washing them down with grog; others buckling on their belts, or making the chambers of their revolvers gyrate; one or two fine young fellows in quiet corners, kissing the lock of hair or the Agnus Dei which some trembling girl or fond old mother far away had pressed round the neck of her darling in the last clinging moments of their partings; others were exchanging sad or laughing reminiscences of the pattern, or the eviction, or the old Abbey, or the Tithe battle, long, long ago, in Ireland, or of some wild brush with Morgan's horse in the brave days of 'Marching to Georgia'—all set to an exhilaratory accompaniment of rattling plates and popping bottles, rollicking laughter, the clanging of swords, the rolling of the vessel, and the mad shrieks and outbreaks of the storm.

'Ken Rohan, the Boys have brought me a bit of news which I may briefly describe as candy-canes, sir,' said the Captain, as he filled for the Lord Harry a moderate measure of grog. 'Our State Treasurer's had a shortage in his accounts—a steal of eighty thousand dollars or thereabouts; he has made a bee line for Montreal, sir, to enjoy the tobogganing a bit. What do the Boys do, but nominate me for State Treasurer by a rising vote? and, gen'lemen, here on board were de-le-gated by the citizens to inform me that a plurality for me is an ironclad certainty at the ballot, if I will only return at once to fix things up a bit with the workers. You see, a little judicious jury-plugging has got to be done in our country, if you want a square verdict. Nobody agen me but some blamed young Copperhead geloot in a buttercracker hat and with no more brains than a yallow dog. So the Boys are de-le-gated to report—I've only to take ship to Worcester, Mass., right away to get on to the swing :—But no, sir !—I guess we've got to go through with this job of twisting the tail of the British Lion fust ! Handsome an arrangement of Providence as was that shortage in Treasurer Liebermann's accounts, it ain't as tempting as a dash on Bantry to-night for Mike MacCarthy, of Coomhōla. There's a big bundle of shekels in that State Treasurership ; but I guess they'll have to bore in with a longer gimlet before they finds a weaker spot in this 'ere ould shot-proof heart than you'll strike whenever there's a job of fighting anywhere around for Ireland. No, sir, my answer to the offer of the citizens—conveyed to me, I must say, in the most flattering and elegant manner by the de-le-gation— my answer,' said Captain Mike, raising his tumbler, and bursting into a song—'my must be, in the words of the poet :

> " Here's dear ould Ireland !
> Brave ould Ireland !
> Ireland, boys—hurrah ! " '

The example was contagious. The bronzed soldiers caught up glasses, and clinked them, and with kindling eyes and lusty throats echoed Mr. T. D. Sullivan's ringing chorus. As the chorus died away, a hoarse shout was heard through the storm from the bridge overhead :

' Boat ahoy ! '

' It's from the General ! It's the order to land !' men shouted all around the table ; and these brawny soldiers, dusky with the smoke of a hundred battlefields, shook and almost sobbed with emotion, as they burst once more into the chorus :

> ' God bless ould Ireland !
> Dear ould Ireland !
> Ireland, boys—hurrah !'

until the very storm seemed to blend in a wild rendering of the soldiers' song.

The last notes had not yet died away when a stern figure in a thick military cloak stood at the foot of the companion-ladder, surveying the choristers with a hard unsympathetic eye. There was a sudden silence. The officers laid down their glasses somewhat awkwardly.

'The General!' exclaimed several voices in a hushed sort of way.

'Gentlemen, this is not a night for revelry. I will ask you to take your seats,' the General said, with a frigid bow, throwing off his dripping cloak, and taking a seat at the head of the table. 'Colonel O'Moran, kindly ask the Skipper to step down.' The officers were now seated, or stood grouped around their commander, leaning on their swords. A singular chill overspead them. Captain Mike himself assumed a grave and business-like air. Uncle Sam's goatee was no sooner seen in the doorway than the General proceeded calmly: 'Captain Silas, if you have more than one anchor down, the sooner you haul up the better.'

'No, sir—only a slip-rope; and I guess not much left of that same if this gale don't quit its bluster,' was Uncle Sam's matter-of-fact reply.

'Then stand by to cut every damned thing, and run out to sea,' said the General, briefly.

'Bully!' said Uncle Sam, disappearing without another word.

'Gentlemen,' he said to his astounded officers, 'I've been through Ireland, right through, and my conclusion is—the only thing we've got to do for this country is to clear out of it, straight away.'

A low rumble of rebellion was heard here and there around the table. The General threw a rapid glance towards the corner where the growl was deepest, and, in his decisive unconcerned way, proceeded:

'If you had been through the country, gentlemen, I should have asked your advice before coming to a decision; but you cannot know what I know—your advice would be uninformed advice; and, as for the people in command on shore'—with a slight, scornful nod—'their opinion upon a military matter is worth that of spring-chickens as to how necks are to be twisted. A week ago, if they had their heads fixed on like men, they might have had half the country in a night. The Pigeon House Fort, Cork Barracks, Clonmel, Fermoy, and Bantry Barracks were all swarming with soldiers ready to hand up the keys and their guns to the first man of grit who came to ask for them. The militia regiments were in training—twenty thousand rebel soldiers, ready-made, rifles and all. The constabulary posts could have been chawed up piecemeal. There was not a day to be lost. If they would give me but five hundred men with guns in their hands, I proposed to organise four simultaneous outbreaks of the four Cork militia regiments, cut up the railways and telegraphs, march upon Cork that night—the City of Cork Militia held one of the forts, and a red-hot Irish regiment furnished the mainguard at the Barracks. With Cork in our grip, Bantry was ours for the asking, or yours for the taking ; your cargo once landed, and your officers distributed, we would have had fifty thousand men in arms in Munster alone—men who hadn't a continent behind them to run away in, like our fellows at Bull Run. We had only to win some one decent engagement with the Britishers, and the heart of America would blaze with gratitude to us for paying off her Alabama claims. I tell you the first gun fired at Fort Sumter did not wake a bigger echo through the States than if the news once flashed across that a victorious Irish army held Cork city, with the flag that floated over Slidell and Mason under their feet. The States would be to our fight what Liverpool was to the Rebels—our arsenal, our base of supplies for privateers and men and money—our raiding-ground across the Canadian frontier. If once the men who carried Gettysburg were thundering at the doors of "Dublin Castle"—don't tell me that with a couple of millions of disbanded soldiers, our old comrades, panting to be even with England for all her open hostilities and secret hate, America could resist the war-fever— she'd have been into it as sure as she went into Georgia, and we would have heard "Yankee Doodle" the day we entered Dublin, as we did the day we entered Richmond.'

'If so last week, why not to-night?' impetuously broke in a young officer, with a pair of burning dark eyes and a heavy sabre-cut across his cheek.

'No, sir—because what would have been a piece of daring soldiership then, and nothing more, would be a piece of criminal idiotcy now. Your civilian conspirators make eyes at England enough for a dime theatre ; but they are incredible idiots when it comes to business. They lay down a plan of campaign for you in a leading article, and expect you to carry it out with pikeheads of the last century, while they themselves bawl for the police and get locked up. Pheugh all that I have seen of that for the past week ! While they were humming and hawing about giving me my orders, some scoundrel—the only practical man of the crowd—sold my idea to the Castle people ; the disaffected regiments were packed off in a single night to India or to England, the militia regiments disembodied, the Channel Fleet ordered round to Bantry Bay, the civilian conspirators sent flying in picturesque attitudes, the pivot men all through the country whisked into jail in scores and hundreds, and I myself obliged to employ more strategy in being here to-night to prevent a landing than would have given us Cork City and fifty thousand men in arms a week ago.'

A deep growl of anger and betrayal broke from the soldiers.

'Then this idea of a Rising to-night is given over!' asked one of the calmest of them—Colonel O'Moran.

'By everybody who knows the stock from the muzzle of a rifle, yes; but these poet-gentlemen in the Fra Diavolo cloaks must have a romantic scene or two with stage shots and blue-fire before they will let down the curtain. They will have the Rising to go on; they have proclamations and a Provisional Government, and everything ready—except powder and shot, or anything to fire them with; they proposed to try me by court-martial for cowardice when I objected to scythes and blackthorn sticks as implements of modern warfare. I have no doubt they could have shot me, if they could have mustered enough of serviceable fire-arms to furnish a firing-party. Gentlemen,' said the West Point veteran, about whose stern mouth lines of scorn had been flitting, ' we are just in time, with this gale on our stern, to save ourselves from being ridiculous for life.'

'Wal, but, General, speaking not as a kicker now, but as a baldpated grizzly with an ould *graw* for a fight on the ould sod when it's to be had so handy,' struck in Captain Mike, 'don't you think 'twould be flying in the face of Providence, having come so far, to quit without giving the Britishers a hug or two that will leave our autograph with them till we call round agen! Here are the boys making for Coomhōla in their thousands this minnit; and here, under the hatches, are the weapons to put in their hands, and here, to the right and left of the Chair, are men with the proper bullion in them to show a good lead. Let us make a night of it, General, anyhow. Bantry will dish us up a supper fit to turn your green turtle, blue-points, and string beans into a five-cent hash for envy. The divvel's in the dice if we don't compose a page of history that we can hand along to the younkers without feeling mean in our graves.'

'Ay, ay, General—let's land, and go for Bantry, anyhow!' the younger officers clamoured, springing to their feet and clustering eagerly around their chief.

'No, sir, I do not undertake this job as a fillibuster,' was the calm reply. 'I have no notion of handing over a defenceless country to martial law and bloodshed for the pleasure of passing an exhilarating evening; and, in any case, the supper you would get at Bantry would be your last supper. Our friends in the garrison sailed out of Cork harbour last night in an Indian troop-ship; there is an English regiment in their place; the whole design is known: instead of being received with open gates and open arms, our bands would be torn to fragments with the combined fire of a thousand breechloaders in front, and of the Channel Fleet in flank. And whoever was unlucky enough to escape would escape with a convict's uniform and penal servitude for life. No, sir, it is soldiers I have led here—to handle rifles, not to pick oakum. As they cannot do what they came for, it only remains to lead them back.'

'Back with their tails between their legs! There's nothing but damnation in it,' cried the young officer with the scarred cheek who had spoken before. 'I guess I'll land, if I've got to swim for it.'

'Is it you are running this show or I?' asked the General, looking up in his cold tranquil way. 'If any man under my command attempts to leave this ship—I'll bore him!'

'That's correct, General. I was wrong. Forgive me!' the young man said, putting out a hand, which the General quietly pressed, remarking : 'That's more like your old Gettysburg form, MacCrossan ; sorry I cannot oblige you with another dash for the guns this time.'

'But do you mean to say,' cried Ken Rohan, who had been an impatient listener to all this—'do you mean to say that a lot of helpless peasant boys are to be allowed to go on and dash themselves against the armed force of England, and that you, who alone could give them arms or advice, are going to desert them?'

'A bloody shame! And such a chance!' chimed in the Lord Harry, from bottomless depths of dejection.

'Our leaders may be all you say—bad conspirators or childish soldiers,' Ken dashed on, with flaming cheek, 'but our men are as unselfish, true, and gallant material as ever a patriot army was built up with. They have risked everything for the sake of the principles you implanted in them—obloquy, treachery, the curse of their Church, the frown of every genteel dastard in the country : they trusted in your promises of help : are they to be left facing the breechloaders and the cannon of the Fleet to-night with empty hands, while an Irish-American ship, full of arms and officers, is cutting its cable and flying for its life at their very doors?'

'Glory!' murmured the deep voice of Con Lehane. Ken had not noticed that Con's massive figure had followed the General down the companion-ladder, and blocked the doorway in grim silence during the council of war.

'That is a sensible observation foolishly put,' replied the General, with a quiet, not unkindly, survey of Ken Rohan. 'It would be the boss meanness of this century if we were to save ourselves without first taking measures to save the men we leave behind us. Our young friend may be reassured. I have spent the better part of this day despatching men through the country to disperse any assembly of the people, and warn them that the whole design is discovered and abandoned. One of my most trusty officers should be at this moment in Coomhöla to send the people to their homes. Nothing worse will come of it than a wetting ; and, if we get back with no greater glory than that of having saved thousands of human sheep from slaughter, it is glory that a soldier will be prouder of over his pipe by-and-by than the glory we might have by a night's cheap buccaneering and getting our names into the papers.'

'Now, then, anybody for shore ?' sang out Captain Silas' sharp voice from above.

'Yes I !' 'And I !' 'And I !' shouted Ken Rohan, Harry Westropp, and Con Lehane, in chorus.

'Young fellows, don't you go doing anything foolish—anything criminal,' said the General solemnly. 'Take the word of an old soldier for it—the only thing to be done for Ireland to-night that isn't criminal lunacy is to get the people into their beds. I have no right to command you, but your foot is on American ground on this deck ; why rush back deliberately to some miserable death, or worse than death, for Irish rebellion cannot afford a man even a decent means of suicide ?'

'Believe me, sir,' said Ken Rohan, who had been warming towards the General, 'we accept your advice, and, in all but quitting the country, will abide by it. But our poor fellows cannot safely be left to themselves on an occasion like this. We would hang our heads all our lives if anything happened and we were not there. There are other reasons— there are private reasons,' he stammered, blushing violently, as visions of a soft, bright aërial figure on Eily's Rock mingled with thoughts of the stricken household at the Mill—'why I, at least, am bound to Ireland.'

'Whatever Ken does, I'll do—if 'twas to scuttle Patsy Driscoll's yawl on the way back,' said Harry, dejectedly. -

'Here's another—let him give the word—devil may care whether 'tis to swim or go to the bottom !' cried Con Lehane, in the first ill-humoured moment of his life.

Tears were trickling down Captain Mike's yellow cheeks. 'Boys,' he said, folding them tenderly in his huge arms, 'I wish an old Ninth Massachusett's man's blessing was worth your having—or his ould carcase worth taking with you. Darned but I'd sooner be on the road to Coomhöla with you to-night than thanking the citizens for giving me a handsome plurality for State Treasurer. Gen'lemen, it's an occasion to make a plain citizen swear bad enough for a basement bar. God bless you boys !—

that's all. Ken Rohan, jest you tell friend Neville, from Mike MacCarthy, that even the British Empire might have its chance of escaping deep damnation, if there was many of his sort visible in that crowd with a powerful lanthorn ; and tell Miss Westropp that if even my ould mother's rosaries smuggles me into Heaven, I'll think I'm handsomely provided for in the article of eternal bliss if I'm set to live in the one continent with those purty eyes of hers—God love her ! Gen'lemen, we've failed to pony up this time ; but Mike MacCarthy don't despair of seeing a line of Irish bayonets charging up the Glen of Coomhōla at the double yet.'

'Not another minnit to oblige the President and Congress,' bellowed Uncle Sam through the storm.

The General put out his hand, with a grave, kind smile. 'Good-bye,' he said, almost softly. 'You lads have made me think better of Ireland. If ever again there's a chance that a soldier may take—who knows ?—we may meet together yet—you will remember the name of —— ——.'

Ken Rohan almost sank to his knees. It was the name of one of the most brilliant of the famous Federal captains. The next moment the wild spray was beating in his face, and Patsy Driscoll's yawl was casting off into the night.

***

CHAPTER THE THIRTY-FIFTH

REJOINING QUISH

THERE was nobody to whom the order for the outbreak came with such blessed relief as it came to Dawley. It offered him escape from an iron cage which he saw contracting to strangle him. Since his interview with Mr. Hans Harman he had been drinking desperately—drinking as if his only care were lest he should not be able to purchase a sufficient quantity of alcohol to kill him. His wife—an enormous, square-shouldered woman, who had been accustomed to trounce him like an impish schoolboy—was daunted by the sparks of hell-fire she saw kindling in his small red eyes. She cowered before him when he spoke, she coaxed him to rest, she saw one piece of household property after another disappear to the pawn-office and return in a whisky-bottle, she even secretly pledged small articles of her own to be in a position to pour libations on the altar of this horrible devil-god that glared at her through her husband's eyes. Perhaps she had heard mutterings in his swinish sleep. Once or twice Hans

Harman's temptation took possession of him, and held fearful converse with the drink-demon. There was treachery eating into the conspiracy on all sides; and those who were not professional spies were drivelling poets, or kid-gloved young cubs who turned up their noses at rough-handed Democracy. Why should he not look out for himself in the crash? A few hours' hot shame in the witness-chair; some scathing denunciations from a counsel fee'd to abuse him, and who would laud him just as eloquently if the retaining-fee were on the other side; one scorching smart of public execration across his cheek, and, with a new name, in a new land, he would be lolling in wealth that would enable him to think of it all simply as an abominable nightmare, like the drudgery of Blackamoor Lane. He could enable the Government to lay their hand on the inmost conspirators of the province— on the General in command himself. He had heard of five thousand pounds being a common price for services of that importance; and with five thousand pounds what visions of a villa-residence, herds, horses, honours, perhaps a seat in some colonial parliament! or, at the worst, what rivers of liquor wherein to drown care! All this flashed before his mind in lurid alcoholic painting; but it brought him no solace. For, in the first place, Dawley was not naturally a bad man, to whom it was a small thing to betray his cause or to stab a comrade; he was only a cranky, half-developed creature, whom the new wine of Democracy, added to the passion for an older tipple, had puffed up with insolence, which he only meant to be independence, and with savagery, which he took to be one of the cardinal virtues which country and the hour demanded. The idea of becoming an informer was to him more absolutely loathsome than the slimy river is to a girl about to throw herself from London Bridge. Besides, the fate he had himself measured out to Quish was there to remind him how much worse than Cain's was the curse of the Irish informer upon the earth; and he asked himself where, from polar circle to polar circle, was the fugitive and vagabond to be free from that awful apparition of an all-pervading Irish eye and a remorseless Irish pistol! Death by whisky, upon the whole, he thought an easier doom than either death upon the gallows or Mr. Hans Harman's alternative of a life haunted by a thousand deaths more cruel. His fear was that either he would not be able to buy alcohol enough, or that death would not come in time, before Mr. Hans Harman should choose to touch the springs of his contracting prison and crush him bone by bone. The most intolerable thought of all was that the iron meshes in which Harman had him caged were a Divine arrangement for avenging Quish's murder—that his entanglement was as irrevocable as fate. The hairy cap and hideous disjoined eyes of the murdered man grinned at him from the bottom of every measure of whisky he swallowed. The more he swallowed the more hideously the eyes bulged out at him. He could no longer get drunk. He could only get delirious. And then a terror seized him lest he should talk in his delirious fits, or lest the fits never should end, but that monstrous gibbering countenance should go on glowering upon him for eternities upon eternities. A singular plan for obtaining the benefits of suicide without incurring its penalties began to shape itself in his mind. He began to calculate how he might lie concealed in Tummulty's taproom after closing-hour, and in the dead of night turn the tap of one of his great whisky-puncheons and put his mouth to the orifice. He argued with his own elastic conscience that it would not necessarily be self-slaughter, if he could keep out of his intention the idea of Death, and limit it to the idea of Drink. If, when his intellect got stupefied by the friendly fumes, the tap still continued flowing, and his gullet continued to gape for it, how was he to be held answerable for results?

He was actually studying at Tummulty's bar, glass in hand, the capabilities of a closet in a sequestered corner of the back-shop for purposes of concealment that day when Danny Delea slapped him on the back with the blessed intelligence of the Rising. Fancy what a change it made for the haunted wretch whose only hope in life or way out of life was Tummulty's spigot! It inebriated him as though the tap were already pouring its fiery flood down his throat. His iron bars flew asunder. His legion of devils flapped away. Quish's bizarre, blood-stained face vanished like a foul spirit before a surge of daylight. A minute before, life resolved itself for him into the choice between death by the rope with a grave of quicklime, and suffocation at the mouth of a whisky-barrel with a grave at some cross-roads. And now, as at the stroke of a bell, here was Freedom, Honour, Vengeance!— the Murderer changed into the Soldier, the haunted madman into a person of consequence in a great cause—Mr. Hans Harman's shivering bondsman into his master and his judge!

'Upon my soul, I'm inclined to apologise to Dawley,' said Georgey O'Meagher's medical brother, Tom, to a select circle in a cabin at Coombóla late that night. Tom, not being as yet provided with any deadlier weapon than his pipe, was practising vigorously with that arm of the service. 'Who could ever have supposed the little devil would turn out such a fire-eater when it came to business? There he is outside flying about like a will-o'-the-wisp in the storm, while we're warming our toes here with a morsel of fire; and the most astonishing thing of all is, he has not been seen so sober this month back! Only for that infernal storm,

and if I was not so comfortable where I am, I would go out and
beg his pardon—I would, upon my soul ! '

And the Doctor (as Tom was semi-reproachfully dubbed in
friendly circles) did not exaggerate.   Dawley was displaying the
courage of a lion and the energy of a hero.   Every body of men
that streamed down with the pitiless sleet from the Bauherla
mountains on one side, or along the wild torrent-bordered path
over Cobhdhuv from the Glengariff direction, he welcomed with
words of good cheer ; he parcelled out the few cabins in the lonesome defile as headquarters for the different sections ; he posted
the best armed dozen men he could find at Snacht Bridge, at the
mouth of the pass ; and when a sentinel ran in with an alarm
that the dragoons were coming, Dawley said, in a businesslike
way : 'Murnaun, go home to your mudder if you're afraid of de
dragoons, or I'll give you a dragoon out of dis,' tapping the barrel of his revolver, 'in de stomach.'   He felt like one of those
criminals into whose jail a riotous mob break in some great commotion, and who, a moment before a felon in irons, in the smashing of a lock becomes a leader, sword and torch in hand.

It was an appalling night.   Swishes of frozen rain struck men
hard in the face, as if they were the blows of dead enemies from
the darkness. Coomhōla is, even in its summer noonday raiment, a
dark and penitential-looking place.   It is a deep narrow gash in
the stony mountains, with just room for a wailful river to moan
its way through the naked haunches of rock on either side of the
road.   The night was pitchy dark.   The icy rain swept the pass
in gusts, like discharges of frozen canister-shot.   The storm
whistled and shrieked about the bleak hillsides with diabolical
glee, and danced around, and hammered, and banged at the crazy
cabin doors, as if nothing but the blood of all in them could content it.   To make matters worse, the river was swollen by the
little torrents that tumbled from every cleft in the hills, and its
normally mournful voice deepened into a thunderous wail which
in the darkness of the narrow pass gave the awful impression of a
deluge that was tearing every living thing along with it.   In spite
of all, men kept pouring in in twos and threes, picking their way
along rocky mountain tracks, where a false step would have immersed them in some waterlogged bog-hole or angry torrent, and
no more regardful of the hailstorm that drenched and buffeted
them than of the terrific power of England.   Even when they
began to coagulate into vague masses in the darkness, and to find
that nobody was regularly armed, and nobody in authoritative
command, and no arrangement for shelter, still less for supper,
the indomitable faith of those brave peasant lads and country
mechanics was not to be damped ; for had not the Americans

actually arrived? and would not the rifles be here presently
by the thousand? and was not the General himself to lead the
attack on Bantry? and where not the very redcoats to
throw open the barrack-gates and run up the flag of the Irish
Republic? Be it for good or ill, our Irish youth are Tertul-
lian's true Faithful, to whom there are things which are
'credible, because they are foolish certain—because they are im·
possible.' By-and-by, as the icy tooth of the storm bit into
their bones, and the horrible concert of wind and waters grew ever
louder, the groups began to congregate more and more under the
sheltered gables of the cabins, and lit immense fires out of the
turf ricks piled beside them ; and, it being a region rich in private
stills, foragers began to pass measures of potheen among the
drenched groups around the bonfires ; and, of all men living,
Dawley took severe measures with the potheen·drinkers in his own
section, and, revolver in hand, took summary possession of the
bottles, to be held until the General should direct their distribu-
tion in regular rations. The strangest thing of all was that they
submitted quietly, while a man whose very nose was a whisky-
still dispossessed them of their only comfort against the downfall
of thawing ice that was piercing and freezing them to the heart.

The dragoons were not coming ; but another scout from
Snacht Bridge ran in with the news that undoubtedly they heard
the noise of galloping on the road from Bantry. Dawley hurried
to the bridge, and reached it just in time to receive the horseman,
as he galloped up, with a row of levelled muskets drawn across
the roadway. The horseman was the young Irish-American
soldier whom the General had left in Bantry with orders for the
dispersal of the insurgents. As he made his way to the cabin in
which the heads of sections were holding counsel with one another
and their pipes, some strange thrill of intelligence seemed to
rush through the pass in the screaming of the wind. Nobody
could tell whence the news came ; nobody repeated it aloud ; but
every group could hear some great voice of disaster as distinctly as
the mysterious lamentation of the river—whispering now of the removal of the disaffected redcoats ; now of the arrival of the Channel
Fleet ; now of the capture of the Americans, arms and all ; now
of failure, treachery, incapacity all along the line—of massacres
of unarmed men, and a flourishing informer trade, and reeking
scaffolds. And now, indeed, a second alarm that the dragoons
were coming sent a thrill through Coomhōla which Dawley's
revolver was no longer adequate to cope with.

'There is no use debating. There is nothing to debate,' said
the American officer to the group assembled in the grimy smoke
of the cabin. 'My orders are summed up in one word—disperse

And the sooner the better. The Flying Column is assembling at Bantry.'

'By God, I don't believe you!' cried Dawley, his eyes burning like live coals. 'We're betrayed by a parcel of liars, cowards, and traitors!'

The young American quietly moved his hand to his breast pocket. 'I am prepared to make allowances; but don't hoe back on that row any more, stranger—do you hear?' he said, almost in a whisper. Then to the rest : '*My* General's a man who's heard shells sing worse nights than this. If he says there's nothing to be done but get home to bed, there *is* nothing, and that's an end of it. A fizzle's bad enough, without its being painted red with honest blood. As soon as you've sent your men home to their families, you're welcome to call me coward for risking penal servitude to come here and tell you so. But first, obey orders—disperse!'

Dawley reeled against the wall as if the order was his death-sentence.

'With all my heart,' said Georgey O'Meagher's brother Tom, lighting his pipe afresh from a sod of red turf. 'It's the most sensible thing I've heard in the whole business. I don't see why we shouldn't be all reasonably happy, if Dawley would only give us a nip of that bottle of potheen I see sticking out of his pocket against the road.'

'Merciful God!' groaned one old man, with a long white beard and a pair of eyes dauntless enough to have been still in their teens, 'I've lived through three different movements and three sentences since John Mitchel's day in the hope of seeing this night, and now—— Well, well, I suppose there's nothing for it but to save the boys—*their* chance may come again, though mine never will.'

As a matter of fact, under the influence of the panic spread by the hoofs of the galloping horse, the masses around the bonfires were already melting off into the night. Men gliding away in twos or threes towards Glengariff in the blinding storm stumbled against other twos or threes making for the Bauherla Mountains, and started back in mutual distrust and terror. Groundless confidence brought its usual penalty of groundless fear. Men who an hour before wanted only rifles in their hands and the word of command to go to their deaths with hearts singing like larks, now started at every scream of the wind, and were ready to fling down their weapons before every figure that bore down on them through the gloom.

Dawley alone grew only the more desperate for the disappointment. He felt like a condemned wretch who had filed through prison bars and climbed over all but impossible stone walls, only to find a policeman's bull's-eye flashed in his face in the very moment when he alighted in liberty. The iron gate, and the damp dungeon, and the gallows-trap yawned for him once more. A fierce thirst for vengeance burned and devoured him. He rushed like a maniac to the hut which his own circle had made their head-quarters. Their bonfire was still burning doggedly in spite of the bombarding hail-stones and the whirling gale. Wild figures still gathered around the blaze or crouched against the neighbouring gable.

' Min,' he cried, in that voice of unflinching purpose, which is always effective, and which made Dawley's fiery cocked nose and half-caste dialect terrible. ' We are betrayed. I always toult you so. I toult you no good would come of your brats of boys sparking up at de Castle by way of organising a revolution. Where are dey to-night ? Are dey afraid some honest man would try whedder a bullet couldn't get inside deir fine clothes for 'em ? Listen, min—we're not going to crawl home to-night widout having some value for our money. We have only to break down Snacht Bridge, and not a redcoat can come west before morning. We'll have dis night at all events, to square accounts wid our tyrants. If dere's a man listening to me dat ever howled under Hans Harman's black whip, now is his time ! '

A yell of execration went up around the fire. Weapons were brandished in the air, the potheen bottles were produced and handed around now freely by Dawley, the devil that courses in all beaten men was blooded, and a wild cry, ' To Stone Hall ! ' mingled with the yelling winds until the crimson blaze, the stormy figures around it, and the background of massive darkness might have been taken for a piece of hell breaking above ground in an eruption. The bulk of the assemblage had by this time disappeared ; even on the verge of Dawley's own fiery circle many dropped silently away. They came for other work than this. Dawley's diabolical look horrified them. The whisky-bottles and the artificial frenzies that followed them simply moved their disgust. But in a land of peasants, whose grievances had been simmering darkly for many a year, and who were maddened by the sense of defeat, outlawry, treachery, and dangers on all sides, Dawley was in no want of desperate recruits—one, a young giant whom Hans Harman had refused to accept as the husband of the daughter of one of the largest tenants ; a second, a poacher whom his merciless fines and imprisonments had driven to beggary and drink ; a third, whose evicted father had sunk down from his comfortable farmhouse into the reeking hut of a town labourer ; a fourth, whose father was under sentence of eviction ; and so on to the merely reckless, who drifted wherever youth, and drink, and the devil chose to drive them. Leaving a party behind to break down Snacht Bridge, and so bar the road from Bantry to the troops, Dawley and his tumultuary forces streamed away towards Drumshaughlin, many of them sticking sods of blazing turf saturated with paraffin on the top of their rude pikeheads, and in their recklessness yelling snatches of song, so that it is not surprising that Miss Deborah Harman, awakened by the thunders at the door, and creeping to the window, should have screamed to her sister :

'Heavens! look, sister! It's not human beings. It's hell broken loose !'

The poor creature cowered and grovelled with terror. Not so Frank. She rushed to her brother's room for a loaded cavalry pistol which she knew he was in the habit of keeping suspended over his bed. Then she flung up the window, and, casting a fearless eye over the smoking torches and the tossing figures underneath their glare, she demanded : 'What do you want ?'

'Hans Harman—we want Hans Harman ! Open the door !' came back cries through the storm that reminded her of a kennel of hounds as she heard them yell at the sight of a carcase.

'He is not here. There is nobody in the house except women,' she returned, unfalteringly.

'You lie! Open the door! Smash it in !' cried Dawley's voice in the momentary lull that followed. Blow followed blow from sledge-hammers. All other noises except the savage chant of the storm ceased while the hollow thuds of the sledge-hammers shook the very heart of the stony house with their sounds of doom. At last came a wild cheer and a deep-echoing crash, which gave some horrible suggestion of breaking in the lid of a coffin. Miss Deborah screamed, and, for the first genuine time in her life, swooned clean away. There was more than the average male's show of undaunted mettle in Frank Harman's composition ; but her heart sickened and grew cold at the awful sound of the human cataract she heard raging through the house, ever nearer and louder. Dawley ran from room to room like a maniac, whirling one of the rude torches above his head. In the half-dark of the study he thought he saw Harman's white face trembling in the gloom. He made a frantic dash at it. It was only Hans Harman's bust in plaster. Dawley put his revolver to its forehead with a frightful oath, and the bullet sent the white fragments flying.

In and out went the eddies of sulphurous torchlights—into each room with the howl of hungry tigers, out again with a deep undergrowl of wild animals beaten back from their prey. Dawley

frantically led the way upstairs ; from room to room, still with the
unsatisfied howl of a hound beating about a cover with its nose
to the ground. He started back from an apparition that suddenly
confronted him. Miss Harman's tall, bony figure stood in ghastly
night-clothes at the door of her bedroom, the levelled cavalry
pistol in one hand and a lighted candle in the other. There was
a dignity about the woman's noble pluck that daunted young
men, most of whom had nothing but a few glasses of fiery spirits
between them and modest manhood. They fell back in silence —
some of them even, I fancy, with blushing cheeks, if the wild flash
of the torches had been steady enough to show them.

'Get out o' the way!' growled Dawley, considerably daunted,
nevertheless, both by the heavy pistol and the pitiless candle-
light in his eyes.

' Not till I'm killed, and I'll kill you first,' she replied, steadily.
Frank Harman was not merely a dead shot in the archery field, but
had practised pistol-shooting as assiduously as she practised most
other manly accomplishments. Dawley would have feared her
pistol much if he had not feared her brother's devil's-grip of him
more. 'I've told you, you have nobody but helpless women to
find in this house. And you call yourselves men ! '

Her scorn cut him like a whip. 'Helpless women, *moryah* !
Bony ould she-divvels like you ! Drop dat pistol, and stand out
o' de road, or by——'

'Stop !' said a voice at his elbow. The young giant already
referred to stepped forward, and having by one skilful movement
wrenched the cavalry pistol out of Miss Harman's hand and placed
his broad shoulders between her and Dawley, coolly turned round
to the latter. 'Lave the woman alone,' he said, with a quiet
emphasis. Then he turned again, and threw open the bedroom
door. 'Go into your room, ma'am,' he said, in the same calm
tone, to Miss Harman. She obeyed him without a word. When
she was within, he threw in the key after her, closed the door,
and placed his gigantic back against it. Was it any tender
memory of his own forbidden espousals that brought that flush of
soft grace into his dark eyes and over his swarthy, Spanish-looking
face ?

Dawley growled again like a baffled wild animal, but turned
away. The women were not his quarry. His passion to find
Harman, to hunt him down, to kill him, and with him kill the
hellish terror that hung on his own life, was now a perfect mania.
'To the Castle !' he ye'led, rushing down stairs. 'As he isn't
here, we're sure to bag him dere, de bloody cunning fox !' In
the hall the poacher was guzzling whisky out of a bottle which
he had lit upon in one of the rooms. The same huge youngster

who had championed Miss Harman dragged the bottle from his lips and sent it crashing out upon the gravel. 'None of that!' he said, fiercely. 'We'll have Harman's life, but we're not going to sile our lips with his liquor, damn him!'

As he again emerged into the storm, a horrid misgiving crossed Dawley's mind lest he should be leaving Harman in safety behind after all. 'Dere's no harm in making sure,' he said, conciliatingly, to the troublesome young giant. 'We'll burn de cover anyway, if 'twas only for a bonfire to warm ourselves dis cowld night.' And pouring a fresh supply of paraffin over his rude blazing cresset, he whirled it about his head, and once more made for the hall.

The young man caught him with a hand of steel. 'With the women inside! No!—do you hear me? No!—or I'll toss you first into the blaze,' he said, in a tone there was no mistaking.

For a moment Dawley's eyes glittered with points as sharp-looking as daggers; but he saw that the scene at Miss Harman's bedroom door had placed the sympathies even of his wildest spirits on the softer side; he yielded with another savage yowl between his teeth, and the weird pageant of smoking torches, flashing here and there upon the point of a pike, or upon a gun-barrel, or upon a desperate face, moved on..

Dawley presently dropped behind to the poacher. 'Go back you,' he whispered, 'and put a match to dat divvel's den, and don't mind dat big bosthoon dat spilt de blessed whisky on you. Give de women tin minnits to lave de house, and if you can find anudder good drop for yourself, drink it; but don't let us be far on de road till you give us a light; and if Hans is widin himself, let him roast till he goes to a place where dey'll roast him a bit hotter.' As he seized the poacher's hand, the poacher thought Dawley's own hand felt hot enough to set fire to Stone Hall by itself. The poacher disappeared. The outlaws had to pass through a suburb of the silent town to reach the Castle. The houses looked like the bodies of houses that were dead and piled up sepulchre-wise at either side of the road. Sub-Inspector Flibbert's orders were to keep his own slender force in their barrack in a distant part of the town, until the strength or weakness of the insurrection should have developed itself. The storm was abating fast, and glimpses of moonlight were beginning to show amidst the rents in the dark gunpowdery clouds. Suddenly, as Dawley's wild company were streaming towards the Castle gates, a great tape of flame shot into the sky in the direction they had just come from. Dawley could not restrain a yell of joy. By some ferocious impulse the yell was taken up through the ranks. It was the first flash of success or vengeance that had

crossed them throughout a night of maddening disappointments.
'Dere, now, you see de divvel has got hoult of his own,
in spite of you,' he cried, turning to the young disappointed
bridegroom. The latter looked at the blazing heavens, and then
scanned Dawley's face fiercely.

'It must be some o' de torches dat set fire to some o' dem
hangings,' said Dawley, by way of answering that uncomfortable
scrutiny,

'God sind it isn't too late to save them unfortunate craytures,
whatever,' was the only reply ; and the gigantic form flew back
towards Stone Hall as if shot from a catapult.

'A good riddance, too,' cried Dawley, savagely. ' 'Tisn't big
babbies, but min we want, whin we've got quarter of a century's
vingeance to pay back before morning. Gate, there !—gate ! and
be damned to you ! ' he shouted, thundering at the lodge-keeper's
door with his boot.

His one purpose in life now was to get hold of Hans Harman.
If he slipped through his fingers now, the morning would bring
the redcoats, and the gallows, or the worst terrors of Harman's
mocking pitiless eye. But Harman once out of the way, his lungs
would once more work as a machinery for breathing, and not for
suffocating. There would hardly be time for dispersal before they
could be fixed with evidence of their night's work, and, at the
worst, flight from the country would give him a fresh start, and,
with a clean slate, in a land of gold, Harman's blood would be his
elixir of life—his magic cup of youth. That once quaffed, he
could imagine his deeply-dinged wrinkles smoothing out, his very
nose losing its malt-worn hue and becoming a reputable credential
again. And then the delight of quaffing that deep draught of
vengeance ! He pictured the agent to himself in a dozen different
attitudes of shameful death ; he gloated over Harman's terror-
stricken look at sight of the flaming brands and the muzzles of the
guns ; he settled with himself that the first judicial proceeding
would have to be to compel him to go on his knees and kiss the
ground at Dawley's feet to beg for mercy ; and then he wavered,
as to subsequent measures, between the pleasure of himself blowing out the agent's brains as he knelt, or of seeing him dangle at
the end of a rope from one of the trees in the Castle avenue ; and
he finally decided that it might be possible to combine the two
plans, after the model of the atrocities perpetrated upon the peasantry in '98, and, after half-hanging him, cut him down for the
additional entertainment of flogging and shooting him at leisure.
These horrible thoughts crowded on his mind with the feelings of
a miser running his hands through heaps of stolen gold. He was,
in a word, a fiend, and his skin felt as if it were already on fire

His most desperate followers, who had bitter grudges against Harman themselves, could not understand Dawley's demoniac fury, and were a bit horrified by it.   But when men are drunk with the sense of disappointment, betrayal, and unslaked vengeance, the man who knows his mind and proceeds unflinchingly to action, is sure to have men to follow him.   As he tore up the avenue to the Castle steps like a Mænad whirling his torch, that mysterious electric blood-fury which burned along his own veins communicated itself to his comrades, and they dashed in at his heels at a mad rush, making the Castle seem to wink with horror under the glare of their dancing cressets, and tremble at the reverberation of their hideous shouts.

The great iron-clamped door could have defied the sledge-hammer for many a bout ; but they need not have thundered so hard.   Only a few blows had been delivered, when the hall-lamp was suddenly seen alight, and the great door swung back—not cautiously, but to its full width.   A girl's slender figure stood alone in the gulf of light thus thrown open to the outlaws.   There was something supernatural-looking about the apparition.   It reminded them of the Madonna surrounded by her lucent nimbus. A sudden awe and silence struck them.   Even Dawley stammered, and his hand went involuntarily to his hat.

'Sorry for troubling you, Miss.   We've come for Harman— Hans Harman,' he said, in a husky voice.

'Mr. Harman is not here,' she replied, calmly, advancing slightly into the doorway.

Her five simple words were so many daggers entering Dawley's flesh.   'No, no, that cannot be !' he cried, writhing as if the steel were actually sticking in the wounds.   'Give him up, de hell-hound !'

'I pledge you my honour,' she said, in a tremulous voice, as her eye fell on the fierce-looking men outside and the torches stuck like hellish eyes in the darkness.   Down below volumes of flame and smoke were ascending into the sky from Stone Hall as from a gigantic brazier.

The fire within the chambers of Stone Hall was no fiercer than that which rushed through Dawley's scorching brain.   'Den, by God, we'll have Lord Drumshaughlin !' he roared, advancing up the steps until his coarse face was so close to Mabel's that she could feel his burning breath on her cheek.

She shrank back in mortal terror.   His face, his very eyes, had a stain of blood.   Her limbs trembled and sank as if her feet stood in pails of ice.   Her voice seemed to have died within her. A feeling came over her that by no possible effort could she make the words audible when she struggled to say—

'My father is not here either.'

But Dawley heard her, and answered with a harsh crackling laugh. 'Ha! anudder rat running! Gone to Bantry to hide behind the sogers, eh! Come, young lady, we've had too much o' dis gammon to-night. We'll just have a look for ourselves. If loyal heroes run away and lave de women behind to look piteous, dis is no time for compliments to purty cheeks, no more'n to plain ones—tisn't de women dey sends to evict de people and flay 'em alive. Come, Miss, we don't want to harm you, but dis is no place for young ladies—giv way dere, or you'll get hurt!'

With unutterable loathing she saw the evil red eyes come nearer. He put out a claw to grasp her wrist. She felt it branding its impression on her flesh like a hot iron. Suddenly he staggered back with a growl of agony. He had lowered the peat torch in his left hand on entering the doorway. In lunging forward to catch her hand, the blazing mass wobbled to the side of his head, frizzling up his red head at a single whiz and stamping into his cheek and scalp a vast blister of charred and crinkling flesh. 'Hell!' he groaned, stumbling back, and, as his foot slipped in the frozen slush left by the hailstorm, he fell down the steps, like a man who had received a death-wound, into some follower's arms.

The release from that nightmare-like clutch gave Mabel Westropp a new draught of life. The cool air on her forehead braced her to one effort more. She advanced again upon the doorstep, her yellow hair blown about by the last eddies of the storm, her fragile form facing that cruel sea of darkly-flaming lights and still more darkly-flaming faces—as pathetic a picture as that of the French child-princess playing under the guillotine while a group of *tireurs à cinq francs* are chaffering over their wages for her father's execution. Her limbs shook and grew cold again, and the torches began to swim faintly before her eyes; but from some well-spring of calm and purity deep within her she received strength to say, with almost superhuman tranquillity:

'You are men and Irishmen. I am alone in this house, with one old woman. I told them I was not afraid to trust my countrymen.' She could not utter a word more for deadly faintness. She leaned against the doorpost. The feeling that she had closed her eyes upon the world came over her with a strange sense of relief. Her few simple words, uttered in that voice of silvery music, had a singular effect. The storm seemed to have died away to listen. So did the angrier storms that scowled from the ferocious faces around her. It was an exorcism so beautiful that the evil spirits themselves were entranced with the music of it. It did not cast them out. It enchanted them.

Dawley alone turned with a despairing rage, to which physical pain now added its torturing dart. He saw the same shame-faced skulking look, the same irresolute lull of passion that the sight of a woman had already produced at Stone Hall, only the effect was as much the more paralysing as Miss Westropp's tender, helpless beauty outshone Miss Harman's bony strength and loaded pistol. He felt that desperation alone could re-establish his credit with his followers and blood their fury. Bellowing with pain and rage, he sprang up the steps, and, waving his torch madly about his head, cried:

'Come on, lads! Whin did dey ever spare de torch to an honest's man's tatch? Whin had you ever before de chance o' being even wid your tyrants! Whin will you ever have it again! We've fired one robber's den to-night. Here's a bigger den, and a bigger robber—come on, and we'll give 'em a blaze to-night dat'll light der sowls to everlasting hell. Out o' de way, you painted hussay!' he cried, grasping the young girl's almost lifeless body with a savage instinct of revenge for his own torturing pain. As he did so, he heard a voice behind that struck on his heart like lead.

'What is this, you demons—what is this?' cried Ken Rohan, pushing his way forward with Harry through the crowd. They instinctively fell back. The sight of the girl's delicate beauty in the ugly little monster's power was too much for them. The young man sprang up the steps, swung Dawley round by the neck and flung him reeling to the bottom of the steps. The torch fell upon the tiled pavement of the hall, and Ken Rohan crushed the smoking embers with his boot. 'You scoundrels!' he said, 'has not Ireland had sorrow enough to-night without staining our cause with devilry like this?' Then he found that it was an unconscious body he held in his arms, and that the softly-carved angel-like face that lay against his shoulder was as white and as cold as marble.

Dawley was more stunned than hurt. His foot was on the steps again, his revolver in his right hand, and a thousand devils caged in his heart. 'Hello! our bloody aristocrats have turned up, have dey? Where were dey skulking to-night?' he hissed, turning round triumphantly to his followers. 'Let 'em answer me dat. You and I, min, am only rubbidge dey wipes der boots in; we have stood to our guns—we don't go shapin' up to lords and ladies—we don't go sellin' de pass, perhaps, like Quish did!'

'What have you got to say against Quish?' suddenly cried Harry Westropp, drawing towards him.

'Dat Quish was a bloody informer,' said Dawley, violently, 'if Quish's master isn't anudder.'

'You lie! Quish was a better man than you. You lie!' repeated Harry, fire shooting from his eyes.

Dawley raised his revolver. A short, vicious crack was heard, and, with a slight spring, Harry fell forward on his face without a groan, and lay still. 'Take back your lie to hell, and a bullet wid it,' said Dawley; but his face was that of a corpse, and the hand that held the smoking pistol almost dropped in a palsy.

Then a moment's deathlike silence. A sound of inarticulate awe like that heard at the Elevation of the Host in a rustic Irish chapel was wrung from the crowd in one great sob. It said 'Dead!' in a deeper tone than any human language. It said something more which told Dawley that his power over the crowd was gone. He looked up in a scared way at the cry of 'Murderer!' as if it must be an avenging angel who had spoken.

The cry came from Ken Rohan. By some instinct he committed the motionless form in his arms to a tall peasant who had crept into the hall, and who stood watching the beautiful face with the reverence with which the lion in the 'Faëry Queen' shuffled up to lick Una's hand. It was the same black-haired, Spanish-skinned young giant who had just been to Stone Hall to prevent murder.

'Murderer!' And Ken Rohan sprang from the steps. By some wild impulse of terror, Dawley turned and attempted to fly. But even as he turned, he felt his neck compressed in an iron hand. Panic did the rest. He felt a rush of cold air as if he were being whirled rapidly about, and he next found himsel dashed on his back to the ground, young Rohan's knee pressed upon his chest and his sinewy hand upon his throat. He tried to cry out, but the attempt nearly strangled him; it seemed to him his eyes must be flying from their sockets into a world of broken lights and fallen stars. Something entangled in his fingers suddenly gave him strength; he pressed the trigger, after struggling in vain to take aim. Ken Rohan felt a stinging, needlelike thrust in the arm; but the revolver had dropped from the murderer's hand, and, without another struggle, his captor wrenched his two hands together over the chest, and called for a rope to bind them.

'Ay, or to hang him!' 'Right!' 'The divil's cure to him!' voices cried on all sides. They had never quite shared Dawley's frenzy, and the insult to Miss Westropp and the murder of Harry had turned their bewilderment into abhorrence.

A man brushed through the crowd and whispered in Rohan's ear, as he still held his captive pinned to the ground. 'The dragoons are coming!' whispered Con Lehane. 'What's to be

done! There are guns enough to hould the Castle agin 'em.
Will I order in the men and bar the door?'

'No, certainly not—on your life, no!' was the answer.
'There is time enough yet. The postern gate we came in by
is still open. Get the men away instantly. They can reach
home by the Glen. I will hold this demon at all hazards. Quick!
Away!'

'And lave you here?' said the stone-mason, rebelliously.

'Con, we have never had an angry word. Let it not be now.
I wish it. I order it. Go!' and he put out his hand. Con
pressed it without a word, and cried: 'The dragoons are coming.
Follow me. It's orders!'

The torches were dashed to the earth. There was a moment's
tumultuous uncertainty; then the trampling of feet and the flash
of weapons began to move away. 'Get to your feet,' he cried to
the prostrate murderer, who, half dead with terror and semi-
strangulation, had to be helped to regain his legs, and then
tottered back, as if he would fall. The face which had been
scarlet and white by turns during the night was now all but
black. 'Don't stir, if you don't want me to strangle you!'
cried young Rohan, relaxing his grasp of the neck. It did not
become necessary to strangle him. The wretch fell to the earth
in a swoon. It was a moment of unutterable lonesomeness and
horror—alone among dead or unconscious forms, with murder in
the air, the gallows looming over his own head as well as
over the murderer's, and now the dreadful clatter of a cavalry
gallop in the night, like the syllables of a chorus of the Fates in
a Greek play. But *was* he alone? A horrible misgiving as to
Mabel's fate crashed through his brain. He glanced around;
but the peasant still stuck to his post with the tenderness of a
Sister of Charity. At the same moment a rattle of dropping
shots mingled with the thunder of hoofs in the avenue, and the
next moment he was in the midst of the steaming horses of the
dragoons, and an officer, waving a sword over his head, shouted,
'Surrender!'

'Stop!' he cried. 'There are bodies lying around.' Just as
he uttered the warning, the horse of a man in civilian dress
shied, as his hoof touched Harry Westropp's body. The horseman brought his animal on its haunches at a tug. The light
from the hall lamp fell upon the horse and upon the rider. The
rider was Lord Drumshaughlin.

Dawley's plan for barring the road against the troops from
Bantry had miscarried. The demoralised party whom he left
behind to break down Snacht Bridge delayed to carouse the
remaining contents of their bottles before beginning operations.

When they did begin, they found that Snacht Bridge was a tougher morsel than, even in a condition of sobriety, they could have anticipated. The first man who wielded a pickaxe did it so unsteadily that a second proposed to relieve him of the weapon, whereupon the first retrieved his character for steadiness by flinging the pickaxe over the parapet into the raging river with an oath ; whereupon it became necessary to beat up distant cabins for a new one, with fresh delays, recriminations, and consolations from the bottles of potheen which it was easier to recruit than pickaxes ; whereupon, in the midst of their maudlin operations the dragoons galloped up, and detached a picket to escort the bridge-wreckers into Bantry, and shoot them if they did not walk as straight as the potheen would allow them. But how did Lord Drumshaughlin come to form part of the dragoon expedition ? Well, it was not with the motive Dawley had suggested of 'hiding behind the soldiers' that he had gone to Bantry. On the contrary, the information in possession of the Government named Bantry as the post of danger—as the point on which the rebel attack would be concentrated—and Lord Drumshaughlin mounted his horse and rode thither to put himself at the head of the county with a blitheness and an appetite for danger which he had never experienced since his hot-blooded bullet-hunt long ago against the Austrians in Lombardo-Venetia. He yielded to his daughter's entreaties to be left at home, all the more easily that no trouble was anticipated in that immediate neighbourhood, and his own knowledge of the peasantry, as well as of her influence with them, relieved him from all apprehension of personal danger to herself. Mr. Hans Harman was either still less apprehensive of insult to his sister's elderly charms, or less disposed to burden himself with the care of two women, for he simply turned his horse's head for Bantry without making the smallest communication to them on the subject, and found himself one of a numerous circle of old ladies with their hysterics and smelling-bottles, panic-stricken matrons with their progenies, qualmish old country squires living in lonesome places, and young bloods only anxious to be wherever there was brandy-and-water and relief from boredom—all of whom flocked within the military lines on the first warning of the rising with as astonishing a passion for scarlet as circus-bulls have an aversion for it. It was in its way characteristic that, while the country squires were turning their eyes to the Government uniforms for protection, the only two English householders in the district stood on the theory of their houses being their castles, and mounted guard for themselves.

'Why should they harm the poor children, in any case ?' said Mrs. Motherwell.

'Of course not, Jane. They've nothing particular to get here except some Books of Common Prayer and baby clothes,' said the Rector, blowing poetic blue spirals of smoke from his pipe. 'All the same, I'll just bolt and lock the back door, and you won't mind if I just leave the gun by the side of the bed, old woman—will you ?'

Joshua Neville, too, looked to his bolts and bars that night in an undemonstrative way; and, although he held strong views of the immorality of war, loaded a revolver and a double-barrelled gun on the sly, and, long after the girls were in bed, patrolled the house clandestinely with a view to possible deeds of prowess for his Queen and country. And we may be quite sure that the Queen's enemies would have fared better against many a fire-eating Whiskerando than if they had come within range of the ironmaster's honest God-fearing double-barrelled gun. His son, however, insisted upon offering his pistol and himself where there was more likelihood of action. By good luck, he found the captain of the dragoon detachment at Bantry to be an old comrade who had sold out of the Life Guards Grey for reasons of domestic economy on his marriage to a parson's penniless daughter; and, side by side with his friend Wanchope, with many a 'Will you ever forget ?' and a 'Don't you remember?' of old Knightsbridge nights, he rode out with the dragoons on receipt of the intelligence that the rebels were dispersing in Coomhóla. The smoky clouds of fire over Stone Hall had directed the cavalry on the insurgents' track; and, reassured as to the fate of the Misses Harman, Wanchope and his troop dashed after the procession of waving brands towards the Castle.

Lord Drumshaughlin had caught a glimpse of the light tangled hair fluttering on the ground. He flung himself from his horse, letting the animal start hither and thither, trembling, with the reins between its legs. He lifted up the face to the light, upon his shoulder. The walls of his chest seemed to break asunder at the sight. It was the face of a happy infant that had gone to sleep. The little rings of light hair in which the forehead was set alone rustled innocently, as if it were only the breath of an angel that was stirring them. There was no stain, no discoloration ; but Lord Drumshaughlin knew at a glance that the pale blue eyes of his boy would never open again. The bullet had gone to his heart. The lad Harry had rejoined Quish in the happy hunting-grounds.

With a roar of pain, like a wild beast's, Lord Drumshaughlin suddenly cried out : 'My daughter ! God of Heaven, my daughter !' and dashed madly into the hall. It was a place large enough to have dined half a regiment. His daughter was lying as motionless as Harry on a white-bearskin-covered couch, the young peasant kneeling and bathing her wrists with water.

'You infernal scoundrel! Who are you? How dare you?' cried the father, in a delirium; and with the stock of his heavy pistol he dealt the young peasant a savage blow on the forehead.

The blow made a horrible, hollow sound. The unfortunate youth, already on his knees, tottered like a sapling pine at some tremendous blow of an axe at its root. He put up his hand to his forehead and brought it down streaming with blood. An oozy current was trickling down his dark skin, and was sopped up by his jet-black hair. He staggered to his feet without a groan. 'I'll take that much for Miss Mabel's sake, and welcome,' the huge towering peasant youth said, quietly.

Dawley's swoon was of short duration. When he opened his eyes, it was with the sensation that the Evil One was blackly overshadowing him and examining him with a hideous eye of fire. He was, if possible, still more horrified to find that it was Mr. Hans Harman who was holding a lantern close to his face to make sure that he was not wounded.

'Kill me! Oh, God, why did you bring me back? For pity sake, kill me and have it over—I do not want to live,' the wretch moaned, still in the nightmare-land of half-consciousness.

'Nonsense, Dawley, you do want to live, and there's no reason why you shouldn't,' whispered the agent. 'You have one chance yet.'

'You are my prisoner!' cried Sub-Inspector Flibbert, who had now come up, with a party of his sombre myrmidons in their long great-coats. He slapped Ken Rohan on the shoulder with the vanity of an Indian Competition Wallah who has brought down his first tiger—'You are my prisoner!'

'That, I presume, you will arrange with a gentleman who has claimed me as his prisoner already,' quietly replied Rohan, through whose arm the slap had sent an intense smart.

Little Flibbert thought he detected some affront—all the more intolerable that it was not altogether intelligible. 'Handcuffs, here, Muldudden—handcuffs,' he cried, loftily.

'None of that, Flibbert—hang it, none of that!' said Neville, coming forward.

'I know my duty,' said the Sub-Inspector, stiffly. 'Captain Neville, I warn you not to interfere with me when engaged in the execution of my duty. Muldudden, you have heard my order.'

'Whenever you are *not* engaged in the execution of your duty, let me know, and I will pull your nose, you wretched cur,' replied Neville, furiously, in a whisper. 'Rohan, I am sorry for you,' he said, pushing little Flibbert aside, to clasp the prisoner's hand in his great palm. 'Why,' he said, starting back, 'you are bleeding!'

'Mister policeman,' said the Captain of Dragoons, who had been a disgusted listener to this colloquy, 'it was not on a pick-pocket hunt my men were brought out to-night. If you know how to treat your prisoner as a soldier should, you shall have him ; but if you don't—pray stand aside, and let us have this wound dressed.'

CHAPTER THE THIRTY-SIXTH

FATHER PHIL FLARES UP

JACK HAROLD knew so little of Dublin that he took it to be a place like Paris, where a human unit added to its multitudinous life could no more be tracked than a West Indian rivulet flowing into the Gulf Stream could be kept under observation until it struck the coast of Ireland. He had not the slightest suspicion that he was followed from the dingy, last-century hotel in a decaying street, where he had discharged himself of his embassy to the revolutionary chiefs, to the Attorney-General's office in the Upper Castle Yard. Still less could he have guessed that the solemn-sided flunkey, like a Chief Justice in reduced circumstances, who glided to the Attorney-General's ear while he was glancing over Mr. Hans Harman's letter of introduction, came with a message from a detective in the ante-room, who had followed our young friend's steps from the headquarters of Treason to the citadel of Government. But when the Attorney-General, with a perfunctory gesture of apology, left the room, it was to receive from the detective a report which steeped his visitor to the lips in suspicion. 'Hum!' soliloquised the Attorney-General, 'they are peopling the whole public service with traitors. This is, I dare say, the beginning of some plot against the judge—perhaps against myself? I've made an army of enemies in prosecuting these fellows. Madden,' he remarked to the detective, 'I think you might as well wait here while this person remains, and—don't you think—ahem!—you might manage to keep an eye on him through the keyhole?' When he returned to the room, the Attorney-General resumed the reading of Mr. Harman's letter, seemingly at the line and word where he had been interrupted. What he was really reading, however, was his visitor's face. 'Doesn't seem the sort of fellow for anything desperate—I rather like him—but you can never tell,' he reflected with a sigh, for Toby Glascock was a man who hated to do unpleasant things, not so much because they were unpleasant for others, as because they were unpleasant for himself—a pea in his patent leather shoes, a crease in his bed of roses.

Like most men of his faith and of his year in Trinity, he had tippled the 'true and blushful Hippocrene' of Young Irelandism. The ghost of his life was a 'Pike Song,' of dubious metre but indubitable treason, which he had contributed anonymously to the *Nation* in its more platonic days, and to which the taunts of Nationalist orators and editors ever since had given a malign immortality that stung like an undying worm the unlucky author of its being. He had been an even warmer Anacreon than he had been a Tyrtæus. But Toby Glascock knew when sentiment became folly, like a Byronic collar upon an elderly Town Councillor. No sooner were the political principles of his callow youth transported to Van Diemen's Land, than he took up as the next best thing the principles which were left flourishing at home in the cosy hot-beds of the Four Courts. He sensibly filed down his rose-wreathed pike into a bread-and-butter knife, and if he still blossomed into Anacreontic quips and transports, kept them for private circulation only. His young Ascendency friends in College used to say to his credit that 'if Toby was a Papist, at all events he was a damned bad one,' but in this matter also he promptly repaired the errors of his youth. He found that the faith, which rather dragged about his legs in Trinity, had fared as well as the Pike Songsters had fared ill in the world ; that red stockings were seen at the private entrée at the Castle levees, and Catholics picked out for their piety scarcely less than for more mundane virtues in the allocation of that splendid public patronage which is an ever-flowing continuation of the bribes by which Lord Castlereagh carried his Act of Union. I do not at all believe that Toby Glascock was a mere hypocrite in his religious observances ; he was at heart a Catholic, as he continued to be in some innermost secret drawer of his heart a Nationalist, even when he was sending Nationalists to lifelong burial in felons' sepulchres ; but he would be the last to see any injustice in the assertion that, when he shook his wise locks as the Cardinal's confidential adviser in weighty matters of trusteeships for hospitals and convents, and, when his resonant voice and vivid rhetoric rang out in defence of the threatened Holy Father against the diabolical forced marches of Garibaldi and his Thousand, his advice was none the less deeply pondered, and his eloquence none the less impassioned, that they were given in a cause which opened up to him a vista of a seat in Parliament as the ante-chamber to the Judicial Bench, and a seat on the Judicial Bench as the ante-chamber to a bed in Heaven. In this way, at all events, our

Tyrtæus-Anacreon had thrown aside his goblet and his garlands of posies and wrapped his patriot limbs in the silk gown of Mister Attorney ; and for the first of his Beatitudes—the seat in Parliament—was only awaiting the completion of a negotiation, now all but concluded, for overcoming the virtuous scruples of the disreputable senior member for the county of Cork, who was accustomed to regale the House of Commons with periodic exhibitions of Irish wit, Irish whisky, and Irish patriotism, in combination, to the high exhilaration of the superior nation and the deep edification of his own.

Such was the handsome, black-haired man, with face of flowing courtesy, and watering bon-vivant lip, who looked across the baize-table of the Law Room at Jack Harold, and in a frank, pleasant manner, said : 'Mr. Harman has delayed so unconscionably long, I am not at all sure that they have not had to fill up this post ; but I am going over to the Courts presently, and I will see the Master myself. If you can call here at twelve o'clock to morrow, I hope you may have something pleasant to hear, though I cannot be too confident.' 'There is no use in making enemies in that part of the country with an election in the offing,' he mused when Jack had been transferred to the care of the efficient Madden. 'I am really sorry, too. There is something taking about the chap. But that is just it—his accent is distinctly foreign—not the remotest flavour of Cork about it—and we have information that the country is flooded with the revolutionists of all nations—Heigho ! our interesting young friend must not be allowed to blow the Four Courts sky-high. I dare say a ten-pound note will send the rascal away in a tolerably good humour, and the money may come back after not too many days if there's a contest for the county. By the way, by Jove ! why shouldn't Monsignor McGrudder have the post in the Pipe Roll Office for that young prodigy of virtue and genius he wrote me about a few days ago ?'

The Attorney-General drew a rack of note-paper towards him, and dashed off two short notes in that large, floriated hand which, like his countenance, made an appearance of giving a great deal, without always passing beyond appearances. One of the notes was directed, with a volley of reverential adjectives, to Monsignor McGrudder. The other, which was placed in Jack Harold's hand by the decayed Chief Justice in the ante-chamber of the Law Room when he called next day, was simply this :

'It is as I apprehended. The Master has been obliged to fill the appointment. I am so sorry. But it is all the fault of Mr. Harman's unaccountable delay. I trust you will do me the justice of acknowledging at least my goodwill by accepting the enclosed note in payment of the expenses of your visit to Dublin. —T. G.'

It was characteristic of the young philosopher of La Mère Médecine that, though the letter was as a thick black curtain falling upon all the stage-glory of the career he had been promising himself, he nevertheless put the crisp bank-note in his pocket along with the Attorney-General's, and, by the time he felt the fresh air blowing on his temples again, was half inclined to think the bank-note the most important part of the communication. Ten pounds *plus* youth was a great deal of present money ; and as for the remote future beyond the ground covered by that dazzling quantity of silver and gold, does the butterfly perched on a luscious summer flower ruffle his pretty wings about equinoctial gales to come ? Dublin was large, and must have more brilliant corners than its workhouses for men of parts ; and in the mean while his ten pounds spread out into an obsequious army of shillings and half-crowns in silver uniforms, obligingly offering to show him the town. Those dusky Irish-American soldiers he had met in the dingy hotel were capital company to begin with ; and the faithless rogue had already remarked that the little girl behind the bar had an uncommonly wicked pair of merry brown eyes and seemed not altogether indisposed to use them. In the airy content of thoughts like these he floated across the frowsy courtyard of the Castle, whose walls of dingy blood-coloured brick, coated with the grimy sweat of ages, habitually suggested the exhalations of an evil conscience in respect of deeds done within. Passing under an arch into the Lower Castle Yard, the prancing of cavalry horses and the hoarse sound of an agitated crowd in motion roused him to the fact that something unusual was astir. The Lower Castle Yard was filled with troops and policemen. A troop of hussars with drawn sabres were keeping back a swaying crowd by backing their horses gently amongst them. Presently a great roar of voices was heard outside and two great prison vans surrounded by mounted constables dashed into the courtyard. A broken multitude surged in after them cheering wildly. The hussars, who had faced around, received a hoarse order, and set their horses and sabres in motion, upon which the rush forward became a rush backward, and the cheers changed into the groans and curses of men slashed at with naked swords, trampled under the hoofs of horses or trampling over one another's bodies.

' What is it ?' asked Jack of a man standing near him.

' Thim's the Fenian prisoners that was took last night,' was the reply.

Harold looked at him inquiringly.

'What, you didn't look at the papers to-day ?' said Madder
the detective, scanning his face slyly. 'They were all grabbed
at the Bull in the middle of the night—eighteen American officers
and the whole Directory in session—so they says. 'Twas the
mischief of a haul, wasn't it ?'

The Bull was the dingy hotel in the decaying street. It did
not tax Madden's keenness much to note what a deadly white
crept over the gay French face.

'And—what is going on now ?'

'Luk it here—they're bringing 'em up at the Po-lis Office for
examination,' said the detective.

A sudden sense of desolation struck upon Jack Harold's heart.
He felt himself a stranger in the great city. The arrests had
deprived him of all his friends at a swoop. They had, at the same
time, brought home to him a sharp sense of personal danger. The
gloomy stone-paved streets were now to him simply so many cor-
ridors of a prison, of which the policemen at the street-corners
were the warders. He crept home to his lodgings in a dirty brick
street on the northern side of the river, oppressed with a nervous
discomfort near the shoulder, as if a heavy hand were going to be
laid there. But what to do next ? He paced up and down the
narrow room till it became a stifling dungeon, till the bed with
its yellow counterpane grew in the foggy twilight into the likeness of a coffin, till a man working in his shirt sleeves in another
grimy brick dungeon over the way seemed to be cutting his
throat, and the bell of the coal-cart rumbling in the street below
sounded horrible as a passing knell. There are natures, like the
sun's, that from their own stores of central heat give out more
than they receive. There are others, like the moon's, which depend
upon light from outside for their brilliancy. Harold was one of
the weaker luminaries. He had little of those reserves of inborn
faith and principle which make your sun-gods glow whether the
winds blow high or low. He would warm at any bright body—
be it wit, wine, music, woman, a good dinner, or even a new thing
in neckties ; but some external brightness had to shine on him or
he was in dead darkness. A terrible craving for this missing sunshine began to attack his soul. It developed in a way that he had
never experienced before, in a way that perturbed him, even while
its novelty fascinated him. It was the first time his thoughts had
ever dwelt on drink for drink's sake. It was the first time also
that he formed a deliberate preference for whisky. Its brutal
strength used to repel him. Now he felt as if no less potent
spirit could drive out the cold and gloom that was settling down
within him. Nevertheless, it was with a horrid feeling of self-
contempt he gave his old charwoman the commission, and with it

the Attorney-General's bank-note.   Mrs. Mullowney was accustomed to take her posset in a small way herself at the latter end
of a sea-coal fire ; but, having boys of her own stretching on
in their teens, the honest old lady was naturally disgusted at the
youthful depravity that could require a whisky-bottle all to its
own cheek in its own clandestine chamber ; and to the indignation thus aroused were added unpleasant suspicions both as to the
genuineness of the Bank of England note and as to the source it
came from.   'What is the world coming to at all, at all,' she
mumbled to herself, ' when a shaver like that goes on a ba-a-tter
of drink just as grand as if he was the fa a-ther of a fam'ly ?   I
humbly hopes there's nawthin' quare about that note, young
man ?' she asked him, plump.   Which was a great relief to Jack
Harold ; for, although he could be a sufficiently checky youth
upon occasion, he was quailing under Mrs. Mullowney's faded old
eyes--partly through a sense of ignominious guilt, partly from a
growing suspicion that the old lady might be in the employment of
an all-seeing detective department, and might be, for all he knew,
comparing his features with a description in the hue-and-cry.
When he found that it was only the genuineness of the Attorney-
General's money that was in question, Mrs. Mullowney was easily
satisfied ; and he dissipated any remaining scruples of hers by
giving her a brand-new half-crown out of the glittering heap of
wealth she brought back to him with the spirits.

As he was stuffing the change into his pocket, a letter which
fell out on the floor caught his eye.   He immediately snatched at
it as at a new idea.   It was a letter from Miss Deborah, full of
the most flamboyant language of the affections.   Truth to tell,
after satisfying himself of this fact from a few opening sentences,
Master Jack had put it aside for more leisurely reading, while the
prospective joys of the clerkship of the Pipe Roll Office were still
titillating him ; but now that those joys had fizzed out in smoke
and darkness, he plunged at the letter as affording highly opportune reading.   It, as it were, supplied him with company over
his bottle ; it took away the uncanny lonesomeness of his carouse.
And so he took Miss Harman's honey vows and the whisky in
alternate sips.   It would be cruel to expose poor Miss Deborah's
love-letter to the gaze of a mocking world.   It was, perhaps, a
more genuine love-letter than most so-called love-letters that come
from young ladies in the heyday of their bloom and blushing
power—a letter flavouring all over with the exuberance of a heart
that thought its soil had for ever ceased to put forth love's rose-red
fancies.   So genuine were its raptures that it (taken, of course, in
combination with the other stimulant) put Jack Harold completely in love, if not with Miss Deborah, at least with the picture

of himself as she painted it ; and the distinction between the two
things was one which a harum-scarum youngster, in a horrible
mess and with the fumes of strong waters in his brain, was not
likely to split straws about.   He remembered that, in one of his
chats with Hans Harman, the agent had mentioned that jointures
of 500l. a year apiece were settled upon his sisters.   With five
hundred a year, in his own bright-coloured Paris, how the Boulevards would blossom !--how distant would seem the mists and horrors of this unhappy island !   Harman's partiality for him seemed
to promise but slight opposition in that quarter ; but, with the
agent's consent or without, Miss Deborah's Sapphic style of correspondence left him in no manner of doubt as to the consent most
immediately important.   And, finally, what else remained, except
a lifelong term of penal servitude, which would be a daily and
hourly act of suicide ?

'I will do it !' he exclaimed, with unnaturally glowing eyes.
'After all, the woman to marry is not the woman you love, but
the woman who loves you.   That makes you the dictator of the
situation.   Deborah is un peu évaporée of course ; but a nurse for a
lifetime vaut mieux than a plaything for six months.   It is finished.
I will write this night even.   It is my betrothal night.   Permit
that I honour it with a ponch d'alléluia.   Yip, yip, yip, tra lalla la
la ! '   And he brightened up his somewhat ghastly-merry chorus
with a deep draught from his tumbler.   When a couple of hours
later Mrs. Mullowney stole up the stairs oppressed with doubts
whether the youthful inebriate might not have fallen into the
fire or set the bedclothes in a blaze, she was greatly relieved to
espy him, pen in hand, scudding over sheets of note-paper with
the elation of an author in a good humour with his own work
of imagination.

It was on a bitter evening, a few days after the abortive Rising,
that Harold walked in by the back door of Father Phil's small
mansion upon his mother, and told his love.   The poor lady's first
conviction was that she was conversing with her darling's ghost.
When she had satisfied herself by solid embraces that this was
not so, the large spectacles on the little nose suddenly lit up with
indignation that it was not his ghost.   'And you dare to come
to tell me this !' said the flashing spectacles.   'I would rather
you came to me laid out in your coffin !   A woman old enough to
be your mother—a persecutor of your holy religion—a wrinkled
witch that has not a drop of sweet blood in her veins—vinegar,
every drop of it.   Oh, oh, why weren't you brought in a corpse to
me, instead of bringing me this sorrowful tale at the end of my
days ? '

'Maybe I soon will, mother.   You have only to go on

bawling like that for a short time, and Head-Constable Mul-dudden will step in and gratify your pious desire for my corpse,' said her hopeful son. He knew his power. He had been in-formed by letter that the police had been searching Father Phil's house with a warrant for his arrest. The memory of the dark-coated policeman's visit hung over the mother's mind like the sight of a flock of vultures flapping their black wings for her son's flesh. She who would not have feared to face the world in arms on any other argument yielded with more than the submissiveness of a baby upon this. The moment it was shown to be an issue between Miss Deborah and the gallows, she accepted and even thirsted for the respite. The one fate did not seem to her much brighter than the other ; but condemned men have been known to go mad with joy even for the boon of lifelong penal servitude. 'Besides, mother,' said Jack, improving his advantage, 'she really loves me to distrac-tion.'

'To be sure she does — as if anyone could help loving my unhappy child !' cried the idolatrous mother ; and a bitter ex-clamation, 'The designing hussy !' followed, which she kept for private consumption. 'Well, well, Jack, it will break my old heart, but that's so pulled and dragged by the world already it is not much that is left to be broken—I suppose we will only have to make the best of this shameless woman's plot against my boy.'

'Come, mother, that is scarcely fair—to my *future*,' said Jack, rallying a smile by way of covering his sense of his own meanness ; 'but,' he added, more nervously, 'what about Father Phil ?'

Mrs. Harold tossed up her sharp nose contemptuously. 'You had better tell him, of course,' she said, 'but—Father Phil does not count.'

Tell him he accordingly did, as soon as Father Phil came in, in his soutane and biretta, after giving out his Litany and his dear old golden-grandfather chat to his Sodality of the Sacred Heart. Encouraged by his success with his mother, and by her tranquil estimate of Father Phil, the young man dashed into a frank account of his relations with the Harman family, and of the object of his journey to Dublin, contriving, before he had finished, to make himself the hero of what he imagined to be as pretty and romantic a tale of penitence as had ever been brought to Father Phil's confessional. The old priest listened, grave and still.

'O-oh ! you unhappy boy !' he cried, rising and pacing the room, after he had finished.

'Well, sir, youth has only a season. All that will pass,'

observed the penitent, in a tolerably comfortable frame of mind. Father Phil's thunderstorms were not used to be more terrible than a hail of kissing-comfits.

'You accepted this post, as I understand, from the Government you were plotting against, because it was to bring you ninety pounds a year?' asked the priest.

'Ninety pounds a year to begin with, sir. I assure you the Pipe Roll Office is premier choix—a first-rate crib,' said Jack, thinking that Father Phil had not altogether understood.

'I am sure ninety pounds a year is very respectable, Philip,' said Mrs. Harold—'as good as a curacy in Drumshaughlin, for that matter,' she added, as a defiant shaft.

'And you were willing for this to desert your comrades, and to save yourself from the danger you brought others into?' proceeded the priest.

'I—I do not comprehend precisely, sir,' stammered his nephew with rising colour.

'I think I do,' resumed the priest, calmly. 'When your project for disposing of yourself to the Government failed, you fall back upon this ignoble plan of selling yourself to this old woman—a woman old enough to be your mother——'

'Indeed, sir, I am sure she has not more than thirty years at worst.'

'Old enough to be your mother,' repeated Father Phil, doggedly.

'Nonsense, Philip, what should you know about a woman's age?' put in Mrs. Harold, bidding defiance to her own phrase, with the heroism of a martyr.

'Having failed in your traffic with the enemy of your country,' resumed the priest, without noticing, 'you have now completed your bargain with the enemy of your religion——'

'Deborah has been a bitter enemy of Catholicism, it is true; but I think I can change all that,' said the nephew, grasping at a happy thought. 'After all, sir, could you desire a victory more triomphateuse for the Church——'

'Stop!' cried the old priest, in a voice of thunder. 'Do not dare to mix up holy things with your own mercenary traffic. Do you think the Church has any need of converts won as you have won this silly woman's heart? God grant me patience!' he cried, resuming his feverish march up and down the room. Then, stopping and facing the drooping bridegroom: 'What has brought you here? Wasn't the world wide enough for you to sin and shame yourself in without darkening my door with such a tale? You haven't come, I presume, for an old man's blessing? That would be of no importance to a philosopher like you. Miss

Deborah Harman has not expressed a desire for a Popish priest
to celebrate her nuptials, I suppose? What do you want from
me?' The whole current of the old man's kindly blood was
changed. It was appalling. Mrs. Harold for the first time in
her life dared not speak.

'Well, sir,' said his nephew, striving to give his tingling face
an aggrieved look. 'If I did want a blessing—if I did want
counsel—if I did want a roof to shelter me from a horrible
fate——'

'Better a thousand times the fate of your comrades who are
dead or in prison than the fate you are preparing for yourself and
for your miserable mother and me.'

'The poorest beggar in the parish would not be treated in my
uncle's house as you are treating me.'

'The poorest beggar in the parish would not have deserved it.
The poorest beggar would not have so perjured himself, so disgraced his name, so betrayed his faith and country for money—
for shameful, filthy, ill-got money.'

'Well, but, Philip, do be reasonable,' pleaded Mrs. Harold,
tremblingly. 'After all, the poor boy——'

'Woman!' exclaimed the old man, raising his hand like one
about to launch some dreadful anathema. 'Hold your tongue!'
She, who had been used to direct him with a wave of her sceptre,
now quailed and shuddered under the eye of one compared with
whom Bow-wow himself had seemed to be a master and ruler of
men. The shorn lamb had all of a sudden faced wolf and shep-
herdess together. She sank upon her knees, under some ghastly
terror, and raised her beseeching hands in agony. 'Oh, don't,'
she cried, 'don't curse him—my boy—my only boy!'

The old man started. He had received a poignant reminder
how fearfully the face at which every beggar urchin used joyously
to sun himself must be transformed when his looks and gesture
bore so appalling a construction. Something like a sob broke
from him. He lifted his sister from the ground, but the stern
lines about the mouth and forehead were not relaxed.

'I did not mean to curse him, Maria,' he said in a more subdued, but still pitiless voice. 'That would have been as wicked
in me as it is wicked in him to barter his purity and manhood in
this selfish, heartless way—to vow at the altar a love he cannot
feel, after his broken vows to a cause which he was willing to
abandon for a Government clerkship. The man who carries
trifling with the most sacred obligations of conscience and affection to that point is a scoundrel—yes, if he were my nephew ten
times over, a scoundrel! I do not curse him, but I blush for
him. I cast him off. Let him never approach me again till he

comes as a penitent to ask God's pardon. I will give him half
an hour to leave this house. It is now half-past eight. If I find
him here at nine o'clock I will call in the police and hand him
over. I will do it! You know if I have ever broken my word.'
Neither mother nor son dared look up to see how that awful figure
vanished. It might have been the Archangel Michael clad in the
lightnings of an angry heaven that had swooped down upon them
in the guise of Father Phil's silvery tonsure and child's blue eyes.

Jack Harold could not draw a free breath until he was out in
the nipping night air. Even then, his uncle's word 'Scoundrel!'
descended upon him again and again like the lashes of a steel-
tipped cat-o'-nine tails. The darkness seemed hardly thick enough
to hide the scarlet welts of shame that were stinging him all over.
What must he have become when the old priest, whose smile was
a Plenary Indulgence beaming on all the sinful children of men,
gnashed his teeth at him? Where was the outcast like unto him
whom his own uncle drove from the door to which Bow-wow's
sores and withered limbs were welcome? He strove hard to persuade himself that the old priest had been unjust as well as cruel—
that nineteen out of every twenty marriages Father Phil himself
celebrated were not love affairs, but marriages of bargain and sale
arranged with much more brutal frankness than his own—that
it was a bigoted dislike of Miss Harman's tracts against Popery
that was really at the bottom of the old man's aversion to the
match—and that he was surely the most irrational and inconse-
quential of men who, after anathematising him for belonging to
a secret society, anathematised him for attempting to quit it,
and reproached him as an unforgivable sin with tasting of those
political flesh-pots of Egypt upon which the Cardinal's devout
friend, the Attorney-General—the ex-Tyrtæus of the *Nation*—
banqueted to repletion. But he could no longer deceive himself
with such flippant pleas as these. He could not shut out from himself that the old priest was right—that selfishness, cowardice, heartlessness, meanness had eaten into his life like maggots into corrupted
flesh. How tawdry all the gay sophistries of the Latin Quarter
looked in the white light of this old man's simple truthfulness!—
how like the daubs and spangles of a gaslit stage when the
honest sun breaks in! As he moved away through the shuddering darkness, a horrible vision occurred to him. The sun of his
First Communion morning shone again. The odour of the sweet
spring flowers exhaled from the lighted altar. He saw himself
kneeling at the communion-rails, a lighted taper in his hands, his
snow-white rosette on his breast, a glow of heaven about him;
when lo! he saw the fresh cheeks and happy smile of the child
change into the deformed limbs and sores of Bow-wow, and the

priest with the uplifted Host recoiling with horror at the transformation. By some irresistible impulse, he passed his hands over his face and then over one another, to make sure that it was a mere fancy—that they were not really festering. He was more effectually recalled to reality by seeing the shrouded forms of a police patrol looming at him out of the darkness, their heavy footfalls sounding like the deep ticking of some unearthly clock. He shrank into the deeper gloom of an archway, his heart beating, it seemed to him, more loudly than the measured tramp of their iron-shod boots. The patrol passed away. It was the spot where he had last shaken hands with Ken Rohan upon the day when he could not repress the presentiment that they would never meet again on the same terms. And they never would ! Barriers higher and thicker than prison walls had risen up between them. Intolerable pictures would keep rushing on his mind of the wounded prisoner, lying on the chilly pallet, to which the oath of that night long ago at St. Fergal's had brought him—of the comrades dead, or in chains, or hunted on the hills, having, at all events, done men's parts:—and these gallant hearts seemed to pursue him with mocking congratulations upon his elderly bride, with condolences upon the eclipse of his brilliant prospects in the Pipe Roll Office.

Yes, there was a sufficient streak of gold in Jack Harold's character to make him feel unutterably false and mean. Once even a passionate idea crossed him of returning to cast himself at the old priest's feet as a penitent. But that of course was only a passing breath of sentiment. His feet kept moving on in the direction of the cottage on the outskirts of Drumshaughlin, where the Harmans took refuge pending the recovery of 8,000*l.* from the barony for the incendiary fire at Stone Hall. Whither, indeed, else was he to drift ? What other friendly light in all that world of night beckoned to him except that which shone out of the Harman windows ? As he came near them, another of his diseased fancies came over him. The lights from the house glimmering out upon the black band of road changed for him into gas-lamps above a dark flowing river into which he was about to fling himself. But who was ever deterred from suicide by the uncomfortable look of the river ? With a heart as cheerless as the night he was leaving behind him, Harold made his plunge— that is to say, opened the wicket and touched the knocker as nervously as if it were one of the brass handles of his own coffin he was touching. Surely a novel sensation for a successful lover under his mistress's window !

Hans Harman was alone in the sitting-room, in the midst of law papers straggling about the table in shackles of red tape.

'Hallo, this is a bad business. You must recollect that I'm a loyal man—not at all ambitious of being sent to the hulks for misprision of treason!' he cried, extending his hand with cordiality, notwithstanding. 'Well, you are welcome, in spite of all the Queen's horses and all the Queen's men. Yes, I am all alone,' he said, in answer to a look of inquiry which his visitor blushed to find discovered. 'Miss Harman is away plotting a Chrysanthemum Show, and Deborah is at some tea-fight at the Church Missions' School—I believe she is bidding them farewell —at least, there is some affecting incident or other. I don't know what has come over the girl of late.' Jack caught his keen eye scrutinising him with a curious rallying and not, he thought, unfriendly look; and he himself flushed scarlet under the scrutiny. Clearly Hans Harman knew that Miss Deborah's thoughts were running on something besides tea-fights. Clearly, also, he was not implacably set against that something. 'If you can find ten minutes' amusement in the morning paper— which is more than I can do—I will be at your service,' said the agent, perceiving his confusion, and diving back into his law papers to give him time for recovery. 'This sale in the Landed Estates Court will be a heavy business. I have the happiness to be receiver, and am half strangled with red tape and sealing-wax.'

'Will it really go to a sale, sir? Are things so bad as that with Lord Drumshaughlin?' asked Harold, with a smart of pain. The Drumshaughlin name had called up memories of an hour of heaven beside the little rivulet at the foot of Mullagh—memories of a love as different from his present sordid, hang-dog show of devotion as the lilies and roses in Mabel Westropp's soft cheek were from Miss Deborah's creased and rigid vellum binding. 'Are things so bad as that with Lord Drumshaughlin?'

'Rotten as last year's pippins,' said the agent. 'Proof of title is all but complete, and we will have the Ordnance Department fellows on the lands in no time for the survey. No child's play settling the rental of such a property as this, I can tell you,' he said, nevertheless toying with the tremendous parchment roll before him, as if it were an engaging baby. In less than ten minutes he folded up the parchment roll—put the baby to bed, as it were—and faced his visitor. 'Now, then,' he said, 'what is to be done? I think you know I have taken to you from the beginning.' He fixed his large eyes upon the young fellow with that frank, caressing air which he had more than once found so fascinating.

The fascination was especially strong at this moment. It was impossible for a friendless outcast to meet that glance of

beaming sympathy unmoved. 'I know it, sir,' Harold answered,
in a low voice, fervently.

'Well, I mean to stand by you still, if you make it possible
for me to do it. But it's a desperately serious matter. I suppose
you know what the breakdown about the Pipe-Roll Office was ?'

'Unfortunately, somebody had been installed,' stammered
the other.

'Pooh ! Nothing of the kind. You were tracked to the
Attorney-General's office straight from some red-hot haunt of
treason.'

This time the colour went instead of coming to Harold's tell-
tale cheek.

'You need not worry about that. Don't imagine I have any
bigoted views on abstract politics. As far as I can see, the only
mistake Cromwell made in Ireland was in stopping at Connaught,
and the mistake of the caitiffs who came after him to this day is
that they'd like to play at Cromwells only they're in dread
'twould get into the papers. But that's neither here nor there.
In a country like this, where one side in politics means a convict
prison, and the other a desk in the Pipe-Roll Office, I'm of the
latter school of politics ; your blunder was in thinking to combine
the two, and a pretty mess it has landed us both in.'

'Both, sir !'

'You don't suppose it is a pleasant thing for me in times like
this to have been caught introducing a rebel into the public
service ? You don't suppose my position would be even tenable,
if—ah—other and closer relations should be established between
us ? In one word, you will have to do me one good turn, if you
want to be forgiven for doing me several ill ones. You will have
to re-establish my credit with the Government by giving them a
helping hand in a matter in which you, and you alone, can help
them.'

'Help them !' exclaimed Harold, with lips the colour of ashes.

'Well, you see, it's just this way. Young Rohan is known
to have been the most pestilent of the rebels about here, and,
between you and me, is a confounded young prig and cub into
the bargain.'

A deep groan was the only comment from his visitor.

'The evidence against him is strong ; but not sufficiently
strong to be conclusive upon any of the graver charges. Now,
you, of course, must be in possession of information that would
decide the matter.'

'I !' said the other, starting to his feet in horror.

'You needn't dress your hair after the manner of the fretful
porcupine, my dear boy,' said the agent, with his most genial

I I

smile. 'It wouldn't be necessary for you to go into the box, or any unpleasantness of the kind. It would be quite sufficient for you to give indications that would enable the Government to lay their hands upon men who could be induced to get over their squeamishness on that point. You must know heaps of such men, and the weak points in their armour. The whole thing could be managed between you and me, without the intervention of any third party, and without even a memorandum of the transaction in any pigeon-hole in the Castle. Pecuniary considerations, of course, are only of secondary importance——'

'For Heaven's sake, spare me!' cried Harold. A fierce light had been kindled in his eyes. He looked around. His eye lighted on the heavy steel knob of the poker resting against the fender. A sudden tigerish temptation to send it crashing through the agent's brain seized him. But his courage failed him. He fell into the chair, sobbing, with his face between his hands, with that helpless moan: 'For Heaven's sake, spare me!'

'That is the way with all you young fellows,' said the agent, with undiminished good-humour. He was quite prepared for all that had happened. He would even have been prepared for the poker. 'The offer of five thousand pounds offends you as much as it would warm the heart of prosaic old stagers like myself. However, that is a detail for hereafter. The important point is that grievous embarrassment overhangs me, and penal servitude for life threatens you, if we have not common sanity enough to adopt the easy, confidential, and not altogether unprofitable mode of deliverance that is open to us. Assuredly, considering the relations that exist between us, and the relations that may exist between us,' he added, with a gentle emphasis, 'if I see no objection to ι king the proposition, it is not you who ought to have much difficulty in accepting it.'

The other started to his feet again, with the scared eyes and panting breath of one who had been buried alive, and was still groping through the fœtid, stifling air of his charnel-house. Harman, who watched him keenly, prepared again for the poker. The precaution was not necessary. The young man threw his arms helplessly above his head, and said, as in soliloquy, 'My uncle was right—a scoundrel! I am a scoundrel—but not such a scoundrel as you!' he hissed, turning fiercely on the agent, who this time winced under his victim's eye, and carried his hand to his breast pocket.

But the agent's calm instantly returned. 'I am a hot-tempered fellow myself, and I always make allowances. I have seen fellows quite as unreasonable as you, who afterwards changed their mind on thinking matters over,' he said, with a not entirely pleasant grin. Then, resuming his former caressing air, and putting out his hand : ' Come, it is for your own sake, after all. I have mentioned all the circumstances in a quarter you will perhaps forgive, and Deborah quite approves——'

He stopped ; for Jack Harold was gone—gone without another word. The young man fled into the open air, still as if he had but just made good his escape from the jaws of the sepulchre. As he left the wicket for the town, he saw a female figure approaching it from the opposite side. He recognised it at once as Deborah Harman's. He had barely time to draw himself into the thick shade of a great ivy hedge which overhung the wall when she came to the wicket. He noticed now for the first time that a man was with her, and that that man was the good Mr. Primshanks. Harold durst not stir while they stood at the gate together.

' And you are really, really going to give us up ? ' groaned Mr. Primshanks—' you who were the soul of our work, the rose of our vineyard, our golden candlestick among the heathen. And nothing, nothing would induce you—nothing that I could say—on my knees—Miss Harman—Deborah——'

' Nothing, Mr. Primshanks. To-night I bid farewell to the Church Missions and to you for ever,' she said, giving him her hand, and passing in.

One last temptation wrestled for an instant with Harold's infirm will. He watched her as she disappeared into the cottage. Would he return ? Even though she was a party to her brother's abominable proposition, might they not agree to drop that topic for ever ?—oh, but to call the woman his wife who had listened to so black a scheme of villainy unshocked—to take her to his arms ! As if enraged with himself for even admitting a thought that had such an intolerable taint of baseness, he struck his hand savagely against his forehead, and strode away towards the town at a speed that almost became a run—as if something horrible was pursuing him.

A few minutes afterwards a knock came to the police-barrack door ; and the constable who opened it admitted a young man, who walked into the midst of a group of policemen assembled around the fire in the day-room, and said :

' I understand you have a warrant for my arrest. Here I am.'

CHAPTER THE THIRTY-SEVENTH

THE IRONMASTER GROWS INQUISITIVE

IT was in a crisis like the present that Joshua Neville's force of character began to make itself felt. As long as it was a question of finding his way amidst the misty labyrinths of Irish life, he stumbled like a child ; but once it came to be a matter of concrete human misfortune, which is of no nation, but is understanded of all the children of men, his kind heart and strong understanding gave him the confidence which a Sister of Charity feels on a battle-field. He took command of the distracted household at Drumshaughlin Castle, and found his orders submitted to without a murmur. Mabel was still insensible when Mr. Neville's carriage whisked her father and herself away to Clanlaurance Castle. When she opened her eyes, it was to feel and yet not to feel Miss Neville's gentle guardianship, and to find herself steeped in a scene of restful English comfort. Alas ! not all the tender cares and drowsy syrups of the Neville household could medicine her into forgetfulness of the appalling sights upon which her eyes last closed. Dawley's fiery eyes swelled till they glared on her like great globes of hellish fire—his head grew to the most monstrous proportions—his arm round her waist crushed her like a band of hot iron contracting, it seemed, to burn and strangle the very soul within her. She trembled and hid her head. Her beautiful limbs shook with cold terror, and then burned with fever. The pupils of her eyes had the distended look of a child seeing some horrible apparition. Then, though she had been mercifully spared the consciousness of the scene of Harry's death, one of those mysterious psychic intimations, which pass from soul to soul by laws which are only now beginning to be faintly perceptible to science, told her that she had not seen the worst of that night of horrors. Her questions about Harry and her other half-expressed clinging anxieties drove poor Miss Neville into looks and changes of colour from which the frightened child drew auguries that put even Dawley's hell-fire face into the background. Mr. Neville had foreseen how it would be. He had the most eminent of the Cork physicians by her bedside before the fever had well declared itself—a man who was a surgeon also, with an iron nerve and an eye like a naked scalpel, and who would have inspired terror only that he inspired confidence still more. He looked at Mabel's showery gold hair in a way that threw the Miss Nevilles into agonies of apprehension.

They would have sunk on their knees and kissed the doctor's
iron hand if it could have softened him.   But even the terrible
doctor had his unguarded point in his professional chain-armour.
As he bent over the soft angel-face resting amidst that silky sea
of gold as on a cloud of glory, it almost seemed to him that
death would be better than the crime of defacing such a picture.

'Well, well, it's saved,' he said, with the sigh of a man who
had struggled hard in vain against a great temptation, 'and
we'll see if we can't save her life as well, though the poor child
has had a deadly fright.'

'Thank you, doctor,' said Joshua Neville, who had waited in
the drawing-room with as much trepidation behind his calm grey
face as if it was the life of the whole Neville family that was
trembling in the balance. 'Thank you. You will save her.'

Lord Drumshaughlin was a patient requiring more pains to
manage.   He was distracted with remorse and grief ; but he
seemed to think that the most creditable way of showing those
natural and praiseworthy dispositions was to make himself as
troublesome as possible to those around him.   The essential flaw
in his character, which was by no means bad in the main, was a
morbid egoism which, by long indulgence, had corrupted both his
power of acting for himself and of feeling for others.   Even at
this moment, when poor Harry's dead face uttered its silent
reproaches, and when the only being who disputed with himself
the empire of his heart was fluttering towards the skies, he
managed to persuade himself that he was the most aggrieved
person under Joshua Neville's roof ; that the circumstances of
Harry's death, just as an indulgent father had obtained for him a
capital career at the Cape, were in some manner a last effort of filial
perversity on his part ; that Mabel's threatening to go off heaven-
wards the moment he had recovered her, was a continuation of
her flight from home into the wilderness, just as all the glories of
London were bursting on her head and upon his ; nay, that the
very perfection of the Nevilles' goodness was in itself a grievance,
since it repressed his craving to make his feelings more stridently
heard and felt.   And what tormented him worst of all was that
he could not always keep up the self-deception as to his wrongs,
but sometimes dashed his gouty foot against something with an
internal confession that he was the most selfish, meanest, and
most worthless of mankind—in which judgment, by the way, he
overshot the mark as much as in his equally unmeasured self-
condolences.   The truth is that Ralph Westropp was one of those
men, of whom army surgeons tell us there are many, who are
lions in battle and whimpering children at the dressing of their
wounds.   Joshua Neville, on the contrary, who made but a poor

show in uniform, could not only stand suffering patiently himself, but (a rarer gift) deal tenderly with the sallies of more impatient sufferers. He took Lord Drumshaughlin's real anguish in charge with his selfishness and his gout as an indulgent nurse would deal with a teething baby, and managed to give his lordship an impression of such unobtrusive considerateness that he quietly accepted the relation, and, from accepting it, characteristically began to make it a merit in himself that he submitted to all this soothing fomentation of his wounds and attention to his bruises.

Once only did the flood of waters from the father's heart quite overflow the sterile egoism of the London clubman. It was while he leaned on Joshua Neville's arm over poor Harry's coffin as it disappeared into the yawning sepulchre in the grey shadow of the moist winter dawn. There was nobody else present except the Rector, young Neville, and two workmen. With an instinct for which Lord Drumshaughlin thanked him by a pressure of the arm, Mr. Neville had taken it upon himself not to invite Mr. Hans Harman to be of the party. . He had more hesitation in deciding against an extraordinary suggestion of his son that Harry should be buried by the side of Quish, the bailiff, whose story had somehow affected father and son in a most unaccountable manner for two prosaic people from the Black Country.—'Poor chap, he never owed much to the Drumshaughlins. I almost think Harry would feel more at home with Quish than in that stuck-up stone vault,' said the most romantic of Guardsmen.—'No, no,' said his father, shaking his head, after a judicial summing-up. 'His father could never be got to consent. Besides, if others were unkind, remember Mabel!'—And here the young Guardsman dropped the subject and flushed scarlet. He had *not* remembered Mabel quite so engrossingly of late.— There was one lonely wreath among the expensive ones which the Misses Neville heaped on poor Harry's coffin—a simply-twined circlet of rustic green with lilies of the valley glistening like angels' tears through it. Where this wreath came from nobody could tell. The Rector, who got it from his wife, and who expressed his wonder where that mother of a family got the lilies of the valley, was told to mind his own business, and could see that there were one or two angels' tears in Mrs. Motherwell's honest eyes as well as in the white chalices of the flowers. I have my own suspicions what took Katie Rohan flitting over to the Rectory like a frightened bird the night before the funeral, with the air of one engaged in the most awful enterprise of her life. She somehow trusted the Rector's wife only little less than Mother Rosalie. I rather suspect also that, for all the timidity of her fluttering heart, she was too honest to soothe herself with the belief that it was on Mabel's part alone she twined the little wreath, but that with all the sweet purity of her soul she offered it as a gratification to the dead boy's shade. May we not go further and assume that when the trembling confession of her daring deed came under Mother Rosalie's eyes, in the next communication from the Mill, a tear from Mother Rosalie's own old heart fell with the wreath upon poor Harry's coffin ? Nay, may we not take one last flight of clairvoyance and make sure that if Harry Westropp's simple spirit hovered at all near his mortal tenement that ghostly winter dawn, the sprays of lily of the valley dropped from the hand he loved made him happier than ever he had been in his lifetime—happier, perhaps, than many a dreary-hearted statesman whose shade beholds the loads of floral lumber with which a nation piles his coffin in West-minster Abbey ? At all events, the Lord Harry's coffin, with its little green and silver crown, vanished from this chilly world to one where kindlier breezes blow, and Lord Drumshaughlin had the first good heart-breaking cry that had ever attacked him since, a little curly-headed blue-eyed boy, he had seen his own mother's coffin disappear into that same vault, upon one of those pure pearly summer mornings that, for Ralph Westropp, never came again.

Miss Westropp's naturally healthy constitution saved her. She emerged at last from the weird fever-world, little more than a beautiful spectre herself, with deep mysterious shadows in her eyes such as the awe-stricken Italians used to remark of 'l' uom ch' è stato all' inferno.' To everybody's relief and wonder it was found that she was aware of all that had happened. Possibly words dropped by her nurses when they thought her delirious had given her the clue ; possibly some more subtle knowledge had come to her in the darksome deathlands she had been traversing of late ; but she spoke of Harry as a mother does of a child who has been long in heaven, and when Miss Neville judged it safe to give her the lock of fair hair she had cut off over the dead boy's brow, Mabel kissed it still with the calm sacred sorrow with which the mother inspects a tiny faded shoe. Lord Drumshaughlin, who had watched by her bedside like a great dog, fell upon his knees in a paroxysm of thankfulness, and fondled the worn outstretched hand as though it had just lifted him out of the very blackness of the pit. A less pleasant surprise was a desire expressed by Mabel to see Katie Rohan— a desire confided in a trembling whisper to Miss Neville when nobody else was by. It was a sore trial for a true-hearted sister, but Miss Neville had heard broken words during her patient's delirium, which seemed to give the key to her present request, and, however her own heart ached, she answered with a kiss of affectionate sympathy on the almost transparent white fore-head, which faintly flushed with joy under her lips. So Katie came, looking almost as white as the worn figure on the bed, and Miss Neville slipped out of the room as from a sacred place—and so, gentle reader, let you and I. But, oh dear, how are we ever to make the roses bloom again on those young, pallid cheeks ?

Having tasted the comfort of seeing his domestic concerns set in order in the ironmaster's sure-footed, noiseless way, Lord Drumshaughlin was more pleased than he cared to own even to himself to find Neville's all-seeing eye directed towards his financial entanglements.

'It's all a hopeless mess, my dear fellow—you'll make nothing of it,' he said, with the slovenly man's sigh of despair at the sight of figures. 'No man living knows his way through the accounts except Hans Harman. The figures and the lawyer's jargon would set you mad.'

'These things are not always so unintelligible as it is the business of the lawyers to make us believe,' said Joshua Neville, with a smile. 'I like figures, and I don't dislike a knotty point. If you have no objection, I should like to try what I can make of it all.'

'Neville, you are a stunning good fellow,' Lord Drumshaughlin answered, shaking his hand in a manner out of which he had been shamed for years by the callous formalism of London club life, where men shake hands like people in a plague.

All things look well in ruins. The broken old lord gave one strongly the impression of a crumbling feudal stronghold by the side of Joshua Neville's flourishing, well-ordered, factory-like mind. There was a picturesque charm about him in his dilapidated fortunes which had never struck the ironmaster when he used to meet him fluttering about Pall Mall in stays and orchid blossoms, in his false spring of second youth. Misfortune had given him a certain pathetic air of dignity, even as his thin grey side-locks and the furrows yawning in his cheeks looked so much more really handsome than when they used to be coated over with dyes and cosmetics. There was a mixture in the man of noble tranquillity in facing ruin and infantile incapacity to avert it which gave Neville something of the same feeling in helping him as a man has in rescuing a brave child who is hanging over a precipice. Besides which, the ironmaster's interest in Mabel Westropp had deepened into a father's idolatry, and in working for her he worked with the sombre enthusiasm of a Quaker saint. Accordingly, he set to work at Lord Drumshaughlin's affairs as he would set to work to decipher a complicated granitic specimen,

His first difficulty was with the floating liabilities, as to which Lord Drumshaughlin could give him but scrappy information, being sensible only that they were for ever and ever crossing him, and blinding him, and stinging him in such numbers that he had given up estimating them, as men who hear lions roar cease to occupy their thoughts with mosquitoes. Neville, believing more in arithmetic than in metaphors, was not impressed at all with this despairful way of looking at things. What he wanted was not opinions, but bills and particulars ; and quite soon he had amassed an alarming pile of documentary evidence, from the wine merchant's civil reminder on his suburban-villa note-paper to the immense blue majesty of debtors' summonses—bills from London livery stables ; bills from Horace's tailors ; judgments marked for mysterious millinery debts, for sporting losses ; bank acceptances and renewals tangled twenty times over ; pressing notes in angular hand from maiden ladies whose jointures were overdue jostling a pork-butcher's bill, scrawled in a hand that suggested he had employed one of his own swine as amanuensis, and the incumbent's timid suggestion of his lordship's unpaid-for (and unused) church sittings—all the flotsam and jetsam of a wrecked and dissipated life.

'A pretty jungle for a man to find his way through, eh ? ' said Lord Drumshaughlin, who, like most men sunk deep in misfortune, sometimes revelled in the immeasurable depth and extent of it, and had a certain pride in impressing Neville with the magnificence of his ruin.

'The only thing that is important about all these is the tot,' said the ironmaster, studying some columns of figures before him. 'And the tot,' he added tranquilly, 'is not formidable in the matter of an estate like this. Now for something more important.'

Having brushed aside the, so to say, accidental incumbrances of the estate, he attacked the real ones. All the liabilities he had been dealing with hitherto had been only so much desert sand which had got so piled and jammed around the Sphinx as almost to bury it. He now proceeded to estimate the true proportions of the naked enigma itself. A celebrated Dublin lawyer arrived at this unseasonable period of the year on a visit to Clanlaurance Castle, and spent some laborious hours with Mr. Neville over the copies of mortgage deeds submitted to the Landed Estates Court amongst the proofs of title. As the result, both gentlemen shook their heads at one another across the table, and Mr. Blaquiere, the eminent lawyer, said, with two several pinches of snuff and a prolonged consultation in the depths of his tawny silk handkerchief :

'Upon my conscience, there seems to be something very queer.'

'So I thought, or I should not have put upon you this dismal journey,' said the ironmaster, quietly.

'Why, the whole arrears of interest overdue do not appear to exceed 15,000*l.*——'

'13,715*l.* and some shillings, I make it.'

'And for this bagatelle an estate of 7,000*l.* a year, mortgaged altogether to not more than sixteen years' purchase of the rental, is to be put up for sale during the panic of a rebellion, and sold for a fourth of its value! Why, it's not merely robbery —it's elementary robbery!—unless, indeed, there's something deeper than plunder at the bottom of it. Has Lord Drumshaughlin an enemy?'

'None that I ever heard of, except himself.'

'Then who is it that has an interest in ruining the estate? Dargan you could understand, but his proceeding appears to be all square and above-board. But who the deuce is Hugg, who has joined in the petition for sale?'

The two men looked at one another cautiously, as if they both had thoughts they did not care to put in words.

'And what was the meaning of a consent to have the order made absolute? Did Lord Drumshaughlin really know he was committing suicide when he signed it?'

'I am afraid he has been committing suicide pretty nearly all his life. So many attempts have failed, he does not seem to attach very much importance to a new one. It appears it was a suggestion of Harman's, the thing being inevitable, to get it over without any wrangle in court about his private affairs, which would get into the papers.'

'A suggestion of Harman's!' repeated Mr. Blaquiere, interrupting the operation of carrying his bandanna to his nose in state and staring across the table at Joshua Neville, who stared back as intently. There was a curious silence for many seconds, when the lawyer proceeded : 'The idea of invoking the authority of the Court of Chancery—the only court that could have questioned or interdicted the sale—was also, I presume, a suggestion of Harman's?'

Neville assumed that his look was a sufficient answer. 'I believe,' he said, 'the idea was that the proceeding in Chancery would act as a check upon any precipitancy in the Landed Estates Court, and would possibly dispose the incumbrancers to come to terms.'

'Quite so, and with that excellent object Mr. Harman is appointed receiver himself, as the landlord's friend and repre-

sentative; and, by way of restraining the impetuosity of the
Landed Estates Court, the receiver comes into court and assents
to the sale in the interest of the landlord, and the Landed Estates
Court, completely reassured as to the *bona fides* of the whole
transaction by the intervention from Chancery, has no alternative but to pass the title, make the order for the survey, and
instruct the Receiver to prepare his rental ; and, with an expedition perfectly unexampled in my experience, the Ordnance Survey
people are already on the ground, and the estate is rushing headlong to a sale in the most panic-stricken year since the Famine.
Now, it seems to me,' said Mr. Blaquiere, after blowing his nose
con spirito, by way of note of admiration, ' Hugg is the missing
link in as rascally——.   Forgive me, Mr. Neville, for being betrayed into an adjective—at least at this stage.'

'I shall have a word with Harman,' said the ironmaster,
thoughtfully, and put on his hat.   The agent was busy with
maps, rentals, and tracings in the Estate Office when Mr. Neville
sauntered in and mentioned that he had undertaken to look into
Lord Drumshaughlin's affairs, as a friend, and that it would
facilitate him very handsomely if he had access to the estate
books.

'Hum, more of this insufferable English meddling,' soliloquised the agent, who had rather a disdainful opinion of his
visitor.   'Thinks he's divinely commissioned to go nosing every
house drain in the universe except his own.   Dare say his inves-
tigations will be as deep as that gold mine he discovered for us in
his interview in the *Banner*.   What amazes me is how a nation
of dull prigs like this fellow ever rose above the sceptre of a
vestry meeting.'   Then aloud: 'Might I ask with what practical
object ?'

'To find out who Hugg is,' said the ironmaster, quietly.

. The agent started.   It was but a moment's quiver through
the sensori-motor apparatus, and was instantly checked by a
strong will ; for Harman was sensible that eyes as sharp as the
words were fixed upon him ; but the quiver had not escaped these
quiet grey eyes.   Never before had six syllables so revolutionised
Harman's opinion of a man.   The contempt of a moment ago was
changed into mortal hate and dread.   'What,' he said, with his
usual jaunty smile, 'Lord Drumshaughlin is not content with
Hugg's money without having his secrets as well.   What if Hugg
answered that he does not lend in that line ?'

'Lord Drumshaughlin has expressed no wish upon the subject.
It was a whim of my own,' said Neville, in the same unim-
passioned tone.

'In which case, Mr. Neville, sorry though I am to seem

uncivil, I am obliged to reply that it is as officer of the Court of Chancery I am now the custodian of those books, and I should not feel at liberty to place them at the disposal of a stranger.'

'Not with Lord Drumshaughlin's authority ?'

'Not without the authority of the Court,' said the agent, shutting his shiny white teeth in a kind of smile that looked like the snapping of a sharp pair of scissors—a smile of triumph and defiance.

'Yes,' said Mr. Neville, meeting Mr. Blaquiere in the drawing-room before Lord Drumslaughlin came down to dinner, 'we are not astray.'

Mr. Blaquiere, who had not said a word or heard a word as to their common search, nevertheless wagged his eminent bald head in gentle token that neither in the present instance nor in any other could it possibly be otherwise.

'Now, my dear sir,' proceeded the other, 'this sale must be stopped at once, but not, you perceive, so precipitately as to endanger our getting to the bottom of this business.'

'I should perceive quite clearly,' said Mr. Blaquiere, who did not altogether like the way in which the stage-managership of this drama was slipping out of his hands, 'if I could perceive where that thirteen thousand odd, instalments of interest overdue, is to come from.'

'Here it is,' said the ironmaster, handing him a cheque of his own for the precise amount, even the shillings being set out in the clear round hand of a man with an easy conscience.

'Bless my soul!' exclaimed the lawyer, who the next moment would have given a handsome fee to recall that gush of unprofessional emotion.

'Lord Drumshaughlin is so unbusinesslike a man that he obliges me to be unbusinesslike,' said the ironmaster, in an apologetic tone. 'He would, no doubt, ruin his family in the grand manner rather than put this thing in the form of an I O U between him and me. You will please accept it as a personal advance of my own on account of your costs in having this petition of sale discharged. What I would now beg of you is to lose no time in placing us in a position to obtain possession of the books, without, you understand, any public proceedings of an alarming character that might possibly have the effect of preventing us from obtaining them in their integrity.'

'My dear sir, perfectly,' said Mr. Blaquiere, whose professional angularities were smoothed out. 'I will set out to-night. We mustn't move in the Landed Estates Court as yet. The Chancellor, I am satisfied, will hear the matter in chamber ; with

an affidavit from Lord Drumshaughlin, and the impounding of
this cheque, he is sure to discharge the Receiver's order; there
won't be a word of it in the papers; and before Harman can
receive the order of the Court, you will be in a position to move
as you may deem desirable.'

Three evenings afterwards Mr. Neville received an official
letter embossed with a great sealing-wax plaster, by special
messenger from Mr. Blaquiere, and after dinner that night he
asked his son Reggy to drive him over to Drumshaughlin.   It
was a bitter-toothed winter night, and, partly owing to this,
partly owing to the terror of martial law which still overhung the
district, there was not a living creature visible, and scarcely a
light burning, when the two men stopped outside the Estate Office,
which was a one-storied, semi-detached building, a little withdrawn from the street.   Mr. Neville was soon at the dark doorway, trying a key which Lord Drumshaughlin had told him
where to find.   The lock turned, but the door did not give way
before several vigorous thrusts. 'It is bolted,' he said, with some
annoyance. 'We must try the windows.'

'By George, governor, this looks uncommonly like a burglary,'
said the Guardsman, half uncomfortably.

'So it is, only the Lord Chancellor is in it with us,' his father
replied, trying a last push at the door. 'Hallo, what have we
here?' he cried, stumbling against a dark body coiled up in the
shadow of the doorway.

'It's only me, sir,' said the mass of rags, rising, and disclosing
the pinched old face of Meehul, the evicted tenant of Cnocaunacurraghcooish, only thinner and bluer than we saw it last.

Neville recognised him, and remembered with a shudder that
he and his son had been charged with Quish's murder. 'How do
you come to be here?' he asked, sternly.

'They turned me out o' gaol yesterday mornin'—they hadn't
a breath agin me—nor agin the poor boy either, though they kep'
him,' was the reply.

'But what are you at here, and at such an hour?'

'Begor, waitin' till mornin' to ketch Hans Harman whin he
comes to the office, an' demand some share of justice.'

'What! you miscreant, you mean more murder, and you have
the hardihood to tell this to me!' cried the ironmaster, grasping
him stoutly by the collar.

'Murdher! wisha, is it the likes of me?' said Meehul, a
ghastly touch of sarcasm playing about his emaciated blue face.
'Amossa! I haven't as much stringth as would murdher a cat
at this present, if the Lord gev me the warrant.'

Joshua Neville could feel how the poor old bones quaked, and penitently let go, a handful of wretched rags coming away in his grasp.

'Oyah, wisha, no, asthore,' continued the old peasant, ''tis only foolish boys that do be thinkin' of the likes of that. I only wanted to show his honour a few ould resates that would prove to the gintlemen of any coort that I ped the gombeen-man back five-and-twinty pound for his tin pound, besides payin' three Griffiths for the ould sthripe of bare mounthaun all the time. All I wants is justice, and Hans Harman was always a pleasant-spoken gintleman to me—that I must say in honesty, no matther if he thrun me out a dozen times for the three Griffiths.'

'But why stay here all night to tell him that in the morning ? '

'Begor, sir, that's simple enough, though I havin't a great deal of English. I had nowhere else to face. The neighbours daren't give a night's shelter to an evicted man. It's agin the rules of the Office. They'd be thrun out theirselves if they were caught, and caught they'd be, for a sow can't litther—with respects to you—that it isn't known at the Office a'most before you could hear the bonnives.'

'Do you mean to say you have nowhere better than this to turn to spend this bitter winter night in ? '

'Well, thin, indeed, sir, I remarked that very thing to 'em at the gaol, but they wouldn't keep me there. The childher's in the workhouse, and I suppose I may as well "take the House" myself to-morrow, if I can't get justice ; but it's a long shore of a road to Banthry—eighteen long Irish miles, they counts it—on an empty stomach ; so I humbly hopes 'twas no offince to make my own o' the doorstep for the night.'

Joshua Neville had almost forgotten his business at the Estate Office. 'Well, well,' he said at last, briskly. 'We will see about those receipts of yours presently, Meehul. Perhaps you'll find that justice is not dead, after all. In the meantime, just lend us a hand in prising open one of these windows.'

'Oyah, sir, if it's to get in you wants, you can do it aisier than that. From the wall of Tummulty's backyard I can aisily get on the roof, an' creep down through the skylight—I was just thinkin' while ago whether a stretch in the loft wouldn't be more comfortin' to my own ould bones than a night in the cowld, only I was afraid they'd think 'twas maybe for robbery or clamper I was there, and, thanks be to Him above, no stink of dishonesty ever came next or near one of my blood, though it's cowld blood enough at the present.'

Cold as it was, it was ardent enough to whisk the old bones on to the roof in a jiffy ; and, after due floundering, Meehul unbolted the front door and flung it open.

'Now, Reggy, good-night—you might take home the trap,' said the ironmaster, striking a match and lighting a taper. 'I am not likely to finish here before morning. They will give me my breakfast at the Mill.'

'Was there ever such a country!' young Neville remarked to his moustache on the way home. 'Everybody seems fated to do something strange—and the stranger the more likely. Who in Sheffield would ever dream of the solemn old governor effecting a burglarious entry in the middle of the night for purposes unknown? And, by Jove! is he doing anything half so unaccountable as his son is doing, or only waiting the chance to do.' At which words he touched the mare into a gay canter, and all the way back through the sable night troops of bright spirits flew and carolled round his head like choirs of singing birds.

Mr. Neville had provided himself with Lord Drumshaughlin's duplicate key of the office safe, without acquainting him too minutely either with his own plans, or with Harman's astounding invocation of the Court of Chancery to secure his refusal to acknowledge Lord Drumshaughlin's authority in his own Rent Office. He was soon foraging industriously among ledgers, deeds, and receipt-blocks. An hour passed away, and his head was never raised. An open letter marked 'Confidential' slipped out of one of the books—a small ledger. He tapped his thumb-nail against his teeth, which was a habit with him when puzzled.— 'Pooh! I'm not here for curiosity—I'm here as an officer of justice,' he said to himself. 'If it's anything really confidential, nobody shall be the worse. If it is otherwise——' Without further hesitation, he read the letter, which was one from Dargan to Harman about arrears of interest on the Hugg loan. As he read his eyes glistened. Under an emotion which he found uncontrollable, he sprang to his feet and paced the room. 'So we are right!' he cried, a gleam of triumphant vanity mingling in the indignant fire of his eyes. 'And this is Hugg! What a rascal!'

He stopped on suddenly meeting the patient, hungry gaze of Meehul, who had waited all this time noiselessly in the passage. 'Forgive me, I had quite forgotten,' he said, drawing the old man kindly into the room. 'Now for your affair.' Meehul began a story scarcely less involved than the tangle of difficulties with the Rent Office and the gombeen-man, in whose meshes he had been struggling for hopeless years on the bleak top of Cnocauna-curraghcooish—poor, ragged, grey-haired, vulture-pecked Prometheus that he was. Whatever obscurity he had as a narrator he plainly felt would be amply cleared up by a dirty bundle of thumbed and frayed receipts, which he produced from the red handkerchief coiled in the airy recesses of his caubeen. The Irish peasant preserves the most insignificant bit of writing connected with his holding as religiously as the Jews did the Golden Candlestick and the brazen laver of the Ark. Joshua Neville set himself in his earnest, dogged way to master the old peasant's financial affairs, and soon understood plainly enough that a loan of ten pounds from the money-lender to pay rent was the beginning of an endless chain of petty payments and increases of interest, the upshot of which was to leave the debt several times greater in the end than it had been in the beginning; while his transactions at the Rent Office had been following a still more complicated course of payments on account, which somehow left the debt greater after every payment. The unfortunate old creature's life for years had been simply one prolonged agony of legal strangulation, with the agent and the money-lender in turn tugging the rope. But there was something in the rent receipts which exercised a curious fascination over the ironmaster. He turned the smeared and ragged dockets over and over again.

'Your rent is stated in the receipts as eleven pounds,' he said, turning over a ledger until he came to Meehul's townland and name. 'I find it is only returned here as nine pounds, and,' turning to the rental which Mr. Hans Harman was engaged in drawing up for the Landed Estates Court, 'I find that eleven pounds is again the figure that is returned to the Landed Estates Court. Did you not obtain the benefit of the general reduction which Lord Drumshaughlin agreed to when Mr. Harman became agent?'

'Oh, sure enough,' said the old man. 'I used to give eighteen days' duty-work in the year at the Castle, and there was two-and sixpence a yard for the turf, and a thrifle of five shillings for the blackweed and redweed we gathers in the tide, and a fine for a weddin' or a christenin', or a thing like that; and Mr. Harman—indeed, to give the divel his due--God bless his honour!—he rid us of all thim things, and we had niver to pay but the eleven pounds ever since -- so 'twas the blessed relief for the tinants. Indeed, for the matther of that, he niver was the man to refuse a thrifle now and a thrifle again from a poor man, though of coorse he kep' the notice-to-quit like a rock of ice over our heads all the while.'

'Meehul, my man, here's a sovereign—go and get a bed for yourself,' said the ironmaster rapidly. 'You can leave these receipts with me. I'll redeem to-morrow morning, and you can fetch back the family to the mountain as fast as wheels can carry them.'

The old man exhibited a comical state of struggle between tho attraction of the gold piece and the danger of abandoning his beloved documents to the custody of a stranger. He had been so accustomed to take it for granted that, in the nature of things, well-dressed people were created to plunder and overreach a poor man, that he might be excused if he either failed to understand his good fortune, or suspected some snare in such incredible benevolence. As the result of a scrutiny in which the dry, withered flesh was puckered up in anxious ridges about the wasted eyes, he remarked, arranging the red handkerchief in the caubeen as a preliminary to putting it on his head : 'Well, your honour has a good face whatever.' There was still some faint sweet odour of a faith in human nature about old Meehul.

'Now I am beginning to understand,' said Joshua Neville, with the deep content of a Huttonian who saw the crux of his life solved by beholding a block of limestone pass into crystalline marble. He had just remembered that the little ledger from which the confidential letter dropped was labelled ' Composition Account.' He pounced upon it, and ferreted out the townland of Cnocaunacurraghcooish, then slapped his knee with a gesture of triumph. 'The very figure—two pounds—the very difference between the rent as paid and the rent as returned ! We must proceed cautiously in this, but I shouldn't be surprised if 'twas the same over the whole estate. This "Composition Account" must be placed in safe keeping. What an—infernal rascal !'

'Lord Drumshaughlin,' he said, in the breakfast-room at Clanlaurance Castle about noon the next day, 'I don't wish to disturb you unnecessarily, but it is time to tell you that the proceedings in the Landed Estates Court are over, and proceedings in a criminal court are in a fair way to commence.'

It was an unlucky way of putting it. Lord Drumshaughlin *was* disturbed, horribly. He grew ghastly pale. There were so many ugly secrets in his wasteful and daredevil·life —so many clamorous duties neglected and lawless passions indulged --that, though he had no reason to believe he had incurred legal guilt, his conscience afforded him no conclusive assurance that in the criminal proceedings announced by this grey-faced, passionless, upright man he himself might not figure as the criminal.

The other took it as a matter of course that he should gasp and grow pale. 'Yes,' he proceeded, 'you have been the victim of a barefaced swindle –a swindle going on for years, and, so far as I can see, eating into every item of your rental.'

A sunbeam of relief played over Lord Drumshaughlin's face. One would have supposed the news of the swindle was a highly gratifying piece of intelligence to the victim. 'Humph,' he said, 'nothing very new with me. Fools like myself are made to be

K K

swindled. I'm not sure that we're of much other use. Who is
it now?' His eyes suddenly kindled, as if he saw the letters
forming on Joshua Neville's lips. 'It's this fellow, Hugg! The
name always sounded like the click of handcuffs on my wrists.
Who the devil is Hugg?'

'That's just it. There's no such person as Hugg. Hugg is
Harman.'

'Harman!' exclaimed Lord Drumshaughlin, falling back in
his chair, his jaws wide apart, his scanty forelock stirring as
though it were about to stand on end. Neville thought it was a
fit. At the same moment Hans Harman himself entered the
room, looking as ghastly as a spectre, but the handsome eyes still
rolling fearlessly around, and his tall figure rather more squarely
set than usual. He had just received by post the official order
in Chancery terminating the Receiver matter, and had boldly
made for headquarters to discover the extent of the disaster.

The old lord sprang to his feet and flew at him like a panther.
'Harman,' he cried, extending his thin white hand, with fore-
finger outstretched, at him. 'Mr. Neville has just been telling
me who Hugg is. Hugg is a scoundrel, and so are you— a
dastardly, treacherous, sneaking scoundrel, do you hear? You
needn't fiddle for your revolver. You have not the courage to get
hanged, damn you! There was a time when I would have asked
you to take one pistol while I took another, and settle it across
the table-cloth, but now—faugh! I'll be treating you too well if
I ring for a groom to kick you out.'

Harman's motion towards his breast-pocket was only momentary. He listened to the rest with a light curl of scorn lurking
around his set teeth and inquiring eyes. He half thought he
knew now what he came to find out—that the discovery went no
further than that he was Humphrey Dargan's real partner in the
incumbrances. 'I am accustomed,' he said, calmly, 'to Lord
Drumshaughlin's fits of outrage. They answer him for fits of
virtue. I am myself to blame for encouraging them. I have
borne his sins for too many years before the public, and his
insults when the public were not looking. If I tried to spare
him pain by pretending that it was not I myself who was pro-
curing him money to stave off ruin many a day ago, I suppose I
have no reason to be astonished if he turns on me now and bites
me. I came on—other business. If there is nothing more to be
said I had better take my leave until Lord Drumshaughlin's
gout departs and his reason returns.'

'There is more to be said,' said Joshua Neville quietly.
'There is a great deal more to be said, but it is not yet quite
time to say it. I have taken charge of the estate books under

an authority from the Court of Chancery, and have already satisfied myself as to their contents.'

Harman reeled as if some frightful blow with a blunt instrument had descended on his head. 'So,' he said, with a desperate attempt to keep his jaws together, 'this is a plot. You have already got as far as burglary. I must go to make sure that you have got no further.' It was not well said. In going to the door he staggered.

Lord Drumshaughlin, who, even yet, had only Hugg before his mind in estimating the character of Harman's villainy, stood blazing with fury. 'The swindling part of the thing I could forgive,' he cried, 'but the deceit, the cunning, the infernal treachery! Harman, you'll take it to your grave with you. You're a scoundrel!' He suddenly marched across the room, seized the agent by the throat in a grasp of steel, and with all his force flung him through the doorway. 'A damned scoundrel!' he repeated, closing the door, and extending his hand cordially to the ironmaster.

CHAPTER THE THIRTY-EIGHTH

THE ELECTION

It was Nomination Day in the Cork County Court-house. O'Shaughnessy had obtained his Governorship of the important island of Tumtum in the South Seas. It afflicted John Jelliland's conscience sorely to do it, but how was he to get on in the House without his Irish Attorney-General, and where was the ministerial seat so safe as O'Shaugh's? O'Shaugh, to be sure, was a disreputable old tippler; but what better qualification in the governor of an island where fire-water was the chief object of adoration? Putting it at the worst, it was no greater scandal to present him in spirits of wine to the South Sea Islanders as their ruler, than to have him representing five hundred thousand more or less civilised people in Cork under the all-seeing eye of a gallery of reporters. Besides, even so passing honest a politician as John Jelliland could scarcely avoid reflecting that, if O'Shaugh's manners and customs in the smoking-room of the Reform Club were continued in the tropics, the Governorship of Tumtum would be soon again a plum at the disposal of the Ministry. So O'Shaugh got his island, and was with difficulty dissuaded from rising in a full after-dinner House to bid a tearful farewell, and the comic journals were agreed that Irish wit and humour were

departing with the ex-member for Cork to the South Seas, and all
the corrupt little coteries in his constituencies who had tasted of the
constitutional advantages of Parliamentary representation, either
in the shape of magistracies or post-offices, or tide-waiterships or
O'Shaugh's whisky-punch, got up dithyrambic addresses recom-
mending the Governor of Tumtum to his unclothed subjects as a
compendium of all the qualities desirable in a king of men.   His
Excellency's seat for the county of Cork was, of course, the only
matter of the smallest Ministerial interest in connection with the
appointment ; and Glascock went down to take up possession of
the seat with as little ceremony as if he were a Sheriff executing a
writ, or a man dropping into an opera-box duly engaged for him.

He stood among his friends to the right of the Sheriff, shed-
ding his beams to right and left like an affable sun and dipping betimes in Monsignor McGrudder's gold snuff-box, which
was a present from Cardinal Rimbomba, and bore His Eminence's
family arms.   Of course, the lively blackguards of Cork turned
up in their thousands to hoot the Attorney-General, whose hands
were imbued up to the armpits in the pending State prosecutions.
That was to be expected.   Glascock referred to them with a
fatherly smile as 'my dear old vivacious Cork friends,' and bowed
with a genial grace when an egg aimed at his head from the gallery diffused its yellow nimbus over a gigantic parish priest behind
him.   Not a word could be heard, of course, in the din ; but that
was no particular disadvantage to a candidate who had nothing in
the least likely to be popular to say ; and all the barbed observations of the gallery glanced lightly off a gentleman who had every
reason to calculate on catching the afternoon train for Dublin
as the elected member for Cork.   There was no other candidate
in the field.   The Bishops, whom he dutifully consulted before
issuing his address, and from whom he ostentatiously adopted a
phrase or two and several adjectives, were entirely favourable to
his candidature.   His personal piety, the Cardinal's known partiality for him, some diplomatic hints at Disestablishment and Disendowment, and the necessity for grappling with the spirit of
Irreligion by co-operating with the Government in stamping out
secret societies – all seemed to unite the clergy in an irresistible
phalanx behind the Attorney-General.   The Tory magnates of
the county, on the other hand, had held a meeting, at which
it was unanimously resolved not to embarrass the Ministerial
candidate with a contest at a moment when the first duty of all
loyal men was to aid in trampling out the smouldering embers of
rebellion.   Finally, the chicane of Parliamentary elections was to
the Nationalists simply a thing of hissing and of scorn. Upon the
whole they preferred to see elections won by antediluvian Tories,

with good old honest-spoken ascendency and bigotry in their blood, rather than by leering lawyers who tricked themselves out in the people's wrongs and creed in order to enhance their attractions in the vile market where political coquettes display their charms. But the best use the young men could see for a Parliamentary candidate of any colour was to hoot him. In any case, they were too much depressed by the abject failure of the Rising, and the pending trials of their leaders, to be formidable. They had assembled simply because the Nomination afforded them the only legal opportunity of giving vent to their feelings which had presented itself since Martial Law laid its ironclad hand on their throats.

A frigid old baronet, with a certain lonesome dignity like that of an iceberg in its own country of eternal ice, proposed the Attorney-General, in a voice that seemed to have been laid up since the days before Catholic Emancipation, and was not yet quite sure that it had returned to life. The iceberg froze the audience into a respectful silence ; but he had no more notion of addressing himself to the rabble in the gallery than of dancing a hornpipe for their amusement. His few haughty sentences were confided to the Sheriff with the air of a Jehovah conversing with Moses in the clouds of Sinai, while the wondering multitude cooled their heels below. Although Glascock pretended to listen with visible edification, and extended his hand at the close with as much effusion as was consistent with a haunting doubt whether it would be accepted, my private opinion is that he did not hear a single sentence What he really said, speaking on the part of the Tory hidalgoes of the county, consisted of oracular half-sentences like—'In times like this—spirit of communism abroad—foundations of property and of society itself menaced—duty of all loyal subjects of the Queen—repress personal and party predilections ;' with much more that was ' faultily faultless, icily regular, splendidly null '—the upshot being that the county gentry were graciously pleased to bestow the seat on the Attorney-General, which he accordingly on their behalf did, bestowing two fingers equally fixedly with it. The chilly baronet was suffered to proceed in awestruck silence, until a compassionate voice from the gallery, 'Yerra, go home, and give yourself a hate of de tire, my poor man !' followed by a roar of laughter, brought his speech to a disastrous peroration.

Monsignor McGrudder stood forth in all the majesty of his thick-rimmed gold spectacles and purple buttons to second the nomination in the name of the clergy. The little knot of Catholic bourgeois, who either had been or hoped to be elevated into magistrates, governors of lunatic asylums, grand jurors, or other such rustic Panjandrums, waved their hats and made unheard-of efforts of enthusiasm ; but the young men, who had tolerated the baronet, rose in instant insurrection against the Monsignor. His altar-denunciations of Fenianism had made him fiercely unpopular. 'No priests in politics !' the young men growled between their teeth, their eyes flashing dangerously. The Monsignor for his part gave them back fire for fire. He could not help feeling saddened with thoughts of former election scenes on that very hustings, when his sonorous voice was as decisive as the Returning Officer's, and when the man who said him nay had better have addressed himself to an unloosed menagerie. But he did not so much mourn the wreck of his own influence in the county as he was scandalised by the insolent growth of a spirit which in his eyes had all the seven heads of the French Revolution, with its *noyades* of priests and its worship of an impure Goddess of Reason. He might be martyred by this Beast, but he was not going to truckle to it.—'Bah !' he said, waving a comminatory arm at the angry crowd. 'The cause of God's Church is not going to be put down by the clamour of ragged brats of boys.'—His great chest and shoulders were thrown back in a fine statuesque posture of defiance, and his right foot was planted as firmly as if it were rooted to the Rock of Ages. The spectacle was one of dignity, and even grandeur. The massive old ecclesiastic stood there clothed around with the tranquil majesty of Divine Right, while the young men bayed at him and glowered at him with the wild hungry flame of Human Liberty in their eyes— 'Yes,' he proceeded, fearlessly, 'I am here to-day as a humble priest of God's sanctuary——'

'Why don't you stay there ?' shouted one pale-faced youth, at which the angry cry swelled up again, 'No priests in politics !'

'I am here to-day,' repeated the Monsignor to their teeth, 'to express the gratitude of all men who love religion and value authority to the Government whose vigorous measures have delivered this land from the most deadly danger that ever threatened our holy faith in this Island of Saints ; and I regard it as the Attorney-General's highest claim upon this Catholic constituency, next to his own well-proved Catholicity and attachment to the Holy See, that he has borne an honourable and conspicuous part in the warfare against those accursed secret societies that were eating into the faith of our people and recruiting souls for hell——'

The crowd were beginning to surge forward ominously.

'Magnificent, but, confound it, it's not war !' muttered Glascock to himself, discontentedly looking at his watch. 'And it's going to lose me the five o'clock train. Don't you think, sir,' he whispered, diffidently, 'that a pleasant word or two to the boys——'

'I'd scorn it!' cried the Monsignor, pronouncing the 'scorn' with a great many r's, and sweeping indignantly round with a glance that made poor Glascock's guilty head bob approvingly, as who should say: 'Certainly. Scorn is the very mildest term for it. I should like to catch the fellow who suggested it, myself.' A trembling little man of peace, who wanted nothing in life except a tide-waitership for a scapegrace nephew, almost died of tears when the Monsignor's eagle eye lighted upon himself. 'A pleasant word, indeed, to the enemies of God's Church, to the desecrators of His temple!'

The angry crowd were swarming on to the witness-table in front of the orator. Some passionate encounter was imminent, when the comic element, which is never lacking in a Cork crowd, came to the rescue. The Cork folk are the Irish Parisians. They have something of the wit and artistic gift of the Boulevardians, with the hankering after barricades of a crowd from the Buttes Chaumont. The orator at a Cork meeting is only one in a merry circle where whoso has anything to say says it *sans gêne*, and when 'Irish potatoes flavoured with Attic salt' (as Father Prout, himself a Corkman, puts it) are always flying about in abundance. A sweep, in the full sable uniform of his profession, had planted himself on the witness-table in front of the Monsignor, in a state of diabolically high spirits. 'Yerra, listen to dat for language!' cried the satirist, pointing his black paw at the Ajax-like figure of the dignitary. 'Dere's ould Paddy McGrudder's son for you!— ould Bottle-de-Broth they used to call him, wasn't it, sir?' he innocently inquired of the Monsignor himself. 'A dacent 'ittle man he was, if he didn't warther de whisky on de people—and he did dat for de people's good, to be sure, de same as de son do be cursin' us. Oh, boys, look at de gold specs of him!' he cried, enjoying intensely the Monsignor's rising colour. 'And look at all de purple and fine linen, for de honour o' God! Begor, ould Bottle-de-Broth wouldn't know his own son in his fine Italian regimentals, so he wouldn't!' The crowd roared at each of these rude thrusts, and the Monsignor winced worse than he would have winced if he had been on a bed of torture and the sweep practising with the thumb-screws.

'This exhibition of scurrilous ribaldry,' he cried, his white hair tossing majestically, 'comes in appositely to remind us how narrow an escape we have had in this Catholic land from the blasphemous teachings of Garibaldi and the Carbonari.'

'Who's dim, your reverence?' asked the sweep. 'Tree cheers for Garrett-de-Dandy and de udder fellow, anyway! Dey

can't be so far wrong whin de Monksinger has de bad word for
'em.'

'Oh, oh!' interposed the scandalised Glascock with eyes
gently directed to the empyrean. 'This is holy Ireland! You
will have them cheering for the devil next.'

'If we did 'imself, we're less in de ould boy's debt dan you
are, Toby, anyhow,' returned the undaunted sweep, who had by
universal acclaim assumed the reins of supreme power for the
moment, and had a whole court hanging on his lightest word and
roaring at his coarsest jest.

'Order, boys, order!' exclaimed Mat Murrin, rising to the
left of the High Sheriff like an eye-glassed Neptune to appease the
waves. Whether it was a wink that lurked behind the eye-glass
the public appeared to be in some doubt, but the rest of his face
was as solemn as a bench of bishops while he said severely:
'Have some respect for the clergy.'

'Holy fly! and is *dat* de clargy?' cried the sweep pointing
the dirty finger of scorn full in the Monsignor's face. 'Boys,
look at de clargy! Begor, if dat's de Church, and if dat'—
pointing to the Attorney-General—'is de State, 'twas a'most
time for de boys to try what a tetch' (touch) 'of physical force
could do to improve tings.'

Monsignor McGrudder's patience was utterly exhausted. He
bent his sturdy body over the bench, and aimed a thundering
blow in the direction of the sweep's black mug. 'Physical force!'
he cried, boiling with indignation. ''Tis well for you I'm a priest
and that you have the police to protect you, or I'd give you a
polthogue in the gob that would teach you what physical force is,
you miserable *sprissaun*!'

This touch of nature, so far from aggravating the situation,
elicited a roar of approving laughter from the crowd. The Monsignor's rough-and-ready prowess threatened to make him almost
popular. Nobody seemed to enjoy it better than the sweep, who,
having by an agile duck of the head dodged the blow, came up
with his white teeth grinning resplendently in their sooty frame-
work. 'Begor, your reverence,' he remarked in a tone of confidential good humour, 'if you were only as good a politician as
you're handy wid de knuckles, we'd be all going to you for
pinances for our sins. Come, Monksinger,' he said suddenly,
'answer me one question, and I'll take de pledge agin openin'
my gob for de rest of de surmonies.'

'I will!' said the Monsignor, seeing a prospect of a respite
from his torturer and facing him boldly.

The diabolical little sweep waited for a moment of dead
silence. 'Was it Dublin Castle or de people ped for de port wine

it took to give your reverence your complexion?' he demanded with a look of triumph, which was his vengeance for the blow.

'Drop that, you little devil!' cried Con Lehane, springing on the table and firing the sweep like a cricket-ball into the body of the court; then, drawing himself up like a massy rampart between Monsignor McGrudder and the audience, he said: 'We won't listen to you, your reverence. That's an end of it. No priests in politics!' And again the young men formed forward with that deep ground-swell cry: 'No priests in politics!'

There was something about Con Lehane's determined reverence which daunted Monsignor McGrudder more than the sweep's flippant blasphemies. He did not attempt to utter another word. With a gesture to the High Sheriff he retired in silence before the stone-mason from the rostrum whence he had so often thundered as a king. He had the feeling that he was doing a solemn thing; and so he was—the Old Order was giving place to the New.

Glascock's rising to speak was, of course, the signal for the breaking up of the fountains of the great deep. Amidst the yells the carcase of a dead cat came sailing down close to the Attorney-General's head. 'Dere's your patriotism, Toby,' said a voice. 'Wouldn't you know it be de smell of it?'

'No, indeed, my dear friend,' said Glascock, with face of flowing courtesy. 'I'd have thought it was one of your own family.'

'Yerra, Toby, what did you do wid "De Pike," agra?' asked voice Number Two. 'Eh, my noble poet?'

'I did what you ought to do with your tongue—I turned it to better account,' was the smiling response.

'You turned it to stab your country for the wages of the Castle!' cried a white-faced, student-like young fellow with burning eyes; and the crowd responded with a roar of 'Renegade!' under which Glascock's affectation of gaiety miserably blenched.

'Boys will be boys,' he said, hoisting signals of benevolent good-humour on his large face.

'And lawyers will sell and hang them,' retorted he of the eyes like glowing coals.

'Men who have no respect for the ministers of our holy religion,' said the Attorney-General, who was becoming solemn, 'can scarcely be expected to do justice to the motives of one who represents mere earthly authority——'

'Is dat what dey calls de rope at de Four Courts?' put in one of his tormentors.

'Ay, ay, Toby de Hangman!' chorused the yelling crowd;

and another egg whizzing past the candidate's ear broke in a star of yellow glory on the High Sheriff's bald expanse of forehead.

'If I were as bad a shot as that I'd never talk of fighting the British Empire,' said Glascock, rallying amidst the merriment caused by the Sheriff's meek agonies ; but it was now plain the young men's wrath was growing dangerous. 'Well, boys,' he said with all the geniality he could command, 'as ye won't let me do anything else to oblige ye, I'll oblige ye by sitting down.' A roar of triumph broke from the crowd. 'That's much more convenient,' he whispered blandly, turning to Mr. Harman, who stood behind him. 'The boys have had their innings, and I will catch my train.' And he passed down to the reporters a packet of manuscript, neatly tied up and addressed, 'With the Attorney-General's compliments.' 'Now, Mr. High Sheriff,' he remarked genially, 'don't you think the sooner we wind up the better ?'

The High Sheriff had just been tying a silk handkerchief over his dishonoured head. 'Is there any elector who has another candidate to propose ?' he asked in a weak voice, for which, however, there was instant silence.

There was a moment's solemn hush.

'Yes, sir, there is !' cried Mat Murrin, arising in majesty on his left, and fixing the eye-glass with the deliberation of a man finding the range of a heavy piece of ordnance which will presently be heard in thunder.

'Ha, ha! a speech from Mat Murrin ! The usual thing !' remarked the Attorney-General to his supporters laughingly. 'That is always capital fun, but I hope he won't run us too close to train-hour.'

'Did I understand you to say you had another candidate to propose ?' timidly squeaked the Sheriff.

'Yes, sir,' said Mat in a voice of thunder. 'And if you didn't understand me up to the present I'll make you and our oleaginous friend, the converted Pikesman, understand me before I sit down, so far as an average allowance of brains and a sound working pair of lungs will serve me.' It was customary at that time to propose unreal candidates for the purpose of enabling partisans on either sides to make speeches on the hustings. The mob, seeing that Mat was in good form, settled themselves down for a treat of this character. There was an encouraging volley of 'Cheers for the *Banner* !' and there were affectionate greetings such as : 'Good man, Mat !' 'Give him lamb-and-salad—de Hangman !' 'Sink your teet in him !' and so on.

'Mister High Sheriff,' said Mat, shaking his grey locks at the Sheriff with a ferocity that gave that unfortunate gentleman sensations of the orator 'sinking his teet' in his own unoffending calves, 'I rise for the purpose of proposing as a fit and proper person to represent this county in the Imperial Parliament, or in any more respectable place, Kennedy Rohan, commonly called Ken Rohan ; profession (and practice), a man and a rebel, every inch of him ; present residence, Her Majesty's Prison, Kilmainham.' The young men, to whom Mat's semi-humorous style was not always acceptable, instantly took fire at the name. It was pretty generally known whose was the pen in the secret press that had made their blood beat and their dreams come, and now that the figure of the writer stood within the shadow of the gallows his bare name went to young hearts like the note of a trumpet. The court-house vibrated with that gallant music of young enthusiasm. Deep in the wilderness of Glascock's heart there whispered a still small voice : 'Once I, too, felt and cheered like that. Is Her Majesty's Attorney-General a happier man ?'

Was it the answer or the dread of listening to the answer that made him turn to Harman, stroking his magnanimous whiskers, with the observation : ' Ha, ha ! what an absurd thing ! But I dare say Mat was bound to let off his squib.'

' You can never make sure with these fellows that there is not a bullet at the tail of it,' remarked Harman, who was in a state of high good humour.

' I have one apology to make in offering this nomination,' proceeded Mat Murrin, ' and that is to Ken Rohan, for condemning him to associate with such an assembly of humbugs and rascals as the Imperial Parliament.' (Yells of assent from the young fellows.) ' I don't know any more respectable position in Irish life than the dock, unless it be the gallows.' (The young fellows positively sang with a fierce joy like the Girondins on their way to the guillotine.) ' Certainly, if you were looking for respectability, you wouldn't look at a Judicial Bench stuffed with patriotic carrion like the poet of the Pike Song, nor in an Imperial Parliament of O'Shaughs, whose only redeeming quality is that they were never seen sober.' (Shouts of scornful laughter.)

' Beggin' your pardon, sir, ould O'Shaugh was sober enough wanst to pass off a fourpenny-bit on myself instead of a tanner after my two mile of a jaunt,' interrupted a jarvey.

' Begor, if de cannibals makes a male of him, dey'll find whisky enough in his 'ittle toe to supply de whole tribe wid refreshments,' said another.

' If I was to consult my personal and private opinion,' resumed the orator, not at all averse to these vulgar variations on his grand manner, ' I should say the fit and proper person for us to present to the Imperial Parliament with our compliments as a colleague would be the ebony gentleman whose brow of Egypt ornamented that witness-table a few moments ago, and who, I hope, will not think too harshly of my unacquaintance with his, I am quite sure, ancient and highly respectable family annals, if I am obliged to describe him briefly in the language of the profession as our friend, the sweep.' ('Ay, ay, the sweep's good enough for them !' was the cry.)

'Oh, great Lord ! did you ever hear de likes of dat ?' cried the sweep, starting up again as at a General Resurrection, with a face of comical indignation. 'Yerra, honest man, when did I ever disgrace my coat dat you should make me out a bloody Mimber of Parliament ?'

'This is becoming too farcical,' said the Attorney-General, laughing, and consulting his watch.

'I perceive that the Attorney-General smiles at the sweep as an antagonist,' roared Mat, who had been leading up to this situation, and who, after passing the eye-glass through his lips and through his handkerchief with incredible rapidity, dashed it into his eye, and proceeded to gorgonise Glascock through it. 'I wonder will that beatific smile continue when I promise him that it is not the sweep, but it is his prisoner, his victim, that will confront him at the door of every honest elector of this county, and will challenge a verdict between the renegade Poet of the Pike and the gallant young Irishman into whose heart he is going to thrust that pike one of these days in Green Street for a government fee ?' (The court-house shook with passion.) 'Where be your smiles now, Toby ?' cried Mat, directing the monocle like a pitiless burning-glass upon the Attorney-General's ashen face. 'Are you as much afraid to meet the ghosts of your prisoners as you are to meet the ghosts of your own songs ? Yes, fellow-countrymen,' he continued, fronting the audience with his mellow, rolling voice, 'we can't honour Ken Rohan by sending him to that Imperial Cesspool in Westminster—we can't serve Ireland by sending him or anybody else there—but we can whip a renegade, we can scourge a humbug, we can avenge our imprisoned comrades if we cannot save them ; and, if you agree with me '—the louvred lights in the roof were set clattering again by the tumultuous sound-waves—'then, by God, we will !' he exclaimed, bringing down his fist with a tremendous bang. The effect was electrical. The young men hugged him, and hugged one another, in a sudden frenzy of delight.

'Does any elector second the nomination ?' piped the Sheriff, hammering the ink-bottle against the desk before him for silence.

Suddenly there was an embarrassed pause. The young men looked at one another uneasily.

'Pooh ! they won't find a seconder,' said the Attorney-General, rapidly recovering his spirits. 'I can still catch the five o'clock.'

There was a painful, choking sort of buzz among the crowd, as of some great animal breathing stertorously. The qualification for county electors was a high one ; the fiery youngsters had no votes ; and most of the householders among them were only electors for the city. Con Lehane would have given his heart's blood to second the nomination ; but his heart's blood was not on the register of voters. Mat Murrin's eye-glass made a circuit of all the fathers of families in court, and fixed the burning glass on the trembling little gentleman whose only craving in life was a tide-waitership and peace. The little man quivered like a reed, but made no response. Another county elector whom he espied, a fat grazier, was seized with a violent attack of influenza.

'I don't exactly see what the delay is about, Mr. Sheriff,' said the Attorney-General, a little testily. 'I ask you to declare the result.'

'It is necessary for me to go through the proper form,' said the High Sheriff, stiffly. He was a bit nettled by this peremptory tone. 'I have to ask once more does any elector of the county second the nomination of Kennedy Rohan ? '

'Yes,' said a voice from the background, 'I do.' All eyes turned to a little scene of commotion behind the group of priests at the back of the bench, where somebody was making his way to the front. All the blood in Monsignor McGrudder's body seemed to rush to his brain in insurrection, when he saw the old withered apple face and weatherbeaten green coat of Father Phil ! 'This is the Doctor's doing,' he gasped to a Vicar Forane sitting next him. Father Phil appeared to be in a mighty state of terror under the eyes of the world while he elbowed his way through ranks of scandalised dignitaries and frowning squires. But once firmly planted in front, he spoke with as much composure as if his foot was on the top of Cnocaunacurraghcooish. 'I am sorry,' he said, 'that there was nobody else to relieve me of this duty. I am an old man, and I am only an humble curate, and it isn't much I can do ; but, no matter what they say, Ken Rohan is a good boy and a brave Irishman, and I'd rather stand by his side before the Great Throne hereafter than with those that are prospering now by prosecuting and defaming him and his cause.' There was a simple earnestness in these words that made them seem almost to come from on high ; their effect was indescribable ; the ministerialists around the Attorney-General shrank back as if a bolt from heaven had passed close to them and scorched them ; the young men tore forward, and kissed the old priest's hands and the green sleeves of his old overcoat.

The show of hands, of course, was all on one side. Not a
hand was raised for the Attorney-General except Monsignor
McGrudder's and the Baronet's from the ice-fields. Hans Harman, who was standing up in a quiet corner behind, exchanged
a benevolent wink with Mat Murrin. The little trembing
gentleman could not have got his hand above his ears for all the
tide-waiterships of Somerset House. The fat grazier's influenza
took a violent turn for the worse. But Monsignor McGrudder
held up his hand like another Moses in a losing battle with a fine
si fractus illabatur orbis air.

'Is a poll demanded for the Attorney-General?' asked the
Sheriff, with a face of the utmost solemnity.

'Yes, of course,' cried the Attorney-General, a little sulkily.
'The thing is really too absurd. Of course they won't be able to
lodge the expenses ; but, confound it, I've missed my train, and
the Special Commission begins next Monday.'

'Now,' remarked Hans Harman to himself, as he rubbed his
long white hands, 'there will be a better chance of bringing
Glascock to business. Mat Murrin,' he said, pleasantly, 'you're
a confounded rebel, and we'll thrash you like old boots ; but all
the same that was a capital hit of yours—capital.'

'Hans Harman,' replied Mat, fixing him with the oracular
eye-glass and speaking with much deliberation, 'you're a confounded scoundrel every inch of you, and you'll be hanged by the
neck some day if there's an ounce of justice going ; but all the
same, you're not quite such a humbug as Toby.'

Mat Murrin had really intended no more, when he entered
the court-house, than, in his own phrase, to 'give Toby a squeeze
in the leg '—to have a rhetorical fling against the ex-patriot and
present Crown Prosecutor. He had been carried away by his
own eloquence, and by the heady enthusiasm of the young men,
into committing himself and them to a contest such as he would
have never in his wildest moments deliberately provoked. Few
as are the years that separate us from those times, it is almost
impossible in our own days of daring and triumphant democracy
to realise what a piece of insanity it seemed to run an unknown
young rebel with one foot on the steps of the gallows for the
immense county of Cork against all the allied influence of the
priests and landlords. When Monsignor McGrudder declared
to a meeting of the Attorney-General's Committee that 'this
wanton contest was being forced on the county by a parcel of
wild boys and drunken men as a sheer bit of blackguardism,' he
expressed the feeling of all sane middle-aged persons with any
pretensions to gentility, or to what is called 'a stake in the
country.' That the conflict at the polls should be anything more

than a sham battle, if not a pure farce, was simply inconceivable. The bulk of the county electors were comfortable farmers of staid and cautious habits, who had been taught to regard Fenianism as a conspiracy, accursed of God and man, to confiscate their farms and undermine their religion. These men had been accustomed to go in flocks like sheep to the polls, either to vote tweedledum under the escort of their clergy, or to vote tweedledee under the whip of their landlords; and now these shepherds of the people were united in directing their flocks to the fold of the Attorney-General. The accepted theory on all sides was that the farmers were a selfish, hard-fisted tribe, to whom Ireland represented no idea except so much grassland and so many head of cattle to graze it. That such men, for a Quixotic sentiment, should set the united clerical and landlord influence at defiance, and of their free will elect an unknown young firebrand from the county gaol, was too absurd for discussion; while as for any violent pressure from the mob, the county was crouching under the terror of an invisible military occupation, and all the more dangerous spirits were in prison or fled. The contest was, of course, a horrible vexation for Glascock. The Special Commission for the trial of the leaders of the Rising was on the point of commencing its sittings; and here he was chained down to the work of canvassing a county as large as a province. Then there was Mr. Hans Harman preparing to constitute himself his agent with plenipotentiary powers, and pressing him unpleasantly as to terms; and attorneys, committee-room-vendors, publicans, and minor sharks rose up in squads, in companies, in regiments to divide his wealth like a horde of diggers making for a new gold-field. The Attorney-General was appalled to think of the thousands of bright gold pieces that were about to be dug out of his bowels.

'There is an easy way out of it,' suggested the invaluable Harman. 'Mat Murrin has a rabbit-warren of children, and is as needy as a Bankruptcy Court beggarman. Let me dump down five hundred if he'll withdraw his man.'

'My dear fellow,' said the Attorney-General, wringing his hand and almost weeping for joy, 'you understand how impossible it is for me in my position——'

'Quite so. I understand,' said Harman, and straightway took a car to Mat Murrin's hotel and made the proposition.

Mat stared hard at him. He had just been cogitating how to pay his hotel bill, as a preliminary to the more grandiose difficulty where to get the large sum the Sheriff would require to have lodged before ordering a poll to be taken. The absolute desperateness of the enterprise he had undertaken did not fully present

itself to his mind until he found that the cash actually on his
p: rson, after paying for his bed and breakfast, with a few humble
items of brandy-and-soda, would not enable him to indulge in the
extravagance of dinner, unless fortune provided him with some
hospitable friend with an idle knife and fork.   He was in a
deeply depressed condition, and just in the mood the Tempter
would have chosen. He hesitated for a few minutes, the greed of
gold plainly glittering through the eye-glass. At last the struggle
was over. 'Done l' he said, doggedly. 'It is a bargain. Down
with the money.'

Harman chuckled ever so discreetly over his own knowledge
of human nature.   Within an hour he had returned from the
bank with the roll of notes. 'Of course,' he said, ' I'll take your
word for it that on receipt of these notes you will go at once to
the Sheriff's office and withdraw your man.'

'You have my word for it,' said the other, gloomily.

Mat counted the notes eagerly.   So much wealth had never
been in his hands except in dreams. He fingered the notes as if
they were godlike spirits that might at any moment flutter away
through the ceiling.   But it was necessary to put a cool face on
things. 'It appears to be all right—them fifty-pound notes are
very handy things,' he remarked, airily, as he folded the bundle
and deposited it in state in the depths of his breast-pocket, like
an East India Company annexing a rich province.   Then he
mounted the eye-glass once more, and directed it upon Harman.
'Now,' said he, 'I'm going to do what Toby Glascock did.'

'And what's that?' asked Harman, delighted to find things
working so gaily.

'I'm going to break my word.'

Harman staggered back, sick.

'Only it will be in a better cause,' proceeded Mat. 'Glascock
broke faith with a confiding people for the sake of his own carcase.
I'm going to break faith with a snivelling renegade to avenge that
same confiding people.'

'You don't mean to say you won't do what you promised
to do?'

'Did the author of the Pike Song do what he promised to do?
I'm going straight to the Sheriff's office, as you stipulated, but I'm
going to lodge Ken Rohan's share of the Sheriff's expenses ; and,
if you want to be laughed out of the county, I'll be happy to explain in a letter to the newspapers to-morrow morning to whom
the National cause is indebted for the necessary supply of bank-
notes.'

Harman looked wretchedly green and downcast. 'Some
cursed ill-luck is coming over me of late,' he said to himself,

grinding his shiny teeth. ‘Who'd ever have thought this blown windbag would have made such a hit? You've got the odd trick this time,' he said aloud, with a ghastly affectation of his usual manner. ‘If you publish it, I'll break every bone in your body. Keep the money, and be damned!'

‘Faith, no—I'll keep the money, and be some day or other the subject for a National Statue,' said Mat, genially. ‘Hans Harman, you were never a sensible man, or I'd invite you to join the boys and myself in a small drain of Toby's own whisky—and, though it's myself that says it, you never read anything purtier in Demosthenes than you'd hear if you'd just step in and hear me propose Toby's health upside down, as the divel reads Scripture.'

And now commenced a battle which, like the irruption of Dumouriez' shoeless, ça-iraing hordes, defied all the rules of regular electoral war. Mat Murrin and his ragged État-Major went ça-iraing over the country, whirling to Mallow by the morning train, breaking the opposition windows in the afternoon, entering Mitchelstown in the thick of a torchlight procession in the evening, and tracked with bonfires all along the borders of Tipperary far into the midnight; then diving into a supper of cold turkey and ham in some friendly ‘strong farmer's' parlour, singing songs, proposing toasts, or stretching themselves in their great frieze coats on the hearthrug, until dawn came again to send them thundering away towards Youghal, with a green flag flying, and a key-bugle waking the glens, and an irregular chorus of wild halloos from the mountain cabins as they passed. Ethan Allen and his Green Mountain Boys never played stranger pranks ‘in the name of the Great Jehovah and the Continental Congress.' There was no conducting-agent; there were no committee rooms but the open market places; the regiment of attorneys, who were supposed to be as indispensable in managing an election as a doctor in dealing with an apoplectic seizure, were represented by one daredevil young solicitor whose only fee was a full share in whatever speech making, bugle-blowing, and punch-drinking was going. But it was noticed that no electors took part in the meetings, except as mute spectators; the farmers remained tongue-tied. In some districts, where ecclesiastics of the old school denounced Mat and his staff roundly from the altars as strolling agitators in the pay of the Castle, even the mob was against them. In one or two rural places they had to fly for their lives.—‘Show me a decent man's name at their meetings,' exclaimed Monsignor McGrudder, triumphantly, in one of his speeches. ‘Whom have they with them except the rag-tag-and-bobtail?'—‘The rag-tag-and-bobtail carried the Bastille,' retorted Mat, quoting the phrase from the top of a wagonette, ‘and

L L

they had all the Monsignors against them as well as the Swiss musketeers.'

Nor was the clergy altogether an unbroken phalanx, either. At a meeting of the Bishops, the new Bishop of Clonard, whose Brief of appointment had just arrived, maintained an obstinate silence while a manifesto denouncing the wickedness and impiety of the opposition to the Attorney-General was being confectioned. The other Bishops were saintly, peace-loving old gentlemen, who could remember what it was to be a Papist in the Pre-Emancipation days, and were lost in thankfulness for a state of government under which Catholic churches, schools, convents, judges, magistrates, and whatnot were multiplying and possessing the land. They could not possibly conceive what object there could be in interrupting this blessed process except that evil men for unhallowed purposes of their own desired to infect the unstained youth of Ireland with the scepticism and irreverence which had wrought such havoc with religion and society in other lands. When it came to a question of signing the manifesto, Dr. O'Harte for the first time broke silence.

'I cannot do it,' he said. 'I am only a newcomer, and I have too much respect for your lordships' venerable character to do anything to oppose your action. I will remain neutral; but that is the utmost I can conscientiously do.'

An Abbot finding barricades thrown up in the cloister could not have been more shocked than those gentle and timid souls. They had always regarded Dr. O'Harte as a staunch partisan of the policy of alliance with the constituted authorities from whom had come Emancipation, and from whom seemed likely to come Disestablishment.

'There are two things that are dearer than life to an Irishman in full health of mind and manhood—his Faith and his Nationality. You used their Nationality as long as it served your purpose, to make the Irish people suffer for their Faith. It would be to my mind madness from the religious, as well as baseness from the human point of view, to think you can now discard and eradicate Nationality after it has served your purpose. You'll simply divide two good forces into opposite camps. That's what they've done over half Europe to religion's cost—goaded young men into thinking that the Faith of the Middle Ages can only co-exist with mediæval tyrannies and thumb-screws. The Faith of the Middle Ages flourishes like a bay-tree in the American Republic, because religious people don't think it necessary to revile George Washington and plot to bring back a king Why should American principles be damnable only when they land on the shores of Ireland? They've landed, my lords, at all events, and all the Queen's troops and judges won't dislodge them ; and, depend upon it, young hearts won't think the less tenderly of them if we persecute them from the altars while the Government is torturing them in its gaols. One thing more I feel bound to remind your lordships of—that there are young hearts under clerical soutanes as well as under frieze coats, and for the one old Father Phil in this diocese I know fifty young Father Phils whom you will never drill into cursing their people's cause in the interest of their people's masters. For my part, I don't intend to try to drill them. My first episcopal act will be to remove Father Phil from Drumshaughlin, in order to avoid the scandal of any open differences between him and so worthy and eminent a priest as Monsignor McGrudder ; but it will not be to banish him into the Siberian mines- it will be to make him my own administrator in Clonard. As for this election —I dare say it is only some tipsy freak of Mat Murrin's ; but if I am asked to brand little Ken Rohan, who served my Mass, and to whom I gave First Communion, as a limb of the devil—I don't believe it, and I won't say it. Candidly, if your lordships must issue any manifesto at all, my advice is that you frankly declare the Attorney-General to be what he is, a political gambler, who has made a dishonest use of his patriotism, and is making a not altogether honest use of his piety ; and if you must denounce armed insurrection in Ireland as the midsummer madness it is— a matter of infants playing at soldiers, so far as England is concerned, but tragic enough for our own poor unarmed boys— then let your lordships not stop there, but point out how other- wise the ineradicable craving for Irish Nationality is to be satisfied, and make the young men feel that in struggling for it they will have our blessing, no matter if we had to take to the wooden chalices and the mountain cabins again with our people.'

' It seems a pity you did not intimate those opinions before,' gravely observed the Archbishop, a noble and courtly figure.

' I tell your lordships frankly I waited until I could give them effect,' said the Coadjutor-Bishop, with perfect composure. ' The Brief for my consecration only arrived yesterday. The opinions that would have been crushed in an humble priest have now some chance of being useful to the Church and to the country.'

The Coadjutor-Bishop, however, was too mindful of the decencies of ecclesiastical differences not to keep his opinions to himself. The manifesto was issued. Monsignor McGrudder, backed by the irresistible Sacred Band of dignitaries of the old school of prerogative, threw himself into the contest with the whole force of his unflinching character, as with a crowning conflict with the Evil One. The landlords,·for their part mustered their own battalions of tenants for the march to the polls, and requisitioned troops of cavalry to escort them. Glascock made one or two speeches in judiciously chosen localities under the broad wings of some powerful dean or canon, and treated the interruptions in a genial bantering manner ; and he was able to set out for the Special Commission with a unanimous chorus of assurances from the canons and attorneys that the opposition would end as harmlessly as the wild halloos that followed Mat Murrin's flying wagonette.

The wagonette and its green flag went on flying nevertheless, and, if the genteel folk of high and low degree fled from Mat and his merry men as from the Headless Coach, there was one wholly unexpected ally who clambered on to the wagonette, and, seeing nothing else that he could do, blew the bugle, until he learned to his amazement that people were as glad to hear his own honest stammering words as the key-bugle. It came about curiously enough. Miss Westropp was lying on a sofa in her room at Clanlaurance Castle, white and weak, with Georgey O'Meagher kneeling beside her. It was one of those tender midwinter days when Nature's sport seems to be playing at spring ― violets and pale-faced roses laughing out in the sun, thrushes and linnets singing their Christmas carols as blithely as if bringing in the May, the infant green buds of the trees peeping out of their tender cradles, as though the woods might at any moment burst into complete woodland costume, even before the generation of dead leaves at their feet were yet rotten. Such rare days there be in Beara—of such flying sunny beauty as makes you forget the storm that was tearing through the country like a maniac only yesterday, and the mists that will enfold it all to-morrow in their wet blankets. Some pale shadow of the sunshine outside seemed to have touched the sick girl. The news of the pending election was the first thing that had drawn her from the deadly languor in which she was wasting. Her beautiful blue eyes, which seemed to have grown darker and larger in illness, filled for the first time with a light that was not like the grave's. Even some faint glow of colour came into the thin white cheeks 'Georgey,' she said, caressing her friend's curly little head fondly, you must do one thing for me after stealing my lover from me.'

The other burst into tears, and covered her hand with tears and kisses. 'Oh, no, no ! Don't !—even in jest,' she cried. 'You know you gave him to me. You know he would die a thousand deaths for you, in comparison with an insignificant chit of a country girl like me.'

Why, how serious you have grown, child!—and how beautiful!' cried the sick girl, holding the pretty head out from her, and examining with wonder the glowing black eyes and flushing cheeks. 'It was well I resigned before you beat me out of the field,' she said, with the sweetest sad smile. 'The young Guardsman who would hesitate between you and me at this moment would—not be a young Guardsman.' The faintest enchanting sigh escaped from her as her eyes fell on the reflection of her own wan face in the mirror opposite where she was lying.

The black eyes flashed with passionate worship. 'Don't—oh, don't—tempt me to tell you what I think—what all the world thinks,' she cried, in her headlong way. 'Yes, but you have tempted me, and I must say it—you were never half so beautiful as you are this moment—I don't know how there can be anything more beautiful in heaven. I could worship you all my life, as well as he—and so he will.'

'You have served me right,' said Mabel, sighing more heavily this time, 'though there was a time when that look in your eyes would have turned my foolish head with joy.'

There was a chord of inexpressible sadness in her voice. Georgey's tears came again. 'Oh, can you forgive me for feeling happy?—it is all your doing; but it seems such heartlessness, such a crime, to think of happiness, while you, and —and—*he*—are suffering torments. Do you really, really think I am such a monster—that Reggy and I are not a pair of monsters—to think of ourselves at all in such a world of sorrow?'

Georgey was certainly an incomprehensible young lady. From the hour when Reggy Neville in his clumsy fashion seized her hand one day and proposed to retain it for life, she who had lived at the highest top sparkle of high spirits, became one of the gravest of womankind. The almost boyish wilfulness which used to scintillate from her eyes as from a pair of gigantic diamonds changed to a diffidence which seemed to tremble and start at every shadow. Miss Neville, who had frankly conceived a prejudice against her as a vulgar little romp, and possibly an adventuress, was astounded to find the wild girl fling herself at her feet in a torrent of tears, and avow that Reggy had proposed to her, and conduct herself as though she were the most guilty and contemptible thing an aristocratic sister had ever spurned from her door. Miss Neville, who had an unspoiled heart herself, was completely melted by the girl's simplicity, sincerity, and agony of artless self-distrust, and took her to her bosom as she might have adopted a tender little wild fawn that she had found in the snow on the mountains. To Joshua Neville it was a sorer blow. Not that he had formed any opinion to the prejudice of

Georgey's wicked dark eyes and tempting little mouth—he had never particularly noticed either. It was the loss of Mabel that weighed upon his soul like a leaden coffin. He had grown to regard her as his own daughter. He had laid up for her love all the wealth of adoring fondness of which his deep, honest heart was capable—and he had more wealth in that heart than in all his red-hot forges and mineral trains. While Lord Drumshaughlin regarded himself as one of the most meritorious of men for dozing asleep for a few hours beside his daughter's bed, Joshua Neville hovered about the door of the sick-chamber night and day with the fidelity of the dog of the Louvre-gate. And now to lose all for a black-eyed country schoolgirl who wore her hair more like a schoolboy ! There was probably only one person in the world who could have kept him from breaking out in a lava-tide of anger terrific as Etna in full glow ; but that one person pleaded, and triumphed. Miss Westropp, in whom her own unhappiness only wrought a deeper longing to save at least the happiness of these two young people from the wreck, used the very first hours of her convalescence to make Georgey's bright eyes shine into Joshua Neville's heart, and ended by, if not reconciling him to his fate, determining him to undergo with cheerfulness whatever fate his adored young guest might be pleased to ordain for him.

Captain Neville himself was puzzled mightily at first by the change in his future wife's behaviour. The gaiety and sparkle which had first dazzled him seemed to be gone ; he seemed never once to have heard her rippling laugh or saucy wit since he proposed to her ; her crisp, curly rings of hair tumbling anyhow about her little pink high-born ears seemed to be undergoing some inexplicable quakerly chastening ; she was timid, constrained—positively dull. And he himself was beginning vaguely to chafe at and resent the change, when he suddenly read the secret one day in the depths of those passionate dark eyes, and in the coming and going scarlet picture-writing on the soft cheeks upheld to his ; and in an ecstasy of joy found that this was love—very love—the ineffable girlish weakness which surrendered up all its pretty arms to its lord paramount—the ravishing, simple-hearted diffidence which trembled with sweet doubt whether she could ever be worthy of his great, strong, masterful affection. For it was only after he had made that astounding proposal that Georgey O'Meagher had really discovered that the strong, stupid Englishman with whom she had flirted only as high-spirited innocent schoolgirls will, was her master, whom she could kneel to, and worship and cling to all the days of her life. The more she studied Reggy's nature she saw that she had hitherto seen only the drab outside of a home in which all the treasures and

joys were kept for a happy fireside circle far within. Or again
she thought of him as of one of those wondrous caverns in the
Arabian Nights, which to the outer world present no appearance
but that of a plain slab of stone with a strong iron ring in it,
but, the stone and iron once lifted, disclose galleries of gems and
gold through which one might wander for a lifetime without ex-
ploring all their golden depths. And in sober earnest, Neville
was one of those simple, honest, manly natures which a woman
would not exchange for all the haunted gold of Samarcand. He
could hardly believe his good luck—that such a clever, dashing
girl as that should not only accept him as a husband, but actually
look up to him, reverence him, tremble with a delightful terror of
him. He for his part found her simply adorable. Happiness
always makes a pure woman beautiful; and, though Georgey
O'Meagher's piquant features and swinging figure were not
exactly of the type of beauty that could be cut in marble, they
were so bright, so unaffected, so suffused with the divine light of
love and happiness, that Reggy Neville's love for her grew with
every hour of every day, and his craving to throw himself down and
live for ever at her feet grew even stronger than her craving to
throw herself down and live for ever at his. Both of them had
commenced their love-making as a matter of only second-bests;
and even still a certain stone cell in Kilmainham Prison was as
a tabernacle enshrining her ideal, as a couch in Clanlaurance
Castle was the Holy of Holies of his; but what had begun in
schoolgirl sport for her, and perhaps to some extent in pique for
him, had ended for both of them in one of those honest, all-in-
all, true-love matches which make the world go round merrily
enough for ordinary mortals, while 'the true gods' and goddesses
are sighing for 'the lost and the pain.' But, for all her happiness—nay, by very reason of her happiness—Georgey's old
frolicsome spirit was utterly tamed; and at this moment she
hated herself when she thought what currents of felicity were
flowing in her own selfish veins while Mabel's all-but-transparent
body was wasting before her eyes, and the knotted rope was
hovering in the gloom of Ken Rohan's cell like a hempen crown.

'Forgive you for feeling happy! Why, to look at you is the
only gleam of happiness that is left me!' said Miss Westropp,
drawing the little head towards her with her delicate white arm.
'And you *are* so happy—and you so deserve to be happy, dear—
that I dread making my petition to you. For it is, that you shall
lend me Reggy—only lend him, mind, and not for very long,'
she added, with a pretty smile.

'And you ask *me*, when you know that a word from you
would make him chop off his right arm with joy!'

'That is your pretty poetry ; but it is *you* who have the right to give the word, now, my dear child—and to see it obeyed,' Mabel answered, with another of her sweet-sad smiles. And the upshot was that Neville was that evening dumbfoundered by a request that he should throw himself into the election struggle in the rebel interest.

'Georgey, your old quizzing ways are coming back,' he said in some bewilderment. 'Miss Westropp cannot desire anything so ridiculous.'

'Miss Westropp desires it, nevertheless, and—and—I do,' she said, timidly.

'But what the deuce could I do in this electioneering business ? Just think. You know yourself I cannot utter a single sentence without breaking down.'

'I know you break down very pleasantly,' she whispered, with a touch of her coquettish malice, thinking of the clumsy strophe of hums and haws in which the Guardsman had stammered out his love—a strophe in which, it must be confessed, she had found more poetry than ever she could find in the works of William Shakespeare.

It would be superfluous to tell what that provocative little observation ended in. All I know is that the soldier received a not altogether mortal wound on the cheek from a small hand, and a young lady with tell-tale cheeks said to him : 'Come, your blandishments will be much more safely employed upon county electors. Upon my word, I don't well know what you are expected to do ; but,' she added, demurely, 'I fancy Mabel thinks that, when all the great and strong are against poor Ken, it can be no harm to have one steadfast English heart for him. I wonder why it is, but somehow or other I could never think of my being on the beaten side while you are near me. I do believe you could beat the whole British army single-handed. Stop, sir !' she cried, in some alarm, drawing back. 'Please remember, you are only being employed as a friendly giant for the rescue of our Prince Prettyman. Poor Ken ! Poor boy !'

'Confound it, Georgey, Mabel and you make a fellow envy Rohan his chance of being hanged. It seems to be the only way to a woman's heart in this extraordinary country of yours. What if I try myself ?'

'You'd better not, sir !' she cried, with an affected gaiety ; but immediately burst into tears and shook with terror, in such a whole-souled, irresistible passion of trembling love, that the Guardsman felt obliged to reassure her as to the nearness of her friendly giant. 'But,' she said, looking up presently out of her radiant tears, 'short of that, you will go and win the county for Mabel's sake, won't you ?—and for mine ? '

'I will go and make a fool of myself to the utmost extent of my capacity,' he said ; and that very night he was installed in Mat Murrin's wagonette, blowing the key-bugle through the glens with the solemn conscientiousness with which he discharged every duty of life ; sharing with the utmost gusto the rashers and eggs and strong waters of Mat's wild bivouacs ; volunteering to head raids for the rescue of terrorised bodies of tenantry from their escorts of hussars ; charming all the women by his honest, clumsy, tender ways, and presently to his amazement finding that even the men were roused to as much enthusiasm by his few short, sharp, downright, volley-of-musketry-like sentences as by Mat Murrin's own soaring soul-flights and honeyed brogue. In the Glascock camp these wild doings were only a subject of derision. In the Drumshaughlin Club the general conclusion was that young Neville was off his head. Mr. Flibbert had reliable private information that it was liquor.

CHAPTER THE THIRTY-NINTH

MR. HANS HARMAN TAKES HIS LEAVE

THE nine o'clock train from King's Cross had gone off northwards into the night, leaving one passenger behind on the platform at Flowerdale, a wayside station in Primroseshire, remarkable for nothing except the garlands of monthly roses and cotoniasters, in which it seemed to be the whole duty of the local railway staff to keep the station-master's house enwreathed. Even this one attraction of Flowerdale was lost to the traveller, for the night was pitchy dark ; nor, judging by the quick, feverish movements of the figure in the heavy Ulster overcoat, would the floral decorations have interested him any the more if the sun had been shining. The station-master, from whom he inquired the exact hour at which the last up train that stopped at Flowerdale was due, and who was strangely struck by his wild look and agitated walk, concluded that he was probably waiting to commit suicide under the wheels of the up express. The station-master, being a man who was himself as happy as a big sunflower, had the strongest objections to suicide, and especially strong objections to the rolling-stock of the Company being used for that purpose · but he did not exactly see how he was to interrogate the gentleman as to his intentions without some more overt act than walking up and down the deserted platform in the dark by himself ; and as at this particular moment the pleasant odour of Mrs. Station-master's slim-cake and the tinkle of many young station-master-kins' laughter reached him through the fire-lit windows of his bower of roses, the station-master came to believe that his duty to the Company and to Society would be sufficiently discharged by ensconcing himself opposite his wife and her tea-kettle at his own fireside, until at all events it was time to look out for the red glims of the up express. The stranger was left alone on the platform with the bleak whistling wind and two shivering gaslights which threatened every minute to go off in a consumption. He had ascertained from the station-master that the up express did not usually stop at Flowerdale, but would be stopped by signal to-night, word having been just received that some of the house-party at The Meads—the Marquis of Asphodei's place (who was lord of the manor) a few miles away —were going to London. 'Precisely. Then it is true !' he muttered to himself, turning away with an ill-smothered oath, which confirmed the station-master's theory that the Evil Spirit was at work within the sombre folds of the Ulster. The gaslights, if they had energy enough left to see his face as he stalked up and down during that awful hour and a half of waiting, would have received a fright that must have finally put out their sickly lives. What a ridiculous thing it is to talk of the passionless impartiality of the exact sciences ! It was an hour and thirty-four minutes precisely that the station-master and the station-masterkins spent romping together in the firelight ; on the most undoubted evidence of horology it was only the same hour and thirty-four minutes precisely that the stranger spent pacing up and down by the death-bed of the consumptive gaslights ; yet who will vouch that they were the same periods of time ? So far as there is anything real at all in this world of shadows, the station-master had only passed through a flash of glowing firelight, while the stranger had been enduring eternities of torments.

'It's not going to be a mash-up on the metals, after all,' the station-master observed to himself with much content, on returning to the platform and seeing the Ulster still doing its dismal sentry-go. 'Yon goods that passed from Blytchley while ago would have done the business for him as well as the express, if 'twas bone-crushing he was after. I am glad. Where's the use of people trespassing on the Company's premises to do away with theirselves ? I do abominate them inquests.' And the good, honest sunflower of a man forgot all about the stranger to look after his own signals.

The sound of wheels on the road outside suddenly caught the
stranger's ears. He concealed himself in the rustic porch of the
station-house while the coach from The Meads drew up, with its
heavy trunks overhead ; and a lady and gentleman descended.
They brushed past him, the lady closely muffled ; passed on to
the platform, and into the tiny waiting-room.   Presently the
man returned to see the luggage disembarked, and to buy the
tickets from the station-master at the little square illuminated
wicket he had just opened in the gloom.   The stranger watched
him with eyes that seemed to burn like lamps in his lurking-
place.   The man threw back the thick fur collar of his coat.   The
light fell on a small, pallid, nervous-looking face, with small eyes
feverishly excited, and white hands that trembled as they fingered
the bank-notes.   It was Lord Amaranth's vicious young face and
rickety figure.   The two eyes that watched him were terrible as
gleaming knives there in the dark behind him.   He was inquiring
what delay there would be in London before the Paris express
would leave Victoria, and the station-master fumbled clumsily
in an old Bradshaw's Guide for the information.   Then Lord
Amaranth returned to the coach, and slipping a piece of gold into
the coachman's hand, despatched him.   Something between a
sigh of relief and a crow of triumph escaped between his sharp
white teeth ; the train was coming up ; humming the chorus of
the music-hall song of the hour, he turned to re-enter the station.
The door was closed, and a tall dark figure barred the way.   A
flash from the station-master's lantern gave Lord Amaranth a
moment's glimpse of the stranger's strong face and terrible eyes.
'Sold, by God !—sold !' cried the depraved young scoundrel,
staggering back as if he had received a blow.

'You cursed cub—you miserable little devil !' hissed the tall
man in the Ulster, catching him by the throat until the young
lad's small weak eyes were starting from their sockets.   The
station was on a high embankment, towards which the road wound
up steeply, the wall alone standing between them and a chasm, at
the bottom of which weltered a dark pool under its treacherous
green coat of slime.   As lightly as if it was a small puppy dog
he held by the throat, the tall man whisked Lord Amaranth's
quivering figure into the air, and hurled it with all his force over
the wall down the embankment.   'Take that—damn you !' he
cried, as he saw the helpless body bump down the slope, and
heard a deep groan of agony from the bottom.

The train had arrived.   The stranger hurried to the waiting-
room.   The lady of the closely-muffled face was standing up
when he entered.   With a cry of deadly terror, she sank to her
knees and crouched abjectly in a corner, holding out her hands

before her face as if her treble black veil was not enough to hide
it from that awful apparition.

'Horace!' she cried. 'O my God!' Her voice quivered
with the anguish of a damned soul.

'Come along, madam. The train is waiting. Come along!'
said Horace Westropp, in a deep, hollow voice, and seizing her
hand with a grip which seemed to be of red-hot steel, half led,
half dragged her, more dead than alive, into the railway-carriage,
where she fell in a terror-stricken heap upon the floor. 'I am
not going to hurt you,' he said, in harsh, pitiless tones, as the
express moved off. 'It will be punishment enough for you to
travel to London with me—with your son.'

Of course Horace Westropp did not think it necessary to acquaint his miserable old father, moping away his time by his
daughter's bedside at Clanlaurance Castle, with the particulars
of the night encounter with the vile young scamp he had left
moaning in the slime at Flowerdale. The particulars remained a
mystery, even to Captain Plynlymmon, who had arranged the
whole affair. It was he who, offended by Lady Drum's repeated
slights, and—who knows?—honestly indignant at the injury
meditated towards his old club-chum, Ralph Westropp, by that
incorrigible brat, Amaranth, dived into all the secrets of the intended flight, and took the fast train to London that morning to
put Horace in possession of them. Of course Plynlymmon, who
could no more have got through his day without hot gossip than
through his dinner without his favourite Indian mango relish,
entertained his club friends with discreet hints of the goings-on at
The Meads; and equally, of course, Mortlake's charitable comment, accompanied by one of his biting laughs, was: 'After all,
where is the difference between a young scamp and an old one?
It was only last May, Lottie slapped Amaranth's face publicly in
the Row for dawdling about Lady Drum; and *en revanche* they
say Lottie and old Drumshaughlin——serve the wretched old
beggar right, say I!' But, beyond hearing that Horace Westropp and his mother had left for Italy, and that Lord Amaranth
had been brought home to The Meads at an advanced hour of the
night on a shutter, and with a broken leg, even Plynlymmon
failed to ascertain the exact details of the curtain-scene in the
drama, of which he had been the stage-manager. And the
Asphodels, for their part, were only too grateful for the broken leg
which kept their worthy son out of a famous prize-fight then
pending, and left him stretched on a sofa at The Meads, at the
mercy of the soft blandishments of Miss Ruysdael. In a week
the Chrysanthemum Club was in the midst of the prize fight, and

had forgotten all about the Drumshaugh'ins.   I have mentioned
that Horace was the only one of her children whom Lady Drumshaughlin loved with a mother's love.   She now quailed like a
depraved child under his stern eye.   She had concealed during all
her married life the fact of her being a Catholic ; it was she herself who now proposed to retire for life into a house of retreat of the
White Penitents in the Milanese, of which her eldest sister was
one of the religious directors ; and thither she was now speeding
with as much penitence as an utterly wretched, crushed, and loveless heart could separate from a sense of guilty disappointment.
' My mother,' wrote Horace Westropp, ' for reasons of which I
approve, has determined to withdraw into an Italian convent on
the borders of her own country, and I do not know that Mabel
need be informed of any more upon the subject.'   The miserable
old man who read these words groaned with the consciousness that,
if there was any convent of Black Penitents dark enough to cover
his own head, he would be more fittingly employed in following
his wife's example than in reprehending her for whatever ugli-
ness lurked between the lines of Horace's blunt letter.   His self-
satisfaction had deserted him as utterly as his hair-dye.   He felt
himself in soul as in body a decrepit, wrinkled, festering thing.
Once selfishness loses its savour at all, decomposition sets rapidly
in.   Long, long ago, as it was, he recalled with miserable self-reproaches how he had soiled that tranquil dove-coloured Swiss
home and left the stain of blood on it, all to fill an idle hour.
Poor Harry's gentle ghost rose at him out of the stone vault, and
out of his weak blue eyes spoke reproofs more intolerable than
fell on the ears of King Richard in his tent the night before the
battle.   Even as to Mabel—and a thousand times a day he desperately assured himself that he had truly loved Mabel, at all
events, and that Mabel loved him—even Mabel's wan face and
fading beauty seemed to be his murderous handiwork.   Hans
Harman's villainy was unmasked, it was true, and the estate was
saved ; but was Harman so very much worse a villain than himself, though in a different line ? and, as to the estate management
itself, the more Joshua Neville's keen eye brought it to light, the
more Lord Drumshaughlin heard the still small voice of neglected
duties, and felt that, among his tenantry, as in his family, he had
flung away treasures of honest affection and well-doing for French
cookery and unhealthy slumbers.   Day by day, Joshua Neville
thought he could almost see Lord Drumshaughlin's cheeks fall in,
and his hair deepen from grey to white.   And as the last touch
of satire upon fashionable ambition, the post one of those mornings while the county elections were pending brought a note from
John Jelliland, in which the Chief Secretary casually mentioned

that Her Majesty had been graciously pleased to include Lord Drumshaughlin in the new batch of peers under the title of Earl of Puddlestone in the Peerage of Great Britain.

'I wish Her Majesty had been graciously pleased to let me die like the miserable dog that I am,' he said, dejectedly, 'or to confer her title upon you, Neville, who have done something better in the world than sponging on it.'

Joshua Neville was too truthful a man to deny that unfortunate Lord Drumshaughlin had given a pretty just estimate of his function in the world, as disclosed by the estate accounts. 'Pooh!' he said, good-humouredly, 'I would no more know what to do with a title than with a suit of mail. You are to the manner born, and as to Miss Mabel—I beg her pardon, Lady Mabel—if Her Majesty had been graciously pleased to abdicate her throne in her favour, all I say is, I don't believe the most dutiful subjects of the House of Hanover would be likely to rebel against their new sovereign.'

'The rascals have done it in the most barefaced way,' said the new earl, following his own train of thought, 'in the very thick of this county election. Jelliland is not a gentleman—never was and never will be. Upon my soul, I have half a mind to send word to the tenants to plump for the Fenian fellow.'

'Are you quite sure that they won't do it without word, my lord?' asked the ironmaster, gently.

'Pooh! am I quite sure my sheep won't agitate against mutton-eating? They are the most docile creatures—the tenants, I mean—not the sheep, though it's all the same—that ever mistook Hans Harman's Rent Office for Mount Sinai and the Rules of the Office for the Tables of the Law.'

'I can easily believe it *has* been so, at all events,' said Neville, gravely, 'judging from the way the books show they have submitted for eighteen years past without a murmur to be swindled in the most glaring fashion by this fellow Harman. The state of things those books reveal is absolutely incredible, and yet there cannot be the smallest mistake about the figures.'

'Damn the books!—or burn them, Neville—there's a good fellow. I'm just as much to blame as Harman.'

'That is not so, my dear lord. I cannot attempt to conceal from you that there appears to have been culpable remissness on your part; but this is now a matter of embezzlement—of wholesale and impudent embezzlement, year after year—and it would be simply a crime—a crime punishable with penal servitude—on your part or on mine to endeavour to conceal or to condone it. I must trouble you to listen to a very brief outline of the proofs I have this morning completed.' His lordship need

not have fidgeted and beaten his forehead so' miserably at sight
of the books and figures, for the story of Harman's thievery was
gross and palpable as a mountain—so gross that it could only
have happened in the case of a man so sovereign as an Irish
agent before the Land Act of 1881 was, and of an absentee to
whom business was so odious and self-indulgence so much a
matter of wild necessity as it was to Lord Drumshaughlin.
When Ringrose, the former agent, was shot, Hans Harman insisted upon a general reduction of rents as the condition of his
taking up the agency; and the revaluation upon which the reductions were based was carried out under his own supervision.
Harman notified the reduction of rents to the tenants, but at the
same time announced that the duty-work, marriage fees, and
other office fines and taxes, which had lain in abeyance during
Ringrose's lax management, would have to be enforced.   These
he at first fixed at so small amounts that the tenantry joyfully
accepted them as the alternative of the percentage of their rents
now remitted; but by degrees, as Lord Drumshaughlin grew accustomed to his reduced rental and the tenantry to the system of
office fines, the agent enlarged this system of supplementary payments until the revenue raised in this way had more than counter-
balanced the amount of rental foregone by Lord Drumshaughlin;
and all this extra revenue he simply turned into his own pockets
half-year after half-year, with the most absolute sense of security.
To the tenants' meek grumblings he only answered by groaning
himself over Lord Drumshaughlin's extravagances in foreign
parts.   To Lord Drumshaughlin he remitted the reduced rental
with punctuality; and by this machine-like punctuality (so enchanting to a lazy man), by his assiduous stories of plots for his
lordship's assassination and his own among the peasantry, and by
a form of receipt which mixed up fines and payments on account
in a form absolutely unintelligible to anybody who did not trace
the details through a complicated set of books, he had long lulled
Lord Drumshaughlin into the belief that he had the most invaluable agent and the most cunning, lying, and bloodthirsty tenantry
in Ireland.   His excuses for raising extra revenues were almost
inexhaustible—the money for which a peasant would commute
his twelve days' duty-work at the Castle in the height of his
potato-digging at home; the fine for which he would commute
his annual tribute of geese to the agent; the price of permission
for his eldest son to marry, or for a baby to be born, or for the
widow to be recognised as tenant; the fine for breaking up more
than an acre of meadow ground, for the trespass of fowl, for a
newly-reclaimed field; the charge for cutting turf off his own
land; the charge for drawing sea sand to give the black bog

mould some consistency; the charge for the red drift-weed which
the peasant waded up to the armpits in the wild waves to gather
for manure—all these, and as many more as he chose, he would
fix on his own whim and enforce with the power of a czar as
Rules of the Office   The peasants bore each successive impost as
dumbly as beasts of burden; were, indeed, mostly inclined to
worship Hans Harman as the intercessory angel who warded off
more merciless burdens which the incessant necessities and greed
of the distant master would, but for him, have imposed upon
them; and whenever discontent (as would happen even among
the mild-eyed hill-folk) became more importunate, the intercessory angel had two ways of dealing with it.   If the discontented peasant had a strapping son handy with firearms, he bribed
him into eternal friendship; when he had only ' a long weak
family ' without any smell of gunpowder about them to deal with,
Mr. Harman transferred the long weak family into the workhouse
as noiselessly as possible, and added their strip of land to his
friend Humphrey Dargan's broad acres.   In this way, for more
than fifteen years now, the agent had been raking nearly two
thousand a year of stolen money into his pocket, and all the while
entangling Lord Drumshaughlin in the system of loans in which
he had contrived to make Dargan his partner; and he was about
to crown his enterprise by forcing a sale which would render him
master of the estate on his own terms, when Joshua Neville's
lynx eyes lighted on the Composition Rent-book and discovered
the key to all this labyrinth of villainy.   The discrepancy between
old Meehul's receipts and the nominal rental had set the ironmaster comparing other tenants' receipts with the rental, with the
result that he had found the difference precisely accounted for by
the entries in the Composition Rent-book, and had found the
scheduled rents prepared by the agent for the Landed Estates
Court to be a tissue of impudent frauds.

' In point of fact, so far as I can see,' said Mr. Neville, ' the
margin of which Harman has been defrauding your lordship and
your tenants made just the difference between happiness and
misery for them and you during all these years.   I don't care to
generalise—that is beyond my ground—but it somehow strikes
me I might go further and say the difference between Irish
comfort and Irish wretchedness is the Irish agent—his salary,
and his callousness, and his professional necessity for poisoning
class against class.'

' Maybe, maybe,' muttered Earl Puddlestone in the Peerage of
Great Britain, his small white hands twitching nervously at his
skull-cap.   ' After all, why should we not all have got on with
the people as well as poor Harry did ?   A pretty verdict of the

Westropps, isn't it? that Harry was the only wise man of the
family! Poor Harry!—Well, well, that's all over.—I'm danmed
if I'm going to begin courting the peasantry at this time of my
life. The question is, Neville, what would you have me do now?'
    'One thing, and one thing only,' said the ironmaster solemnly.
'Let me send for a policeman.'

    It was only that morning Hans Harman had finally satisfied
himself that the Composition Account was in the hands of the all-
seeing Englishman. Things had been going horribly wrong with
him all round. A superstitious belief in luck was the agent's
religion. His belief in his own star had hitherto been indomitable. But now that the run of luck was against him he had the
gambler's usual cowardly conviction that if red was breaking the
bank he had only to lay a napoleon on it to transfer the luck to
black. His latest great scheme had been to make himself the
Attorney-General's chief bottle-holder, with a view to obtaining
the vacant seat at the Local Government Board by way of recom-
pense. His agency at Drumshaughlin had, of course, become
untenable; but, on the other hand, Lord Drumshaughlin could
have no interest in provoking a public exposure of his own family
skeletons; and what with the 8,000l. he would receive from the
county for the burning of Stone Hall, and the income he might
hope to derive from the reinvestment of the Hugg loan and his
own, he was able to map out a career of opulence and splendour
for himself in Dublin, where a seat at the Local Government
Board was the blue ribbon of place-hunting ambition. But,
though he threatened in his own daring way to throw himself
into the Fenian camp, he could not bring Toby Glascock to
business about the vacancy in the Local Government Board.
The fact of it is, the Attorney-General, who never liked the
agent's cynical air, had heard rumours of the relations between
Harman and his principal; and was so satisfied that the Puddlestone peerage had made the Drumshaughlin tenantry secure, and
so universally assured that the whole contest would be a mere
matter of form, that he flatly rejected Harman's terms, and was
even emboldened (out of hearing of the reverend clergy) to tell
the agent that he might go to the Fenians, or go to the devil, if
upon mature consideration he felt so disposed. The agent *did*
quietly arrange a little revenge by giving Mat Murrin a secret
letter to the tenantry; but he no longer felt as if his revenge
had much sting in it. He felt like a beaten general who could
look for no higher satisfaction than gouging a wounded enemy's
eye out for mere mischief's sake on his line of flight. And now
he had learned for certain that the Composition Account, the key

to his life of fraud, had fallen into the iron grip of Joshua Neville. This book he had usually kept locked up in his own cabinet at Stone Hall. But, so completely secure seemed the triumph of his plans for forcing a sale of the estate, that in sitting up late at night, preparing the Rental for the Court, he had transferred the Composition Account-book to the Rent Office for the purpose of readier reference as to the difference between the nominal and real rental, and had overlooked it among the other books which he locked into the safe upon the night of Joshua Neville's mid-night visit to the office. He had not at first remembered the circumstance, and had searched for the private account book like a maniac in all sorts of possible and impossible places; but this morning the recollection of having seen its red-and-gold-lettered title on the white vellum among the pile of estate-books he had bundled into the safe, suddenly flashed upon him clear as day; and he started up, ashen-coloured as a corpse, with the horrible thought that a policeman had just grasped him by the collar and hissed 'Felon!' in his ear.

'Neville is quite capable of doing it—those infernal virtuous fellows always are merciless—but I dare say they would scarcely search me, and ten minutes would do it,' he said, opening his cabi-net and placing a small phial of laudanum in his breast-pocket. 'Poor Deb!' he said, as he saw his sister's green and shrunken face on the garden-path outside. There is no such thing as a perfect villain. Hans Harman was about as bad a scoundrel as I could find in nature; but it was impossible not to feel some touch of human kinship with him as he stood there by the win-dow, like a chained and doomed wild animal, softening towards the one human creature who had been able to make tendrils of affection cling round his lonely heart. 'There is the insurance for five thousand on my life. She must have that at all events, in spite of all the hell-hounds that will tear my carcase,' and he spent half an hour over some legal instrument, which he then called in Deborah and a servant to witness; and, without the slightest word of explanation, kissed Deborah on the forehead. 'If I had only a trifle of ready money,' he said, after bundling his sister out as unceremoniously as he had embraced her. 'But, curse it!—there is no time to realise, and any application at the bank might only precipitate matters. What if I try old Dargan? He is to a certain extent in the same boat.'

It was a novel sensation to Hans Harman to feel his heart go pit-a-pat in a sickening way as he saw Head-Constable Mul-dudden's great-coated figure approach his gig on the way to Dargan's. The horse felt a sudden jerk at its jaws and nearly stumbled. The handsome spectre that held the reins hardly dared to raise his eyes out of their dark circles. 'Has he the warrant ?' was the question that every drop of blood seemed to ask as it jostled towards his heart. Head-Constable Muldudden had not the warrant, however, and had the usual full-dress salute for the agent. Muldudden had just been informed that he had been awarded 'a record' for distinguished service against the Rebels, and could not conceive how anybody could be thinking of anything else in the world this morning.

Humphrey had but a frosty welcome for his old patron. The money-lender was sitting in the back parlour at the bank counting over sovereigns and bank-notes, which he was building into solid ramparts and pyramids in front of him. It was an immense sum —being in full discharge of all interest due on the Drumshaughlin loans ; and Joshua Neville himself had just been with him to deliver the notes and gold and receive his receipt. Neville had also frightened him out of his senses by hints that a colossal fraud had been discovered, and that the degree to which criminal responsibility attached to the several parties thereto was still a subject of painful investigation. A violation of the criminal law was the very last thing Dargan's cautious soul had contemplated. That he should have pinched and schemed all his life to end his days in a convict's jacket was an idea altogether insupportable. He had reposed implicit confidence in Hans Harman's astuteness and knowledge of law ; but if Harman's own feet were in the snare was he likely to be over-nice about exculpating his confederate ? Ever since his failure to carry His Worship for the Club, Mrs. Dargan had conceived a distrust of, and contempt for, the agent. She blamed him for the wreck of all her ambitious dreams —for the unpleasant sensation made by her own sky-blue silk and emerald-green sunshade at the archery tournament—for little Flibbert's insolent demand of an additional thousand pounds with Lily's fortune —for the ugly cough contracted by poor Lily herself during that secret night mission to the Mill —for the three thousand pounds' worth of bills Lord Shinrone's son had inveigled Lionel into 'doing' for him before bolting for the Colonies. And now that she learned that the fallen agent was himself within measurable distance of a police-cell, the worthy lady observed to His Worship, with a chaste virtuousness all her own : 'Serve him quite right too. And I have to request, Humphrey, that you will give all the assistance possible to the ministers of justice. He will possibly be brought before yourself,' she added, with a last touch of feminine satisfaction.

'The truth of the matter is, Mr. Harman, sir,' remarked Shaunyaun, kneading his hands together as if rubbing them with an unusually heavy lather of soap, 'I'm the feether of a family, sir—humble people, sir, but still in their own way have managed by humble industhering to keep a clane sleet, so to say, sir, as between man and man ; and altogether apart from the disgreece, sir, as Mrs. D. remarked : "You're getting on in years, Humphrey," she says, "and how do you think a flagged cell would agree with your rheumatism in the end of your days ?" That's the way women do be talking, Mr. Harman, and in short, sir——'

'Devil take your cant ! You mean that you're afraid your own crooked neck is in danger, and that if tightening the rope round my neck can save you, you'll do the strangling.'

The money-lender bobbed in his chair, as if an electric battery were playing under his long nails. There was something in the agent's face that frightened him ; it gave him a thrill of relief when he saw a policeman pass the window. 'Well, Mr. Harman, sir, you do put things in strong language—in powerful strong language, sir ; but that was always a pleasant way of yours—he, he !' he sniggered, with a ghastly assumption of gaiety. 'All that I ventured to submit—submission I always do hold by as a man that knows his pleece, sir, and ever did—all I so far trespassed as to submit was that this affair in the Landed Estates Court seems to have been, sir, ahem !—in short, a narrow squeak, sir— and now I'm told there's something behind, Mr. Harman, sir— something worse, they really do be telling me, sir—something —ahem !—in short, sir, too onpleasant to be mintioned among gintlemen, so to say, Mr. Harman, sir——'

'Fiddlesticks, Dargan, you moneyed men are always afraid of your shadows,' said Harman, in his old jaunty way, appropriating the fire with his spread coat-tails as he used to do at Stone Hall, and laughing down over the shoulder of the money-lender, who was sitting in front of him. 'This meddlesome Englishman has got under some damned Fenian influence or other, and has a plot on foot to get rid of me by cooking the estate accounts against me. I've got to remove myself out of the fellow's power for a while, or he may give you and me trouble ; but it's a mere question of my quitting the country for six months, and of your giving me the means to quit it.' He left the fire and walked to the opposite side of the table for the purpose of looking Dargan full in the face.

'Me, sir !' exclaimed the money-lender, bounding in the air.

'Two thousand will do it—half that heap of money you have there on the table before you. It is the merest matter of accommodation. You have got the Hugg loan secured, and I will give you a lien on the 8,000l. that will be coming to me from the Grand Jury at the Spring Assizes. I could raise it at the bank myself within half an hour, only that I don't care to be drawing large sums there publicly at this moment. Hell and furies ! Dargan, you don't mean to say you hesitate ? Will it take a legal argument to hammer it into your stupid skull that you will be running absolutely no risk, and that you will be saving yourself as well as me from very substantial risk by putting me out of harm's way ? '

'A stupid old skull it is, I must allow, though it served you well enough in a small way in its time, Mr. Harman, sir,' said the money-lender, with that feline movement of his long nails from under their velvet sheath with which his humbler clients were familiar enough, and which even his most powerful ones had once in a way made uncomfortable acquaintance with. 'My knowledge of law is not much, sir, to be sure ; but they do be telling me—they reelly do, sir—Head-Constable Muldudden now, for example, is a deep man about the sections of an Act of Parliament——'

'Has Muldudden been talking of my name ?' gasped the agent.

'Not exactly that, sir, but I once heard Head-Constable Muldudden referring the Bench to the section that makes it—in short, Mr. Harman, sir, a felony—yes, reelly !—to conspire for the purpose of—of course, it's a funny thing to say, sir - for the purpose of screening a criminal from justice, so to say, Mr. Harman, sir.'

'May the devil roast you on a slow fire !' muttered Harman walking round to his former position between the fire and the money-lender's chair. For a moment there was silence in the room. Harman's eyes rested on the barricade of money which Dargan had just been building up in sections. The dull gleam of the gold fascinated him, made him giddy. Suddenly a wild, bloodshot-like light flamed into his eyes. His tall figure towered up behind the money-lender like a handsome panther ready to spring. 'Make it one thousand, Dargan,' he said, almost caressingly. 'I have been your friend. It is to me you owe your endless farms, your loan transactions with Lord Drumshaughlin, your magistracy. Make it one thousand. It will enable me to start a ranche in a small way. It will save my life, and you will have security ten times over at your mercy.'

Humphrey thanked his stars that he had not to face his visitor this time. He could not for worlds have turned around and met his confederate's eye when answering this piteous appeal. 'I am an old man, Mr. Harman, sir, and I never bargained for getting into collision with the law —you know I never did, sir, he whimpered in a feeble whine, instinctively plunging his long bony fingers into the pyramids of gold, and drawing them silently towards him as if they clung to his flesh.

The panther-like look on Harman's face changed to one of eager intelligence. He turned his face to the fire, and the phial of laudanum suddenly flashed in his hand in the firelight. At the same moment he pulled out his vast silk handkerchief and made a parade of blowing his nose with the utmost coolness. 'And that is really your final answer to an old friend, Dargan?' he said, quietly, as he plunged the contents of the phial into his handkerchief, and turned once more to look down upon the money-lender and his armful of wealth.

Calmly though the words were spoken, there was a certain quiver in them which made old Dargan's skeleton fingers tighten upon the gold, and caused him involuntarily to look around with a choking sensation at the throat. As he did so, all grew dark as night before his eyes. He had a vague, horrible feeling of something thrust down his throat which was stifling him; of some thick veil dropped all in an instant between the living world and himself. A great cry of terror which burst from his heart seemed to be strangled within him. There was a moment's singing in his ears, as though the voice trying to escape in that way was being smothered in the passages. His nostrils, too, seemed to be a battle-ground in which pungent spirits were engaged in some vague nightmare-like struggle of darkness; and then all was mist, blackness, silence, nothingness.

'He's all right now for a dozen hours, anyhow,' said Hans Harman, propping the insensible figure up in a comfortable attitude on the arm-chair, with the chloroformed handkerchief still covering the face of the sleeper. Then he calmly walked to the window, and saw the policeman pass tranquilly on the other side of the street on his beat. 'That's all right,' he said, pulling out his revolver, and, click after click, methodically refilling the empty chambers. 'I should not advise any police-officer for whom I had a regard to come in my way this afternoon. 'Twas a devilish happy thought—killing oneself, after all, is only the resource of a booby,' he cried, as he papered up the parcels of gold and Bank of England notes in a leisurely manner and stored them away in the leathern pouch which he usually carried for Rent-Office purposes under his great-coat. 'The Irish paper I am almost inclined to burn, as I can make no other use of it, to spite the old miscreant. No, we had better do everything in a businesslike way. But how about Deb?' he suddenly bethought himself. 'Now that that suicide is not to come off, the insurance won't do. I've got it!' he cried, jumping up, and seizing Dargan's keys, with which he opened the safe and dived upon a deed which he had often seen him stow away in a well-remembered corner. He opened the deed, and examined the signatures to make sure that it was the original ; then stuffed it carefully into his breast-pocket. Then he coolly raked over a sheet of letter-paper from under the insensible man's elbow, and wrote :—

'You behaved like the miser, coward, and traitor that you are. If I left a bullet in your heart in exchange for the gold I am taking from you, you would only get your deserts. I am taking a loan of 1,850*l.* in gold, and 1,500*l.* in notes—total 3,350*l.* (say three thousand three hundred and fifty pounds), for which amount I herewith enclose I O U. I enclose also my promissory note for a further sum of 2,000*l.* (say two thousand pounds), which I require you to advance within seven days to my sister, Miss Deborah Harman, for her sole use and disposition. To ensure this advance, I have taken possession of your deed covering your advances to me in respect of the Hugg loans. If my instructions herein are faithfully observed by you, you shall receive prompt repayment of every shilling now appropriated by me or advanced to my sister ; and, upon my learning that the advance to Miss Deborah Harman has been completed, you shall immediately recover possession of the deed which will place you in a position to realise the amount of the Hugg mortgages. I would further suggest to you the advisability, from your own point of view as well as from mine, of observing silence as to the circumstances under which this letter is written and the advances now in question have been negotiated. If within one month from date I do not learn that you have honourably fulfilled the conditions herein specified, I shall burn the deed which gives you your sole title to claim under the Hugg mortgages, and I shall take such steps as may seem most advisable either to inflict chastisement upon you myself, or to denounce you to the criminal law as the principal in the conspiracy for the confiscation of the Drumshaughlin estates.'

He folded the letter neatly and addressed it.

'That, I should say, completes our business together for the present, Humphrey,' said Hans Harman, with a grin and a mock bow towards the motionless body of the money-lender. Something suggested by the rigidity of the body seemed to strike him, and he tore away the handkerchief from the face. It exhaled the cold grey mystery of a corpse—the features tightly drawn, the teeth set, the nostrils still. 'By Jove, it looks as if it had been overmuch,' Harman cried, bending down with his ear close to the money-lender's heart. 'Pooh ! I don't think so—action not too, bad. In any case, that is a detail. Upon the whole better be than I !—at least, perhaps '—added the broken criminal, with a weary sigh as he buttoned up his great-coat.

CHAPTER THE FORTIETH

IS THE BANSHEE TO HAVE HER BRIDEGROOM ?

As Ken Rohan was passing through the dark stone passage from the cells to the dock of the Green Street Court-house, he stumbled against a figure coming the other way, with a turnkey's heavy shoulders looming up close behind him. A smoky gas-jet was sputtering against one of the clammy walls. He immediately recognised Mahon's old-fashioned cloak and long grey-black locks, and knew that the poet's trial for high treason must have finished. —'What luck ?' Ken whispered, as they clasped hands.—The poet's large, melancholy eyes filled with a luminous glow, and the sweetest smile came over the deep-dug lines that curved from his nostrils around the corners of his mouth. 'The best of all luck— death for Ireland !' he whispered, softly ; then laying his delicate white hand tenderly on the other's shoulder, 'but you—at your age ——' 'Mustn't talk,' muttered the turnkey, hustling the old cloak and the silvering locks into the gloom ; an iron door opened in front of Ken Rohan, and he found the mid-day sun and a thousand human eyes beating blindingly down upon him.

In Ireland, gaols are popular shrines, like the ruined Abbeys and the Holy Wells. The only really venerated part of a court of justice is the dock. The judge's ermine inspires respect to the same extent, and for the same reason, as the loaded guns of the policemen in all the passages. Let me not scare those who may have been wiled thus far by recalling the woful explanation why Ken Rohan's first sensation in the dock was that of being in a sacred place—some such delicate *frissonnement* of the nervous and spiritual apparatus as he used to experience in strewing the flowers and lighting the tapers on the altar of the Blessed Sacrament on Corpus Christi Day, so long, long dreamy ages ago. The dock in Green Street is a curious sunken well in the centre of the court, through which prisoners seem to rise out of the bowels of the earth and disappear again into the pit as suddenly. High overhead in front, with only the witness-table between, looms the canopied tribunal on which the two Special Commission judges, in blood-red gowns, looked threateningly down upon the prisoner ; at the side, in a high-pitched gallery, which seemed to be in danger of falling from the roof, the jury sat like beings hopelessly removed from fellowship with the unhappy wretch below and menaced him every hour of the day with falling on him and crushing him under the ruins of gallery, verdict, and all ; the seats for the public rose in steep semicircles behind the dock up to the roof, so that the prisoner seemed to have left all worldly friends and hopes behind him, and to see nothing in front of him but wood-carved lawyers' visages, a jury-gallery as darkly threatening as Damocles' sword, and blood-red judges, whose slightly faded robes seemed to be waiting for the fresh young blood at present in the dock to restore them to their pristine dye. The dock was, in fact, for all the world like a cockpit, in which the prisoner had to make his forlorn fight for life against desperate odds, sinking down when all was over into the Tophet which yawned for him amidst the cells below. And yet Ken Rohan was not thinking of cockpits, wigs, verdicts, nor black caps at this moment. He was thinking that it was from this very dock, from this very spot Robert Emmett gave up his young life two generations before in words over which Irish maidens still weep, and Irish youths wring their weaponless hands. From this very dock, and from this very spot, a generation later, John Mitchel uttered his fierce hymn of scorn while the irresistible Juggernaut-car thundered down upon him to break him limb by limb. An heir examining his Crusading ancestors in some baronial hall—a novice treading the cloisters of Monte Cassino or Clairvaux on the very stones pressed by a St. Benedict or a St. Bernard— could not have felt more reverential pride than Ken Rohan in finding himself heir to that sad, sad royal house of Irish Patriotism, of which the gallows is the genealogical tree. Underneath was the vault by which Emmett passed from the dock to die at break of day. Cause, scene, actors, issue, always the same throughout the rolling generations—the only change wrought by a dreary century being that, for the work of draining the most gallant young hearts in the land of their life-blood, Catholic Emancipation had substituted two spiteful Catholic judges for one stern Protestant one. Just such another audience, long ago dead and gone, must have hedged Emmett in with pitiless eyes. Ah ! but the hapless, happy love which irradiated young Emmett's life —which made it at once so easy and so hard to die ! How easy to bear the stare of all those callous faces if one could only know that among them all there was one crystal-pure heart where one's shrine would glow for ever and for ever ! How sweet to die in the soft break of day, if one could only be sure that the love of one adored being would be buried with him in his unknown prison grave ! A dreadful chill of loneliness shot through Ken

Rohan's limbs while the wood-carved lawyers were going through their preliminary abracadabra. The fashionable ladies, who, as the reporters would say, 'were accommodated with seats on the Bench near their lordships,' and paid their lordships with nosegays of flowers, thought they could, through their lorgnettes, see the prisoner trembling. And yet some instinct more powerful than their lorgnettes softened the fashionable ladies in spite of themselves towards the prisoner, with his fresh tint of youth and frankness—possibly some subtle touch of that magnetism that always betrays a man in love to women and always ranges them on his side. He could not himself exactly tell what this sense of forsakenness meant. He was an unknown stripling in Dublin, and could scarcely have expected friendly faces among the audience, even if the audiences who would have looked friendly were not kept far from the precincts of the court by pickets of cavalry and battalions of police. His mother and Katie, who had seen him in turn in prison, had been mercifully summoned back to Drumshaughlin by news of the miller's growing worse. Father Phil had burst upon him also like a sudden gush of sunshine through a stormy December sky.

'The boy can get in Christian's food till the trial,' the Coadjutor-Bishop remarked to him before he set out, and something as closely resembling a tear as anything ever seen trembling in that stern eye trembled there as he added : 'I don't suppose food or any other of this world's cares will trouble him for very long after it. There's my blank cheque. Arrange for everything, Father Phil—tell him I will never say Mass without remembering him—and tell him—oh, bother !—tell him first of all, and last of all, God bless him !'

Nor was the Coadjutor-Bishop's message the only shaft of brightness Father Phil's sunny old face projected into the cell. Father Phil had been to visit his scapegrace nephew. There was no substantial evidence against Jack Harold. He had been transferred to Mountjoy Prison in the category of 'suspects' detained under the Habeas Corpus Suspension, and had to his disgust received an intimation that he would be released on his consenting to be conveyed on board an American-bound steamer at Queenstown.

'Tell Ken I have done all my possible to be hanged—truly,' he said, with a half-comic whole-earnest pathos, 'but I am doomed not to succeed in anything—not even in being cravated with hemp. All I want him and you to know is that I have tried.'

'That you have, boy. I am proud of you,' said the old priest, with moistening eyes, squeezing his hand.

'Poor Jack!' his friend exclaimed, when he received the message. 'I am so glad he has tried—and I am so much gladder that he has failed. As if the world were so gay a place that it could find nothing better to do with Jack Harold than to hang him!'

'Or so noble a place that it can find nothing better to do with you,' said the old priest, who was blubbering like a child; which was, perhaps, the less shameful that the cast-iron turnkey, who was standing between them, had a painful facial struggle to keep from blubbering too.

'Ah, that is a different matter, Father Phil,' said the prisoner, colouring and smiling. 'If there is any one thing in life I flatter myself I can do well, it is to die. The world is simply taking me at my word; and—will I tell you candidly?—I find dying is by no means so simple an operation as it looked.'

But now that the priest's old weather beaten seraph face was gone (for Father Phil had been obliged to depart to give his vote at the county election) there was a vast aching void in Ken Rohan's heart which neither friend's grasp, nor Bishop's blessing, nor even the full tide of a mother's love could fill; he scarcely dared to ask himself whence this sense of lonesomeness and soul hunger. I dare say one of the reasons why Ireland can command a love so passionately tender is that Erin is pictured as a woman—a weak as well as beautiful one. You may be sure it was not in this moment of distress she appeared less ravishing to one who felt the wine of youth and strength rushing to his brain. But deny it as he would, shut his eyes to it as he would, his mistress was no longer to him a mere dazzling abstraction; her eyes were deep and her flesh was palpitating; her features always ran into the same image, and that image not framed in the blue-black hair of the traditional 'Dark Rosaleen,' but in a flood of showery gold. He was haunted by a vague vision of a Presence which summed up all his greedy Imagination could conceive of beauty, goodness, love, and country—summed them all up in human all-too-well-known shape; and yet the unreality of his vision forced itself upon him, mocked him, left him cold and desolate. At this moment he had to put his hands before his eyes to keep out the haunting, maddening sense of finding the air thrill with Mabel Westropp's presence, of actually seeing her before him, there in that foul, dingy place of doom. 'Am I going mad?' he asked himself.

As a matter of fact his eyes were not in the least deceiving him. Lady Mabel was sitting by Joshua Neville's side in a scarcely visible seat amidst the gloom cast by the shadow of the gallery overhead. She was dressed in deep mourning, with a heavy black veil drawn completely down over her face and throat, but he could not be mistaken as to the exquisite lines of that sylph-like figure; he thought he could even distinguish a pale, pale face, and eyes of heavenly blue shining out of that black shroud of hers as the bodies of saints have sometimes shone through their tombs. The paleness was there at all events, woful to see; and her head sometimes swayed towards Joshua Neville's shoulder as though it could no longer support itself, light and flower-like enough though it looked on its delicate stem. The iron-master could not spare one thought for the youth in the dock away from the shrinking creature beside him. He felt miserably guilty. She had made him her confidant, placing her small white hand in his as a child might; and he had yielded, as he would have yielded if her request had been to open the largest vein in his arm. 'Don't be afraid of me,' she whispered, 'I won't cry out. I won't do anything wrong. Trust me, I will live through it, and—and—I am not sure how I am to live unless you help me.' And, of course, he pressed his lips on the lily-white hand, and fobbed off the Earl (whose gout was rising to his knees) with the miserable pretext of bringing Mabel to consult a Dublin doctor. Her sweet courage on the journey had enchanted him more than all her loveliness; it was not her determination he doubted, but her whiteness and her supernatural calm terrified him beyond description. He felt like one in charge of one of those vases of Venetian glass which crumbled in the hands of a clumsy holder. As for Ken Rohan, he no longer heard the challenges to the array, the rejoinders, surrebutters, and other solemn gibberish with which the lawyers were celebrating their Witches' Sabbath around him. He did not even dare to lift his eyes again. They were blinded with light and happiness. The fœtid court-room expanded into a rosy summerland, in which the blood-red judges, bewigged lawyers, and blue-bottle policemen were only so many midges buzzing in the resplendent sun. He pinched himself again and again to make sure that it was all real. He felt that if he could only die at this moment by one swift bullet stroke, he would die a million million times a happier man than the judge who sentenced him. The ladies who watched him through their lorgnettes did not well know what to make of him, but agreed that he wore an uncommonly pretty blush—a blush such as one only sees in a young nun or a true lover.

The trial went on, as Irish State Trials go on age after age, as regularly as Famines, in dark and creepy ways such as the steaming fog that laid its slimy touch on everything in the Green Street Court-house furnished an appropriate atmosphere for

Every juror of the prisoner's creed, which was also the judges
creed and the Attorney-General's creed, was thrust aside like a
Jew in a mediæval city, the sleek Jews in the judges' and
Attorney-General's gaberdines piously turning up their eyes at
the atrocious suggestion that the coincidence of all the rejected
jurors being of one creed, and all the accepted ones of another,
could be anything more than a coincidence. Twelve jurors were
sworn who might as well have been twelve policemen turned out
to throttle a burglar. Irish State Trials finish with the swearing
of the jury, not with their verdict. All the rest is a prosy novel,
of which the last chapter is placed first. In the present instance
the aspect of the jury-box was so unmistakable, and the evidence,
moreover, so overwhelming, that the Attorney-General could
afford to sail along in balmy regions of judicial calm. 'There
were reasons they could all understand,' he observed, with a smile
of gentle pity, 'why he was specially desirous not to overstrain
his duty by the turning of a hair against the unhappy young man
at the Bar.' Everybody agreed that nothing could have been
handsomer, and that Glascock was really a good fellow—also that
he must be sure of his election, or he would never wear such an
expression of genial beatitude when referring to his preposterous
young adversary. There was some ground for the sarcasm of the
legal wits around the library fire that Toby Glascock had thriven
more by reason of what was outside his head than by reason of what
was within. His sunny smile, frank face, bounteous whiskers, and
hearty caressing voice were a better stock-in-trade than any he
had been able to find in calf-bound Croke-Charleses; and he was
as careful never, in good or evil fortune, to take this attractive
stock out of his windows as other lawyers are to cram their
mental shelves with the learned lumber of the Law Reports. The
truth is that the Attorney-General was sufficiently ill at ease at
this moment. The polling had taken place the previous day.
Owing to the vast extent of the county, and the difficulty of communications in those times, the declaration of the poll could not
be made until late to-day. There were no telegraph wires to
many of the polling-places, and such accounts as had reached him
were uncomfortably conflicting. Some entirely unlooked-for things
had happened. The Drumshaughlin tenantry, who were counted
the most lamblike serfs in the county had broken away from
their hussar escort en masse, hooted Monsignor McGrudder in the
streets, and rushed to the polls for the young rebel with flaming
eyes and whirling shillelaghs. A mob led by young Neville, the
Guardsman, had broken into the hotel yard where Lord Clanlaurance's agent had his tenants stabled like so many stalled oxen, and
had borne them off through a volley of musketry from the police

with trumpets sounding. There had been serious rioting elsewhere, through which Mat Murrin's hoarse voice could be heard
thundering and his eye-glass seen flashing. Those silent, inscrutable
farmers had displayed the most unaccountable tenderness for the
young rebel when the moment came to speak out. Many of the
young priests had openly sided with him. But most of this was
in the neighbourhood where local favouritism would naturally
come into play. In other districts the canons and agents had
victoriously headed their battalions to the polls. There were
other extensive regions still to be heard from, and the Attorney-
General's agents were as sanguine as ever of a thumping majority,
though the contest had undeniably been a more serious one than
they could have anticipated.

'What about this trial in the other venue, Attorney?'
maliciously asked one of the judges, meeting him at the door of
the judges' room that morning. 'Wouldn't it be a funny thing
if your Song of the Pike lost you the county?'

'Not a bit of it, judge,' retorted genial Mr. Attorney—'no
more than your lordship's hint to the Westmeath Ribbonmen
lost you your judgeship.' For Mr. Justice Murrorty in his
popularity-hunting days had made a speech which sounded
perilously like a Song of the Blunderbuss, and was making atone-
ment by a life of savage ferocity towards all who took his hints.
Such is life in Ireland. The two judges from whose red robes
the offended majesty of the law glared at Ken Rohan had both
of them purchased their red robes by putting up Ken Rohan's
principles for sale in market overt; and the bland Attorney-
General who uttered his brief-ful of well-fed horror of the
prisoner's treasons against his sovereign had a sneaking feeling
somewhere in the very innermost recesses of his heart that if this
were not a world of humbug the prisoner would be stepping out
of the dock to kick him.

The Attorney-General, undoubtedly, did his spiriting gently.
His sleek platitudes about the criminality of rebellion and the
sacred interests of society were delivered with an apologetic
drooping of the eyelids and a certain genial, semi-demi-wink-like
eye upon the dock, as who should say : 'My dear fellow, you
understand, of course, that all this twaddle is briefed to me and
has to be got through ; it will involve unpleasant consequences,
no doubt, for you ; but I am sure you are too good a fellow not
to feel how much more uncomfortable a business it must be for
me, with that infernal Pike Song for ever ringing in my ears—
and a devilish good thing it was, by the way, if those rascals
wouldn't insist upon making it immortal.' The principal evidence
consisted of letters in Ken Rohan's handwriting found on the

premises of the suppressed newspaper, and tracing to him the authorship of the fiery rebel ballad which had precipitated the suppression.

'You don't intend to rely upon the writing of a rebel ballad alone as conclusive evidence of high treason, Attorney?' growled Mr. Justice Murrorty, who had not forgiven the thrust about the whirling rhetoric of his own Bohemian days. The junior bar grinned furtively, and looked at Toby Glascock's face.

'Certainly not, m' lud; your ludship, with the perspicacity which distinguishes you among judges in a scarcely less remarkable degree than the kindheartedness which endears you among friends, has quite accurately anticipated what I was about to say,' said the Attorney-General with undiminished sweetness. 'This correspondence we rely upon as establishing the prisoner's connection with the leaders of this abominable conspiracy; but we do not stop there. Out of the mouth of one of his own accomplices—one of his own dupes—it will be our melancholy duty to establish the prisoner's actual participation in scenes of insurrection and of bloodshed.'

The prisoner became vaguely conscious of a deep susurrus of popular interest such as might have thrilled the Roman Amphitheatre when a fasting lion was turned into the arena. He felt himself wrenched painfully out of his beautiful dreams. The lucent empyrean heaven in which he had been floating faded out, and in its place loomed up through the clammy yellow fog a figure in the witness-chair which seemed to have risen like an ugly exhalation. The eyes had a gleam of blood in them; the teeth were those of a wild animal fresh from some bloody prey; the very hair of the monster seemed to have been steeped in murder. Perhaps it was indignation at being torn from his delicious dreamland that moved Ken Rohan, even more than his repulsion for the trade of the informer; but he thought he had never before seen an object so loathsome, so satanic. He had seen precisely the same object often before, however; for the squat figure, blazing hair, and vermilion bulb of nose now dully burning through the sodden air were those of Dawley.

.   .   .   .   .   .

From the moment the informer, horrible-looking as if the hell of remorse and alcohol within him were oozing through the pores of his flesh, began his story, all was over. Mr. Justice Murrorty, whose handsome, imperious, cruel-jawed head resembled one of those seen on the coins of the later Roman Emperors, was subject to keen internal torments, and dashed into the work of hunting down the prisoner as other men take morning gallops to stir up a torpid liver. I have not the heart to tell how he sniffed and fumed in a holy rage for the interests of justice—how he championed the informer against every uncomfortable raid of the cross-examining counsel—how he bedaubed the double-dyed murderer and perjurer with praises, and actually saluted the red-headed little demon with the title of 'saviour of his country' —and what an abyss of horror and ruin suddenly opened under Ken Rohan's feet—what torturing pictures of a dying father, of a weeping mother, of a lost cause, and of a hideous black frame- work and a strangling body, and a grave underneath the flags of the little exercise-yard where he had learned with a curious fascination fourteen murderers were already sleeping in their quicklime shrouds. Pray Heaven, gracious reader, that nobody you love may ever know what dismal eternities may be crushed into the moments after twelve men retire into their jury-room to write down the word which, in our own land and in our own day, has bruised many a thousand young lives as fairly blossoming as Ken Rohan's, and lacerated many a thousand hearts as tender as his mother's, and broken many a thousand as stalwart forms as that of the stout old miller !

Not that everybody in court could not have written down the verdict before the jury retired, and sworn to it. But, in a country where judicial decency, like certain simple-minded African belles, is more particular about its necklaces than about more important articles of toilette, a political jury always pride themselves on writing the word 'Guilty' with as much leisurely dignity as if they were engaged in illuminating it in gold and colours. They were illuminating it with their glowing tobacco- pipes, at all events, and while they were so engaged a telegraph messenger arrived with two messages, one of which was handed from policeman to policeman into the dock, and the other into the hands of the Attorney-General. A buzz of excitement went through the court-room. Everybody felt the telegrams announced the verdict in the other venue. A mist swam before Ken Rohan's eyes. The address upon the envelope appeared to dance and stagger before him. It was :

'KENNEDY ROHAN, ESQUIRE M.P., THE DOCK, GREEN ST.'

His hand trembled with incredulous joy as he tore it open. The telegram was from Mat Murrin, and was in these words :

'Declaration of the Poll—Rohan, 7,245 ; Glascock, 1,360. God bless you, old boy ! That is a verdict worth living for, and worth dying for.'

A delicious rush, whether of humiliation or of joy, or of both

commingled, came over him like a great wave of golden water.
The ladies through their lorgnettes noticed that he read the message as though it were a love-letter—with that tender trembling
delight with which a man hears a woman's soul faltering forth
its love. And it did affect him precisely as did the sight of
Mabel Westropp's angel-face in his desolation ; for was not this
also a shy, sad, unlooked-for, enrapturing declaration of love ?—
the melting, thrilling love of a nation ?—and it is only those who
entered as passionately as he into the genius and sorrows of his
race who can understand how preternaturally like a woman's
voice of love is that wild sob of clinging affection with which the
saddest but tenderest of the nations repays her soldiers for all
their losing battles and doomed hopes. The victory was to him
all but incomprehensible. For fear of adding the pang of a
disheartening defeat, Father Phil had only acquainted him in a
vague, jocular way with the contest as one of Mat Murrin's
pranks. It had never once occurred to him as a matter of sane
possibility that he, a penniless unknown lad with one foot on the
gallows, should be lifted to this impossible height by a constituency
of close-fisted, closer-minded farmers ; yet, by one of those electric impulses which now and again set the veins of a nation
tingling with a fine frenzy, up those dumb, cautious, terrorised,
crushed farmers rose, with their blood afire, and, oversetting all
calculations and barriers, dashing aside the Monsignors' gold-
knobbed sticks, and the agents' whips, and the Castle's bribes,
and the hussars' sabres, shook the young rebel by the hand at the
gallows' foot in the face of the world, and declared that his were
the wild hopes which were whispered in sacred moments round their
firesides—his the immortal longings which nestled in their heart of
hearts ! Ken Rohan's face was one of those rustic old-fashioned
ones which made no more effort to conceal emotion than the Caha
Mountains did to frown while the sun was smiling in their face.
He looked as if ten thousand beaming eyes of affection had
suddenly shone out upon him from the yellow, guilty gloom.

The Attorney-General's smile was no less seraphic. 'Curse
it, there goes a cool eight thousand to divert Mat Murrin on a
spree !' he muttered in the sanctuary underneath his silk gown ;
but the junior bar, cruelly though their eyes sought to get inside
Toby's thin varnish of bonhomie, found it hard to make sure
that his telegram was not some capital stroke of wit, over which
he was only restrained by the solemnity of the occasion from
bursting out laughing.

'Well ?' inquired Judge Murrorty, bobbing his red gills discreetly over the ink-bottle.

'The boys have been having their practical joke, my lord—

N N

that's all,' whispered the Attorney-General, furtively passing up the telegram.

The red gills swelled scarlet. Convulsions of rage passed over the bold, handsome face, whose firmly-chiselled features were only just losing their contour in the fat underhung layers of flesh which follow sensual indulgence as surely as an eager outlooking of the eyes follows asceticism. Except that he used his sword in the opposite camp, the judge was no more squeamish about his words in a temple of justice than he had been about his words in a Ribbon Lodge. He burned to commit the whole 7,245 electors to prison for a wicked and audacious contempt of court. He found it hard even to subdue his voice to a whisper as he bent over and said to the Attorney-General, with a snort of triumph :

'You'll soon have another vacancy, anyhow. Here comes the jury !'

Joshua Neville felt his hand gripped with a sudden convulsive energy. He glanced in terror at his companion. 'Don't be afraid,' she said, faintly. 'I won't scream.' A cold, sick feeling crept through her limbs. She heard vaguely as through a rushing of waves a deep groan of pity rising amidst the clammy shadows ; saw, as through some dim cold film, the erect figure in the dock bow graciously with the brightest happy light playing over the pallid face ; saw the judge's stormy, cruel face flashing as blood-red as his gown, heard him utter bitter raging words, and suddenly saw all the world turn black with the blackness of the tiny silk skull-cap that was drawn over the judge's poll. Then the fierce grip upon Joshua Neville's hand relaxed ; the white fingers fell coldly away ; the beautiful head rolled helplessly against his shoulder. She had kept her word. She had fainted—but without a cry.

The turnkey tapped Ken Rohan on the shoulder, and pointed to the dark trap-door underneath, through which he was to pass for ever from the light of human eyes—through which thousands as young as he had passed before him and have followed after him. As he stood up, another telegram was passed into his hands, but was instantly snatched out of them by the gaoler.

'Condemned—can't receive communications,' was his gruff apology.

The condemned youth bowed, smiled slightly, and disappeared.

'For once the law is merciful,' said his lawyer, to whom the telegram had been made over. 'Better he should never know.'

The message was from the Coadjutor-Bishop of Clonard : 'My brave old friend is gone to heaven. He died in blessing you. Your mother and sister will be my charge for life.'

'You are not going to hang that boy,' said Joshua Neville, sitting opposite the miserable Chief Secretary in his dismal study at the Lodge that night. There was a winter storm moaning through the trees in the Phœnix Park, keeping up a mournful tattoo upon the neglected window-frames, and careering about the ill-warmed room in shivery little currents. 'It is a perfect infamy. To my own knowledge, instead of causing bloodshed, he risked his life to prevent it; the wretch who swore against him is reeking with the guilt of two diabolical murders, besides the murder resolved upon to-day. Erect your gallows as quickly as you like for him; if you hang the judge who called him saviour of his country along with him, a gallows was never put to better use. But to reward these and strangle the other — gracious heavens ! if this is how we have been ruling Ireland for half a dozen centuries, it makes a man inclined to toss his Bible in the fire to think of a God of Justice who could witness such things without raining down fire and brimstone on our heads !'

John Jelliland passed his hands despairingly over his bald skull as though the fire and brimstone would not find much in the way of devastation left for it to do there. A kind, hard-working, unimaginative man, he had taken up the Irish Problem with the full persuasion that it was a mere affair of punctual office work, and arterial drainage, and such things ; and here was his arterial drainage turning to crimson blood-letting, and hecatombs of young lives marked down in his police reports for slaughter or transportation. A respectable butler engaging with an interesting family, and finding that the first duty expected of him was to cut the throats of the younger members of the family with a carving-knife, could not have been more horrified than John Jelliland to find his honest Quaker hands dripping blood, and a chorus of heart-broken mothers' cries loading the air around him.

'What would you have ?' he groaned, helplessly. 'We must either hang these men, or hand over Ireland to them.'

'And why not ?' cried the ironmaster, hotly. 'Have we done so much more brilliantly by handing it over to the place-hunters and informers ? You will gain nothing by strangling young Rohan, unless you go on and strangle the seven thousand electors who subscribed to his treason yesterday, and the seven millions who would be just as fiery rebels as young Rohan if they were not older, or meaner, or more selfish. Has it ever occurred to you that it might be nobler, and even cheaper, to bribe the Irish people into affection for us, than to bribe landlords, placemen, and informers to make us detested and detestable ?'

The Secretary's head remained buried in his hands. 'That is

a dream !' he said, at last, with a deep groan. 'All I know is that there is one unhappier place in Ireland than the condemned cell, and that is, the Chief Secretary's Lodge.'

A few mornings afterwards it was announced to Ken Rohan that His Excellency the Lord-Lieutenant had been pleased to commute the capital sentence into one of penal servitude for life. 'I am afraid,' said the chaplain, who communicated the news, 'it will not be altogether a pleasant surprise.'

'It realises an old dream of mine, that is all,' he answered, with a mournful smile. 'I used once to rave of the life of St. Finn Barr's old monks in their stone-box cells in Gougaun Barra. I am going to have an opportunity of tasting the reality. A convict prison is a monastery under three locks in place of The Three Vows, and, as the sentence is for life, I dare say there will be no fear of a breakdown in my vocation.'

A greasy wintry dawn on the river below Dublin ; a steamer belching black steam like the breathing of an ugly monster awaking from a nap ; policemen and infantry in their great-coats daubed here and there on the dank fog, like the blotches on an Impressionist picture. A clatter of horses' hoofs, and out of the womb of the unwholesome darkness a black prison-van with its hedge of naked sabres rolled heavily. Two civilian figures pressed close to the gangway—one of them a woman in deep black—whom the rough soldiers shrank pityingly back from. The convicts came out two by two : each of the political felons being handcuffed to a professional convict for better security in their transfer to an English convict station. There passed one whose dreamy eyes we know, though the fading cloak and rolling sable locks are gone. Then came another upon whose lithe young figure even the hideous felon's jacket and cap sat with a picturesque gracefulness ; the bright colour in his cheeks sadly dimmed, but his eyes glowing more luminously than ever with that sad winning smile of a soul at peace within ; his right wrist clasped with steel to the wrist of a man whose hair sprouted down almost to his eyes, and whose awful mouth yawned in the gaps between black wolfish teeth. The dingy wet fog extin-guished the struggling morning light outside a radius of a few yards. As the youth with his wolfish comrade stepped on the gangway, a piercing shriek just beside him went like a poniard to his heart. He started back, with a jerk that made the hand-cuff cut into his wrist ; he turned, and, with eyes and cheeks aflame, beheld the slight black apparition through the fog.—
'Forward there, Number Five-hundred and seventy-five ! Now, then, get along !' cried a burly prison-officer, pushing him for-

ward brusquely on the gangway. He stumbled down a steep ladder, knocking his head against an iron stanchion; when he recovered consciousness he was under stifling hatches below, and the heavy piston-rods of the steamer were commencing their dull, cruel thuds. 'Courage!' whispered the deep, true voice of Joshua Neville, bending down over the slender white-faced creature he held in his arms like a baby. 'Courage! This is

'NOT THE END.'

A word as to how these pages came to be written. During large portions of the writer's two latest terms of imprisonment under the Coercion Act, he was, owing to the influence of British public opinion, proffered the use of books and writing materials. It was with no higher purpose than that of beguiling weary hours that the story just completed was commenced. With the exception of four chapters it was written wholly in prison. The writer is aware that, however relevant these circumstances may be as an apology for writing the book, they constitute no valid plea for publishing it, with all the blemishes of a work of fiction so produced upon its head, and with the further blemishes which it must possess in consequence of the fact that eight of the early chapters, the manuscript of which was lost while he was last in prison, had to be re-written, and that he has been forced, through absence from England, to let the book pass through the press without his personal revision. The truth is, that the sketch idly begun grew insensibly into something like a picture of the transformation which the progress of American democratic ideas has brought about in Irish society, and it seemed as if clumsiness on the part of the artist alone could fail to impart some interest to a revolution so fertile in novel and wide-reaching results. If the reading of the story should happily brighten even a small portion of the time that was brightened in writing it, the experiment will have been sufficiently rewarded. It was a painful, as well as dangerous, duty to affront the time-honoured and entirely human demand of novel readers for a happy ending. Upon this topic two things have to be said. In the first place, the woeful thing about the closing scene is that it is true, and that any more joyous closing scene would be a falsehood. Within our own generation, innumerable Irish hearts as young and lightsome as Ken Rohan's have been quenched in penal servitude, and innumerable Irish mothers, sweethearts, and sisters have wept at the prison gates. An Irish novelist, if he loved his youths or maidens, had only to make them die or suffer. The writer's besetting difficulty throughout was how to soften for strangers' ears those minor chords of sorrow which haunt Irish life like night-winds sighing through one of our ruined shrines. The second excuse touches happier ground. It is, that we have not come to the end at all. Irishmen have discovered a saner resource than the wild weapons of boyish insurrection, and Englishmen a more glorious revenge than a handcuffed wrist and a convict's brand. The issue between Humanity and Barbarism—between Love and Hate—is even at this moment trembling in the balance. Readers, who shrink from the thought of a tale of youth and love ending with the sailing away of a dark-browed convict-ship, and the heart-breaking cry upon the quay behind, will in an approaching hour be summoned to exercise the all-but-heavenly high prerogative of settling for themselves what shall really be

THE END.

Haverhill Public Library.

This book, unless marked "Seven day book," may be kept four weeks, and, if non-fiction, may be renewed once for four weeks. If it is fiction, or on the reserve list, it may nõt be renewed. It may not be transferred.

If this book is kept overtime, a fine of two cents a day will be charged. If sent for by messenger, the fine and twenty cents additional will be charged.

Borrowers finding this book mutilated or defaced will please report it.   .

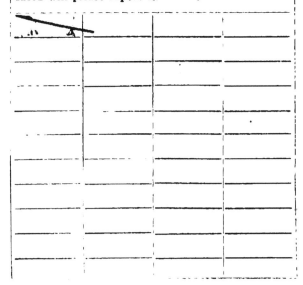